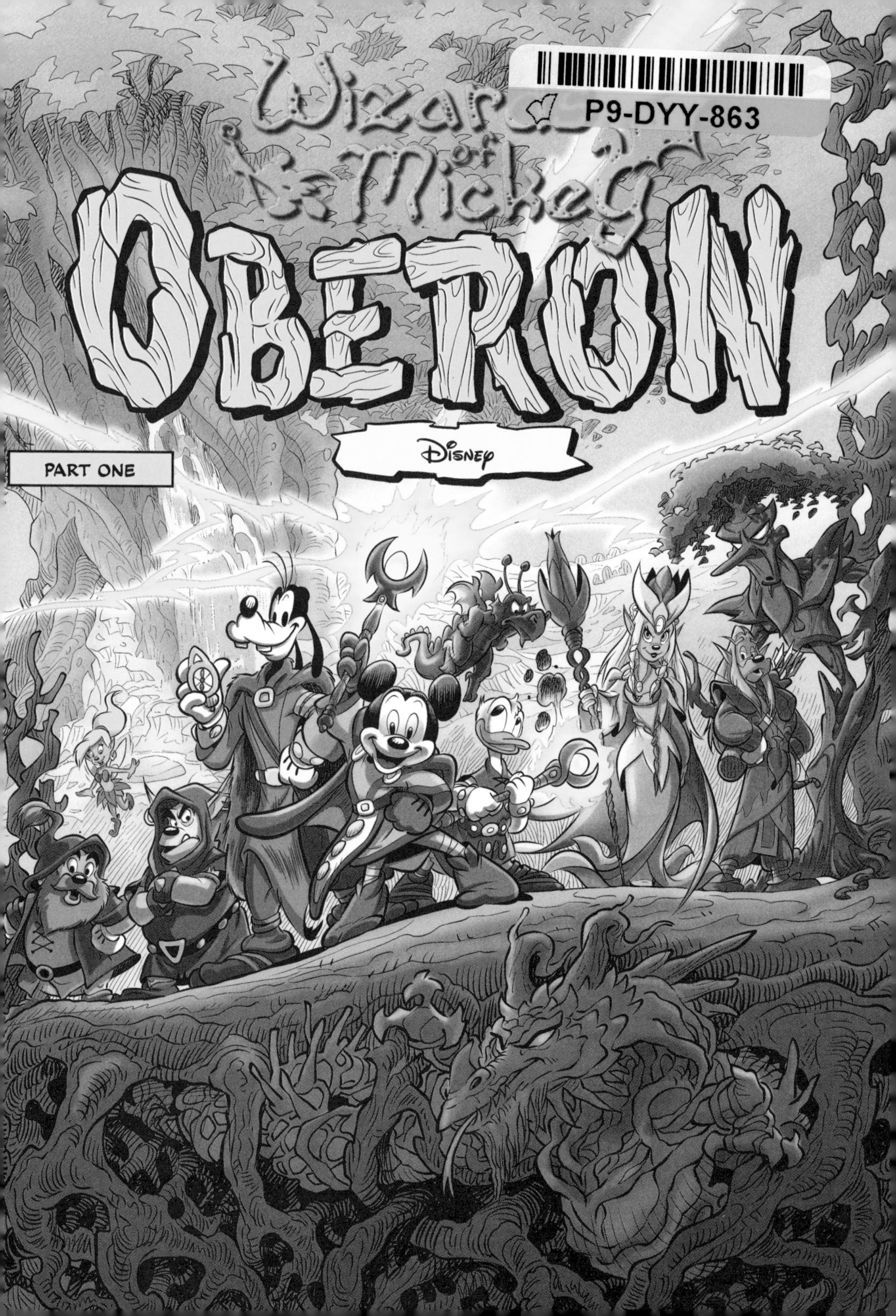
Wizards of Mickey
OBERON
DISNEY
PART ONE

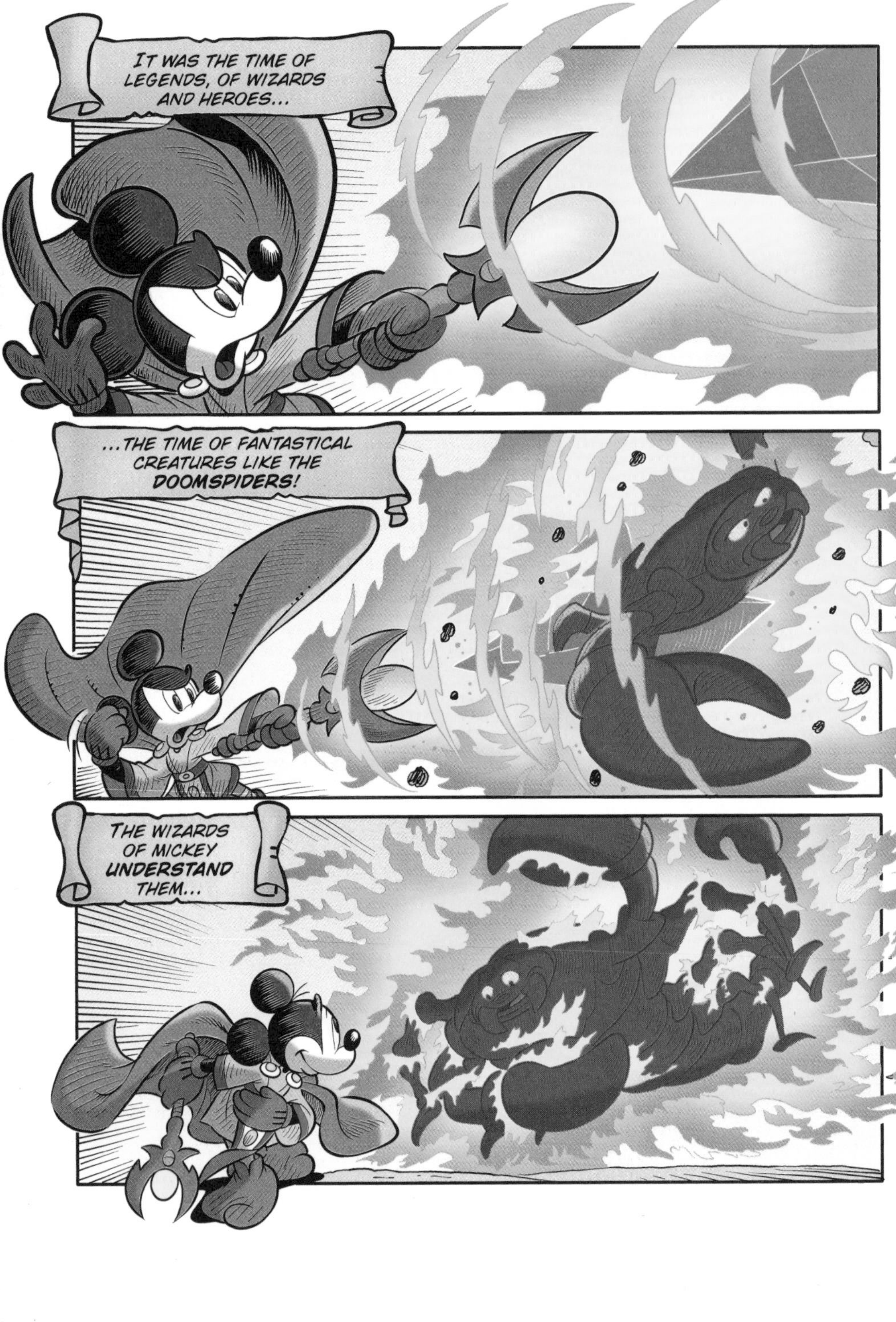
IT WAS THE TIME OF LEGENDS, OF WIZARDS AND HEROES...
...THE TIME OF FANTASTICAL CREATURES LIKE THE DOOMSPIDERS!
THE WIZARDS OF MICKEY UNDERSTAND THEM...

THE GRAPHIC NOVEL

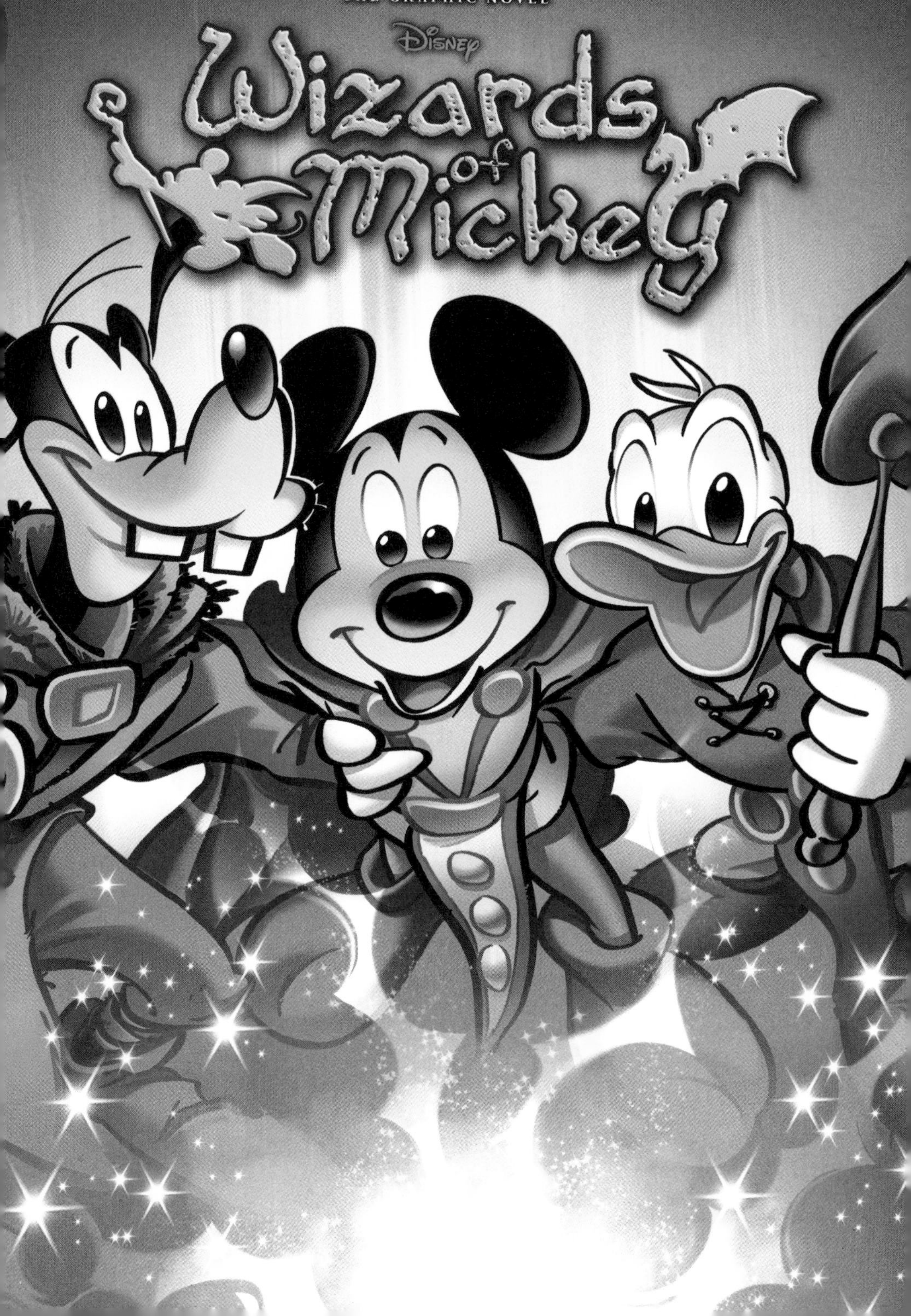
Disney
Wizards of Mickey

Wizards of Mickey

6

Contents

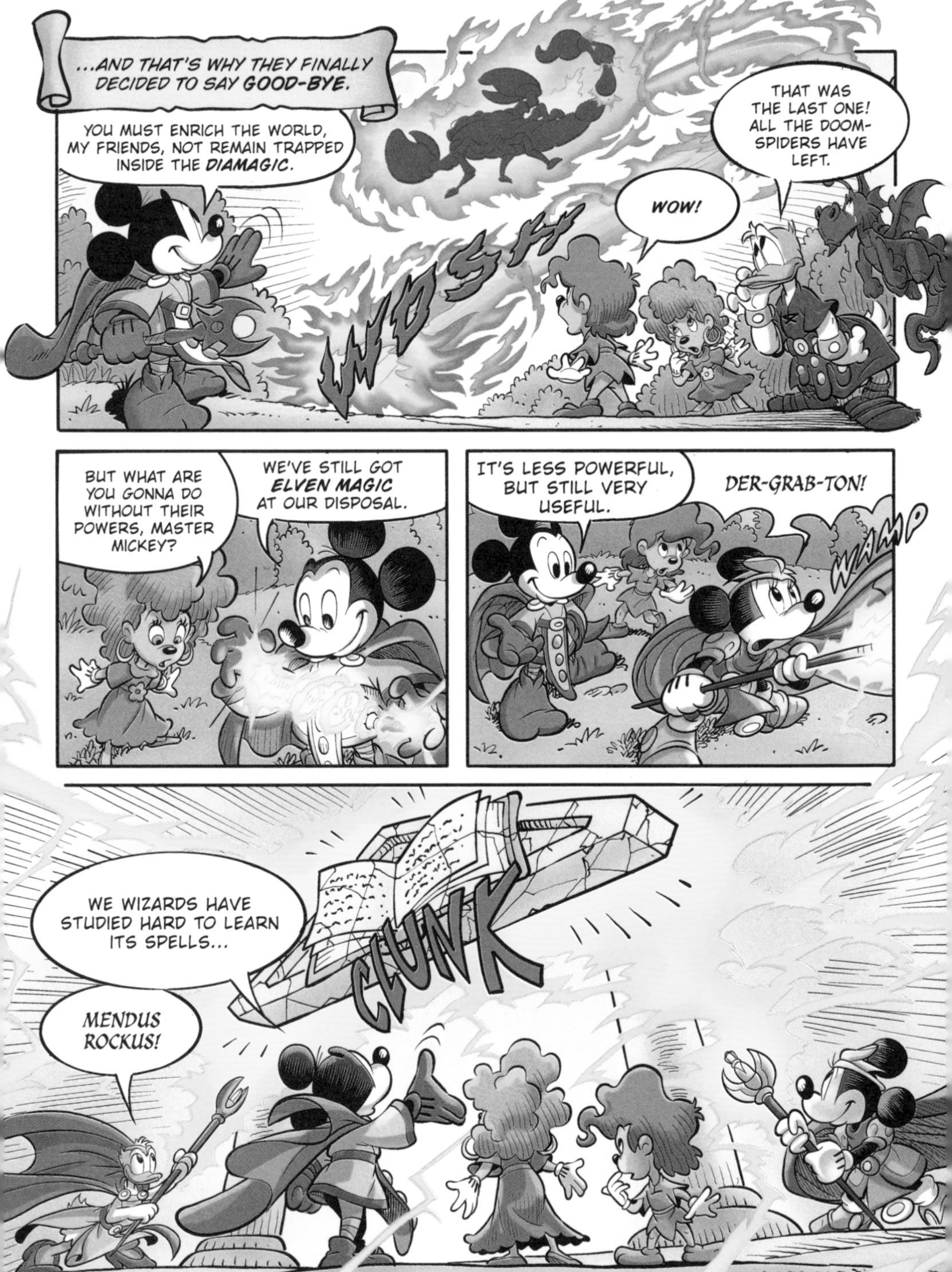
...AND THAT'S WHY THEY FINALLY DECIDED TO SAY GOOD-BYE.
YOU MUST ENRICH THE WORLD, MY FRIENDS, NOT REMAIN TRAPPED INSIDE THE DIAMAGIC.
WOOSH
WOW!
THAT WAS THE LAST ONE! ALL THE DOOM-SPIDERS HAVE LEFT.
BUT WHAT ARE YOU GONNA DO WITHOUT THEIR POWERS, MASTER MICKEY?
WE'VE STILL GOT ELVEN MAGIC AT OUR DISPOSAL.
IT'S LESS POWERFUL, BUT STILL VERY USEFUL.
DER-GRAB-TON!
WAMP
WE WIZARDS HAVE STUDIED HARD TO LEARN ITS SPELLS...
MENDUS ROCKUS!
CLUNK

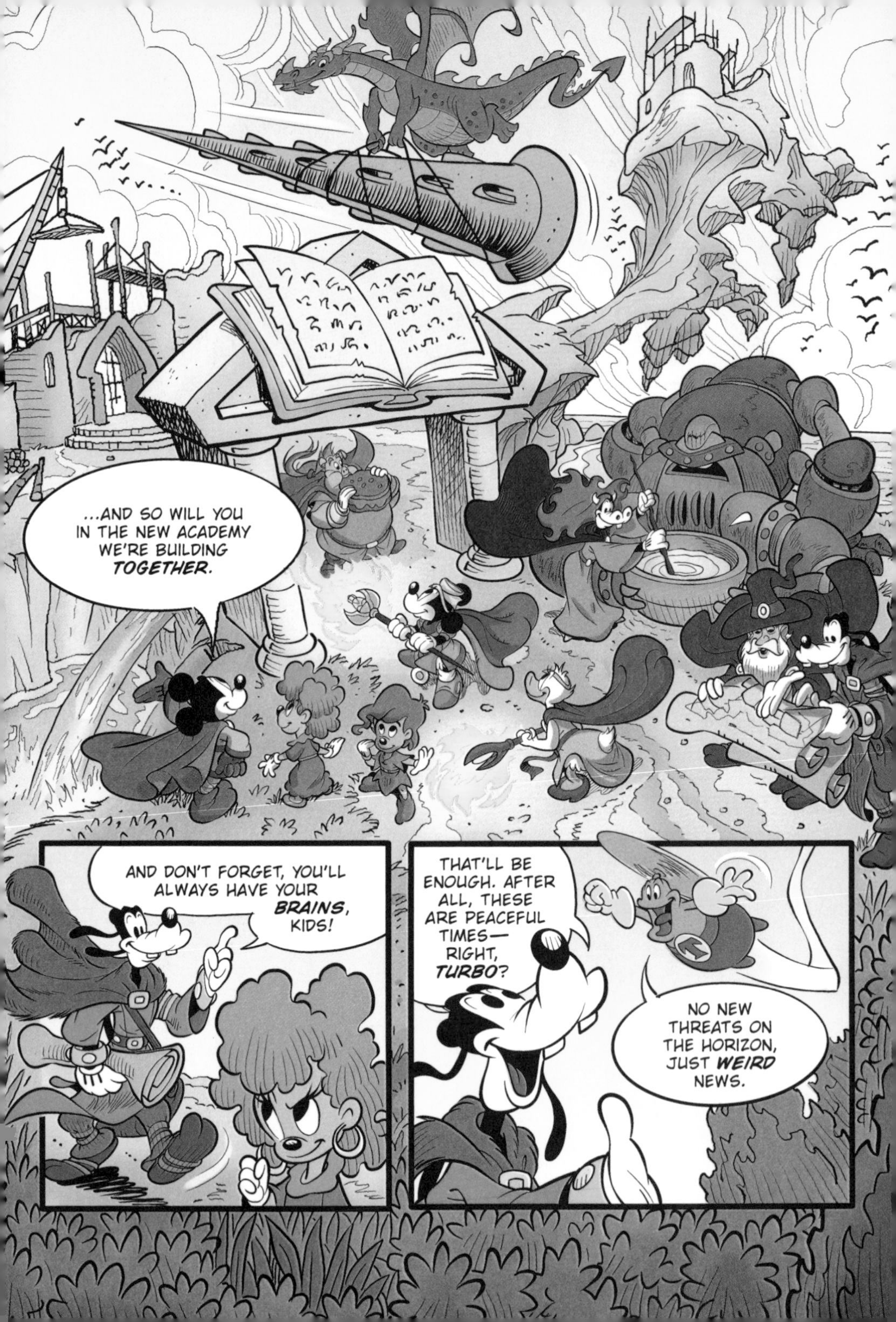
...AND SO WILL YOU IN THE NEW ACADEMY WE'RE BUILDING *TOGETHER*.
AND DON'T FORGET, YOU'LL ALWAYS HAVE YOUR *BRAINS*, KIDS!
THAT'LL BE ENOUGH. AFTER ALL, THESE ARE PEACEFUL TIMES— RIGHT, *TURBO*?
NO NEW THREATS ON THE HORIZON, JUST *WEIRD* NEWS.

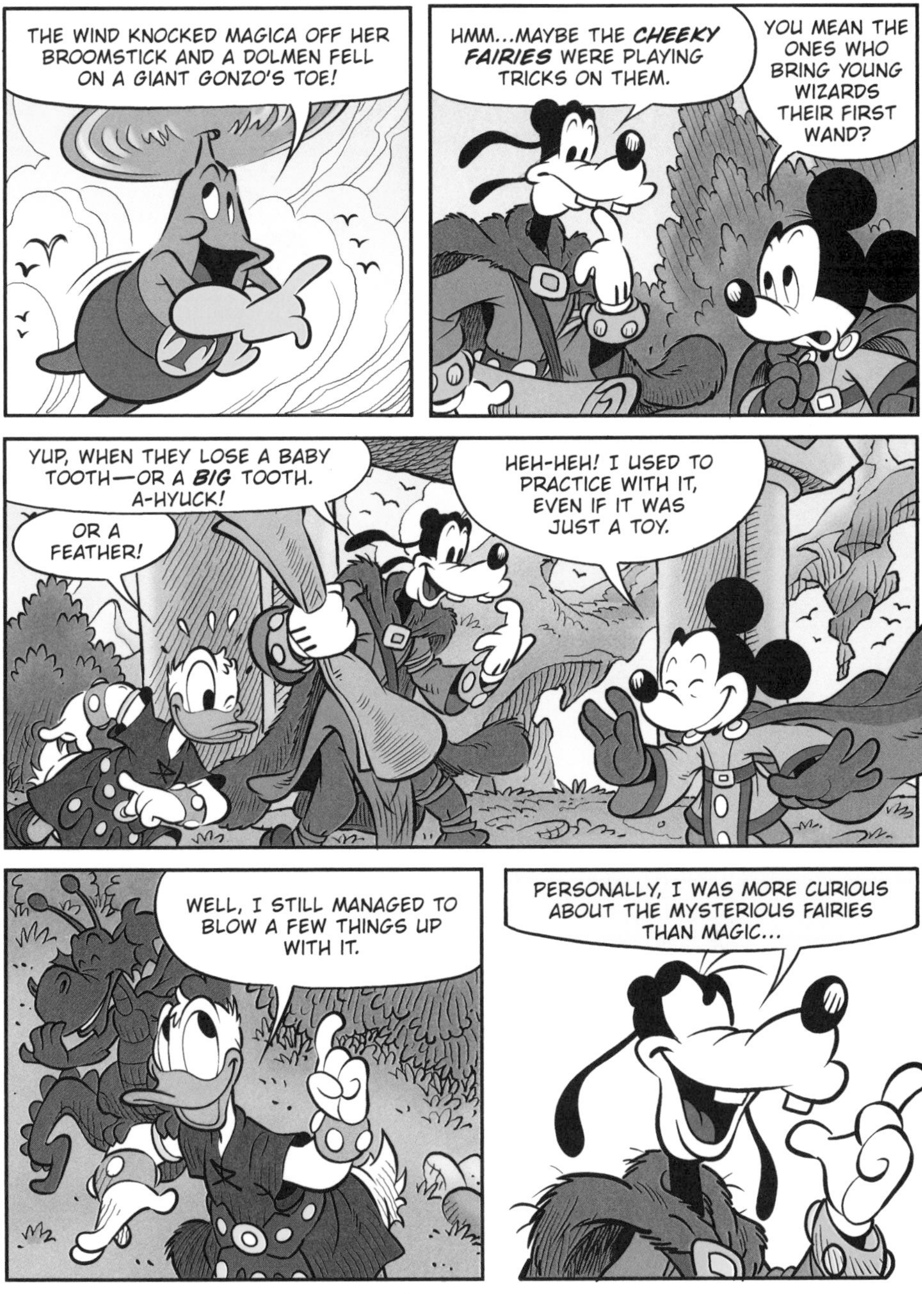
THE WIND KNOCKED MAGICA OFF HER BROOMSTICK AND A DOLMEN FELL ON A GIANT GONZO'S TOE!
HMM...MAYBE THE *CHEEKY FAIRIES* WERE PLAYING TRICKS ON THEM.
YOU MEAN THE ONES WHO BRING YOUNG WIZARDS THEIR FIRST WAND?
YUP, WHEN THEY LOSE A BABY TOOTH—OR A *BIG* TOOTH. A-HYUCK!
OR A FEATHER!
HEH-HEH! I USED TO PRACTICE WITH IT, EVEN IF IT WAS JUST A TOY.
WELL, I STILL MANAGED TO BLOW A FEW THINGS UP WITH IT.
PERSONALLY, I WAS MORE CURIOUS ABOUT THE MYSTERIOUS FAIRIES THAN MAGIC...

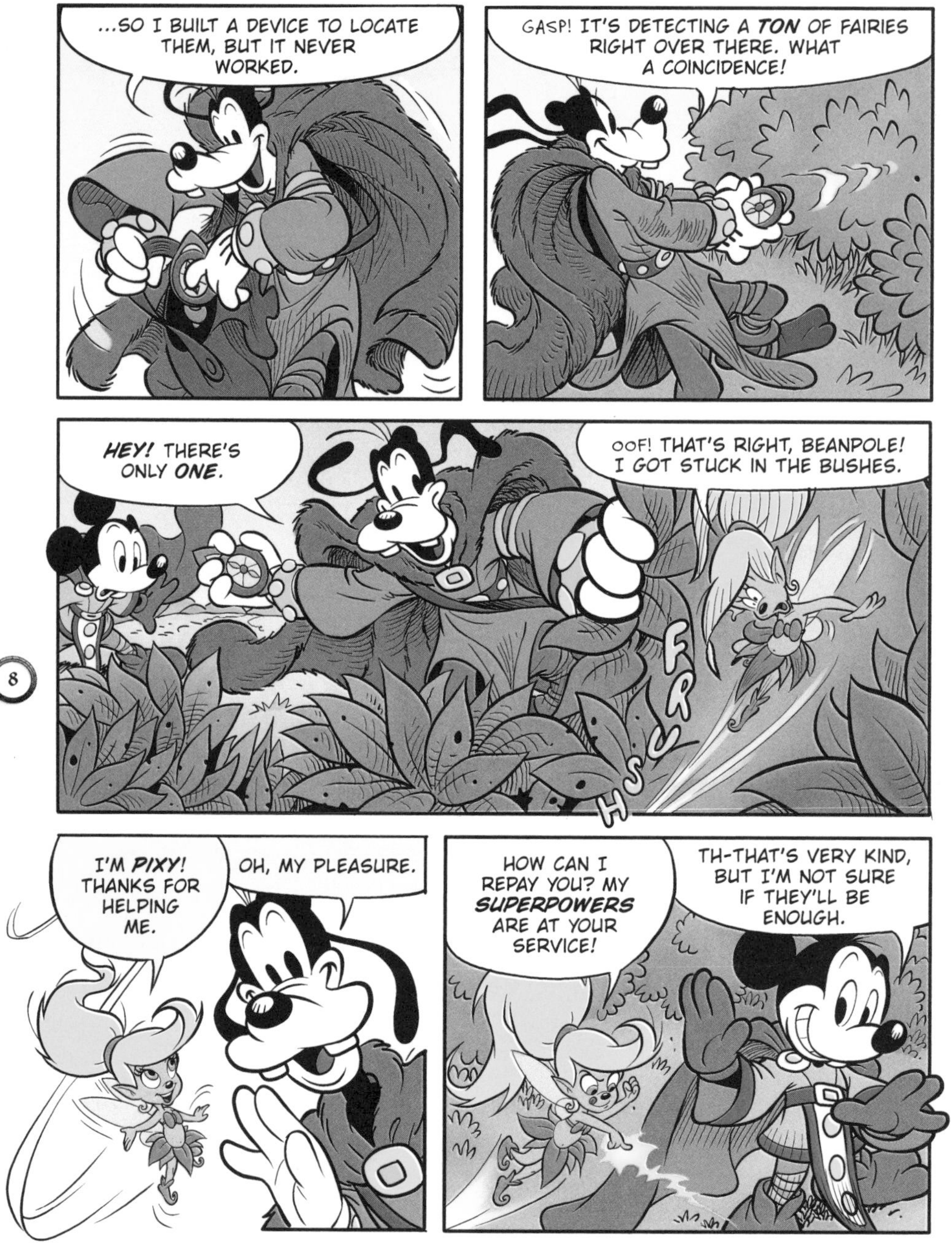

...SO I BUILT A DEVICE TO LOCATE THEM, BUT IT NEVER WORKED.
GASP! IT'S DETECTING A **TON** OF FAIRIES RIGHT OVER THERE. WHAT A COINCIDENCE!
HEY! THERE'S ONLY **ONE**.
OOF! THAT'S RIGHT, BEANPOLE! I GOT STUCK IN THE BUSHES.
FRSCHSH
I'M **PIXY**! THANKS FOR HELPING ME.
OH, MY PLEASURE.
HOW CAN I REPAY YOU? MY **SUPERPOWERS** ARE AT YOUR SERVICE!
TH-THAT'S VERY KIND, BUT I'M NOT SURE IF THEY'LL BE ENOUGH.

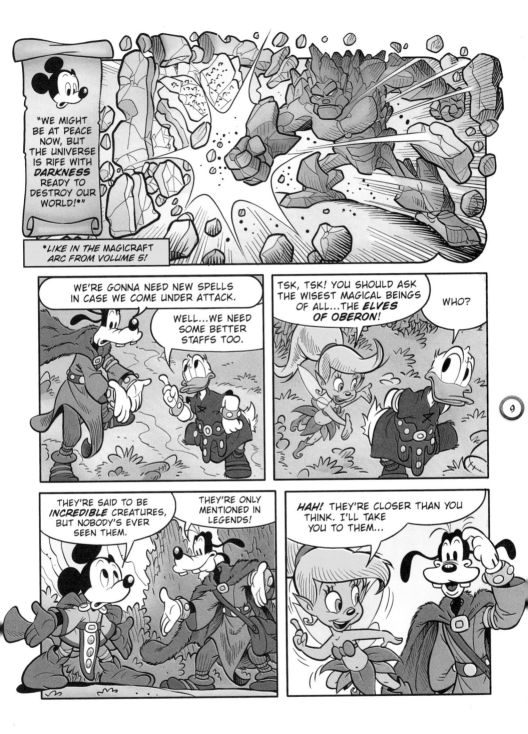

"WE MIGHT BE AT PEACE NOW, BUT THE UNIVERSE IS RIFE WITH *DARKNESS* READY TO DESTROY OUR WORLD!*"

*LIKE IN THE MAGICRAFT ARC FROM VOLUME 5!

WE'RE GONNA NEED NEW SPELLS IN CASE WE COME UNDER ATTACK.

WELL...WE NEED SOME BETTER STAFFS TOO.

TSK, TSK! YOU SHOULD ASK THE WISEST MAGICAL BEINGS OF ALL...THE *ELVES OF OBERON!*

WHO?

THEY'RE SAID TO BE *INCREDIBLE* CREATURES, BUT NOBODY'S EVER SEEN THEM.

THEY'RE ONLY MENTIONED IN LEGENDS!

HAH! THEY'RE CLOSER THAN YOU THINK. I'LL TAKE YOU TO THEM...

9

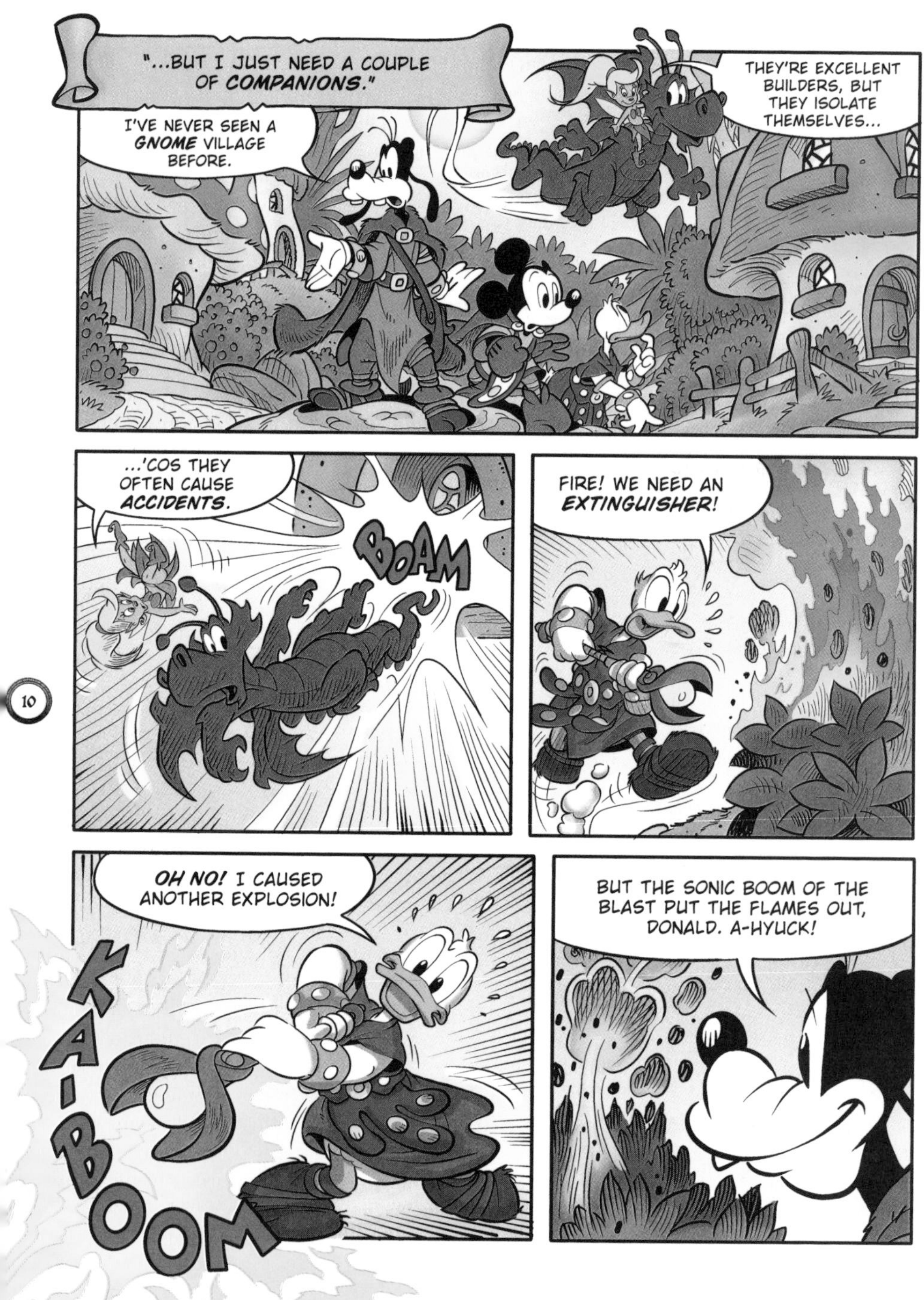
"...BUT I JUST NEED A COUPLE OF **COMPANIONS**."
I'VE NEVER SEEN A **GNOME** VILLAGE BEFORE.
THEY'RE EXCELLENT BUILDERS, BUT THEY ISOLATE THEMSELVES...
...'COS THEY OFTEN CAUSE **ACCIDENTS**.
BOAM
FIRE! WE NEED AN **EXTINGUISHER**!
OH NO! I CAUSED ANOTHER EXPLOSION!
KA-BOOM
BUT THE SONIC BOOM OF THE BLAST PUT THE FLAMES OUT, DONALD. A-HYUCK!

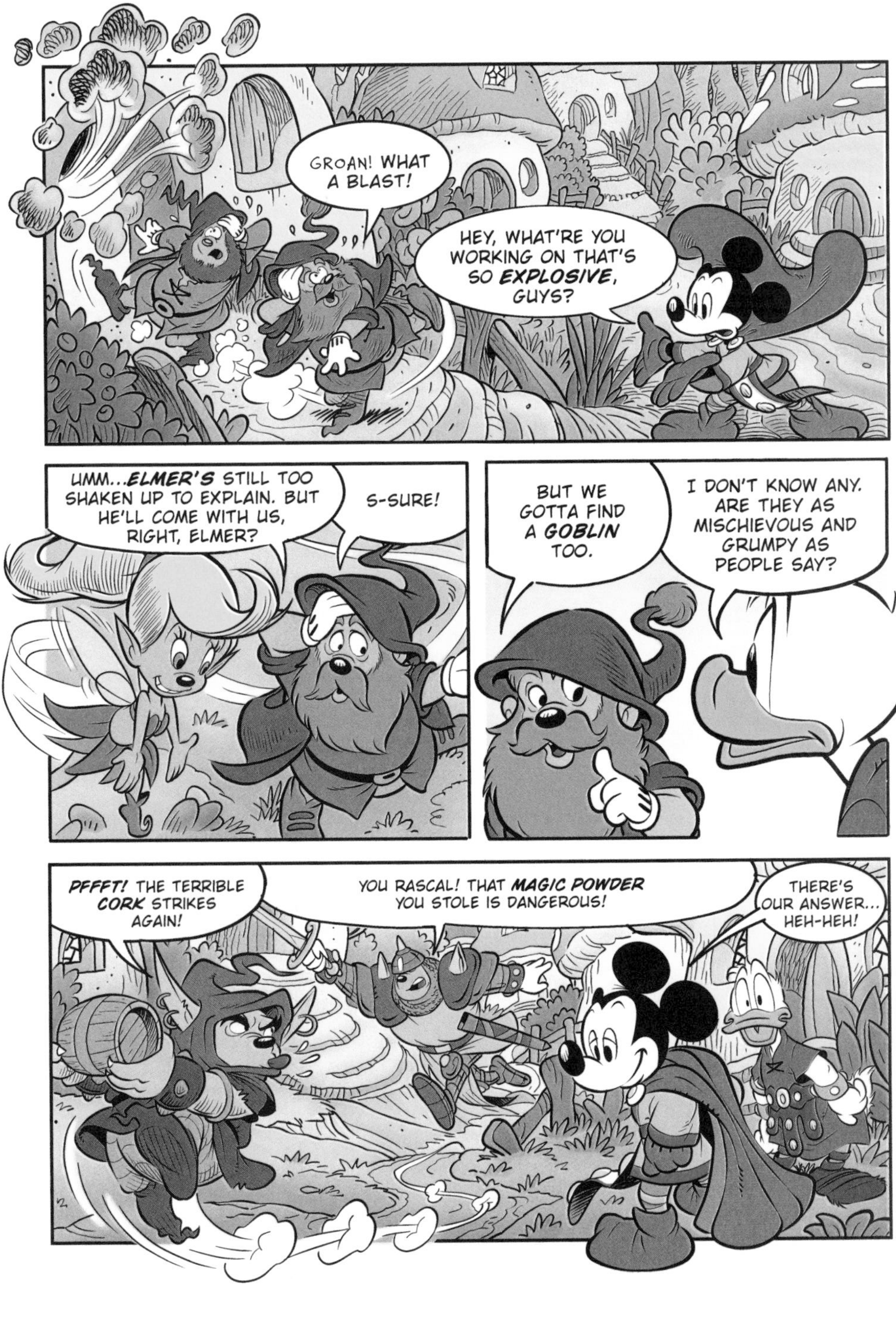
GROAN! WHAT A BLAST!
HEY, WHAT'RE YOU WORKING ON THAT'S SO EXPLOSIVE, GUYS?
UMM... ELMER'S STILL TOO SHAKEN UP TO EXPLAIN. BUT HE'LL COME WITH US, RIGHT, ELMER?
S-SURE!
BUT WE GOTTA FIND A GOBLIN TOO.
I DON'T KNOW ANY. ARE THEY AS MISCHIEVOUS AND GRUMPY AS PEOPLE SAY?
PFFFT! THE TERRIBLE CORK STRIKES AGAIN!
YOU RASCAL! THAT MAGIC POWDER YOU STOLE IS DANGEROUS!
THERE'S OUR ANSWER... HEH-HEH!

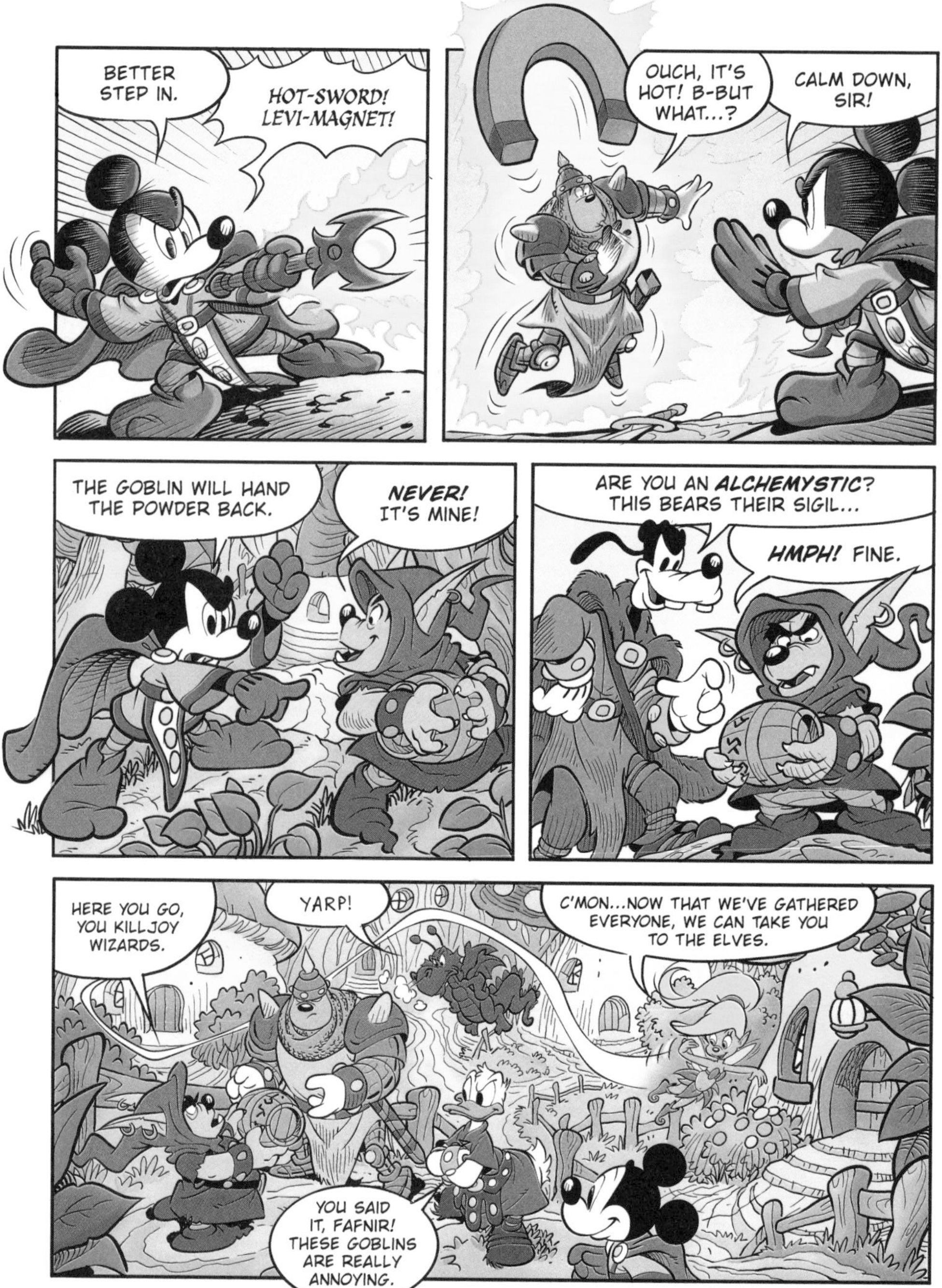
BETTER STEP IN.
HOT-SWORD! LEVI-MAGNET!
OUCH, IT'S HOT! B-BUT WHAT...?
CALM DOWN, SIR!
THE GOBLIN WILL HAND THE POWDER BACK.
NEVER! IT'S MINE!
ARE YOU AN ALCHEMYSTIC? THIS BEARS THEIR SIGIL...
HMPH! FINE.
HERE YOU GO, YOU KILLJOY WIZARDS.
YARP!
C'MON...NOW THAT WE'VE GATHERED EVERYONE, WE CAN TAKE YOU TO THE ELVES.
YOU SAID IT, FAFNIR! THESE GOBLINS ARE REALLY ANNOYING.

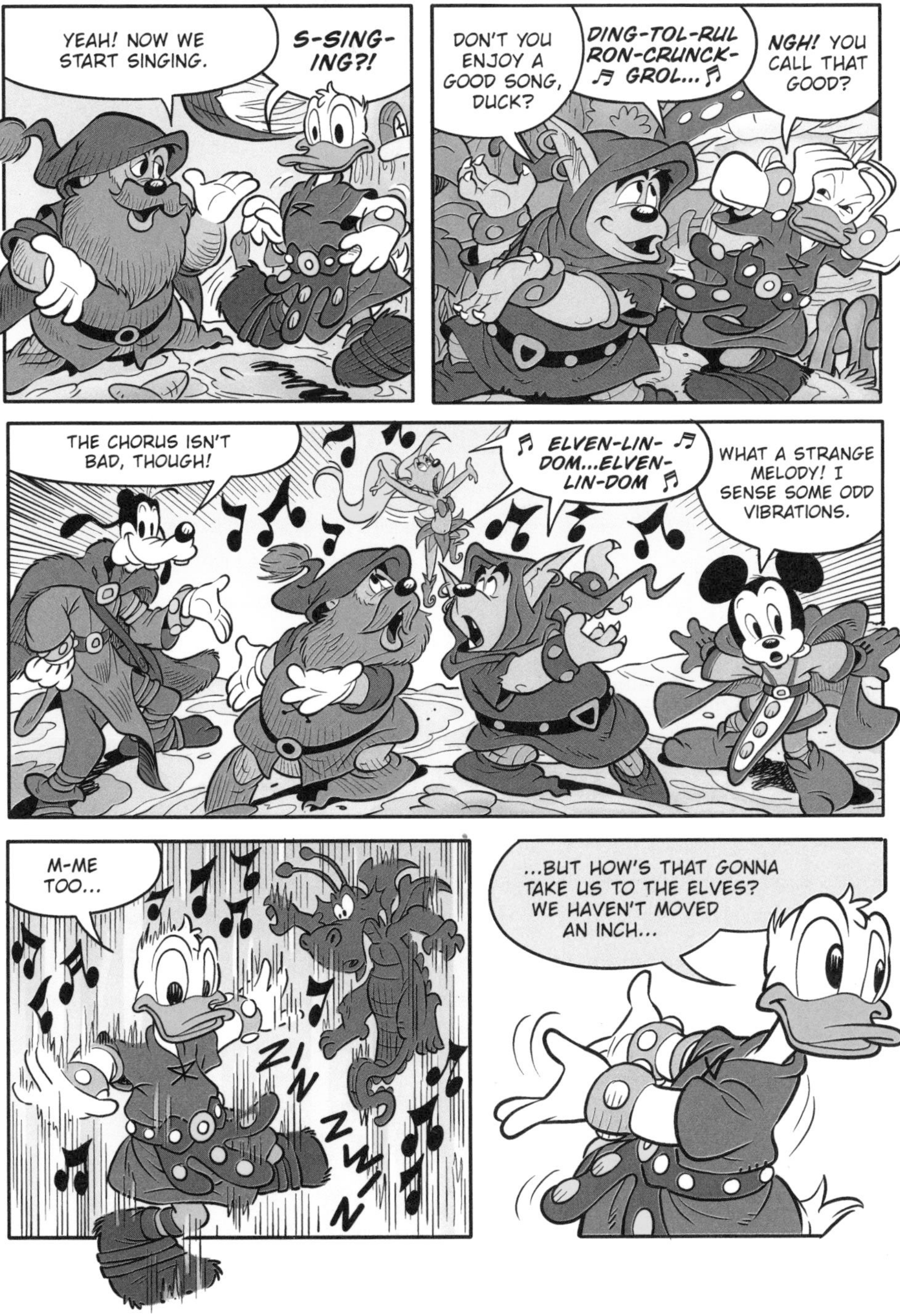
YEAH! NOW WE START SINGING.
S-SING-ING?!
DON'T YOU ENJOY A GOOD SONG, DUCK?
DING-TOL-RUL RON-CRUNCK-GROL...
NGH! YOU CALL THAT GOOD?
THE CHORUS ISN'T BAD, THOUGH!
ELVEN-LIN-DOM...ELVEN-LIN-DOM
WHAT A STRANGE MELODY! I SENSE SOME ODD VIBRATIONS.
M-ME TOO...
ZIN ZWIN
...BUT HOW'S THAT GONNA TAKE US TO THE ELVES? WE HAVEN'T MOVED AN INCH...

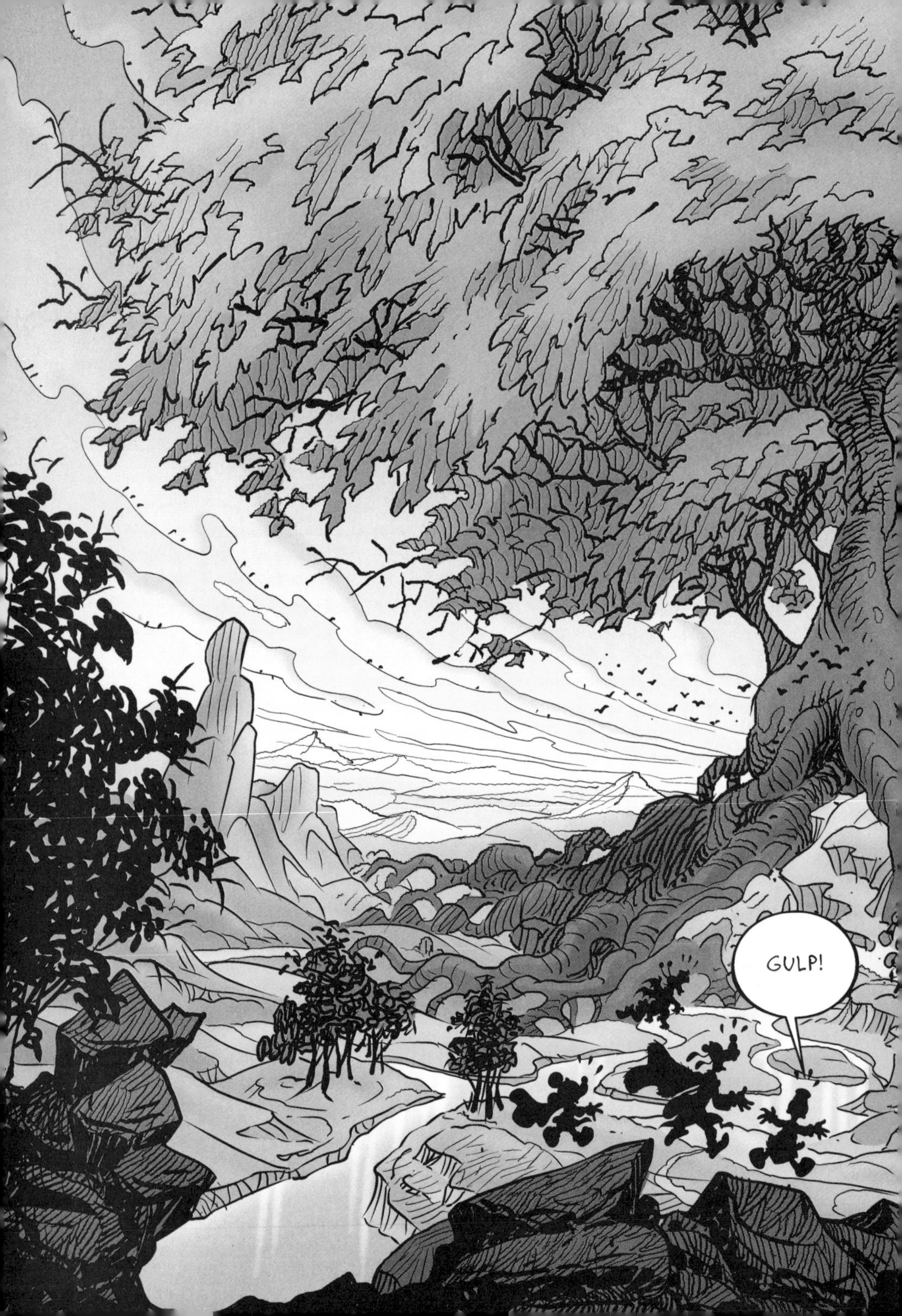
GULP!

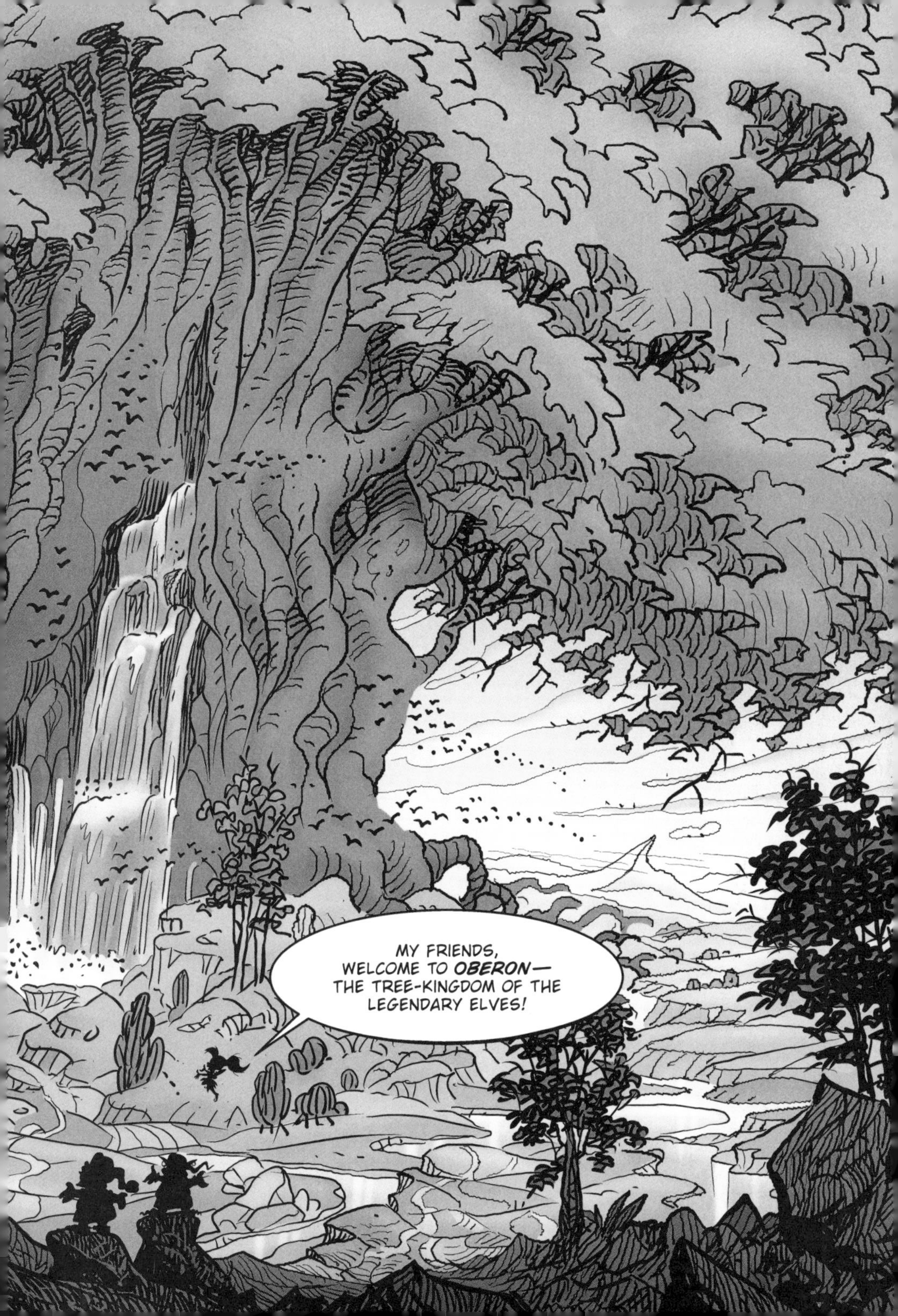
MY FRIENDS, WELCOME TO OBERON— THE TREE-KINGDOM OF THE LEGENDARY ELVES!

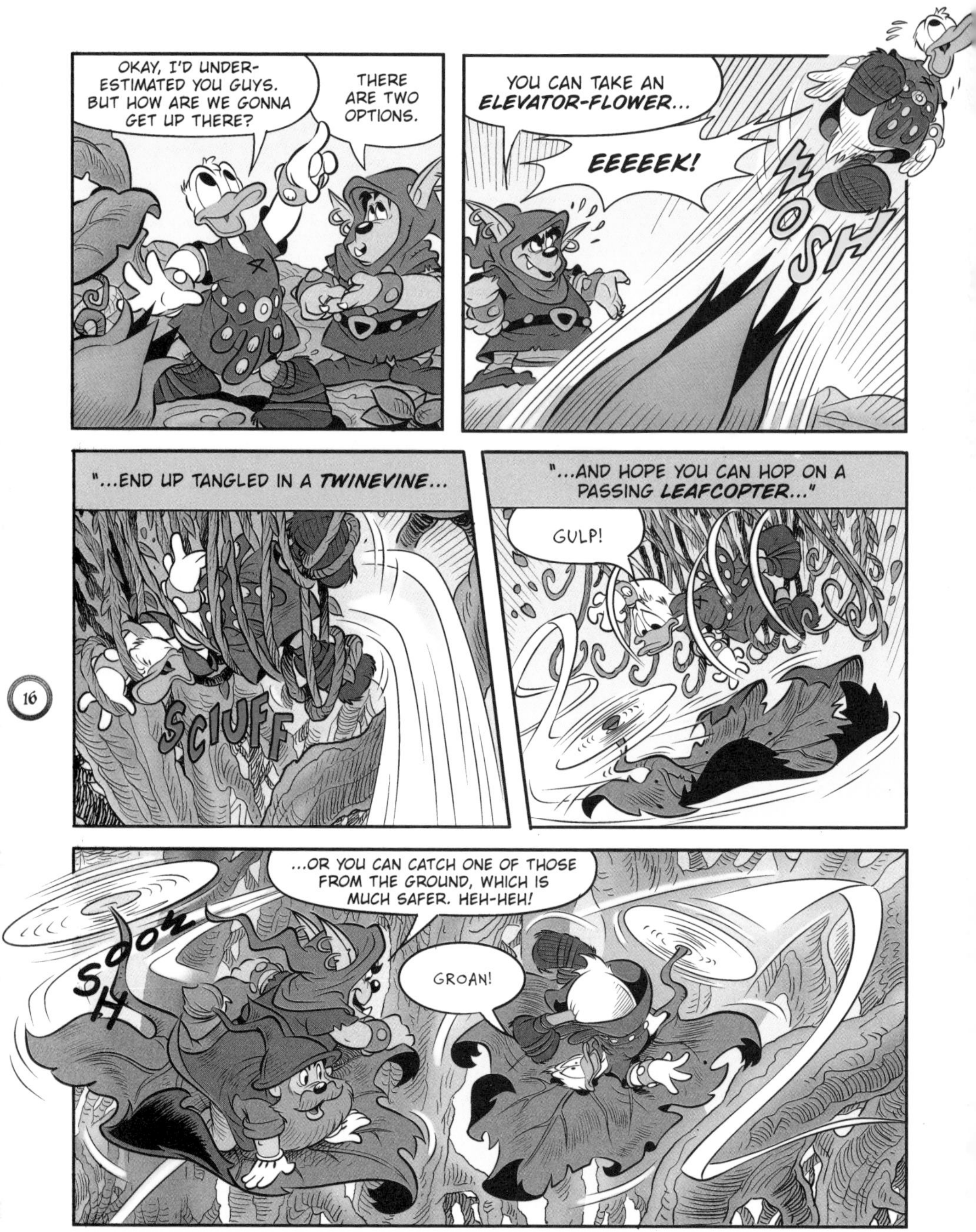

OKAY, I'D UNDER-ESTIMATED YOU GUYS. BUT HOW ARE WE GONNA GET UP THERE?
THERE ARE TWO OPTIONS.
YOU CAN TAKE AN ELEVATOR-FLOWER...
EEEEEK!
WOOSH
"...END UP TANGLED IN A TWINEVINE...
SCIUFF
"...AND HOPE YOU CAN HOP ON A PASSING LEAFCOPTER..."
GULP!
...OR YOU CAN CATCH ONE OF THOSE FROM THE GROUND, WHICH IS MUCH SAFER. HEH-HEH!
SWOOOSH
GROAN!

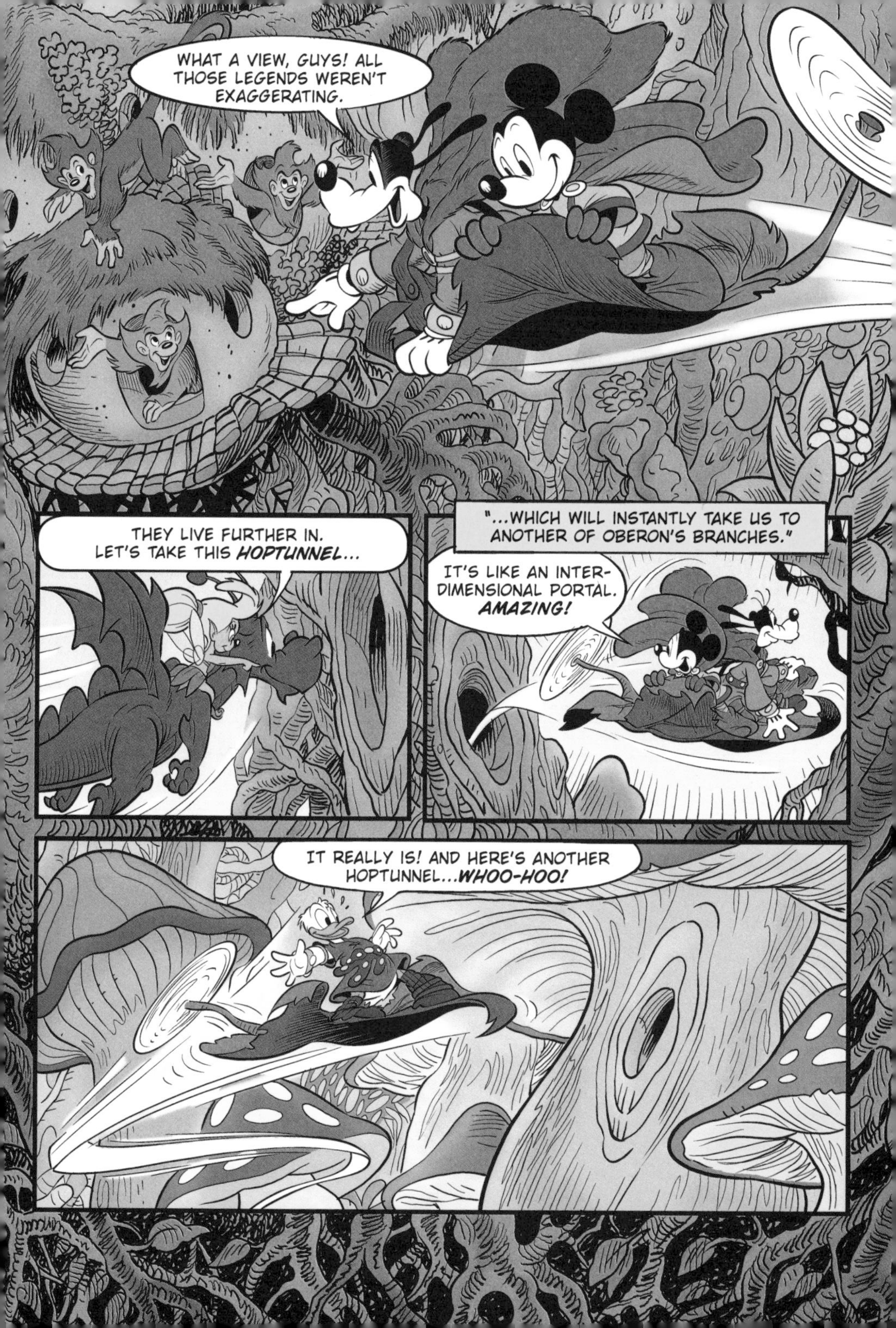
WHAT A VIEW, GUYS! ALL THOSE LEGENDS WEREN'T EXAGGERATING.
THEY LIVE FURTHER IN. LET'S TAKE THIS *HOPTUNNEL*...
"...WHICH WILL INSTANTLY TAKE US TO ANOTHER OF OBERON'S BRANCHES."
IT'S LIKE AN INTER-DIMENSIONAL PORTAL. *AMAZING!*
IT REALLY IS! AND HERE'S ANOTHER HOPTUNNEL...*WHOO-HOO!*

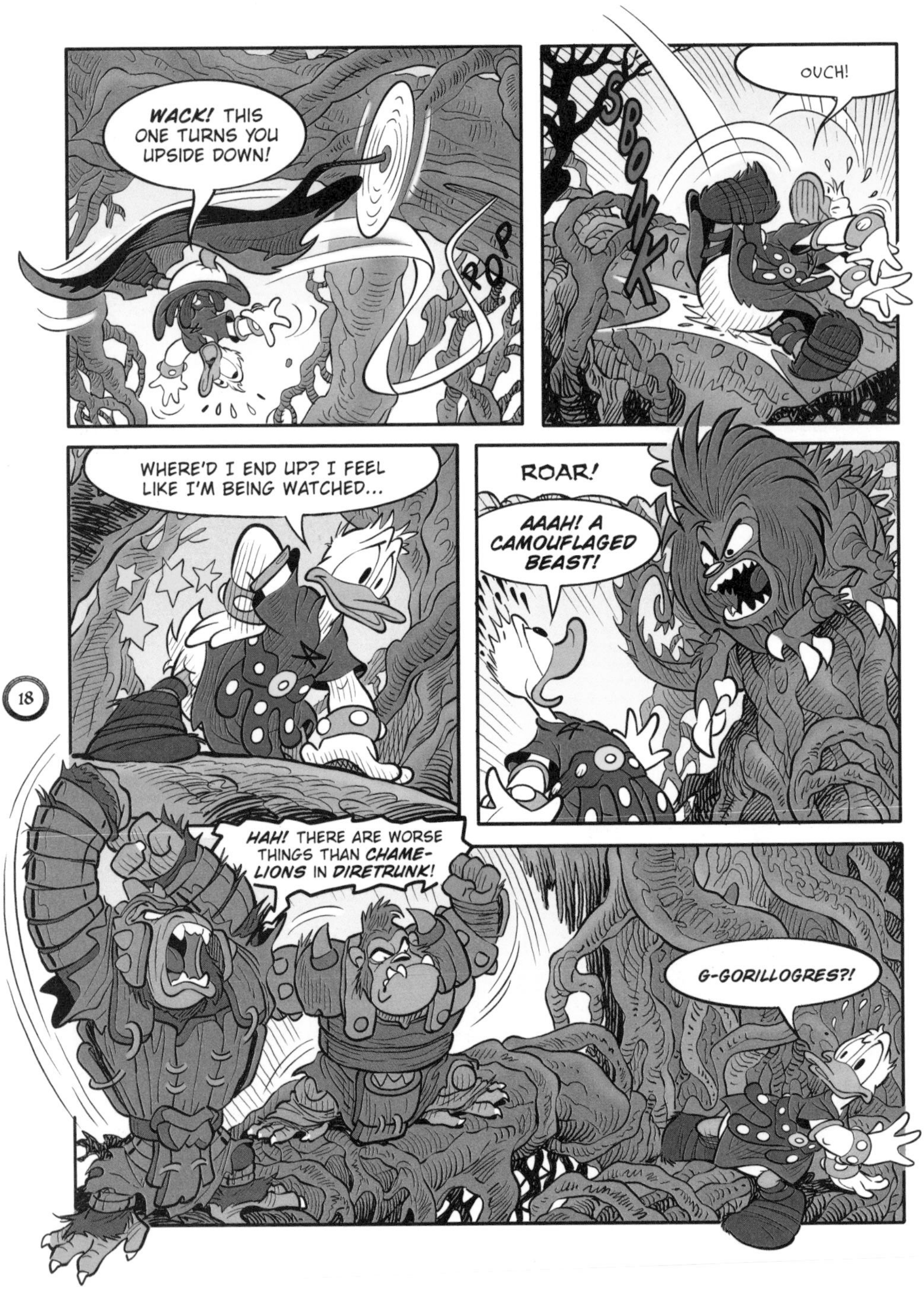
WACK! THIS ONE TURNS YOU UPSIDE DOWN!
POP
SBONK
OUCH!
WHERE'D I END UP? I FEEL LIKE I'M BEING WATCHED...
ROAR!
AAAH! A CAMOUFLAGED BEAST!
HAH! THERE ARE WORSE THINGS THAN CHAME-LIONS IN DIRETRUNK!
G-GORILLOGRES?!

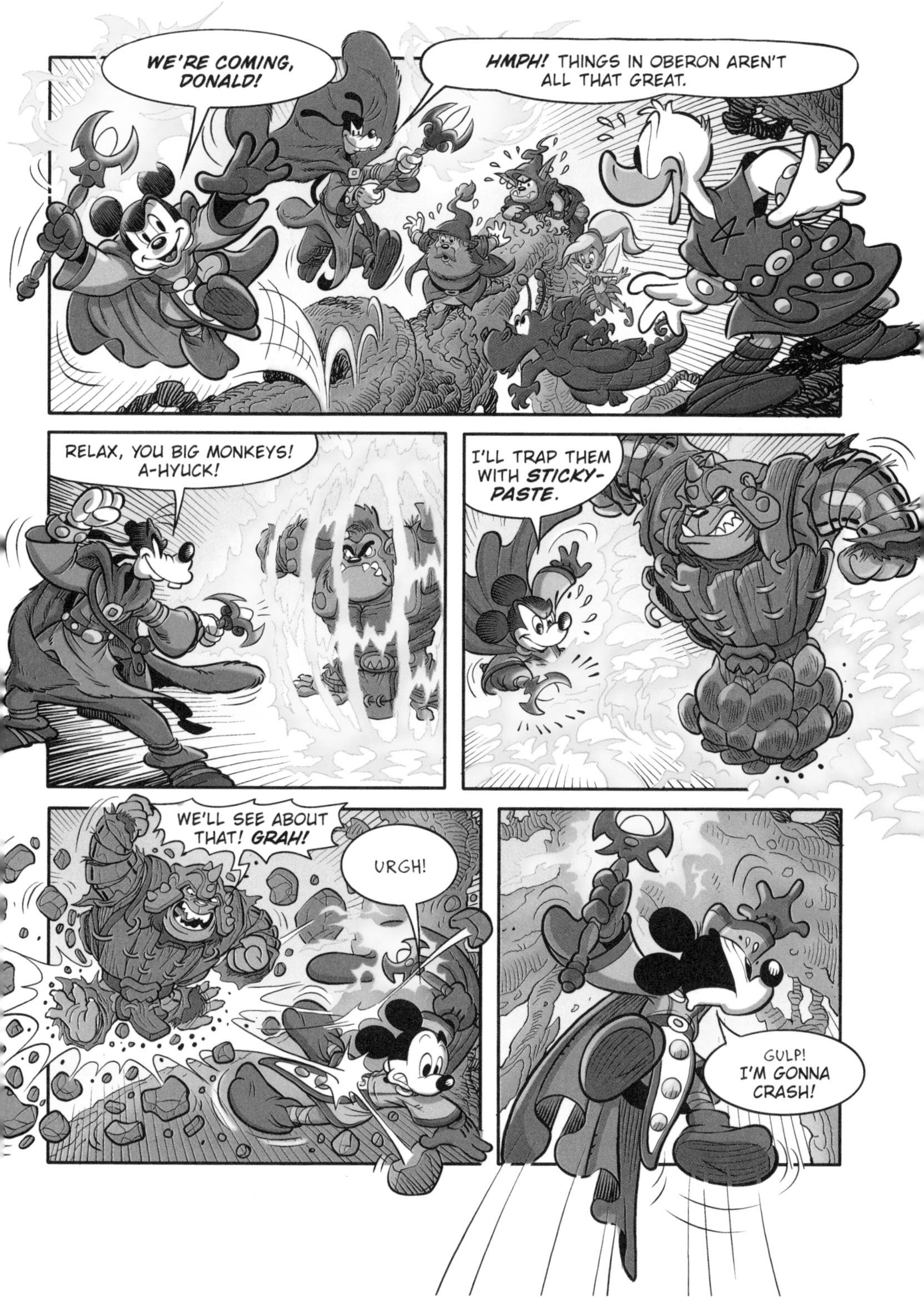
WE'RE COMING, DONALD!
HMPH! THINGS IN OBERON AREN'T ALL THAT GREAT.
RELAX, YOU BIG MONKEYS! A-HYUCK!
I'LL TRAP THEM WITH STICKY-PASTE.
WE'LL SEE ABOUT THAT! GRAH!
URGH!
GULP! I'M GONNA CRASH!

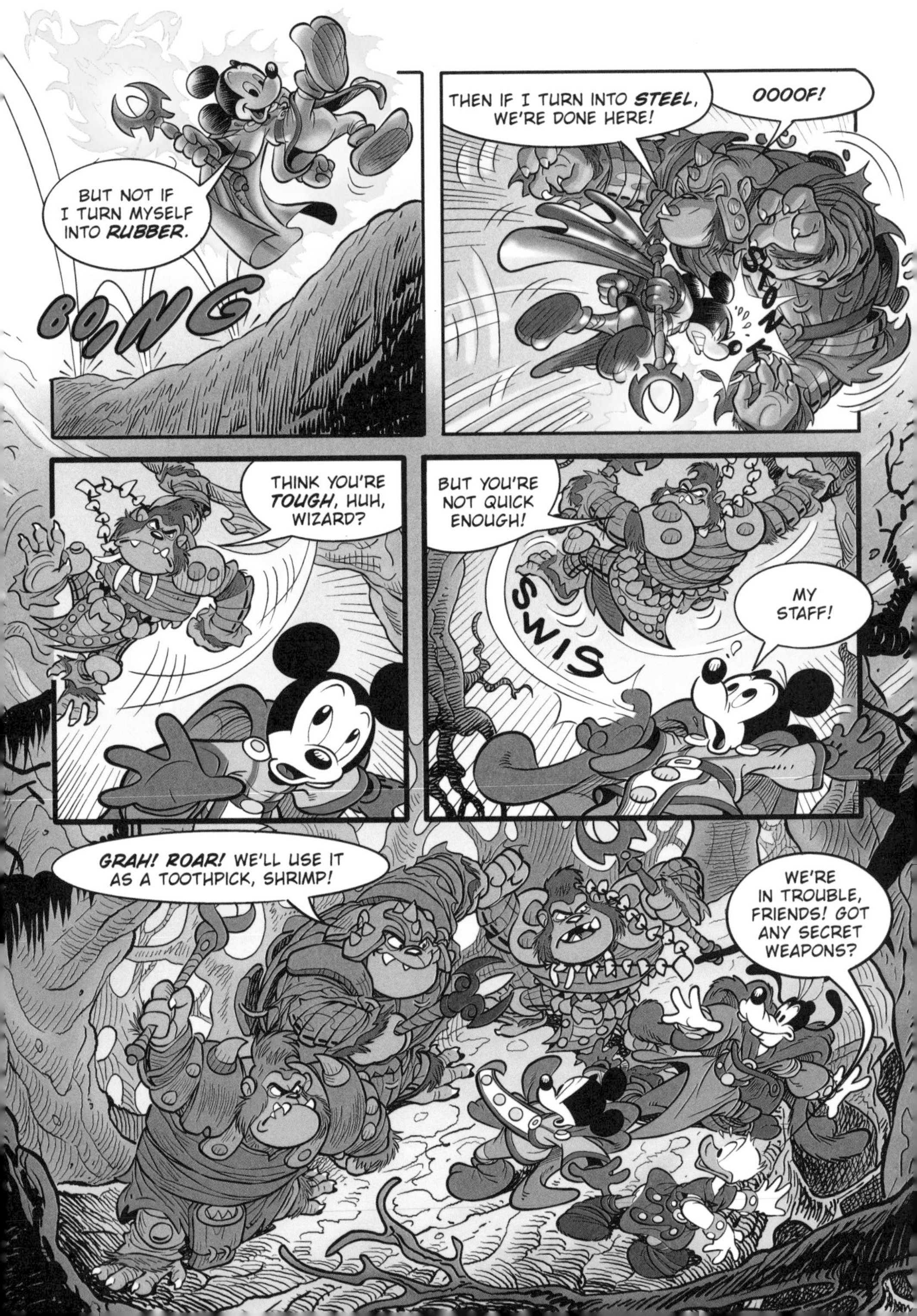
BUT NOT IF I TURN MYSELF INTO RUBBER.
BOING
THEN IF I TURN INTO STEEL, WE'RE DONE HERE!
OOOOF!
STONK
THINK YOU'RE TOUGH, HUH, WIZARD?
BUT YOU'RE NOT QUICK ENOUGH!
SWIS
MY STAFF!
GRAH! ROAR! WE'LL USE IT AS A TOOTHPICK, SHRIMP!
WE'RE IN TROUBLE, FRIENDS! GOT ANY SECRET WEAPONS?

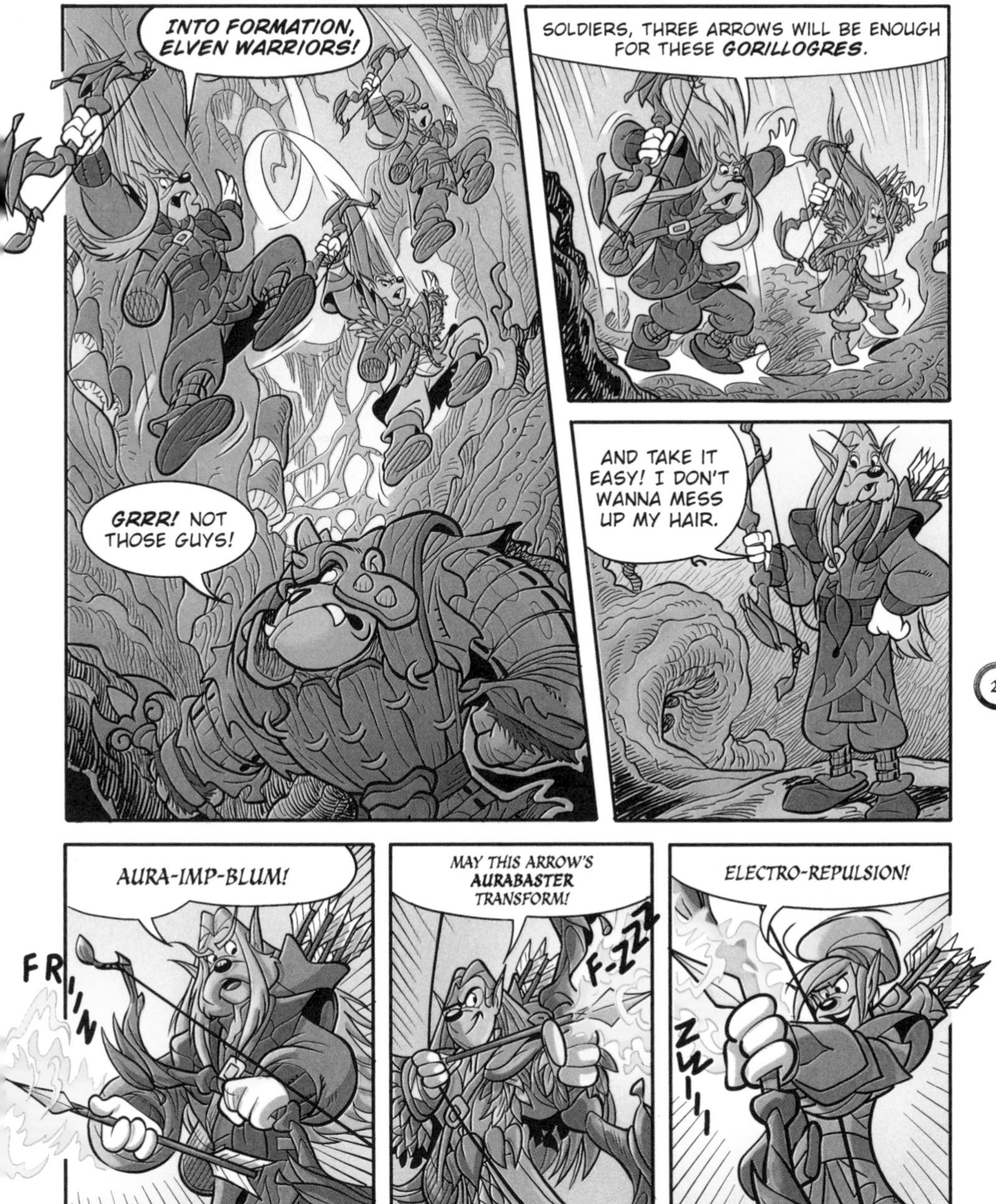
INTO FORMATION, ELVEN WARRIORS!
GRRR! NOT THOSE GUYS!
SOLDIERS, THREE ARROWS WILL BE ENOUGH FOR THESE GORILLOGRES.
AND TAKE IT EASY! I DON'T WANNA MESS UP MY HAIR.
AURA-IMP-BLUM!
FRIIIN
MAY THIS ARROW'S AURABASTER TRANSFORM!
F-ZZZ
ELECTRO-REPULSION!
ZWIIII

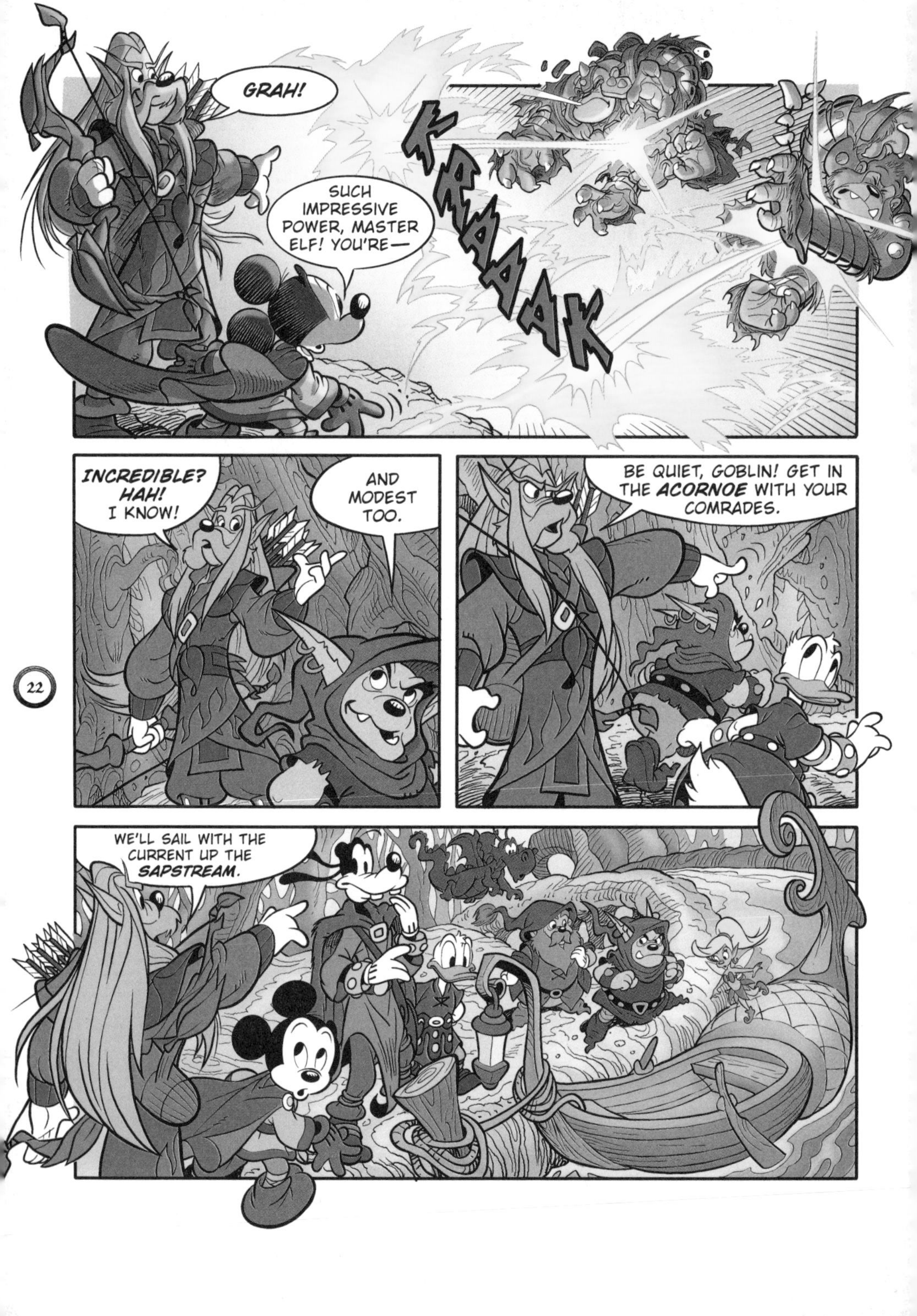

GRAH!
SUCH IMPRESSIVE POWER, MASTER ELF! YOU'RE—
KRAAAAK
INCREDIBLE? HAH! I KNOW!
AND MODEST TOO.
BE QUIET, GOBLIN! GET IN THE ACORNOE WITH YOUR COMRADES.
WE'LL SAIL WITH THE CURRENT UP THE SAPSTREAM.

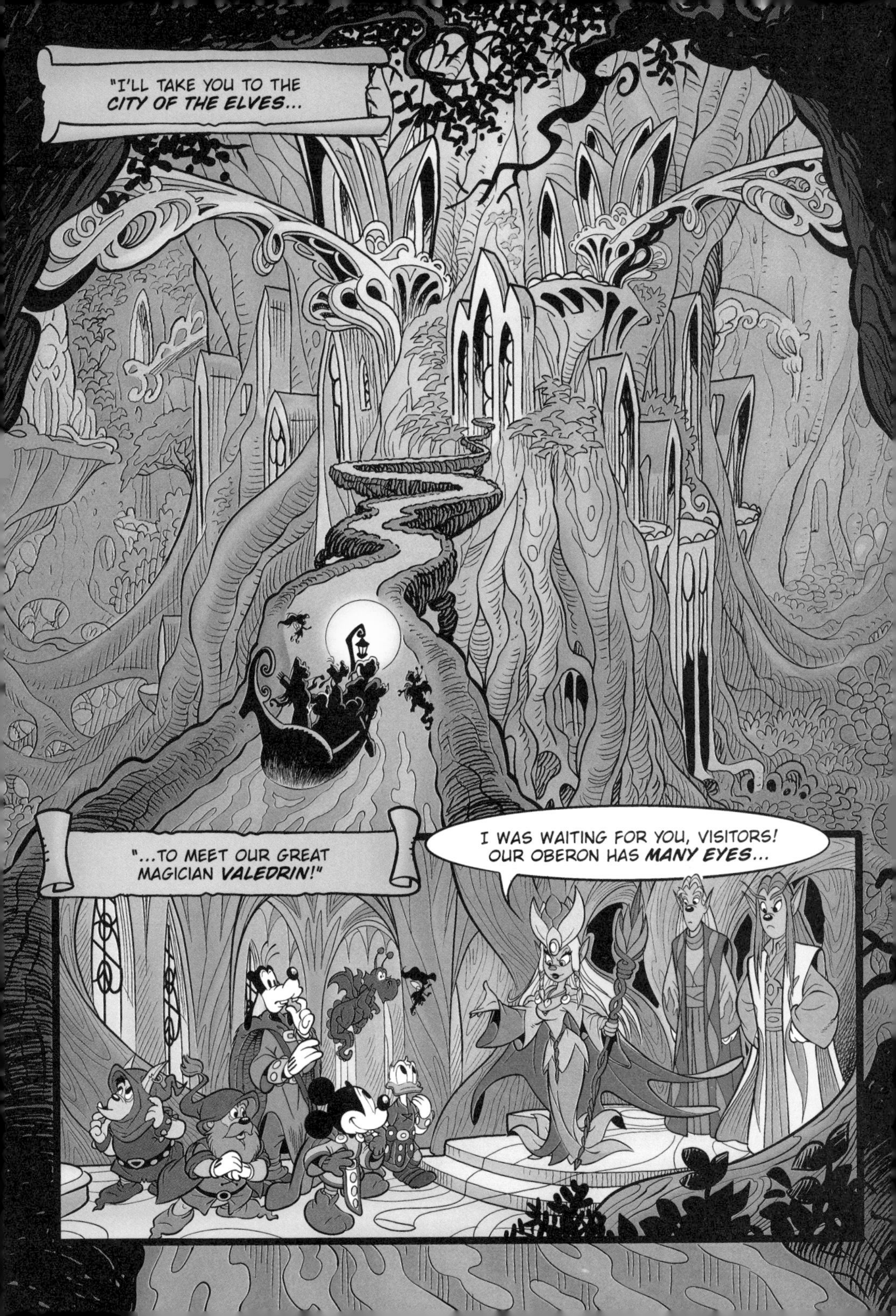
"I'LL TAKE YOU TO THE *CITY OF THE ELVES*...
"...TO MEET OUR GREAT MAGICIAN *VALEDRIN*!"
I WAS WAITING FOR YOU, VISITORS! OUR OBERON HAS *MANY EYES*...

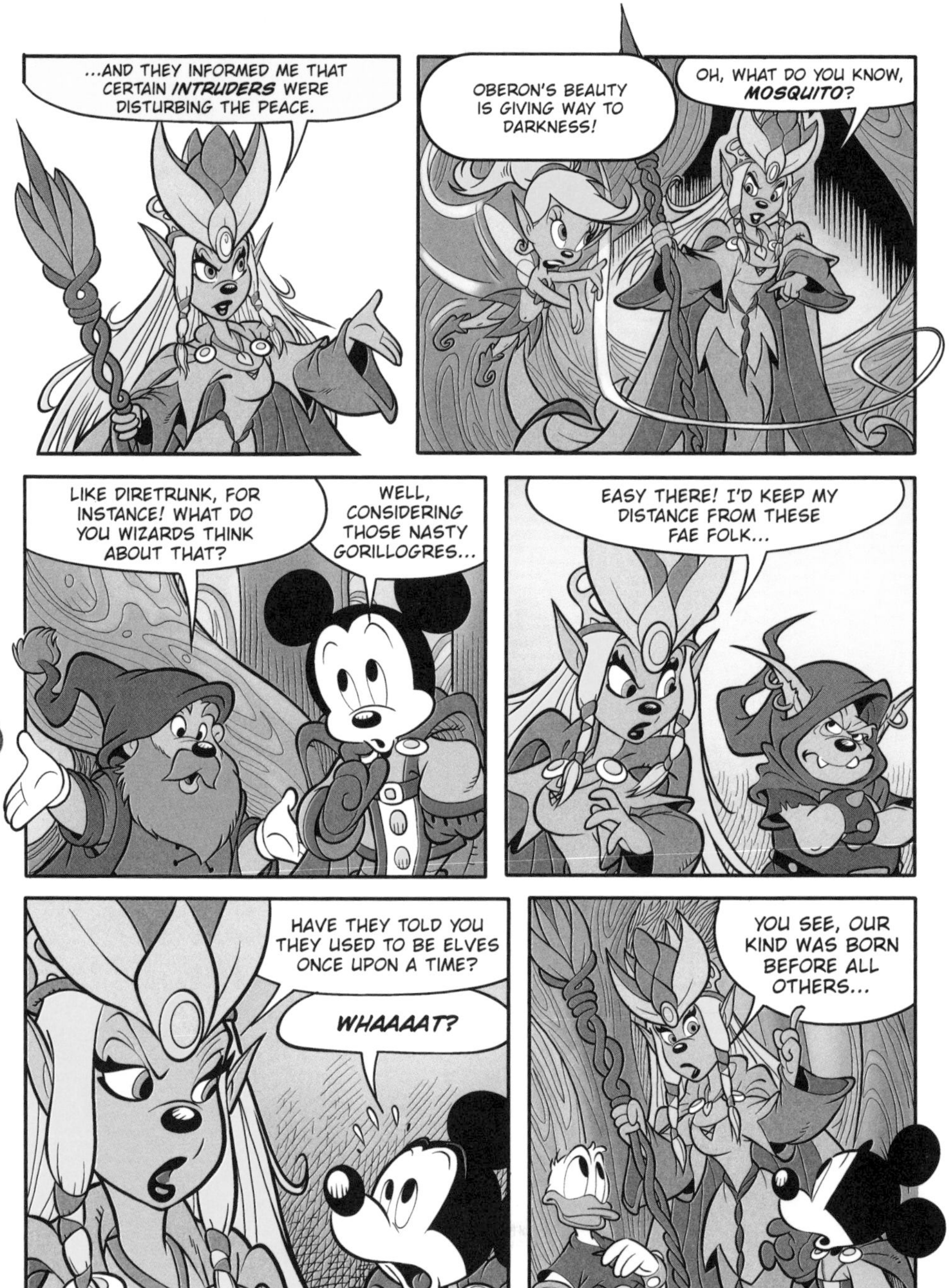

...AND THEY INFORMED ME THAT CERTAIN **INTRUDERS** WERE DISTURBING THE PEACE.
OBERON'S BEAUTY IS GIVING WAY TO DARKNESS!
OH, WHAT DO YOU KNOW, **MOSQUITO**?
LIKE DIRETRUNK, FOR INSTANCE! WHAT DO YOU WIZARDS THINK ABOUT THAT?
WELL, CONSIDERING THOSE NASTY GORILLOGRES...
EASY THERE! I'D KEEP MY DISTANCE FROM THESE FAE FOLK...
HAVE THEY TOLD YOU THEY USED TO BE ELVES ONCE UPON A TIME?
WHAAAAT?
YOU SEE, OUR KIND WAS BORN BEFORE ALL OTHERS...

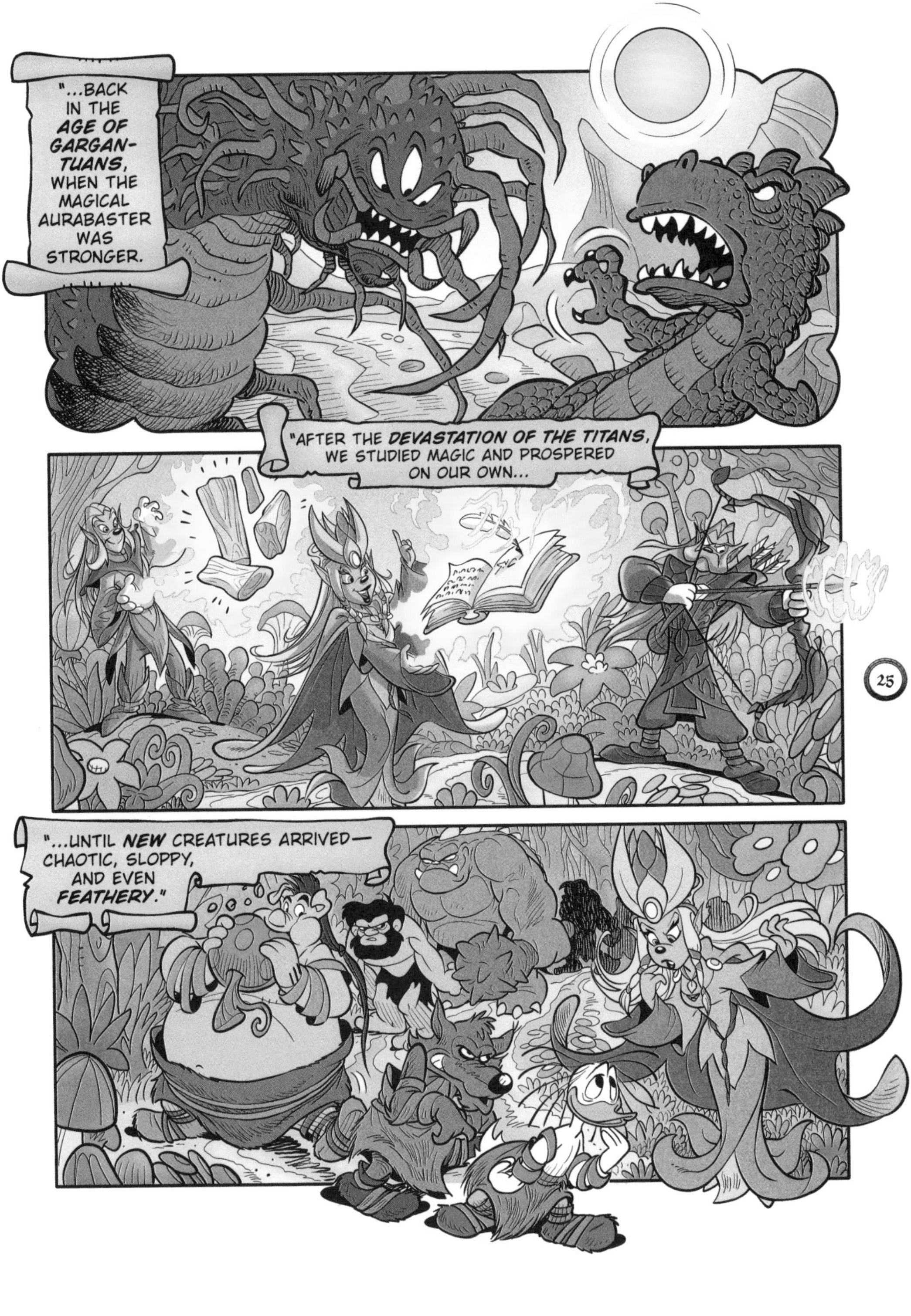
"...BACK IN THE AGE OF GARGAN-TUANS, WHEN THE MAGICAL AURABASTER WAS STRONGER.
"AFTER THE DEVASTATION OF THE TITANS, WE STUDIED MAGIC AND PROSPERED ON OUR OWN...
"...UNTIL NEW CREATURES ARRIVED— CHAOTIC, SLOPPY, AND EVEN FEATHERY."

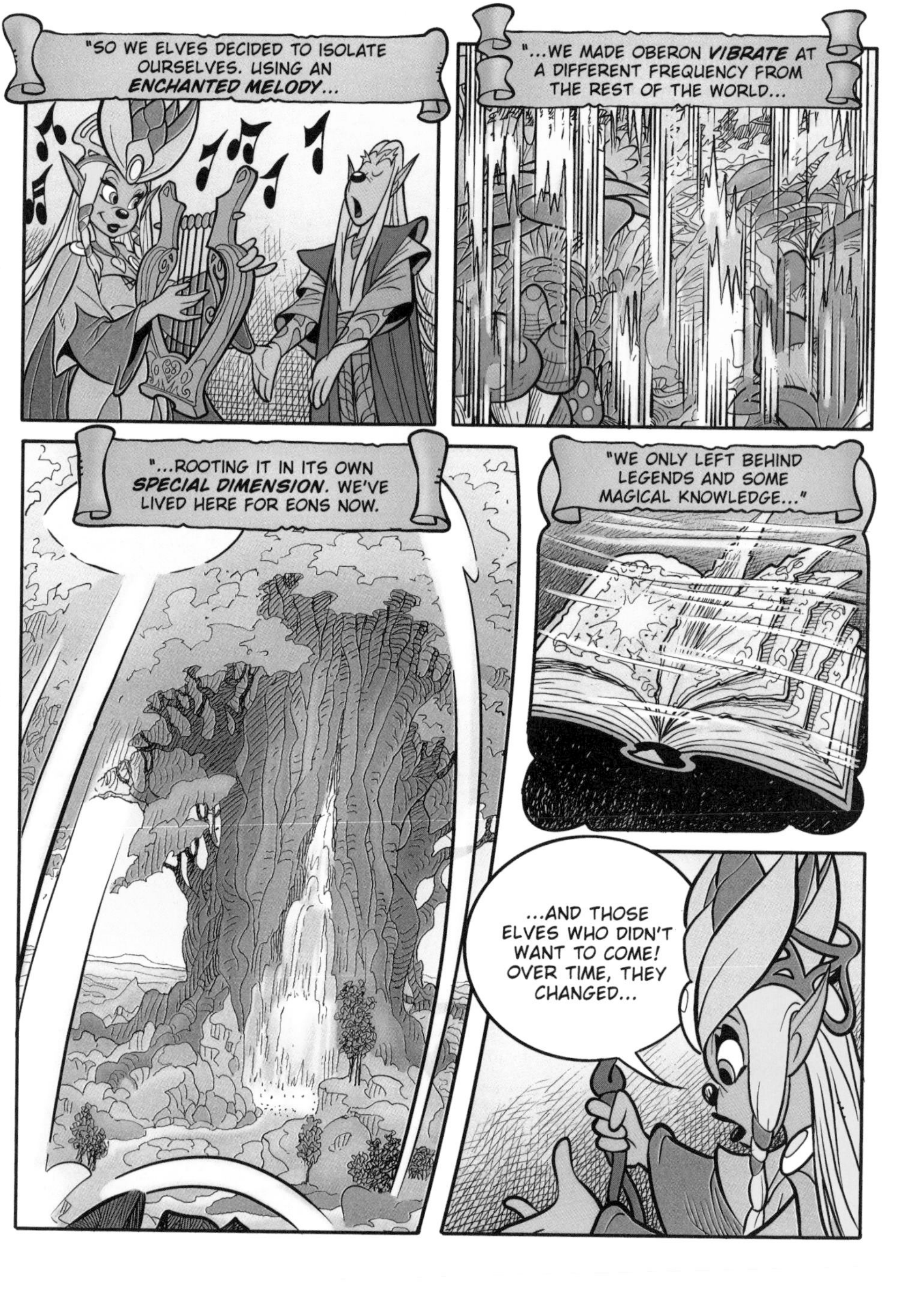
"SO WE ELVES DECIDED TO ISOLATE OURSELVES. USING AN ENCHANTED MELODY...
"...WE MADE OBERON VIBRATE AT A DIFFERENT FREQUENCY FROM THE REST OF THE WORLD...
"...ROOTING IT IN ITS OWN SPECIAL DIMENSION. WE'VE LIVED HERE FOR EONS NOW.
"WE ONLY LEFT BEHIND LEGENDS AND SOME MAGICAL KNOWLEDGE..."
...AND THOSE ELVES WHO DIDN'T WANT TO COME! OVER TIME, THEY CHANGED...

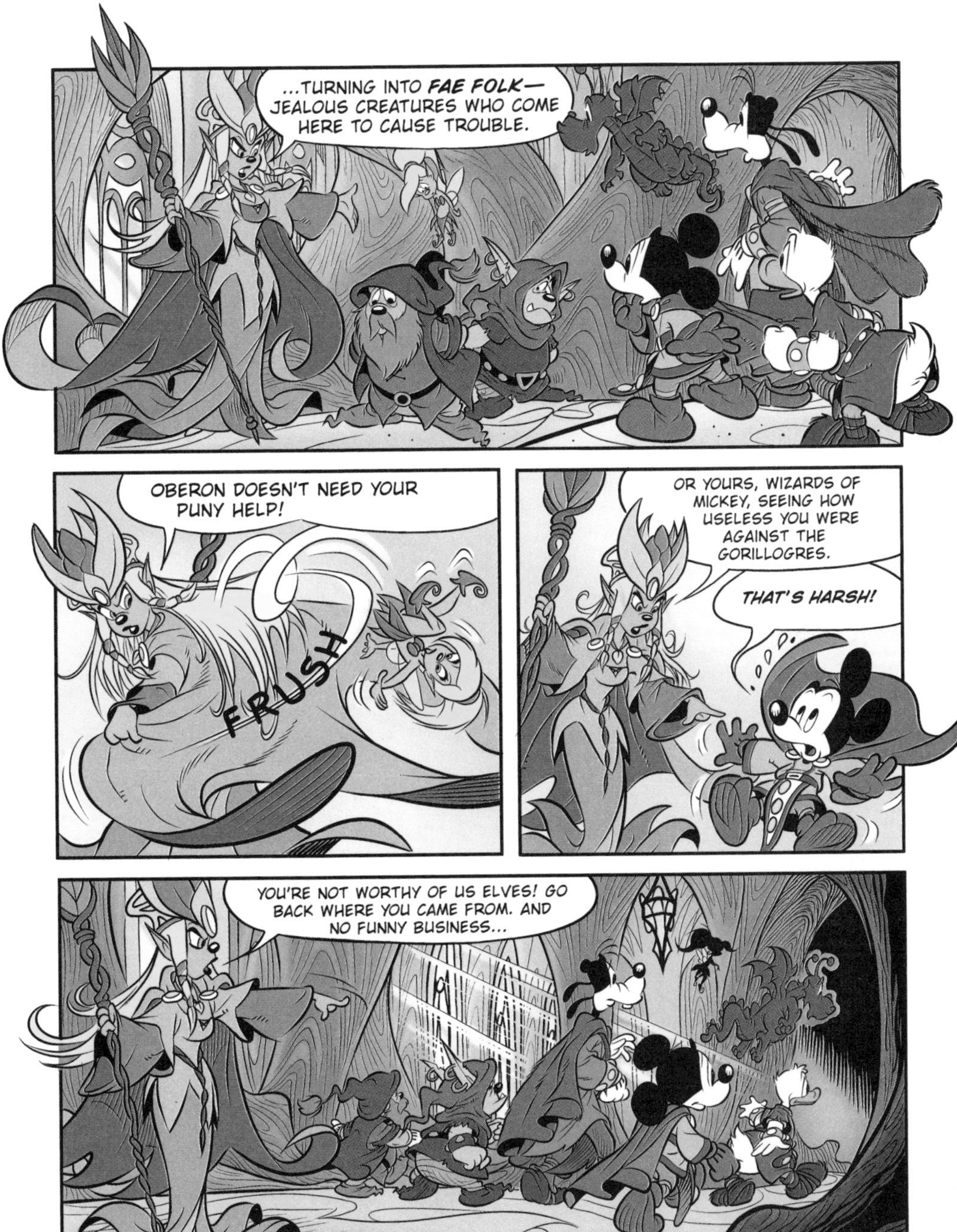
...TURNING INTO FAE FOLK—JEALOUS CREATURES WHO COME HERE TO CAUSE TROUBLE.
OBERON DOESN'T NEED YOUR PUNY HELP!
FRUSH
OR YOURS, WIZARDS OF MICKEY, SEEING HOW USELESS YOU WERE AGAINST THE GORILLOGRES.
THAT'S HARSH!
YOU'RE NOT WORTHY OF US ELVES! GO BACK WHERE YOU CAME FROM. AND NO FUNNY BUSINESS...

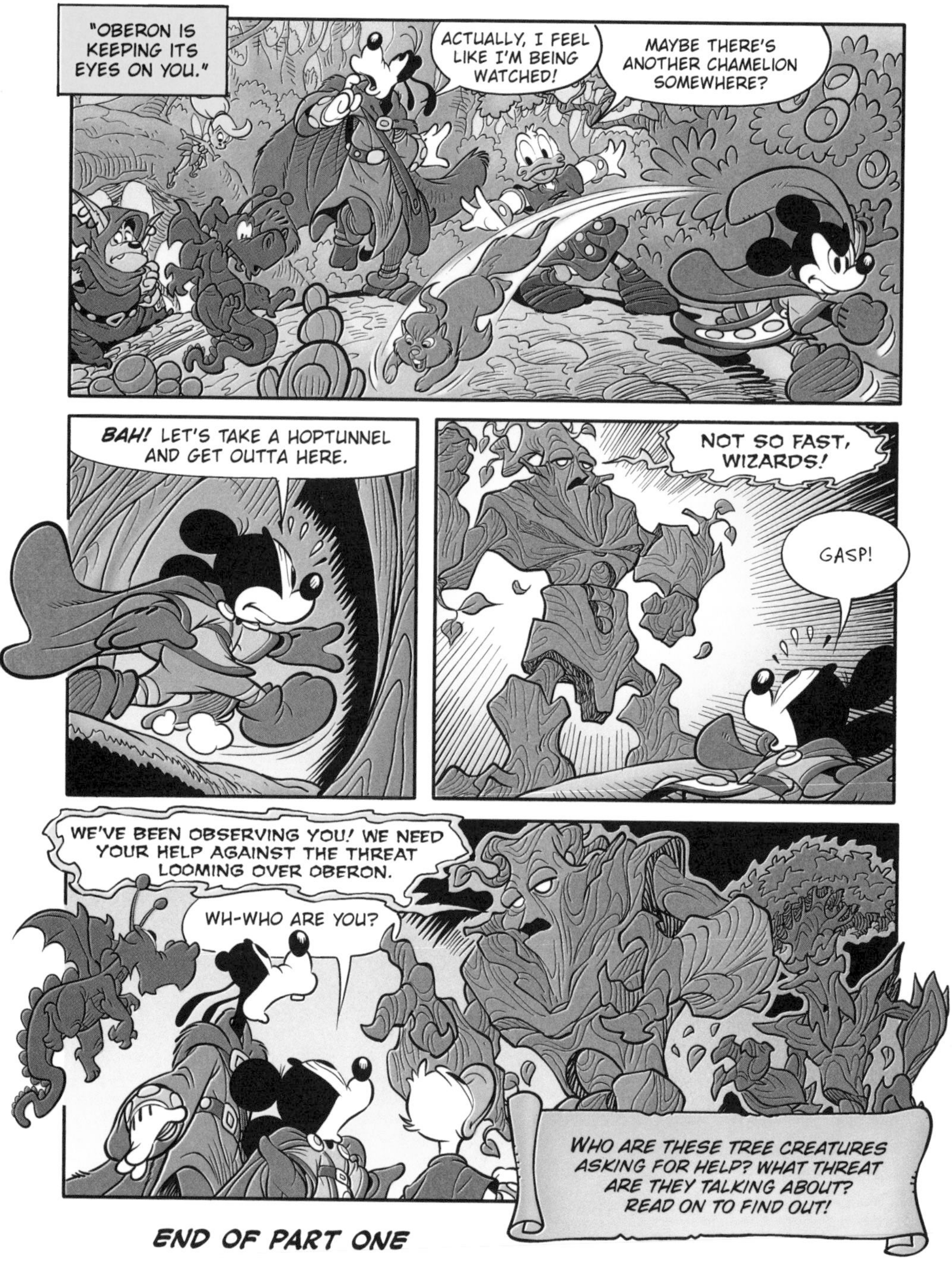
"OBERON IS KEEPING ITS EYES ON YOU."
ACTUALLY, I FEEL LIKE I'M BEING WATCHED!
MAYBE THERE'S ANOTHER CHAMELION SOMEWHERE?
BAH! LET'S TAKE A HOPTUNNEL AND GET OUTTA HERE.
NOT SO FAST, WIZARDS!
GASP!
WE'VE BEEN OBSERVING YOU! WE NEED YOUR HELP AGAINST THE THREAT LOOMING OVER OBERON.
WH-WHO ARE YOU?
WHO ARE THESE TREE CREATURES ASKING FOR HELP? WHAT THREAT ARE THEY TALKING ABOUT? READ ON TO FIND OUT!

END OF PART ONE

Wizards of Mickey

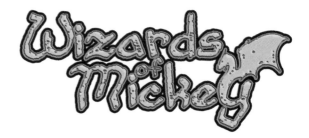

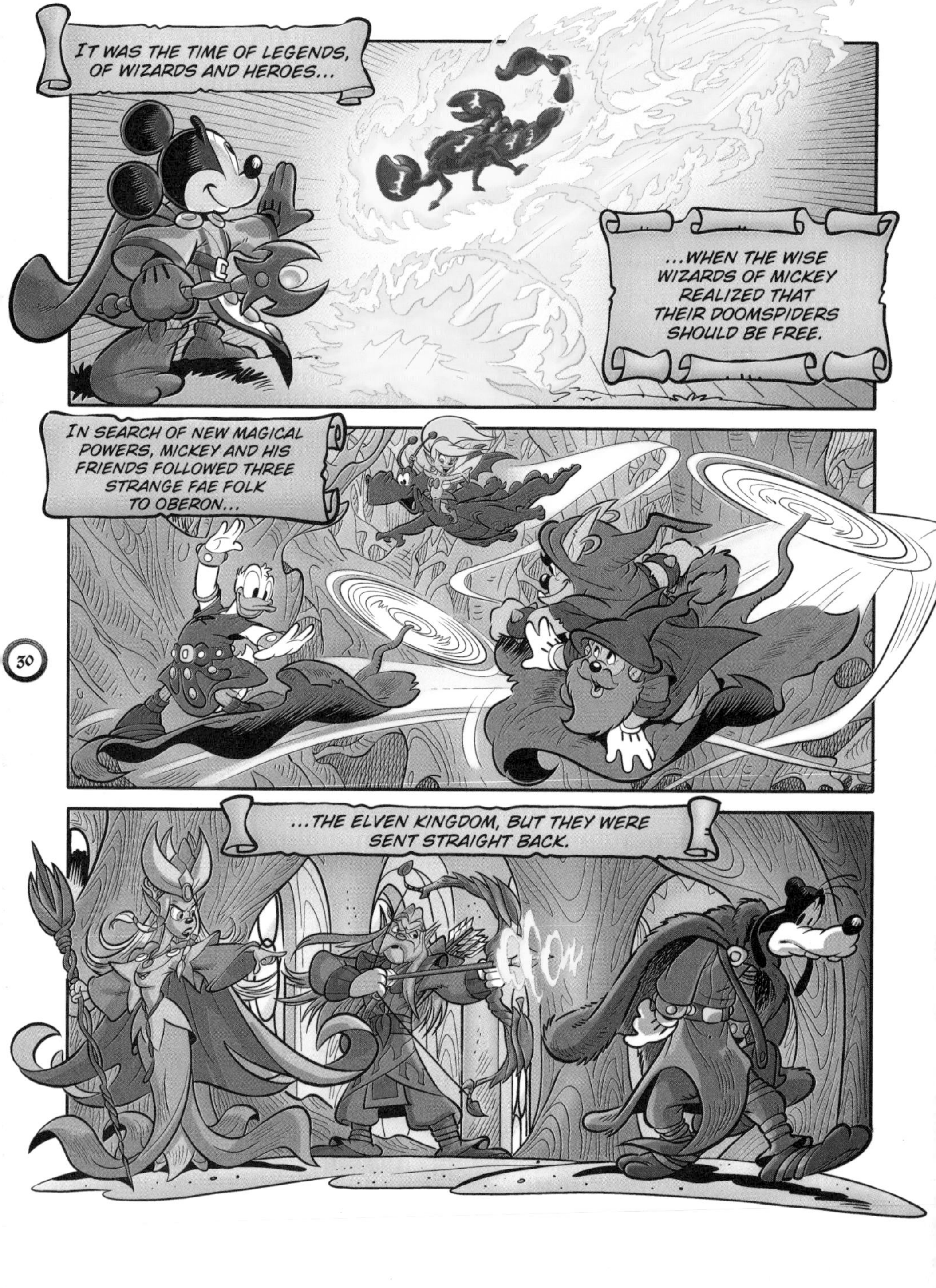

IT WAS THE TIME OF LEGENDS, OF WIZARDS AND HEROES...
...WHEN THE WISE WIZARDS OF MICKEY REALIZED THAT THEIR DOOMSPIDERS SHOULD BE FREE.
IN SEARCH OF NEW MAGICAL POWERS, MICKEY AND HIS FRIENDS FOLLOWED THREE STRANGE FAE FOLK TO OBERON...
...THE ELVEN KINGDOM, BUT THEY WERE SENT STRAIGHT BACK.

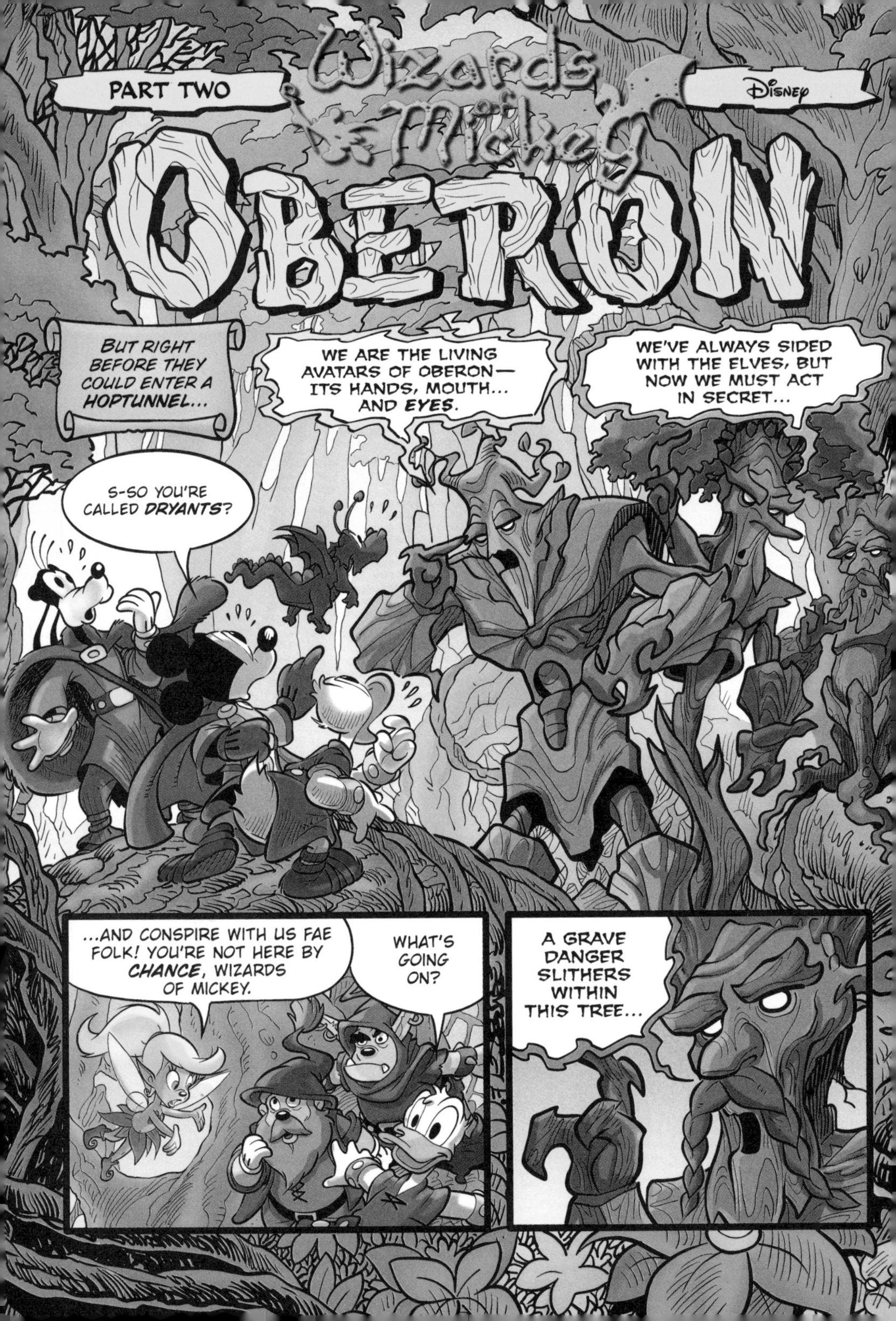
PART TWO
Wizards of Mickey
Disney
OBERON
BUT RIGHT BEFORE THEY COULD ENTER A HOPTUNNEL...
WE ARE THE LIVING AVATARS OF OBERON— ITS HANDS, MOUTH... AND EYES.
WE'VE ALWAYS SIDED WITH THE ELVES, BUT NOW WE MUST ACT IN SECRET...
S-SO YOU'RE CALLED DRYANTS?
...AND CONSPIRE WITH US FAE FOLK! YOU'RE NOT HERE BY CHANCE, WIZARDS OF MICKEY.
WHAT'S GOING ON?
A GRAVE DANGER SLITHERS WITHIN THIS TREE...

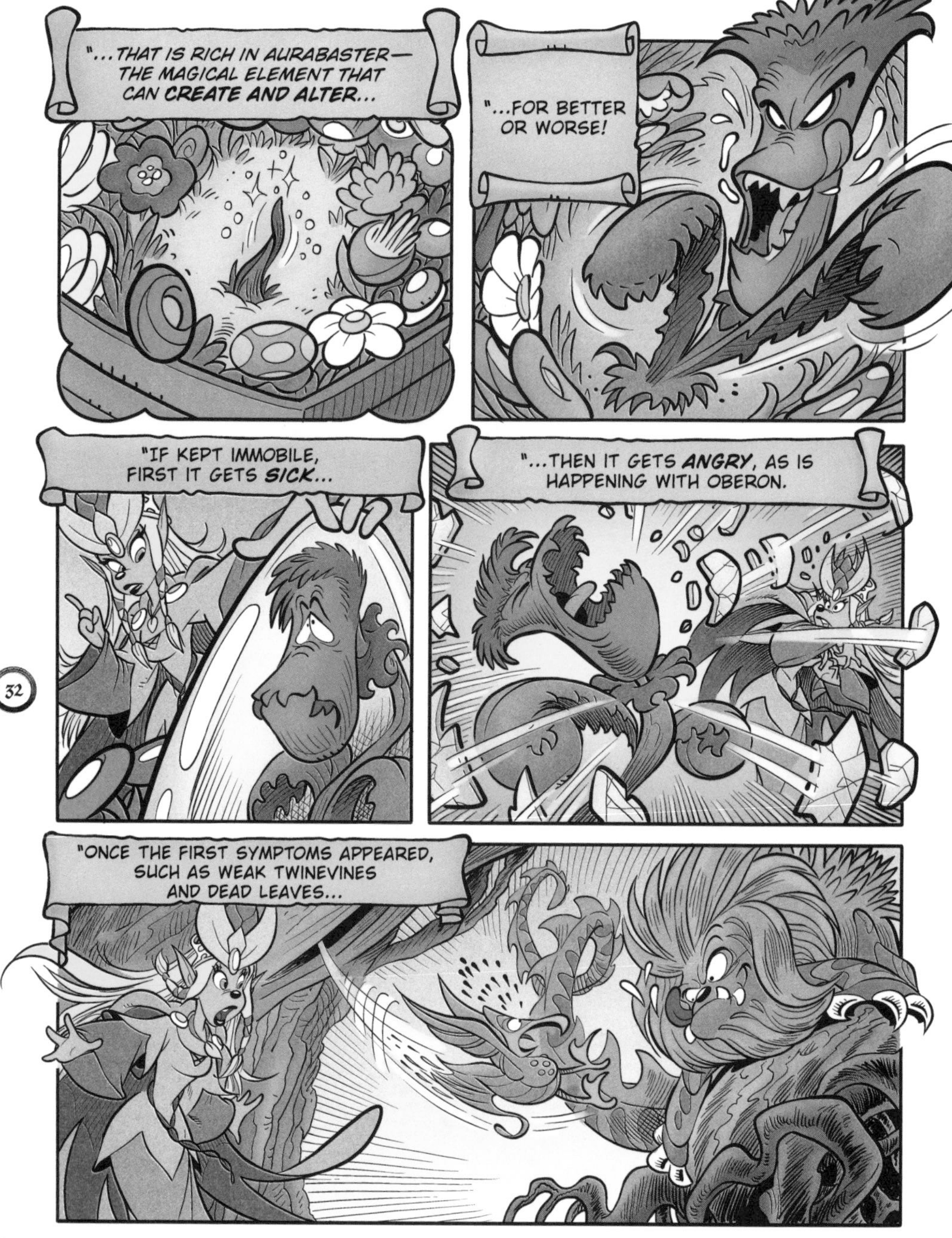
"...THAT IS RICH IN AURABASTER— THE MAGICAL ELEMENT THAT CAN CREATE AND ALTER...
"...FOR BETTER OR WORSE!
"IF KEPT IMMOBILE, FIRST IT GETS SICK...
"...THEN IT GETS ANGRY, AS IS HAPPENING WITH OBERON.
"ONCE THE FIRST SYMPTOMS APPEARED, SUCH AS WEAK TWINEVINES AND DEAD LEAVES...

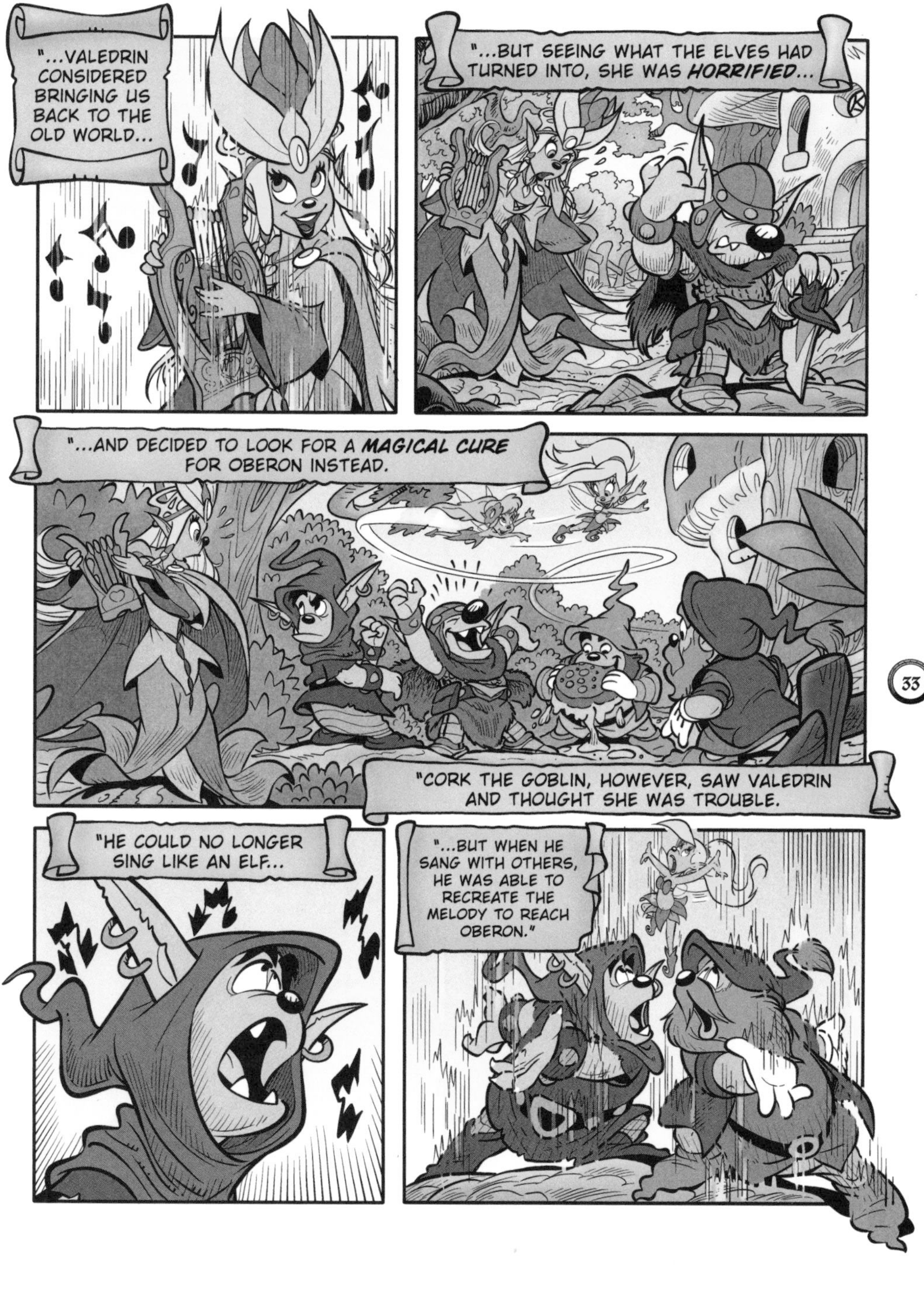
"...VALEDRIN CONSIDERED BRINGING US BACK TO THE OLD WORLD...
"...BUT SEEING WHAT THE ELVES HAD TURNED INTO, SHE WAS HORRIFIED...
"...AND DECIDED TO LOOK FOR A MAGICAL CURE FOR OBERON INSTEAD.
"CORK THE GOBLIN, HOWEVER, SAW VALEDRIN AND THOUGHT SHE WAS TROUBLE.
"HE COULD NO LONGER SING LIKE AN ELF...
"...BUT WHEN HE SANG WITH OTHERS, HE WAS ABLE TO RECREATE THE MELODY TO REACH OBERON."

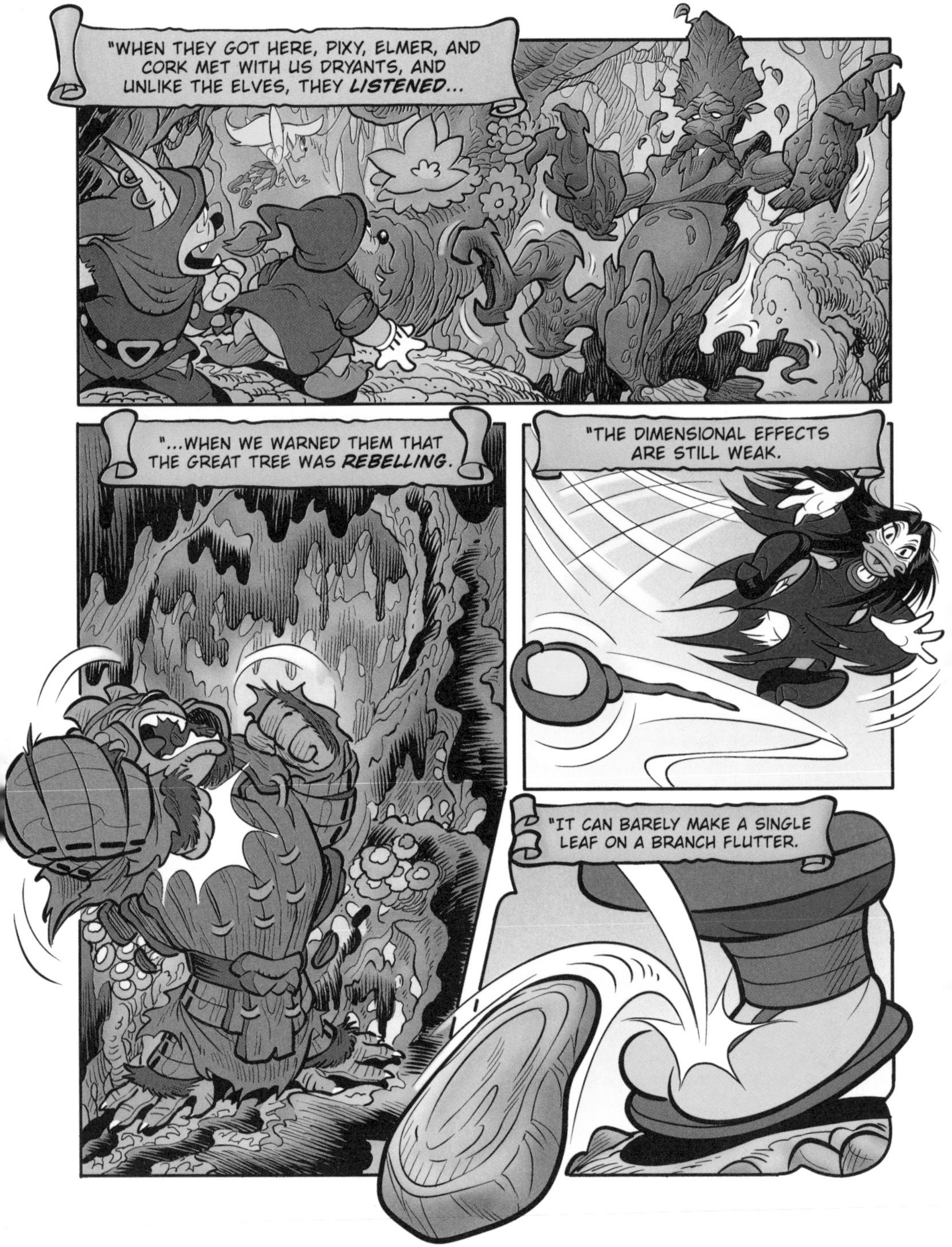
"WHEN THEY GOT HERE, PIXY, ELMER, AND CORK MET WITH US DRYANTS, AND UNLIKE THE ELVES, THEY LISTENED...
"...WHEN WE WARNED THEM THAT THE GREAT TREE WAS REBELLING.
"THE DIMENSIONAL EFFECTS ARE STILL WEAK.
"IT CAN BARELY MAKE A SINGLE LEAF ON A BRANCH FLUTTER.

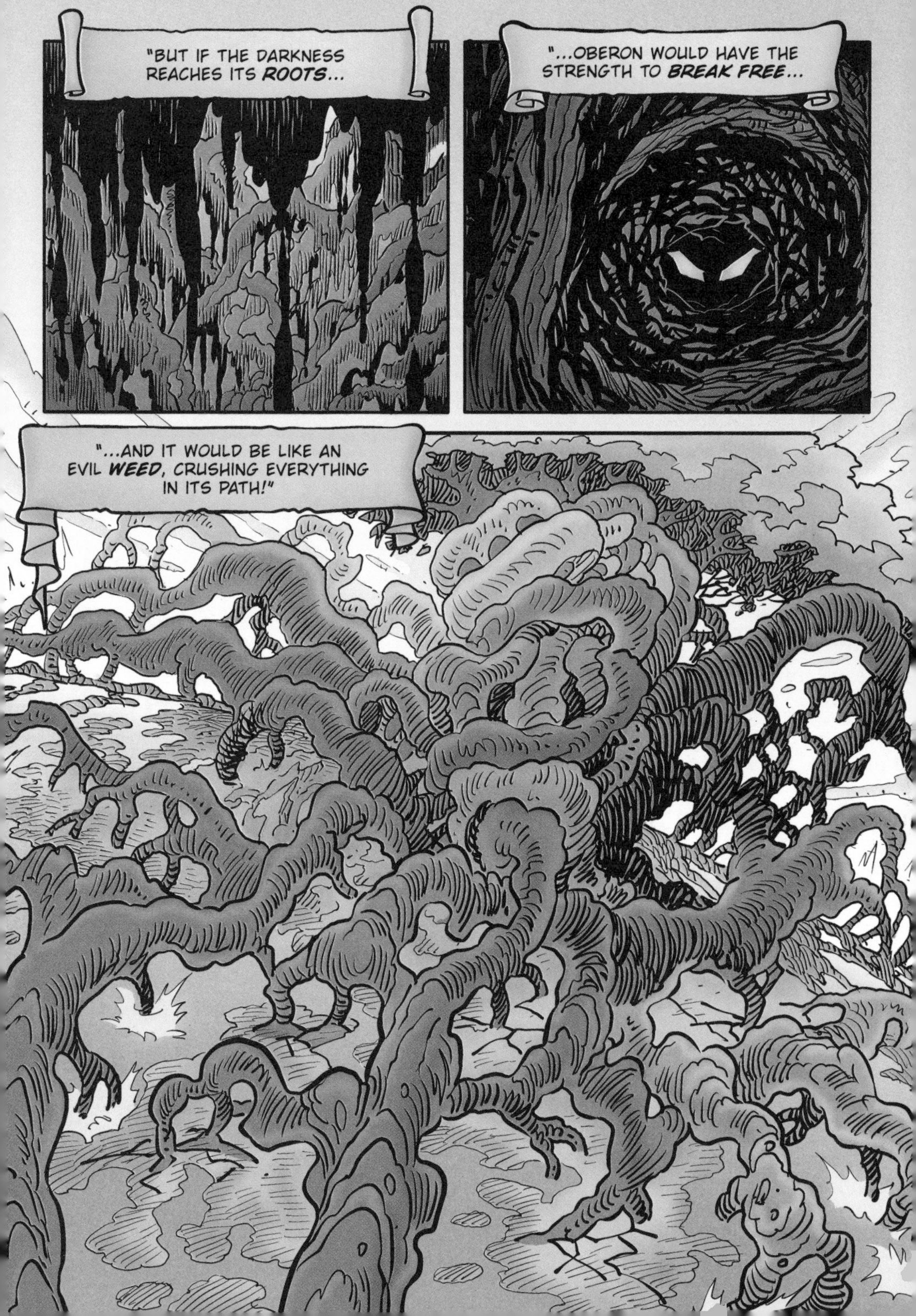
"BUT IF THE DARKNESS REACHES ITS ROOTS...
"...OBERON WOULD HAVE THE STRENGTH TO BREAK FREE...
"...AND IT WOULD BE LIKE AN EVIL WEED, CRUSHING EVERYTHING IN ITS PATH!"

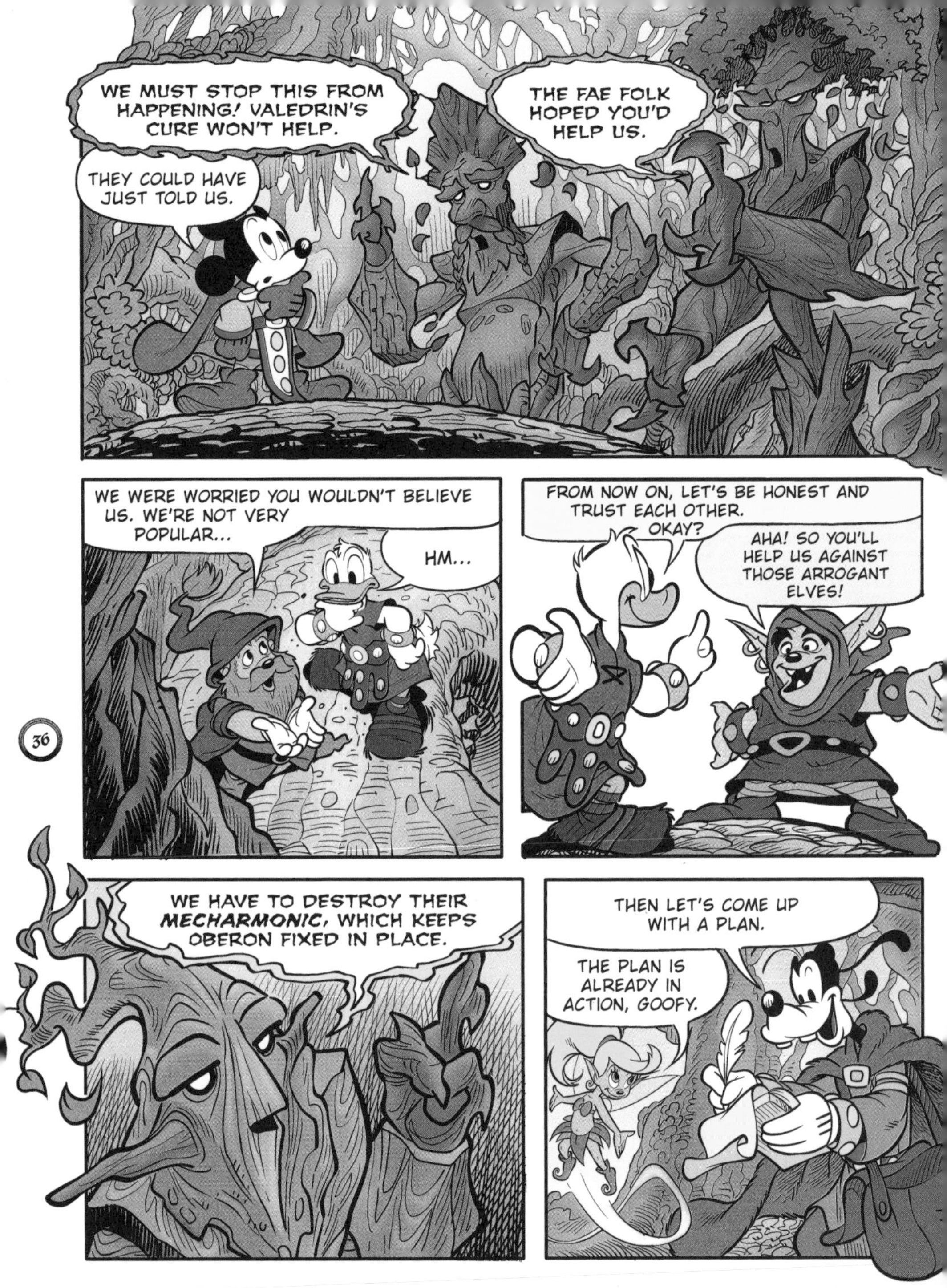
WE MUST STOP THIS FROM HAPPENING! VALEDRIN'S CURE WON'T HELP.
THE FAE FOLK HOPED YOU'D HELP US.
THEY COULD HAVE JUST TOLD US.
WE WERE WORRIED YOU WOULDN'T BELIEVE US. WE'RE NOT VERY POPULAR...
HM...
FROM NOW ON, LET'S BE HONEST AND TRUST EACH OTHER. OKAY?
AHA! SO YOU'LL HELP US AGAINST THOSE ARROGANT ELVES!
WE HAVE TO DESTROY THEIR *MECHARMONIC*, WHICH KEEPS OBERON FIXED IN PLACE.
THEN LET'S COME UP WITH A PLAN.
THE PLAN IS ALREADY IN ACTION, GOOFY.

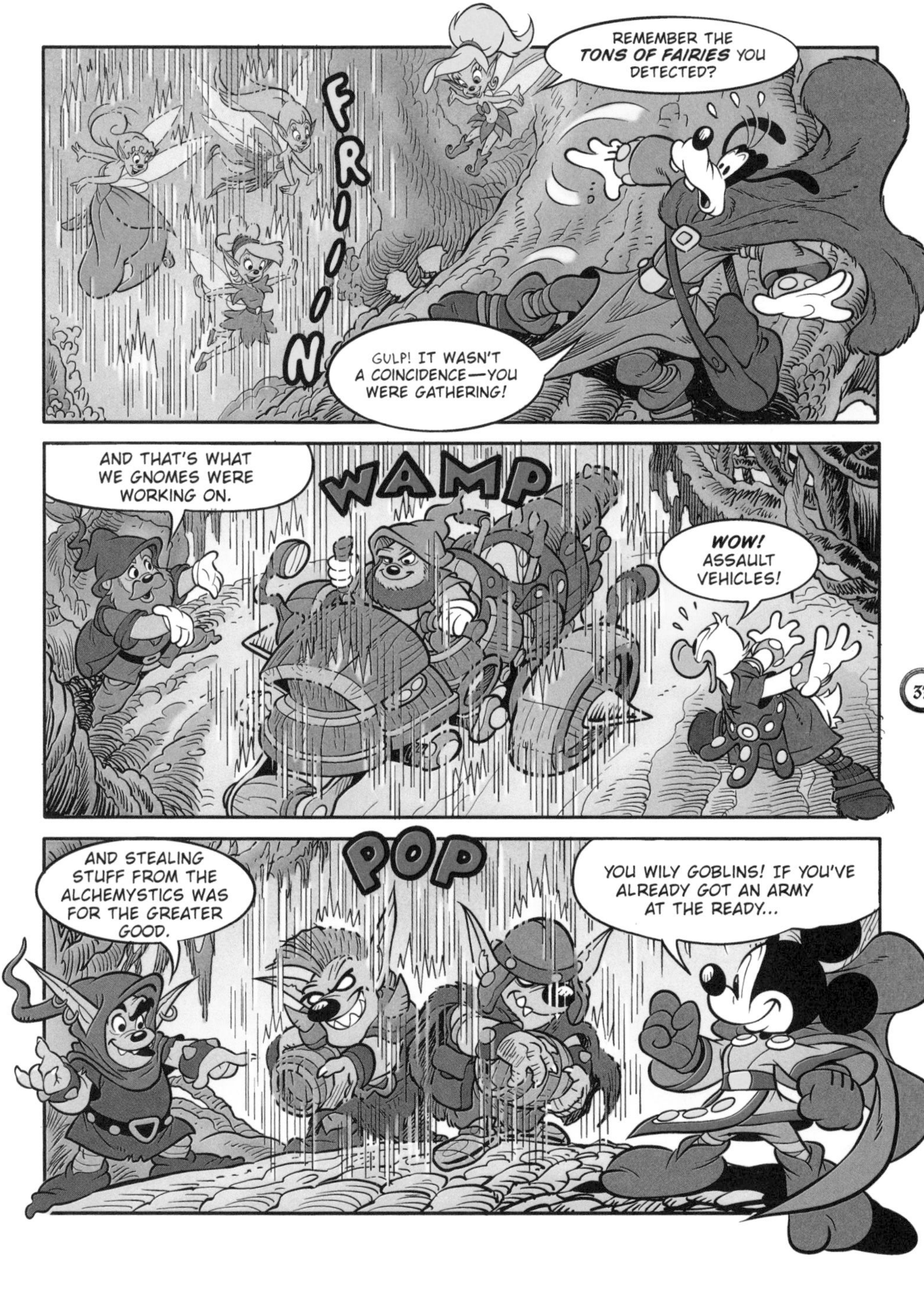

REMEMBER THE *TONS OF FAIRIES* YOU DETECTED?
FRIIIIN
GULP! IT WASN'T A COINCIDENCE—YOU WERE GATHERING!
AND THAT'S WHAT WE GNOMES WERE WORKING ON.
WAMP
WOW! ASSAULT VEHICLES!
POP
AND STEALING STUFF FROM THE ALCHEMYSTICS WAS FOR THE GREATER GOOD.
YOU WILY GOBLINS! IF YOU'VE ALREADY GOT AN ARMY AT THE READY...

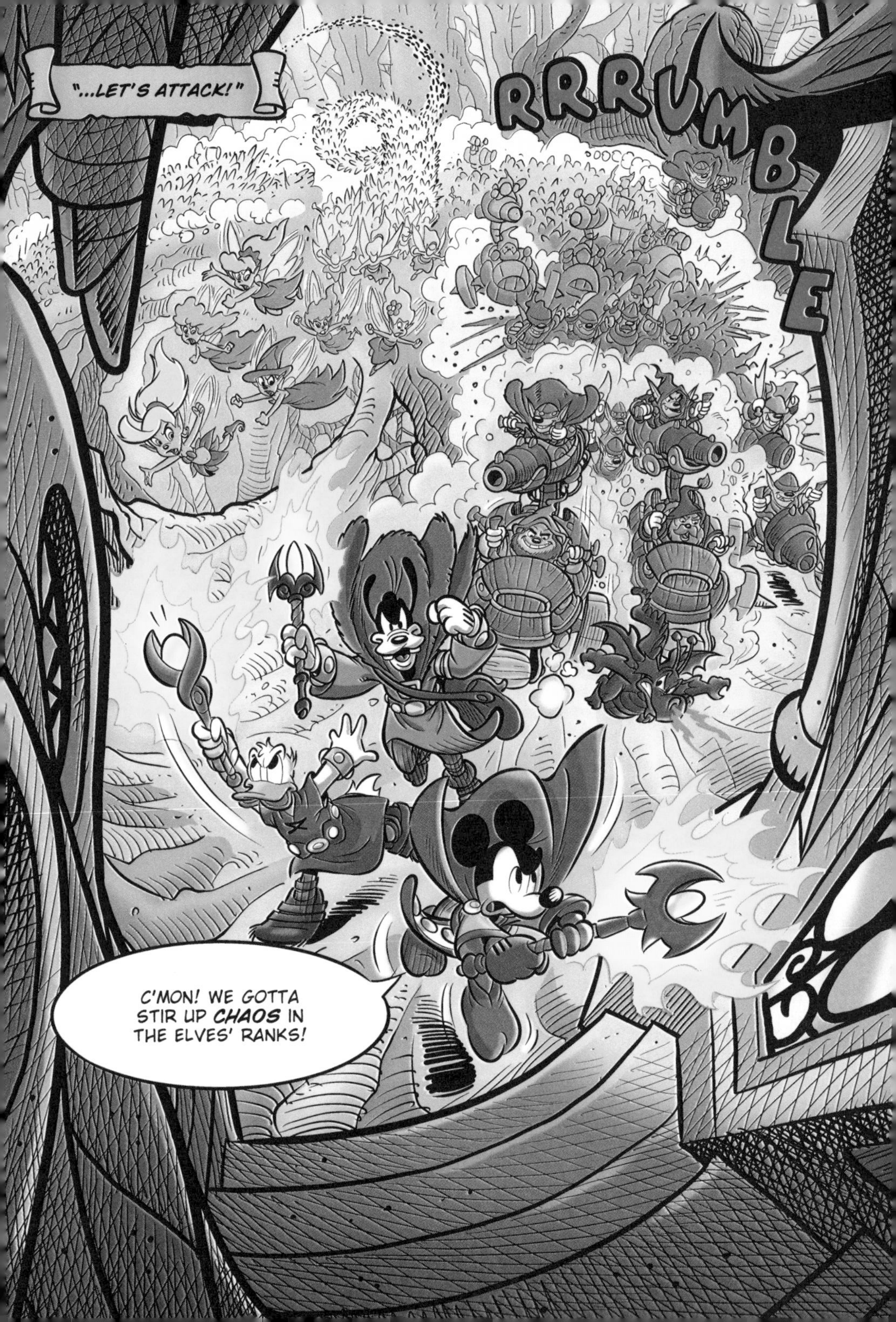
"...LET'S ATTACK!"
RRRUMBLE
C'MON! WE GOTTA STIR UP CHAOS IN THE ELVES' RANKS!

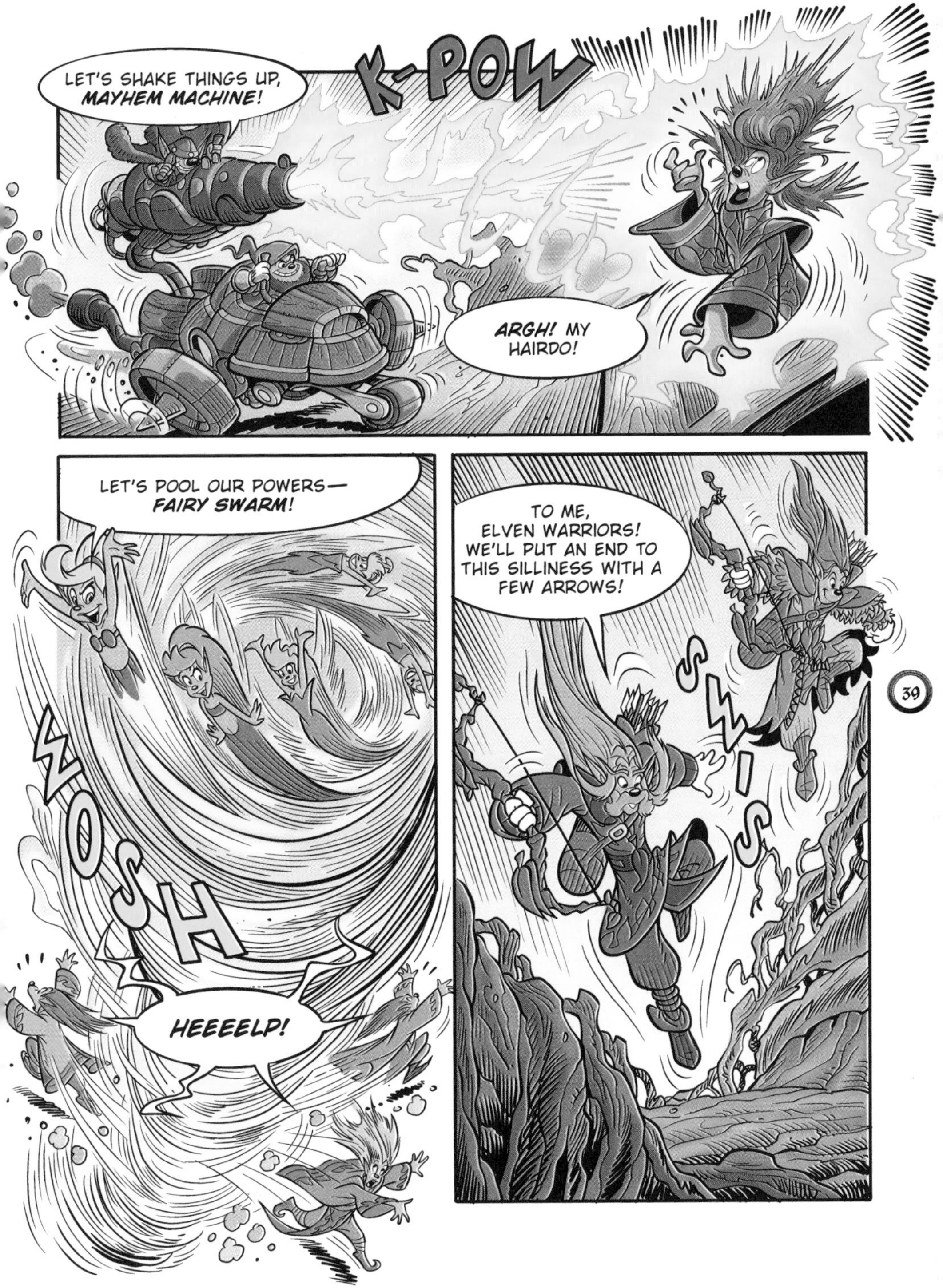
LET'S SHAKE THINGS UP, MAYHEM MACHINE!
K-POW
ARGH! MY HAIRDO!
LET'S POOL OUR POWERS—FAIRY SWARM!
WOOSH
HEEEELP!
TO ME, ELVEN WARRIORS! WE'LL PUT AN END TO THIS SILLINESS WITH A FEW ARROWS!
SWISS

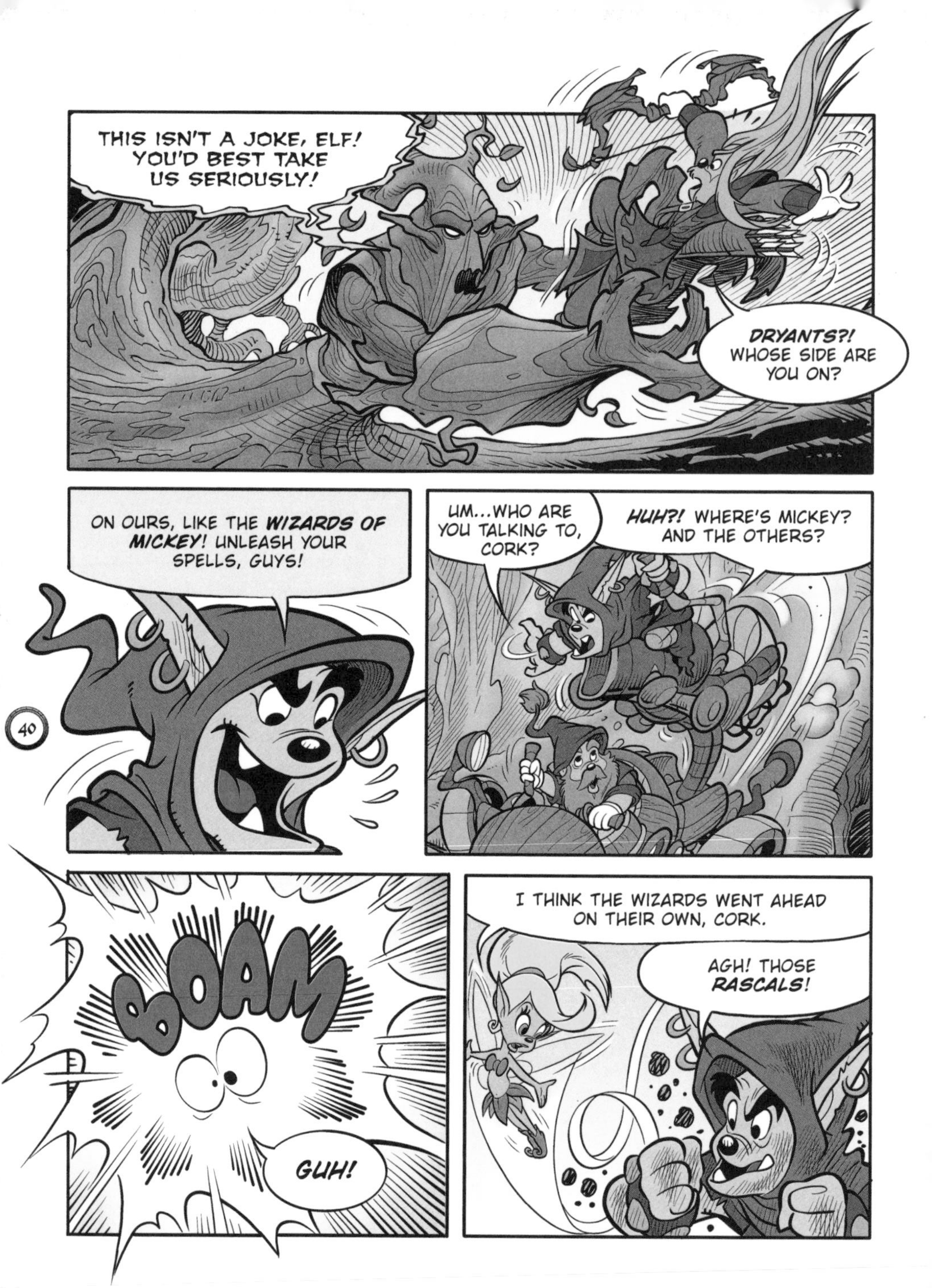
THIS ISN'T A JOKE, ELF! YOU'D BEST TAKE US SERIOUSLY!
DRYANTS?! WHOSE SIDE ARE YOU ON?
ON OURS, LIKE THE WIZARDS OF MICKEY! UNLEASH YOUR SPELLS, GUYS!
UM...WHO ARE YOU TALKING TO, CORK?
HUH?! WHERE'S MICKEY? AND THE OTHERS?
BOAM
GUH!
I THINK THE WIZARDS WENT AHEAD ON THEIR OWN, CORK.
AGH! THOSE RASCALS!

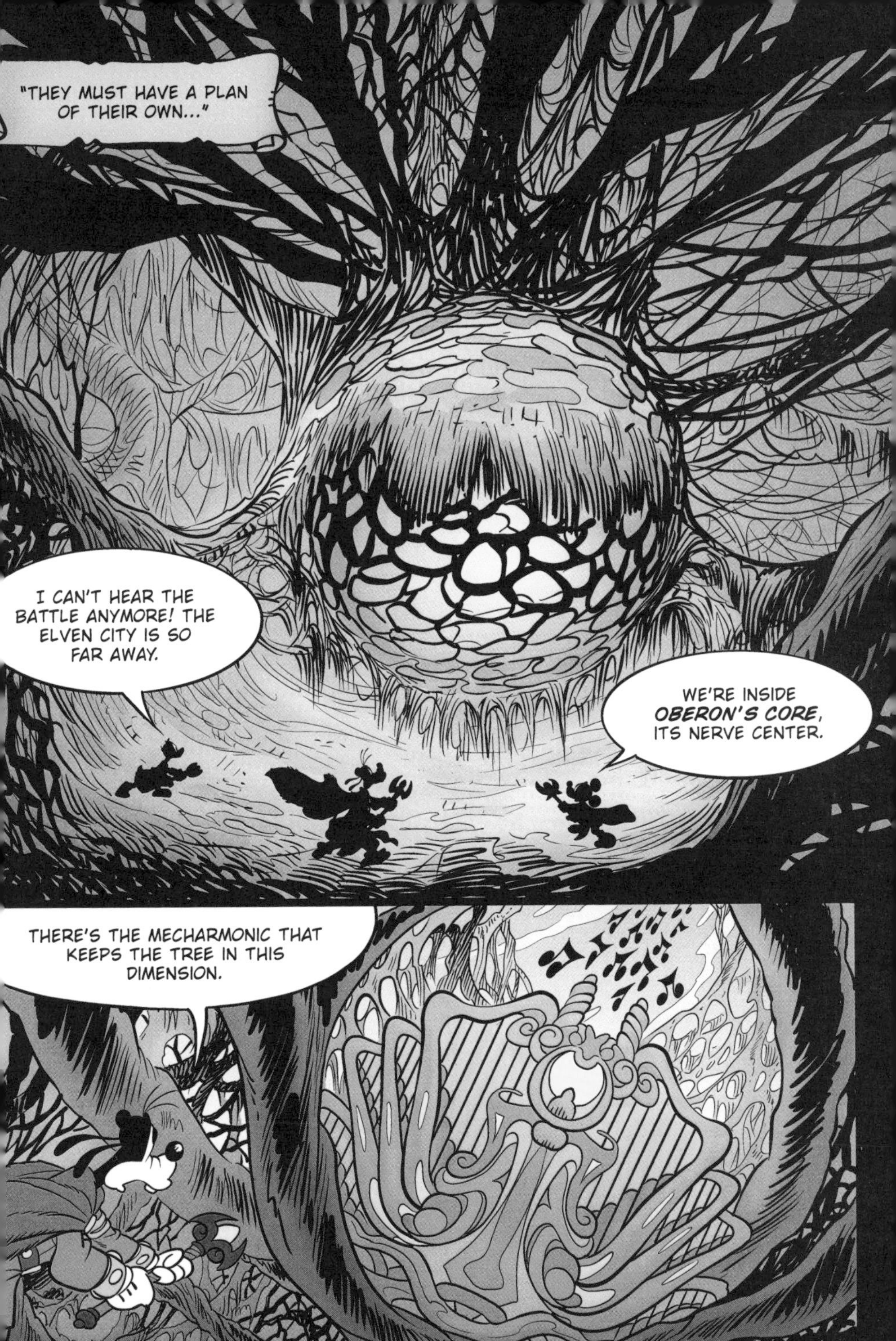
"THEY MUST HAVE A PLAN OF THEIR OWN..."
I CAN'T HEAR THE BATTLE ANYMORE! THE ELVEN CITY IS SO FAR AWAY.
WE'RE INSIDE OBERON'S CORE, ITS NERVE CENTER.
THERE'S THE MECHARMONIC THAT KEEPS THE TREE IN THIS DIMENSION.

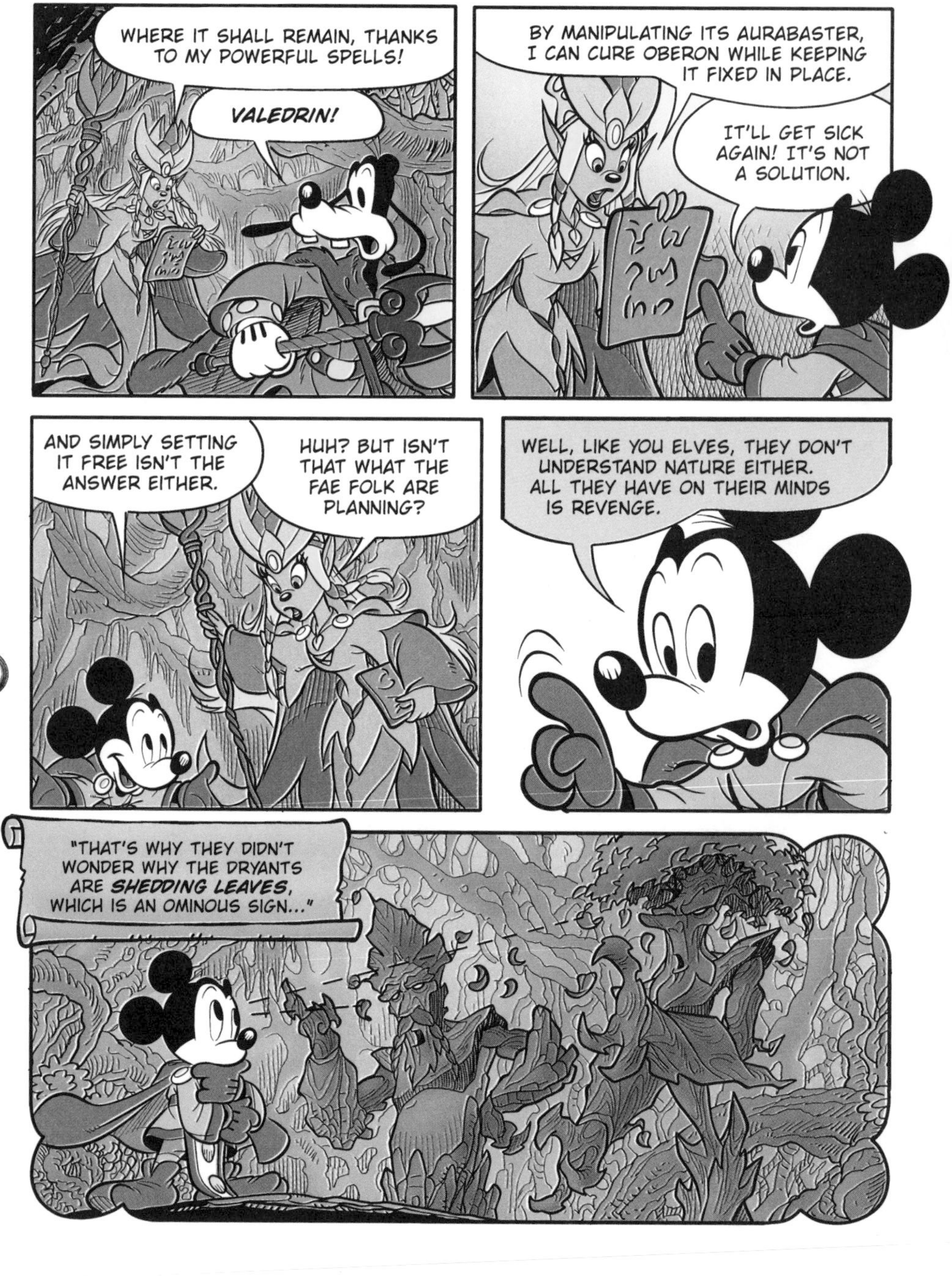
WHERE IT SHALL REMAIN, THANKS TO MY POWERFUL SPELLS!
VALEDRIN!
BY MANIPULATING ITS AURABASTER, I CAN CURE OBERON WHILE KEEPING IT FIXED IN PLACE.
IT'LL GET SICK AGAIN! IT'S NOT A SOLUTION.
AND SIMPLY SETTING IT FREE ISN'T THE ANSWER EITHER.
HUH? BUT ISN'T THAT WHAT THE FAE FOLK ARE PLANNING?
WELL, LIKE YOU ELVES, THEY DON'T UNDERSTAND NATURE EITHER. ALL THEY HAVE ON THEIR MINDS IS REVENGE.
"THAT'S WHY THEY DIDN'T WONDER WHY THE DRYANTS ARE SHEDDING LEAVES, WHICH IS AN OMINOUS SIGN..."

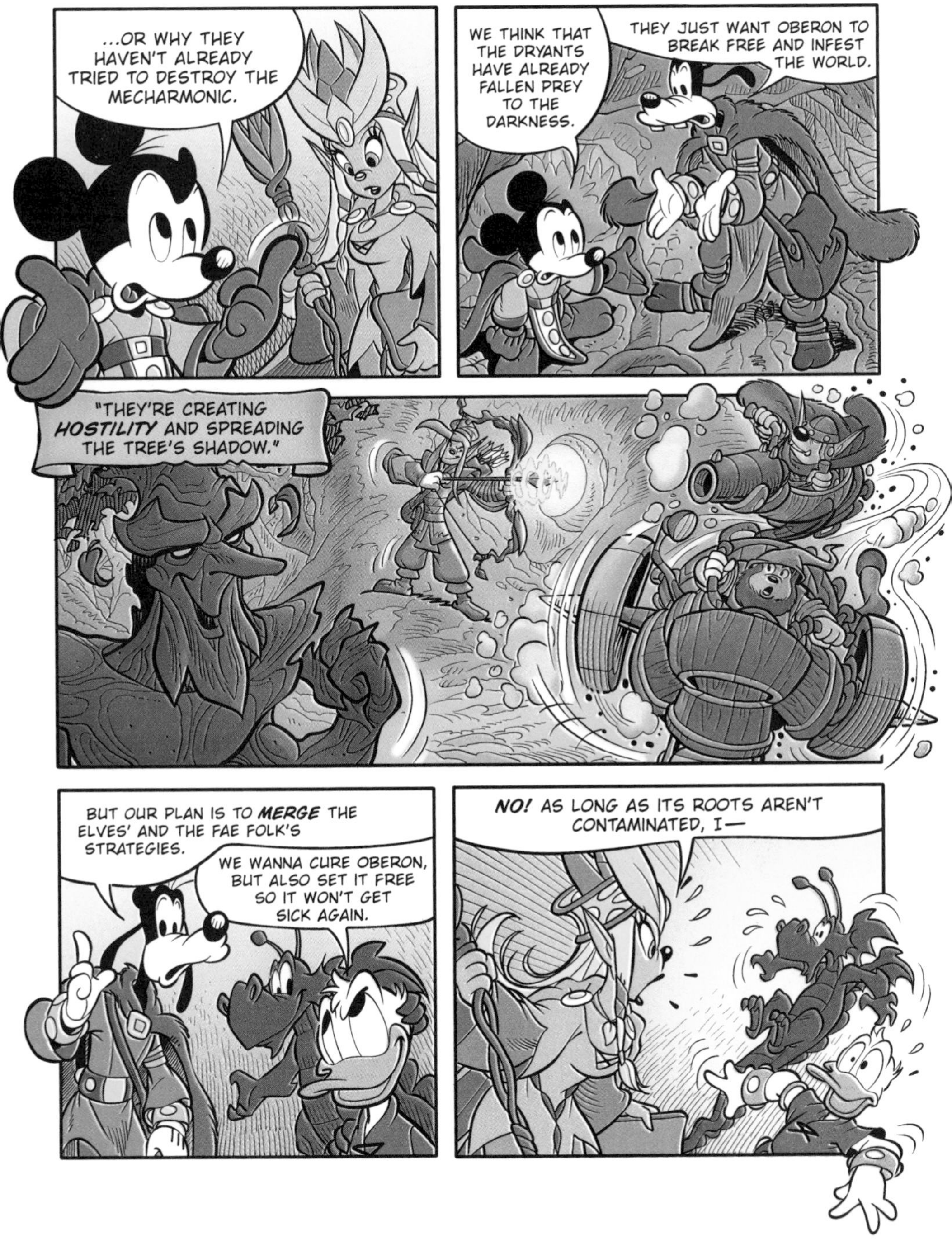
...OR WHY THEY HAVEN'T ALREADY TRIED TO DESTROY THE MECHARMONIC.
WE THINK THAT THE DRYANTS HAVE ALREADY FALLEN PREY TO THE DARKNESS.
THEY JUST WANT OBERON TO BREAK FREE AND INFEST THE WORLD.
"THEY'RE CREATING ***HOSTILITY*** AND SPREADING THE TREE'S SHADOW."
BUT OUR PLAN IS TO ***MERGE*** THE ELVES' AND THE FAE FOLK'S STRATEGIES.
WE WANNA CURE OBERON, BUT ALSO SET IT FREE SO IT WON'T GET SICK AGAIN.
NO! AS LONG AS ITS ROOTS AREN'T CONTAMINATED, I—

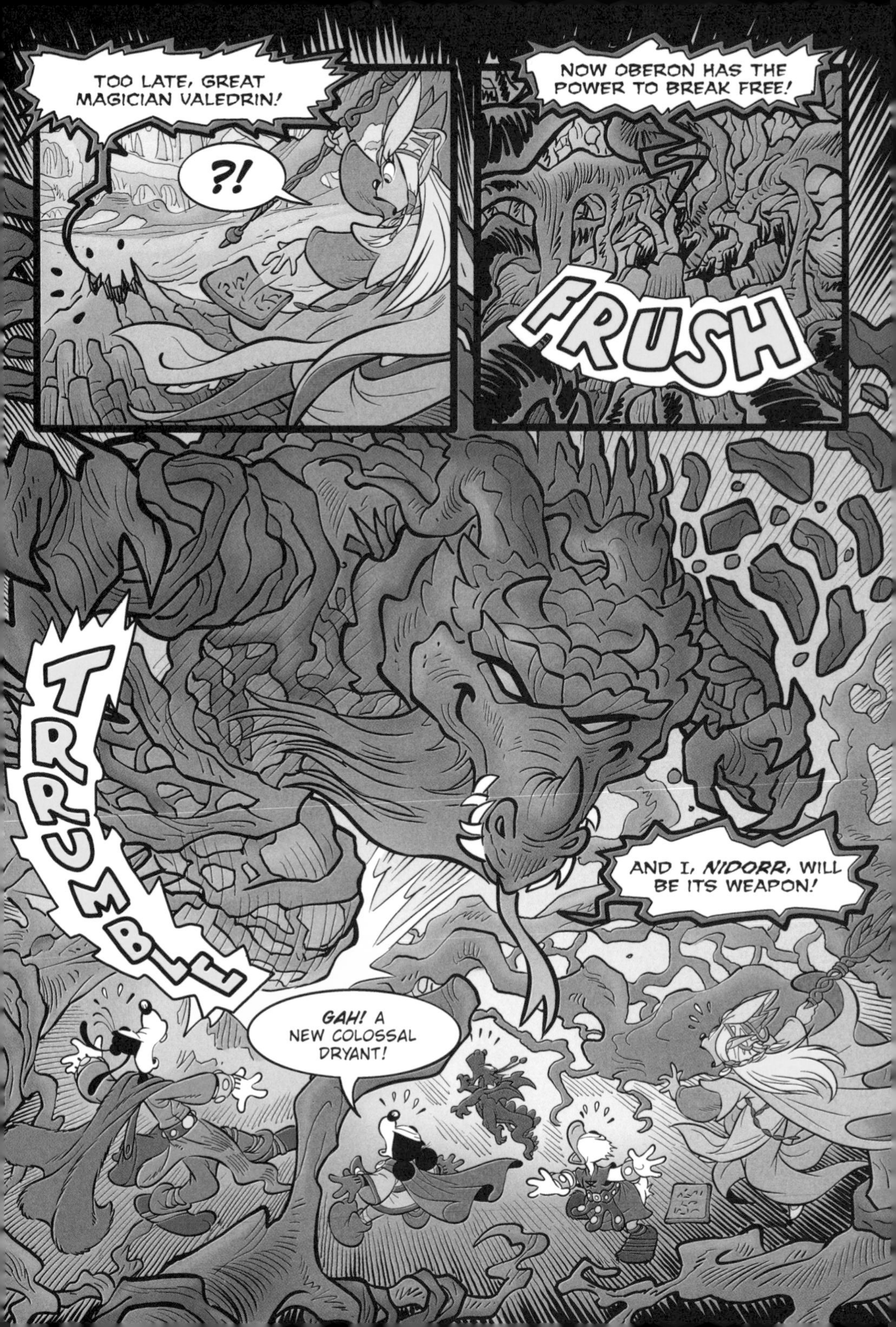
TOO LATE, GREAT MAGICIAN VALEDRIN!
?!
NOW OBERON HAS THE POWER TO BREAK FREE!
FRUSH
TRRUMBLE
AND I, *NIDORR*, WILL BE ITS WEAPON!
GAH! A NEW COLOSSAL DRYANT!

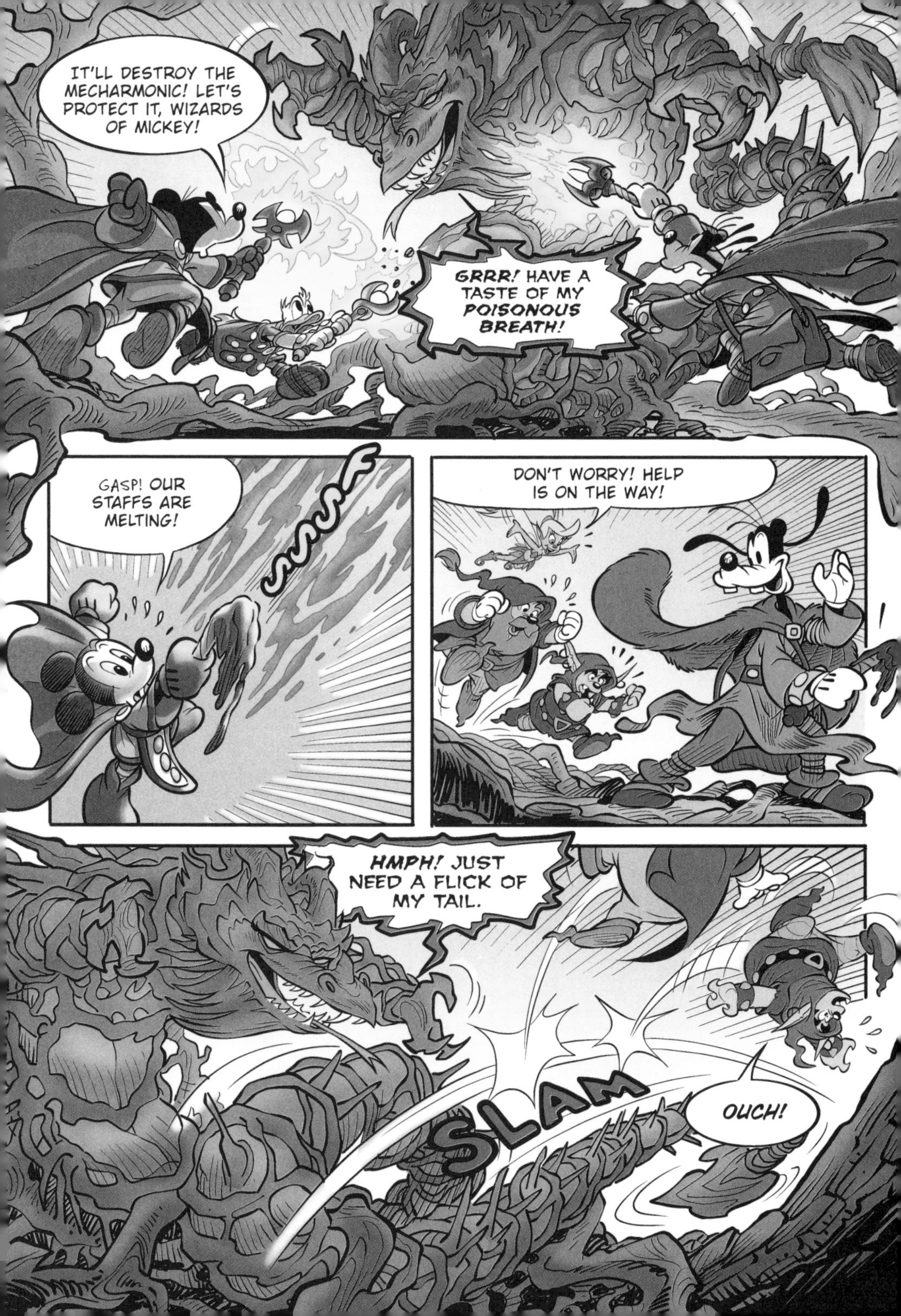
IT'LL DESTROY THE MECHARMONIC! LET'S PROTECT IT, WIZARDS OF MICKEY!
GRRR! HAVE A TASTE OF MY POISONOUS BREATH!
GASP! OUR STAFFS ARE MELTING!
WUUUF
DON'T WORRY! HELP IS ON THE WAY!
HMPH! JUST NEED A FLICK OF MY TAIL.
SLAM
OUCH!

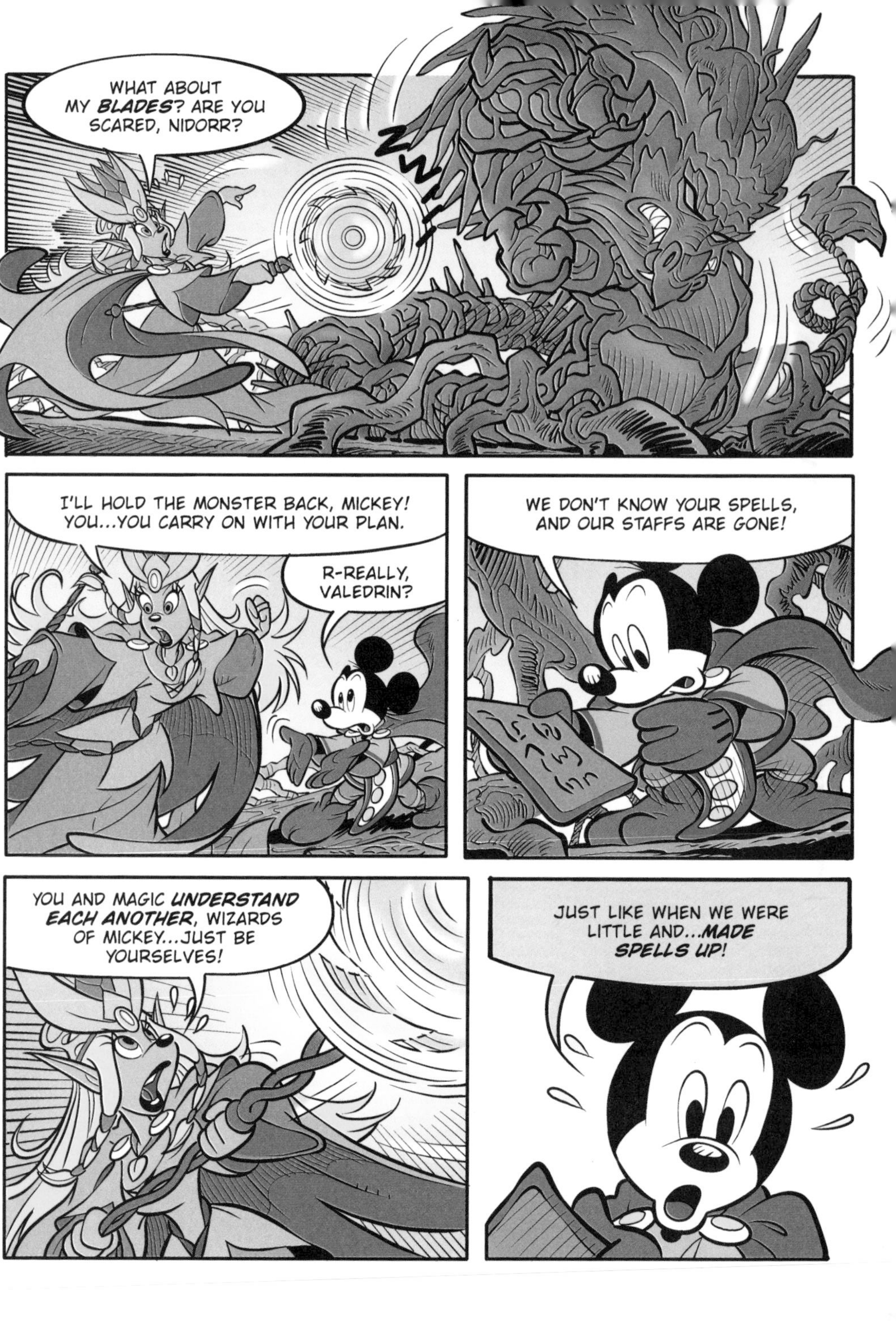
WHAT ABOUT MY BLADES? ARE YOU SCARED, NIDORR?
ZWIII
I'LL HOLD THE MONSTER BACK, MICKEY! YOU...YOU CARRY ON WITH YOUR PLAN.
R-REALLY, VALEDRIN?
WE DON'T KNOW YOUR SPELLS, AND OUR STAFFS ARE GONE!
YOU AND MAGIC UNDERSTAND EACH ANOTHER, WIZARDS OF MICKEY...JUST BE YOURSELVES!
JUST LIKE WHEN WE WERE LITTLE AND...MADE SPELLS UP!

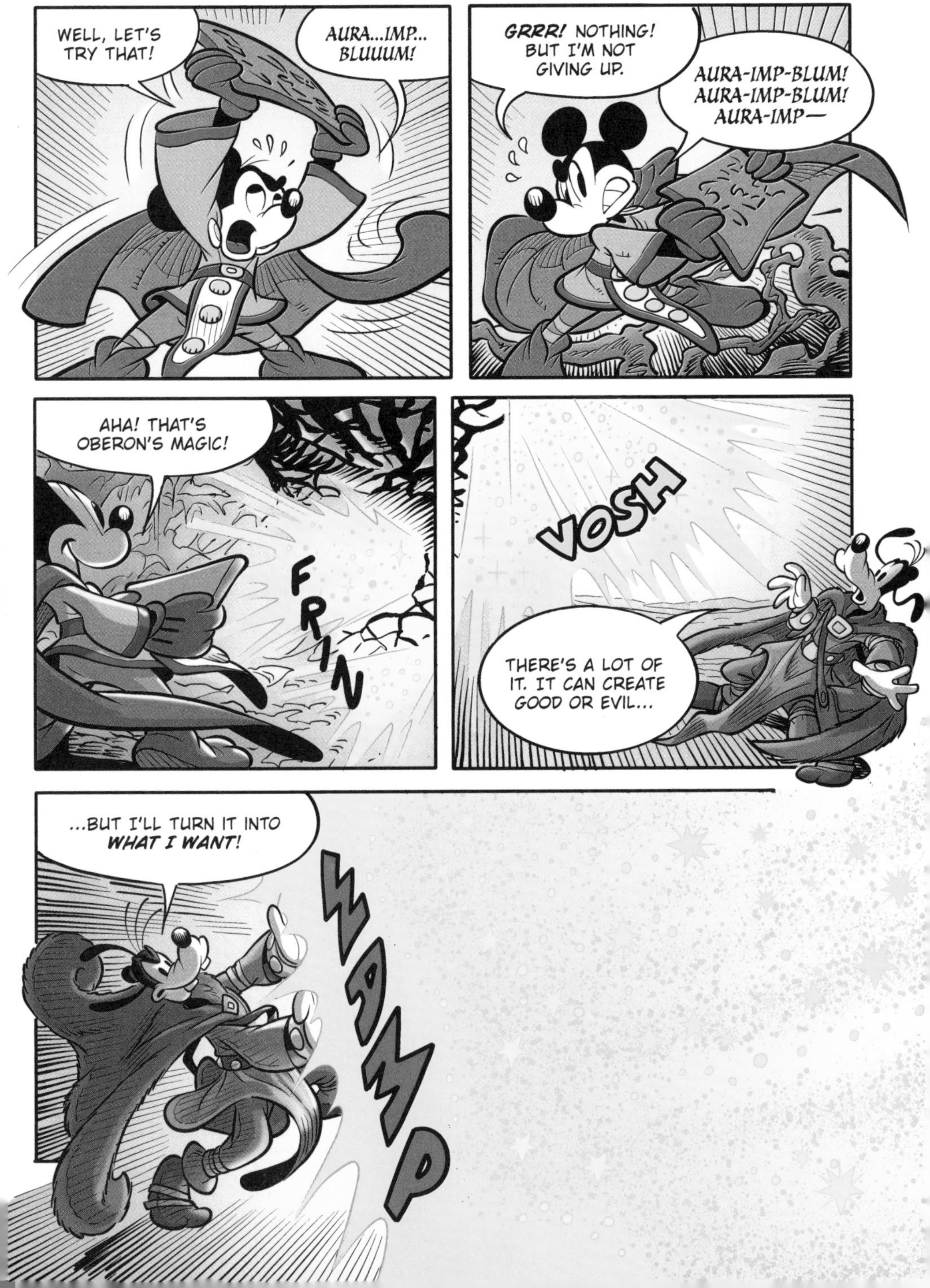
WELL, LET'S TRY THAT!
AURA...IMP... BLUUUM!
GRRR! NOTHING! BUT I'M NOT GIVING UP.
AURA-IMP-BLUM! AURA-IMP-BLUM! AURA-IMP—
AHA! THAT'S OBERON'S MAGIC!
FRIN
VOSH
THERE'S A LOT OF IT. IT CAN CREATE GOOD OR EVIL...
...BUT I'LL TURN IT INTO WHAT I WANT!
WAMP

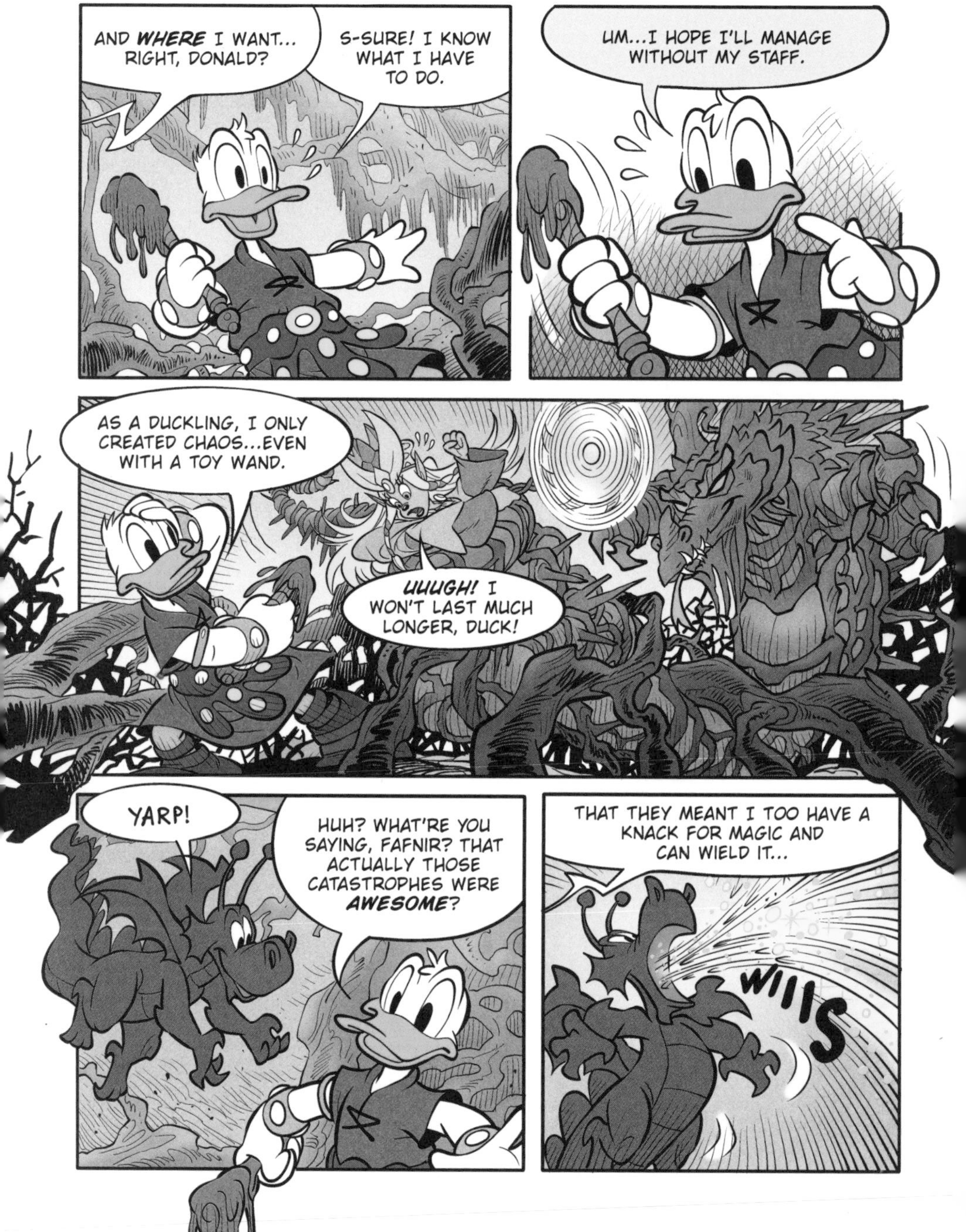
AND *WHERE* I WANT... RIGHT, DONALD?
S-SURE! I KNOW WHAT I HAVE TO DO.
UM...I HOPE I'LL MANAGE WITHOUT MY STAFF.
AS A DUCKLING, I ONLY CREATED CHAOS...EVEN WITH A TOY WAND.
UUUGH! I WON'T LAST MUCH LONGER, DUCK!
YARP!
HUH? WHAT'RE YOU SAYING, FAFNIR? THAT ACTUALLY THOSE CATASTROPHES WERE *AWESOME*?
THAT THEY MEANT I TOO HAVE A KNACK FOR MAGIC AND CAN WIELD IT...
WIIIS

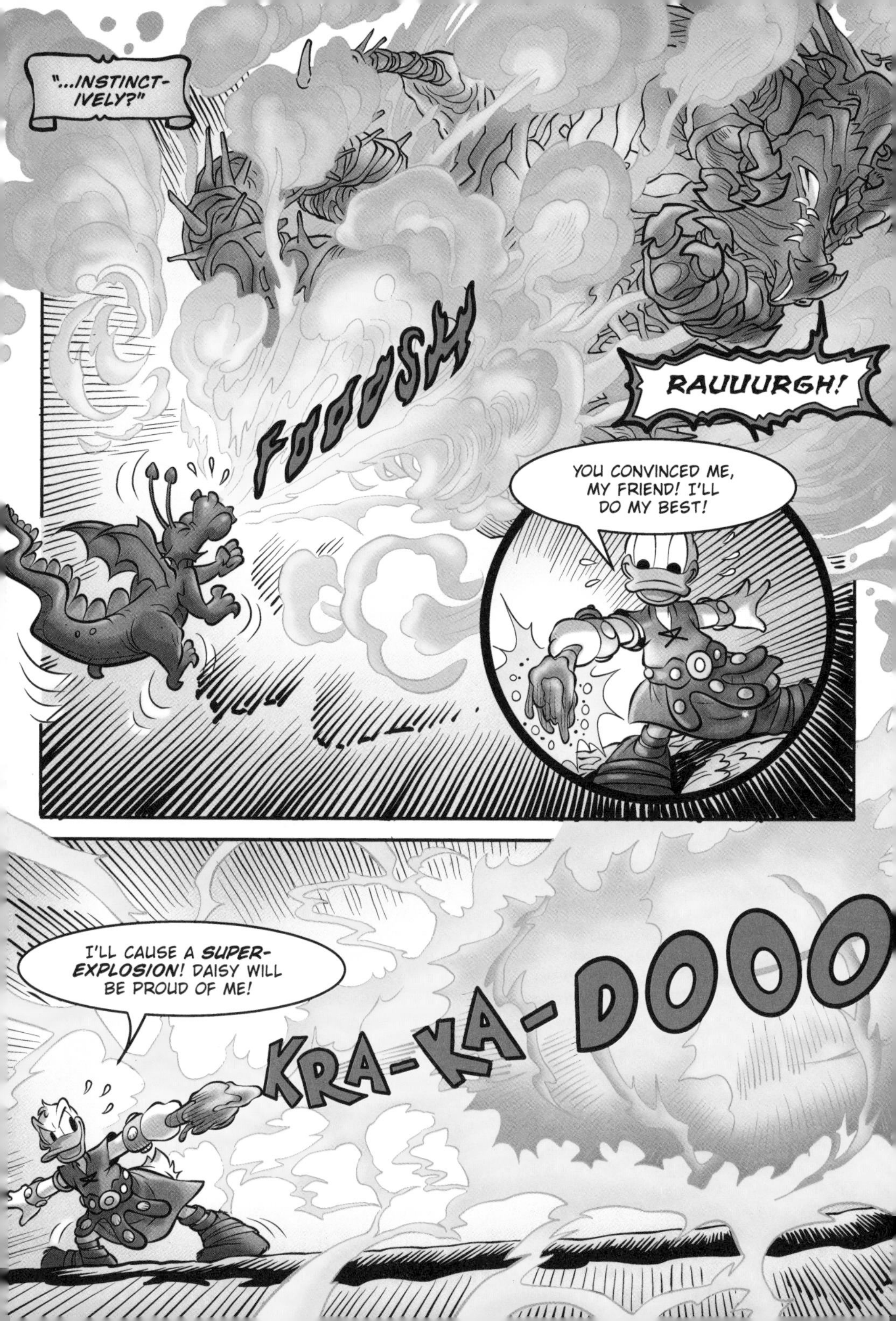
"...INSTINCT-IVELY?"
FOOOSH
RAUUURGH!
YOU CONVINCED ME, MY FRIEND! I'LL DO MY BEST!
I'LL CAUSE A *SUPER-EXPLOSION*! DAISY WILL BE PROUD OF ME!
KRA-KA-DOOO

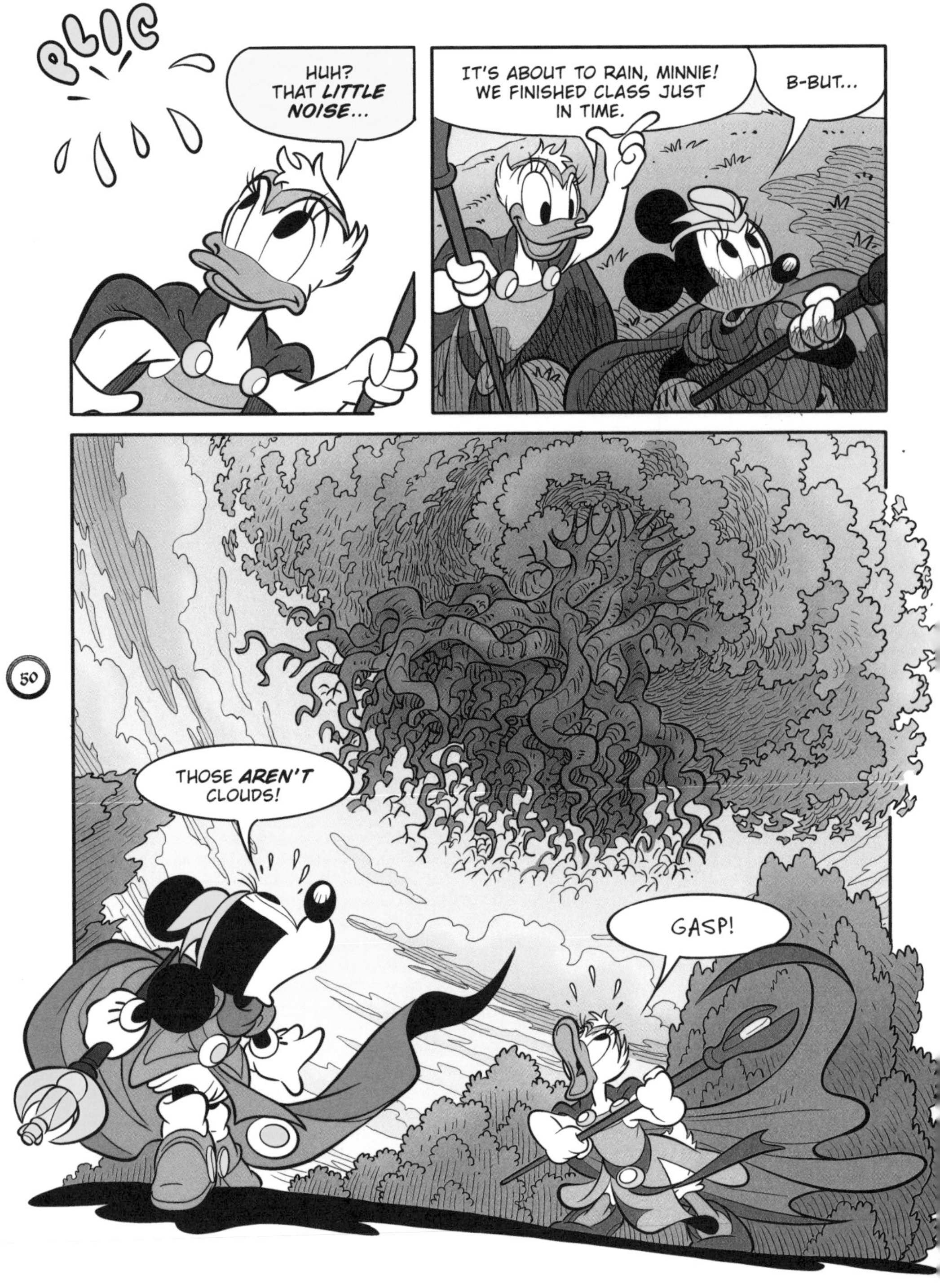
PLIC
HUH? THAT LITTLE NOISE...
IT'S ABOUT TO RAIN, MINNIE! WE FINISHED CLASS JUST IN TIME.
B-BUT...
THOSE AREN'T CLOUDS!
GASP!

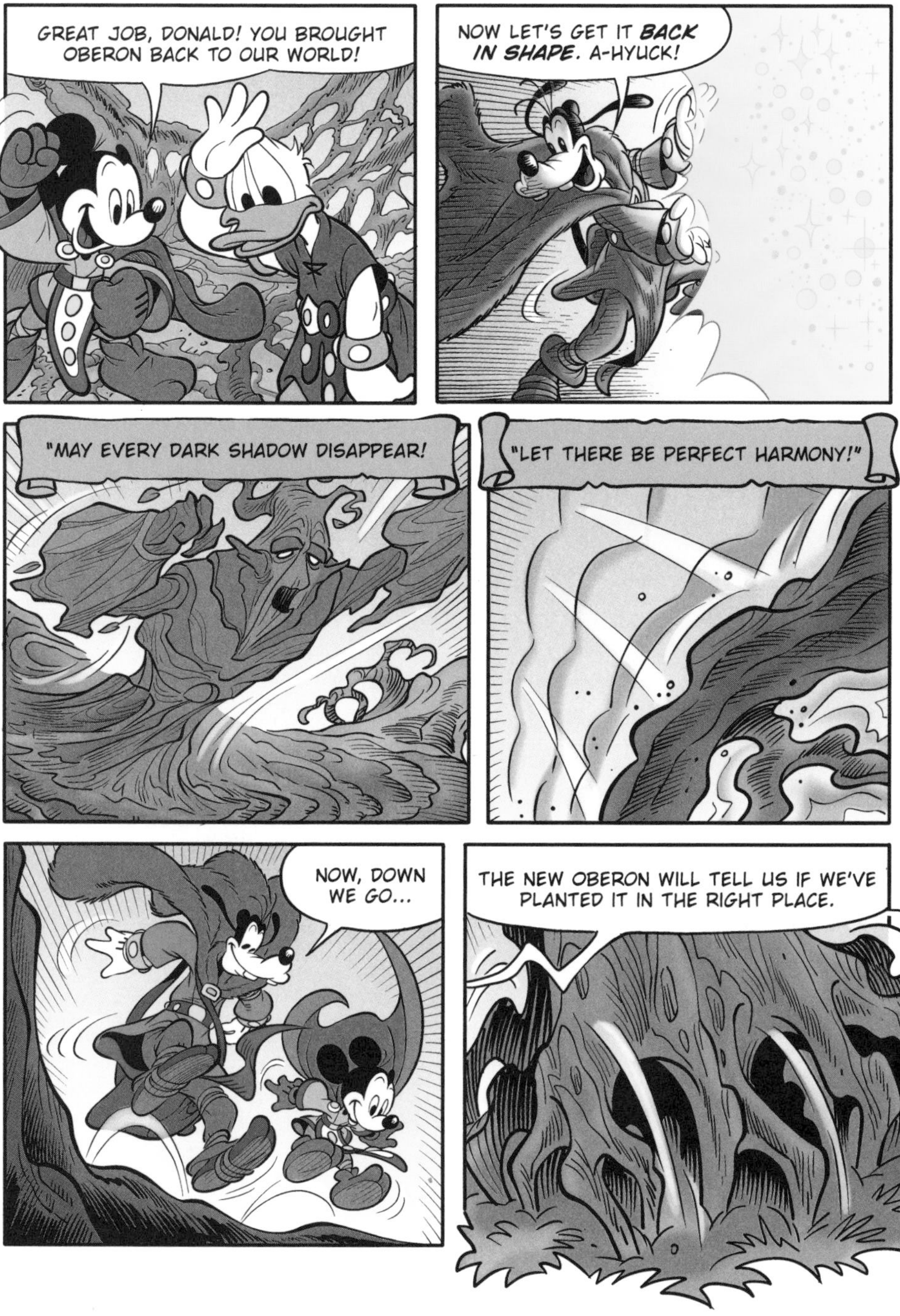
GREAT JOB, DONALD! YOU BROUGHT OBERON BACK TO OUR WORLD!
NOW LET'S GET IT **BACK IN SHAPE**. A-HYUCK!
"MAY EVERY DARK SHADOW DISAPPEAR!
"LET THERE BE PERFECT HARMONY!"
NOW, DOWN WE GO...
THE NEW OBERON WILL TELL US IF WE'VE PLANTED IT IN THE RIGHT PLACE.

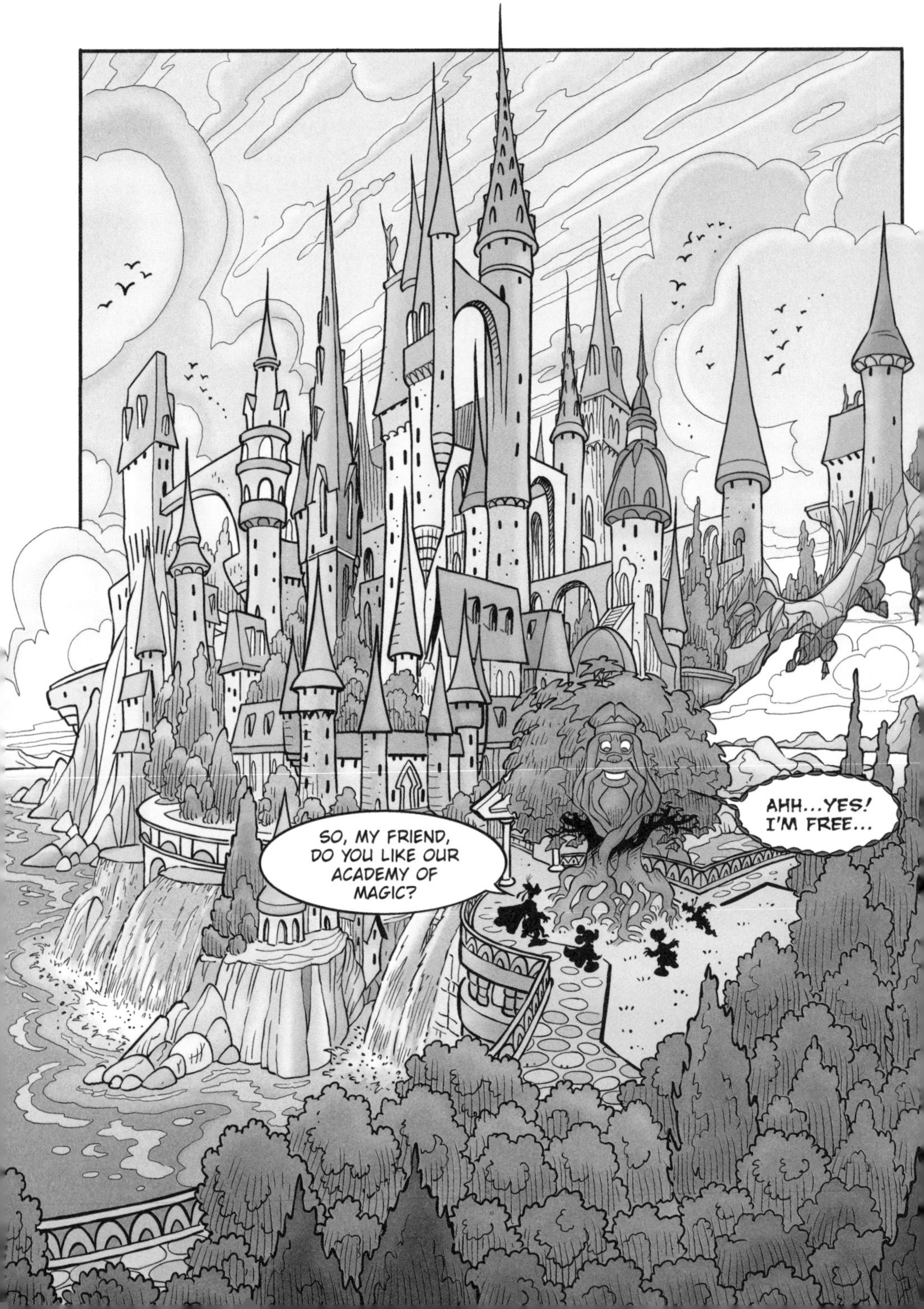
SO, MY FRIEND, DO YOU LIKE OUR ACADEMY OF MAGIC?
AHH...YES! I'M FREE...

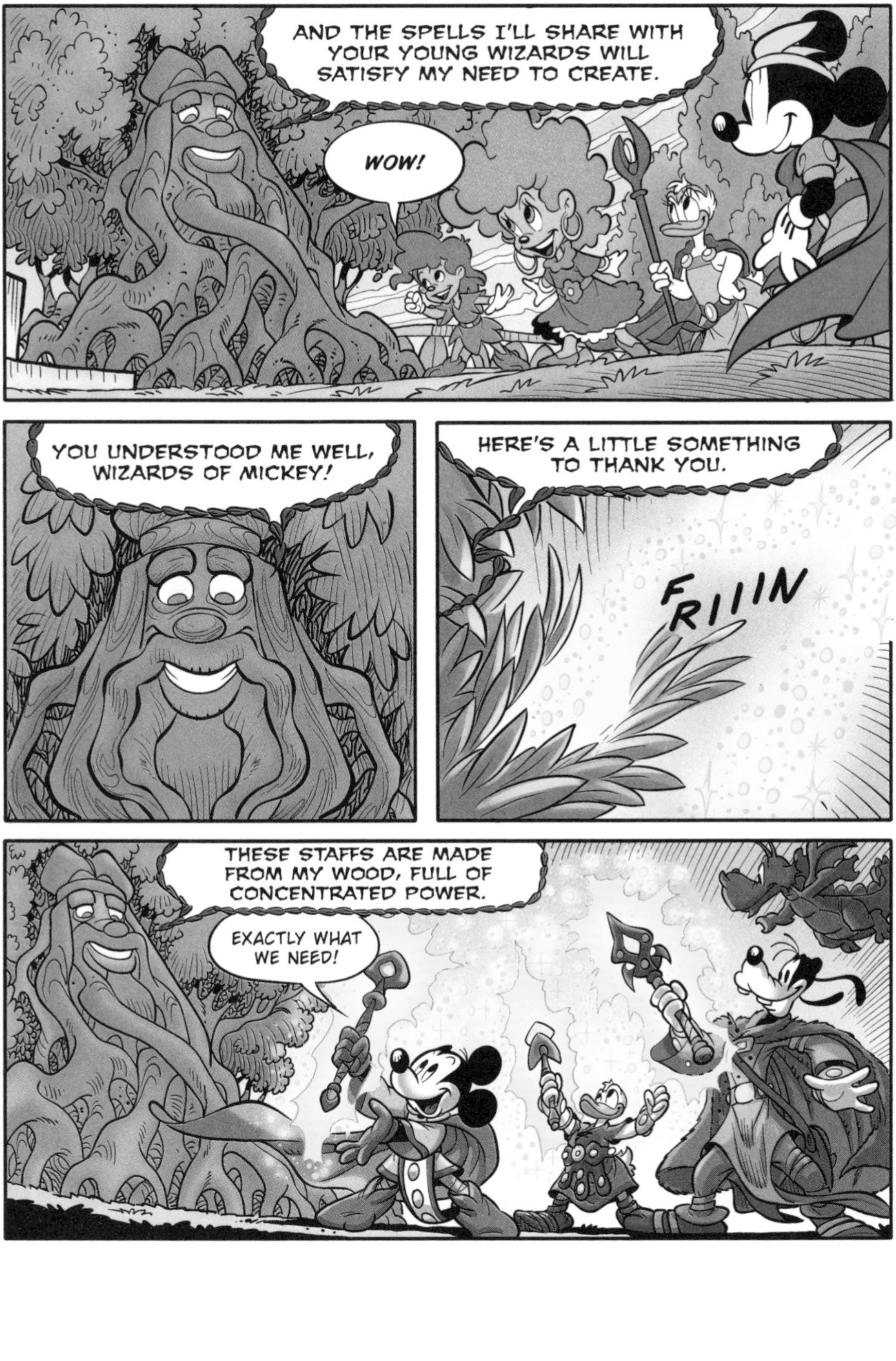
AND THE SPELLS I'LL SHARE WITH YOUR YOUNG WIZARDS WILL SATISFY MY NEED TO CREATE.
WOW!
YOU UNDERSTOOD ME WELL, WIZARDS OF MICKEY!
HERE'S A LITTLE SOMETHING TO THANK YOU.
FRIIIN
THESE STAFFS ARE MADE FROM MY WOOD, FULL OF CONCENTRATED POWER.
EXACTLY WHAT WE NEED!

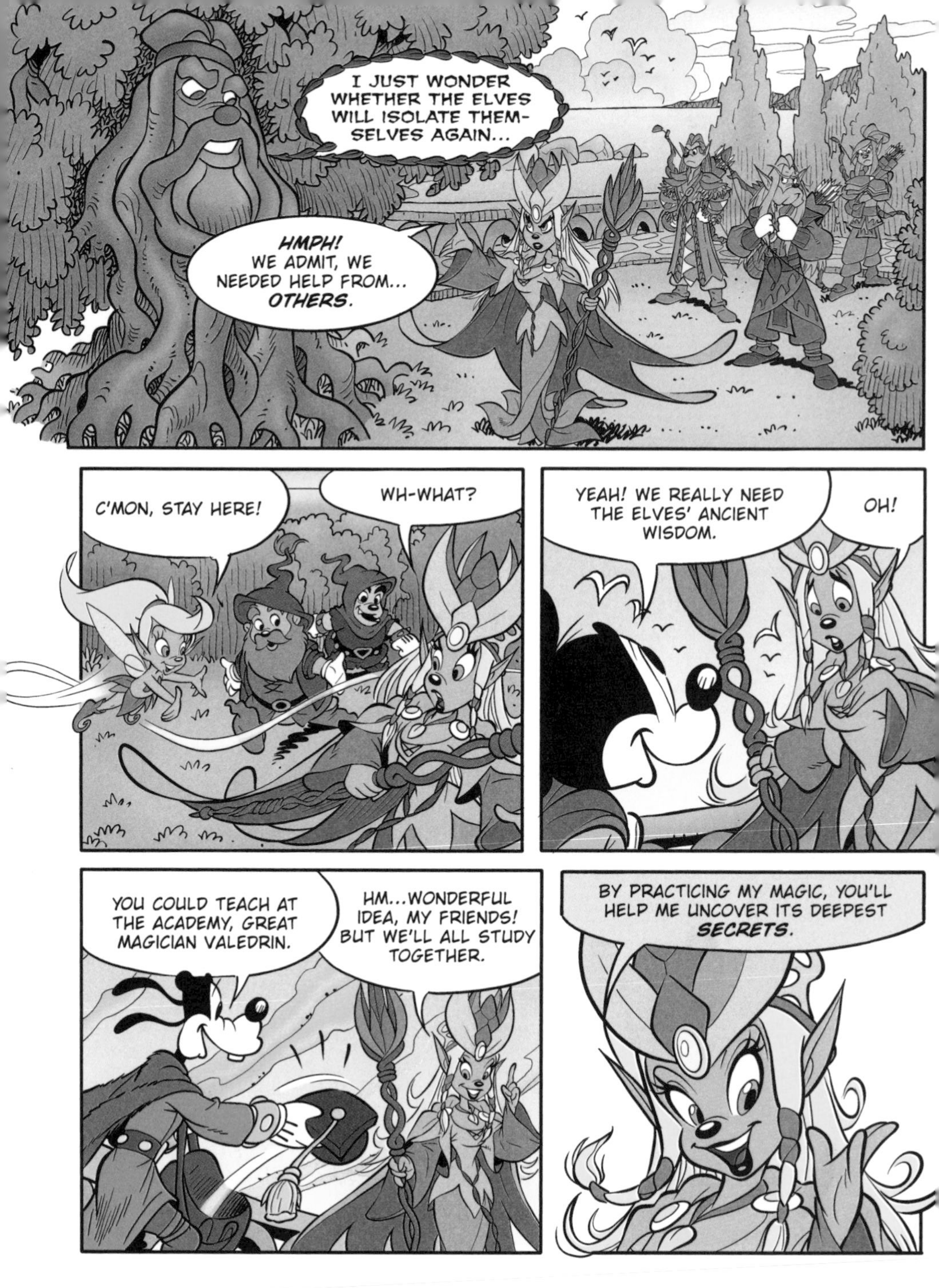
I JUST WONDER WHETHER THE ELVES WILL ISOLATE THEM-SELVES AGAIN...
HMPH! WE ADMIT, WE NEEDED HELP FROM... OTHERS.
C'MON, STAY HERE!
WH-WHAT?
YEAH! WE REALLY NEED THE ELVES' ANCIENT WISDOM.
OH!
YOU COULD TEACH AT THE ACADEMY, GREAT MAGICIAN VALEDRIN.
HM...WONDERFUL IDEA, MY FRIENDS! BUT WE'LL ALL STUDY TOGETHER.
BY PRACTICING MY MAGIC, YOU'LL HELP ME UNCOVER ITS DEEPEST SECRETS.

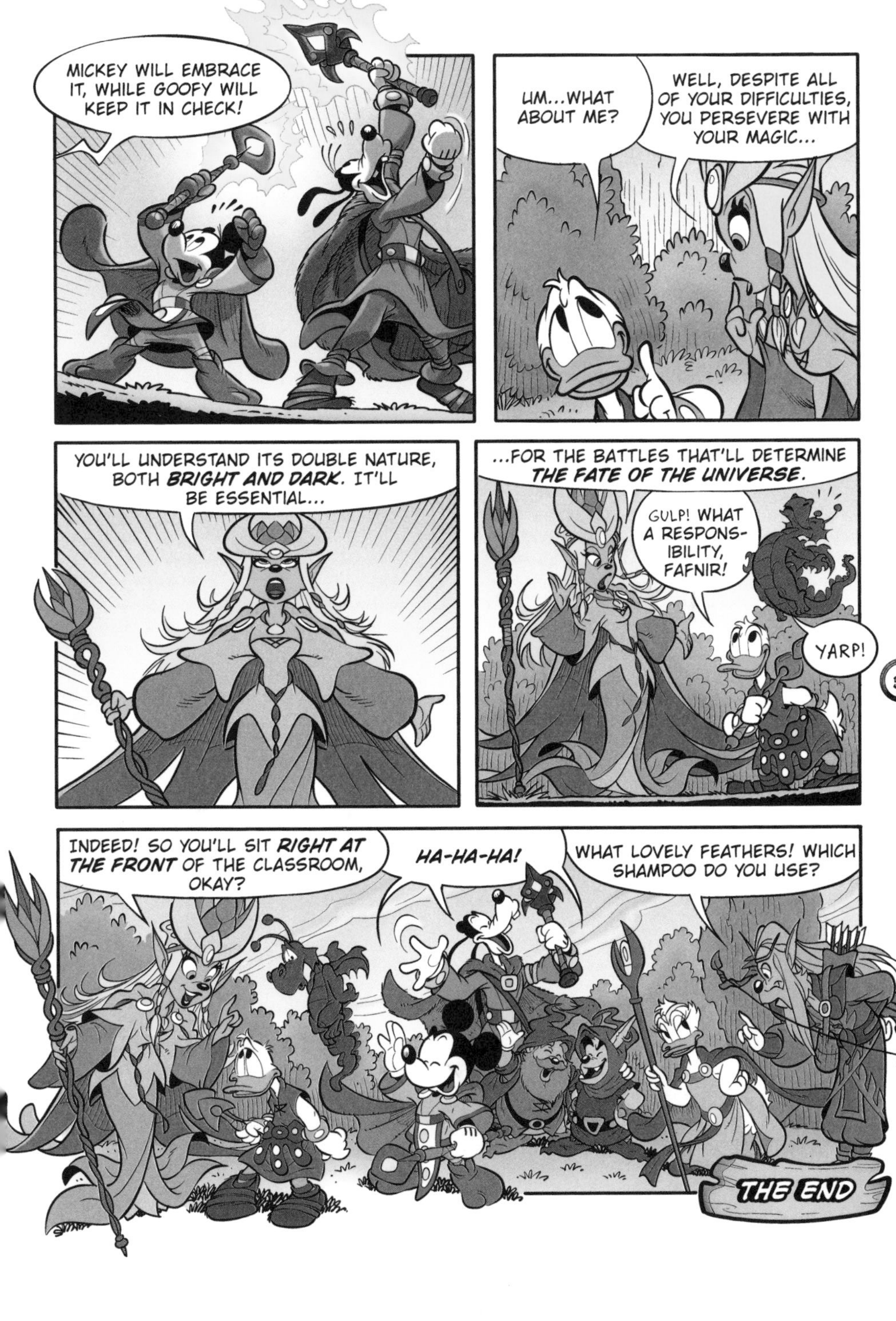
MICKEY WILL EMBRACE IT, WHILE GOOFY WILL KEEP IT IN CHECK!
UM...WHAT ABOUT ME?
WELL, DESPITE ALL OF YOUR DIFFICULTIES, YOU PERSEVERE WITH YOUR MAGIC...
YOU'LL UNDERSTAND ITS DOUBLE NATURE, BOTH BRIGHT AND DARK. IT'LL BE ESSENTIAL...
...FOR THE BATTLES THAT'LL DETERMINE THE FATE OF THE UNIVERSE.
GULP! WHAT A RESPONS-IBILITY, FAFNIR!
YARP!
INDEED! SO YOU'LL SIT RIGHT AT THE FRONT OF THE CLASSROOM, OKAY?
HA-HA-HA!
WHAT LOVELY FEATHERS! WHICH SHAMPOO DO YOU USE?
THE END

Wizards of Mickey

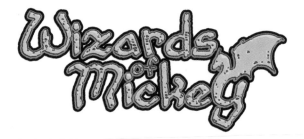

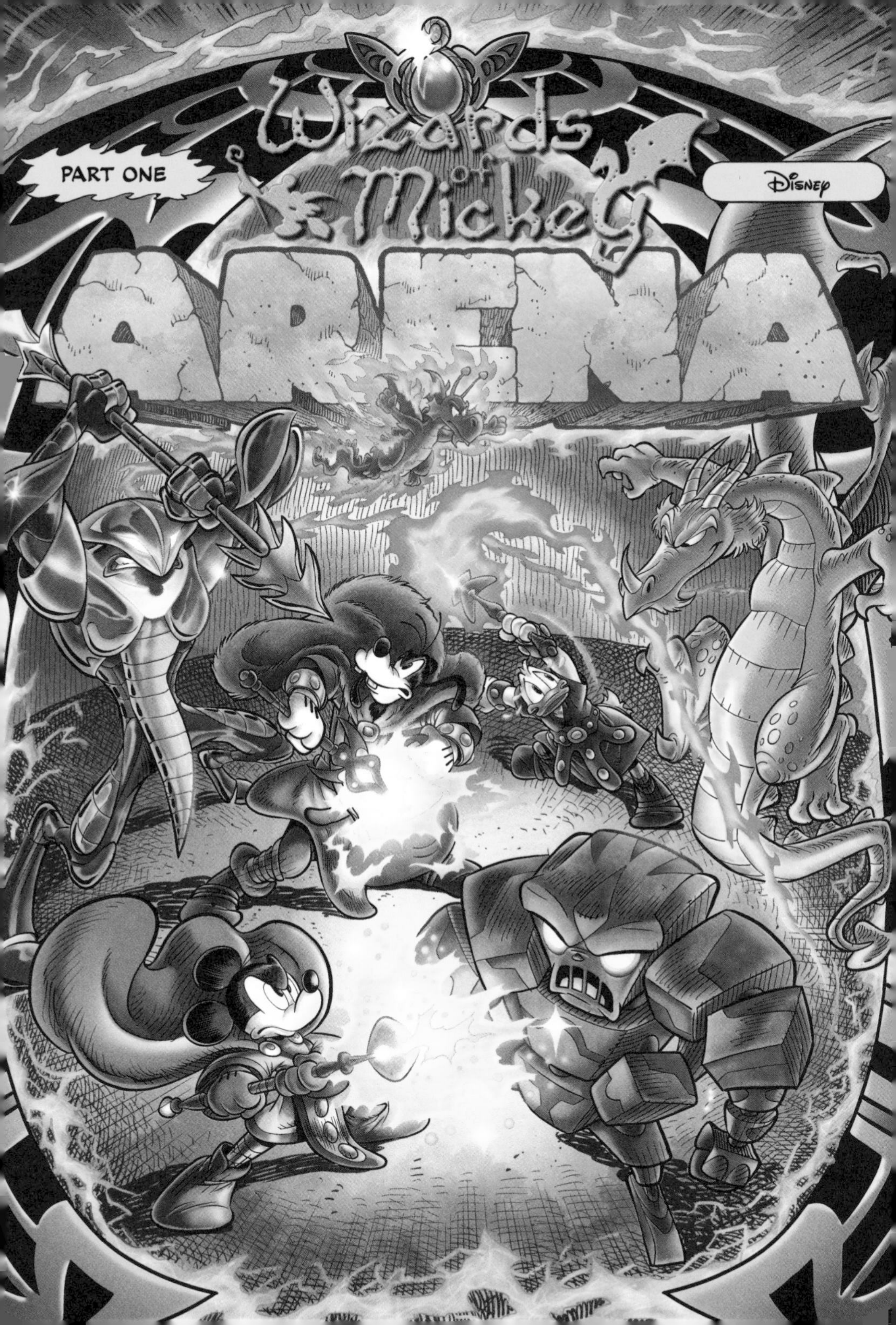
Wizards of Mickey
PART ONE
Disney
ARENA

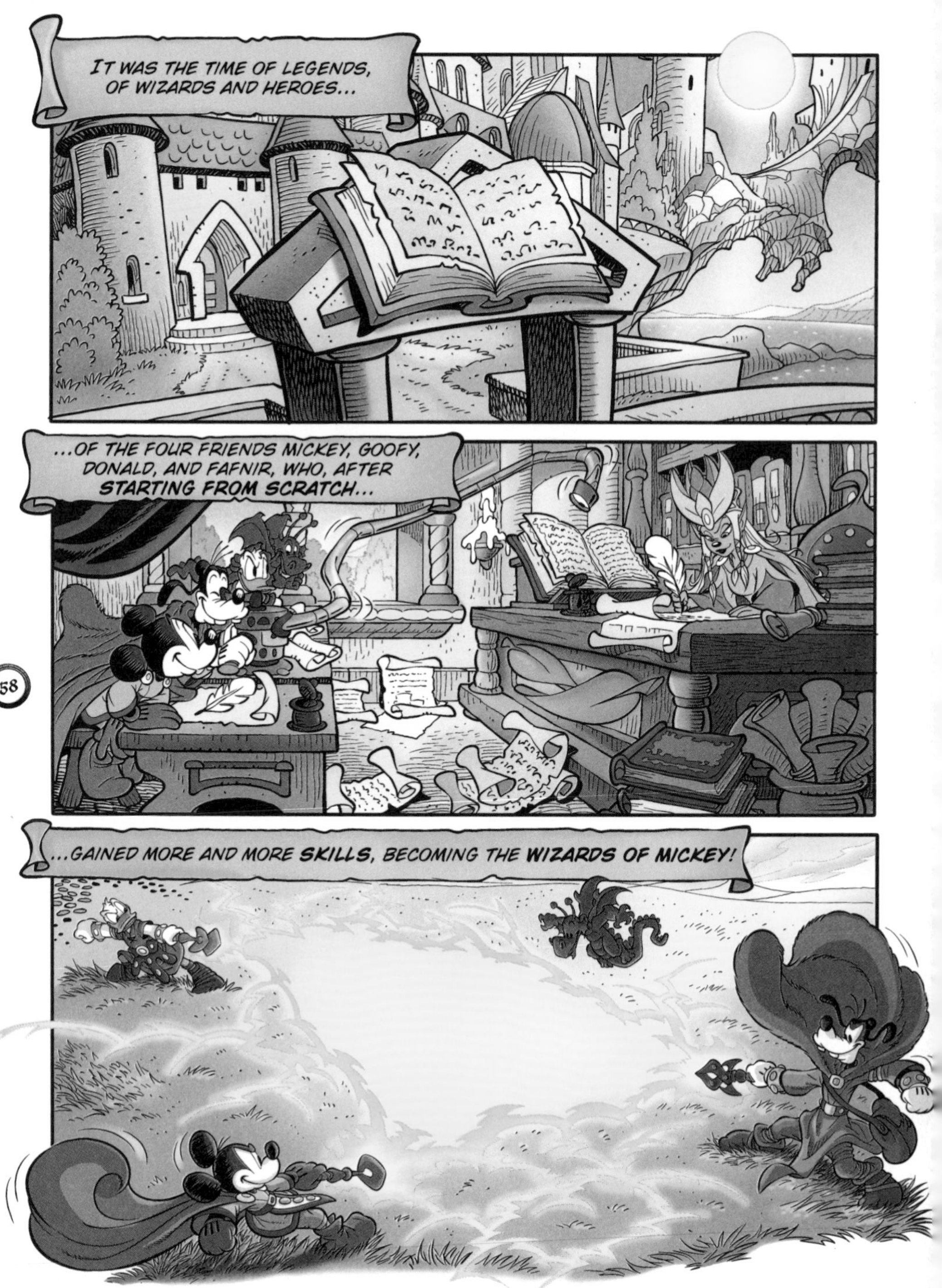
IT WAS THE TIME OF LEGENDS, OF WIZARDS AND HEROES...
...OF THE FOUR FRIENDS MICKEY, GOOFY, DONALD, AND FAFNIR, WHO, AFTER STARTING FROM SCRATCH...
...GAINED MORE AND MORE SKILLS, BECOMING THE WIZARDS OF MICKEY!

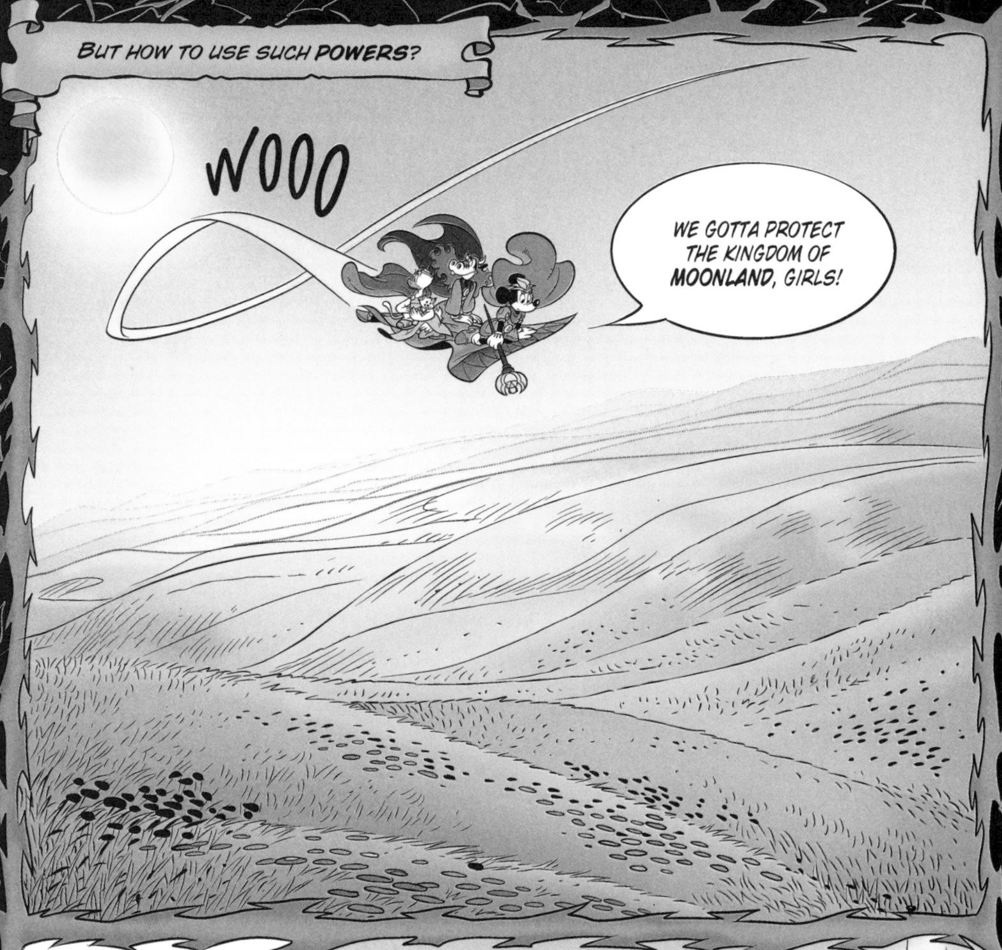
BUT HOW TO USE SUCH POWERS?
WOOO
WE GOTTA PROTECT THE KINGDOM OF MOONLAND, GIRLS!

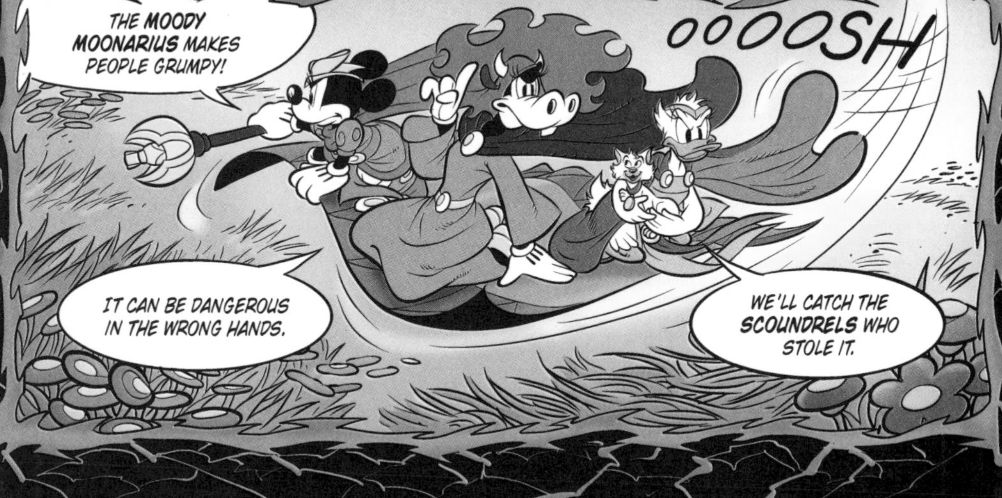
THE MOODY MOONARIUS MAKES PEOPLE GRUMPY!
OOOOSH
IT CAN BE DANGEROUS IN THE WRONG HANDS.
WE'LL CATCH THE SCOUNDRELS WHO STOLE IT.

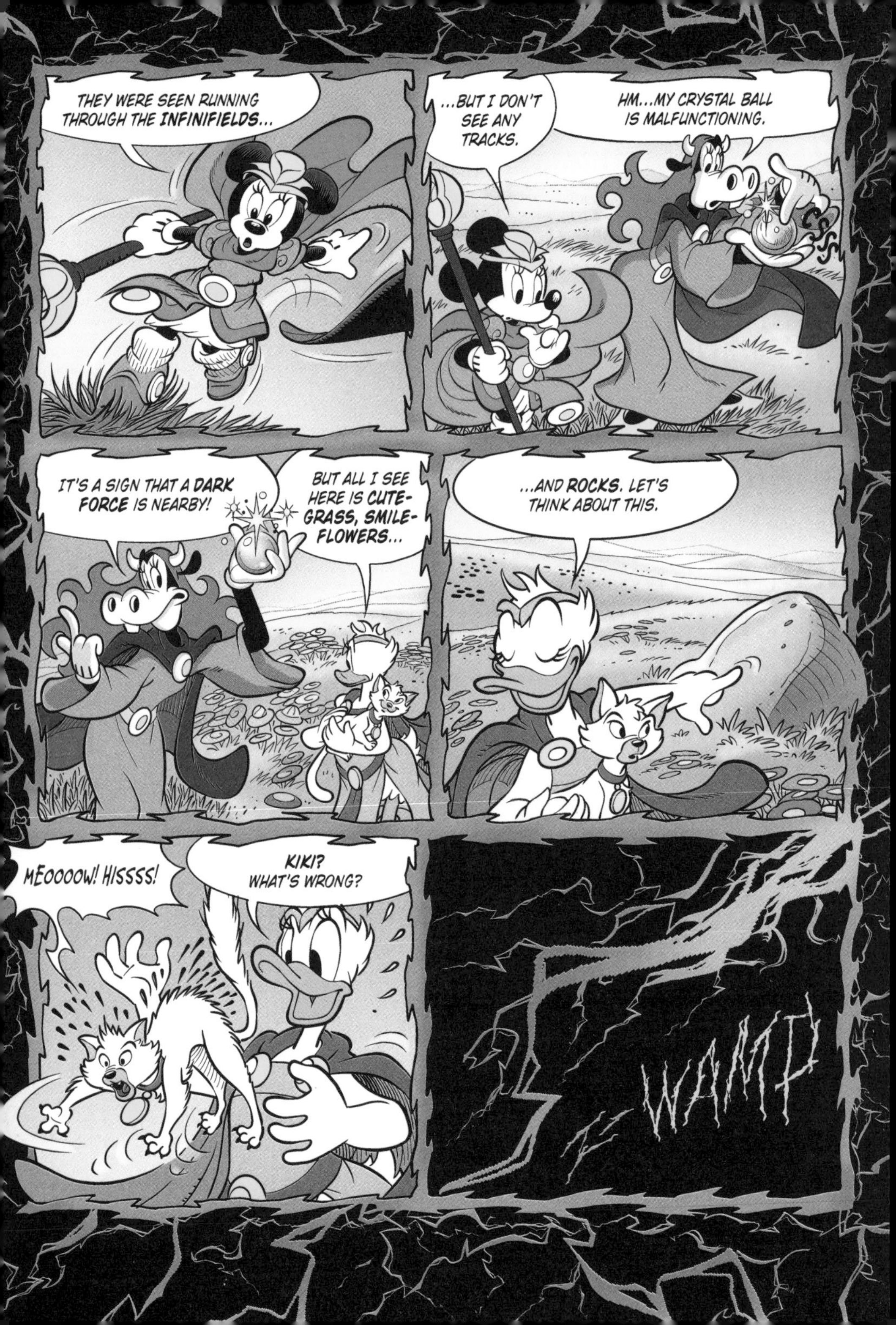
THEY WERE SEEN RUNNING THROUGH THE INFINIFIELDS...
HM...MY CRYSTAL BALL IS MALFUNCTIONING.
...BUT I DON'T SEE ANY TRACKS.
IT'S A SIGN THAT A DARK FORCE IS NEARBY!
BUT ALL I SEE HERE IS CUTE-GRASS, SMILE-FLOWERS...
...AND ROCKS. LET'S THINK ABOUT THIS.
MEOOOOW! HISSSS!
KIKI? WHAT'S WRONG?
WAMP!

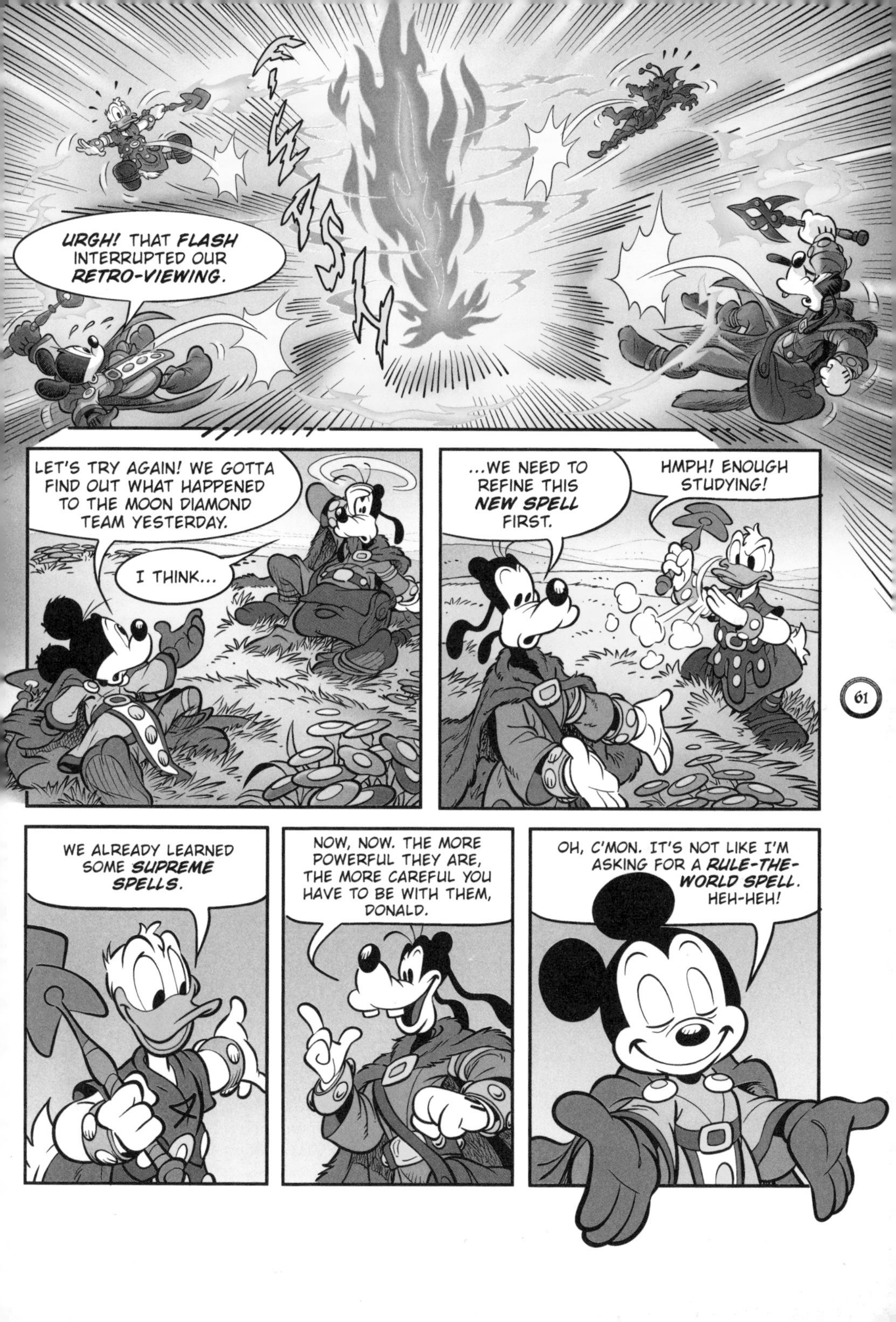
FLASH
URGH! THAT FLASH INTERRUPTED OUR RETRO-VIEWING.
LET'S TRY AGAIN! WE GOTTA FIND OUT WHAT HAPPENED TO THE MOON DIAMOND TEAM YESTERDAY.
I THINK...
...WE NEED TO REFINE THIS NEW SPELL FIRST.
HMPH! ENOUGH STUDYING!
WE ALREADY LEARNED SOME SUPREME SPELLS.
NOW, NOW. THE MORE POWERFUL THEY ARE, THE MORE CAREFUL YOU HAVE TO BE WITH THEM, DONALD.
OH, C'MON. IT'S NOT LIKE I'M ASKING FOR A RULE-THE-WORLD SPELL. HEH-HEH!

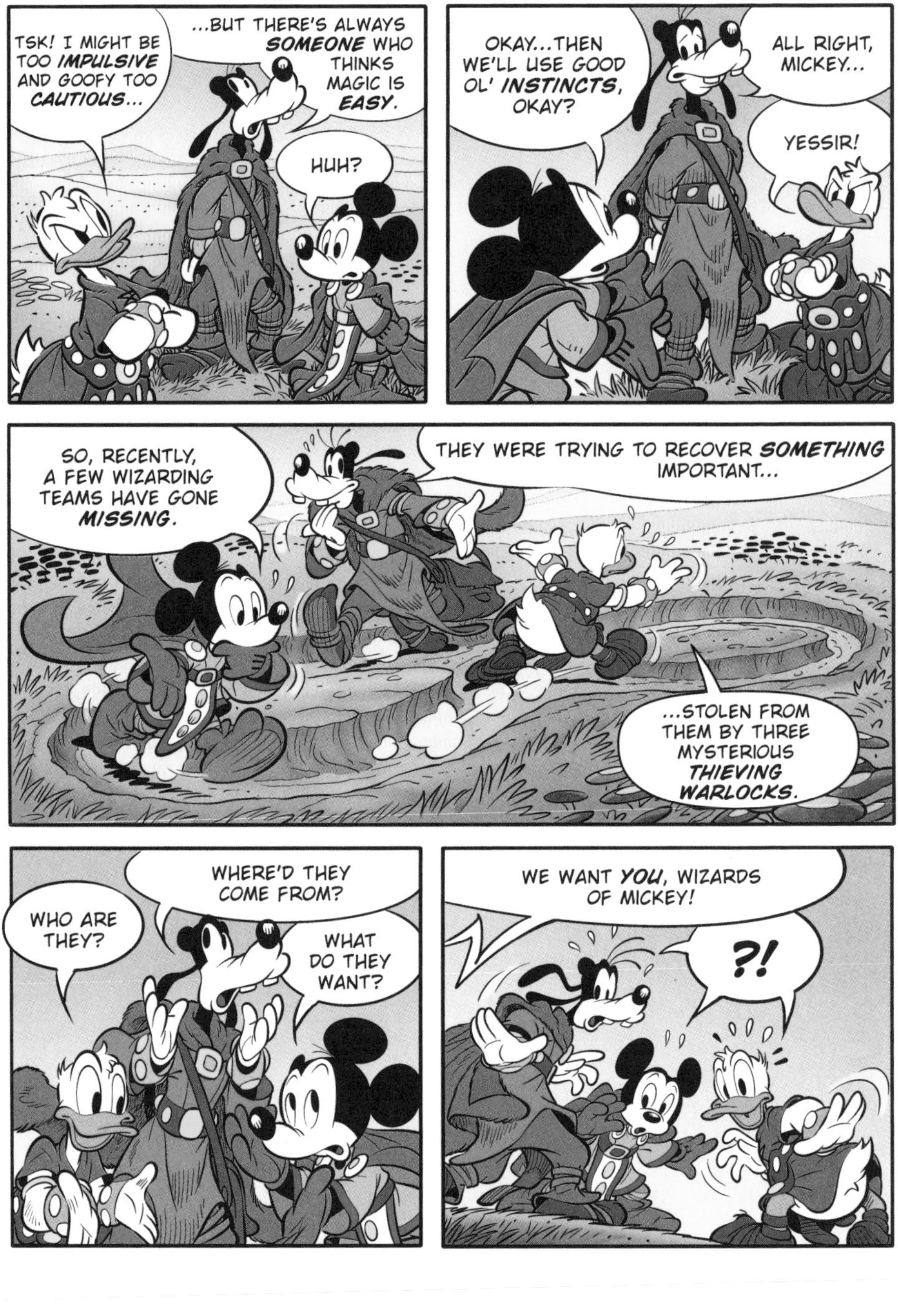
TSK! I MIGHT BE TOO IMPULSIVE AND GOOFY TOO CAUTIOUS...
...BUT THERE'S ALWAYS SOMEONE WHO THINKS MAGIC IS EASY.
HUH?
OKAY...THEN WE'LL USE GOOD OL' INSTINCTS, OKAY?
ALL RIGHT, MICKEY...
YESSIR!
SO, RECENTLY, A FEW WIZARDING TEAMS HAVE GONE MISSING.
THEY WERE TRYING TO RECOVER SOMETHING IMPORTANT...
...STOLEN FROM THEM BY THREE MYSTERIOUS THIEVING WARLOCKS.
WHO ARE THEY?
WHERE'D THEY COME FROM?
WHAT DO THEY WANT?
WE WANT YOU, WIZARDS OF MICKEY!
?!

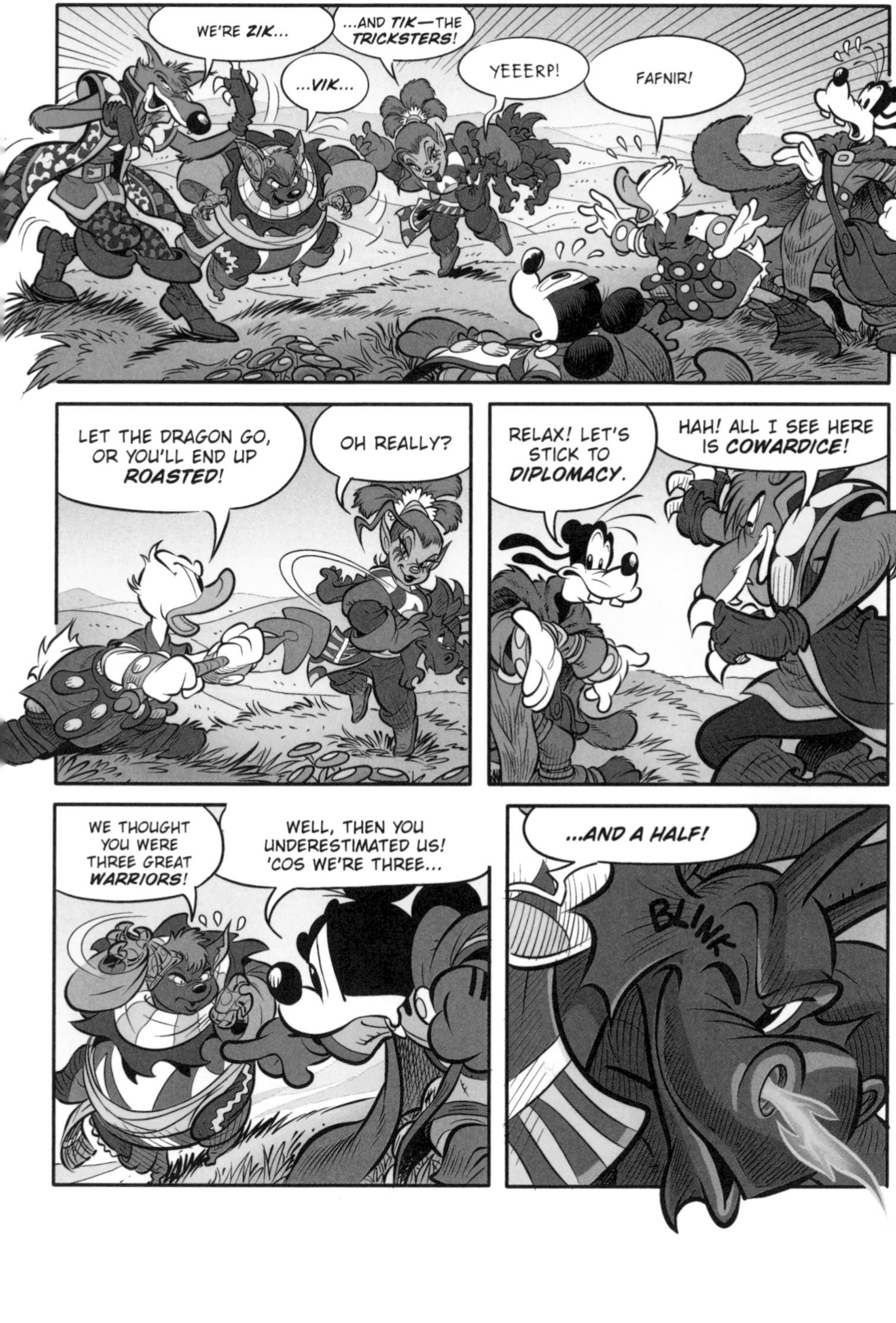
WE'RE ZIK...
...VIK...
...AND TIK—THE TRICKSTERS!
YEEERP!
FAFNIR!
LET THE DRAGON GO, OR YOU'LL END UP ROASTED!
OH REALLY?
RELAX! LET'S STICK TO DIPLOMACY.
HAH! ALL I SEE HERE IS COWARDICE!
WE THOUGHT YOU WERE THREE GREAT WARRIORS!
WELL, THEN YOU UNDERESTIMATED US! 'COS WE'RE THREE...
...AND A HALF!
BLINK

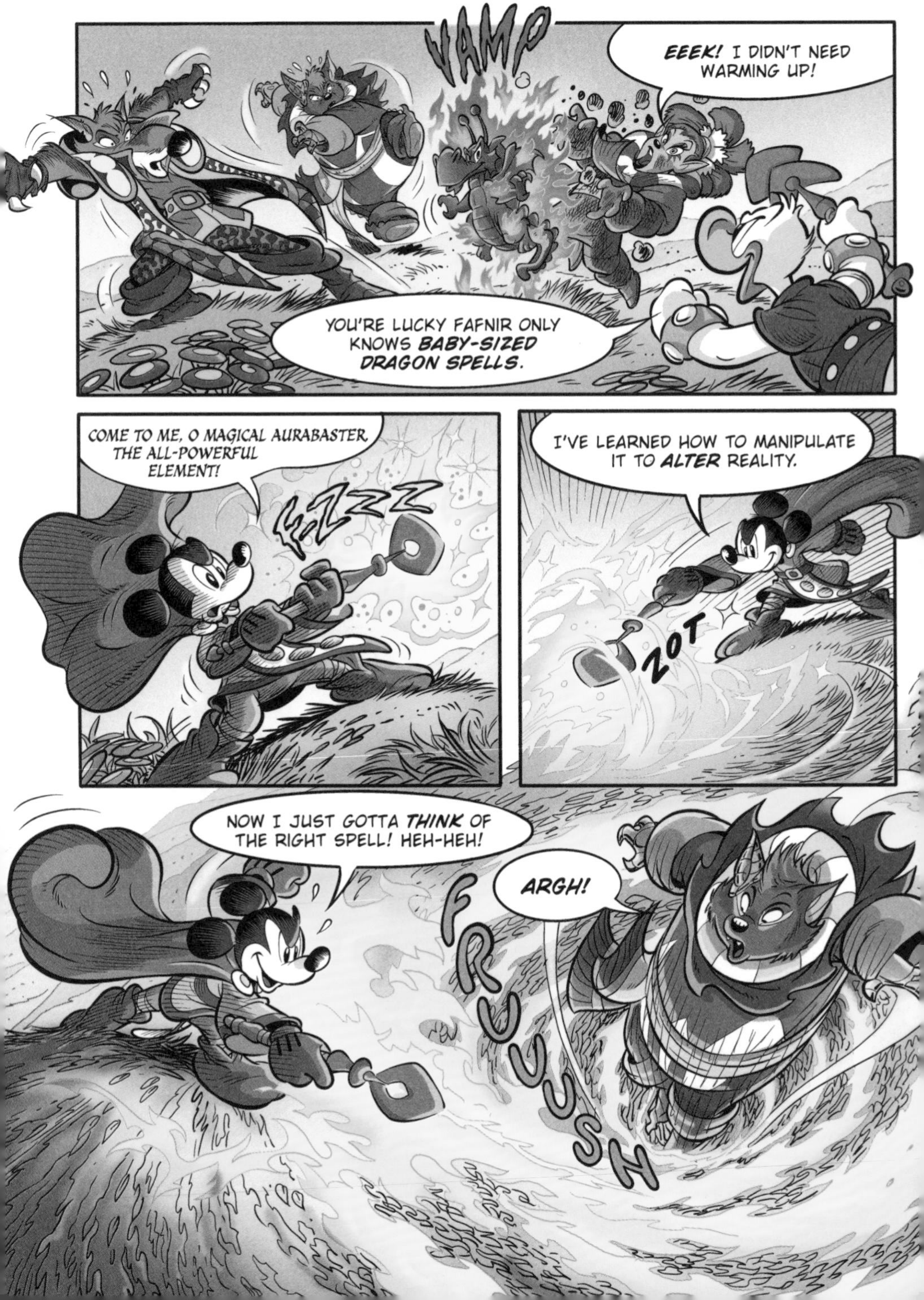
VAMP
EEEK! I DIDN'T NEED WARMING UP!
YOU'RE LUCKY FAFNIR ONLY KNOWS BABY-SIZED DRAGON SPELLS.
COME TO ME, O MAGICAL AURABASTER, THE ALL-POWERFUL ELEMENT!
FZZZZ
I'VE LEARNED HOW TO MANIPULATE IT TO ALTER REALITY.
ZOT
NOW I JUST GOTTA THINK OF THE RIGHT SPELL! HEH-HEH!
ARGH!
FRUUUSH

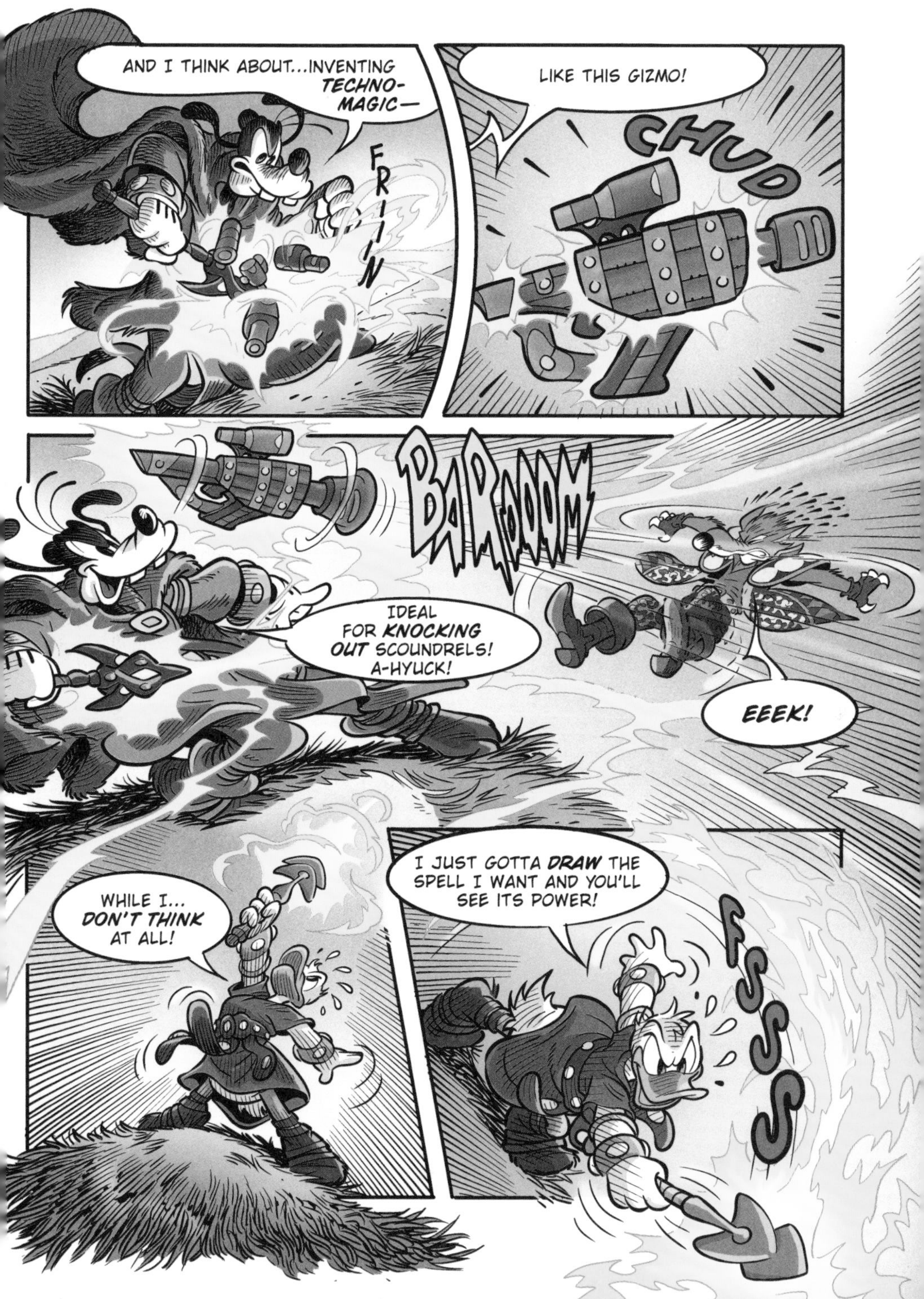
AND I THINK ABOUT...INVENTING TECHNO-MAGIC—
FRIIIN
LIKE THIS GIZMO!
CHUD
BaROOOM
IDEAL FOR KNOCKING OUT SCOUNDRELS! A-HYUCK!
EEEK!
WHILE I... DON'T THINK AT ALL!
I JUST GOTTA DRAW THE SPELL I WANT AND YOU'LL SEE ITS POWER!
FSSSS

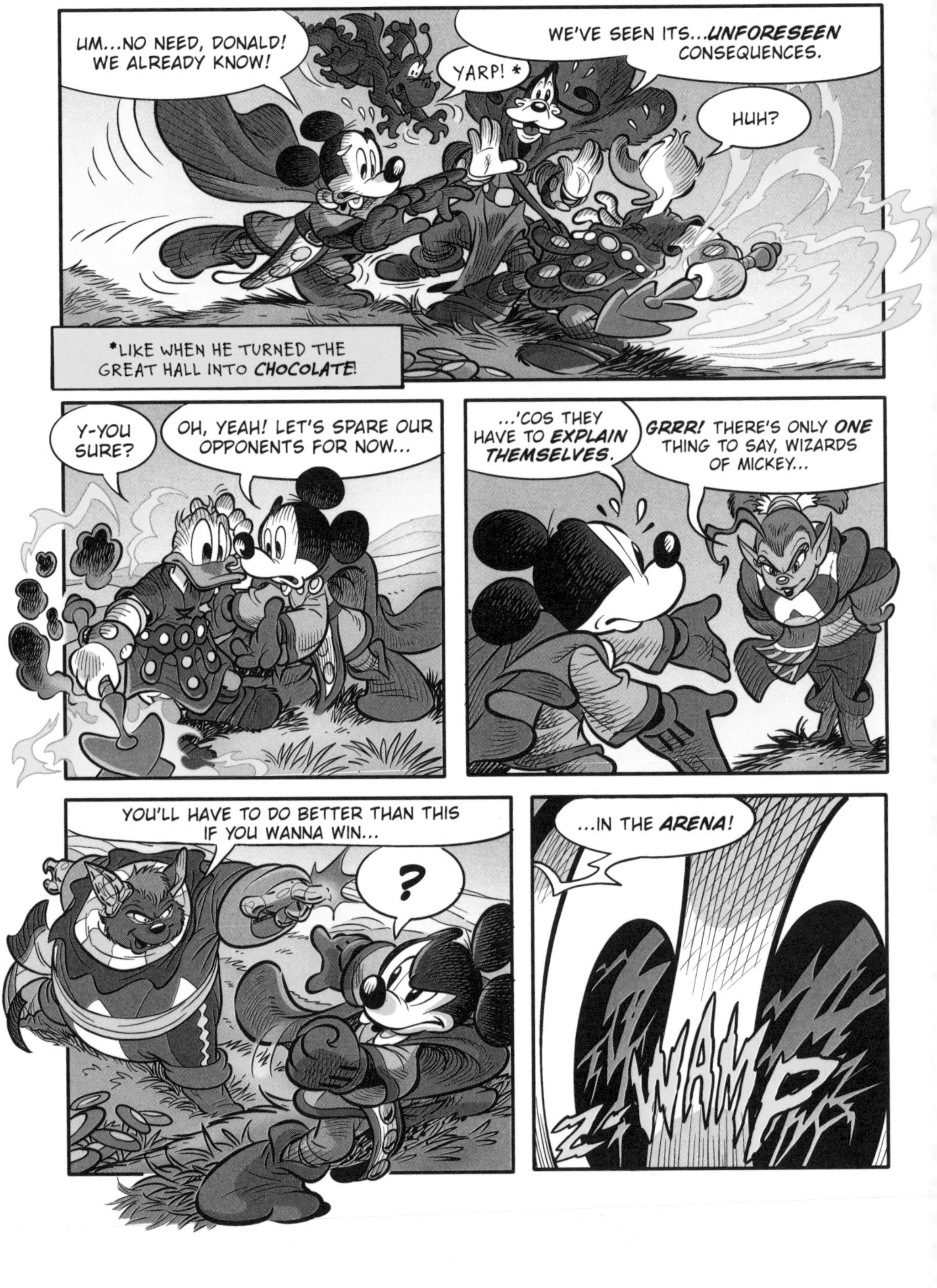
UM...NO NEED, DONALD! WE ALREADY KNOW!
WE'VE SEEN ITS...UNFORESEEN CONSEQUENCES.
YARP! *
HUH?
*LIKE WHEN HE TURNED THE GREAT HALL INTO CHOCOLATE!
Y-YOU SURE?
OH, YEAH! LET'S SPARE OUR OPPONENTS FOR NOW...
...'COS THEY HAVE TO EXPLAIN THEMSELVES.
GRRR! THERE'S ONLY ONE THING TO SAY, WIZARDS OF MICKEY...
YOU'LL HAVE TO DO BETTER THAN THIS IF YOU WANNA WIN...
?
...IN THE ARENA!
WAMP

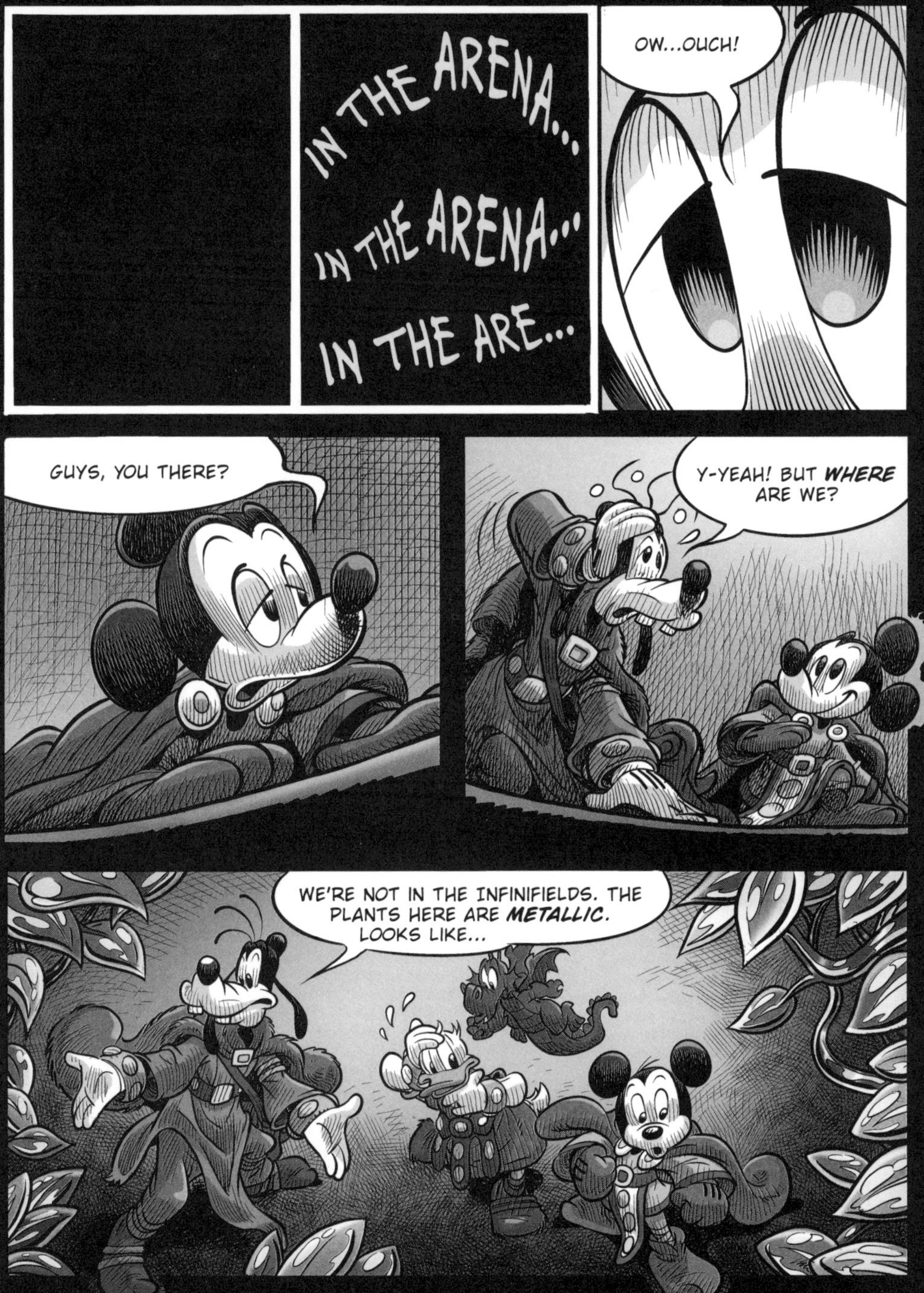
IN THE ARENA...
IN THE ARENA...
IN THE ARE...
OW...OUCH!
GUYS, YOU THERE?
Y-YEAH! BUT WHERE ARE WE?
WE'RE NOT IN THE INFINIFIELDS. THE PLANTS HERE ARE METALLIC. LOOKS LIKE...

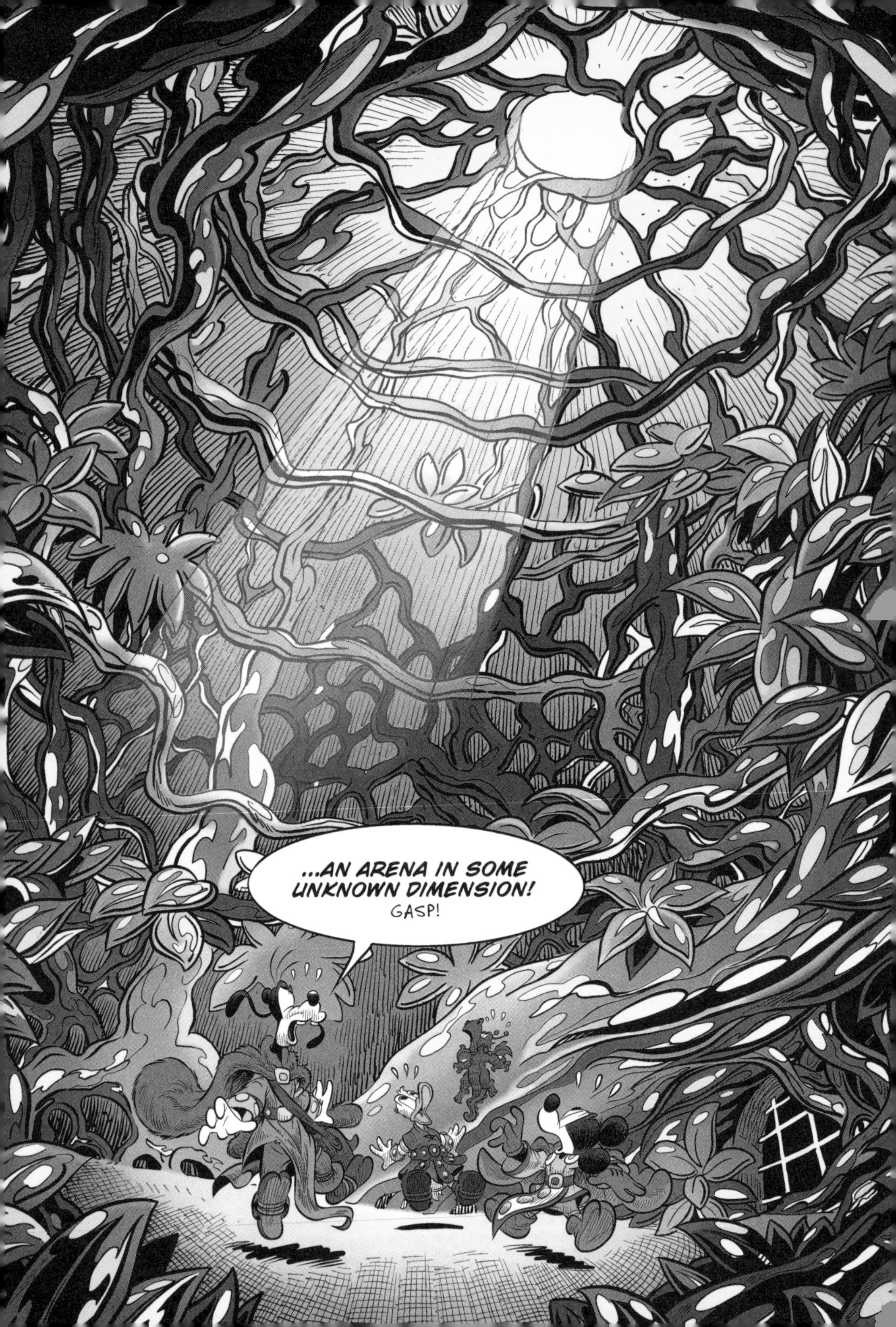
...AN ARENA IN SOME UNKNOWN DIMENSION!
GASP!

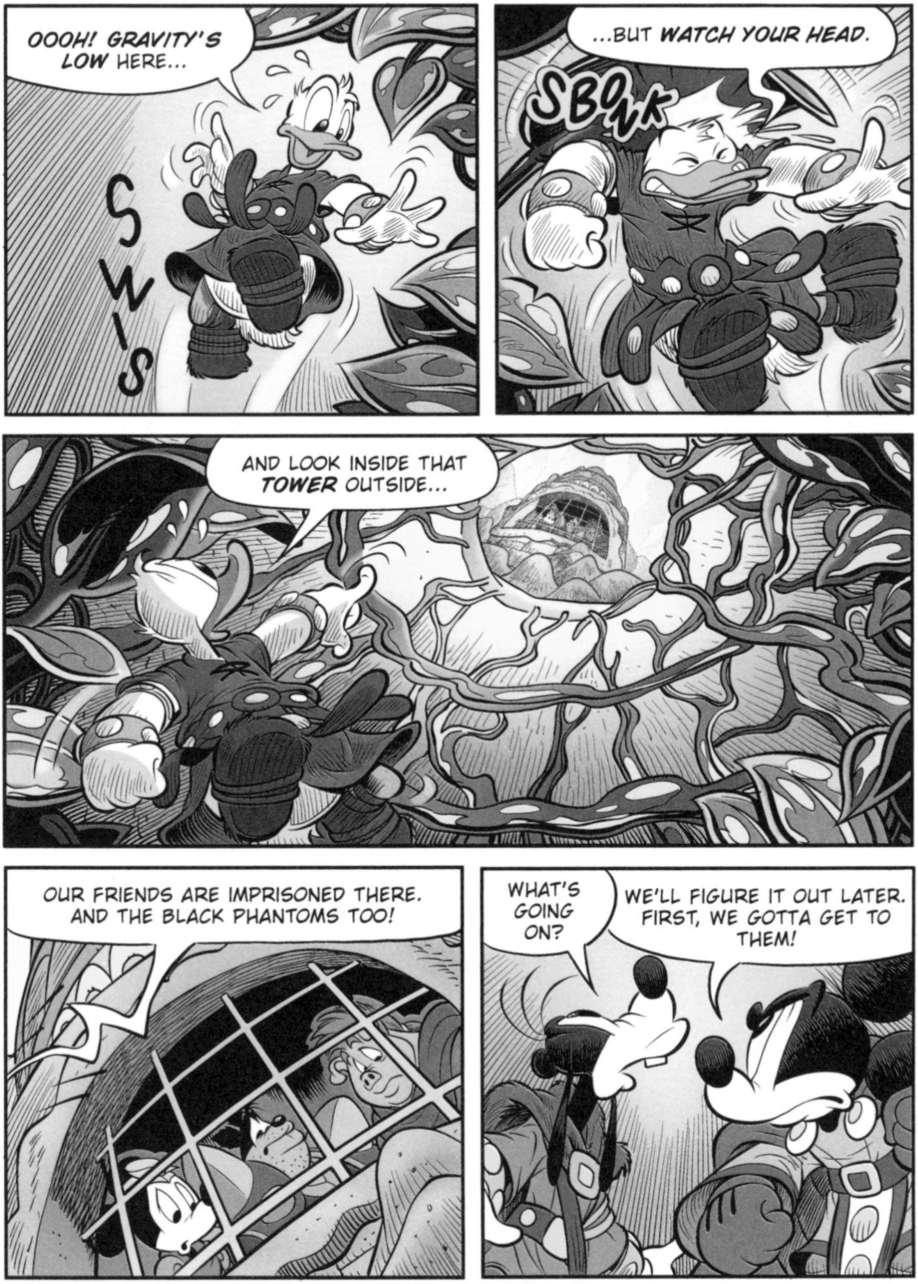
OOOH! GRAVITY'S LOW HERE...
SWIS
...BUT WATCH YOUR HEAD.
SBONK
AND LOOK INSIDE THAT TOWER OUTSIDE...
OUR FRIENDS ARE IMPRISONED THERE. AND THE BLACK PHANTOMS TOO!
WHAT'S GOING ON?
WE'LL FIGURE IT OUT LATER. FIRST, WE GOTTA GET TO THEM!

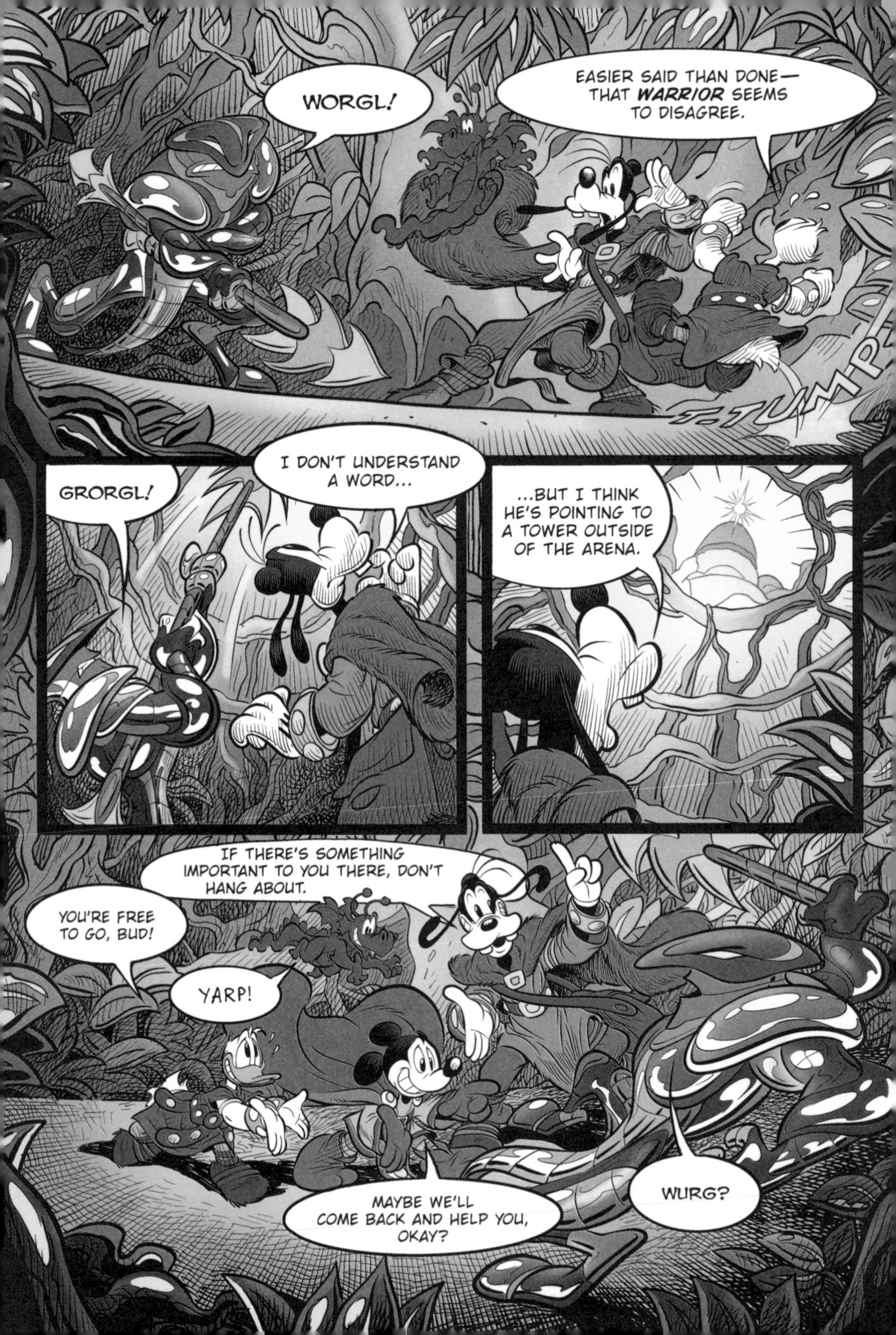

WORGL!
EASIER SAID THAN DONE— THAT WARRIOR SEEMS TO DISAGREE.
T-TUMP
GRORGL!
I DON'T UNDERSTAND A WORD...
...BUT I THINK HE'S POINTING TO A TOWER OUTSIDE OF THE ARENA.
IF THERE'S SOMETHING IMPORTANT TO YOU THERE, DON'T HANG ABOUT.
YOU'RE FREE TO GO, BUD!
YARP!
MAYBE WE'LL COME BACK AND HELP YOU, OKAY?
WURG?

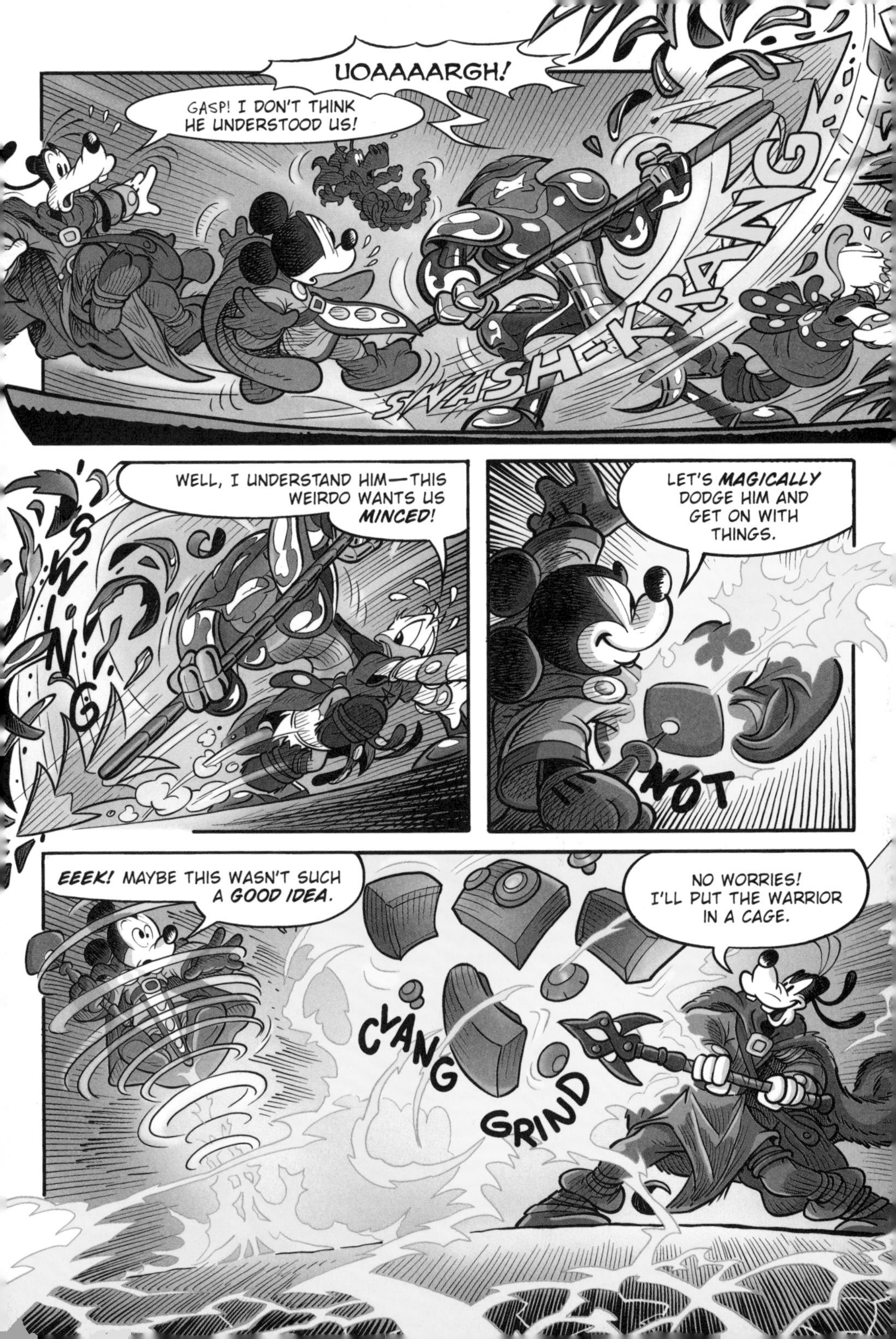
UOAAAARGH!
GASP! I DON'T THINK HE UNDERSTOOD US!
SWASH-KRANG
SWING
WELL, I UNDERSTAND HIM—THIS WEIRDO WANTS US *MINCED*!
LET'S *MAGICALLY* DODGE HIM AND GET ON WITH THINGS.
NOT
EEEK! MAYBE THIS WASN'T SUCH A *GOOD IDEA*.
NO WORRIES! I'LL PUT THE WARRIOR IN A CAGE.
CLANG
GRIND

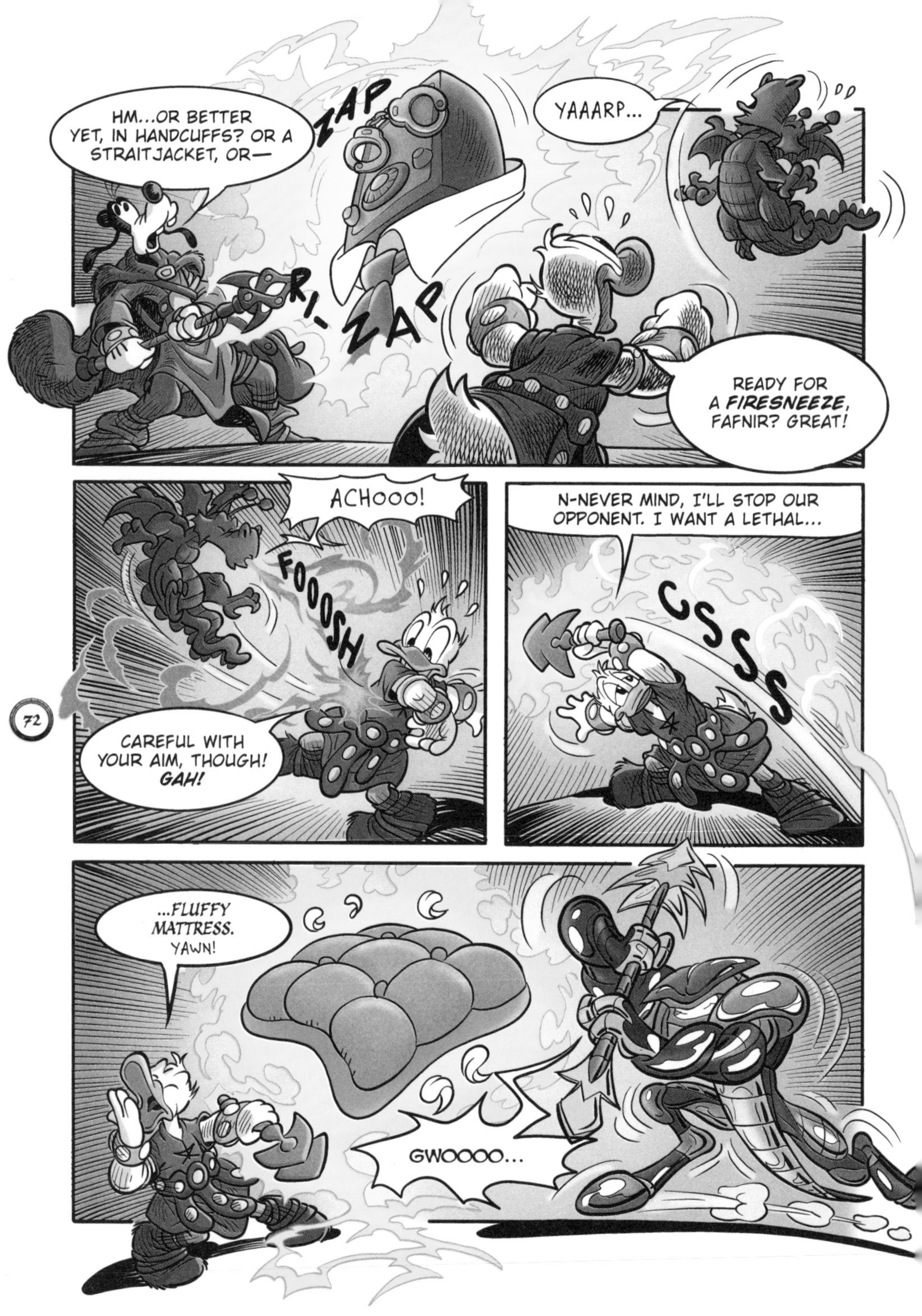
HM...OR BETTER YET, IN HANDCUFFS? OR A STRAITJACKET, OR—
ZAP
RI-ZAP
YAAARP...
READY FOR A ***FIRESNEEZE***, FAFNIR? GREAT!
ACHOOO!
FOOOOSH
CAREFUL WITH YOUR AIM, THOUGH! ***GAH!***
N-NEVER MIND, I'LL STOP OUR OPPONENT. I WANT A LETHAL...
CSSSS
...FLUFFY MATTRESS. YAWN!
GWOOOO...

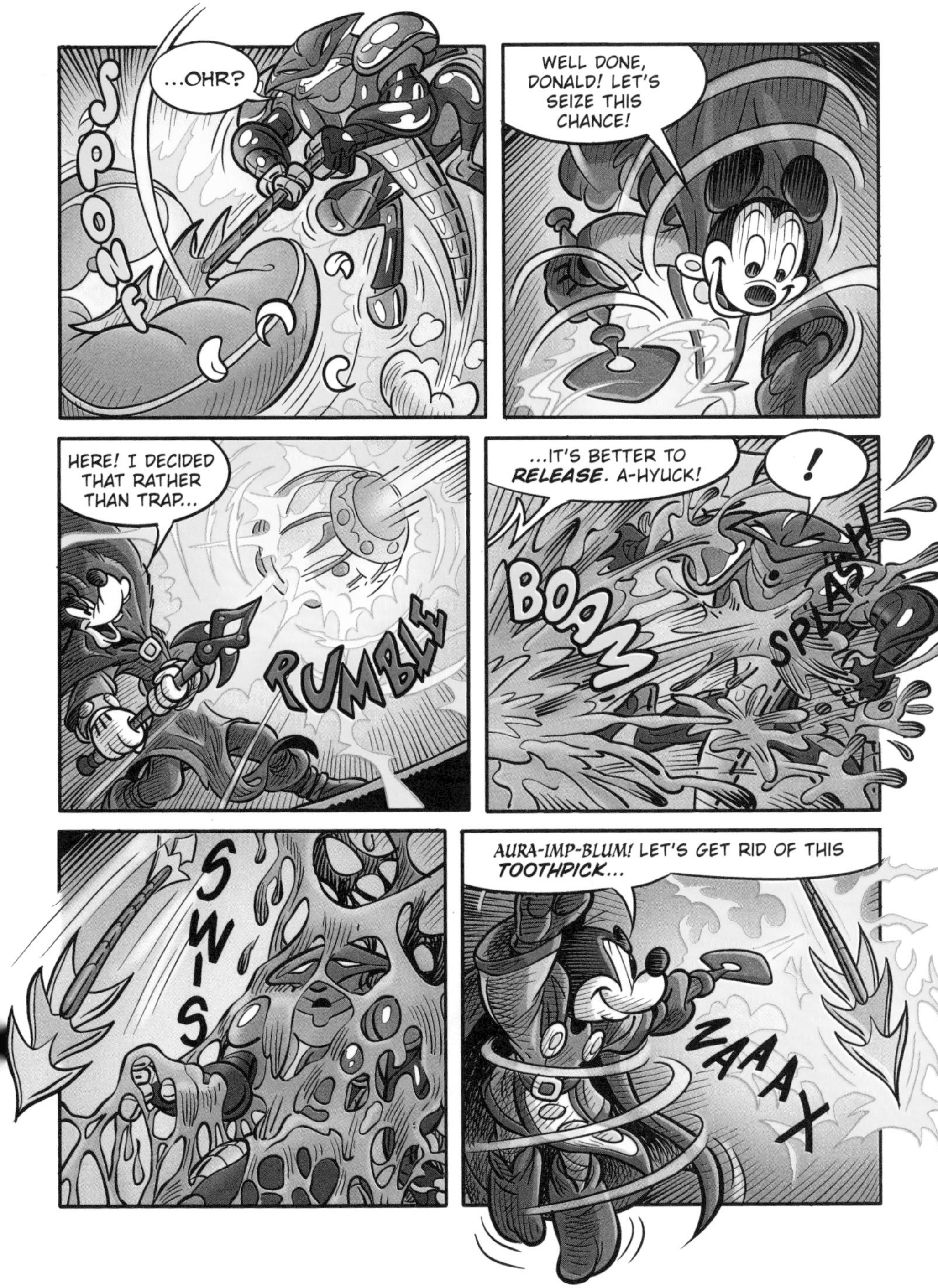
SPONF
...OHR?
WELL DONE, DONALD! LET'S SEIZE THIS CHANCE!
HERE! I DECIDED THAT RATHER THAN TRAP...
RUMBLE
...IT'S BETTER TO *RELEASE*. A-HYUCK!
!
BOAM
SPLASH
SWIS
AURA-IMP-BLUM! LET'S GET RID OF THIS *TOOTHPICK*...
ZAAAX

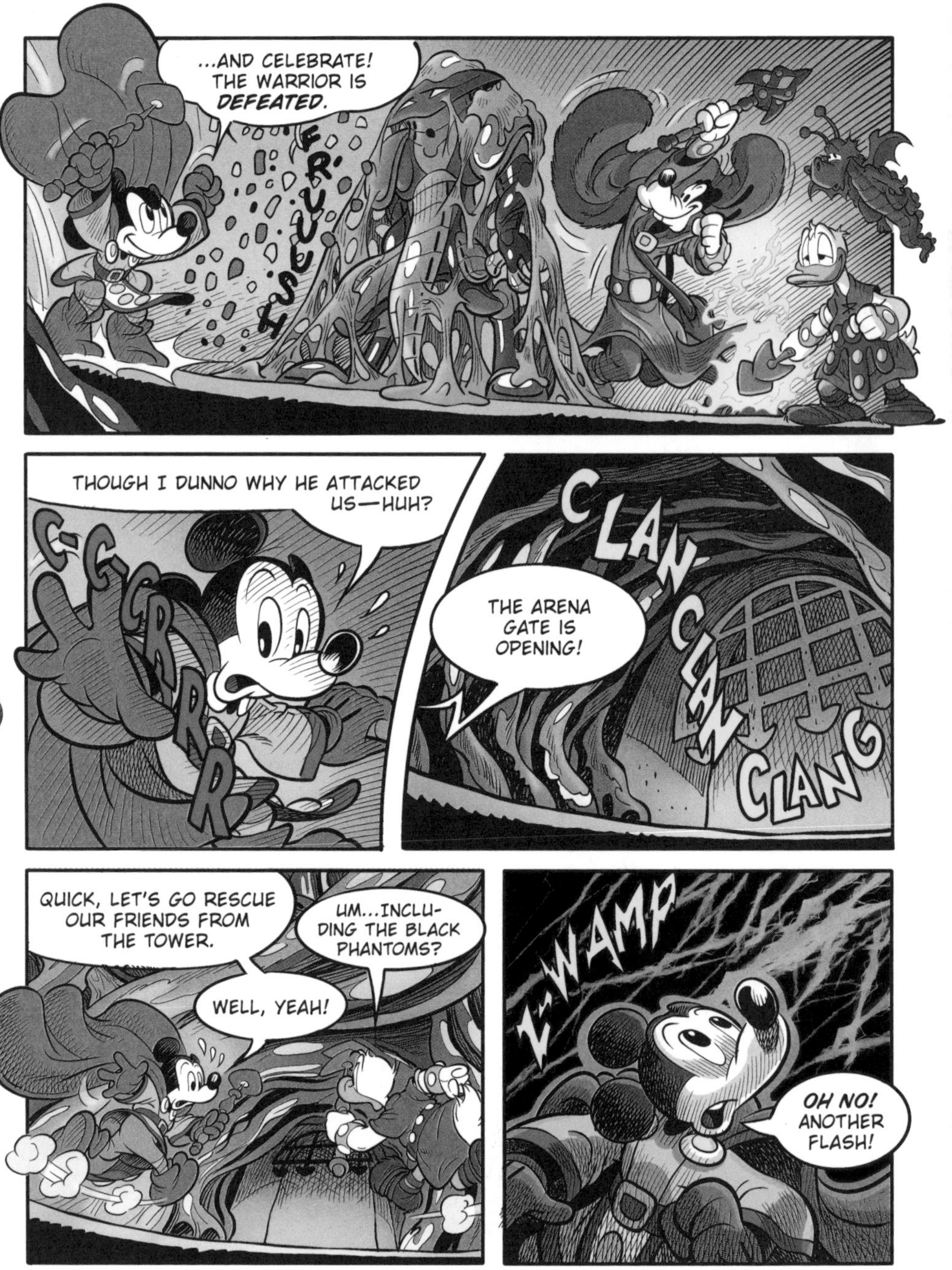
...AND CELEBRATE! THE WARRIOR IS DEFEATED.
FRRUUSHH
THOUGH I DUNNO WHY HE ATTACKED US—HUH?
C-C-CRRRR
CLAN-CLAN-CLAN CLANG
THE ARENA GATE IS OPENING!
QUICK, LET'S GO RESCUE OUR FRIENDS FROM THE TOWER.
UM...INCLU-DING THE BLACK PHANTOMS?
WELL, YEAH!
Z-WAMP
OH NO! ANOTHER FLASH!

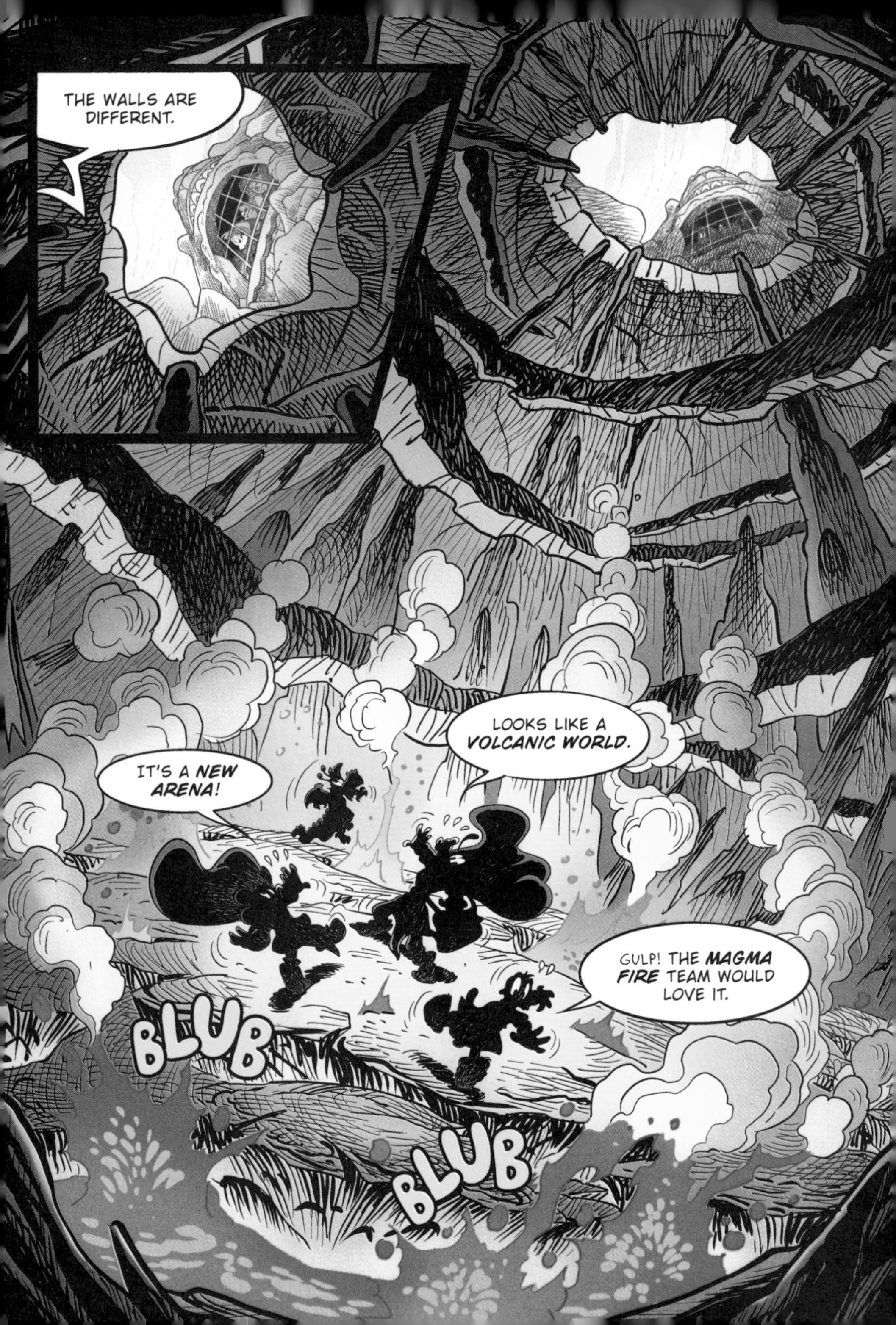
THE WALLS ARE DIFFERENT.
IT'S A NEW ARENA!
LOOKS LIKE A VOLCANIC WORLD.
GULP! THE MAGMA FIRE TEAM WOULD LOVE IT.
BLUB
BLUB

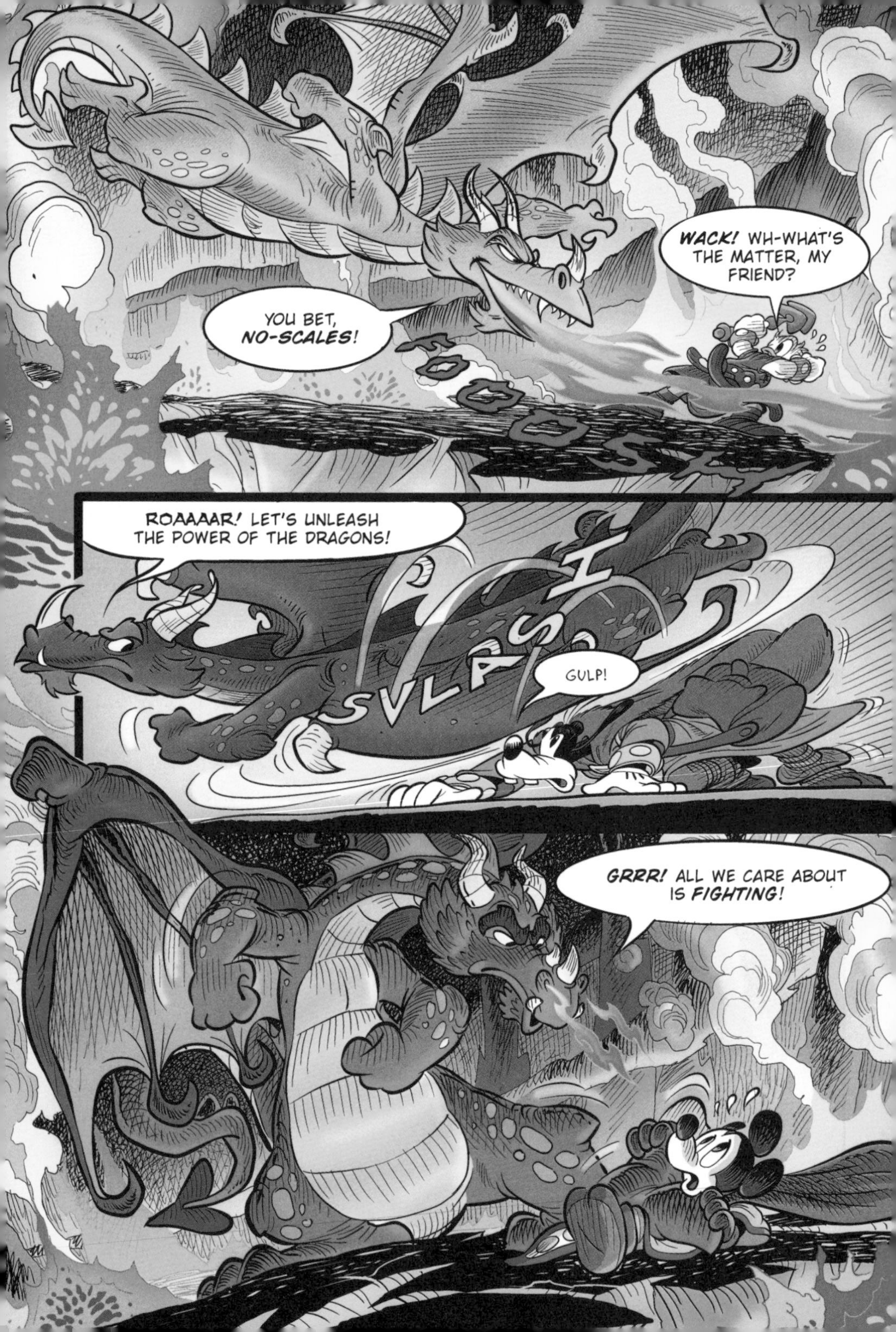
WACK! WH-WHAT'S THE MATTER, MY FRIEND?
YOU BET, NO-SCALES!
ROAAAAR! LET'S UNLEASH THE POWER OF THE DRAGONS!
GULP!
GRRR! ALL WE CARE ABOUT IS FIGHTING!

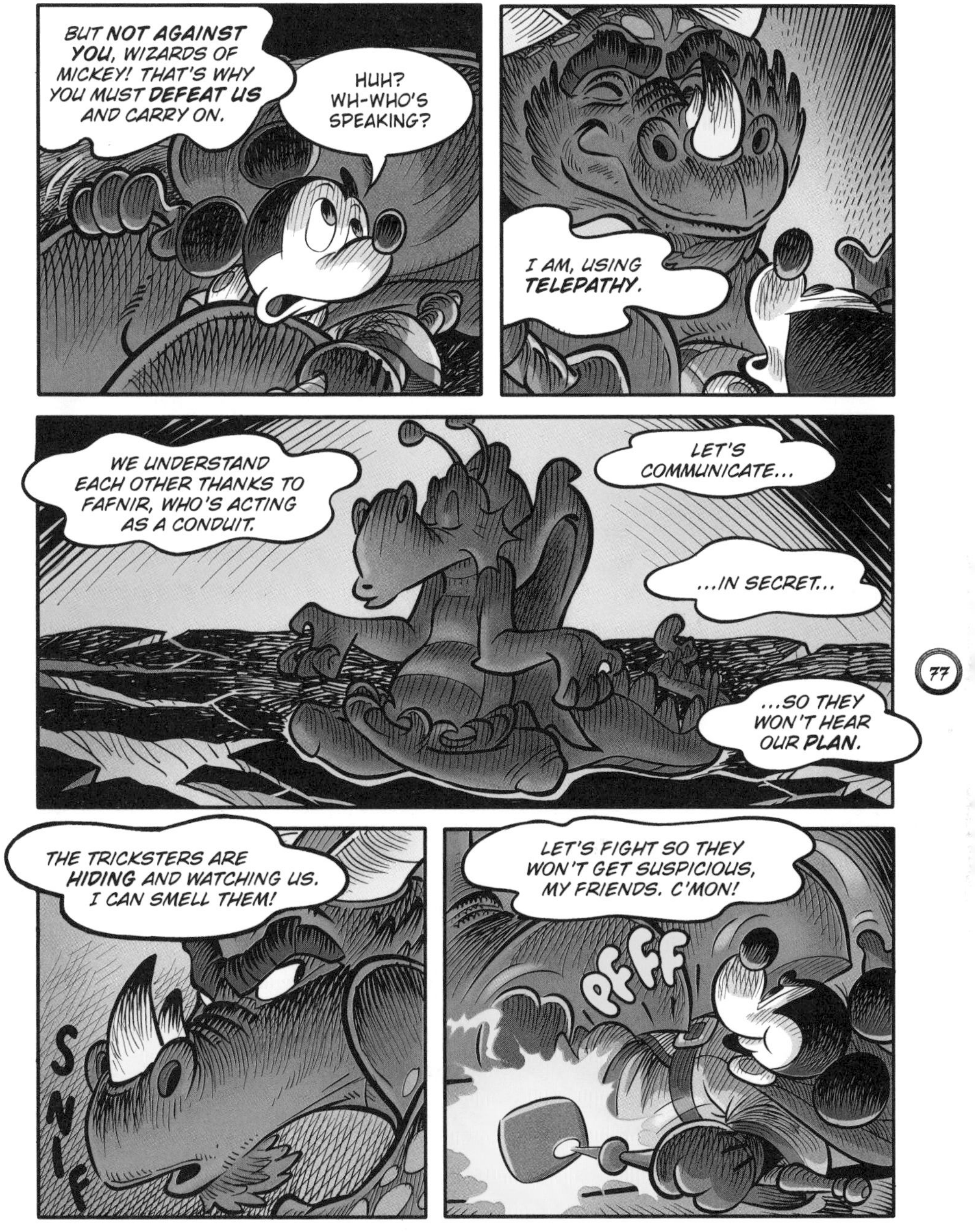
BUT NOT AGAINST YOU, WIZARDS OF MICKEY! THAT'S WHY YOU MUST DEFEAT US AND CARRY ON.
HUH? WH-WHO'S SPEAKING?
I AM, USING TELEPATHY.
WE UNDERSTAND EACH OTHER THANKS TO FAFNIR, WHO'S ACTING AS A CONDUIT.
LET'S COMMUNICATE...
...IN SECRET...
...SO THEY WON'T HEAR OUR PLAN.
THE TRICKSTERS ARE HIDING AND WATCHING US. I CAN SMELL THEM!
SNIF
LET'S FIGHT SO THEY WON'T GET SUSPICIOUS, MY FRIENDS. C'MON!
PFFF

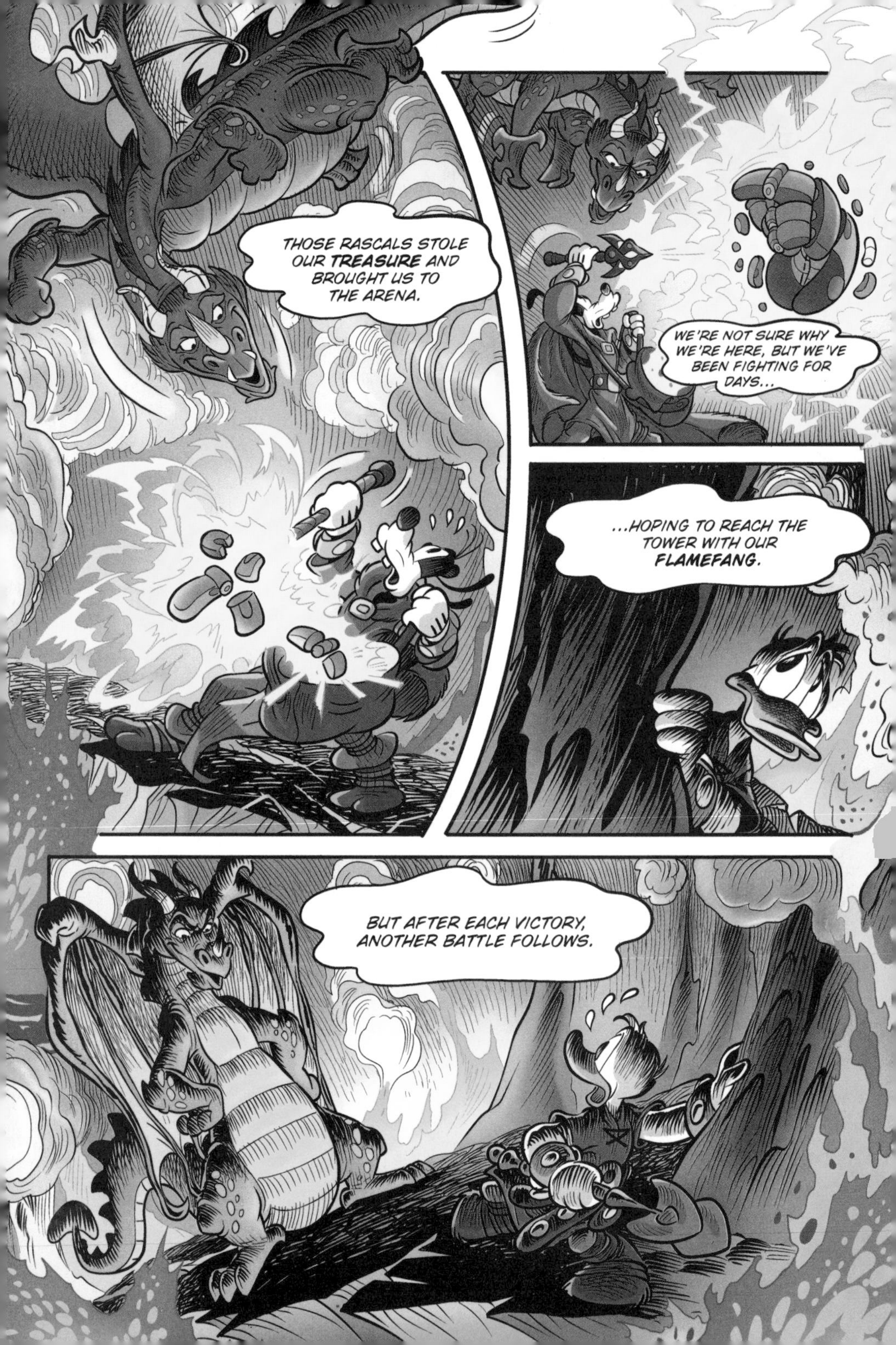
THOSE RASCALS STOLE OUR TREASURE AND BROUGHT US TO THE ARENA.
WE'RE NOT SURE WHY WE'RE HERE, BUT WE'VE BEEN FIGHTING FOR DAYS...
...HOPING TO REACH THE TOWER WITH OUR FLAMEFANG.
BUT AFTER EACH VICTORY, ANOTHER BATTLE FOLLOWS.

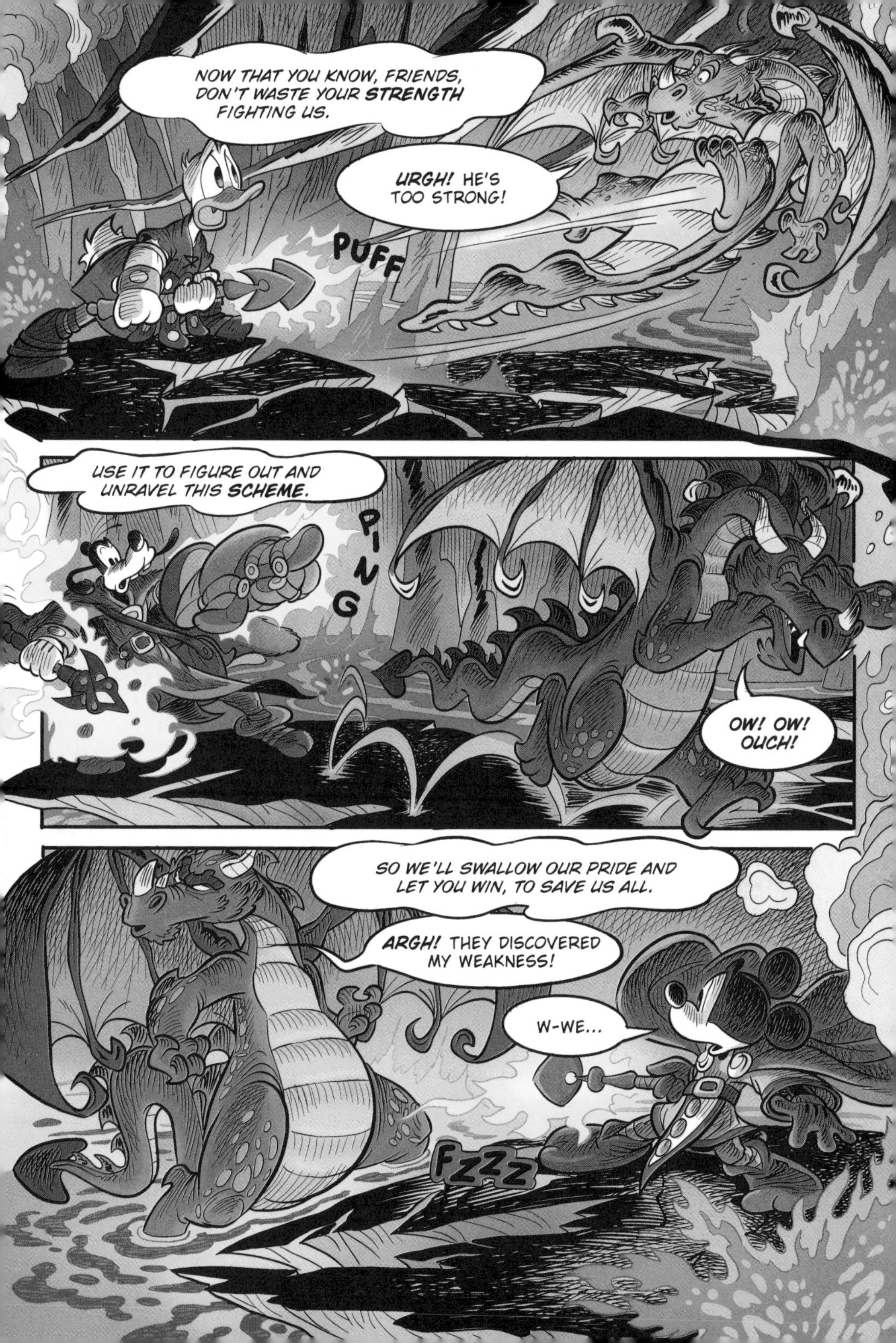
NOW THAT YOU KNOW, FRIENDS, DON'T WASTE YOUR STRENGTH FIGHTING US.
URGH! HE'S TOO STRONG!
PUFF
USE IT TO FIGURE OUT AND UNRAVEL THIS SCHEME.
PING
OW! OW! OUCH!
SO WE'LL SWALLOW OUR PRIDE AND LET YOU WIN, TO SAVE US ALL.
ARGH! THEY DISCOVERED MY WEAKNESS!
W-WE...
FZZZ

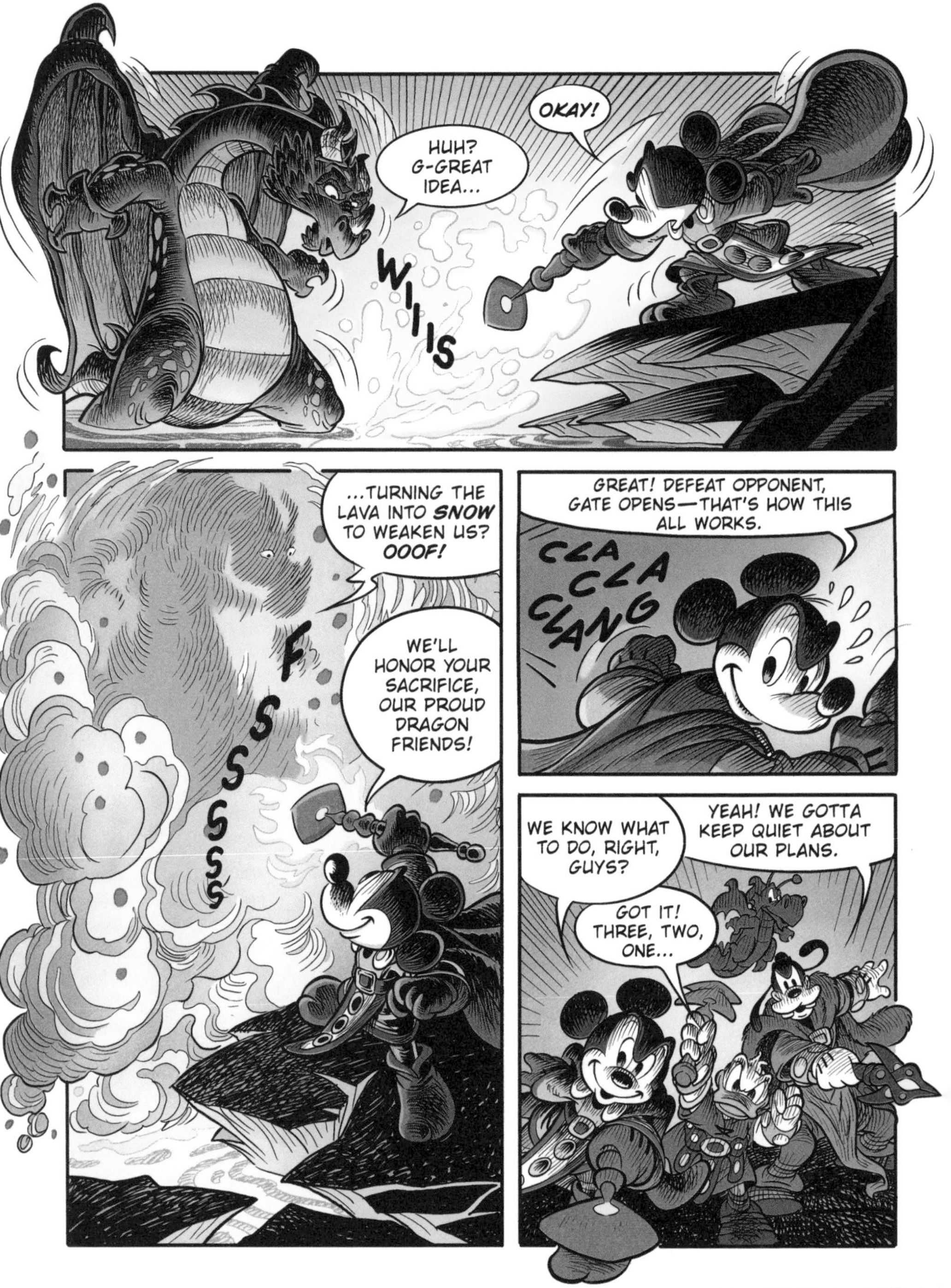
HUH? G-GREAT IDEA...
OKAY!
WIIIS
...TURNING THE LAVA INTO **SNOW** TO WEAKEN US? ***OOOF!***
FSSSSSS
WE'LL HONOR YOUR SACRIFICE, OUR PROUD DRAGON FRIENDS!
GREAT! DEFEAT OPPONENT, GATE OPENS—THAT'S HOW THIS ALL WORKS.
CLA CLA CLANG
WE KNOW WHAT TO DO, RIGHT, GUYS?
YEAH! WE GOTTA KEEP QUIET ABOUT OUR PLANS.
GOT IT! THREE, TWO, ONE...

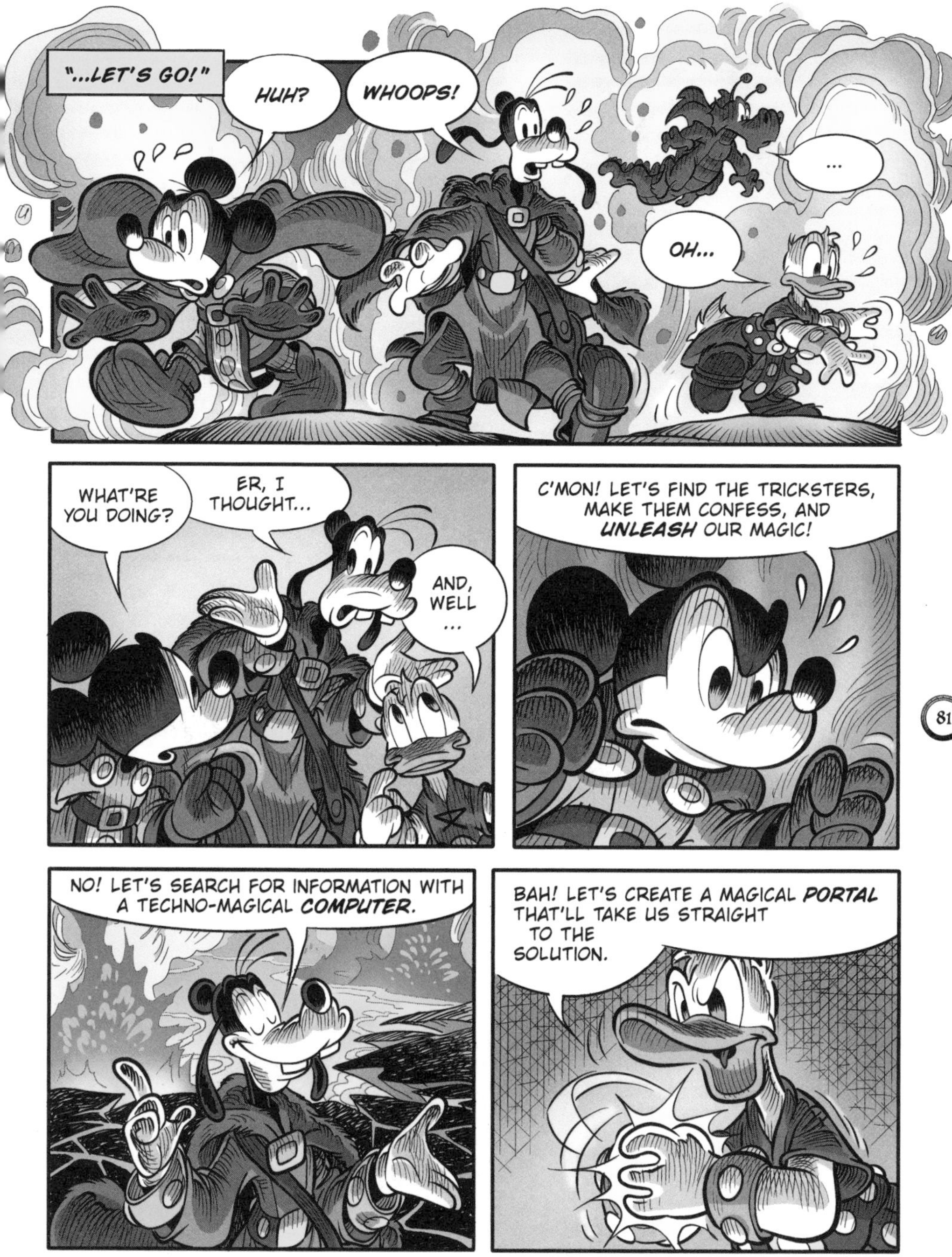
"...LET'S GO!"
HUH?
WHOOPS!
...
OH...
WHAT'RE YOU DOING?
ER, I THOUGHT...
AND, WELL ...
C'MON! LET'S FIND THE TRICKSTERS, MAKE THEM CONFESS, AND UNLEASH OUR MAGIC!
NO! LET'S SEARCH FOR INFORMATION WITH A TECHNO-MAGICAL COMPUTER.
BAH! LET'S CREATE A MAGICAL PORTAL THAT'LL TAKE US STRAIGHT TO THE SOLUTION.

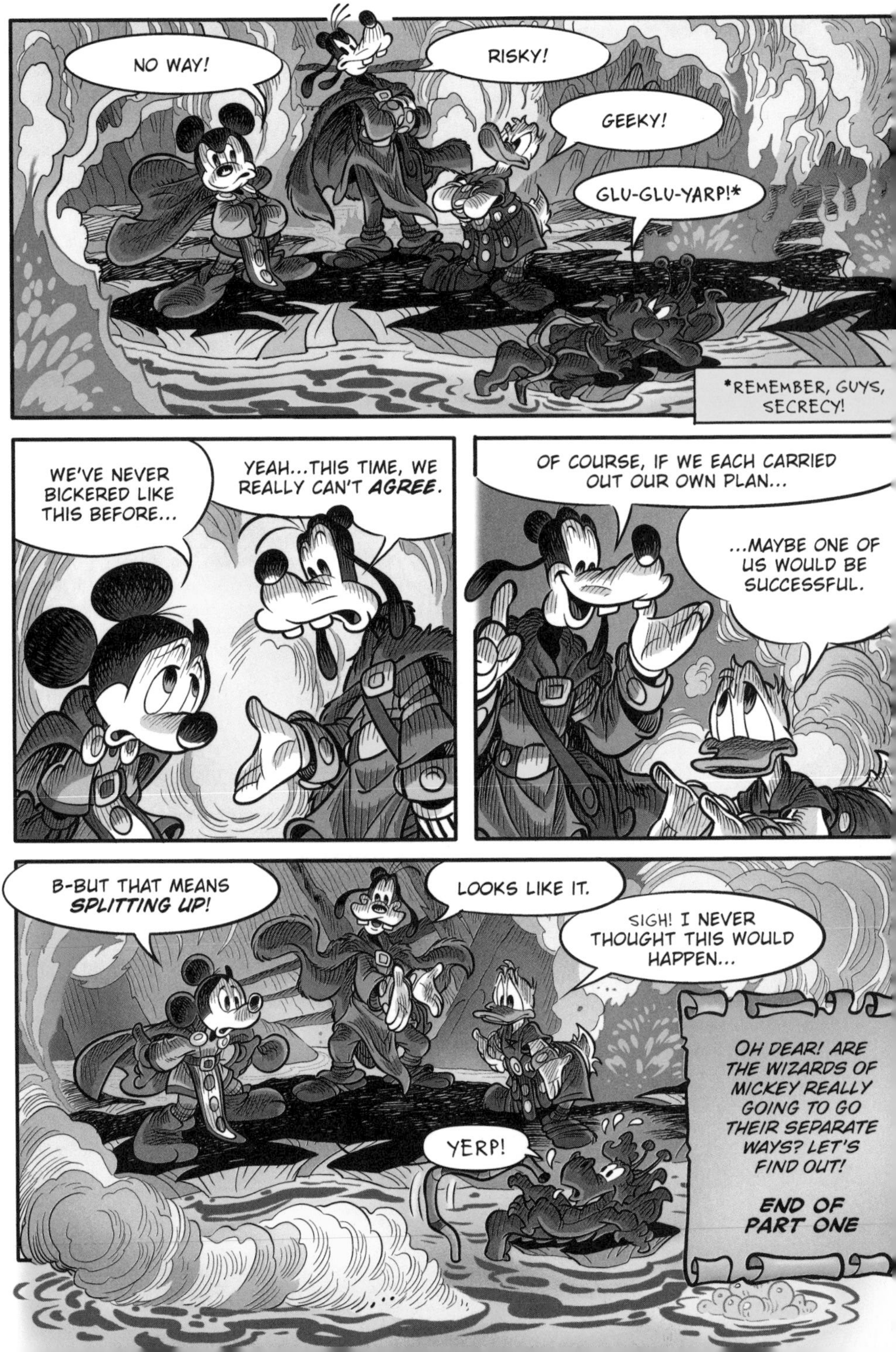
NO WAY!
RISKY!
GEEKY!
GLU-GLU-YARP!*
*REMEMBER, GUYS, SECRECY!
WE'VE NEVER BICKERED LIKE THIS BEFORE...
YEAH...THIS TIME, WE REALLY CAN'T AGREE.
OF COURSE, IF WE EACH CARRIED OUT OUR OWN PLAN...
...MAYBE ONE OF US WOULD BE SUCCESSFUL.
B-BUT THAT MEANS SPLITTING UP!
LOOKS LIKE IT.
SIGH! I NEVER THOUGHT THIS WOULD HAPPEN...
YERP!
OH DEAR! ARE THE WIZARDS OF MICKEY REALLY GOING TO GO THEIR SEPARATE WAYS? LET'S FIND OUT!
END OF PART ONE

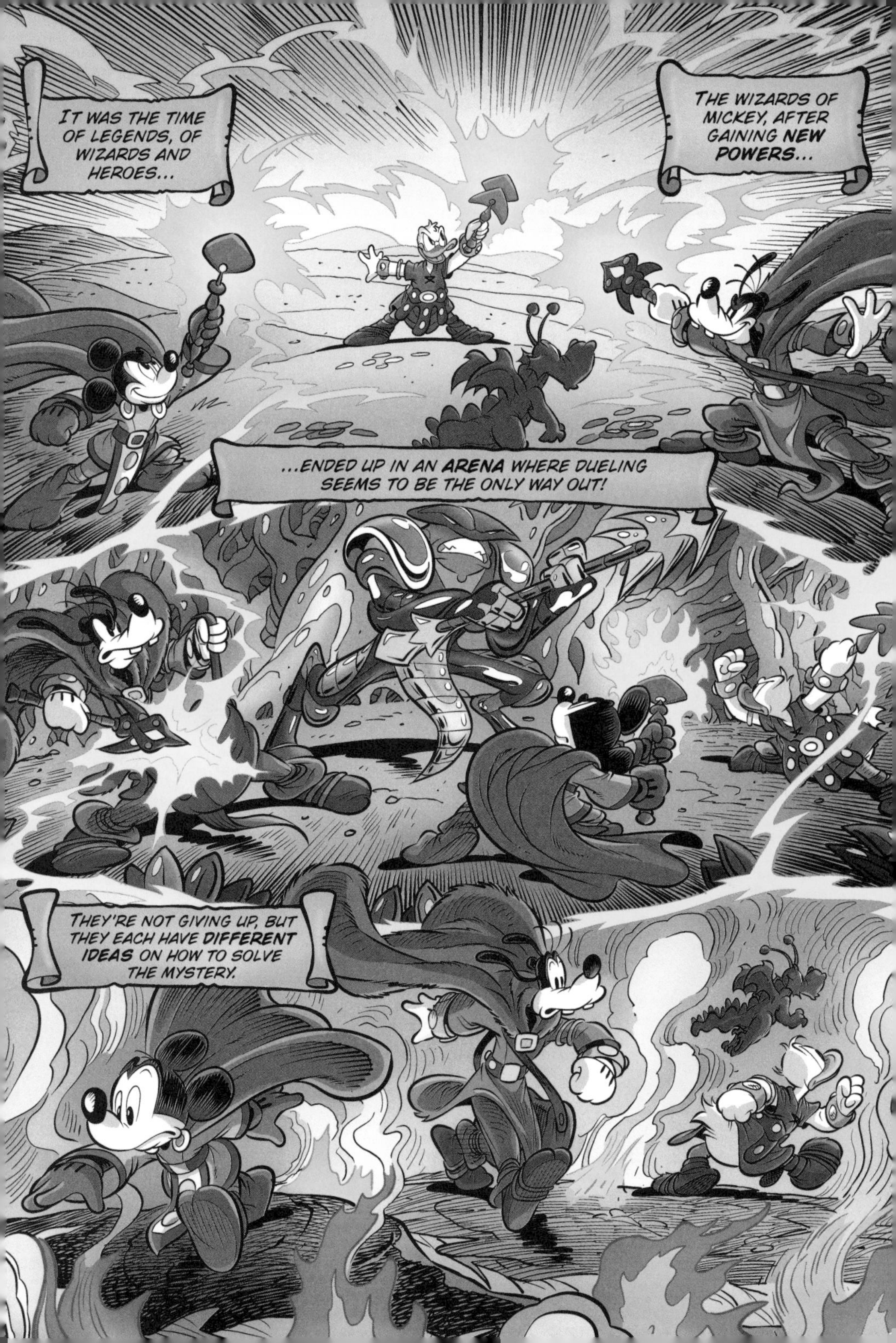
IT WAS THE TIME OF LEGENDS, OF WIZARDS AND HEROES...
THE WIZARDS OF MICKEY, AFTER GAINING NEW POWERS...
...ENDED UP IN AN ARENA WHERE DUELING SEEMS TO BE THE ONLY WAY OUT!
THEY'RE NOT GIVING UP, BUT THEY EACH HAVE DIFFERENT IDEAS ON HOW TO SOLVE THE MYSTERY.

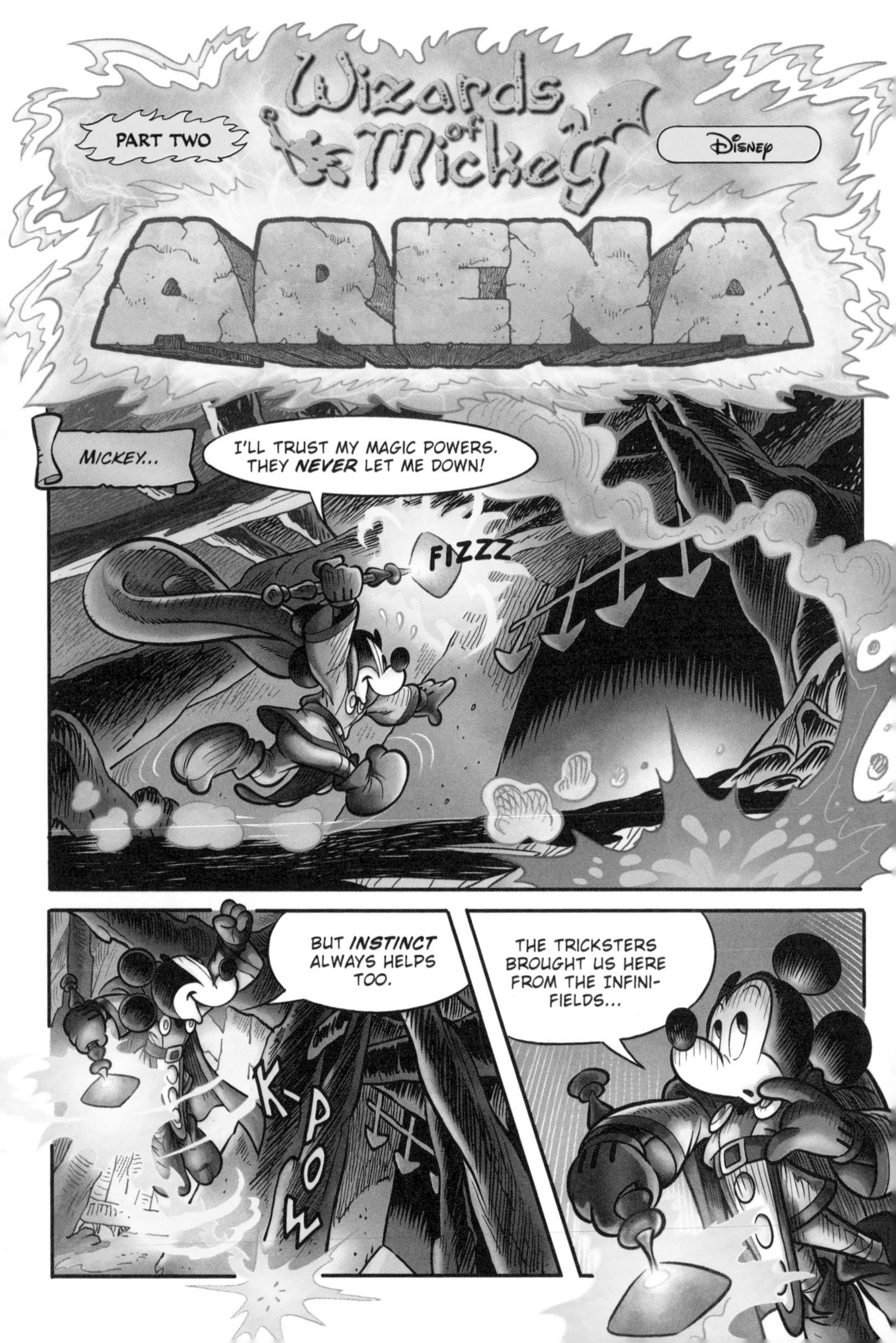
PART TWO
Wizards of Mickey
DISNEY
ARENA
MICKEY...
I'LL TRUST MY MAGIC POWERS. THEY NEVER LET ME DOWN!
FIZZZ
BUT INSTINCT ALWAYS HELPS TOO.
K-POW
THE TRICKSTERS BROUGHT US HERE FROM THE INFINI-FIELDS...

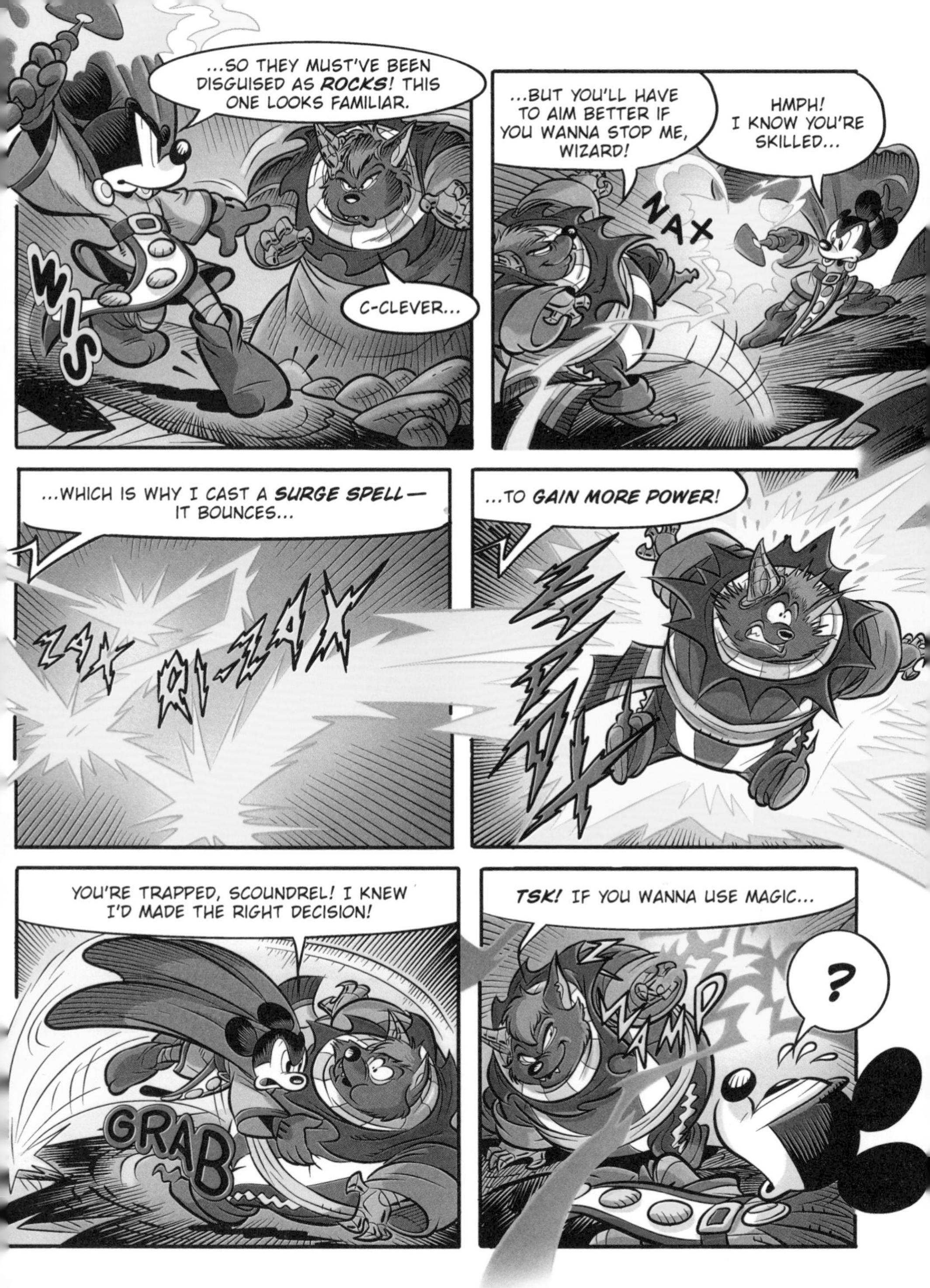

...SO THEY MUST'VE BEEN DISGUISED AS ROCKS! THIS ONE LOOKS FAMILIAR.
WIIS
C-CLEVER...
HMPH! I KNOW YOU'RE SKILLED...
...BUT YOU'LL HAVE TO AIM BETTER IF YOU WANNA STOP ME, WIZARD!
ZAX
...WHICH IS WHY I CAST A SURGE SPELL— IT BOUNCES...
ZAX RI-ZAX
...TO GAIN MORE POWER!
YOU'RE TRAPPED, SCOUNDREL! I KNEW I'D MADE THE RIGHT DECISION!
GRAB
TSK! IF YOU WANNA USE MAGIC...
WAMP
?

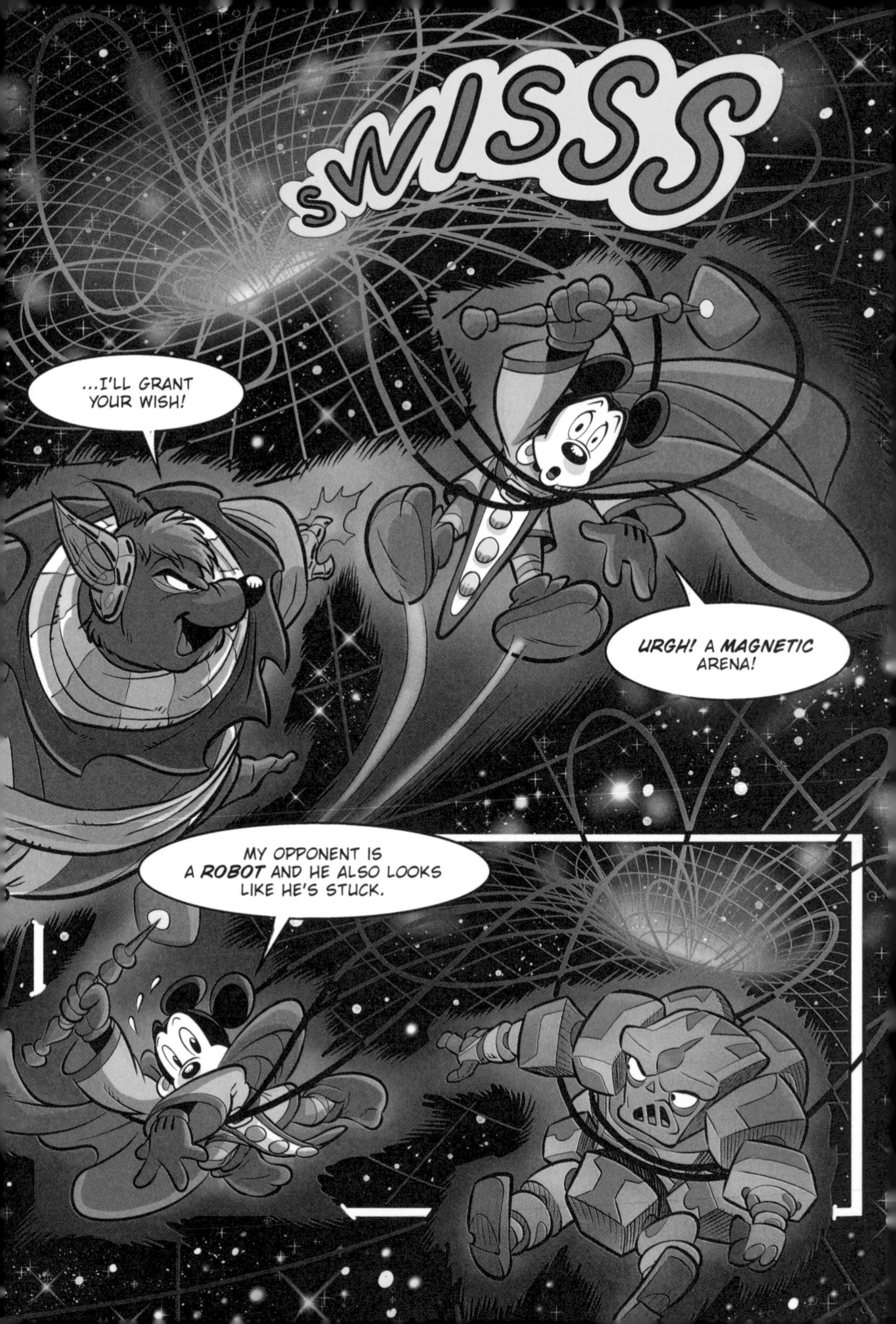
SWISSS
...I'LL GRANT YOUR WISH!
URGH! A MAGNETIC ARENA!
MY OPPONENT IS A ROBOT AND HE ALSO LOOKS LIKE HE'S STUCK.

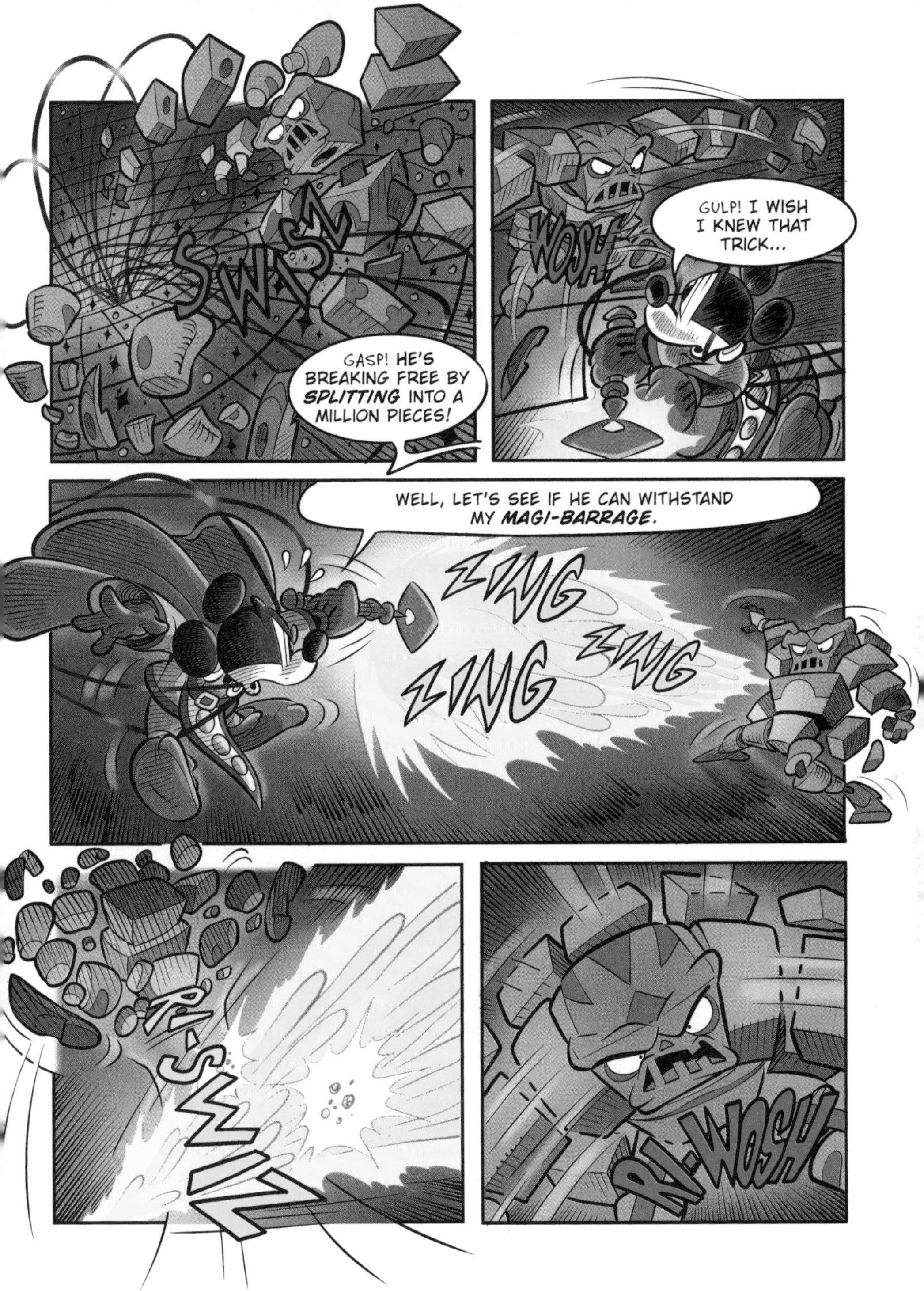

SWISH
GASP! HE'S BREAKING FREE BY SPLITTING INTO A MILLION PIECES!
WOSH
GULP! I WISH I KNEW THAT TRICK...
WELL, LET'S SEE IF HE CAN WITHSTAND MY MAGI-BARRAGE.
ZING
ZING
ZING
RI-SWIZZ
RI-WOSH

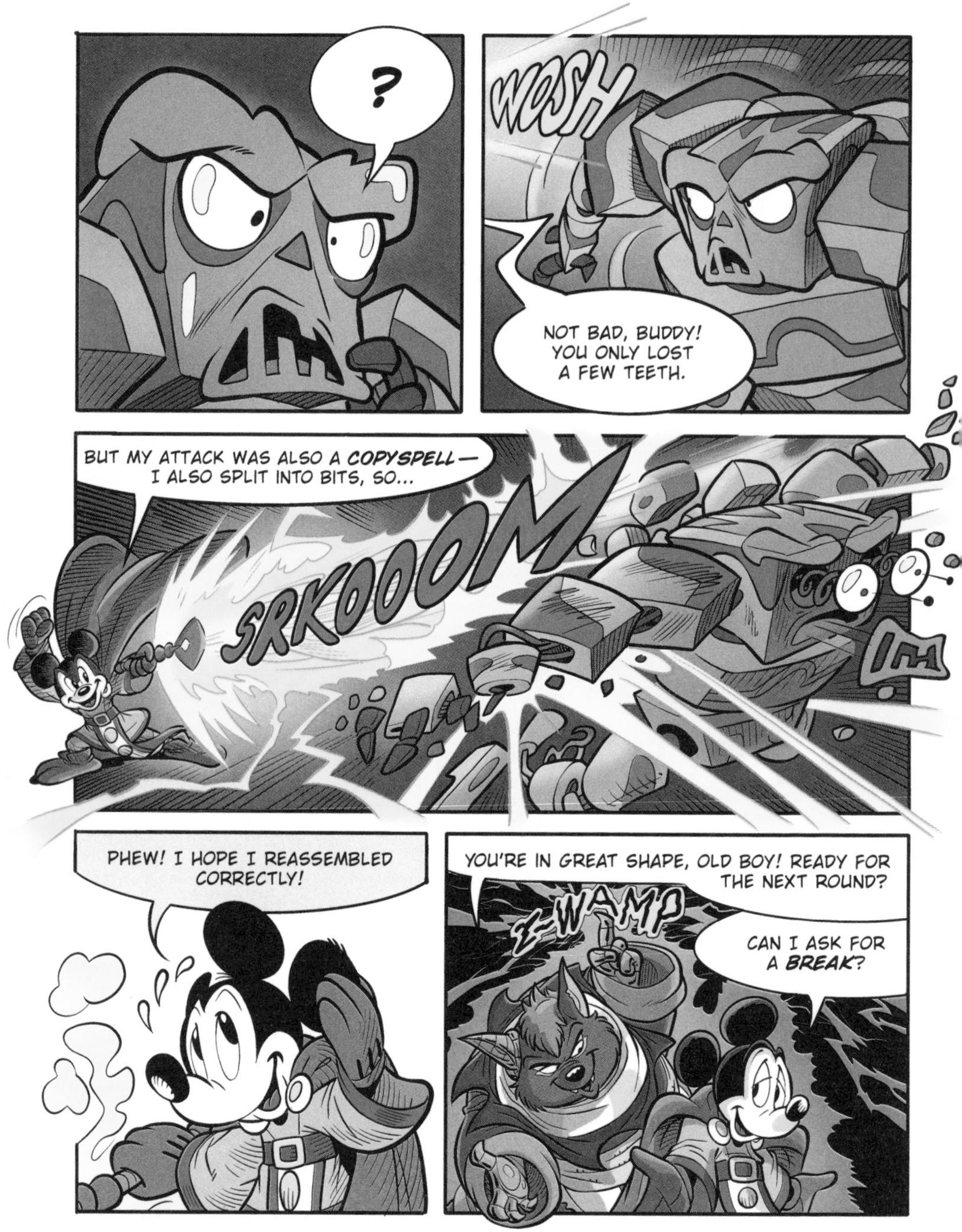
?
WOSH
NOT BAD, BUDDY! YOU ONLY LOST A FEW TEETH.
BUT MY ATTACK WAS ALSO A *COPYSPELL*— I ALSO SPLIT INTO BITS, SO...
SRKOOOM
PHEW! I HOPE I REASSEMBLED CORRECTLY!
YOU'RE IN GREAT SHAPE, OLD BOY! READY FOR THE NEXT ROUND?
ZWAMP
CAN I ASK FOR A *BREAK*?

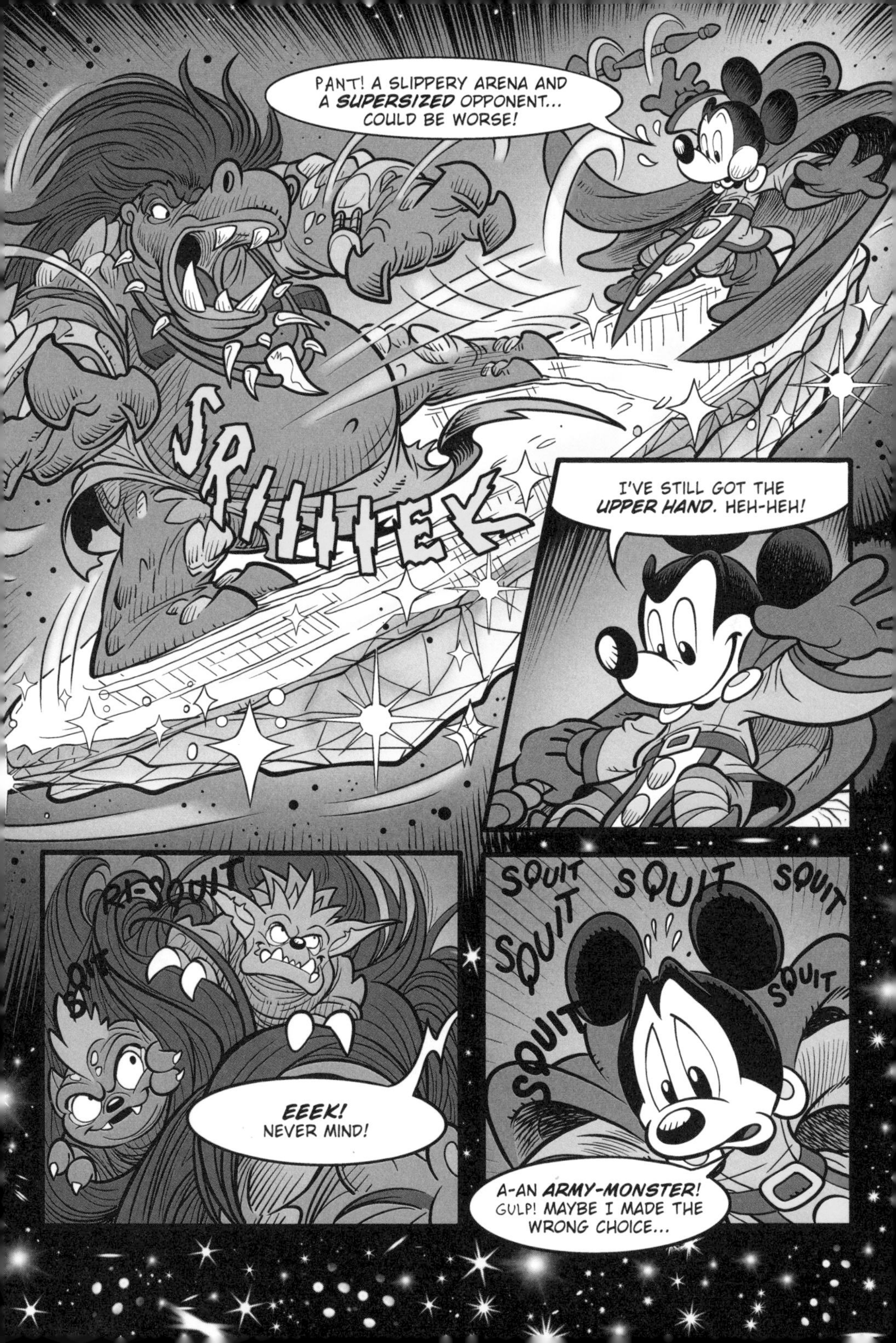
PANT! A SLIPPERY ARENA AND A SUPERSIZED OPPONENT... COULD BE WORSE!
SRIIIIEK
I'VE STILL GOT THE UPPER HAND. HEH-HEH!
RI-SQUIT
EEEK! NEVER MIND!
SQUIT SQUIT SQUIT SQUIT SQUIT SQUIT SQUIT
A-AN ARMY-MONSTER! GULP! MAYBE I MADE THE WRONG CHOICE...

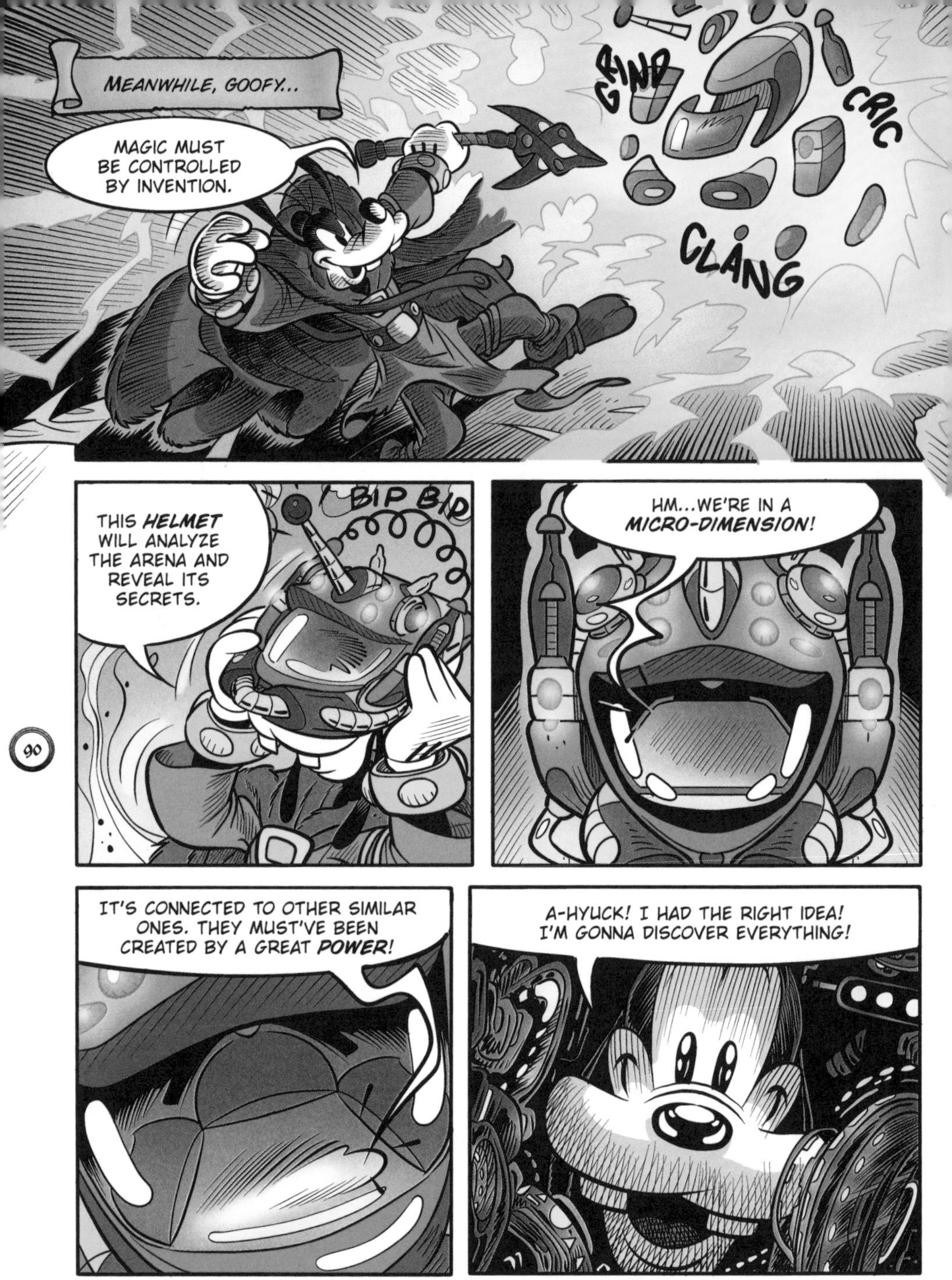
MEANWHILE, GOOFY...
MAGIC MUST BE CONTROLLED BY INVENTION.
GRIND
CRIC
CLANG
BIP BIP
THIS HELMET WILL ANALYZE THE ARENA AND REVEAL ITS SECRETS.
HM...WE'RE IN A MICRO-DIMENSION!
IT'S CONNECTED TO OTHER SIMILAR ONES. THEY MUST'VE BEEN CREATED BY A GREAT POWER!
A-HYUCK! I HAD THE RIGHT IDEA! I'M GONNA DISCOVER EVERYTHING!

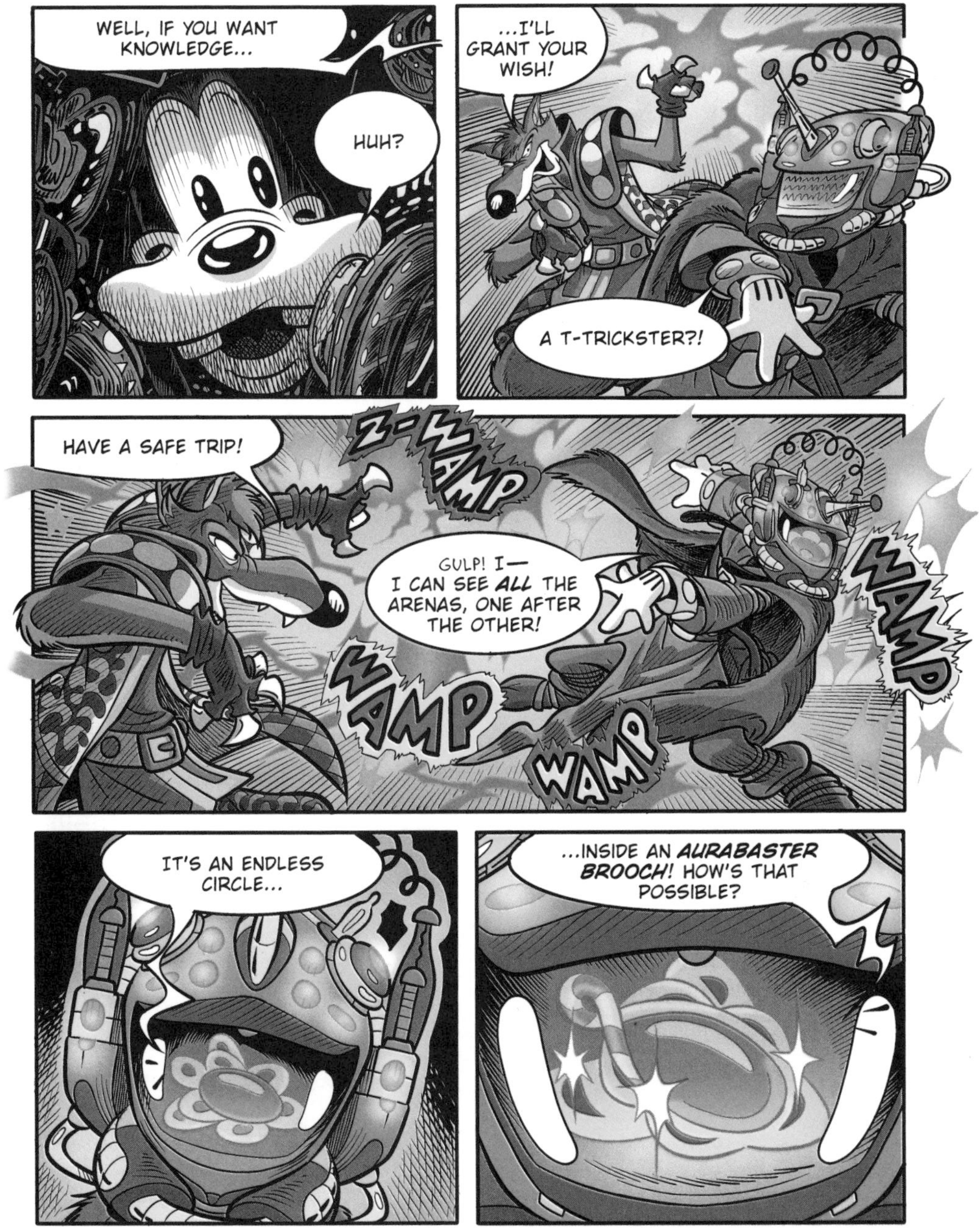

WELL, IF YOU WANT KNOWLEDGE...
HUH?
...I'LL GRANT YOUR WISH!
A T-TRICKSTER?!
HAVE A SAFE TRIP!
Z-WAMP
GULP! I— I CAN SEE ALL THE ARENAS, ONE AFTER THE OTHER!
WAMP
WAMP
WAMP
IT'S AN ENDLESS CIRCLE...
...INSIDE AN AURABASTER BROOCH! HOW'S THAT POSSIBLE?

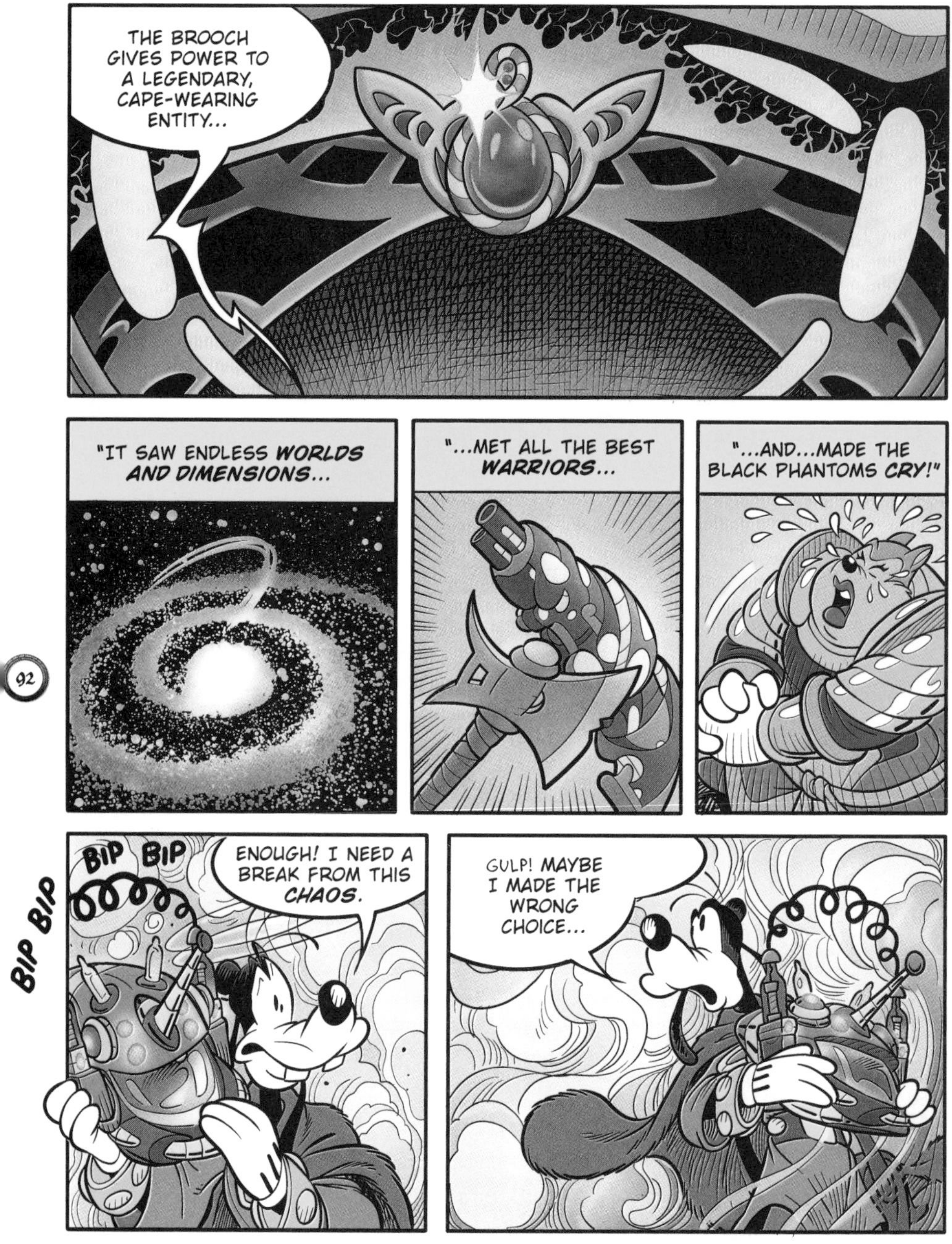
THE BROOCH GIVES POWER TO A LEGENDARY, CAPE-WEARING ENTITY...
"IT SAW ENDLESS WORLDS AND DIMENSIONS...
"...MET ALL THE BEST WARRIORS...
"...AND...MADE THE BLACK PHANTOMS CRY!"
BIP BIP
BIP BIP
ENOUGH! I NEED A BREAK FROM THIS CHAOS.
GULP! MAYBE I MADE THE WRONG CHOICE...

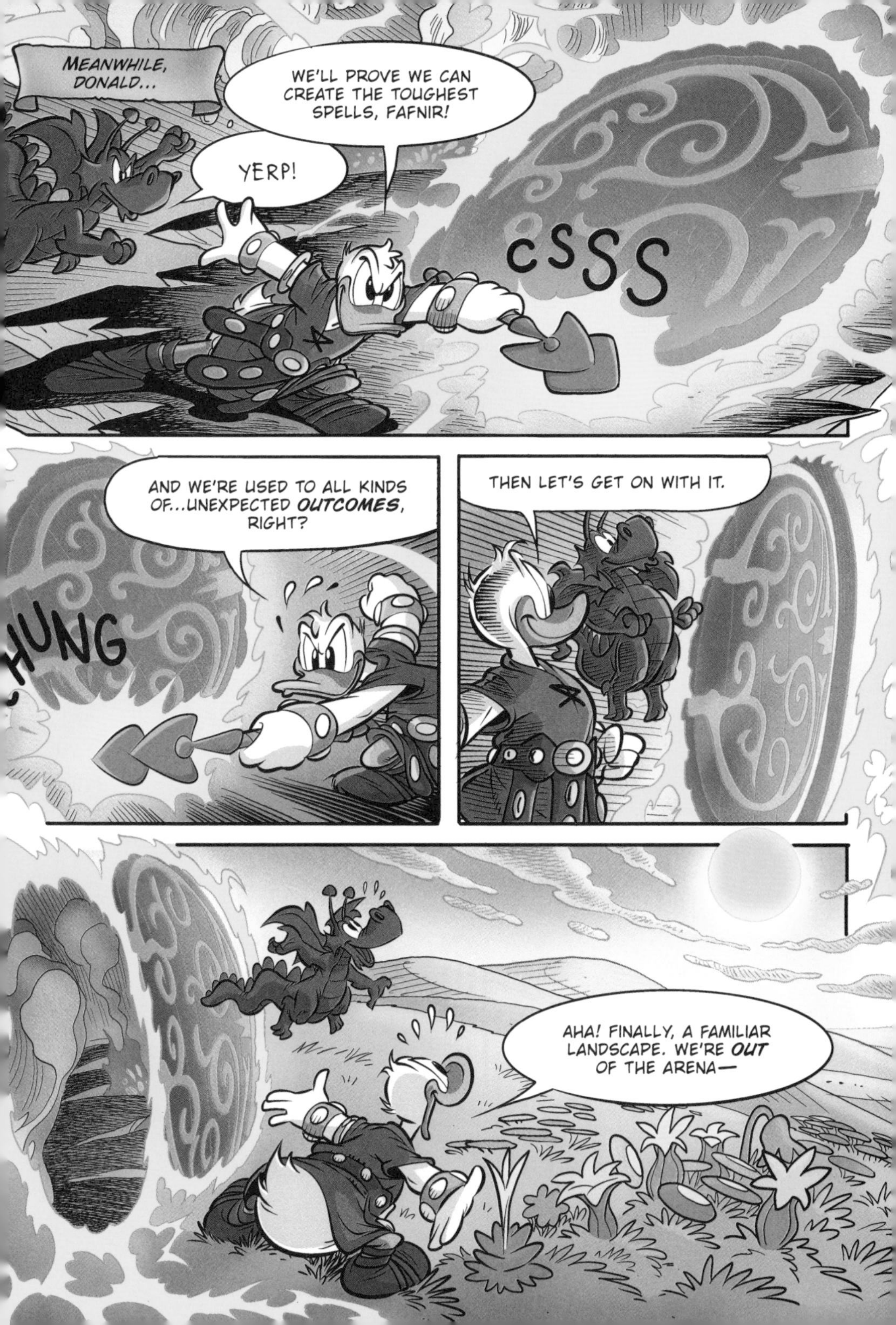
MEANWHILE, DONALD...
WE'LL PROVE WE CAN CREATE THE TOUGHEST SPELLS, FAFNIR!
YERP!
CSSS
AND WE'RE USED TO ALL KINDS OF...UNEXPECTED OUTCOMES, RIGHT?
HUNG
THEN LET'S GET ON WITH IT.
AHA! FINALLY, A FAMILIAR LANDSCAPE. WE'RE OUT OF THE ARENA—

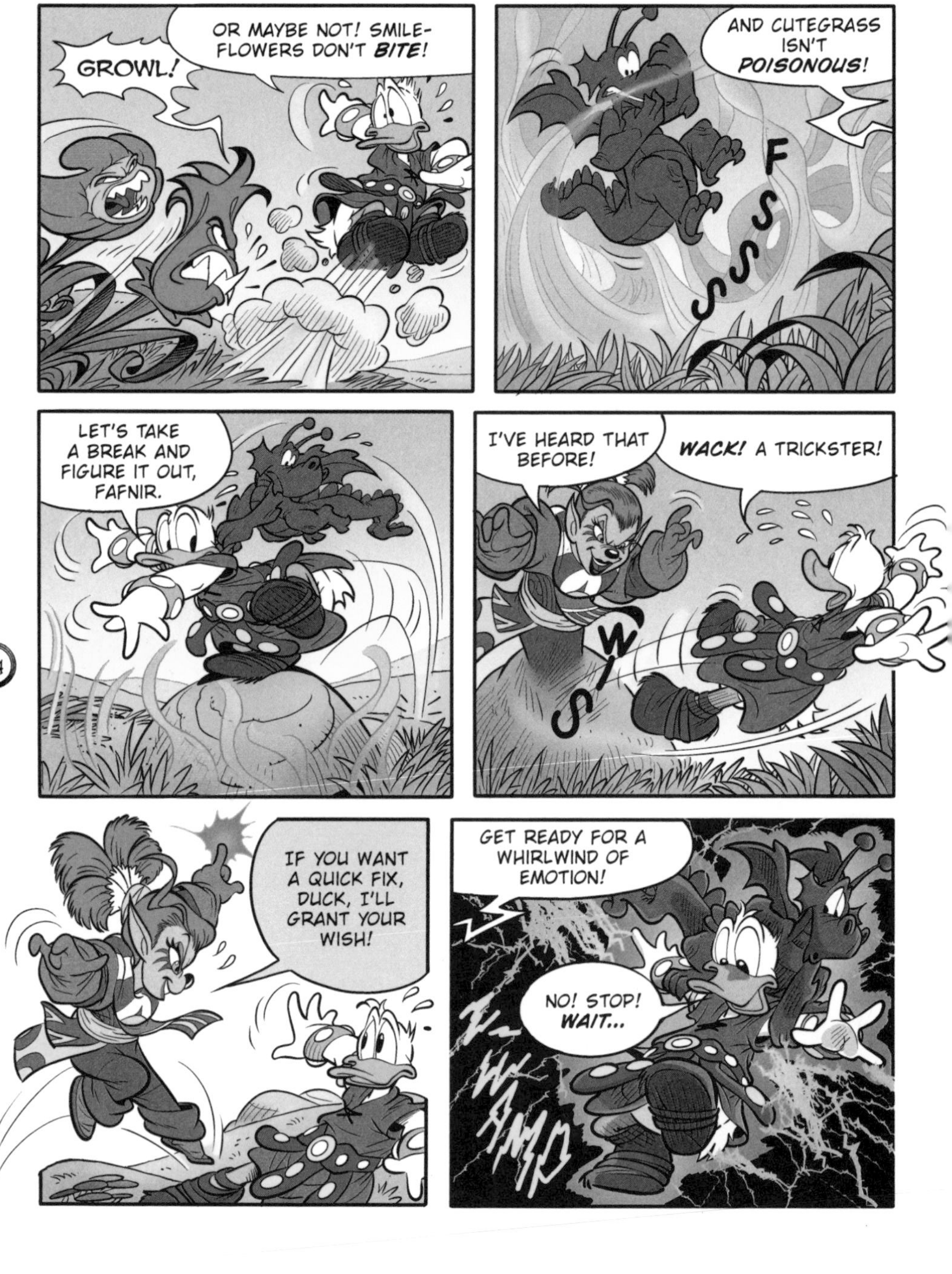
GROWL!
OR MAYBE NOT! SMILE-FLOWERS DON'T **BITE**!
AND CUTEGRASS ISN'T **POISONOUS**!
FSSSS
LET'S TAKE A BREAK AND FIGURE IT OUT, FAFNIR.
I'VE HEARD THAT BEFORE!
WACK! A TRICKSTER!
SWISS
IF YOU WANT A QUICK FIX, DUCK, I'LL GRANT YOUR WISH!
GET READY FOR A WHIRLWIND OF EMOTION!
NO! STOP! **WAIT...**

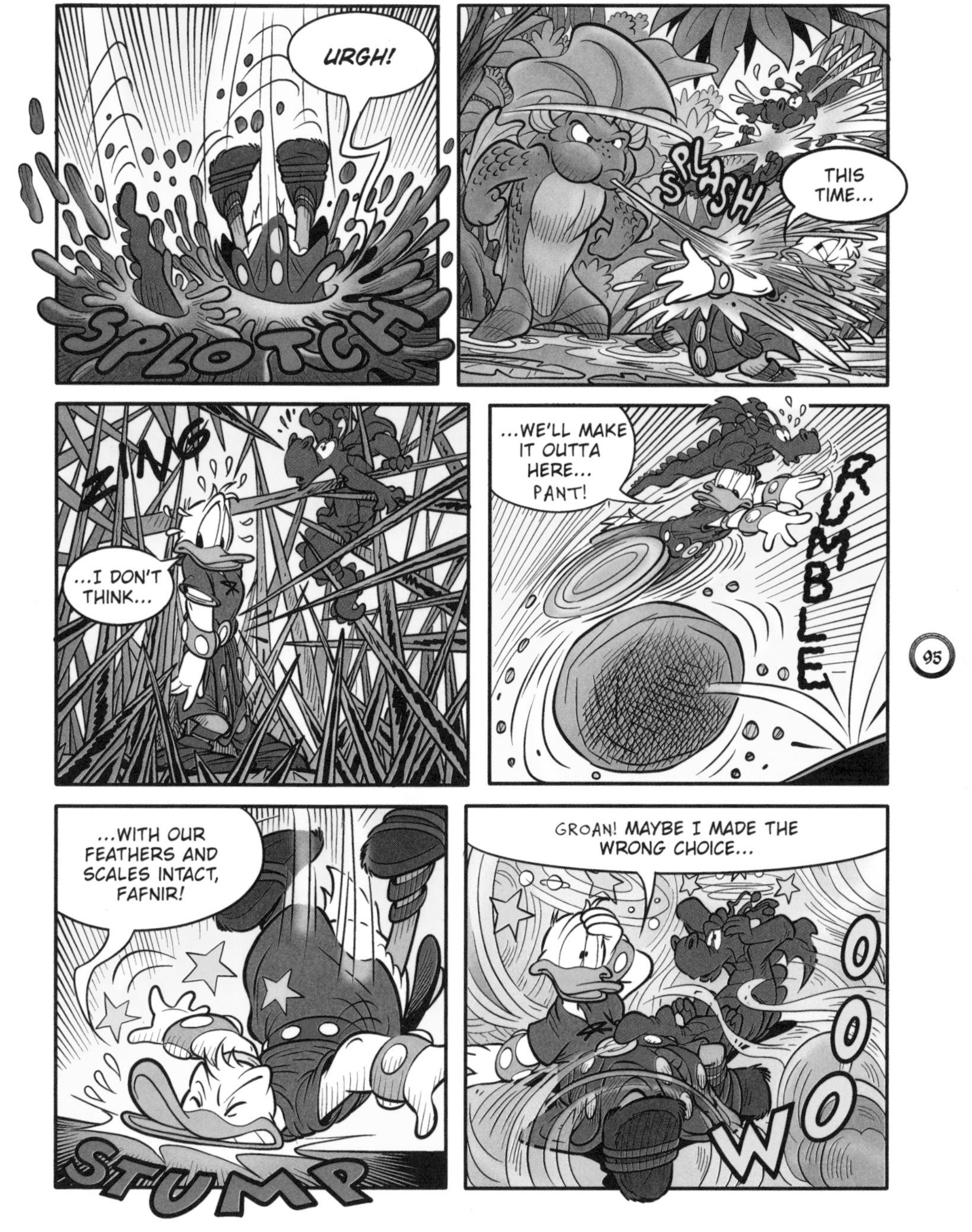
URGH!
SPLOTCH
SPLASH
THIS TIME...
ZING
...I DON'T THINK...
...WE'LL MAKE IT OUTTA HERE... PANT!
RUMBLE
...WITH OUR FEATHERS AND SCALES INTACT, FAFNIR!
STUMP
GROAN! MAYBE I MADE THE WRONG CHOICE...
WOOOO

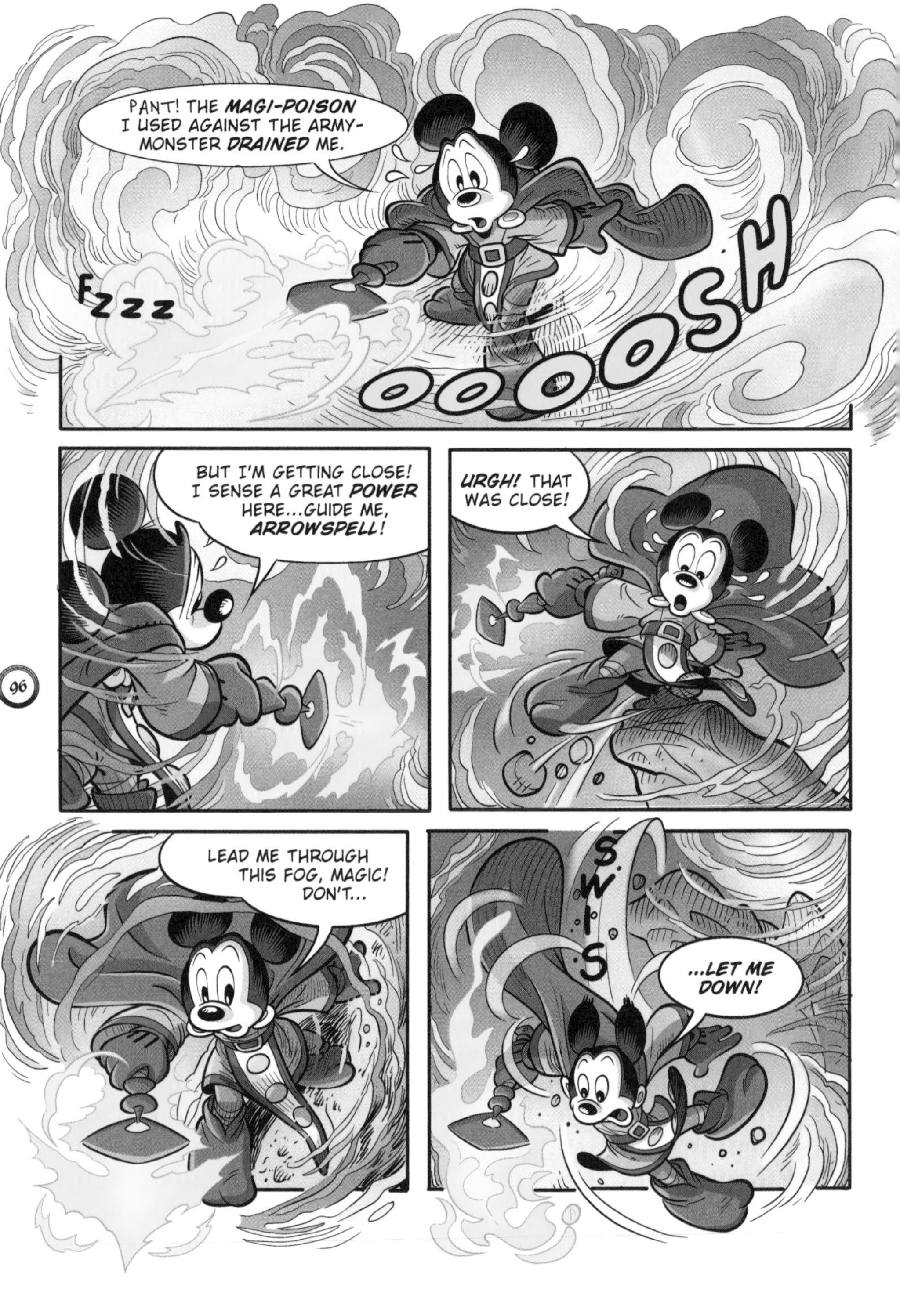

PANT! THE MAGI-POISON I USED AGAINST THE ARMY-MONSTER DRAINED ME.
FZZZ
OOOOOSH
BUT I'M GETTING CLOSE! I SENSE A GREAT POWER HERE...GUIDE ME, ARROWSPELL!
URGH! THAT WAS CLOSE!
LEAD ME THROUGH THIS FOG, MAGIC! DON'T...
SWIS
...LET ME DOWN!

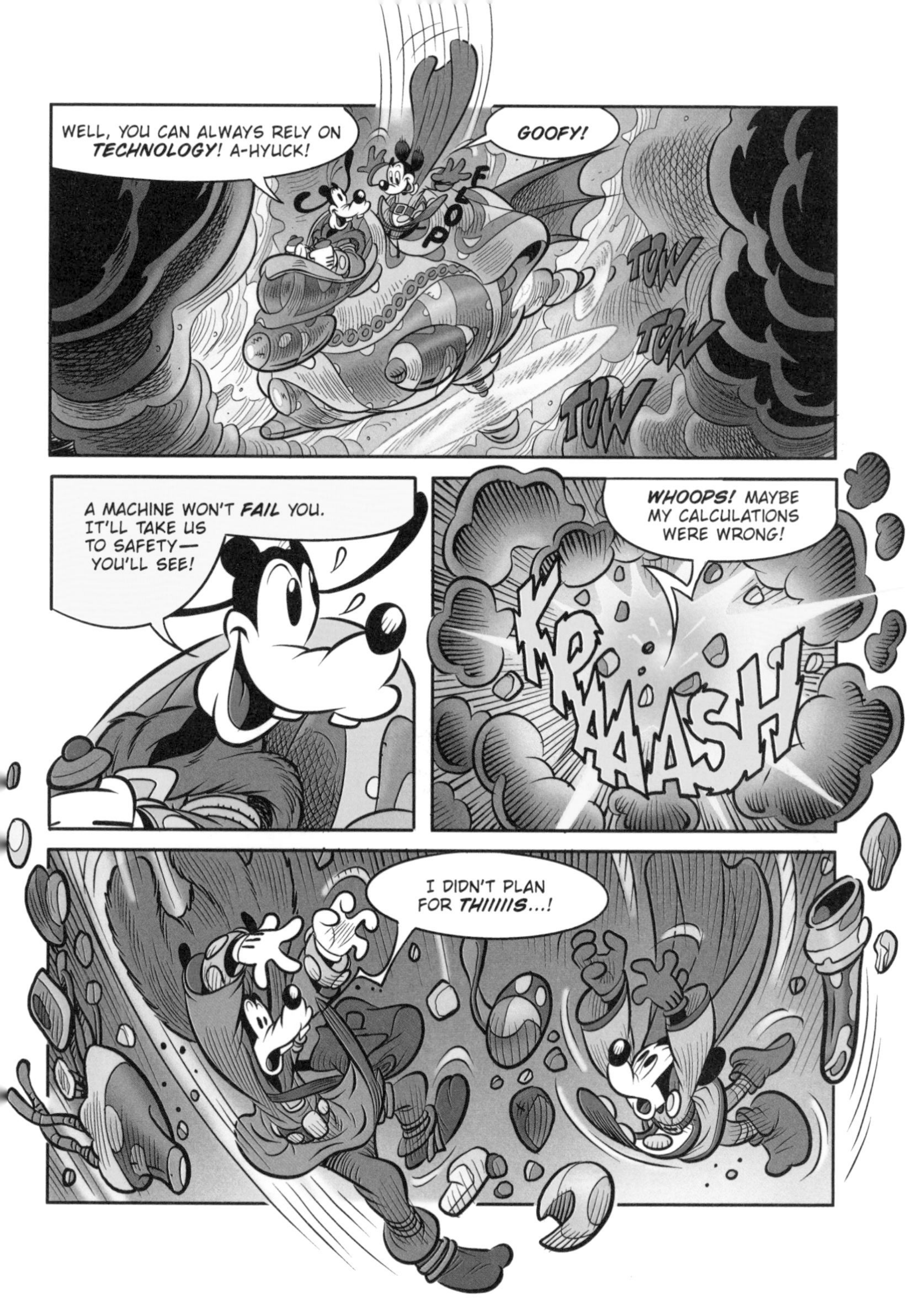
WELL, YOU CAN ALWAYS RELY ON TECHNOLOGY! A-HYUCK!
GOOFY!
FLOP
TOW
TOW
TOW
A MACHINE WON'T FAIL YOU. IT'LL TAKE US TO SAFETY— YOU'LL SEE!
WHOOPS! MAYBE MY CALCULATIONS WERE WRONG!
KRAAASH
I DIDN'T PLAN FOR THIIIIIS...!

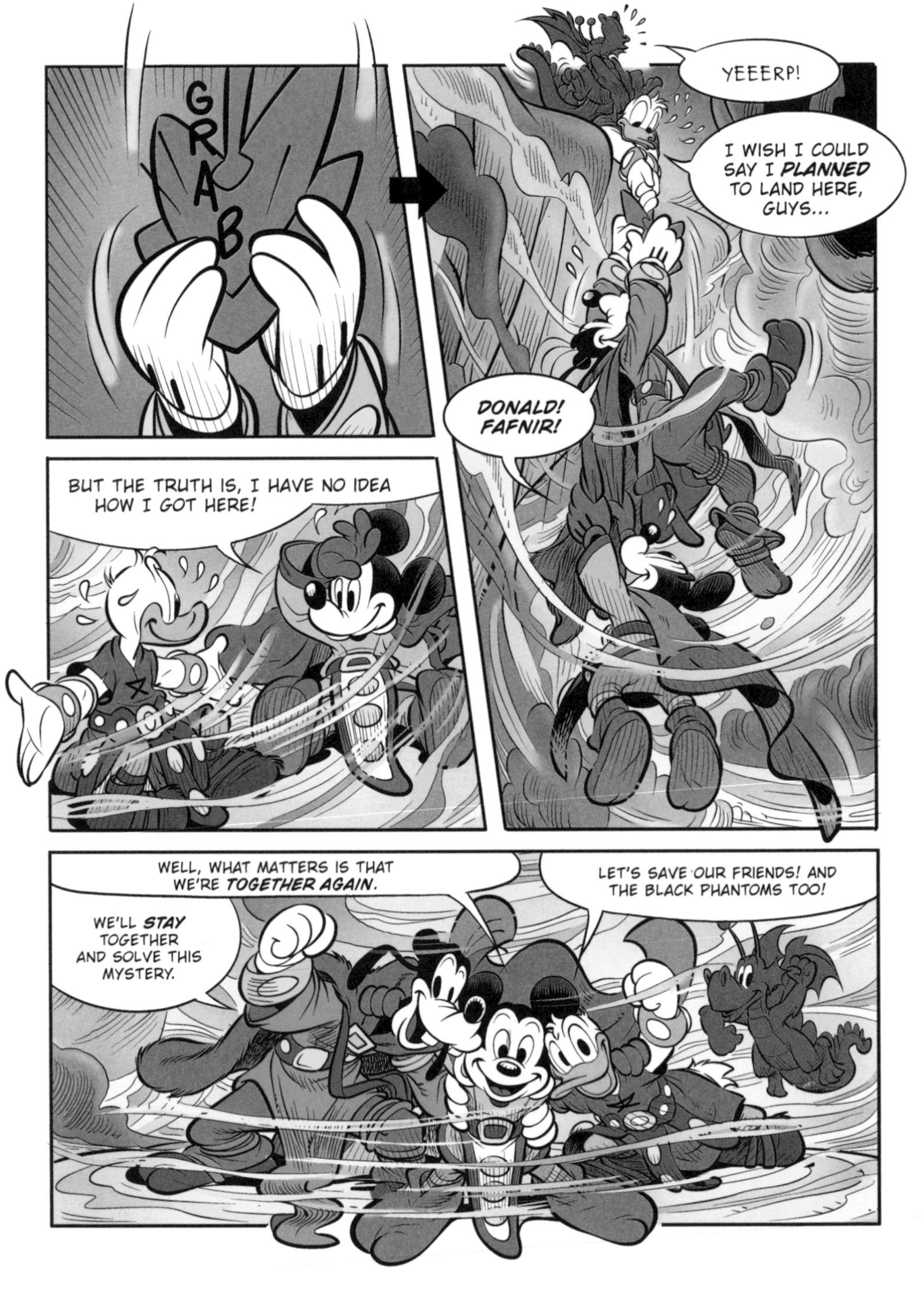
GRAB
YEEERP!
I WISH I COULD SAY I PLANNED TO LAND HERE, GUYS...
BUT THE TRUTH IS, I HAVE NO IDEA HOW I GOT HERE!
DONALD! FAFNIR!
WELL, WHAT MATTERS IS THAT WE'RE TOGETHER AGAIN.
WE'LL STAY TOGETHER AND SOLVE THIS MYSTERY.
LET'S SAVE OUR FRIENDS! AND THE BLACK PHANTOMS TOO!

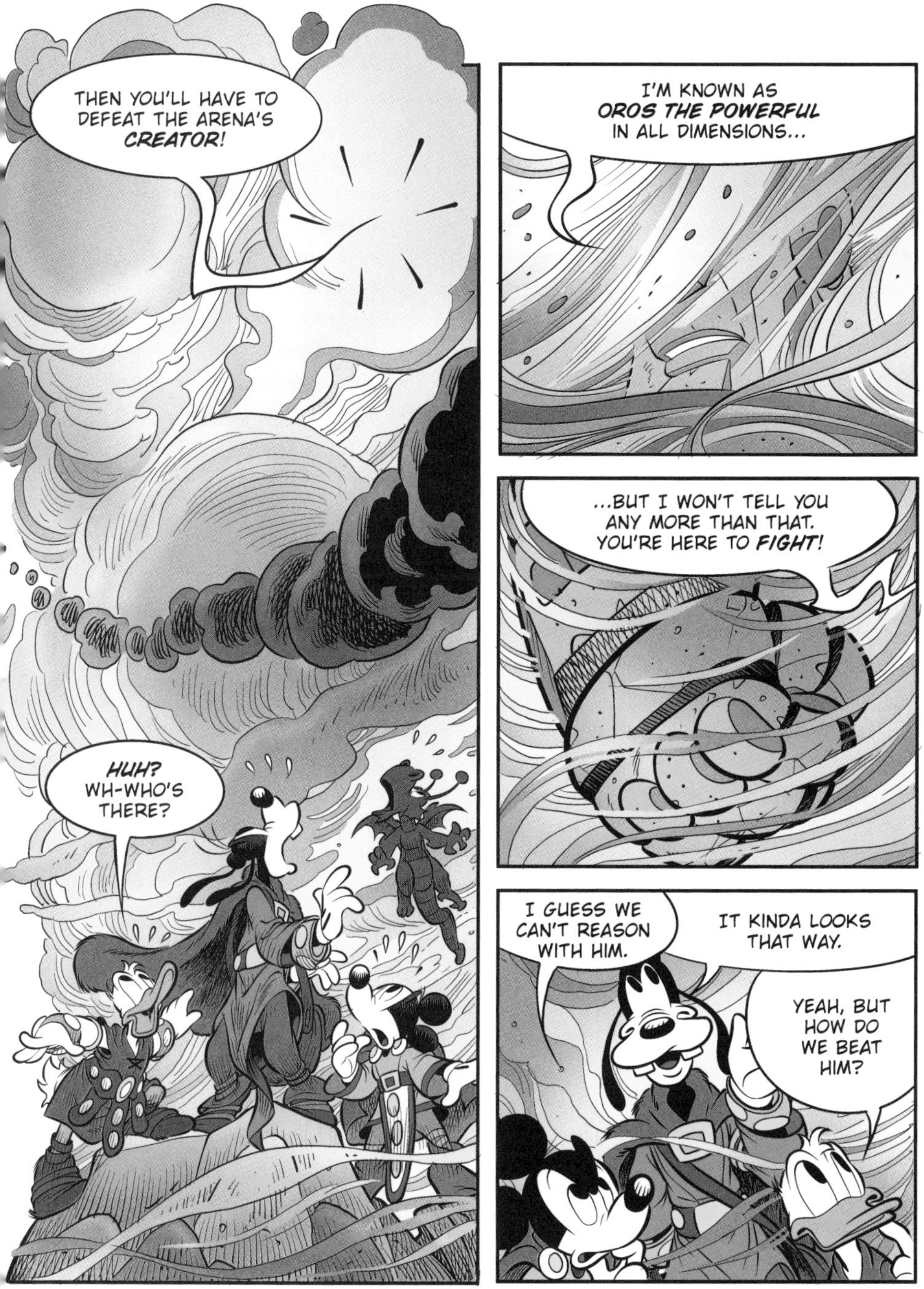
THEN YOU'LL HAVE TO DEFEAT THE ARENA'S **CREATOR**!
HUH? WH-WHO'S THERE?
I'M KNOWN AS **OROS THE POWERFUL** IN ALL DIMENSIONS...
...BUT I WON'T TELL YOU ANY MORE THAN THAT. YOU'RE HERE TO **FIGHT**!
I GUESS WE CAN'T REASON WITH HIM.
IT KINDA LOOKS THAT WAY.
YEAH, BUT HOW DO WE BEAT HIM?

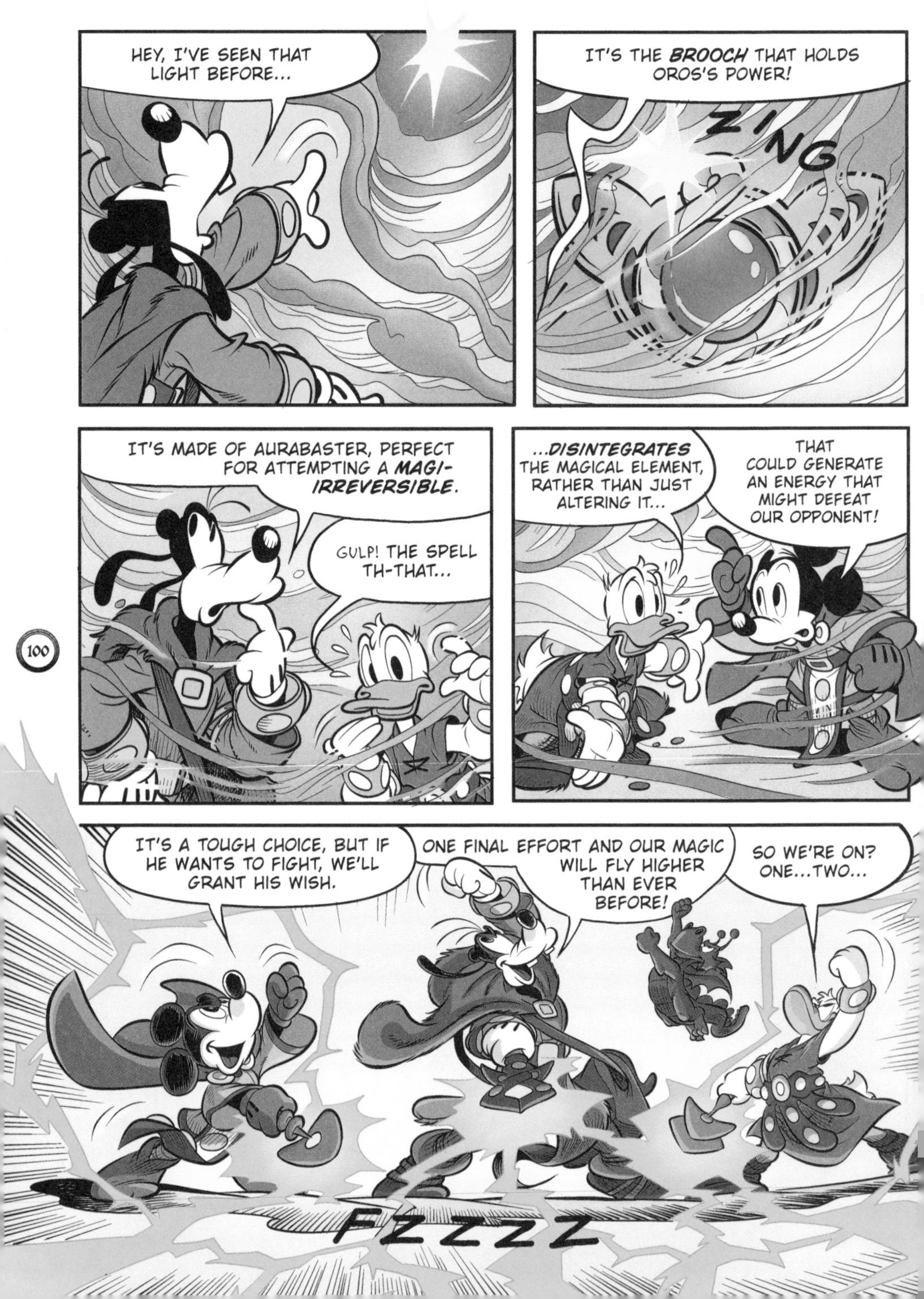
HEY, I'VE SEEN THAT LIGHT BEFORE...
IT'S THE BROOCH THAT HOLDS OROS'S POWER!
ZING
IT'S MADE OF AURABASTER, PERFECT FOR ATTEMPTING A MAGI-IRREVERSIBLE.
GULP! THE SPELL TH-THAT...
...DISINTEGRATES THE MAGICAL ELEMENT, RATHER THAN JUST ALTERING IT...
THAT COULD GENERATE AN ENERGY THAT MIGHT DEFEAT OUR OPPONENT!
IT'S A TOUGH CHOICE, BUT IF HE WANTS TO FIGHT, WE'LL GRANT HIS WISH.
ONE FINAL EFFORT AND OUR MAGIC WILL FLY HIGHER THAN EVER BEFORE!
SO WE'RE ON? ONE...TWO...
FZZZZZ

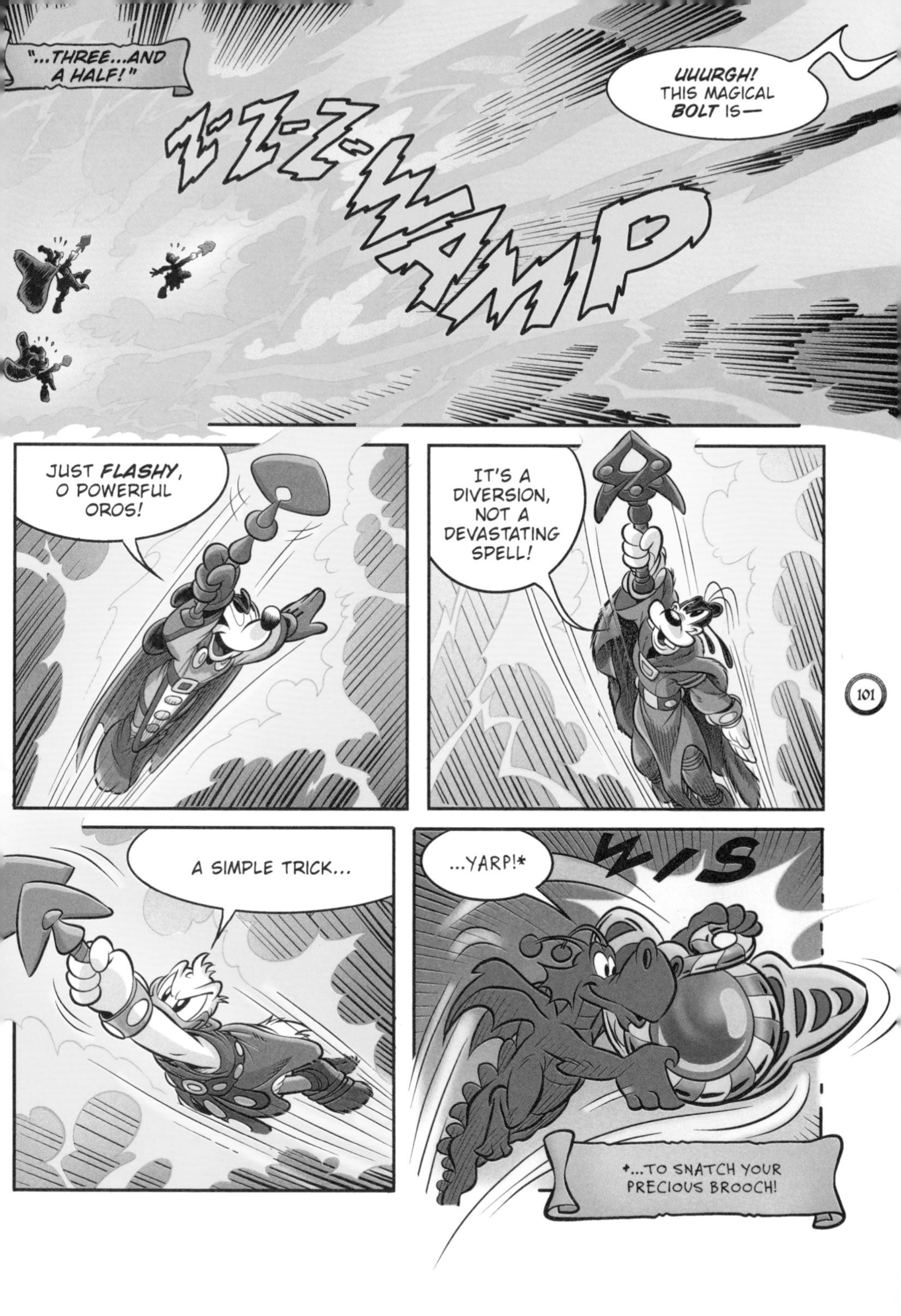
"...THREE...AND A HALF!"
UUURGH! THIS MAGICAL BOLT IS—
TZZ-ZAMP
JUST FLASHY, O POWERFUL OROS!
IT'S A DIVERSION, NOT A DEVASTATING SPELL!
A SIMPLE TRICK...
...YARP!*
WIS
*...TO SNATCH YOUR PRECIOUS BROOCH!

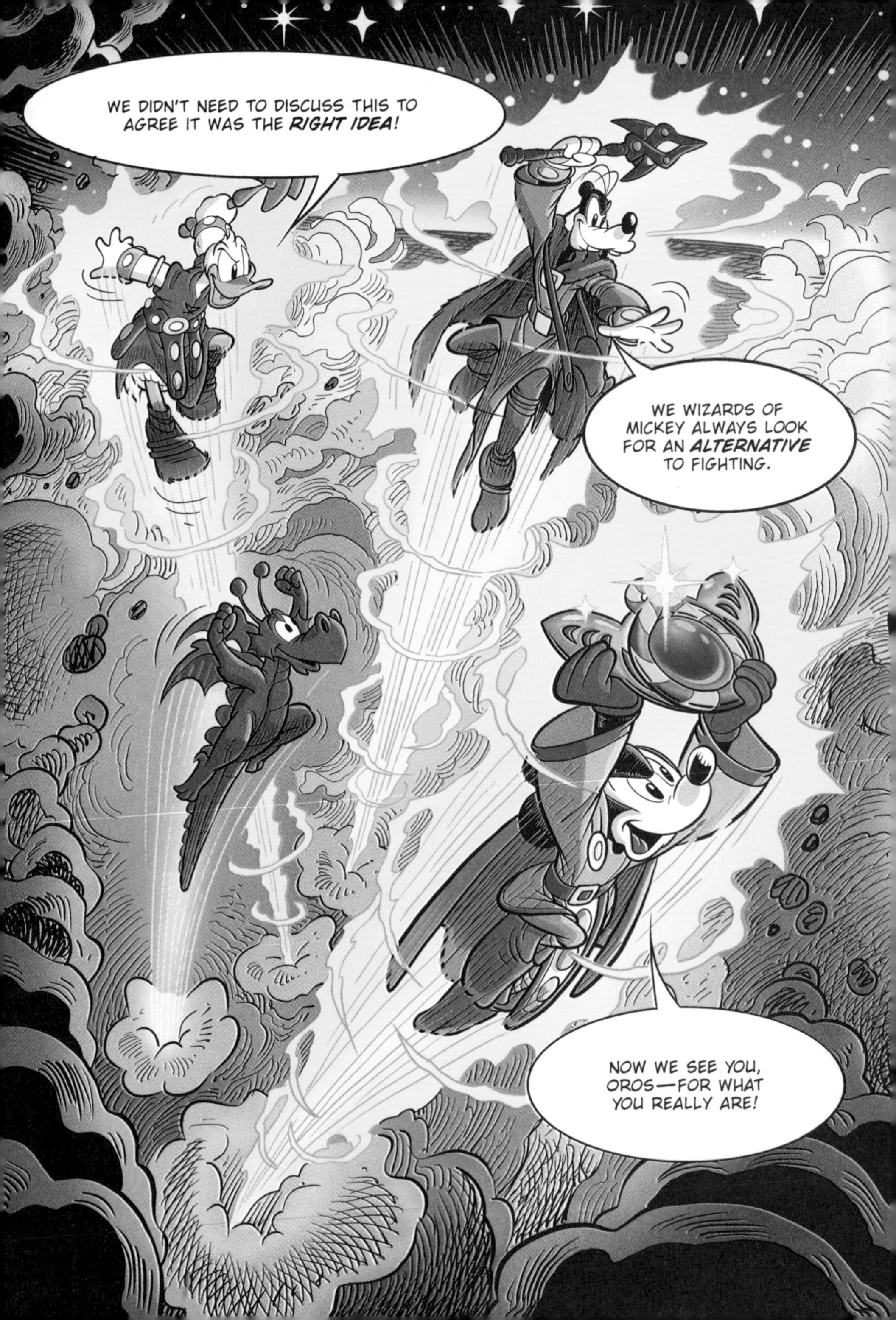
WE DIDN'T NEED TO DISCUSS THIS TO AGREE IT WAS THE ***RIGHT IDEA***!
WE WIZARDS OF MICKEY ALWAYS LOOK FOR AN ***ALTERNATIVE*** TO FIGHTING.
NOW WE SEE YOU, OROS—FOR WHAT YOU REALLY ARE!

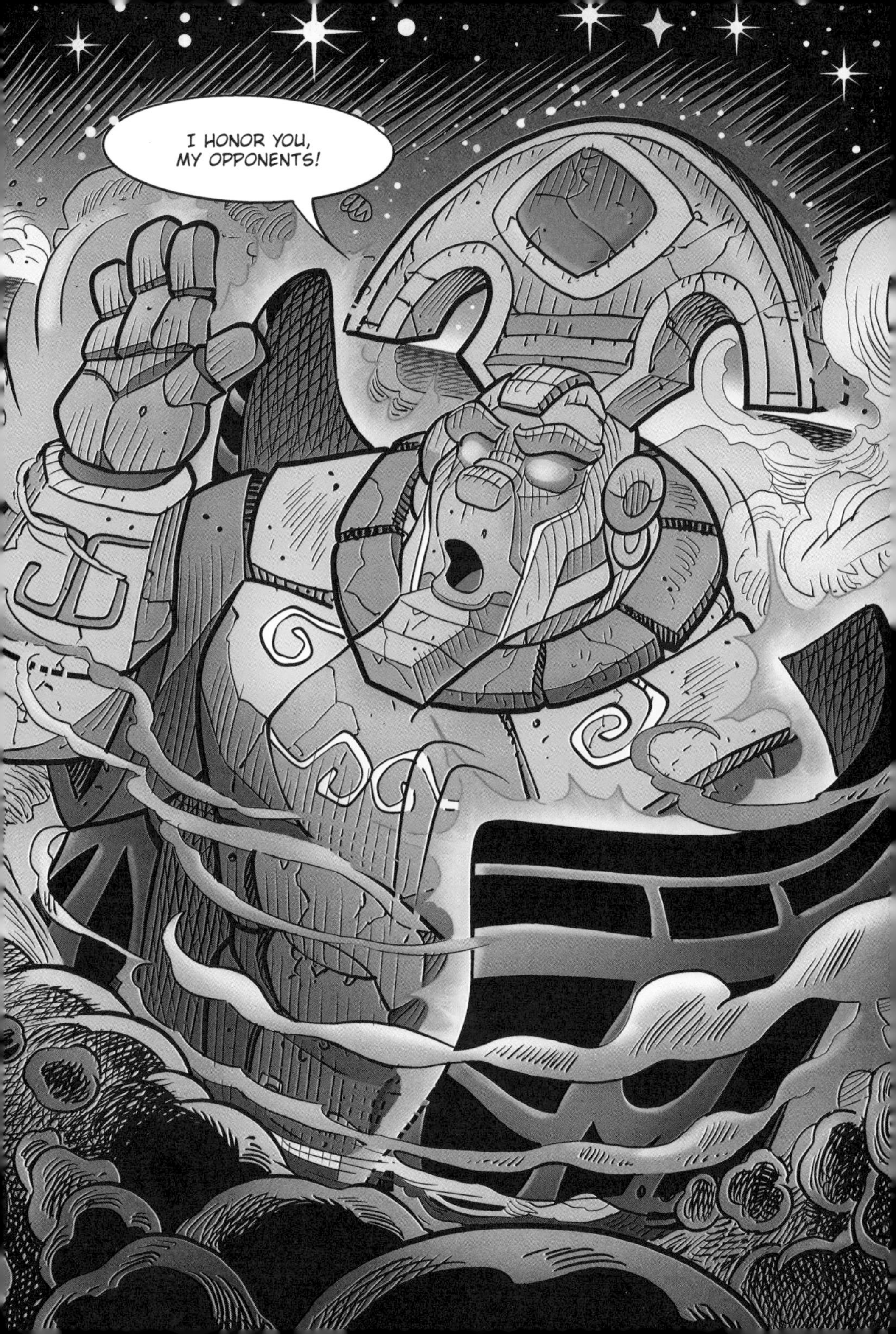
I HONOR YOU, MY OPPONENTS!

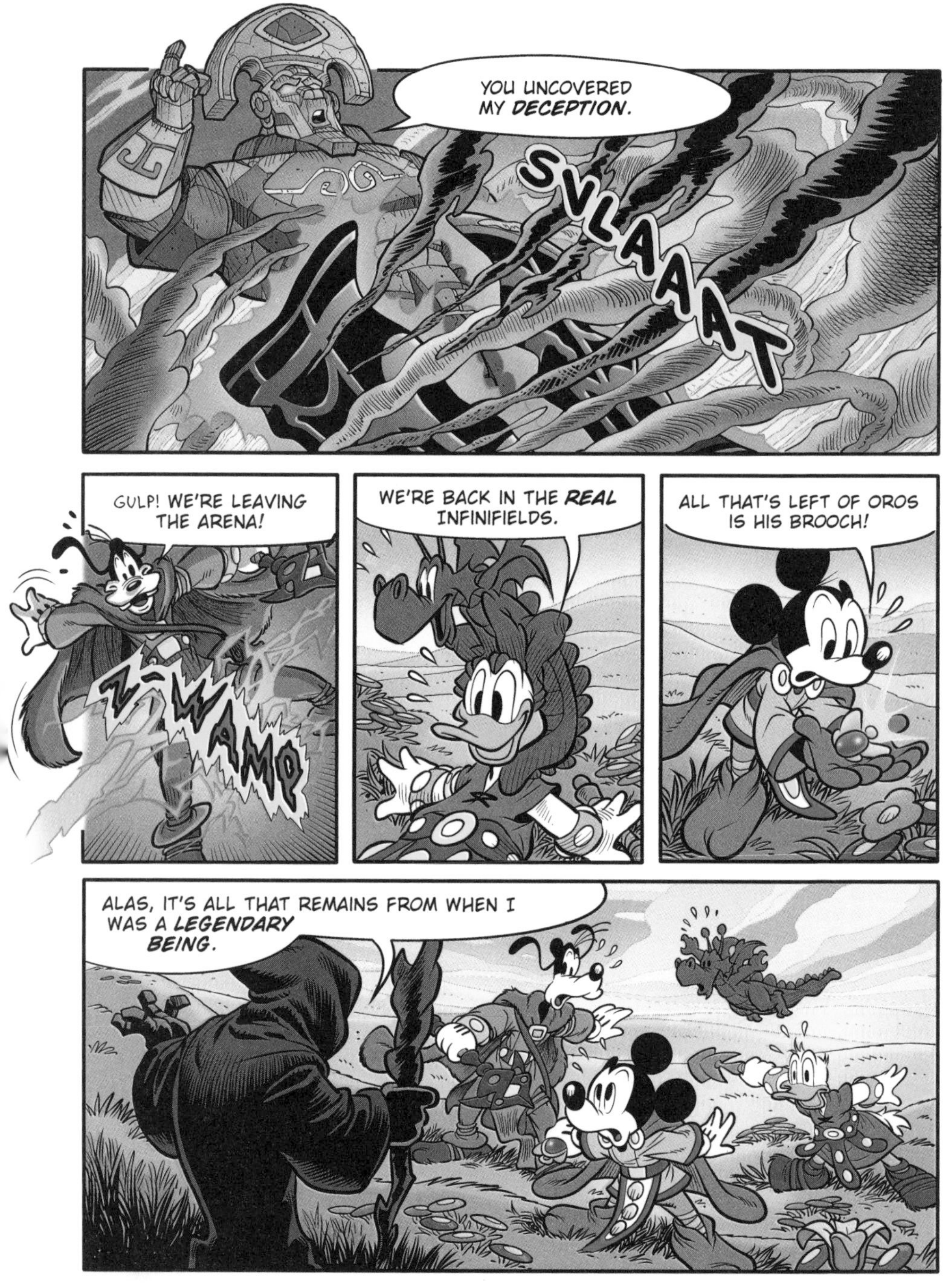
YOU UNCOVERED MY DECEPTION.
SVLAAAT
GULP! WE'RE LEAVING THE ARENA!
Z-WAMP
WE'RE BACK IN THE REAL INFINIFIELDS.
ALL THAT'S LEFT OF OROS IS HIS BROOCH!
ALAS, IT'S ALL THAT REMAINS FROM WHEN I WAS A LEGENDARY BEING.

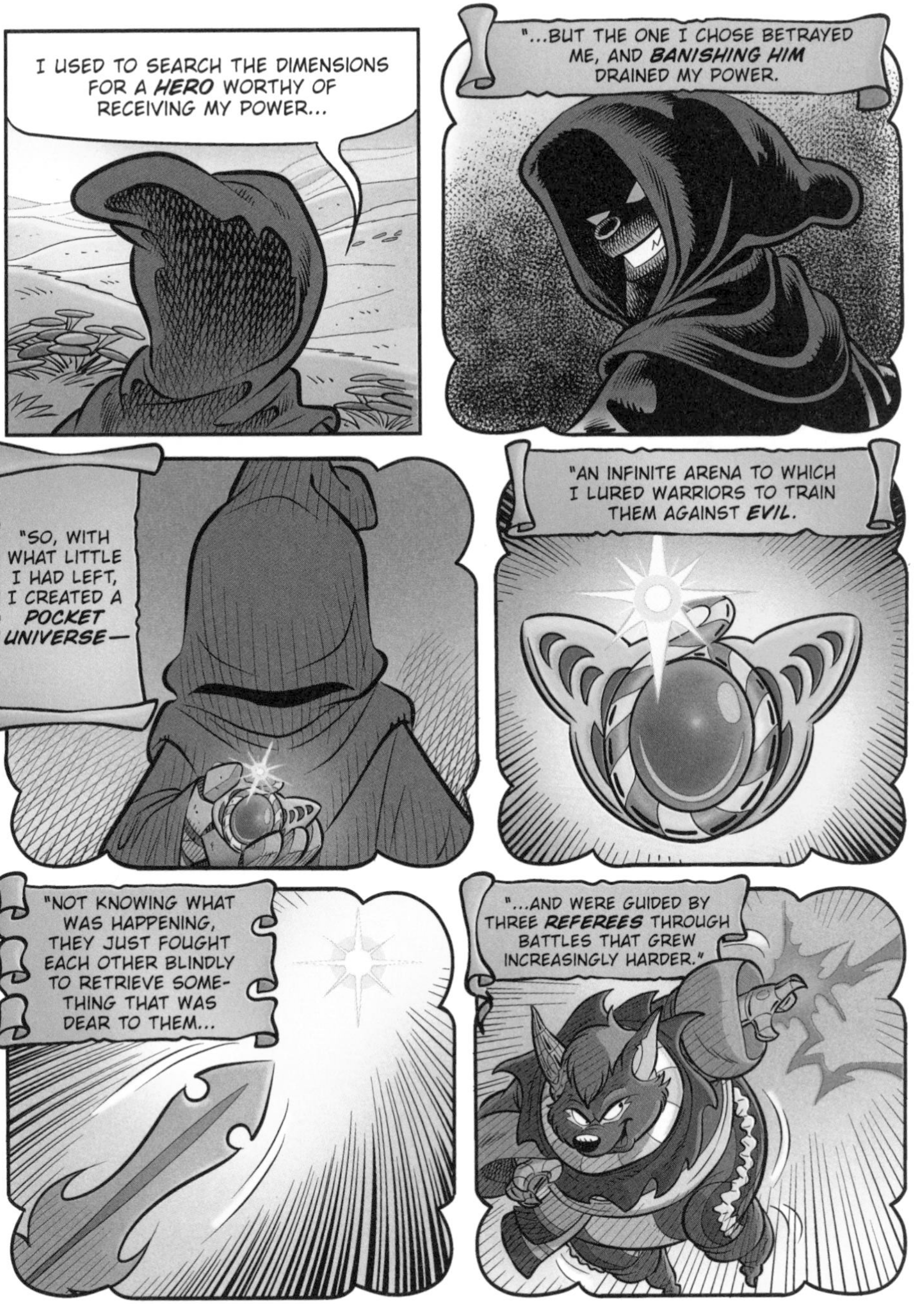
I USED TO SEARCH THE DIMENSIONS FOR A HERO WORTHY OF RECEIVING MY POWER...
"...BUT THE ONE I CHOSE BETRAYED ME, AND BANISHING HIM DRAINED MY POWER.
"SO, WITH WHAT LITTLE I HAD LEFT, I CREATED A POCKET UNIVERSE—
"AN INFINITE ARENA TO WHICH I LURED WARRIORS TO TRAIN THEM AGAINST EVIL.
"NOT KNOWING WHAT WAS HAPPENING, THEY JUST FOUGHT EACH OTHER BLINDLY TO RETRIEVE SOME-THING THAT WAS DEAR TO THEM...
"...AND WERE GUIDED BY THREE REFEREES THROUGH BATTLES THAT GREW INCREASINGLY HARDER."

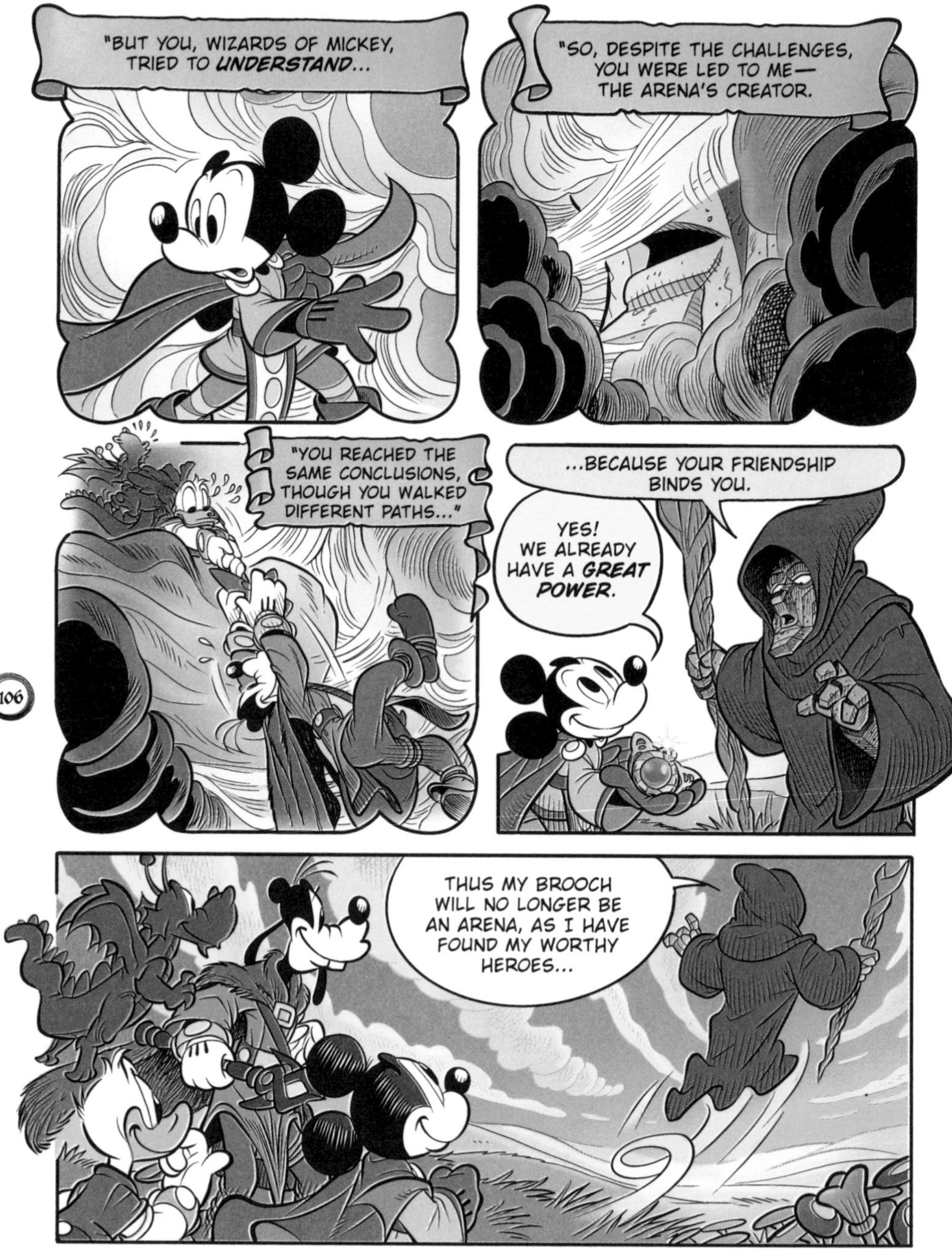

"BUT YOU, WIZARDS OF MICKEY, TRIED TO UNDERSTAND...
"SO, DESPITE THE CHALLENGES, YOU WERE LED TO ME— THE ARENA'S CREATOR.
"YOU REACHED THE SAME CONCLUSIONS, THOUGH YOU WALKED DIFFERENT PATHS..."
...BECAUSE YOUR FRIENDSHIP BINDS YOU.
YES! WE ALREADY HAVE A GREAT POWER.
THUS MY BROOCH WILL NO LONGER BE AN ARENA, AS I HAVE FOUND MY WORTHY HEROES...

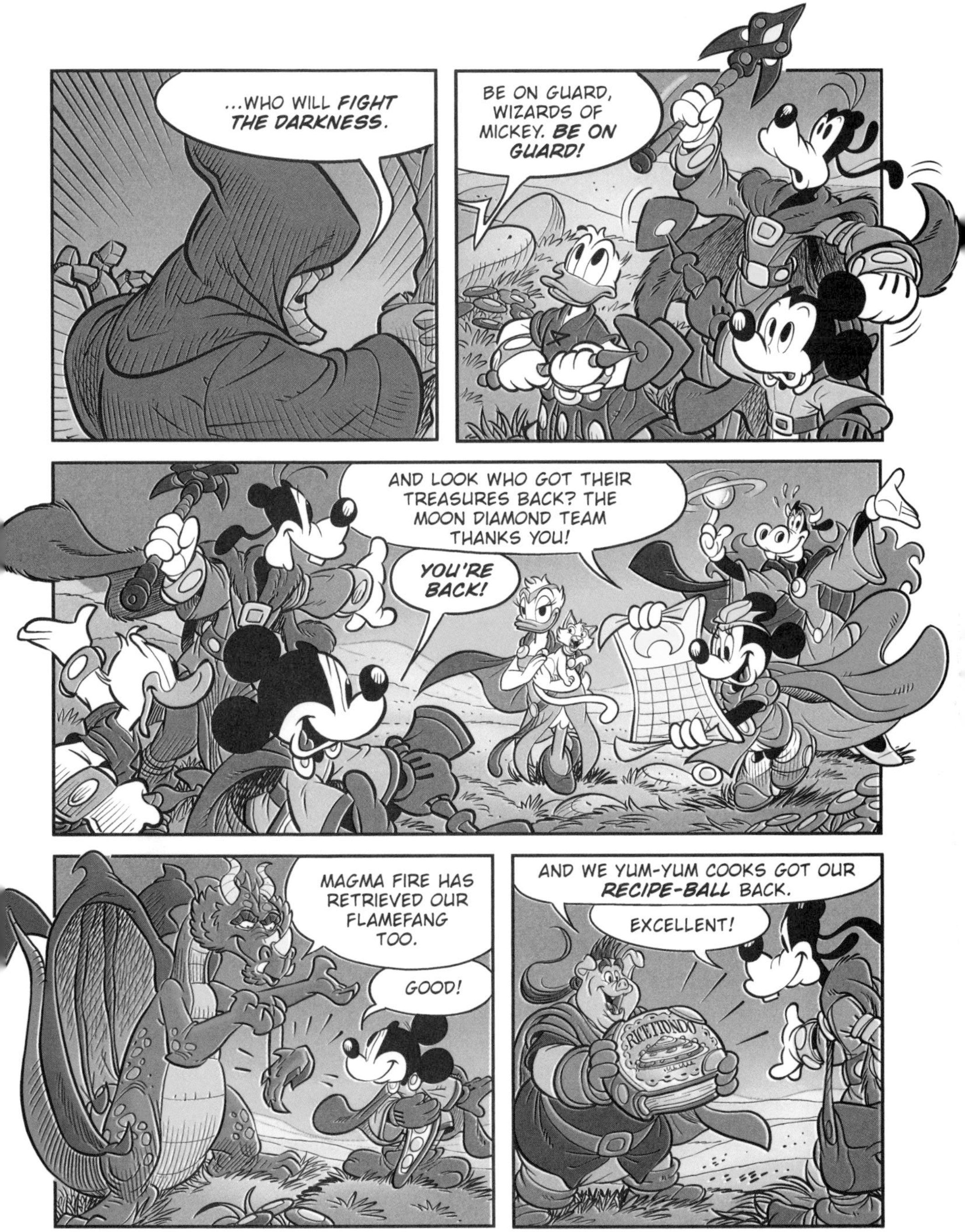

...WHO WILL FIGHT THE DARKNESS.
BE ON GUARD, WIZARDS OF MICKEY. BE ON GUARD!
AND LOOK WHO GOT THEIR TREASURES BACK? THE MOON DIAMOND TEAM THANKS YOU!
YOU'RE BACK!
MAGMA FIRE HAS RETRIEVED OUR FLAMEFANG TOO.
GOOD!
AND WE YUM-YUM COOKS GOT OUR RECIPE-BALL BACK.
EXCELLENT!
RICETTONDO

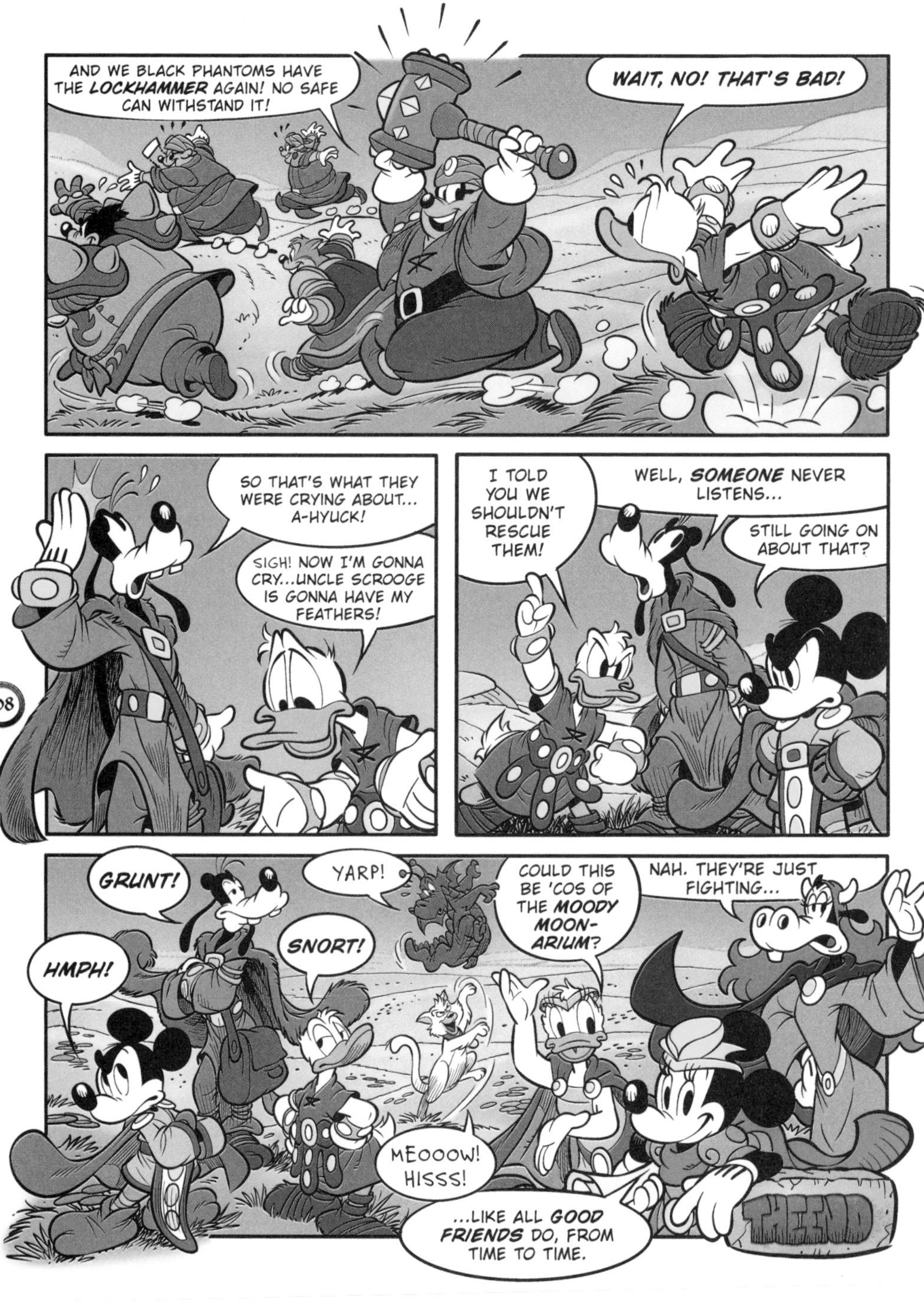
AND WE BLACK PHANTOMS HAVE THE LOCKHAMMER AGAIN! NO SAFE CAN WITHSTAND IT!
WAIT, NO! THAT'S BAD!
SO THAT'S WHAT THEY WERE CRYING ABOUT... A-HYUCK!
SIGH! NOW I'M GONNA CRY...UNCLE SCROOGE IS GONNA HAVE MY FEATHERS!
I TOLD YOU WE SHOULDN'T RESCUE THEM!
WELL, SOMEONE NEVER LISTENS...
STILL GOING ON ABOUT THAT?
GRUNT!
HMPH!
YARP!
SNORT!
COULD THIS BE 'COS OF THE MOODY MOON-ARIUM?
NAH. THEY'RE JUST FIGHTING...
MEOOOW! HISSS!
...LIKE ALL GOOD FRIENDS DO, FROM TIME TO TIME.
THE END

Wizards of Mickey

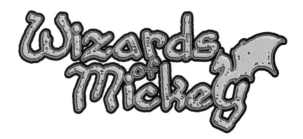

Wizards of Mickey

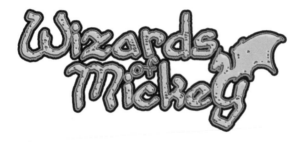

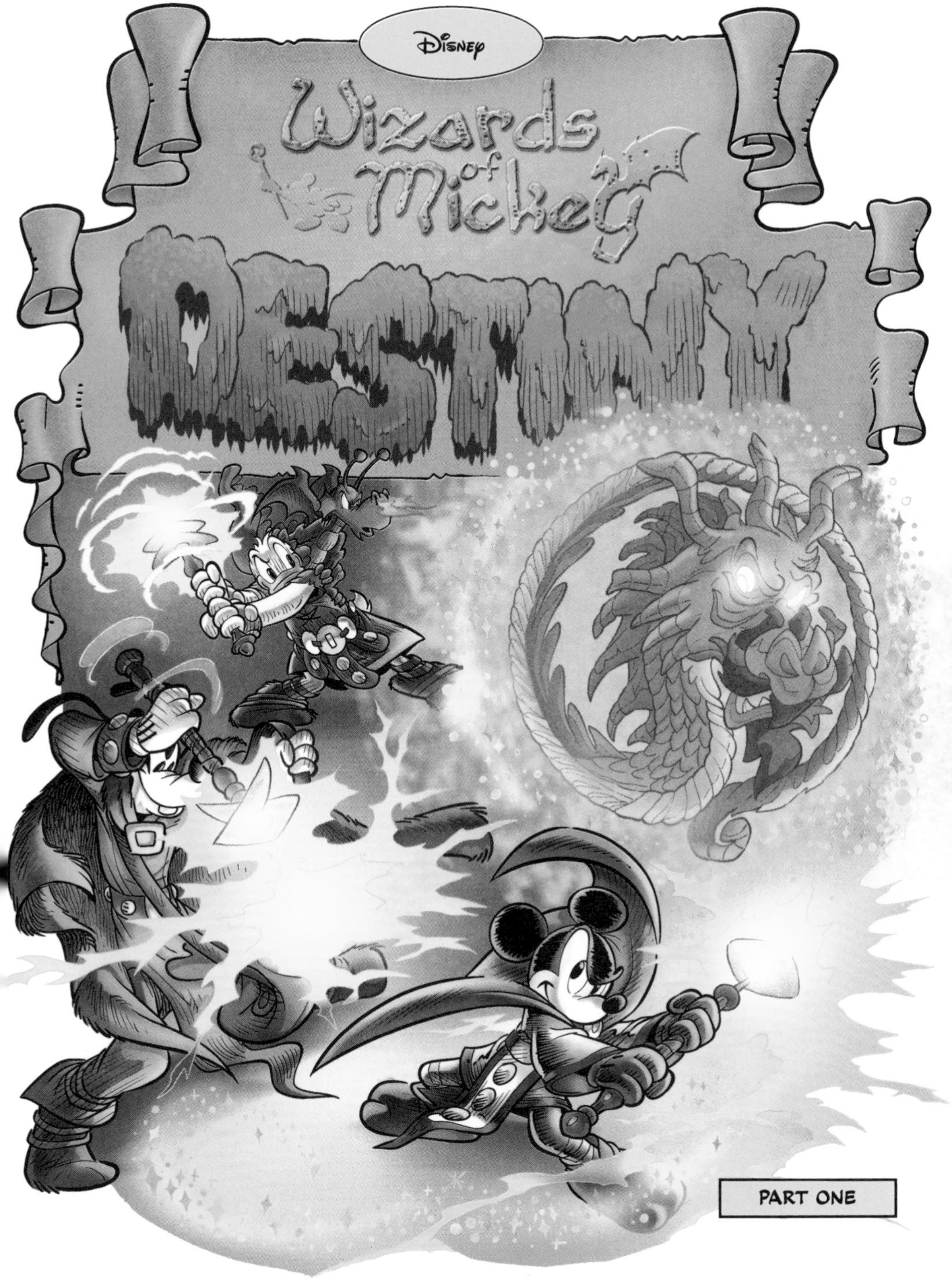
Disney
Wizards of Mickey
DESTINY
PART ONE

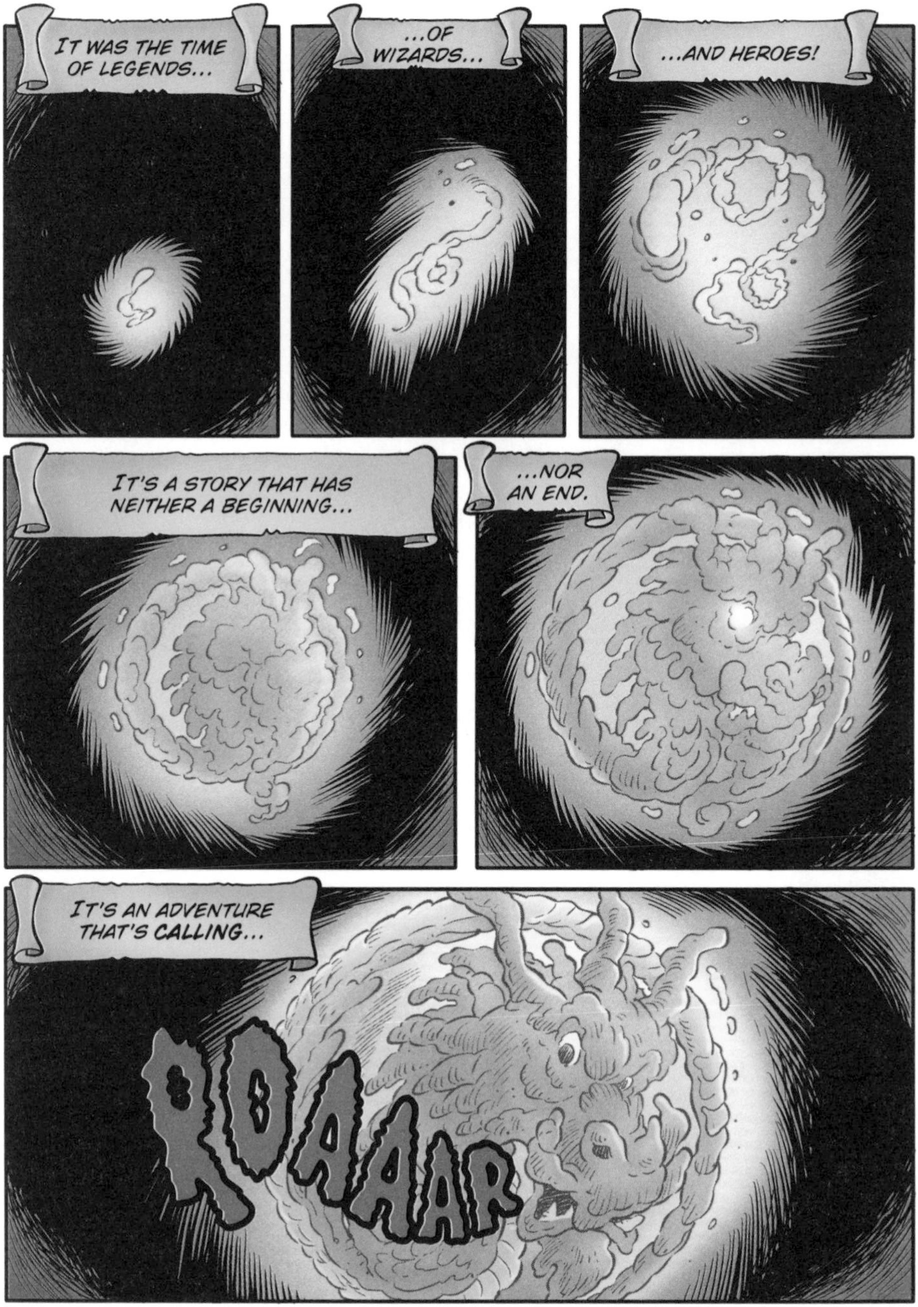
IT WAS THE TIME OF LEGENDS...
...OF WIZARDS...
...AND HEROES!
IT'S A STORY THAT HAS NEITHER A BEGINNING...
...NOR AN END.
IT'S AN ADVENTURE THAT'S CALLING...
ROAAAR

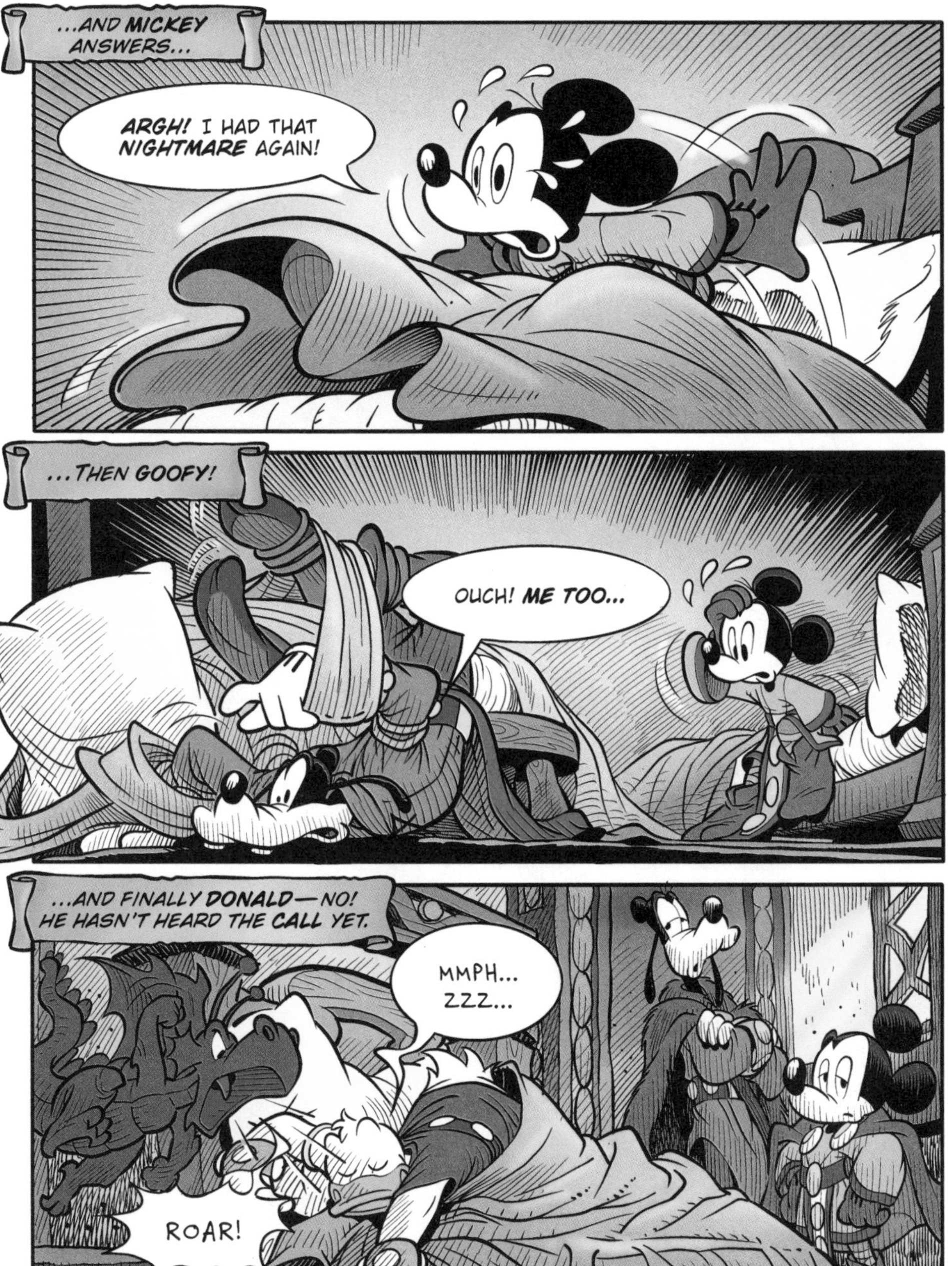
...AND MICKEY ANSWERS...
ARGH! I HAD THAT NIGHTMARE AGAIN!
...THEN GOOFY!
OUCH! ME TOO...
...AND FINALLY DONALD—NO! HE HASN'T HEARD THE CALL YET.
MMPH... ZZZ...
ROAR!

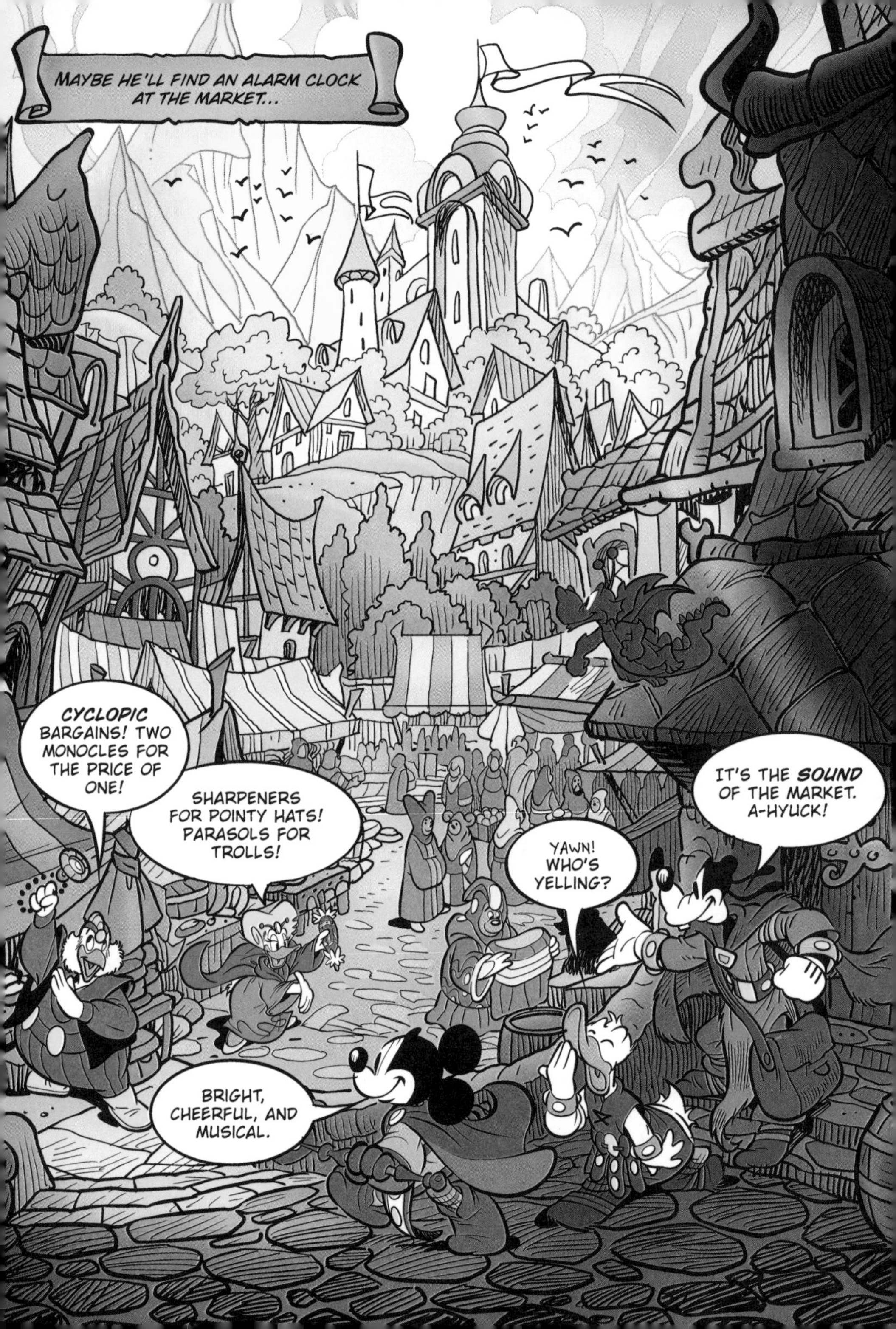
MAYBE HE'LL FIND AN ALARM CLOCK AT THE MARKET...
CYCLOPIC BARGAINS! TWO MONOCLES FOR THE PRICE OF ONE!
SHARPENERS FOR POINTY HATS! PARASOLS FOR TROLLS!
YAWN! WHO'S YELLING?
IT'S THE SOUND OF THE MARKET. A-HYUCK!
BRIGHT, CHEERFUL, AND MUSICAL.

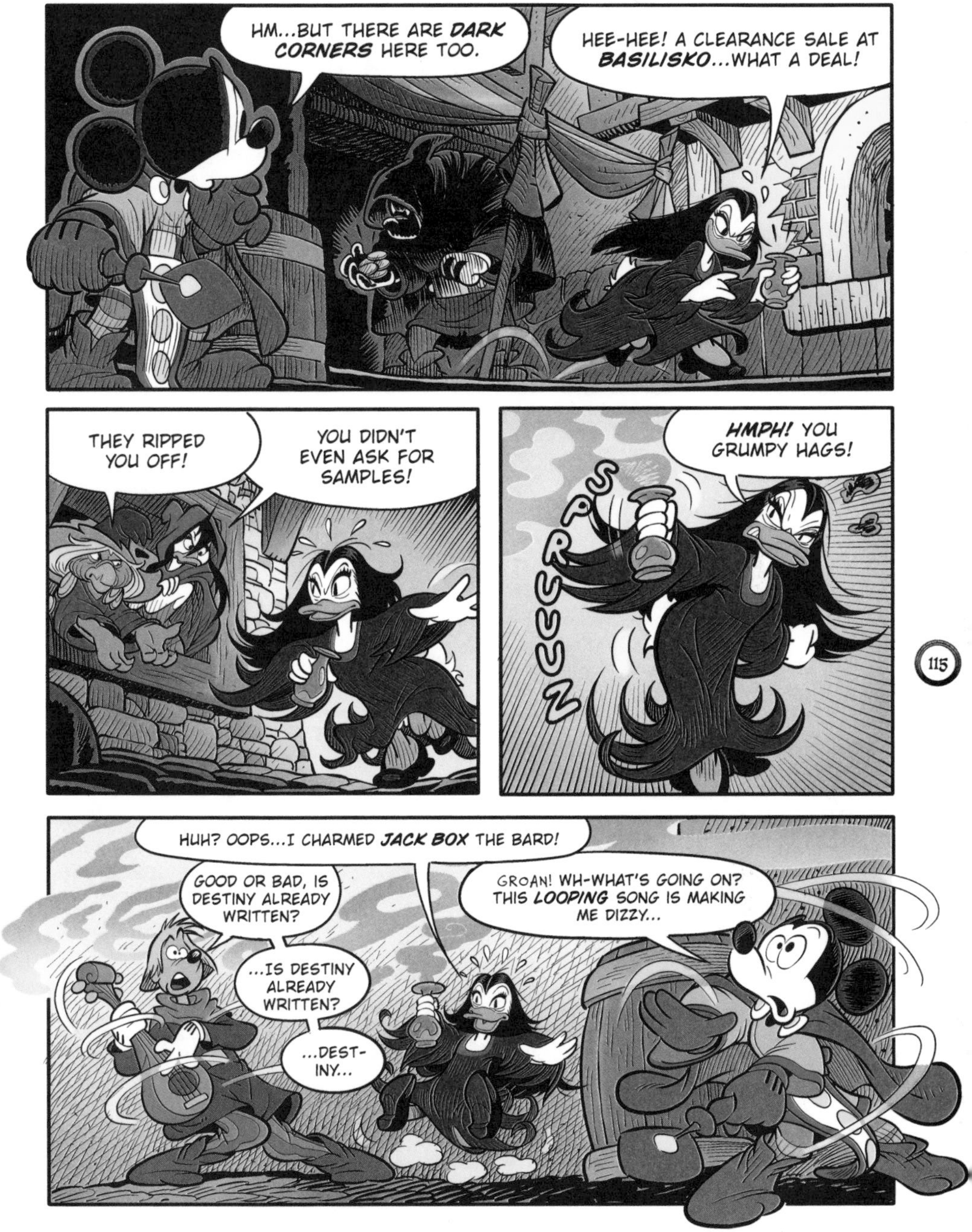
HM...BUT THERE ARE DARK CORNERS HERE TOO.
HEE-HEE! A CLEARANCE SALE AT BASILISKO...WHAT A DEAL!
THEY RIPPED YOU OFF!
YOU DIDN'T EVEN ASK FOR SAMPLES!
HMPH! YOU GRUMPY HAGS!
SPRUUUZ
HUH? OOPS...I CHARMED JACK BOX THE BARD!
GOOD OR BAD, IS DESTINY ALREADY WRITTEN?
...IS DESTINY ALREADY WRITTEN?
...DEST-INY...
GROAN! WH-WHAT'S GOING ON? THIS LOOPING SONG IS MAKING ME DIZZY...

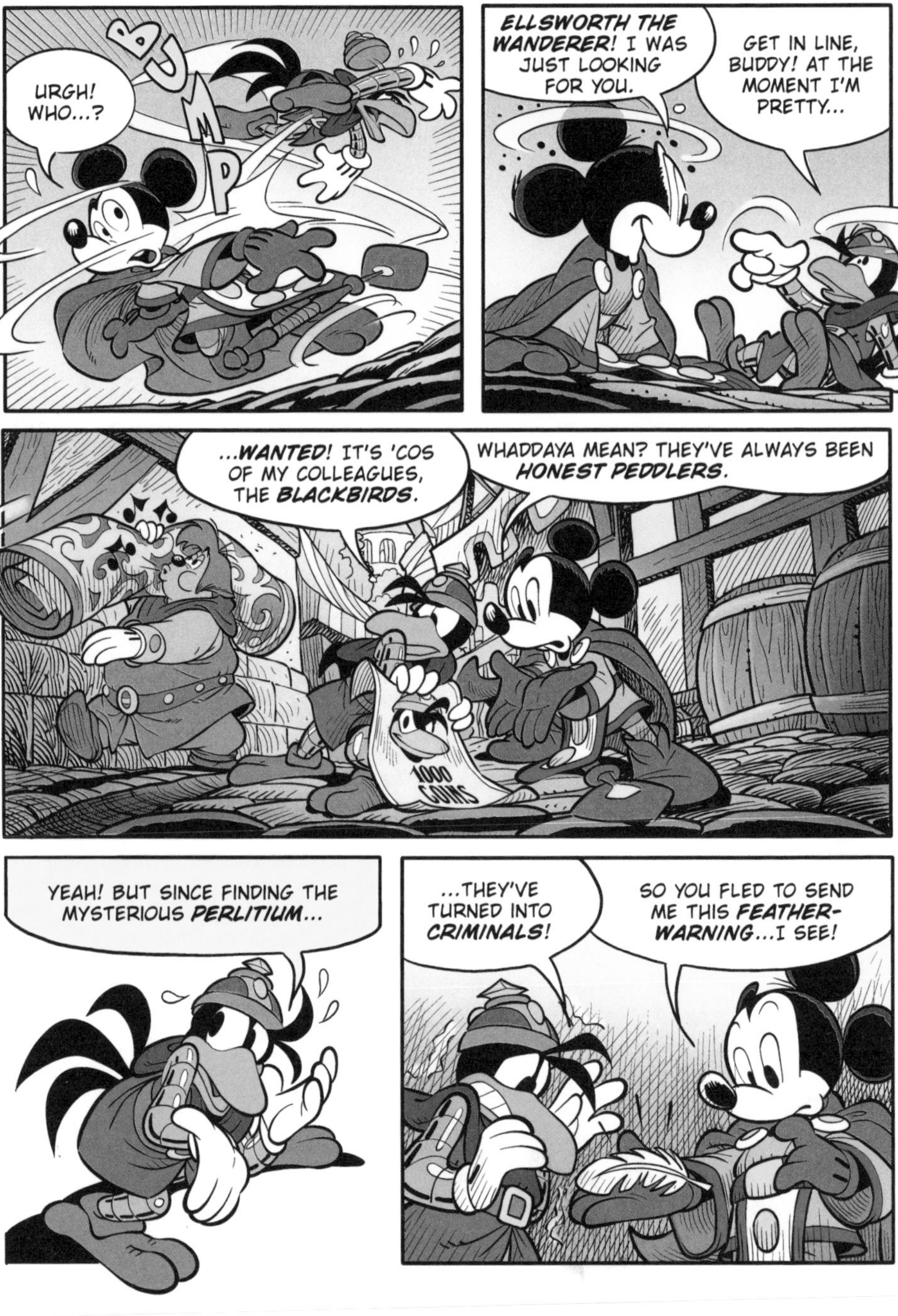

BJMMP
URGH! WHO...?
ELLSWORTH THE WANDERER! I WAS JUST LOOKING FOR YOU.
GET IN LINE, BUDDY! AT THE MOMENT I'M PRETTY...
...WANTED! IT'S 'COS OF MY COLLEAGUES, THE BLACKBIRDS.
WHADDAYA MEAN? THEY'VE ALWAYS BEEN HONEST PEDDLERS.
1000 COINS
YEAH! BUT SINCE FINDING THE MYSTERIOUS PERLITIUM...
...THEY'VE TURNED INTO CRIMINALS!
SO YOU FLED TO SEND ME THIS FEATHER-WARNING...I SEE!

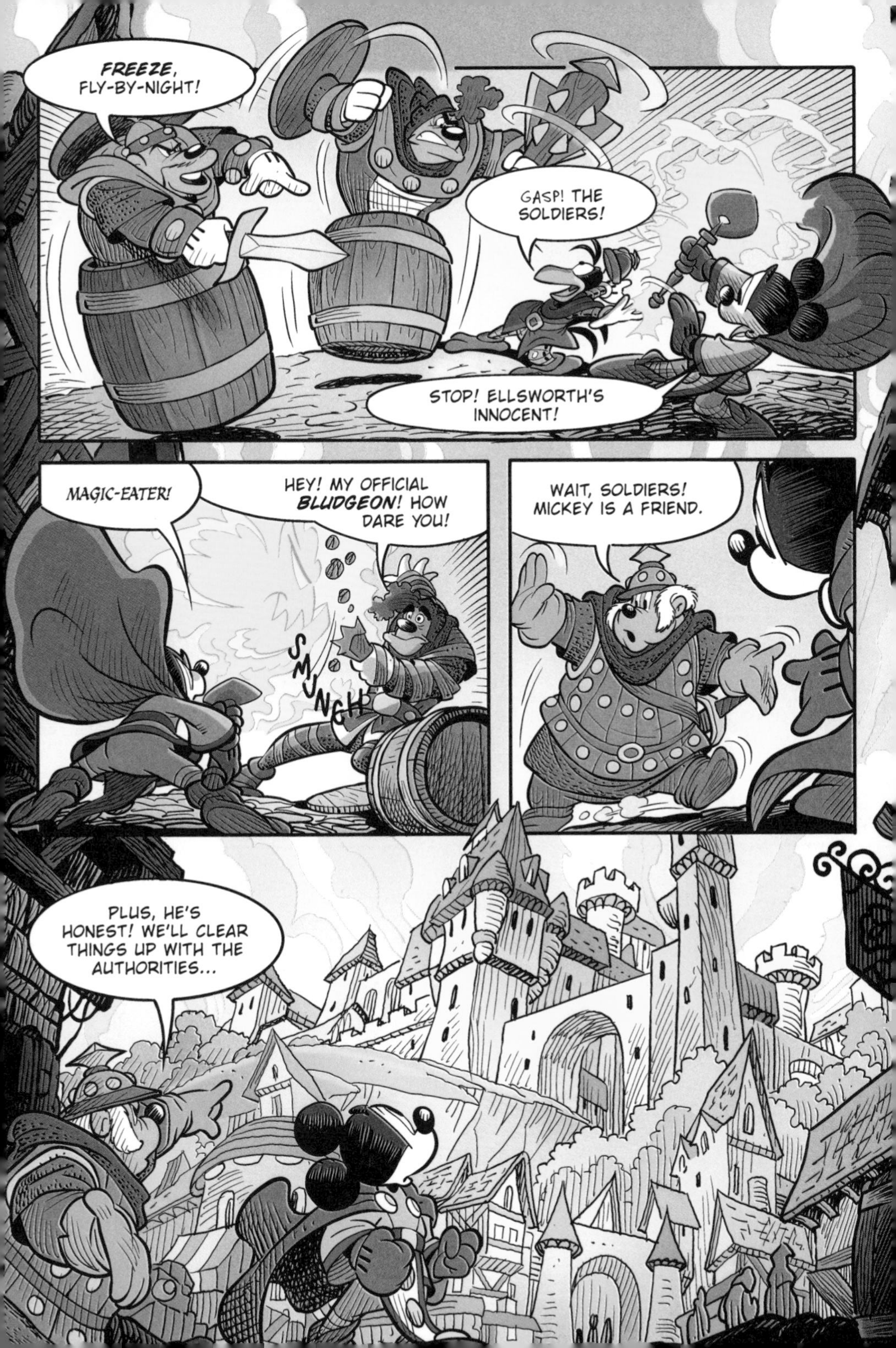

FREEZE, FLY-BY-NIGHT!
GASP! THE SOLDIERS!
STOP! ELLSWORTH'S INNOCENT!
MAGIC-EATER!
HEY! MY OFFICIAL BLUDGEON! HOW DARE YOU!
SMUNCH
WAIT, SOLDIERS! MICKEY IS A FRIEND.
PLUS, HE'S HONEST! WE'LL CLEAR THINGS UP WITH THE AUTHORITIES...

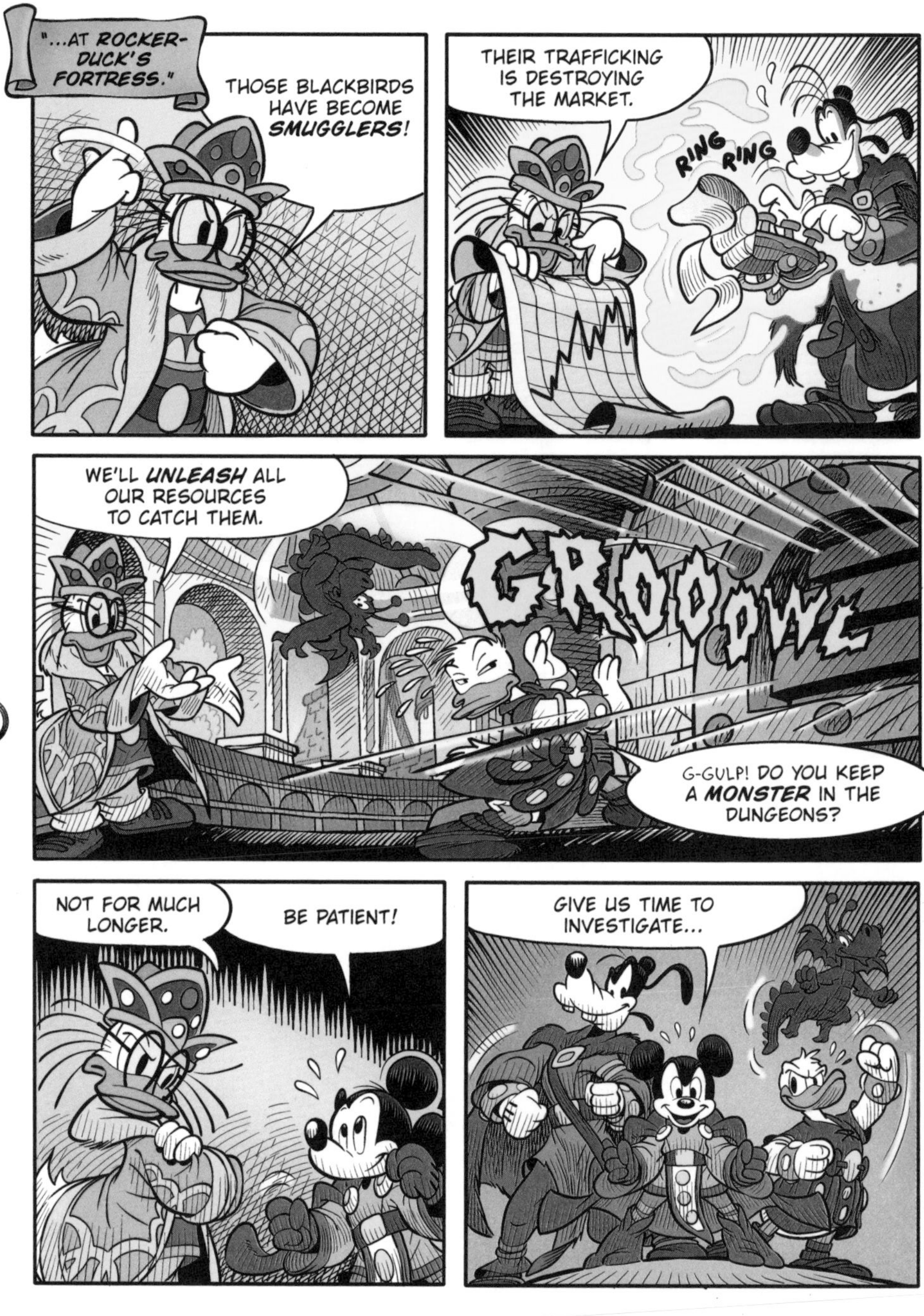
"...AT ROCKER-DUCK'S FORTRESS."
THOSE BLACKBIRDS HAVE BECOME SMUGGLERS!
THEIR TRAFFICKING IS DESTROYING THE MARKET.
RING RING
WE'LL UNLEASH ALL OUR RESOURCES TO CATCH THEM.
GROOOOWL
G-GULP! DO YOU KEEP A MONSTER IN THE DUNGEONS?
NOT FOR MUCH LONGER.
BE PATIENT!
GIVE US TIME TO INVESTIGATE...

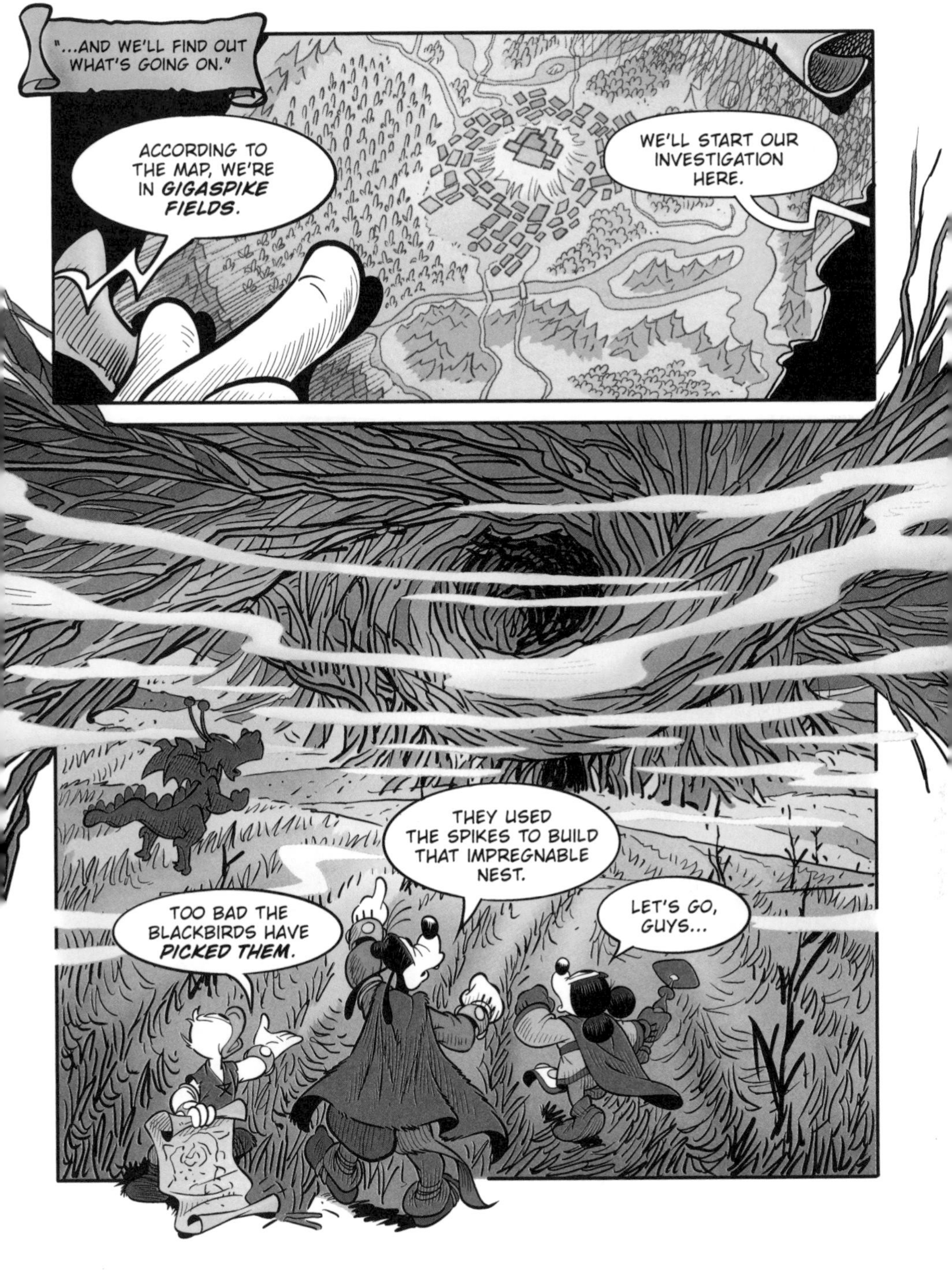
"...AND WE'LL FIND OUT WHAT'S GOING ON."
ACCORDING TO THE MAP, WE'RE IN *GIGASPIKE FIELDS*.
WE'LL START OUR INVESTIGATION HERE.
THEY USED THE SPIKES TO BUILD THAT IMPREGNABLE NEST.
TOO BAD THE BLACKBIRDS HAVE *PICKED THEM*.
LET'S GO, GUYS...

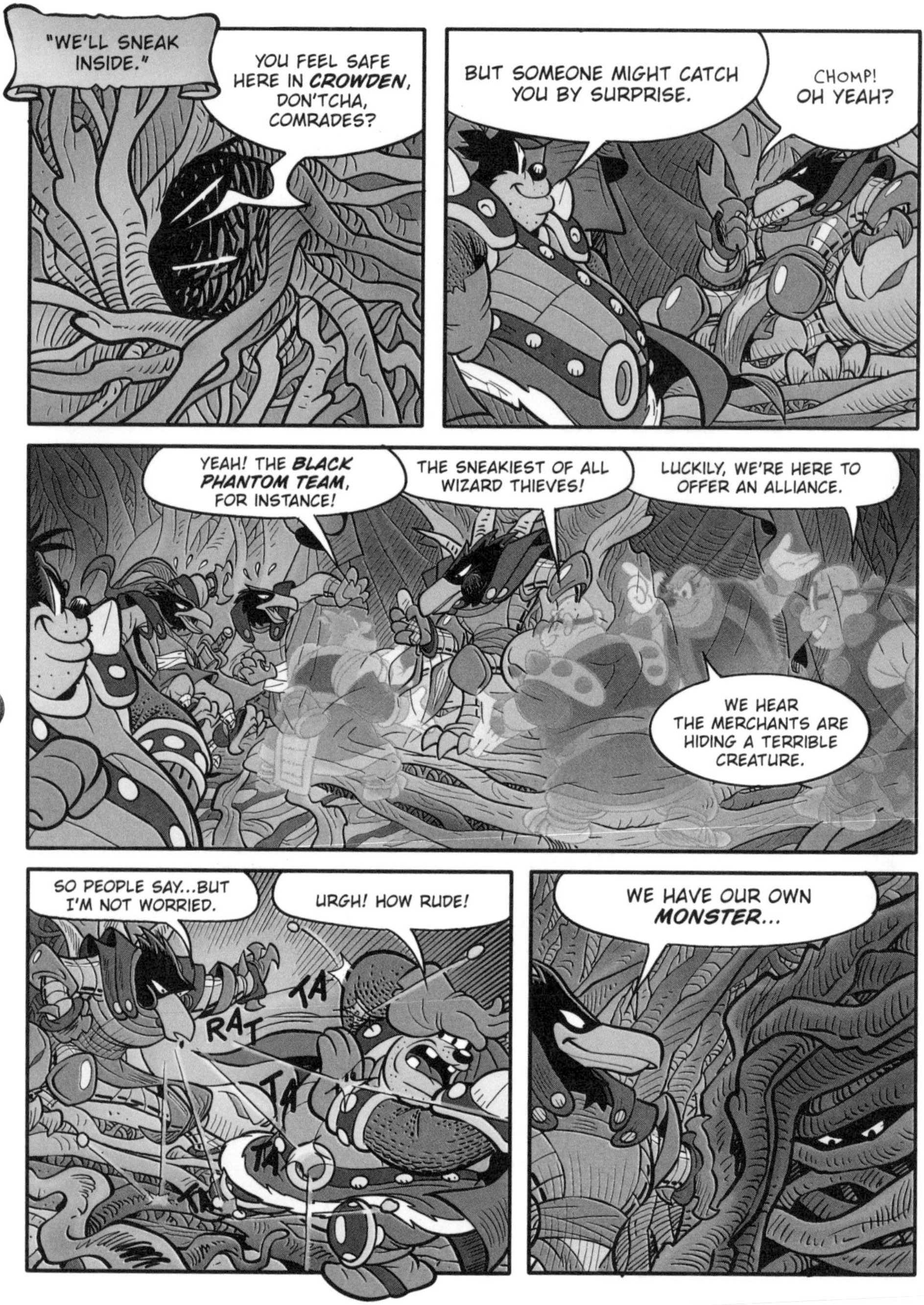

"WE'LL SNEAK INSIDE."
YOU FEEL SAFE HERE IN CROWDEN, DON'TCHA, COMRADES?
BUT SOMEONE MIGHT CATCH YOU BY SURPRISE.
CHOMP! OH YEAH?
YEAH! THE BLACK PHANTOM TEAM, FOR INSTANCE!
THE SNEAKIEST OF ALL WIZARD THIEVES!
LUCKILY, WE'RE HERE TO OFFER AN ALLIANCE.
WE HEAR THE MERCHANTS ARE HIDING A TERRIBLE CREATURE.
SO PEOPLE SAY...BUT I'M NOT WORRIED.
URGH! HOW RUDE!
RAT TA TA TA TA
WE HAVE OUR OWN MONSTER...

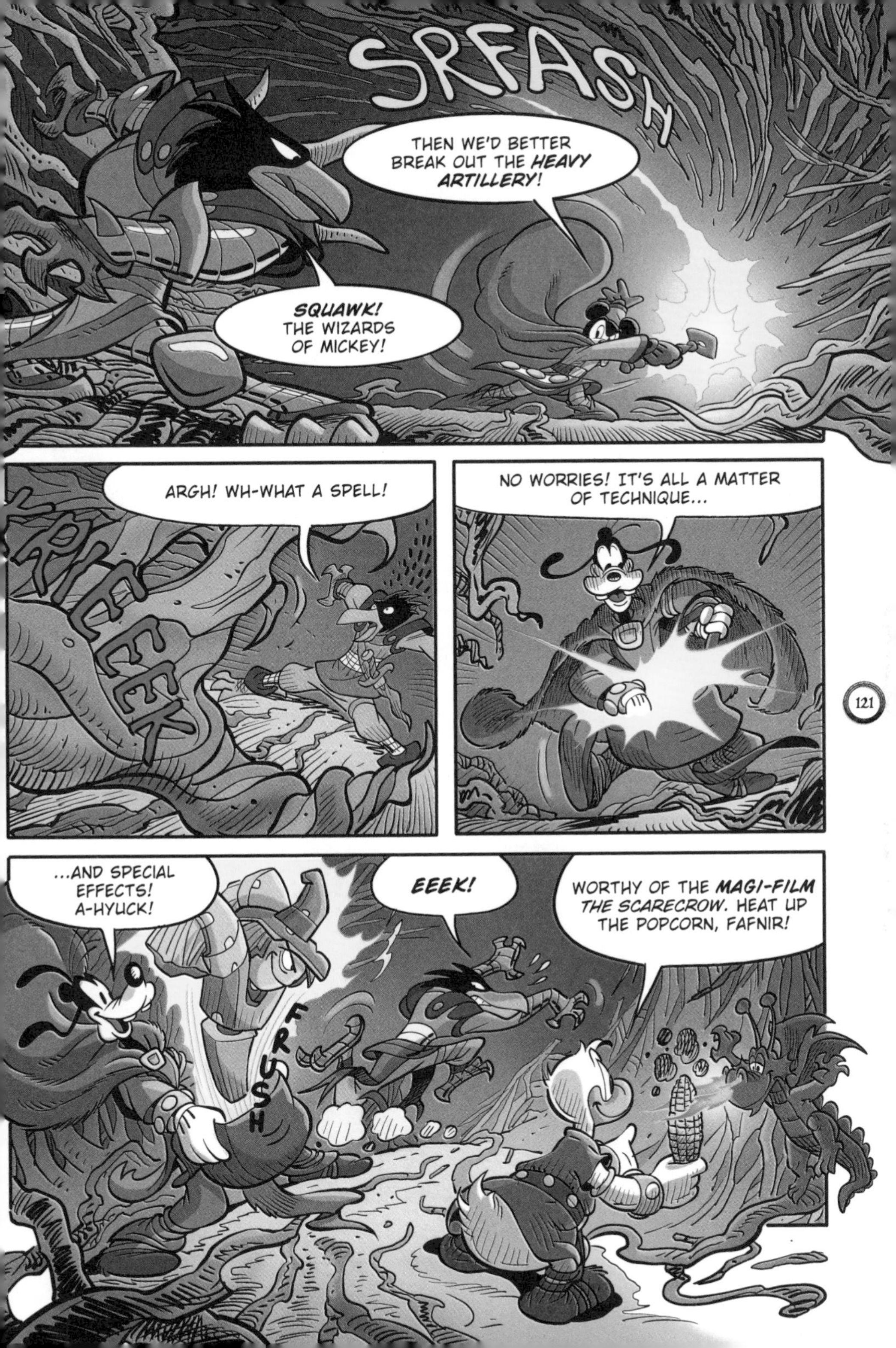
SRFASH
THEN WE'D BETTER BREAK OUT THE HEAVY ARTILLERY!
SQUAWK! THE WIZARDS OF MICKEY!
ARGH! WH-WHAT A SPELL!
SKRIEEEK
NO WORRIES! IT'S ALL A MATTER OF TECHNIQUE...
...AND SPECIAL EFFECTS! A-HYUCK!
FRUSSH
EEEK!
WORTHY OF THE MAGI-FILM THE SCARECROW. HEAT UP THE POPCORN, FAFNIR!

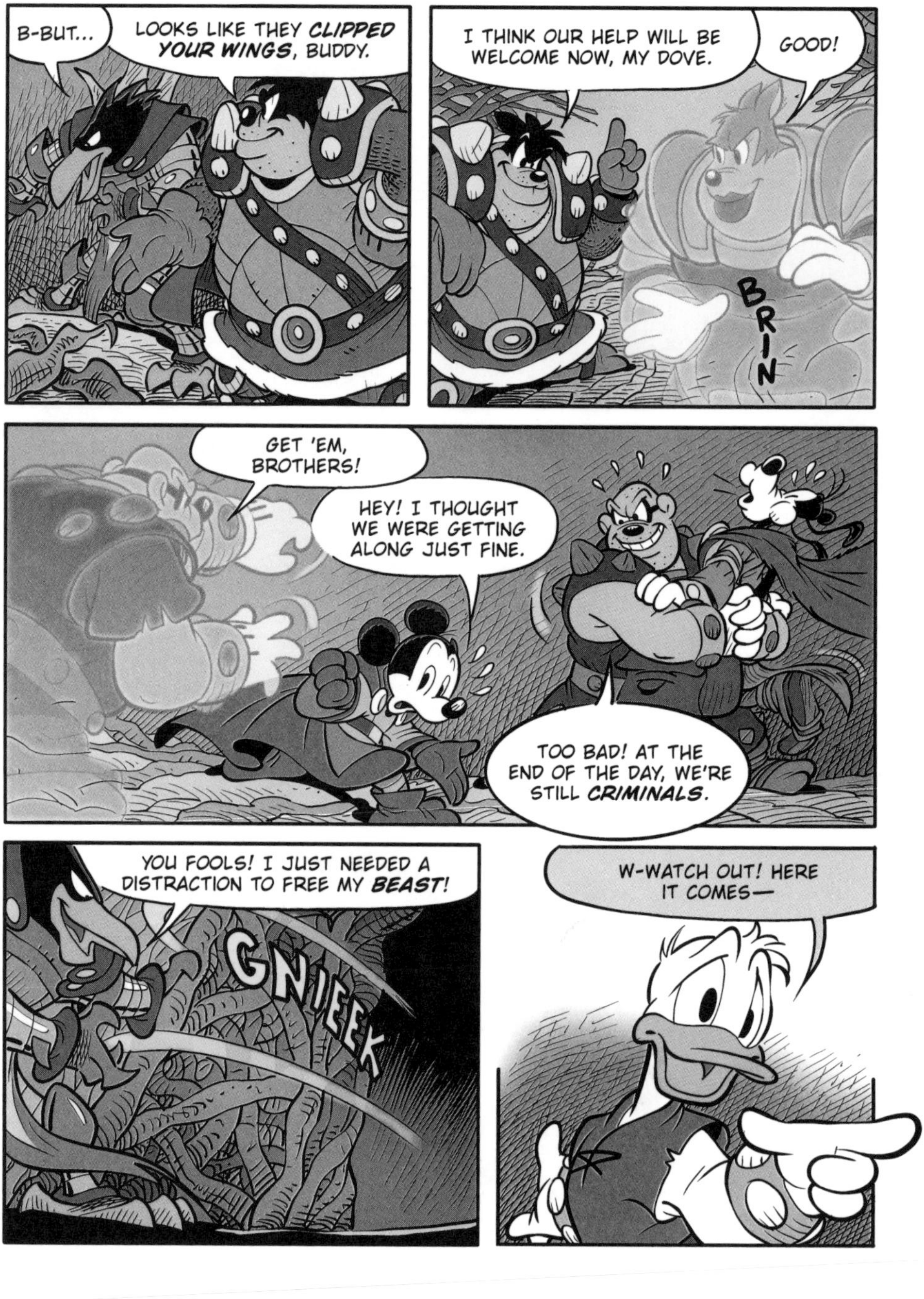

B-BUT...
LOOKS LIKE THEY CLIPPED YOUR WINGS, BUDDY.
I THINK OUR HELP WILL BE WELCOME NOW, MY DOVE.
GOOD!
BRIN
GET 'EM, BROTHERS!
HEY! I THOUGHT WE WERE GETTING ALONG JUST FINE.
TOO BAD! AT THE END OF THE DAY, WE'RE STILL CRIMINALS.
YOU FOOLS! I JUST NEEDED A DISTRACTION TO FREE MY BEAST!
GNIEEK
W-WATCH OUT! HERE IT COMES—

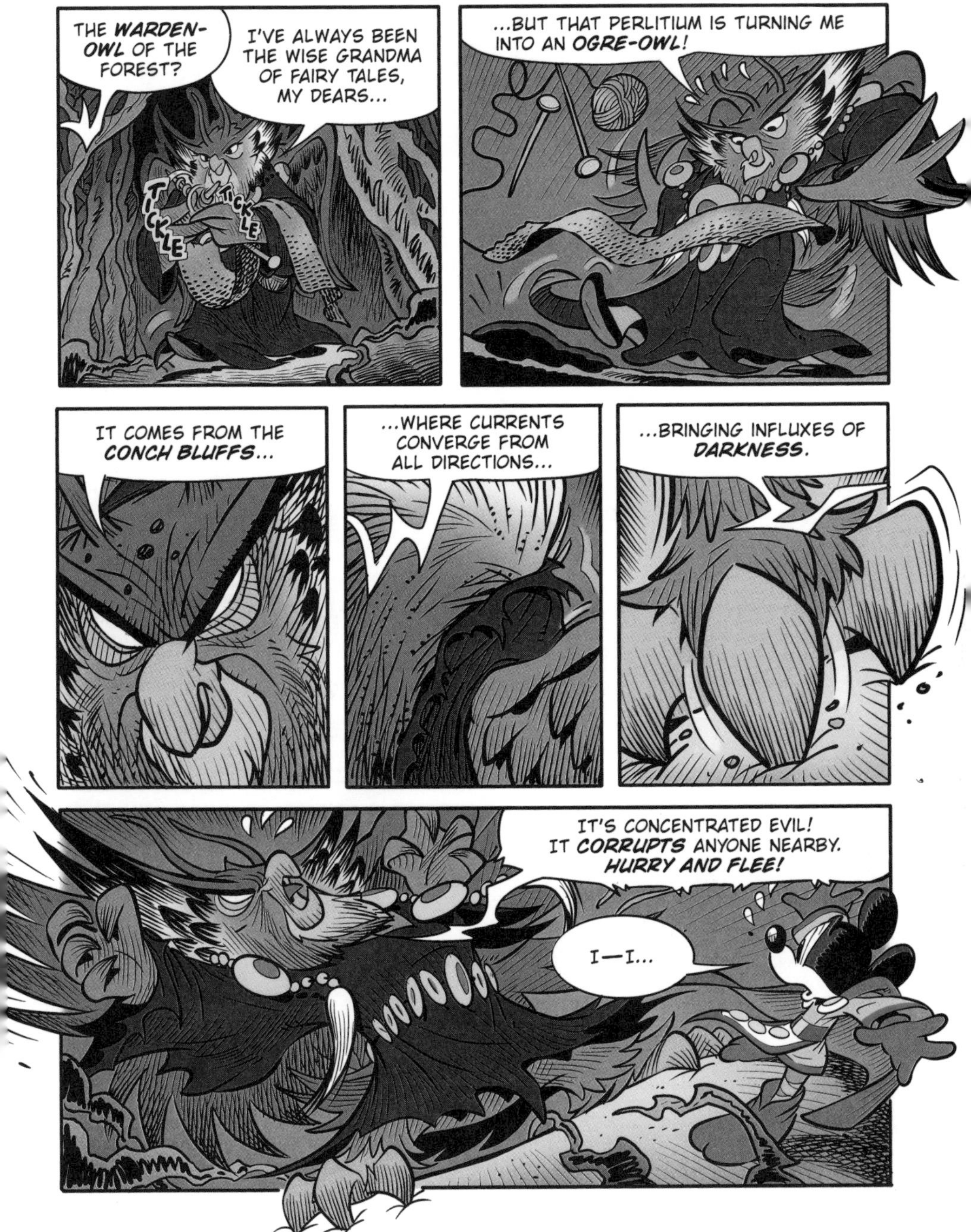
THE WARDEN-OWL OF THE FOREST?
I'VE ALWAYS BEEN THE WISE GRANDMA OF FAIRY TALES, MY DEARS...
TICKLE
TICKLE
...BUT THAT PERLITIUM IS TURNING ME INTO AN OGRE-OWL!
IT COMES FROM THE CONCH BLUFFS...
...WHERE CURRENTS CONVERGE FROM ALL DIRECTIONS...
...BRINGING INFLUXES OF DARKNESS.
IT'S CONCENTRATED EVIL! IT CORRUPTS ANYONE NEARBY. HURRY AND FLEE!
I—I...

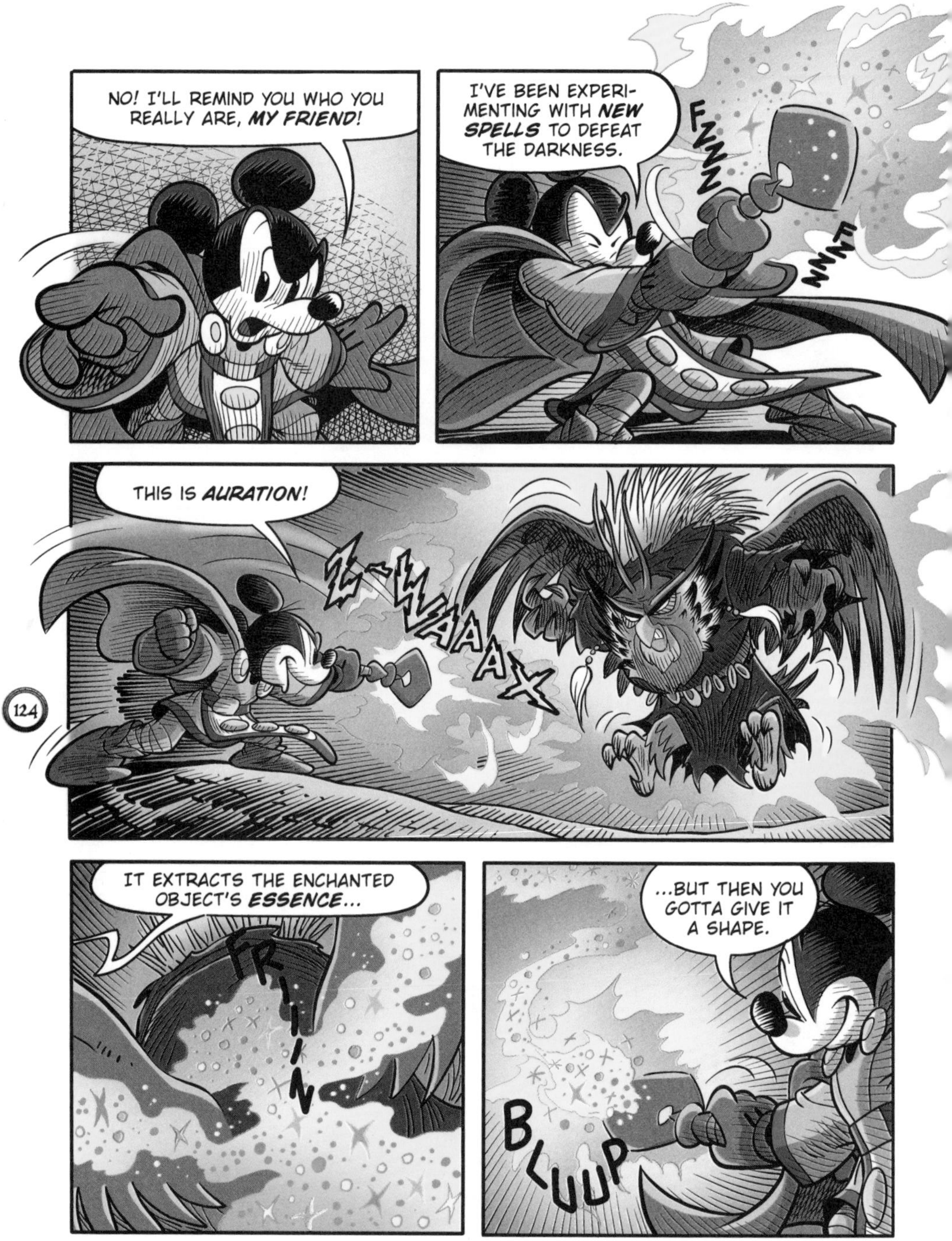
NO! I'LL REMIND YOU WHO YOU REALLY ARE, MY FRIEND!
I'VE BEEN EXPERI-MENTING WITH NEW SPELLS TO DEFEAT THE DARKNESS.
FZZZ
FZZZZ
THIS IS AURATION!
Z-WAAAAX
IT EXTRACTS THE ENCHANTED OBJECT'S ESSENCE...
FRIIIN
...BUT THEN YOU GOTTA GIVE IT A SHAPE.
BLUUP

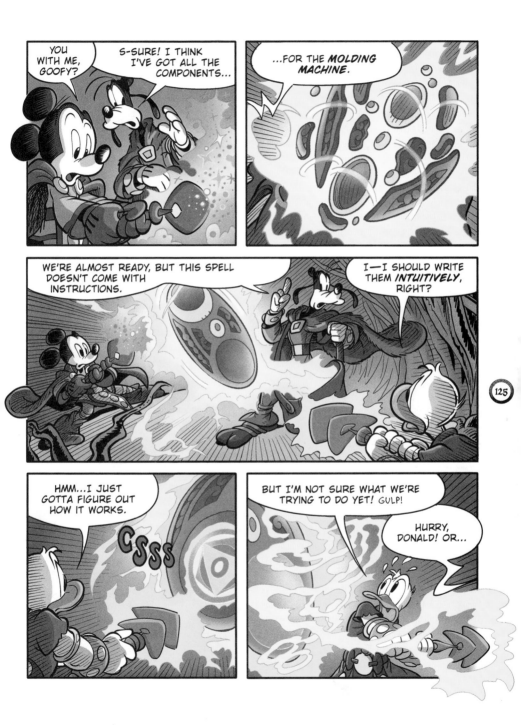

YOU WITH ME, GOOFY?

S-SURE! I THINK I'VE GOT ALL THE COMPONENTS...

...FOR THE *MOLDING MACHINE*.

WE'RE ALMOST READY, BUT THIS SPELL DOESN'T COME WITH INSTRUCTIONS.

I—I SHOULD WRITE THEM *INTUITIVELY*, RIGHT?

125

HMM...I JUST GOTTA FIGURE OUT HOW IT WORKS.

CSSS

BUT I'M NOT SURE WHAT WE'RE TRYING TO DO YET! *GULP!*

HURRY, DONALD! OR...

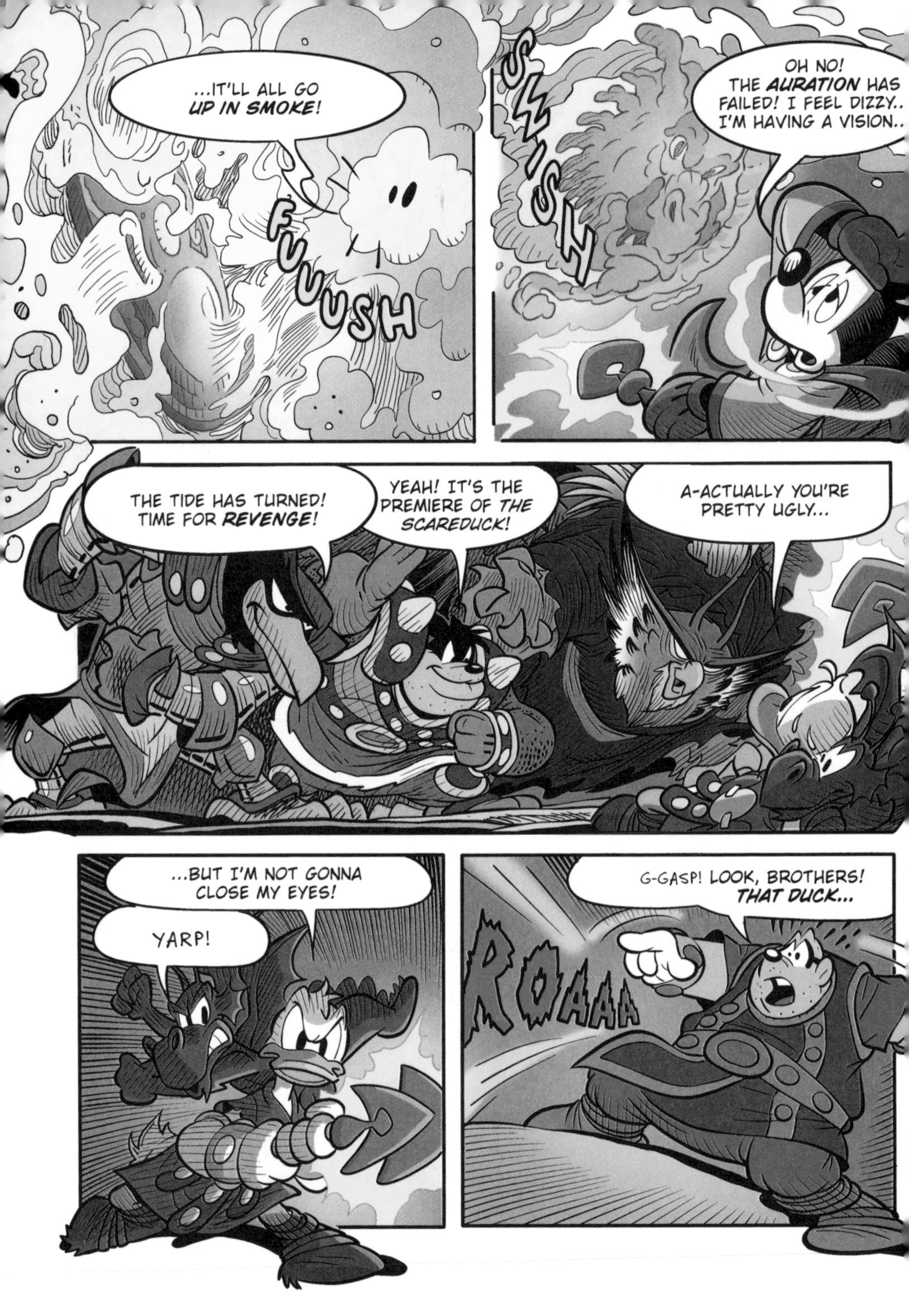

...IT'LL ALL GO UP IN SMOKE!
FUUUSH
SWISH
OH NO! THE AURATION HAS FAILED! I FEEL DIZZY.. I'M HAVING A VISION..
THE TIDE HAS TURNED! TIME FOR REVENGE!
YEAH! IT'S THE PREMIERE OF THE SCAREDUCK!
A-ACTUALLY YOU'RE PRETTY UGLY...
...BUT I'M NOT GONNA CLOSE MY EYES!
YARP!
G-GASP! LOOK, BROTHERS! THAT DUCK...
ROAAA

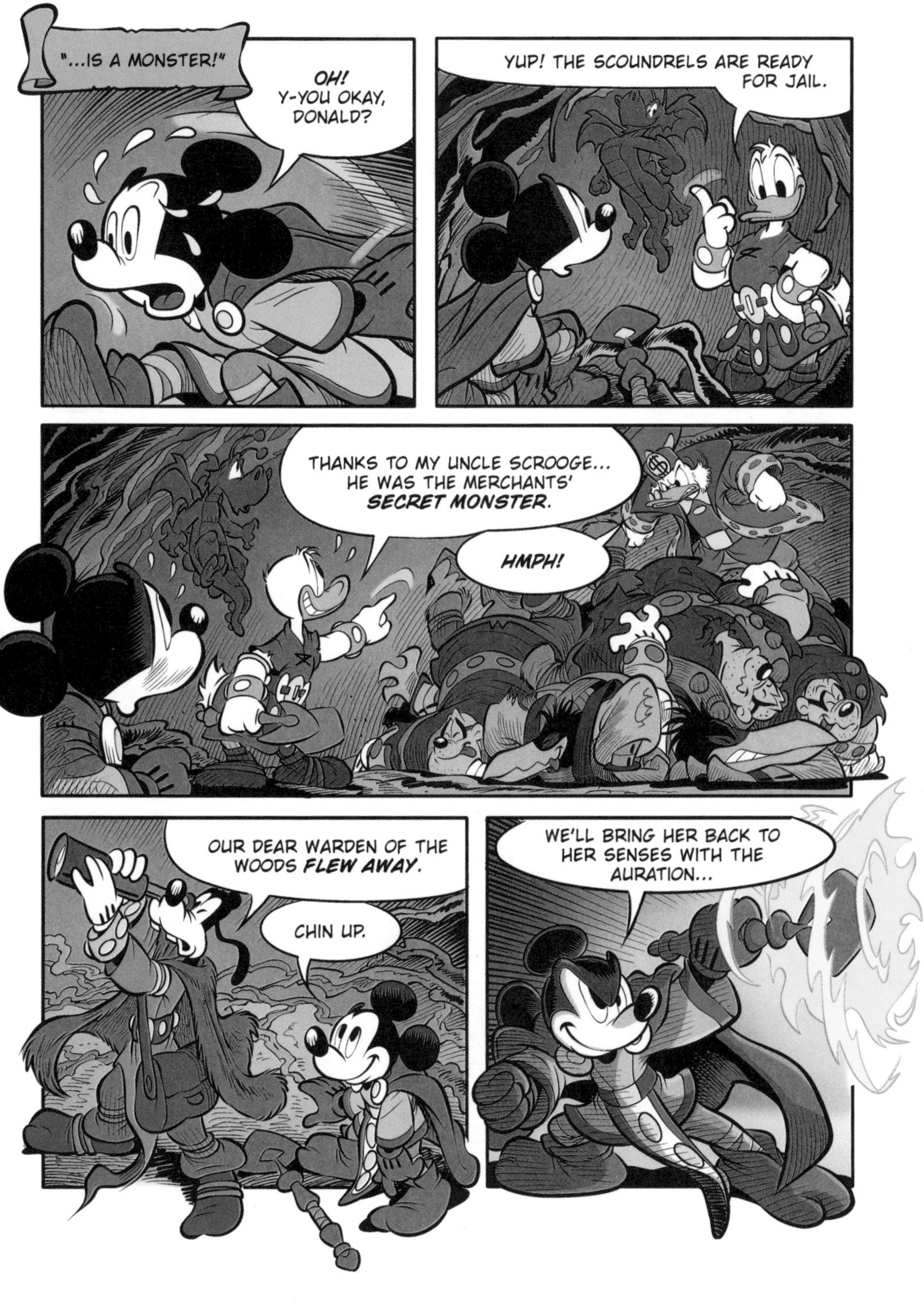
"...IS A MONSTER!"
OH! Y-YOU OKAY, DONALD?
YUP! THE SCOUNDRELS ARE READY FOR JAIL.
THANKS TO MY UNCLE SCROOGE... HE WAS THE MERCHANTS' SECRET MONSTER.
HMPH!
OUR DEAR WARDEN OF THE WOODS FLEW AWAY.
CHIN UP.
WE'LL BRING HER BACK TO HER SENSES WITH THE AURATION...

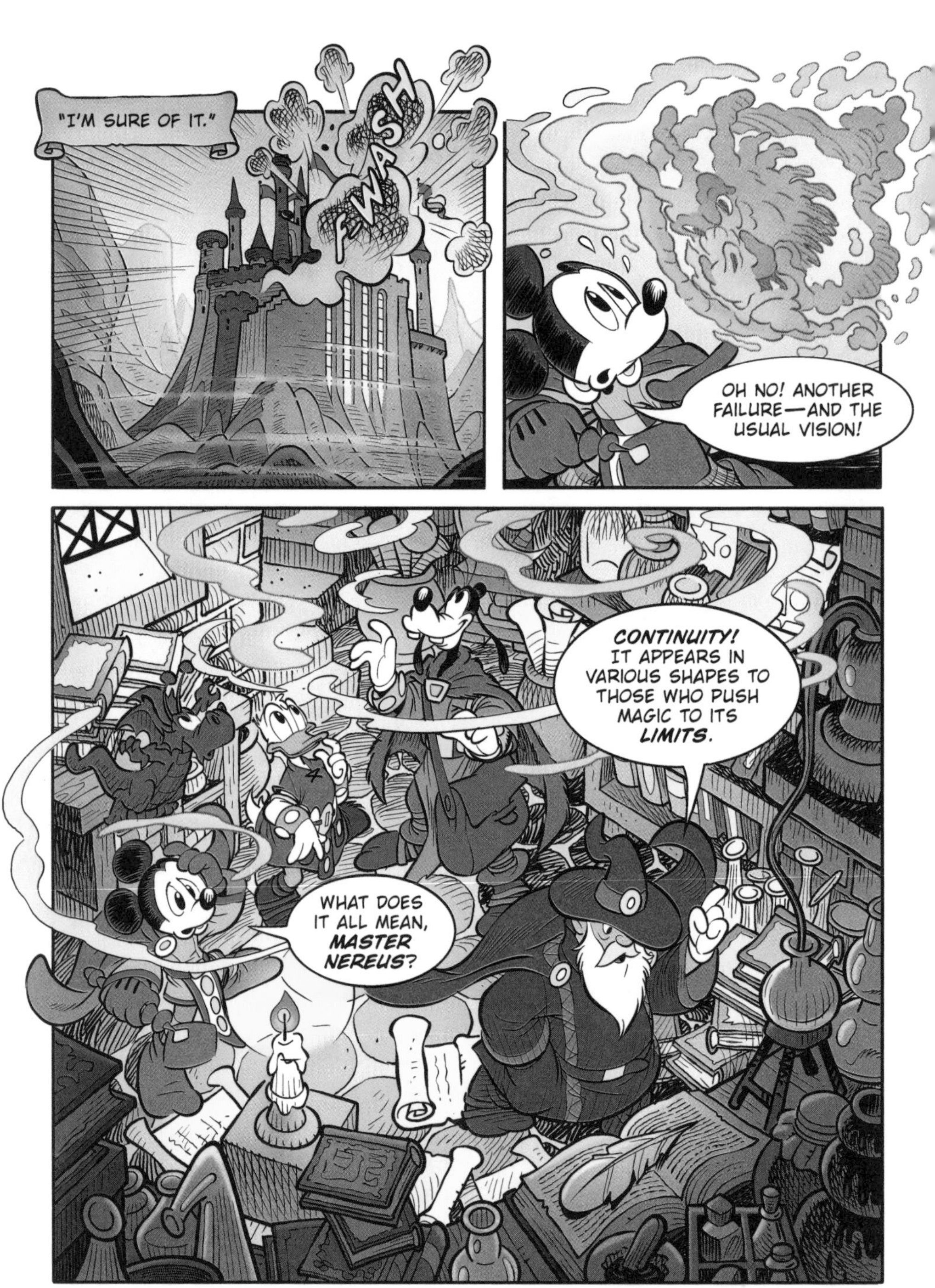

"I'M SURE OF IT."
FWASH
OH NO! ANOTHER FAILURE—AND THE USUAL VISION!
WHAT DOES IT ALL MEAN, MASTER NEREUS?
CONTINUITY! IT APPEARS IN VARIOUS SHAPES TO THOSE WHO PUSH MAGIC TO ITS LIMITS.

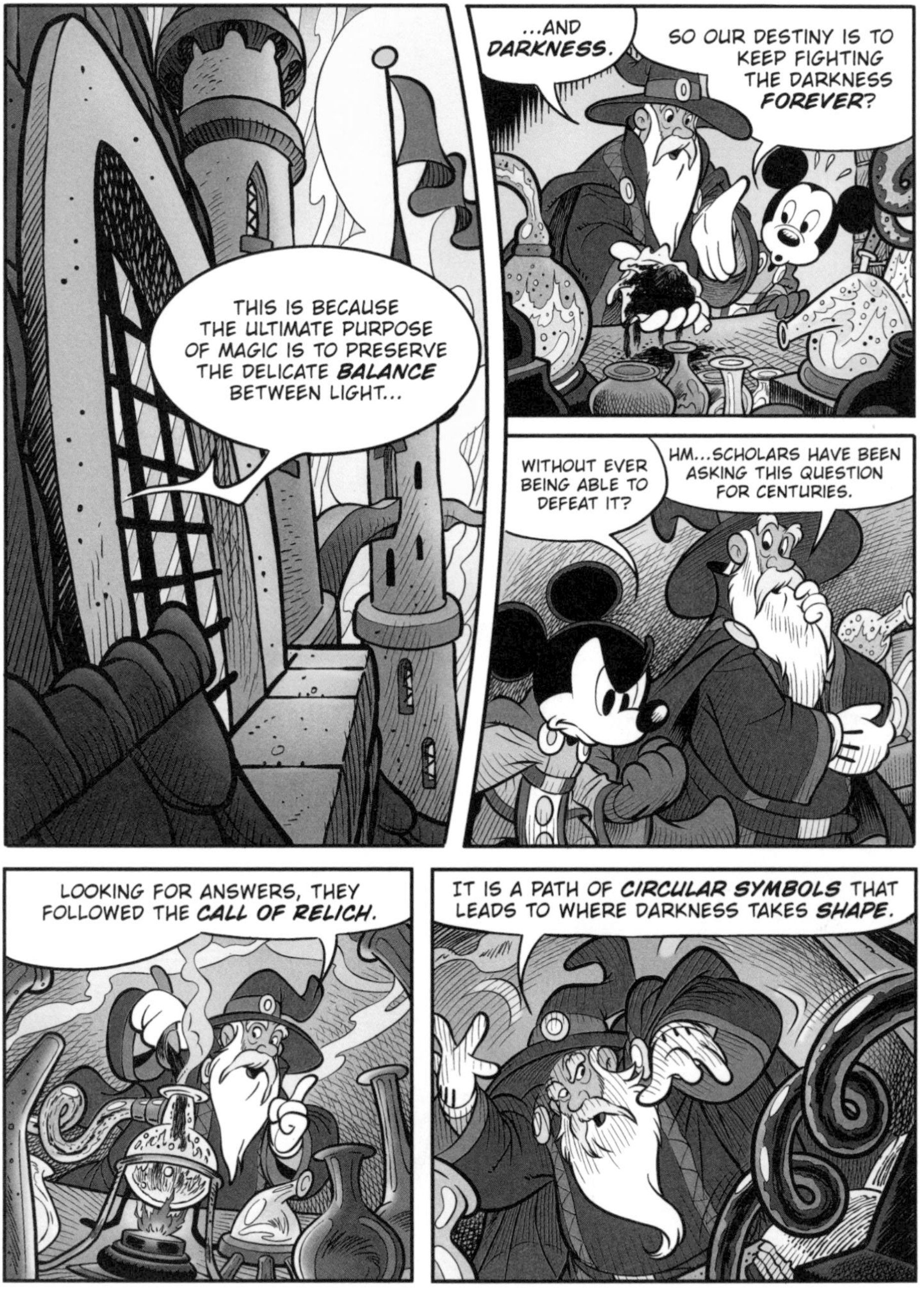
THIS IS BECAUSE THE ULTIMATE PURPOSE OF MAGIC IS TO PRESERVE THE DELICATE BALANCE BETWEEN LIGHT...
...AND DARKNESS.
SO OUR DESTINY IS TO KEEP FIGHTING THE DARKNESS FOREVER?
WITHOUT EVER BEING ABLE TO DEFEAT IT?
HM...SCHOLARS HAVE BEEN ASKING THIS QUESTION FOR CENTURIES.
LOOKING FOR ANSWERS, THEY FOLLOWED THE CALL OF RELICH.
IT IS A PATH OF CIRCULAR SYMBOLS THAT LEADS TO WHERE DARKNESS TAKES SHAPE.

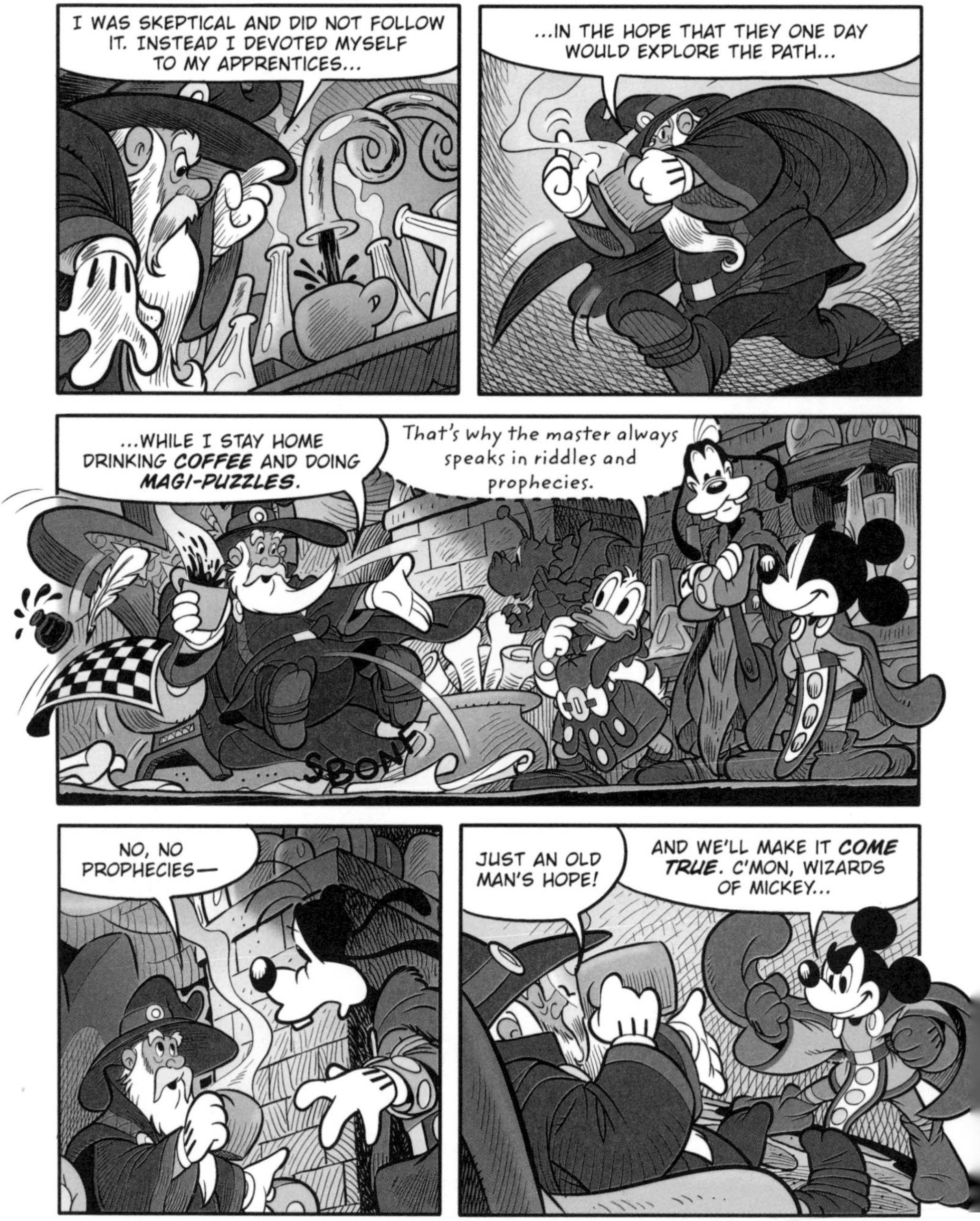
I WAS SKEPTICAL AND DID NOT FOLLOW IT. INSTEAD I DEVOTED MYSELF TO MY APPRENTICES...
...IN THE HOPE THAT THEY ONE DAY WOULD EXPLORE THE PATH...
...WHILE I STAY HOME DRINKING COFFEE AND DOING MAGI-PUZZLES.
That's why the master always speaks in riddles and prophecies.
SBONF
NO, NO PROPHECIES—
JUST AN OLD MAN'S HOPE!
AND WE'LL MAKE IT COME TRUE. C'MON, WIZARDS OF MICKEY...

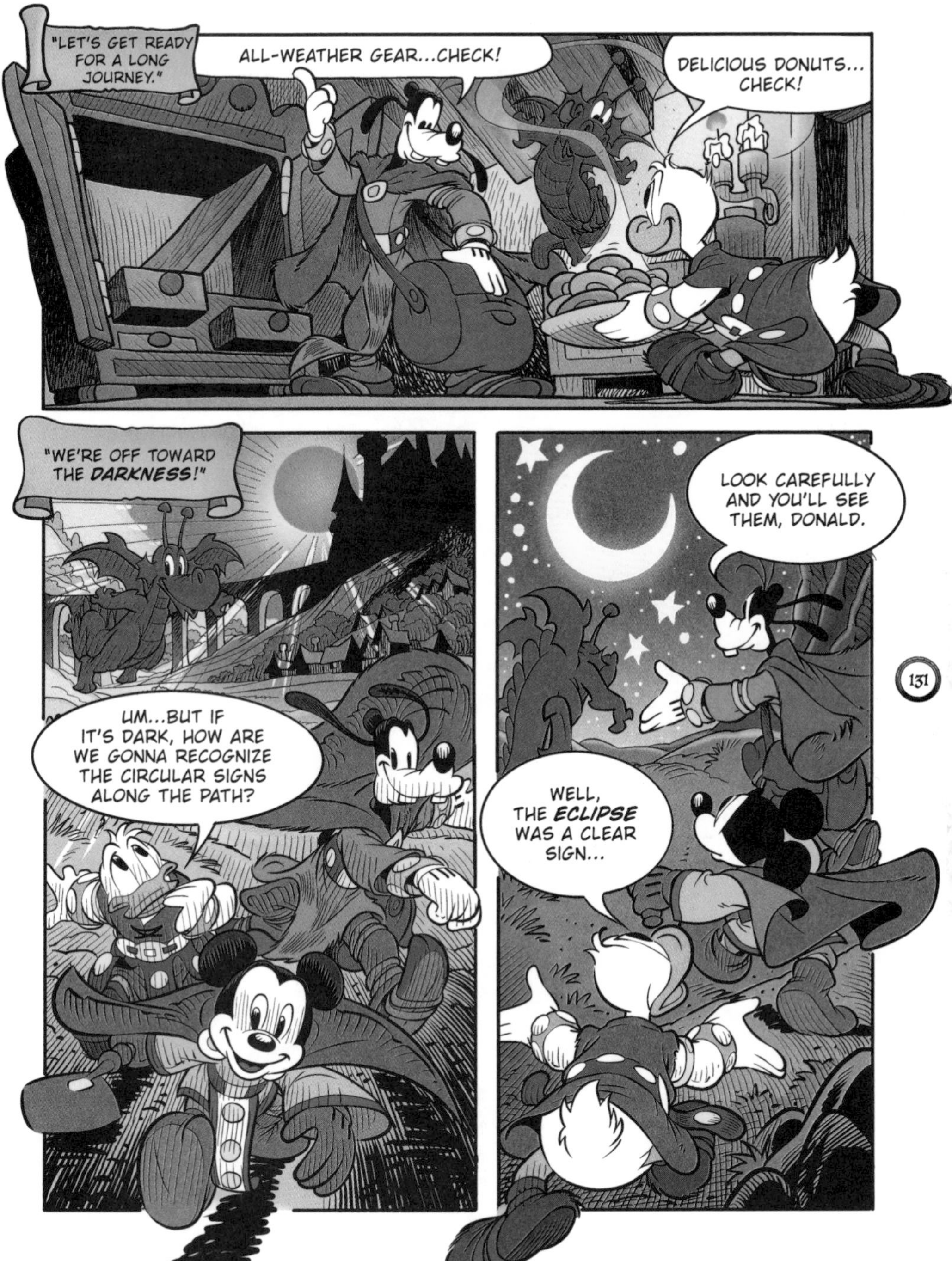
"LET'S GET READY FOR A LONG JOURNEY."
ALL-WEATHER GEAR...CHECK!
DELICIOUS DONUTS... CHECK!
"WE'RE OFF TOWARD THE DARKNESS!"
UM...BUT IF IT'S DARK, HOW ARE WE GONNA RECOGNIZE THE CIRCULAR SIGNS ALONG THE PATH?
LOOK CAREFULLY AND YOU'LL SEE THEM, DONALD.
WELL, THE ECLIPSE WAS A CLEAR SIGN...

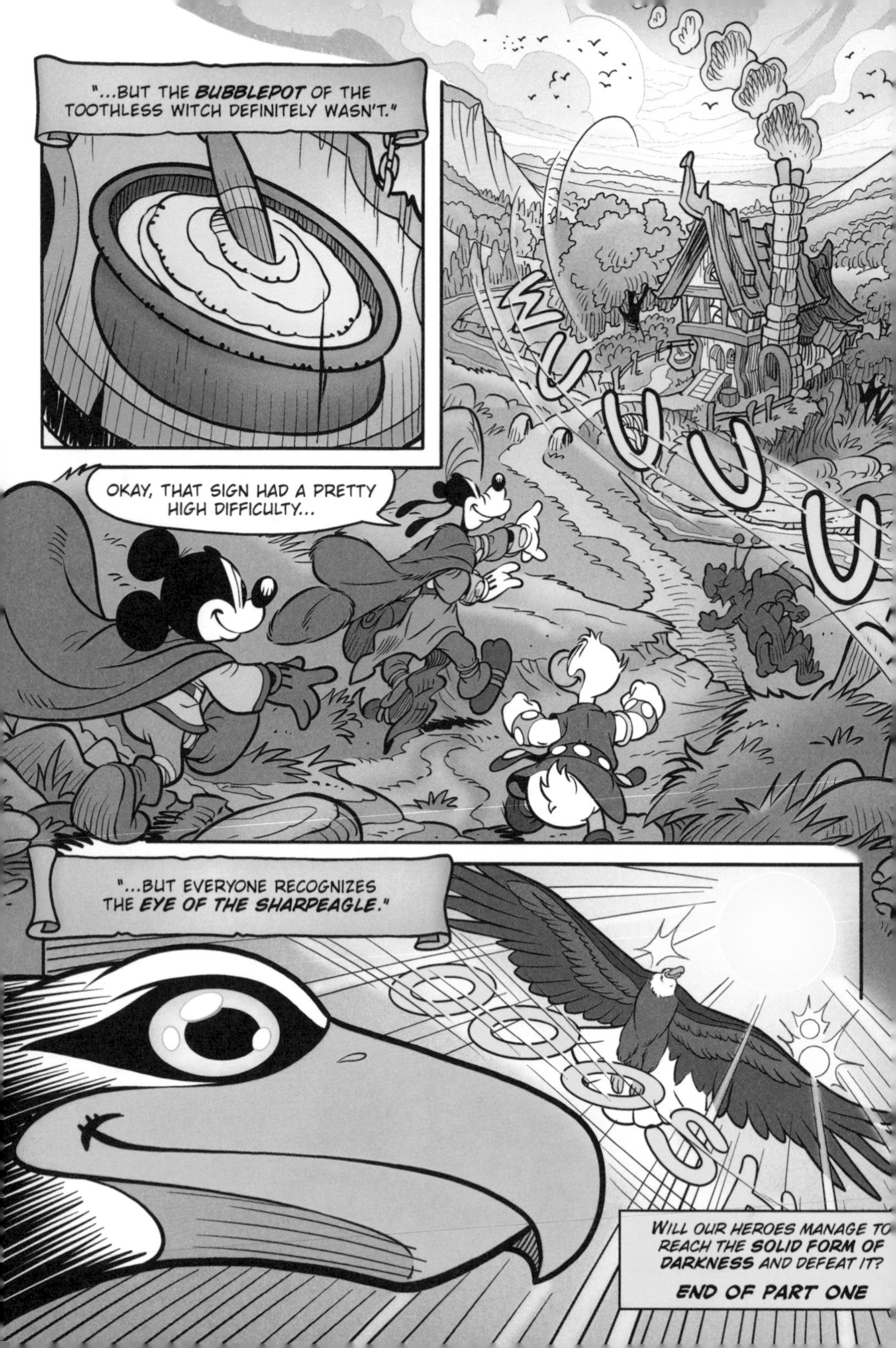
"...BUT THE BUBBLEPOT OF THE TOOTHLESS WITCH DEFINITELY WASN'T."
OKAY, THAT SIGN HAD A PRETTY HIGH DIFFICULTY...
"...BUT EVERYONE RECOGNIZES THE EYE OF THE SHARPEAGLE."
WILL OUR HEROES MANAGE TO REACH THE SOLID FORM OF DARKNESS AND DEFEAT IT?
END OF PART ONE

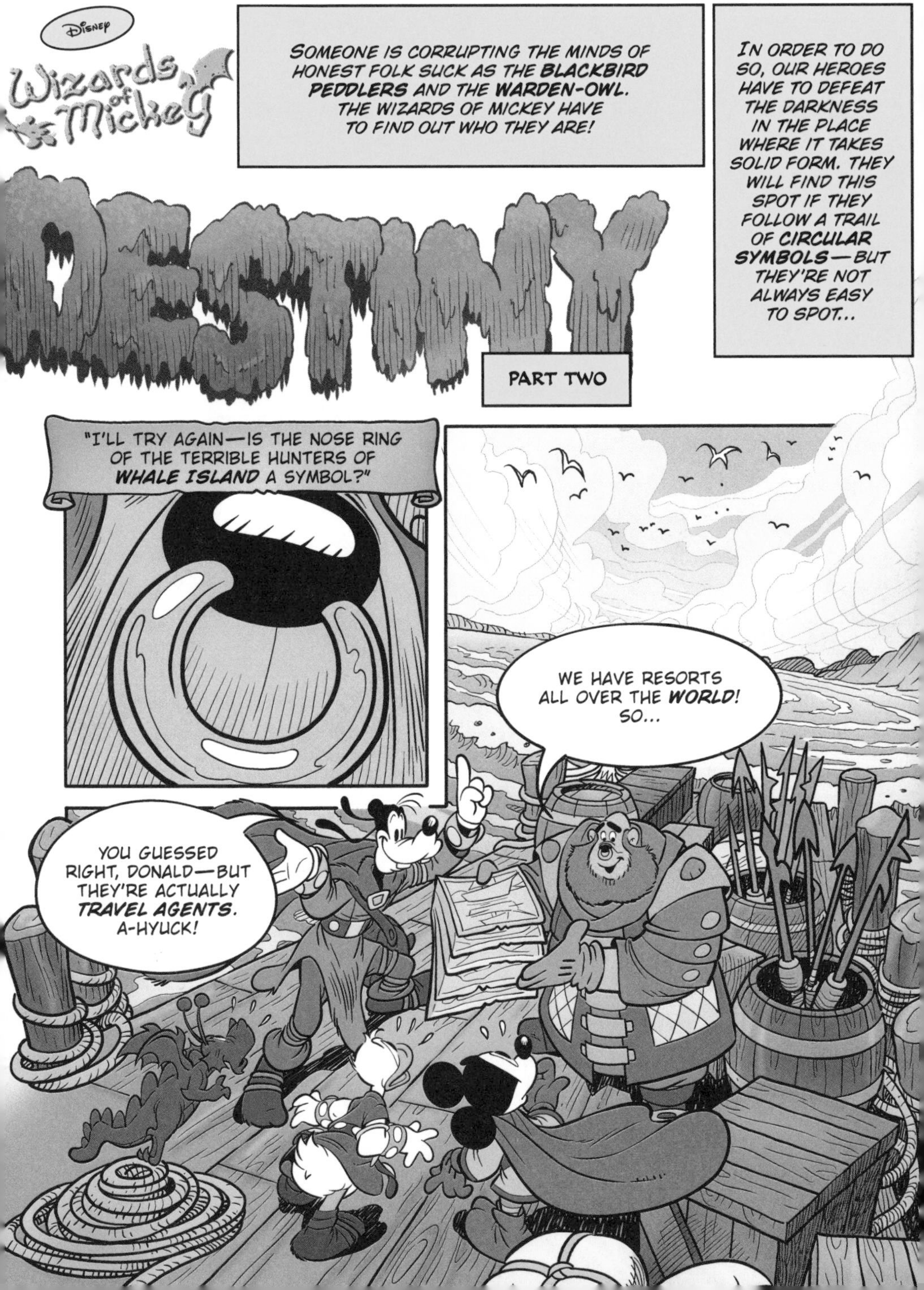
Disney
Wizards of Mickey
SOMEONE IS CORRUPTING THE MINDS OF HONEST FOLK SUCK AS THE BLACKBIRD PEDDLERS AND THE WARDEN-OWL. THE WIZARDS OF MICKEY HAVE TO FIND OUT WHO THEY ARE!
IN ORDER TO DO SO, OUR HEROES HAVE TO DEFEAT THE DARKNESS IN THE PLACE WHERE IT TAKES SOLID FORM. THEY WILL FIND THIS SPOT IF THEY FOLLOW A TRAIL OF CIRCULAR SYMBOLS—BUT THEY'RE NOT ALWAYS EASY TO SPOT...
DESTINY
PART TWO
"I'LL TRY AGAIN—IS THE NOSE RING OF THE TERRIBLE HUNTERS OF WHALE ISLAND A SYMBOL?"
WE HAVE RESORTS ALL OVER THE WORLD! SO...
YOU GUESSED RIGHT, DONALD—BUT THEY'RE ACTUALLY TRAVEL AGENTS. A-HYUCK!

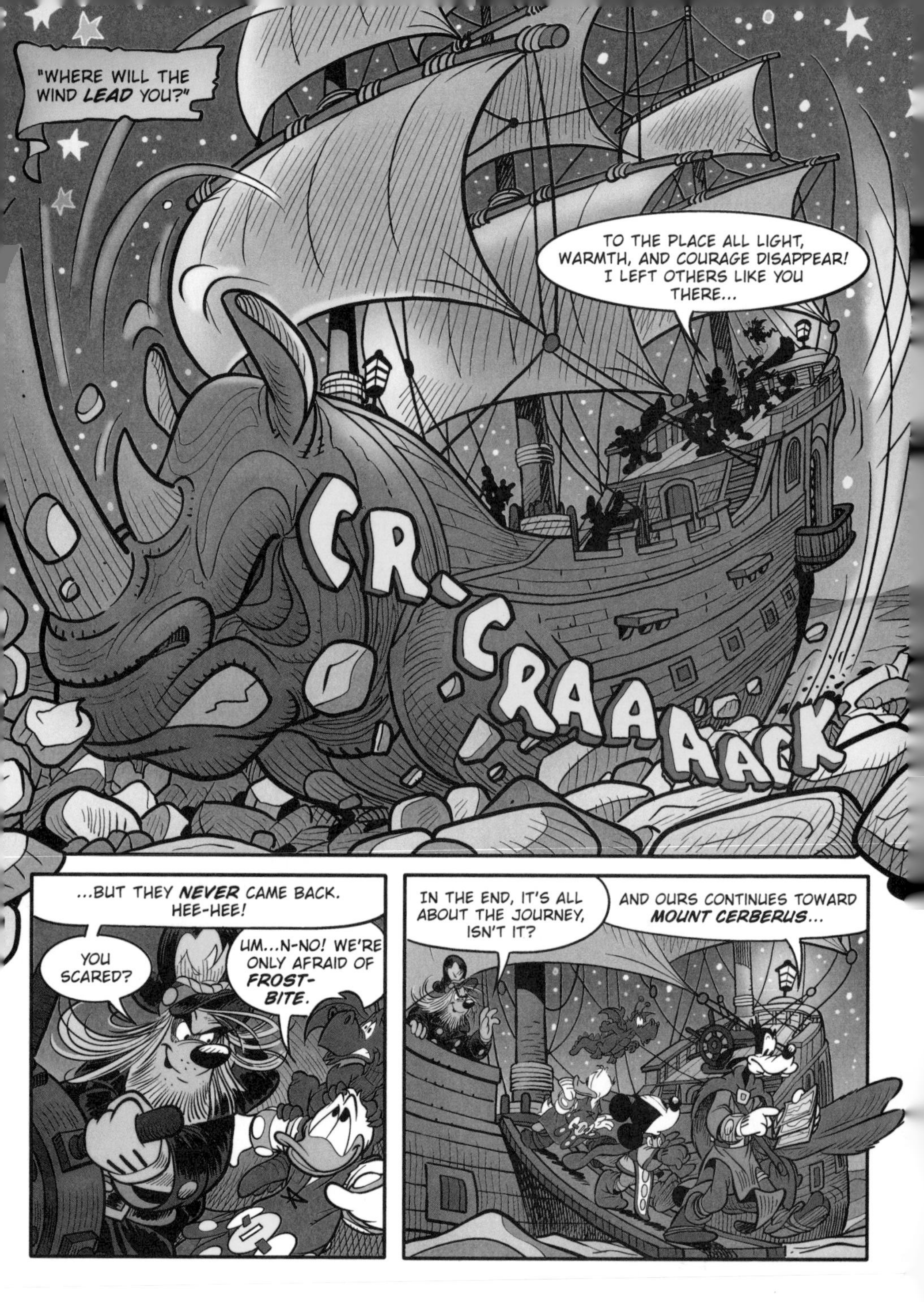
"WHERE WILL THE WIND LEAD YOU?"
TO THE PLACE ALL LIGHT, WARMTH, AND COURAGE DISAPPEAR! I LEFT OTHERS LIKE YOU THERE...
CR-CRAAAACK
...BUT THEY NEVER CAME BACK. HEE-HEE!
YOU SCARED?
UM...N-NO! WE'RE ONLY AFRAID OF FROST-BITE.
IN THE END, IT'S ALL ABOUT THE JOURNEY, ISN'T IT?
AND OURS CONTINUES TOWARD MOUNT CERBERUS...

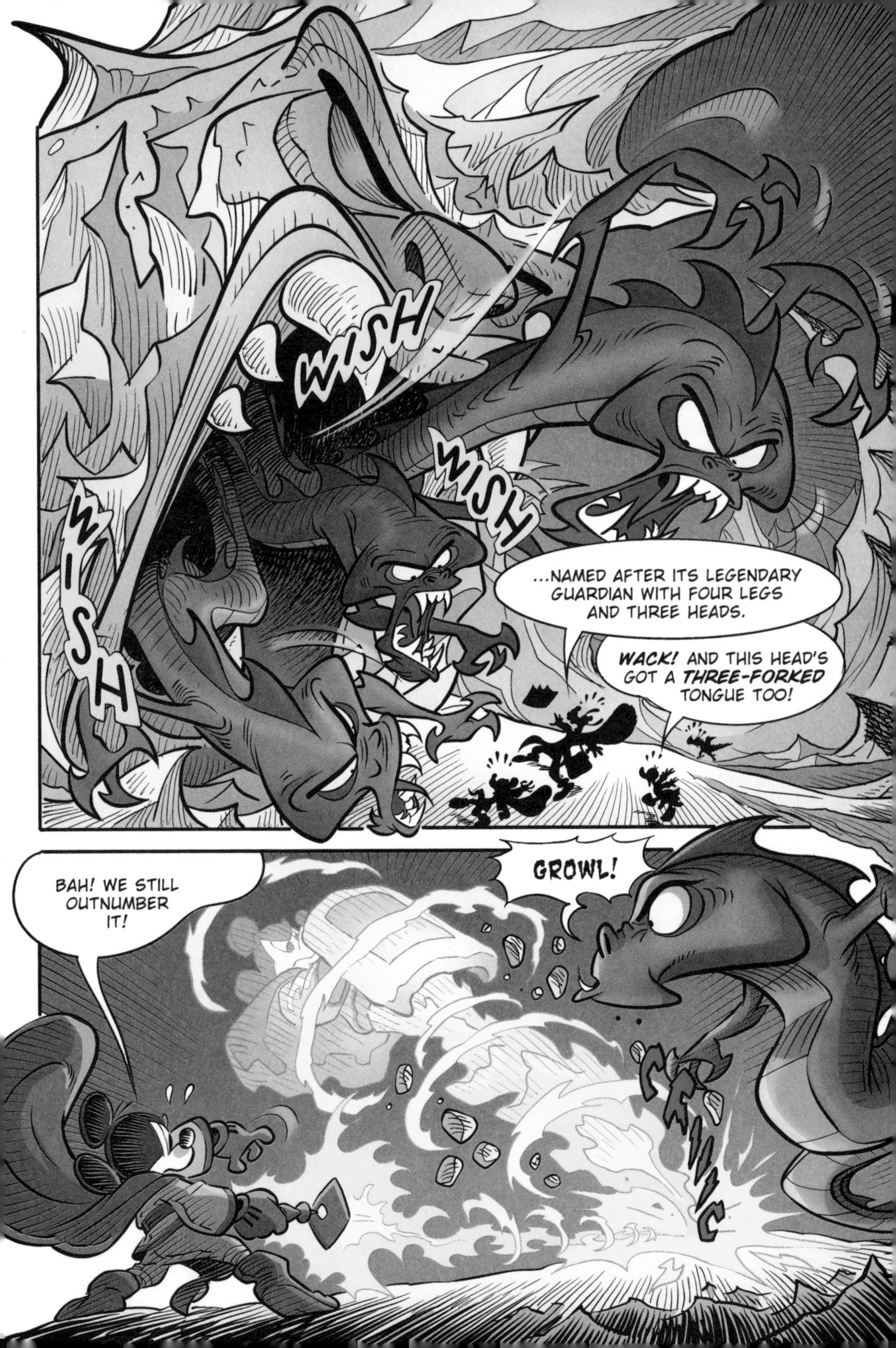
WISH
WISH
W-I-S-H
...NAMED AFTER ITS LEGENDARY GUARDIAN WITH FOUR LEGS AND THREE HEADS.
WACK! AND THIS HEAD'S GOT A THREE-FORKED TONGUE TOO!
BAH! WE STILL OUTNUMBER IT!
GROWL!

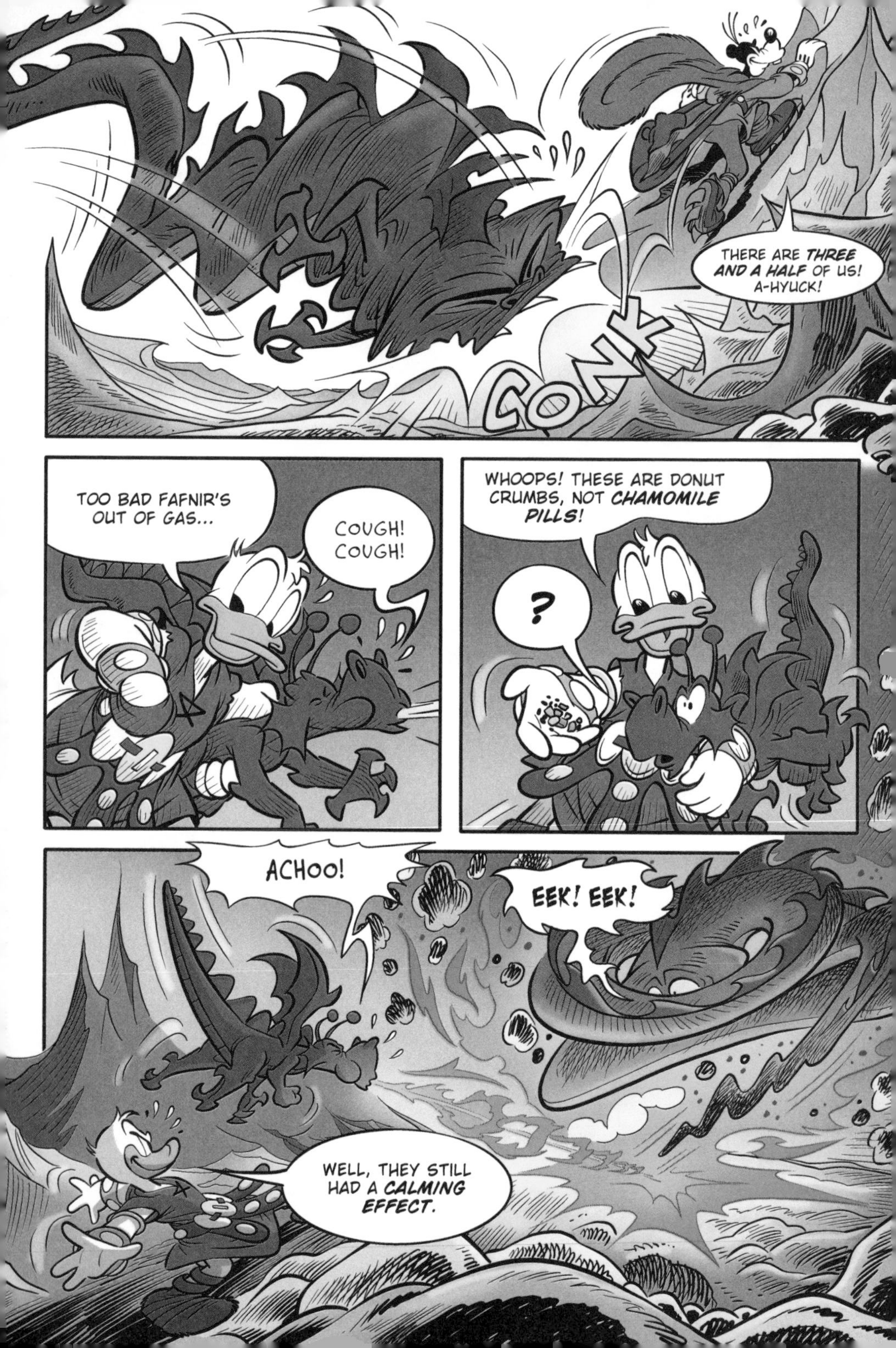
THERE ARE THREE AND A HALF OF US! A-HYUCK!
CONK
TOO BAD FAFNIR'S OUT OF GAS...
COUGH! COUGH!
WHOOPS! THESE ARE DONUT CRUMBS, NOT CHAMOMILE PILLS!
?
ACHOO!
EEK! EEK!
WELL, THEY STILL HAD A CALMING EFFECT.

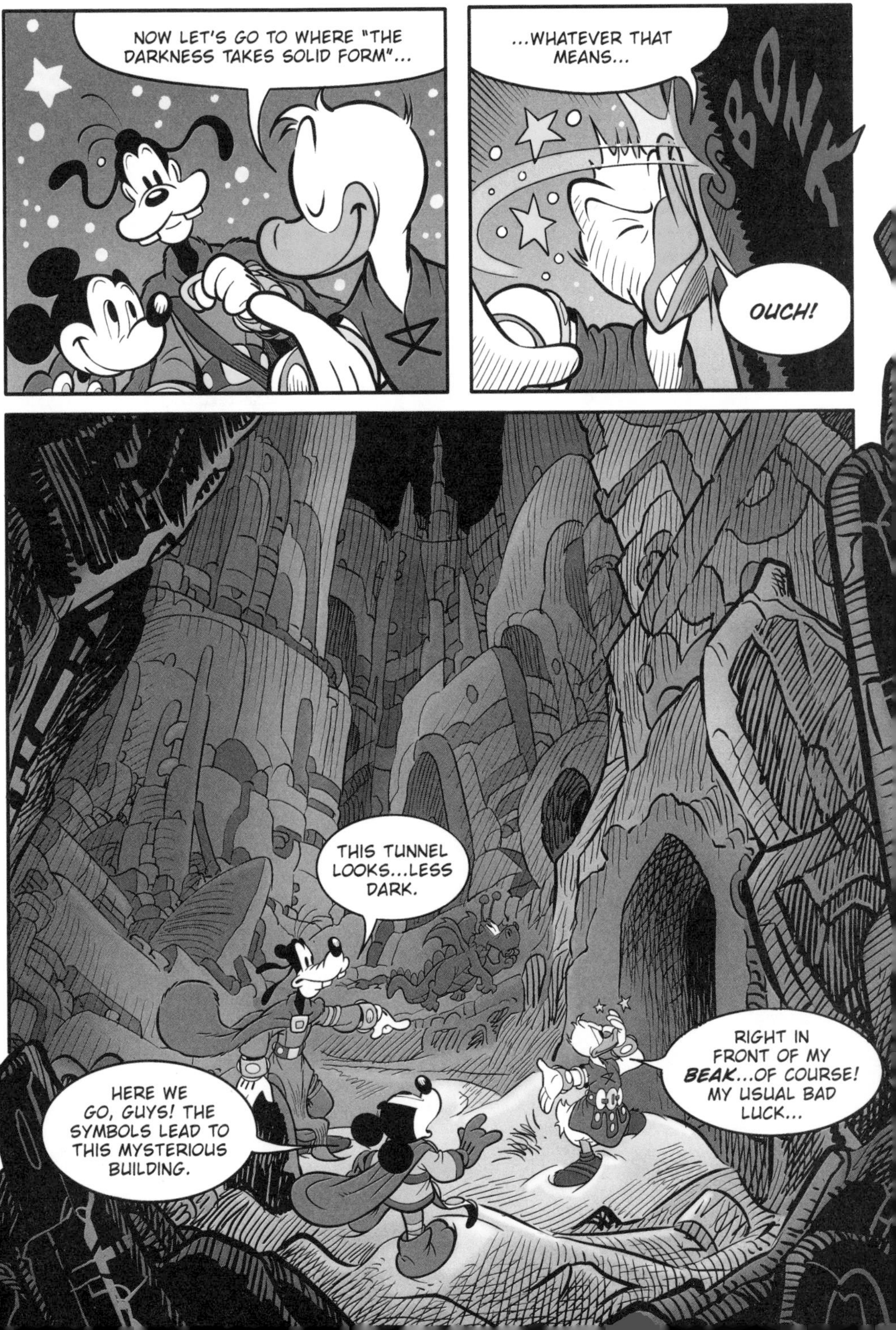
NOW LET'S GO TO WHERE "THE DARKNESS TAKES SOLID FORM"...
...WHATEVER THAT MEANS...
BONK
OUCH!
THIS TUNNEL LOOKS...LESS DARK.
HERE WE GO, GUYS! THE SYMBOLS LEAD TO THIS MYSTERIOUS BUILDING.
RIGHT IN FRONT OF MY BEAK...OF COURSE! MY USUAL BAD LUCK...

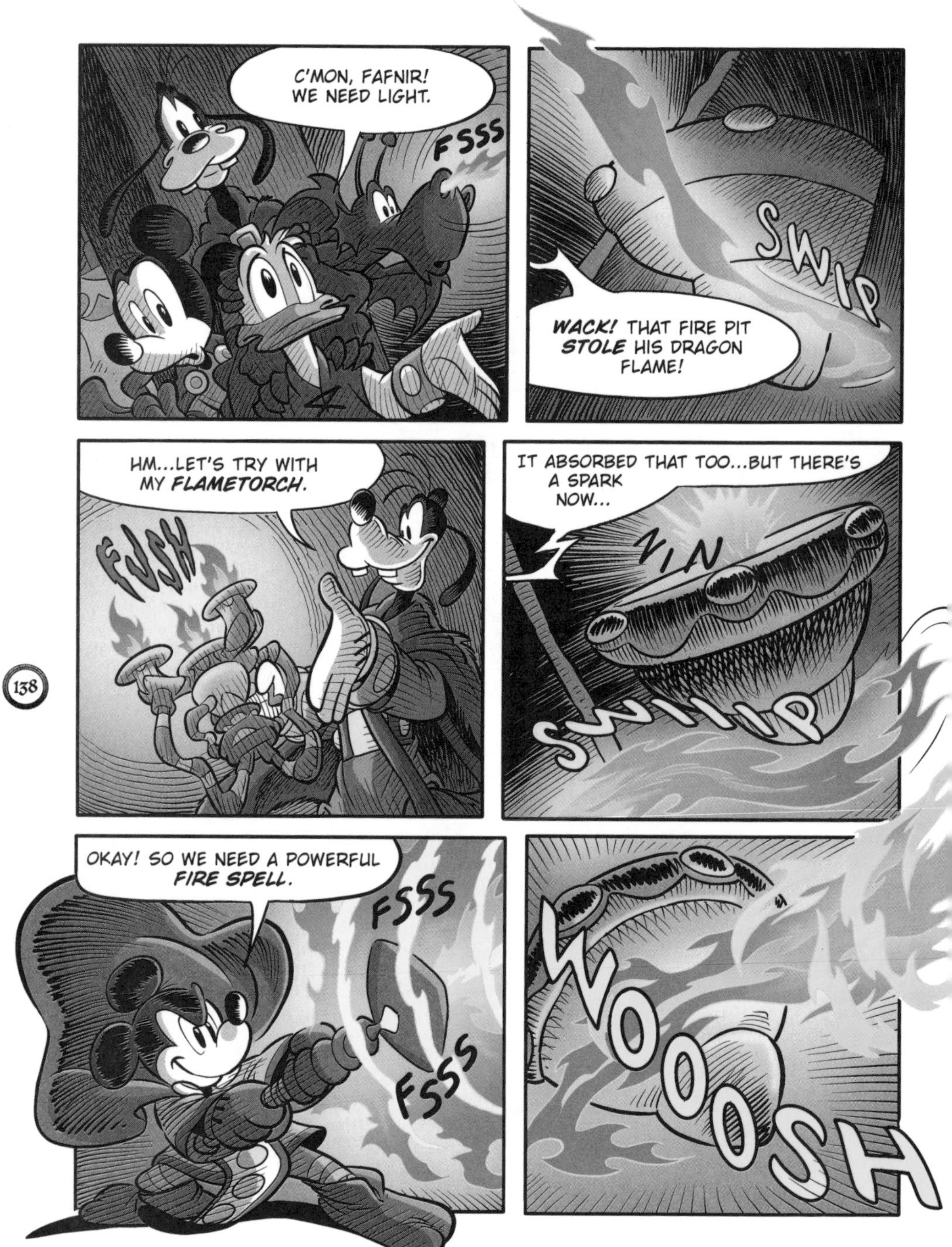
C'MON, FAFNIR! WE NEED LIGHT.
FSSS
SWIP
WACK! THAT FIRE PIT STOLE HIS DRAGON FLAME!
HM...LET'S TRY WITH MY FLAMETORCH.
FJSH
IT ABSORBED THAT TOO...BUT THERE'S A SPARK NOW...
ZIN
SWIIIP
OKAY! SO WE NEED A POWERFUL FIRE SPELL.
FSSS
FSSS
WOOOOSH

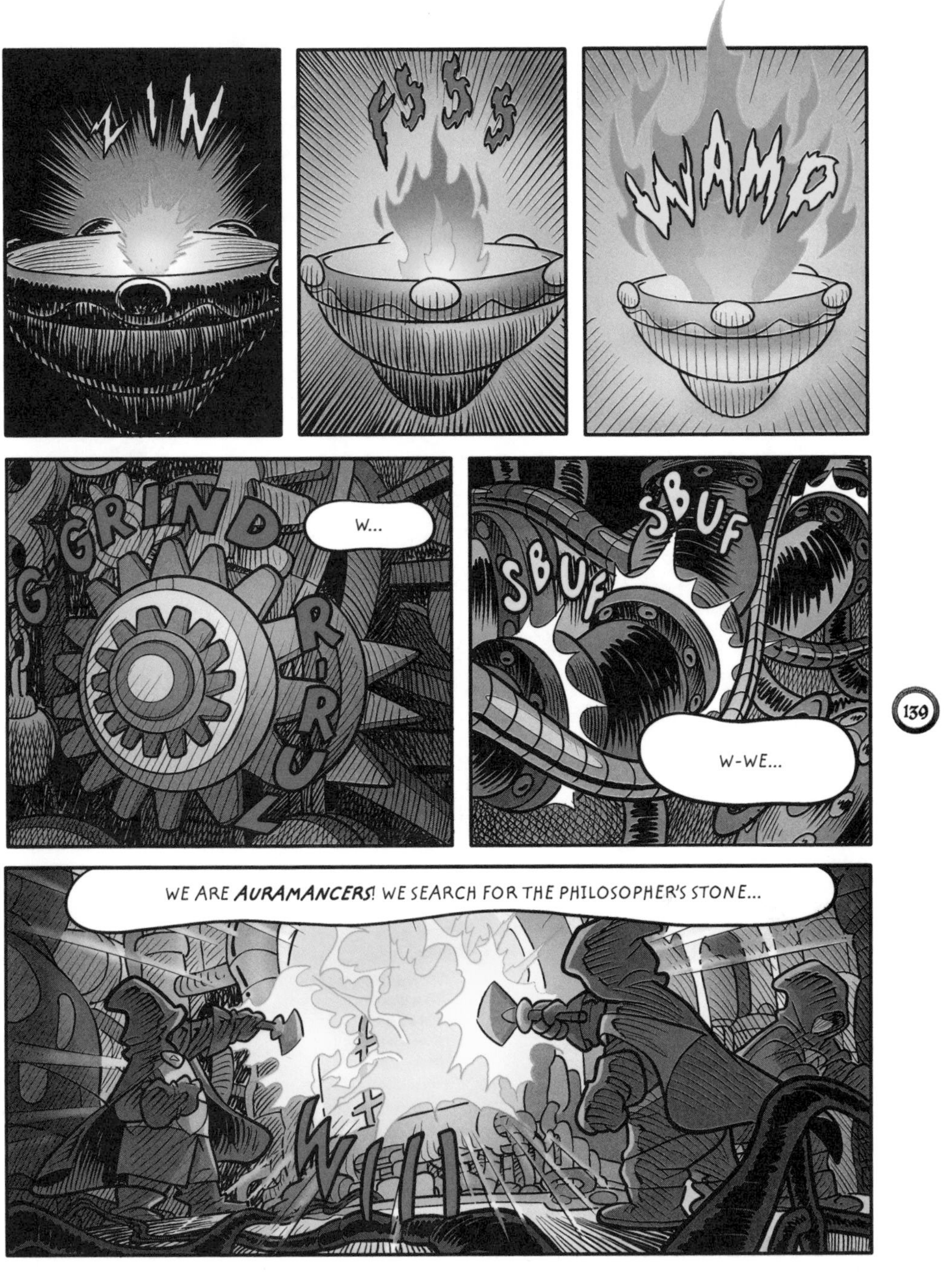
ZIN
FSSS
WAMP
G-GRIND
W...
RRRUL
SBUF
SBUF
W-WE...
WE ARE AURAMANCERS! WE SEARCH FOR THE PHILOSOPHER'S STONE...
WIII

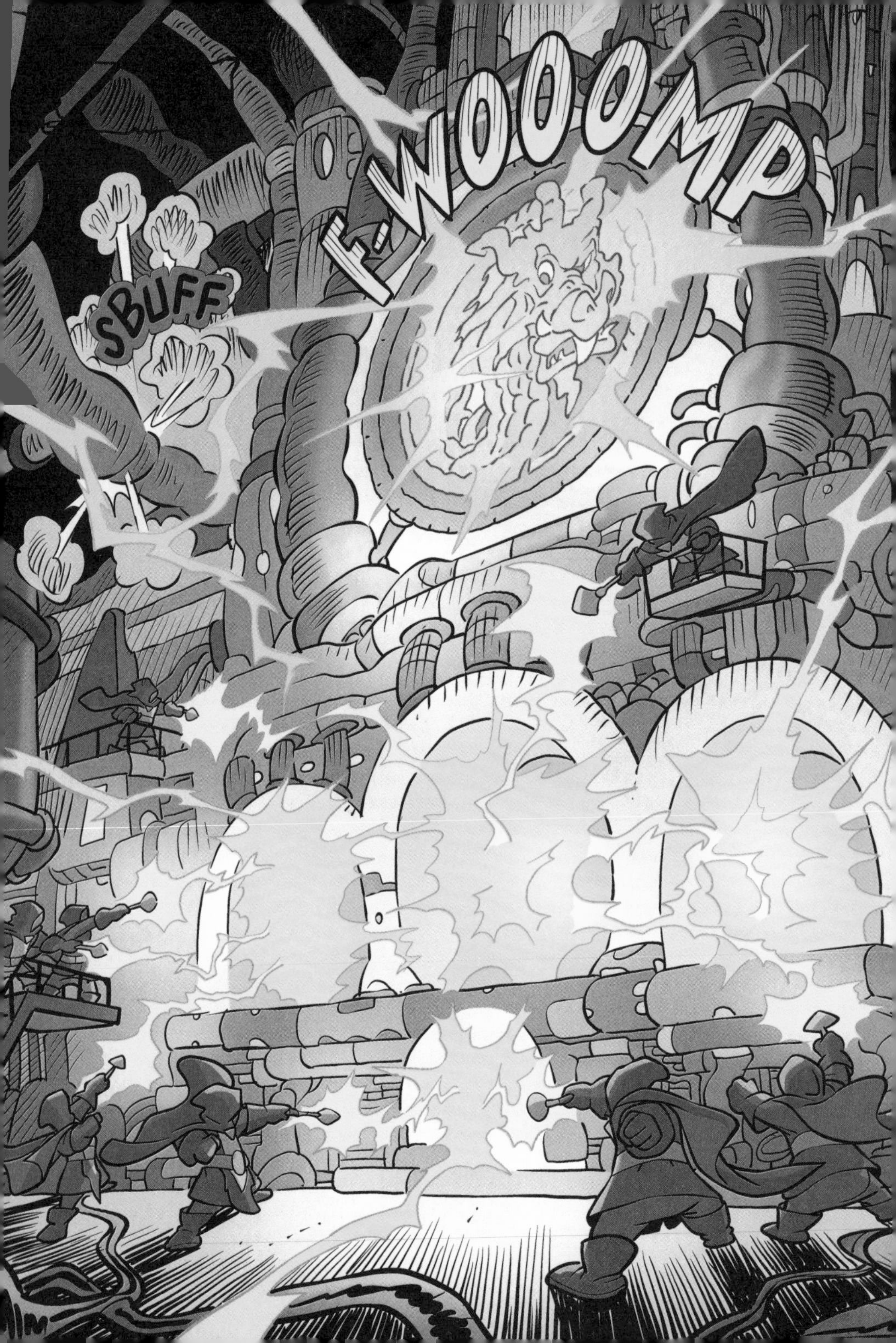
SBUFF
WOOOMP

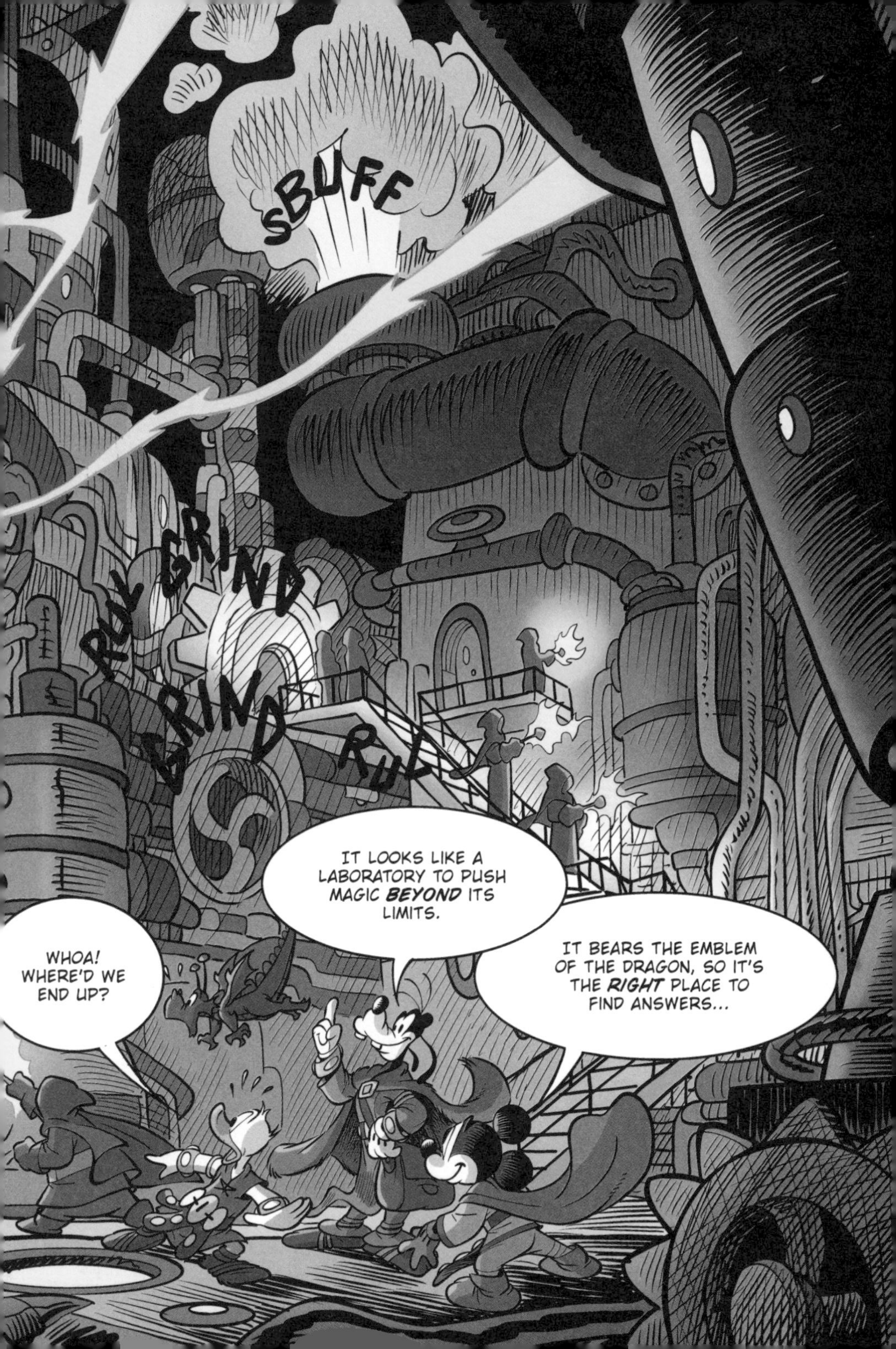
SBUFF
RUL GRIND
GRIND RUL
WHOA! WHERE'D WE END UP?
IT LOOKS LIKE A LABORATORY TO PUSH MAGIC BEYOND ITS LIMITS.
IT BEARS THE EMBLEM OF THE DRAGON, SO IT'S THE RIGHT PLACE TO FIND ANSWERS...

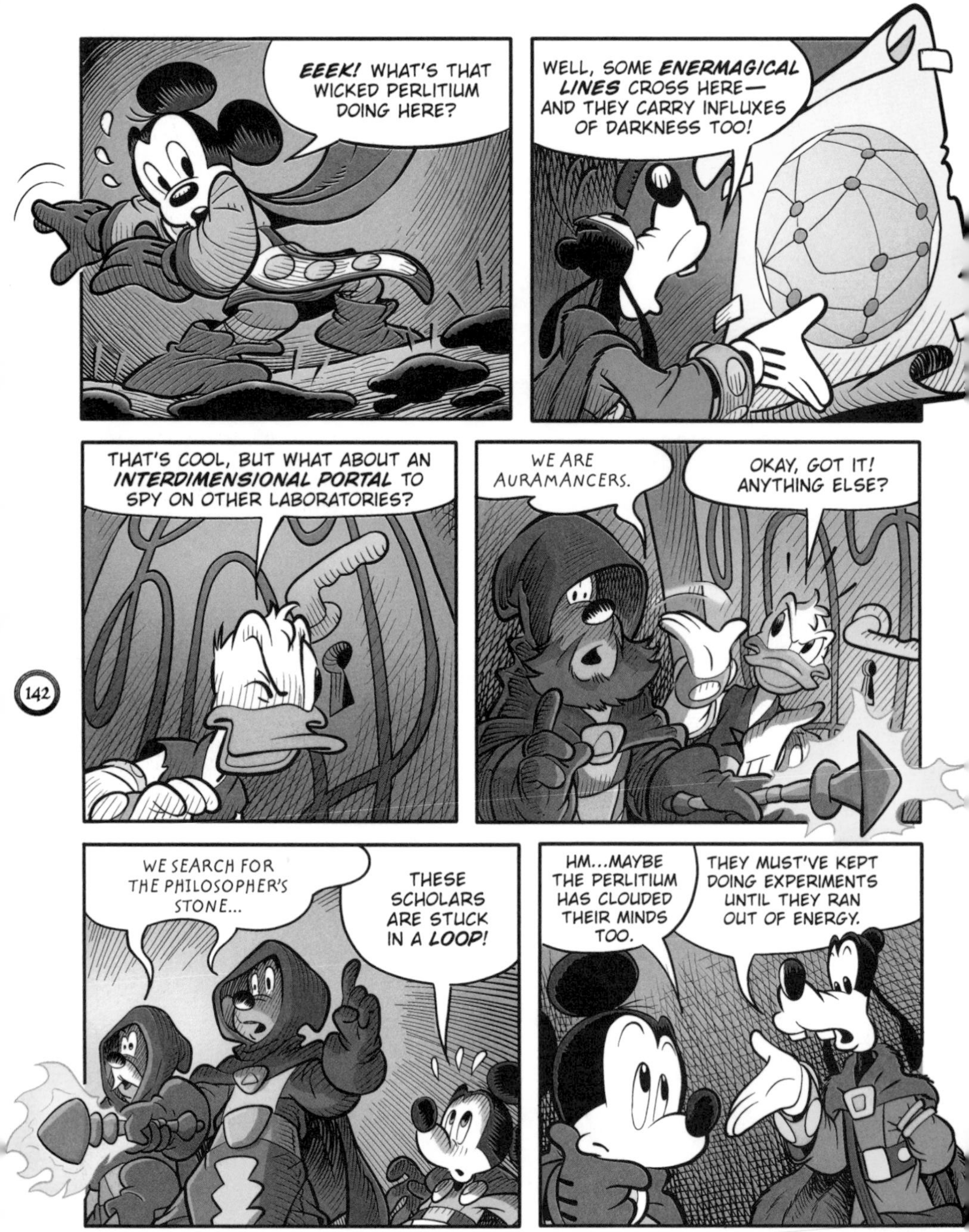
EEEK! WHAT'S THAT WICKED PERLITIUM DOING HERE?
WELL, SOME ENERMAGICAL LINES CROSS HERE— AND THEY CARRY INFLUXES OF DARKNESS TOO!
THAT'S COOL, BUT WHAT ABOUT AN INTERDIMENSIONAL PORTAL TO SPY ON OTHER LABORATORIES?
WE ARE AURAMANCERS.
OKAY, GOT IT! ANYTHING ELSE?
WE SEARCH FOR THE PHILOSOPHER'S STONE...
THESE SCHOLARS ARE STUCK IN A LOOP!
HM...MAYBE THE PERLITIUM HAS CLOUDED THEIR MINDS TOO.
THEY MUST'VE KEPT DOING EXPERIMENTS UNTIL THEY RAN OUT OF ENERGY.

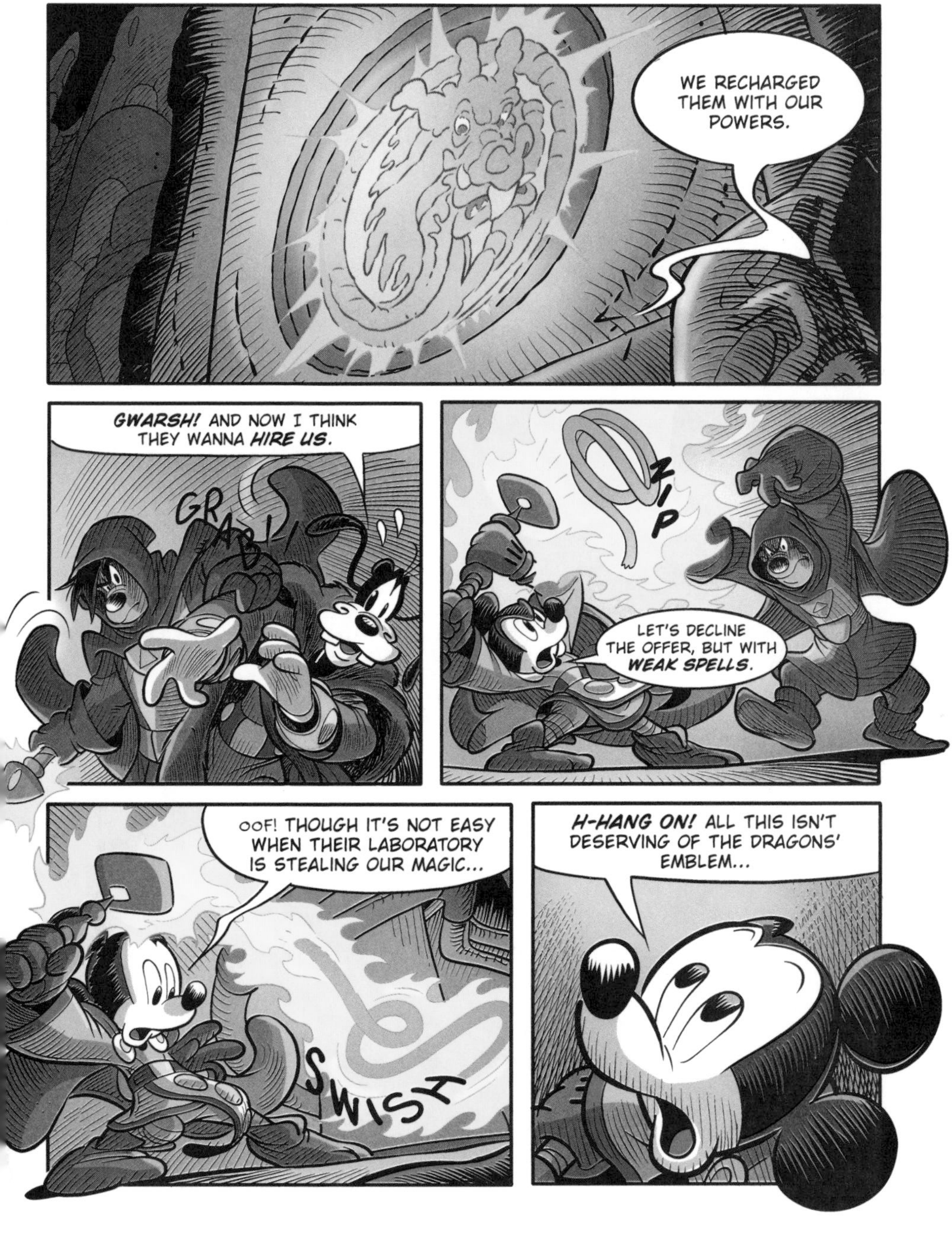

WE RECHARGED THEM WITH OUR POWERS.
GWARSH! AND NOW I THINK THEY WANNA HIRE US.
GRAB!!
ZIP
LET'S DECLINE THE OFFER, BUT WITH WEAK SPELLS.
OOF! THOUGH IT'S NOT EASY WHEN THEIR LABORATORY IS STEALING OUR MAGIC...
SWISH
H-HANG ON! ALL THIS ISN'T DESERVING OF THE DRAGONS' EMBLEM...

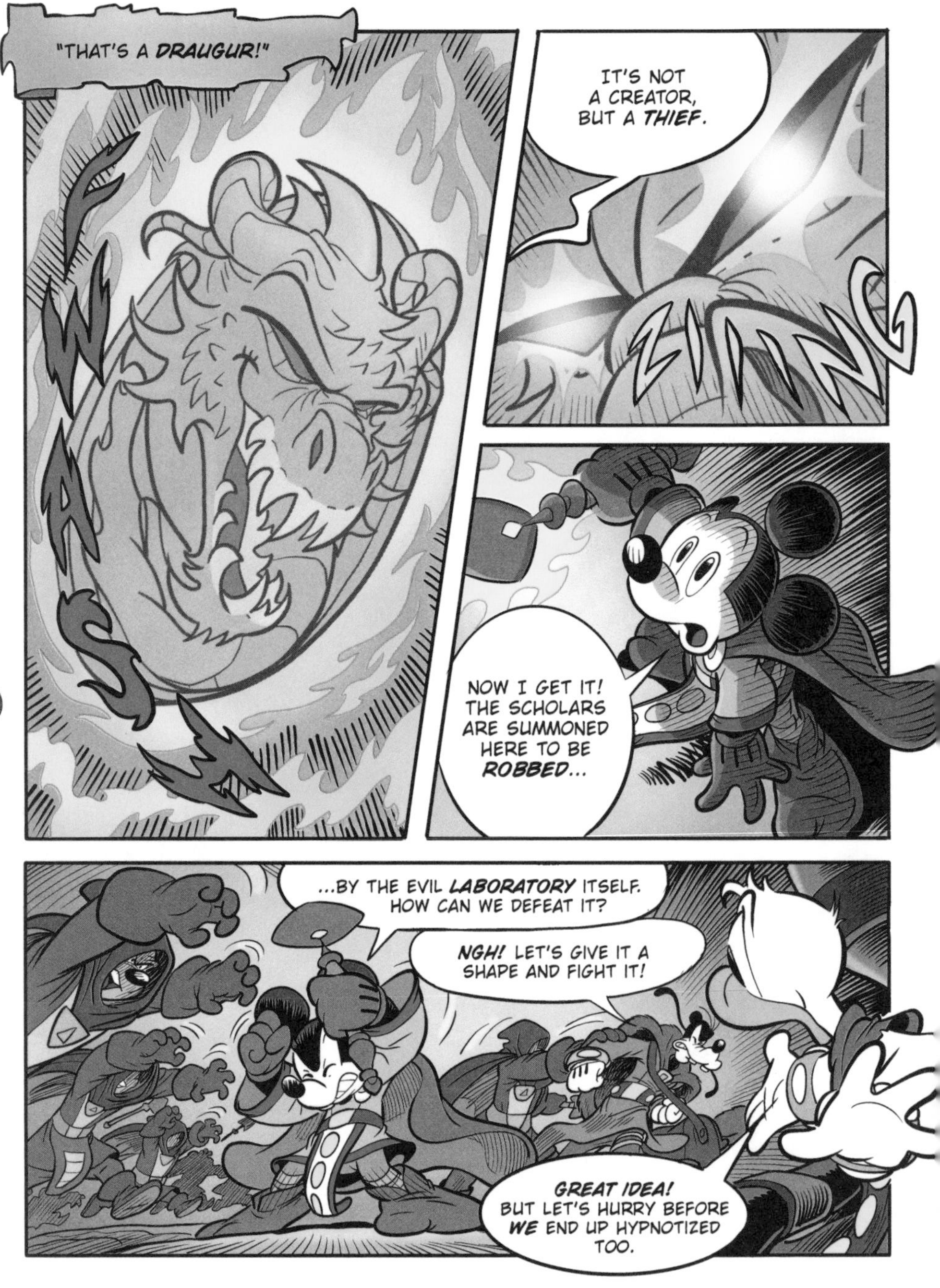
"THAT'S A DRAUGUR!"
FWASS
IT'S NOT A CREATOR, BUT A THIEF.
ZIIING
NOW I GET IT! THE SCHOLARS ARE SUMMONED HERE TO BE ROBBED...
...BY THE EVIL LABORATORY ITSELF. HOW CAN WE DEFEAT IT?
NGH! LET'S GIVE IT A SHAPE AND FIGHT IT!
GREAT IDEA! BUT LET'S HURRY BEFORE WE END UP HYPNOTIZED TOO.

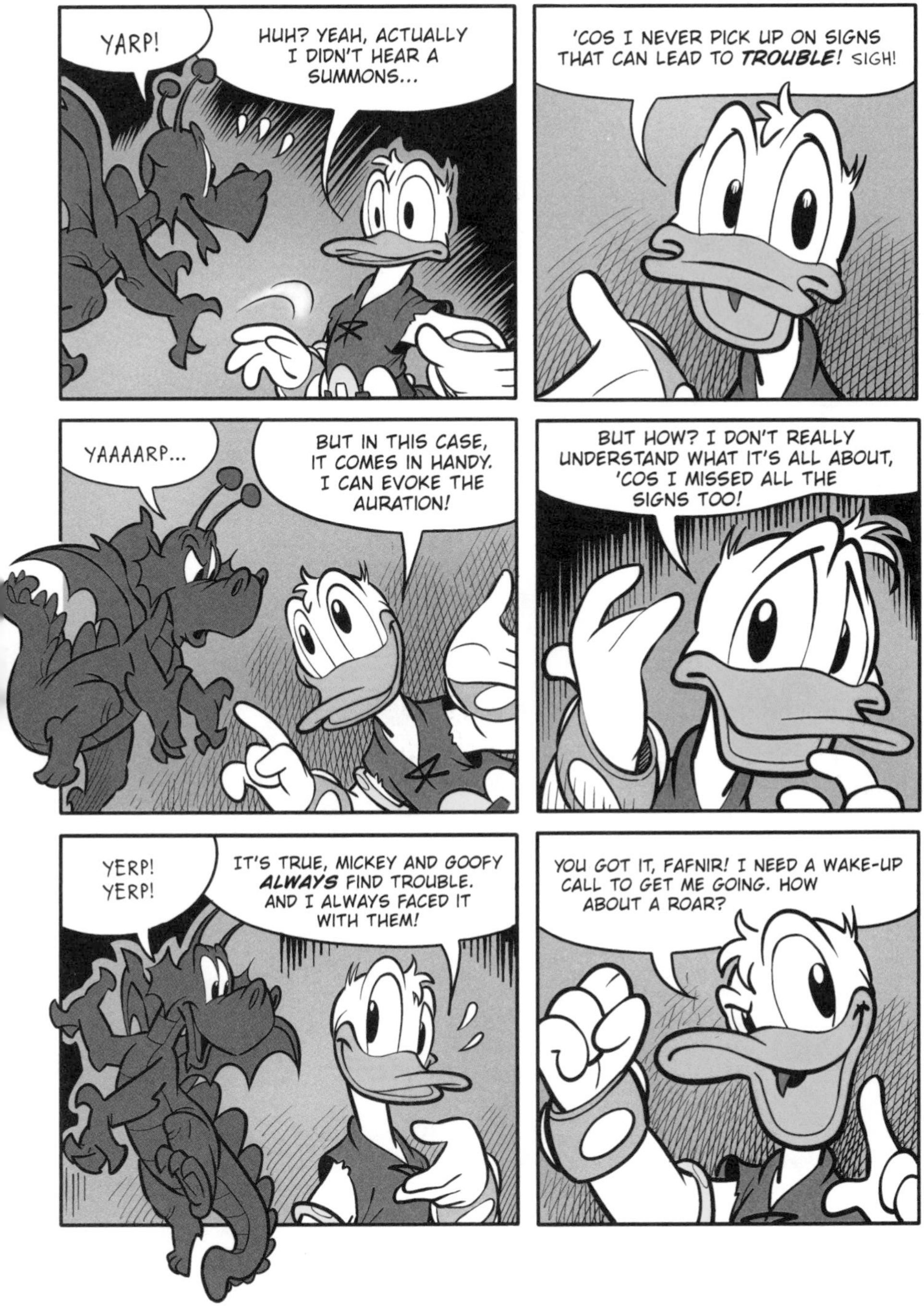
YARP!
HUH? YEAH, ACTUALLY I DIDN'T HEAR A SUMMONS...
'COS I NEVER PICK UP ON SIGNS THAT CAN LEAD TO TROUBLE! SIGH!
YAAAARP...
BUT IN THIS CASE, IT COMES IN HANDY. I CAN EVOKE THE AURATION!
BUT HOW? I DON'T REALLY UNDERSTAND WHAT IT'S ALL ABOUT, 'COS I MISSED ALL THE SIGNS TOO!
YERP! YERP!
IT'S TRUE, MICKEY AND GOOFY ALWAYS FIND TROUBLE. AND I ALWAYS FACED IT WITH THEM!
YOU GOT IT, FAFNIR! I NEED A WAKE-UP CALL TO GET ME GOING. HOW ABOUT A ROAR?

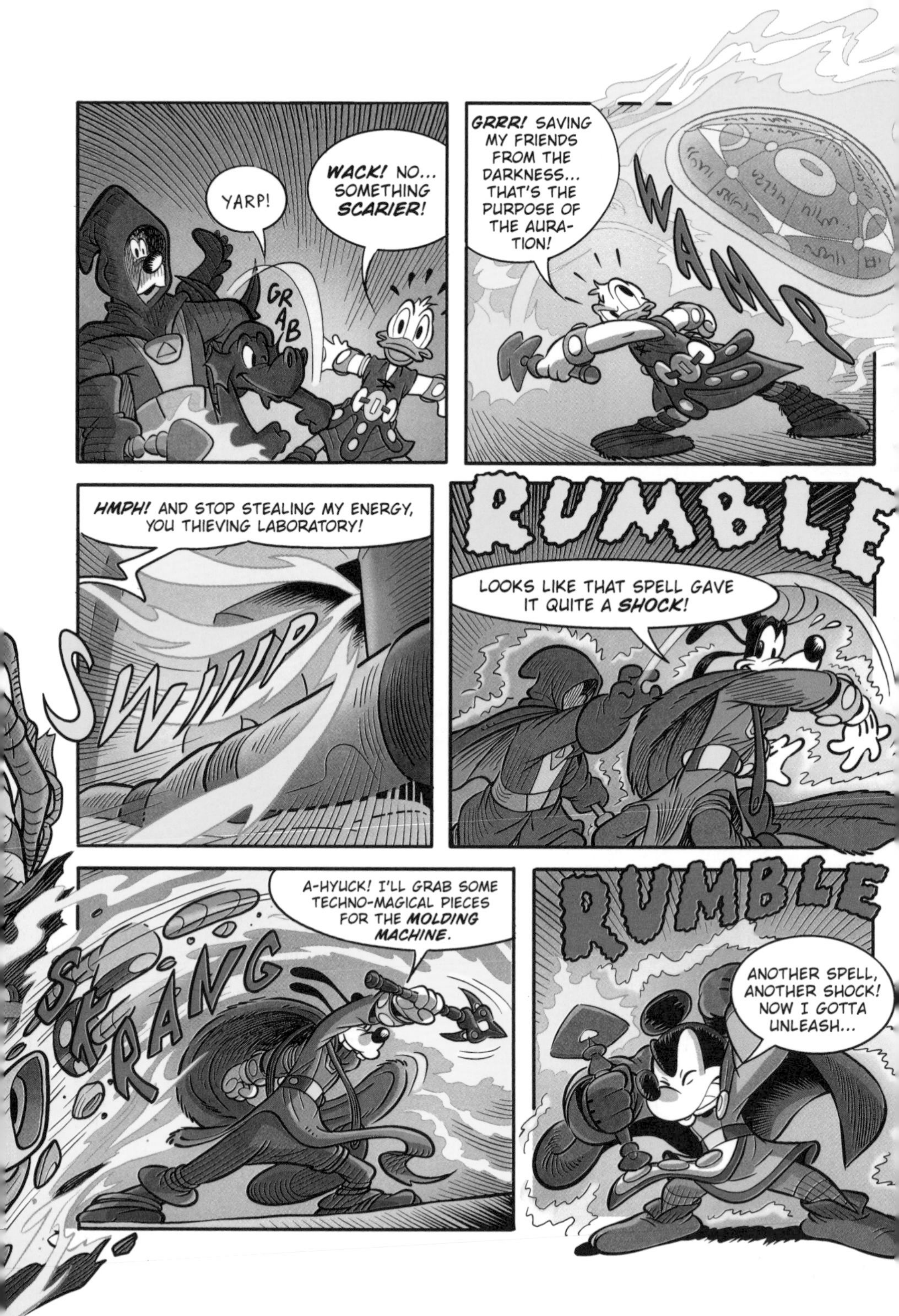
YARP!
WACK! NO... SOMETHING SCARIER!
GRAB
GRRR! SAVING MY FRIENDS FROM THE DARKNESS... THAT'S THE PURPOSE OF THE AURATION!
WAMP
HMPH! AND STOP STEALING MY ENERGY, YOU THIEVING LABORATORY!
SWIIIP
RUMBLE
LOOKS LIKE THAT SPELL GAVE IT QUITE A SHOCK!
A-HYUCK! I'LL GRAB SOME TECHNO-MAGICAL PIECES FOR THE MOLDING MACHINE.
SKRANG
RUMBLE
ANOTHER SPELL, ANOTHER SHOCK! NOW I GOTTA UNLEASH...

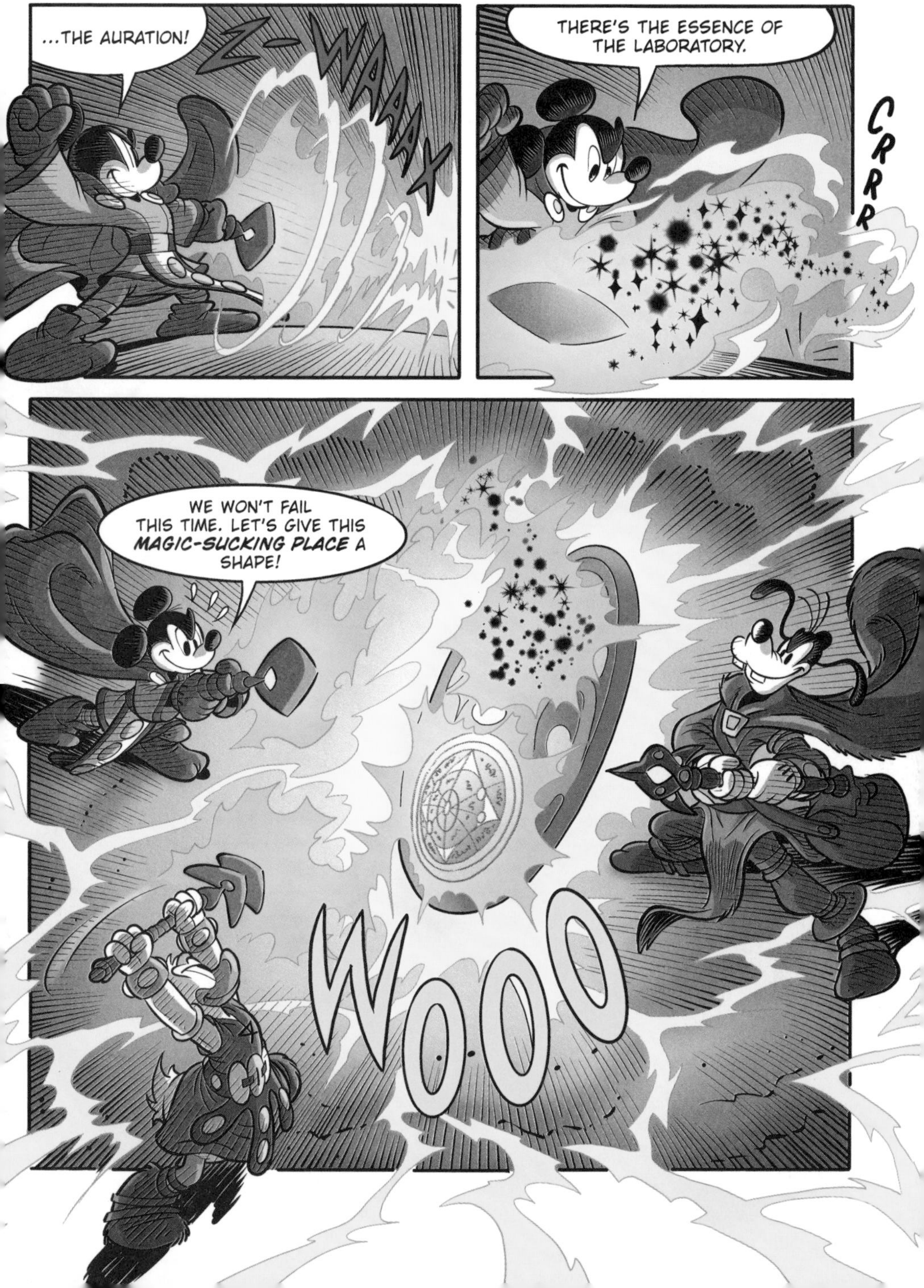

...THE AURATION!
Z-WAAAX
THERE'S THE ESSENCE OF THE LABORATORY.
CRRRR
WE WON'T FAIL THIS TIME. LET'S GIVE THIS *MAGIC-SUCKING PLACE* A SHAPE!
WOOO

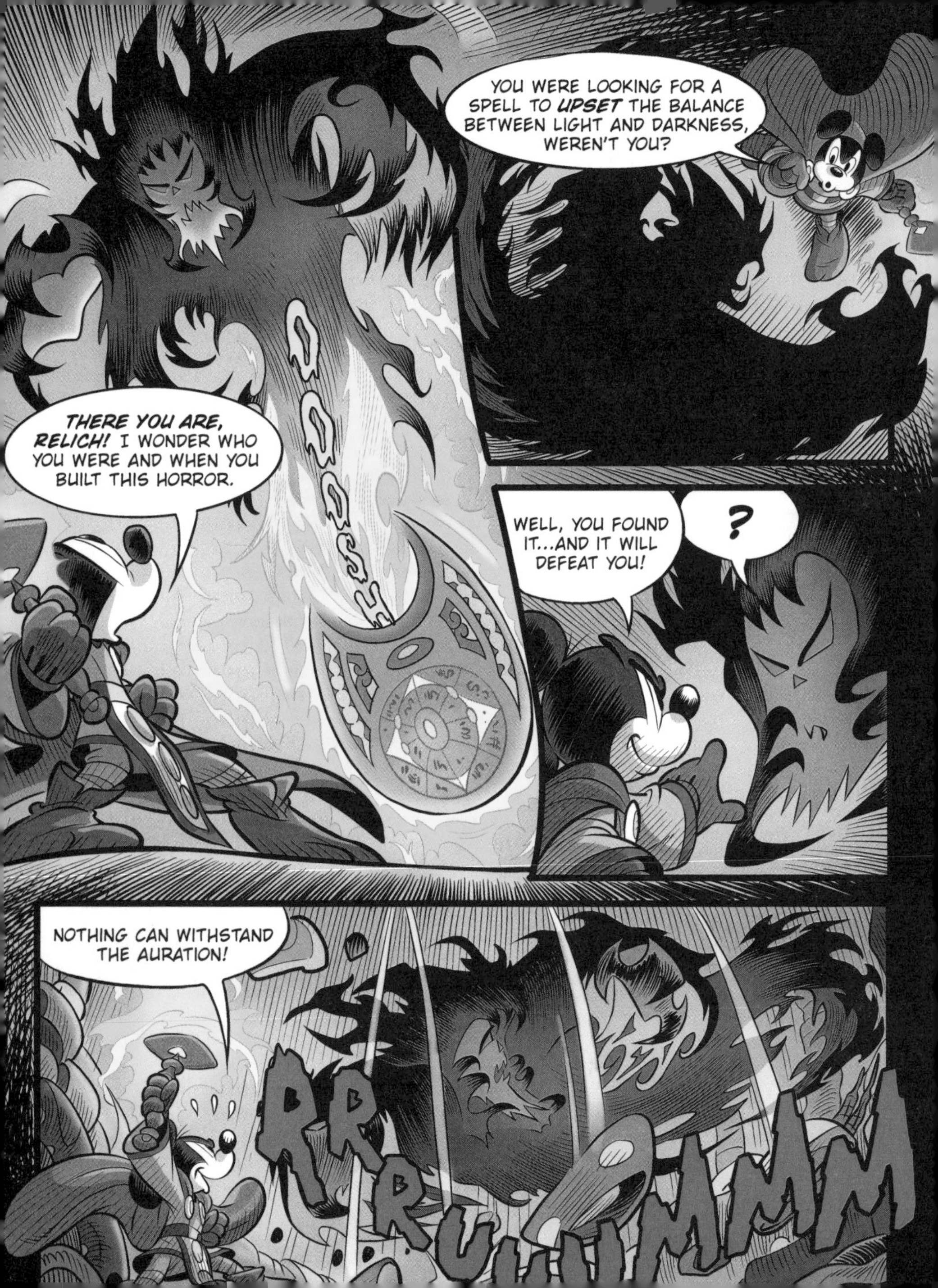
YOU WERE LOOKING FOR A SPELL TO UPSET THE BALANCE BETWEEN LIGHT AND DARKNESS, WEREN'T YOU?
THERE YOU ARE, RELICH! I WONDER WHO YOU WERE AND WHEN YOU BUILT THIS HORROR.
WELL, YOU FOUND IT...AND IT WILL DEFEAT YOU!
?
NOTHING CAN WITHSTAND THE AURATION!
RRRUMMMM

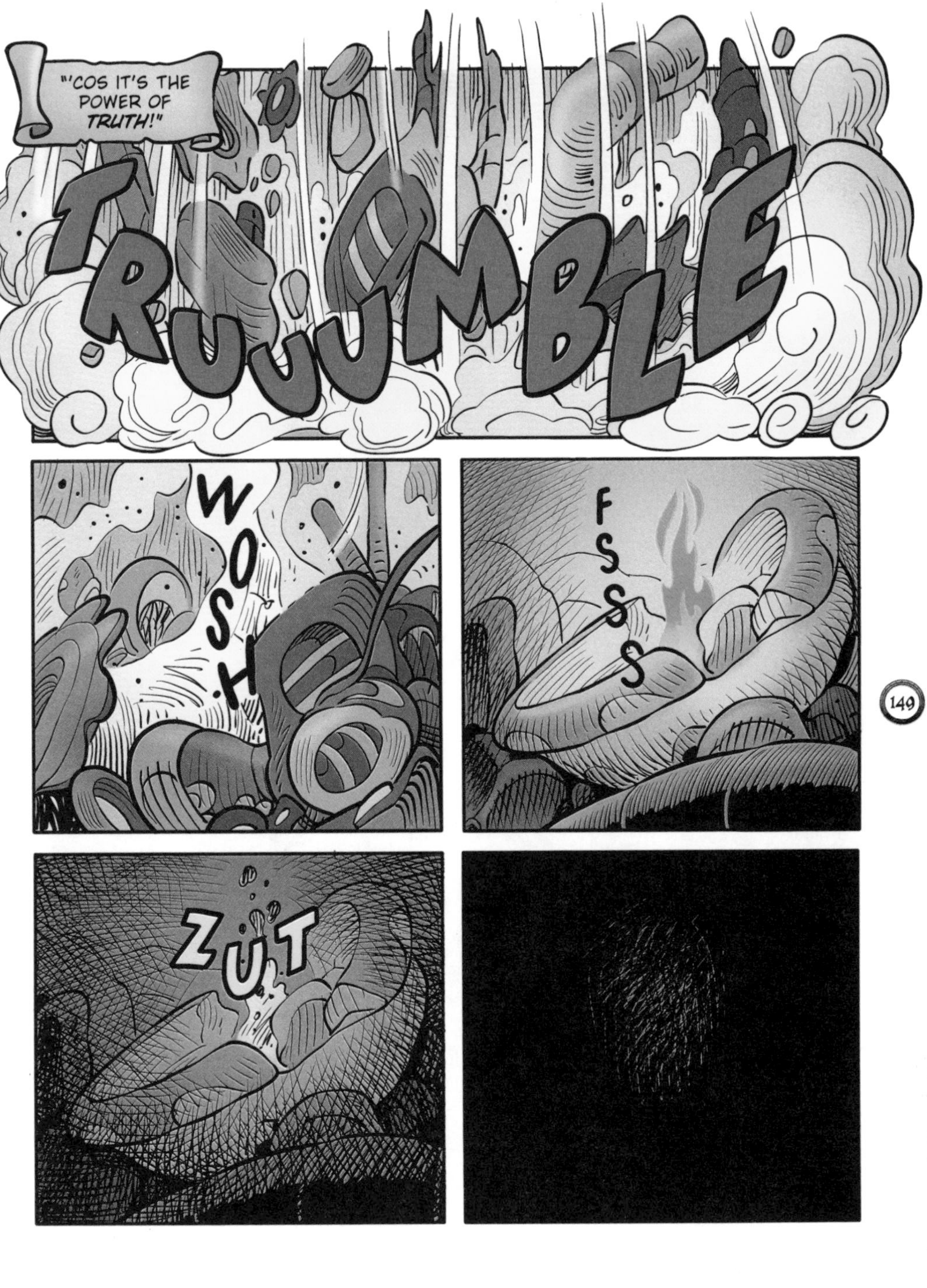
"COS IT'S THE POWER OF TRUTH!"
TRUUUMBLE
WOOSH
FSSSS
ZUT

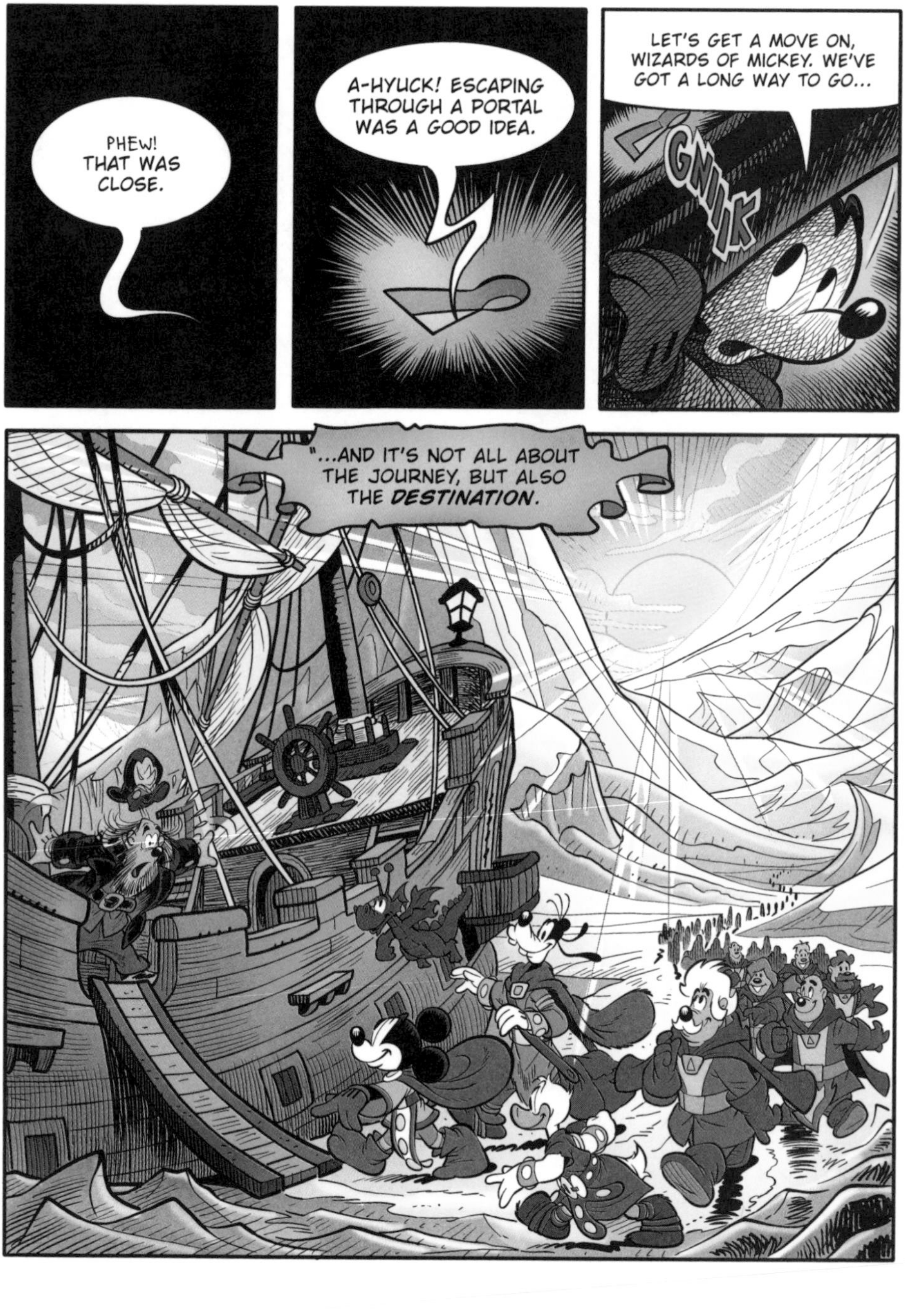
PHEW! THAT WAS CLOSE.
A-HYUCK! ESCAPING THROUGH A PORTAL WAS A GOOD IDEA.
LET'S GET A MOVE ON, WIZARDS OF MICKEY. WE'VE GOT A LONG WAY TO GO...
GNIIK
"...AND IT'S NOT ALL ABOUT THE JOURNEY, BUT ALSO THE *DESTINATION*.

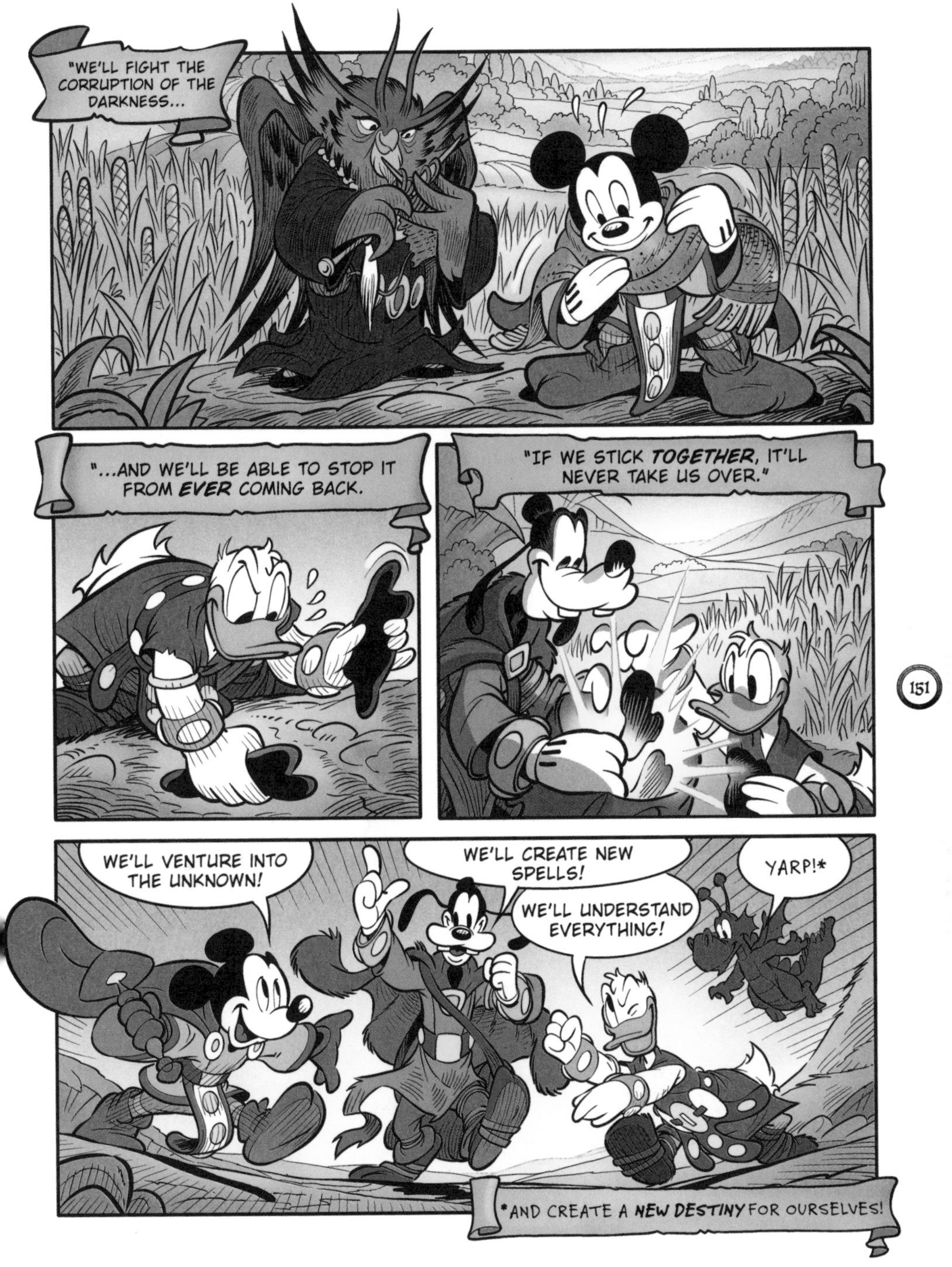

"WE'LL FIGHT THE CORRUPTION OF THE DARKNESS...
"...AND WE'LL BE ABLE TO STOP IT FROM EVER COMING BACK.
"IF WE STICK TOGETHER, IT'LL NEVER TAKE US OVER."
WE'LL VENTURE INTO THE UNKNOWN!
WE'LL CREATE NEW SPELLS!
WE'LL UNDERSTAND EVERYTHING!
YARP!*
*AND CREATE A NEW DESTINY FOR OURSELVES!

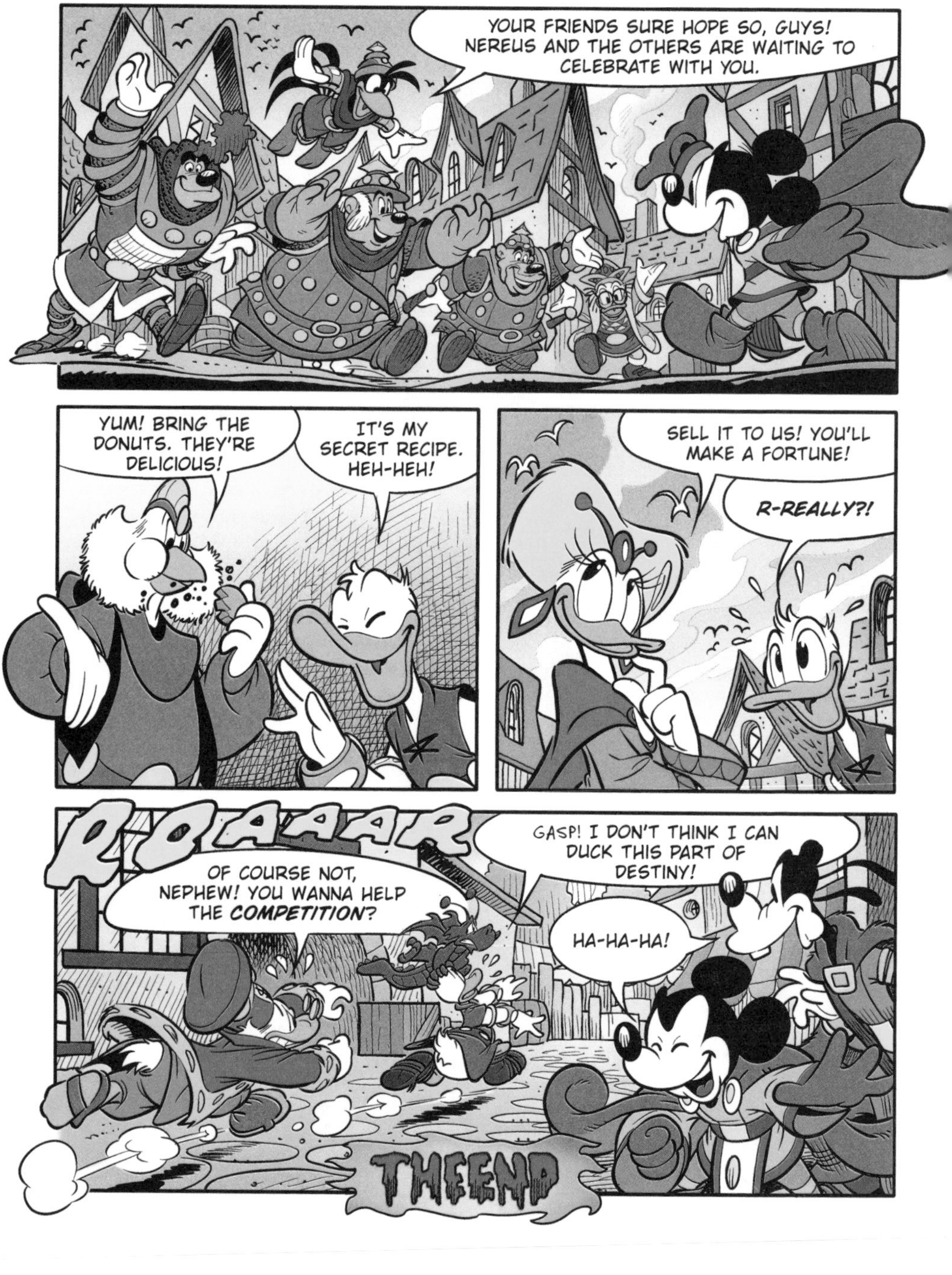
YOUR FRIENDS SURE HOPE SO, GUYS! NEREUS AND THE OTHERS ARE WAITING TO CELEBRATE WITH YOU.
YUM! BRING THE DONUTS. THEY'RE DELICIOUS!
IT'S MY SECRET RECIPE. HEH-HEH!
SELL IT TO US! YOU'LL MAKE A FORTUNE!
R-REALLY?!
ROAAAR
OF COURSE NOT, NEPHEW! YOU WANNA HELP THE COMPETITION?
GASP! I DON'T THINK I CAN DUCK THIS PART OF DESTINY!
HA-HA-HA!
THE END

Wizards of Mickey

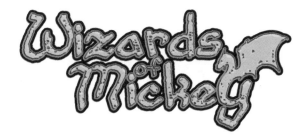

Wizards of Mickey

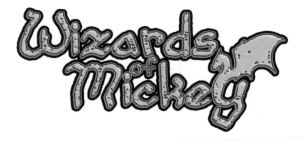

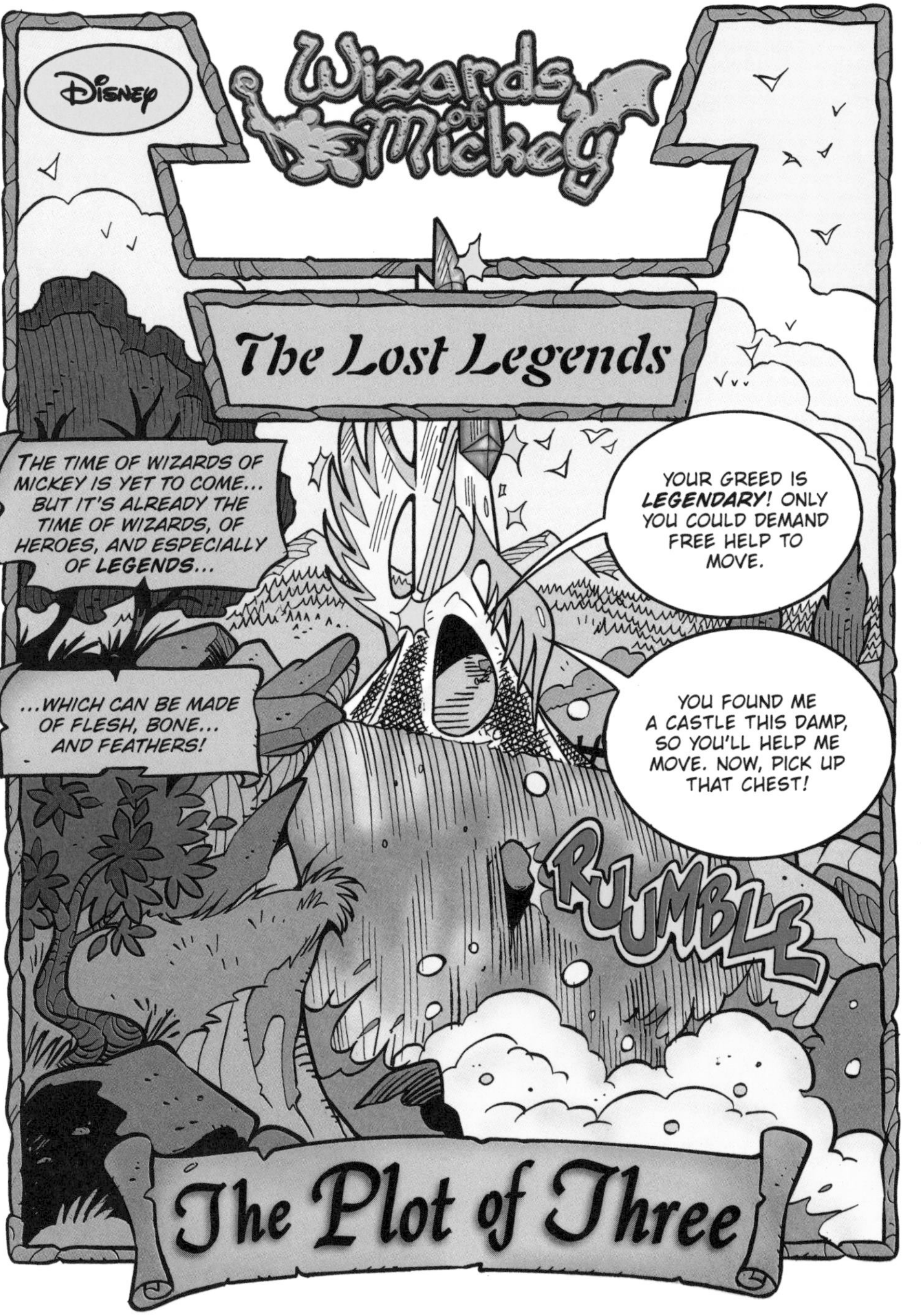
Disney
Wizards of Mickey
The Lost Legends
THE TIME OF WIZARDS OF MICKEY IS YET TO COME... BUT IT'S ALREADY THE TIME OF WIZARDS, OF HEROES, AND ESPECIALLY OF LEGENDS...
...WHICH CAN BE MADE OF FLESH, BONE... AND FEATHERS!
YOUR GREED IS LEGENDARY! ONLY YOU COULD DEMAND FREE HELP TO MOVE.
YOU FOUND ME A CASTLE THIS DAMP, SO YOU'LL HELP ME MOVE. NOW, PICK UP THAT CHEST!
RUUMBLE
The Plot of Three

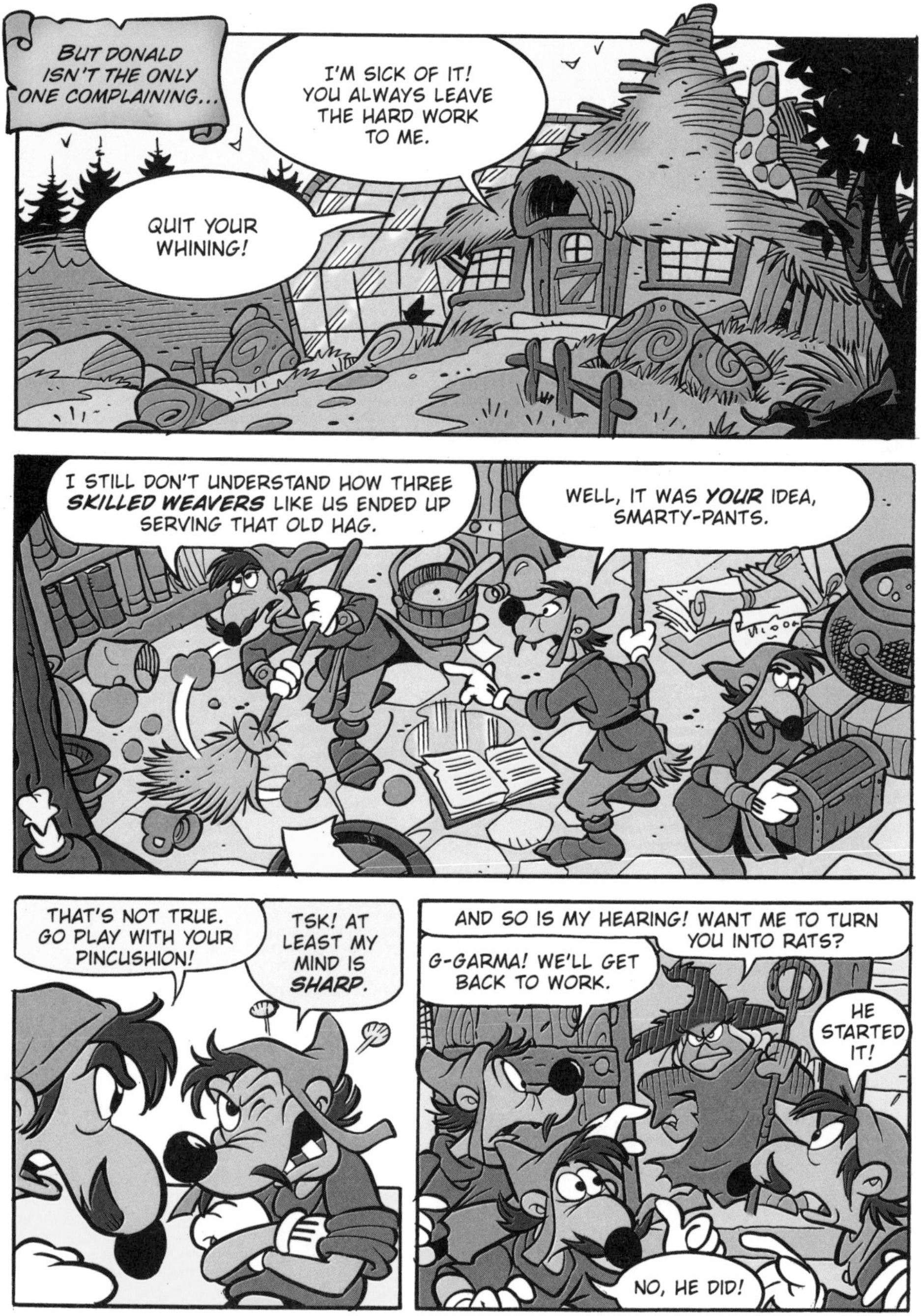
BUT DONALD ISN'T THE ONLY ONE COMPLAINING...
I'M SICK OF IT! YOU ALWAYS LEAVE THE HARD WORK TO ME.
QUIT YOUR WHINING!
I STILL DON'T UNDERSTAND HOW THREE SKILLED WEAVERS LIKE US ENDED UP SERVING THAT OLD HAG.
WELL, IT WAS YOUR IDEA, SMARTY-PANTS.
THAT'S NOT TRUE. GO PLAY WITH YOUR PINCUSHION!
TSK! AT LEAST MY MIND IS SHARP.
AND SO IS MY HEARING! WANT ME TO TURN YOU INTO RATS?
G-GARMA! WE'LL GET BACK TO WORK.
HE STARTED IT!
NO, HE DID!

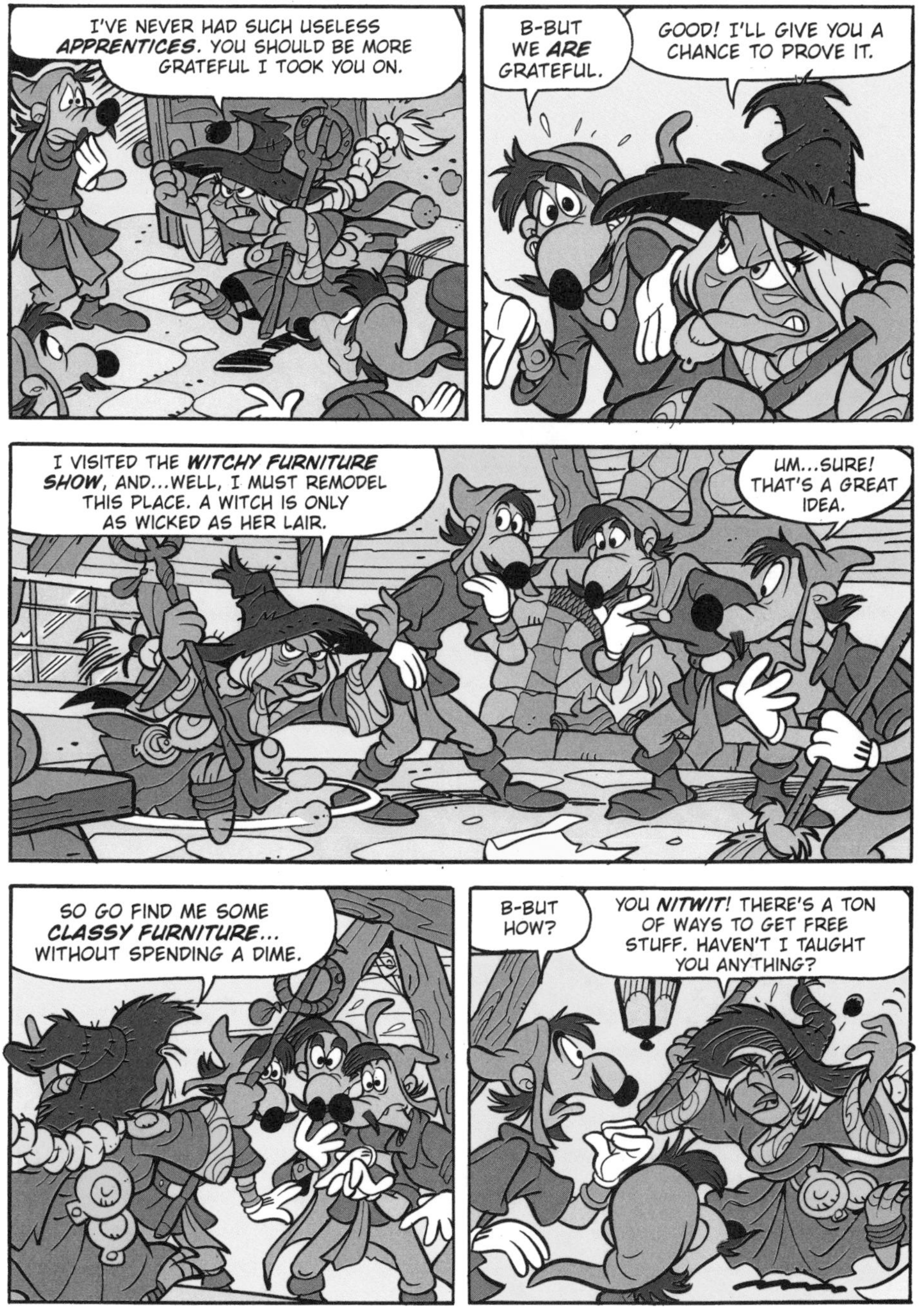
I'VE NEVER HAD SUCH USELESS APPRENTICES. YOU SHOULD BE MORE GRATEFUL I TOOK YOU ON.
B-BUT WE ARE GRATEFUL.
GOOD! I'LL GIVE YOU A CHANCE TO PROVE IT.
I VISITED THE WITCHY FURNITURE SHOW, AND...WELL, I MUST REMODEL THIS PLACE. A WITCH IS ONLY AS WICKED AS HER LAIR.
UM...SURE! THAT'S A GREAT IDEA.
SO GO FIND ME SOME CLASSY FURNITURE... WITHOUT SPENDING A DIME.
B-BUT HOW?
YOU NITWIT! THERE'S A TON OF WAYS TO GET FREE STUFF. HAVEN'T I TAUGHT YOU ANYTHING?

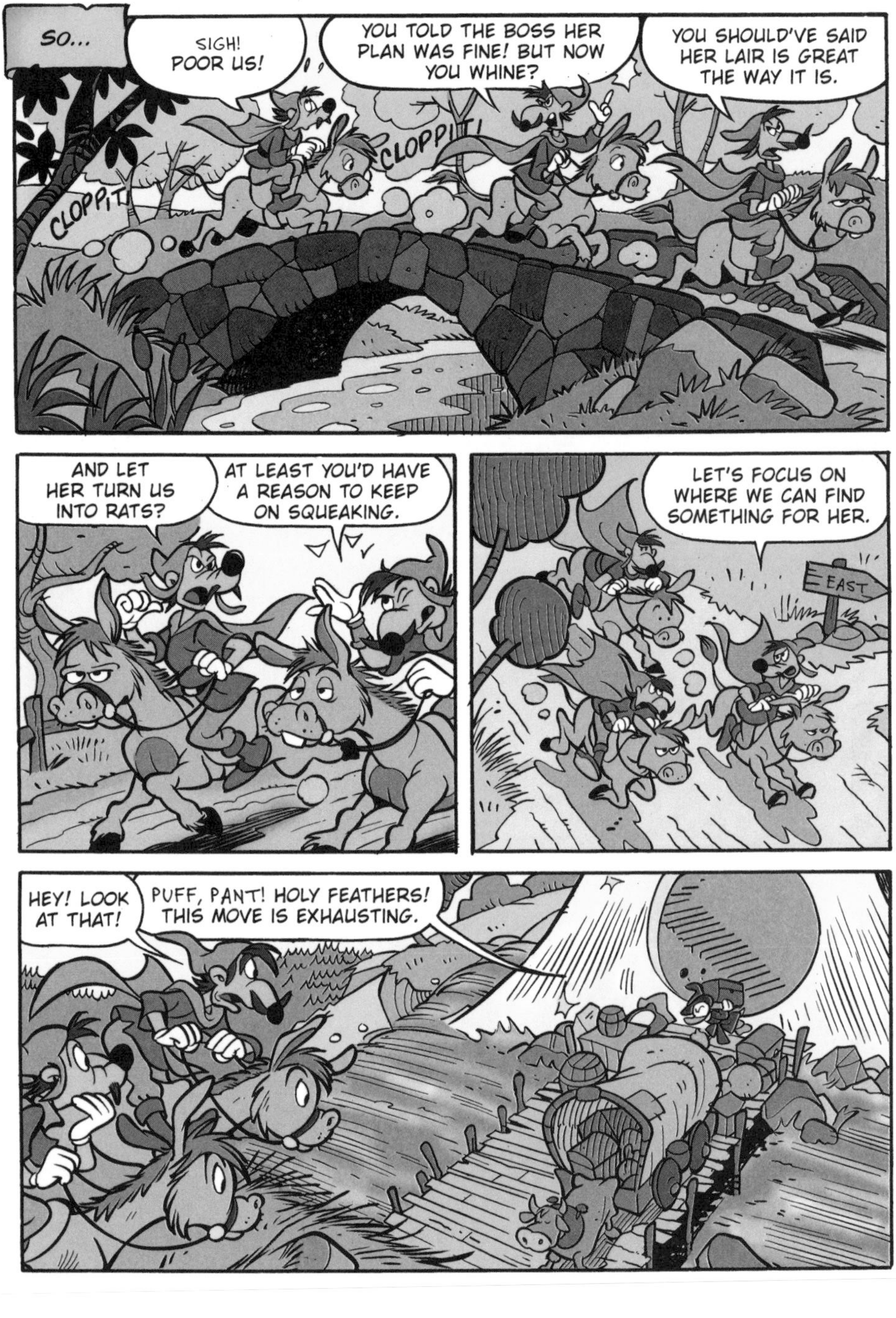
SO...
SIGH! POOR US!
YOU TOLD THE BOSS HER PLAN WAS FINE! BUT NOW YOU WHINE?
YOU SHOULD'VE SAID HER LAIR IS GREAT THE WAY IT IS.
CLOPPIT!
CLOPPIT!
AND LET HER TURN US INTO RATS?
AT LEAST YOU'D HAVE A REASON TO KEEP ON SQUEAKING.
LET'S FOCUS ON WHERE WE CAN FIND SOMETHING FOR HER.
EAST
HEY! LOOK AT THAT!
PUFF, PANT! HOLY FEATHERS! THIS MOVE IS EXHAUSTING.

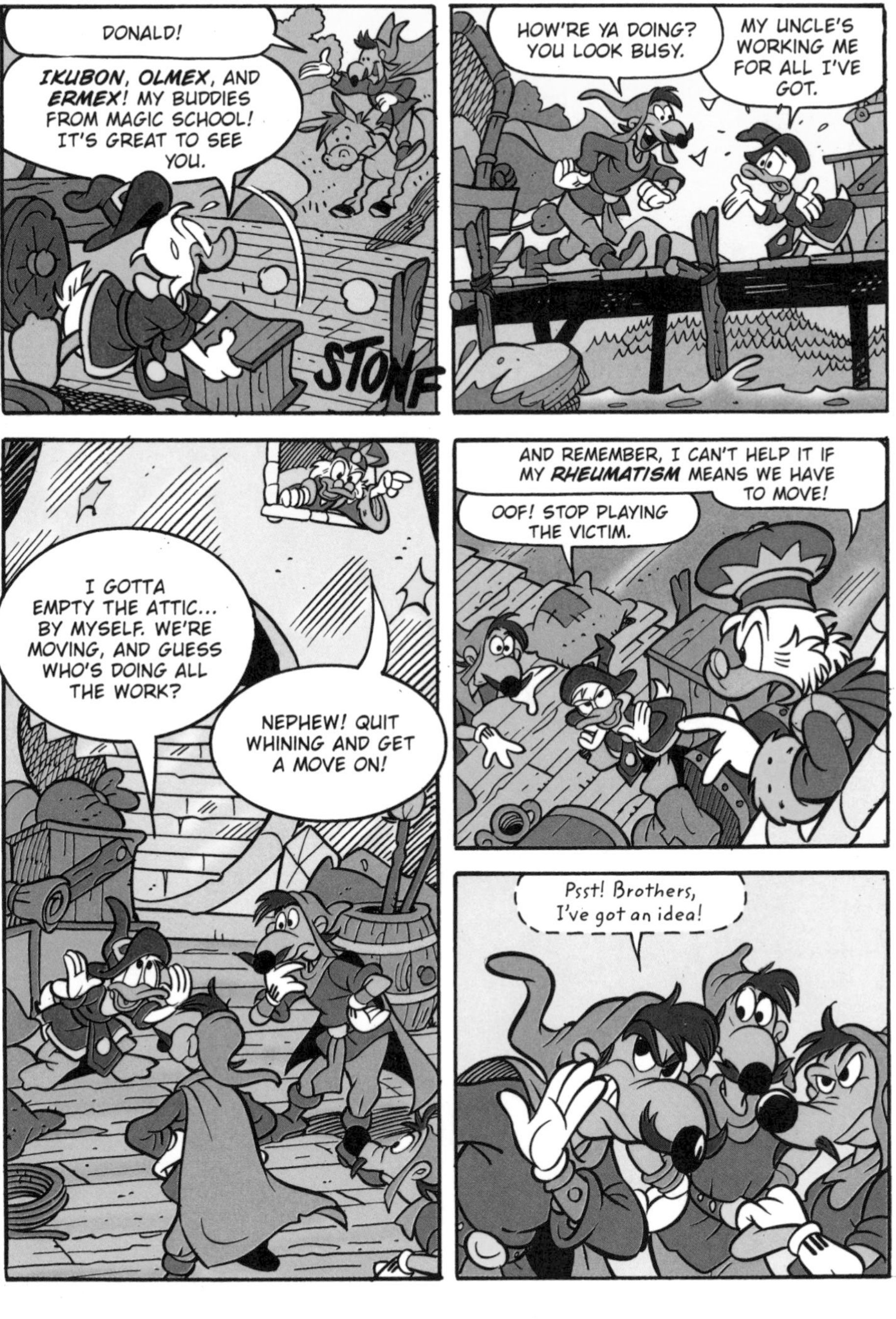
DONALD!
IKUBON, **OLMEX**, AND **ERMEX**! MY BUDDIES FROM MAGIC SCHOOL! IT'S GREAT TO SEE YOU.
STONF
HOW'RE YA DOING? YOU LOOK BUSY.
MY UNCLE'S WORKING ME FOR ALL I'VE GOT.
I GOTTA EMPTY THE ATTIC... BY MYSELF. WE'RE MOVING, AND GUESS WHO'S DOING ALL THE WORK?
NEPHEW! QUIT WHINING AND GET A MOVE ON!
AND REMEMBER, I CAN'T HELP IT IF MY **RHEUMATISM** MEANS WE HAVE TO MOVE!
OOF! STOP PLAYING THE VICTIM.
Psst! Brothers, I've got an idea!

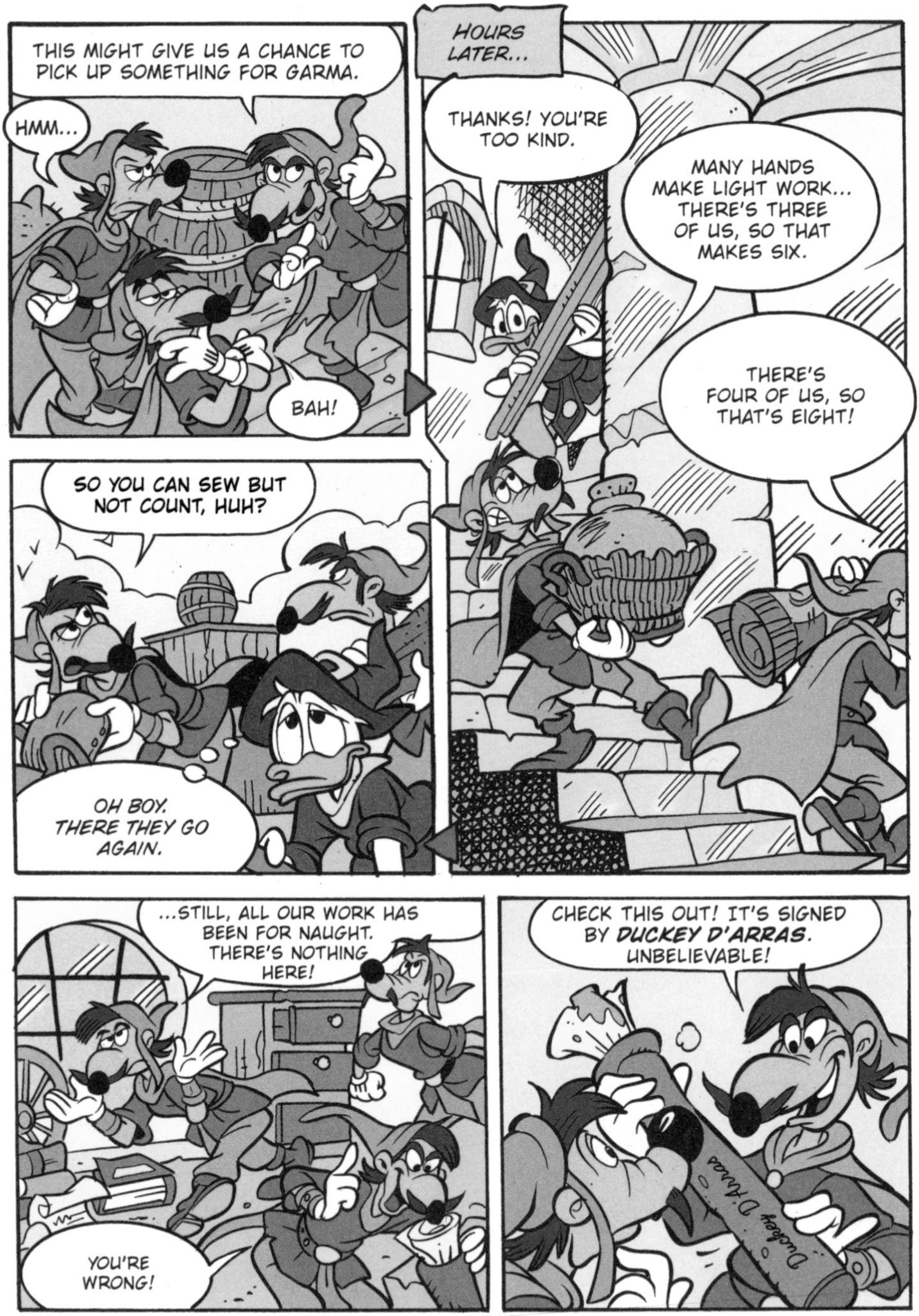
THIS MIGHT GIVE US A CHANCE TO PICK UP SOMETHING FOR GARMA.
HMM...
BAH!
HOURS LATER...
THANKS! YOU'RE TOO KIND.
MANY HANDS MAKE LIGHT WORK... THERE'S THREE OF US, SO THAT MAKES SIX.
THERE'S FOUR OF US, SO THAT'S EIGHT!
SO YOU CAN SEW BUT NOT COUNT, HUH?
OH BOY. THERE THEY GO AGAIN.
...STILL, ALL OUR WORK HAS BEEN FOR NAUGHT. THERE'S NOTHING HERE!
YOU'RE WRONG!
CHECK THIS OUT! IT'S SIGNED BY DUCKEY D'ARRAS. UNBELIEVABLE!
Duckey D'Arras

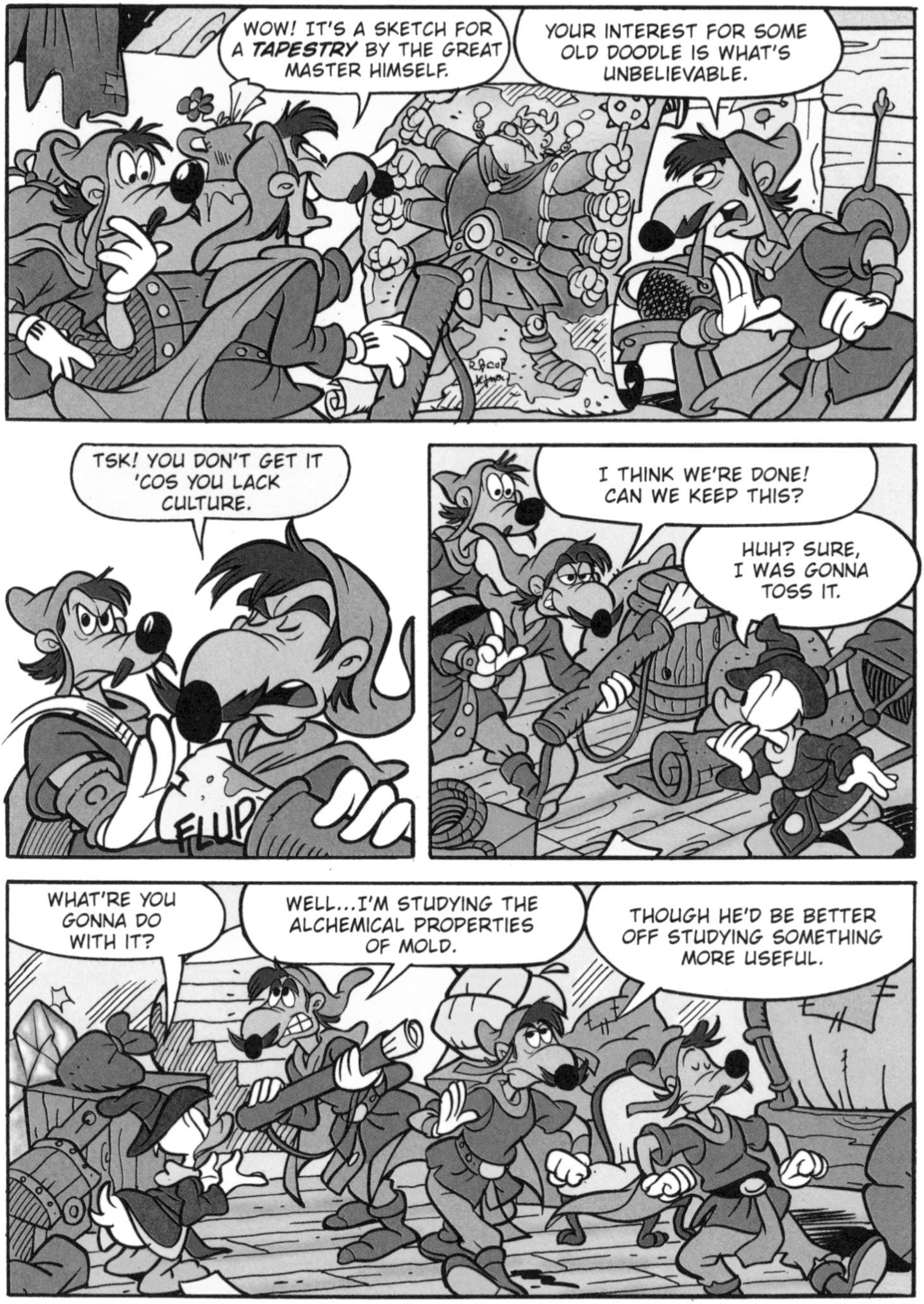
WOW! IT'S A SKETCH FOR A TAPESTRY BY THE GREAT MASTER HIMSELF.
YOUR INTEREST FOR SOME OLD DOODLE IS WHAT'S UNBELIEVABLE.
TSK! YOU DON'T GET IT 'COS YOU LACK CULTURE.
FLUP
I THINK WE'RE DONE! CAN WE KEEP THIS?
HUH? SURE, I WAS GONNA TOSS IT.
WHAT'RE YOU GONNA DO WITH IT?
WELL...I'M STUDYING THE ALCHEMICAL PROPERTIES OF MOLD.
THOUGH HE'D BE BETTER OFF STUDYING SOMETHING MORE USEFUL.

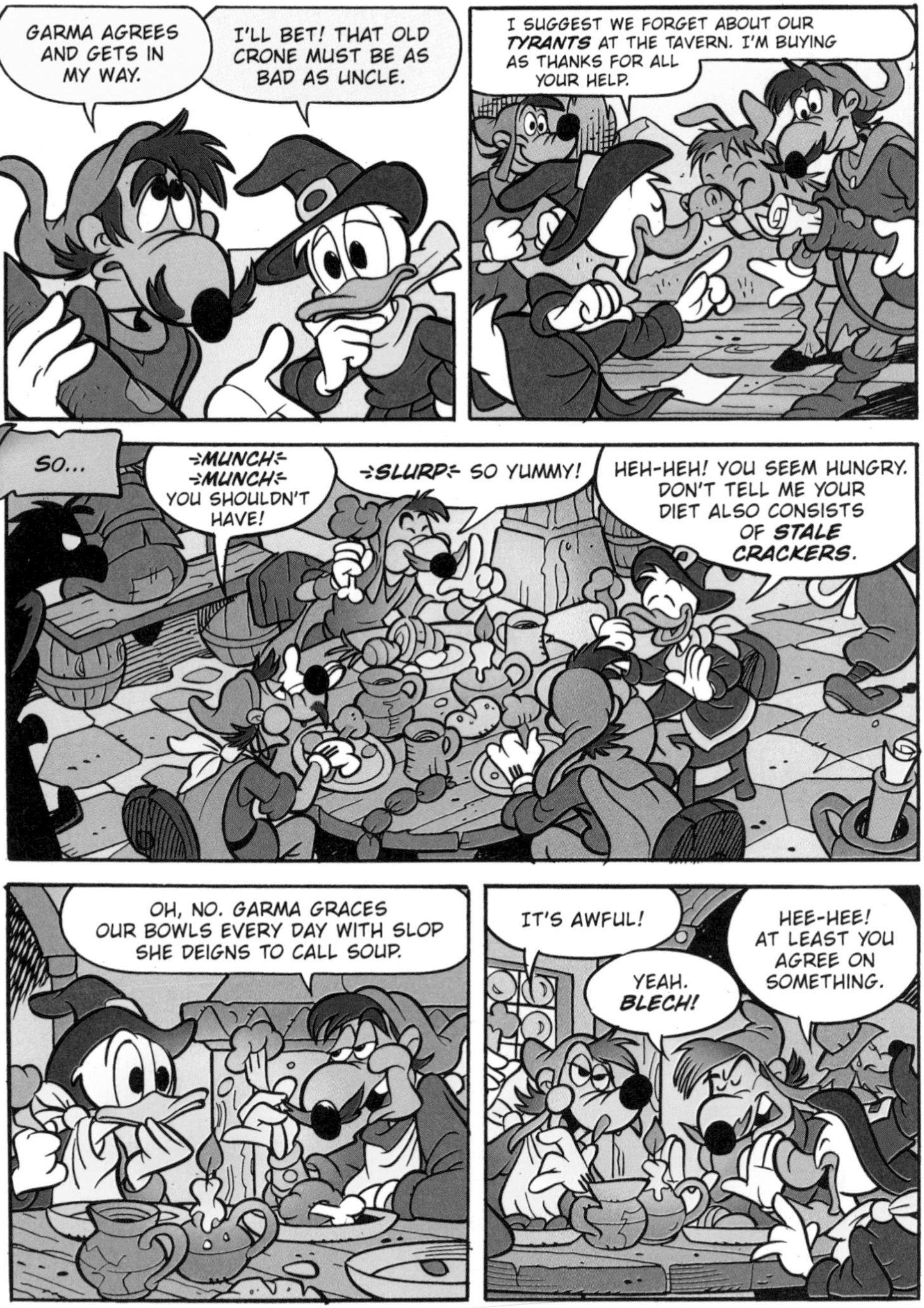
GARMA AGREES AND GETS IN MY WAY.
I'LL BET! THAT OLD CRONE MUST BE AS BAD AS UNCLE.
I SUGGEST WE FORGET ABOUT OUR TYRANTS AT THE TAVERN. I'M BUYING AS THANKS FOR ALL YOUR HELP.
SO...
MUNCH MUNCH YOU SHOULDN'T HAVE!
SLURP SO YUMMY!
HEH-HEH! YOU SEEM HUNGRY. DON'T TELL ME YOUR DIET ALSO CONSISTS OF STALE CRACKERS.
OH, NO. GARMA GRACES OUR BOWLS EVERY DAY WITH SLOP SHE DEIGNS TO CALL SOUP.
IT'S AWFUL!
YEAH. BLECH!
HEE-HEE! AT LEAST YOU AGREE ON SOMETHING.

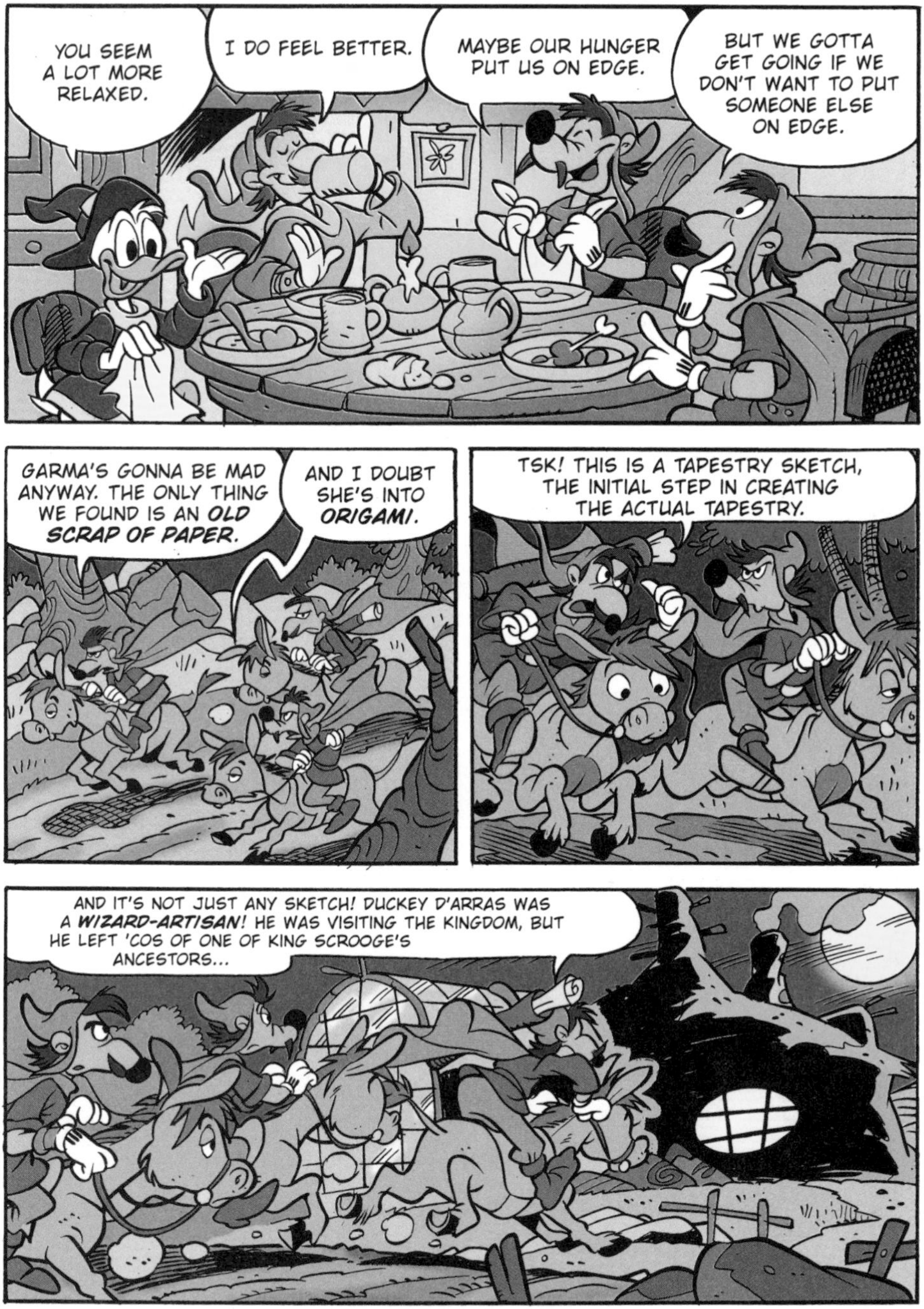
YOU SEEM A LOT MORE RELAXED.
I DO FEEL BETTER.
MAYBE OUR HUNGER PUT US ON EDGE.
BUT WE GOTTA GET GOING IF WE DON'T WANT TO PUT SOMEONE ELSE ON EDGE.
GARMA'S GONNA BE MAD ANYWAY. THE ONLY THING WE FOUND IS AN OLD SCRAP OF PAPER.
AND I DOUBT SHE'S INTO ORIGAMI.
TSK! THIS IS A TAPESTRY SKETCH, THE INITIAL STEP IN CREATING THE ACTUAL TAPESTRY.
AND IT'S NOT JUST ANY SKETCH! DUCKEY D'ARRAS WAS A WIZARD-ARTISAN! HE WAS VISITING THE KINGDOM, BUT HE LEFT 'COS OF ONE OF KING SCROOGE'S ANCESTORS...

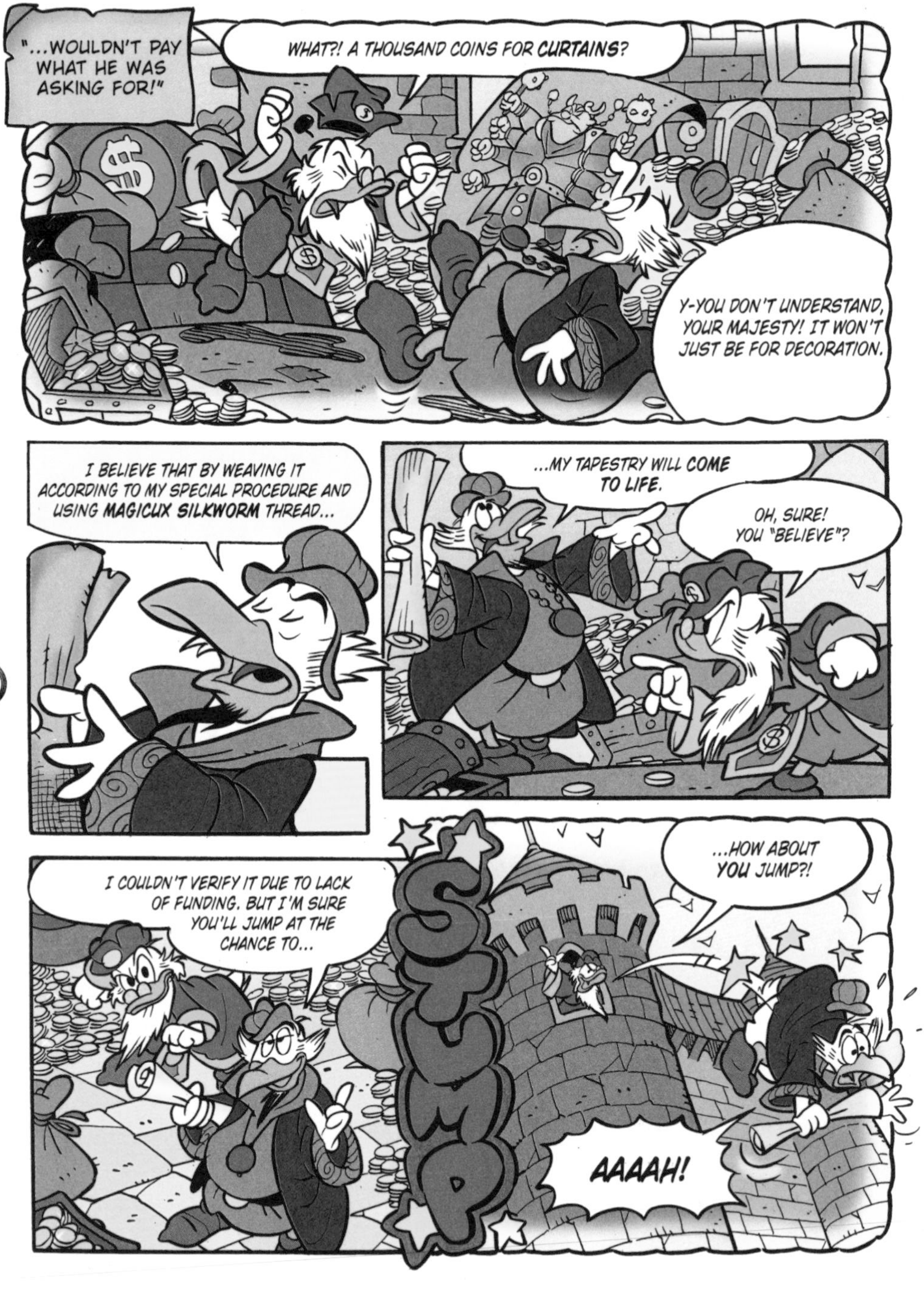

"...WOULDN'T PAY WHAT HE WAS ASKING FOR!"
WHAT?! A THOUSAND COINS FOR CURTAINS?
Y-YOU DON'T UNDERSTAND, YOUR MAJESTY! IT WON'T JUST BE FOR DECORATION.
I BELIEVE THAT BY WEAVING IT ACCORDING TO MY SPECIAL PROCEDURE AND USING MAGICUX SILKWORM THREAD...
...MY TAPESTRY WILL COME TO LIFE.
OH, SURE! YOU "BELIEVE"?
I COULDN'T VERIFY IT DUE TO LACK OF FUNDING. BUT I'M SURE YOU'LL JUMP AT THE CHANCE TO...
STUMP
...HOW ABOUT YOU JUMP?!
AAAAH!

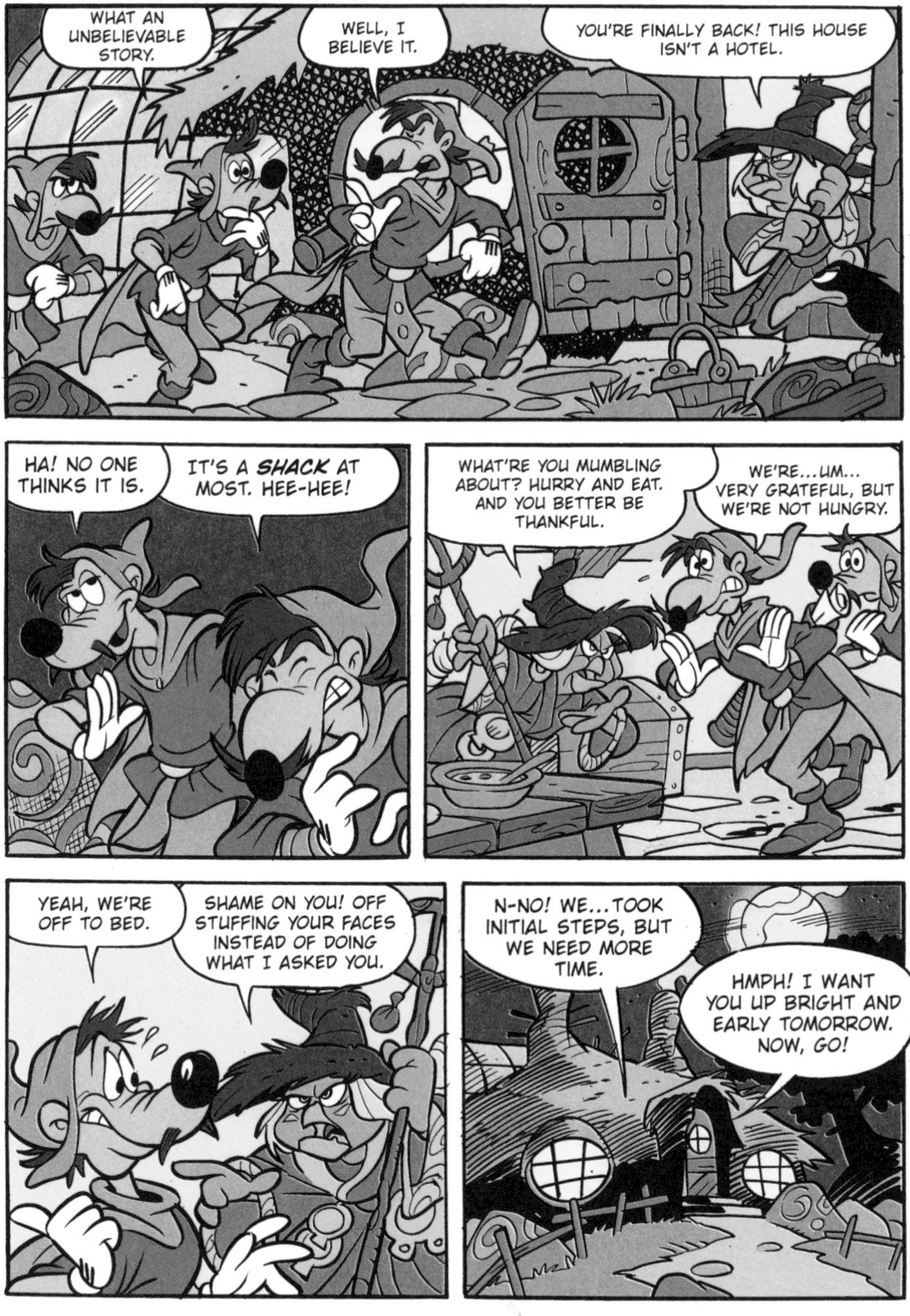
WHAT AN UNBELIEVABLE STORY.
WELL, I BELIEVE IT.
YOU'RE FINALLY BACK! THIS HOUSE ISN'T A HOTEL.
HA! NO ONE THINKS IT IS.
IT'S A SHACK AT MOST. HEE-HEE!
WHAT'RE YOU MUMBLING ABOUT? HURRY AND EAT. AND YOU BETTER BE THANKFUL.
WE'RE...UM... VERY GRATEFUL, BUT WE'RE NOT HUNGRY.
YEAH, WE'RE OFF TO BED.
SHAME ON YOU! OFF STUFFING YOUR FACES INSTEAD OF DOING WHAT I ASKED YOU.
N-NO! WE...TOOK INITIAL STEPS, BUT WE NEED MORE TIME.
HMPH! I WANT YOU UP BRIGHT AND EARLY TOMORROW. NOW, GO!

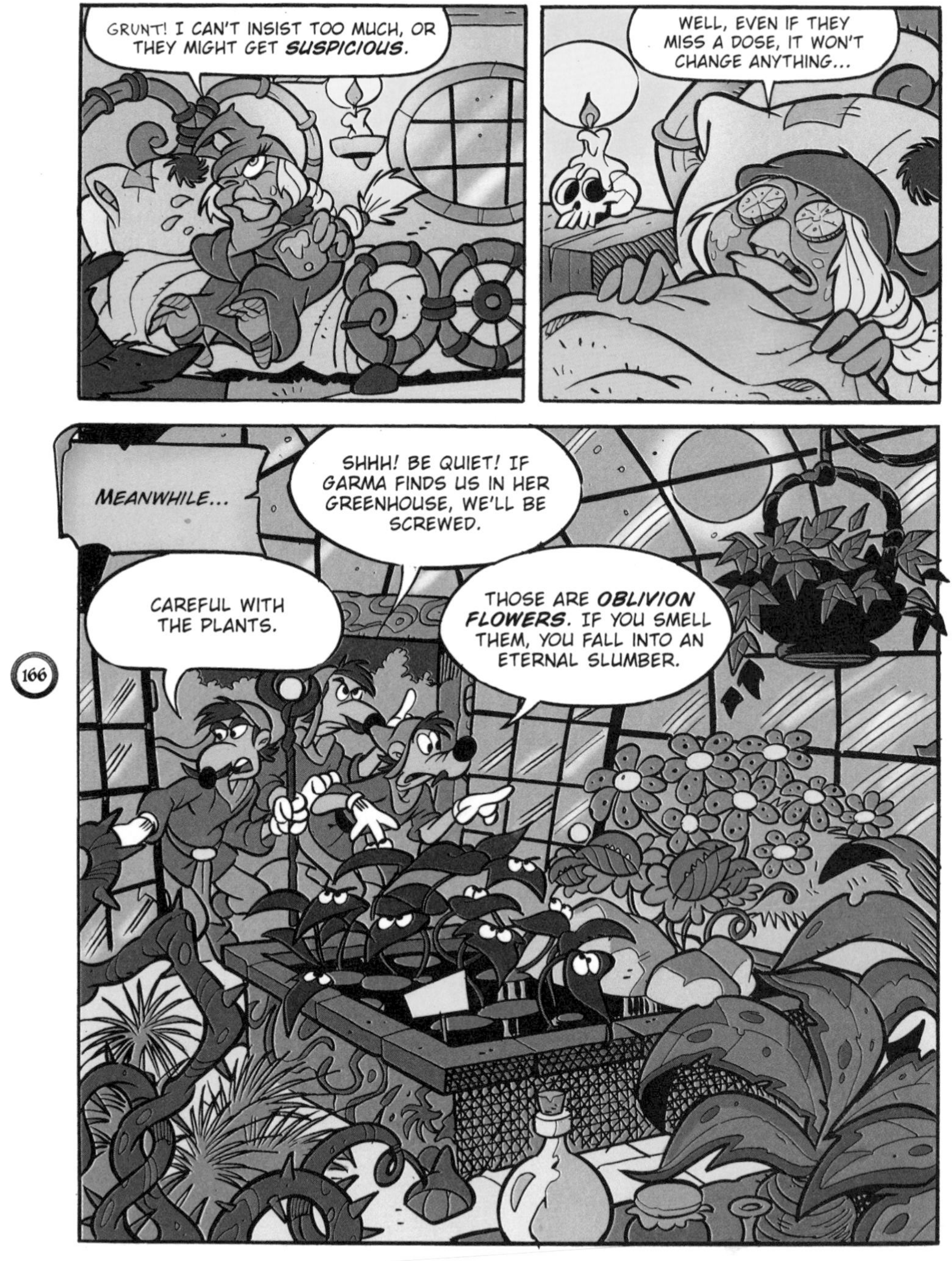
GRUNT! I CAN'T INSIST TOO MUCH, OR THEY MIGHT GET SUSPICIOUS.
WELL, EVEN IF THEY MISS A DOSE, IT WON'T CHANGE ANYTHING...
MEANWHILE...
SHHH! BE QUIET! IF GARMA FINDS US IN HER GREENHOUSE, WE'LL BE SCREWED.
CAREFUL WITH THE PLANTS.
THOSE ARE OBLIVION FLOWERS. IF YOU SMELL THEM, YOU FALL INTO AN ETERNAL SLUMBER.

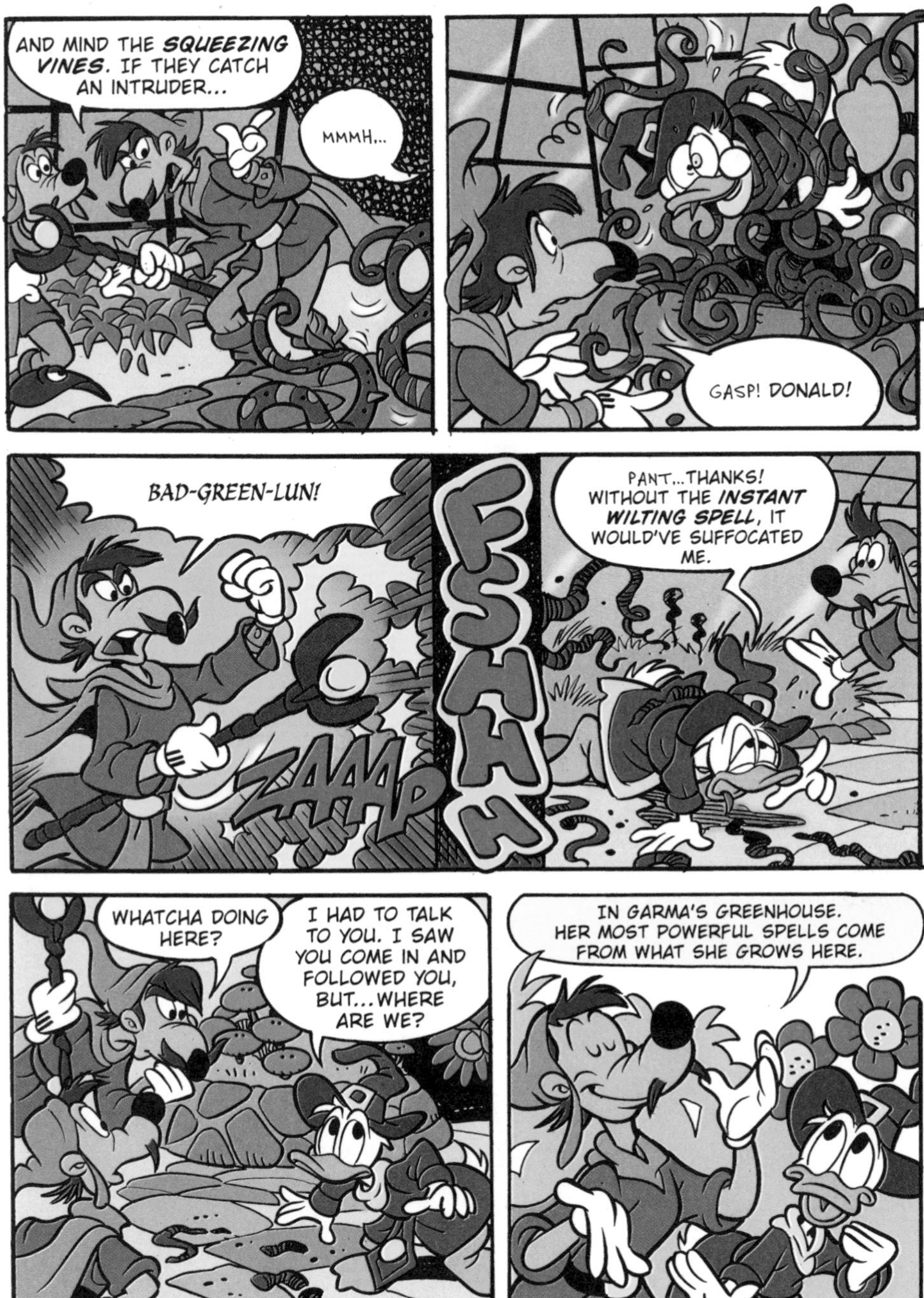

AND MIND THE SQUEEZING VINES. IF THEY CATCH AN INTRUDER...
MMMH...
GASP! DONALD!
BAD-GREEN-LUN!
ZAAAP
FSHHHH
PANT...THANKS! WITHOUT THE INSTANT WILTING SPELL, IT WOULD'VE SUFFOCATED ME.
WHATCHA DOING HERE?
I HAD TO TALK TO YOU. I SAW YOU COME IN AND FOLLOWED YOU, BUT...WHERE ARE WE?
IN GARMA'S GREENHOUSE. HER MOST POWERFUL SPELLS COME FROM WHAT SHE GROWS HERE.

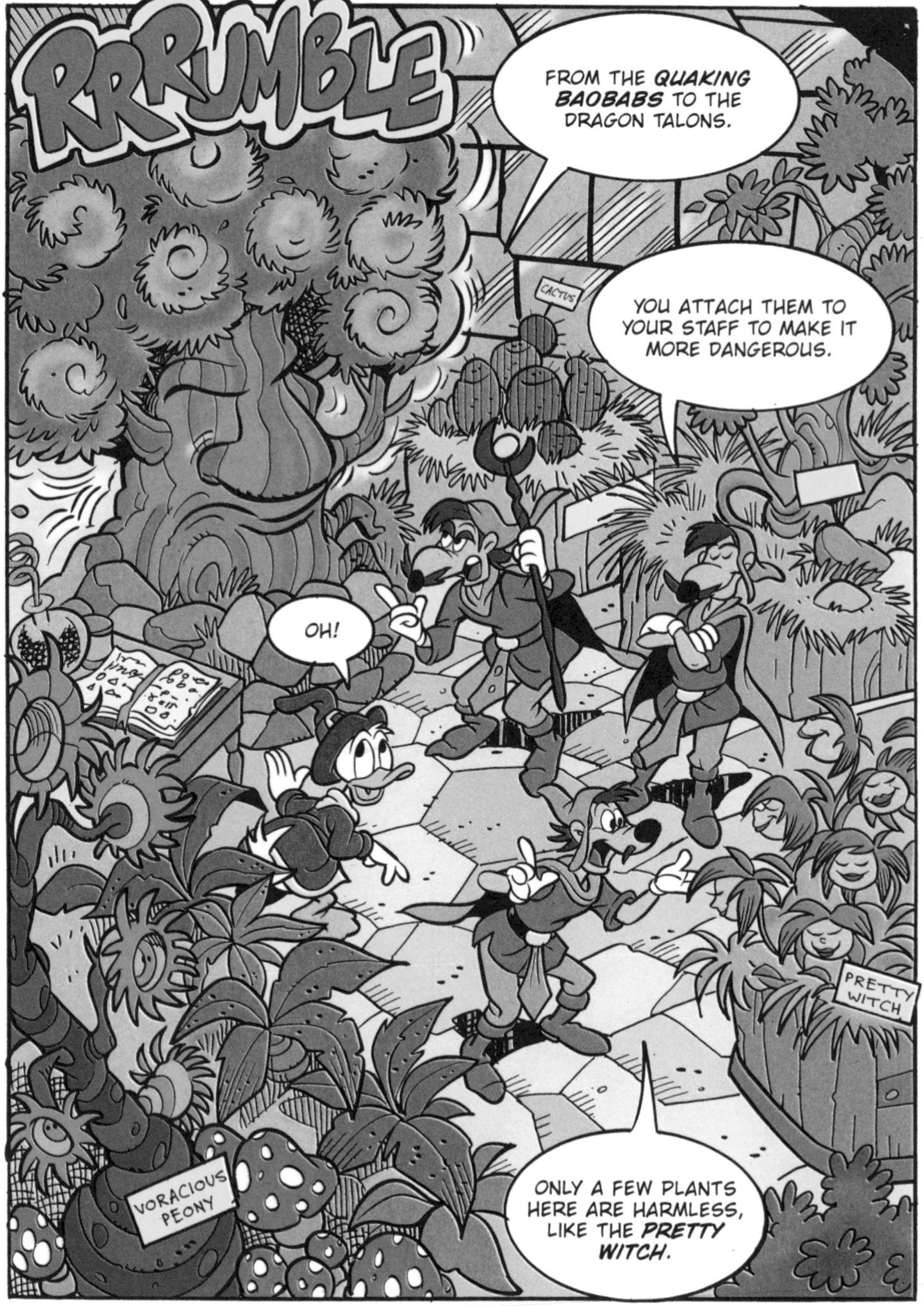
RRRUMBLE
FROM THE QUAKING BAOBABS TO THE DRAGON TALONS.
CACTUS
YOU ATTACH THEM TO YOUR STAFF TO MAKE IT MORE DANGEROUS.
OH!
PRETTY WITCH
VORACIOUS PEONY
ONLY A FEW PLANTS HERE ARE HARMLESS, LIKE THE PRETTY WITCH.

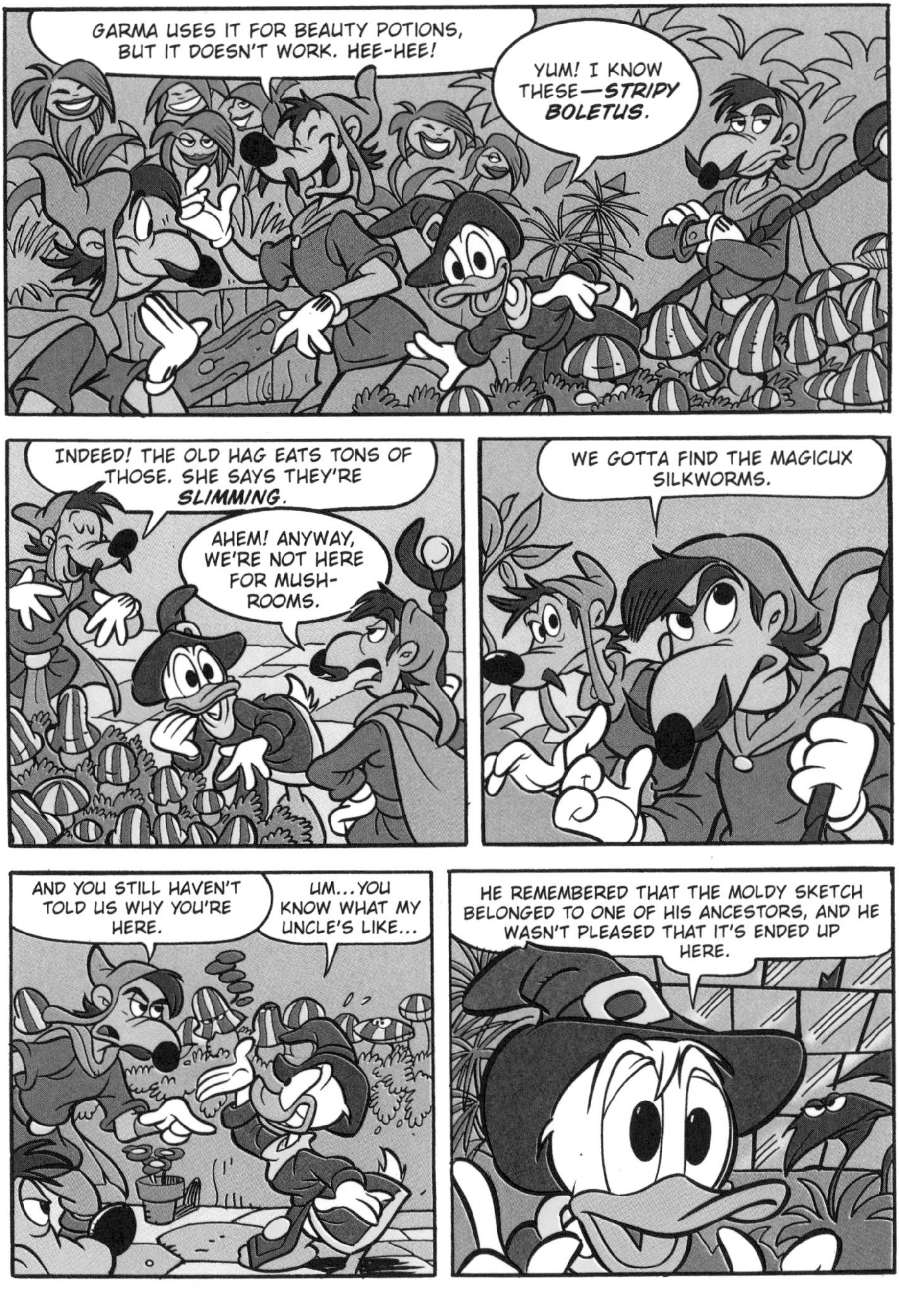
GARMA USES IT FOR BEAUTY POTIONS, BUT IT DOESN'T WORK. HEE-HEE!
YUM! I KNOW THESE—STRIPY BOLETUS.
INDEED! THE OLD HAG EATS TONS OF THOSE. SHE SAYS THEY'RE SLIMMING.
AHEM! ANYWAY, WE'RE NOT HERE FOR MUSH-ROOMS.
WE GOTTA FIND THE MAGICUX SILKWORMS.
AND YOU STILL HAVEN'T TOLD US WHY YOU'RE HERE.
UM...YOU KNOW WHAT MY UNCLE'S LIKE...
HE REMEMBERED THAT THE MOLDY SKETCH BELONGED TO ONE OF HIS ANCESTORS, AND HE WASN'T PLEASED THAT IT'S ENDED UP HERE.

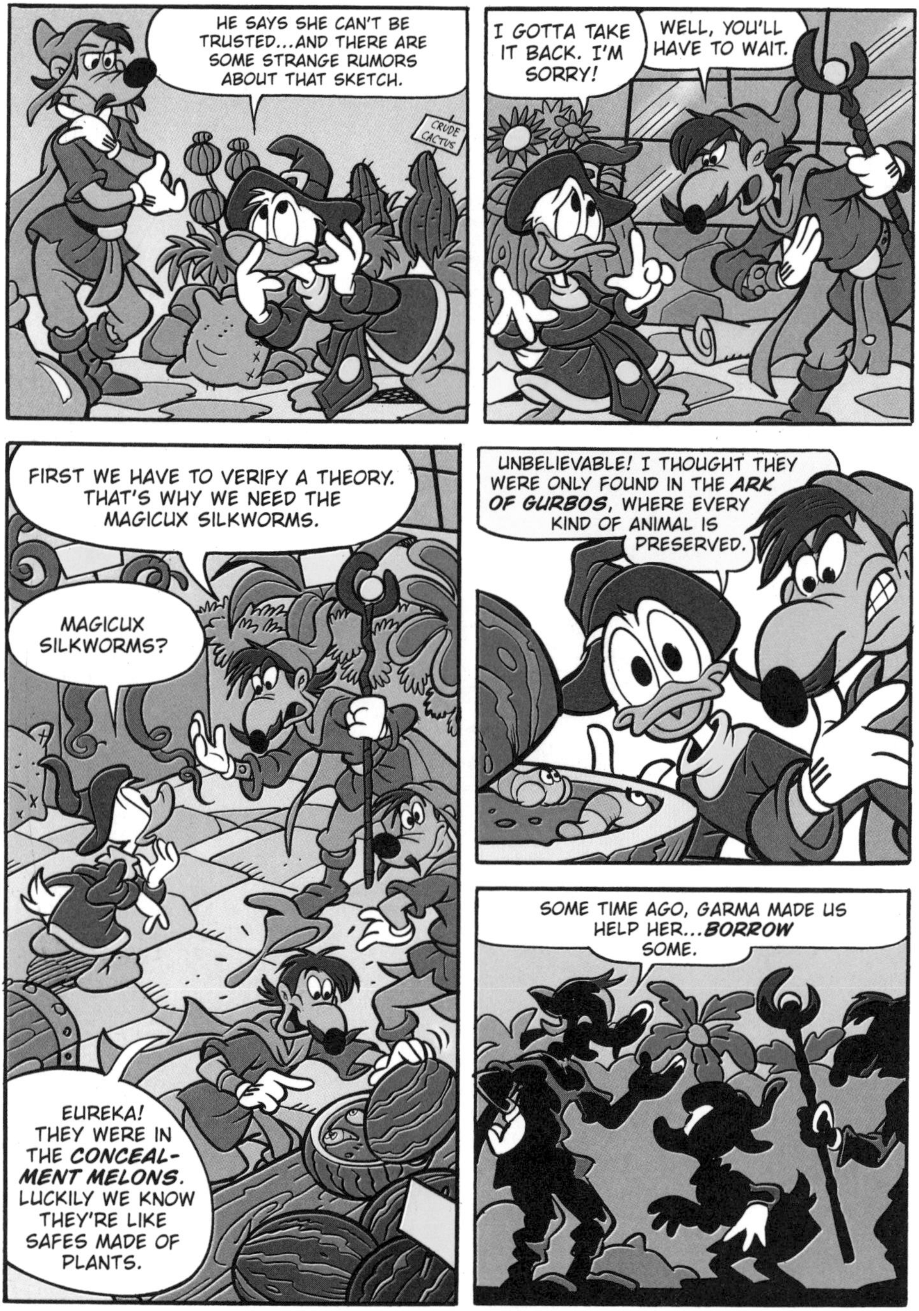
HE SAYS SHE CAN'T BE TRUSTED...AND THERE ARE SOME STRANGE RUMORS ABOUT THAT SKETCH.
CRUDE CACTUS
I GOTTA TAKE IT BACK. I'M SORRY!
WELL, YOU'LL HAVE TO WAIT.
FIRST WE HAVE TO VERIFY A THEORY. THAT'S WHY WE NEED THE MAGICUX SILKWORMS.
MAGICUX SILKWORMS?
EUREKA! THEY WERE IN THE ***CONCEALMENT MELONS***. LUCKILY WE KNOW THEY'RE LIKE SAFES MADE OF PLANTS.
UNBELIEVABLE! I THOUGHT THEY WERE ONLY FOUND IN THE ***ARK OF GURBOS***, WHERE EVERY KIND OF ANIMAL IS PRESERVED.
SOME TIME AGO, GARMA MADE US HELP HER...***BORROW*** SOME.

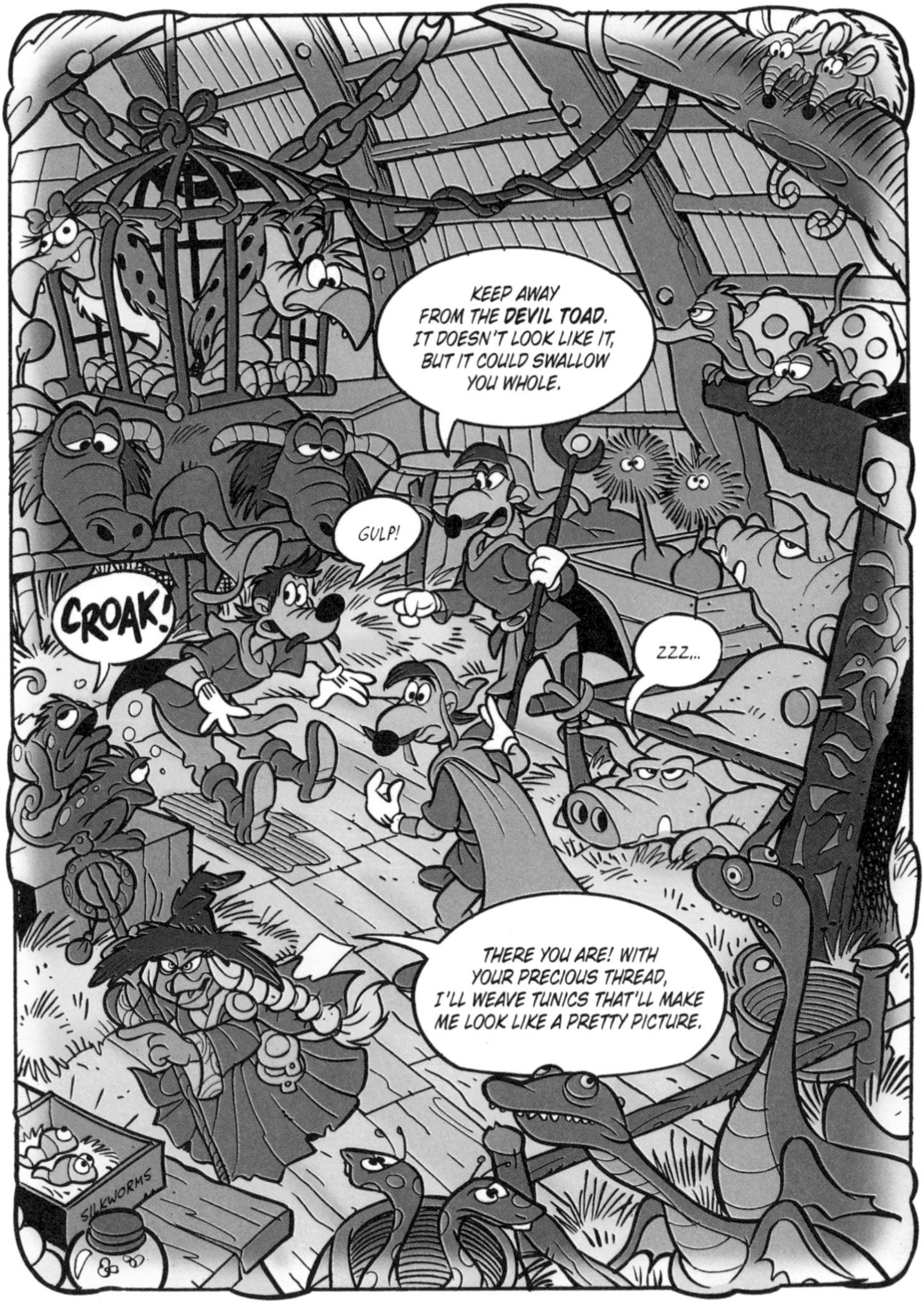
KEEP AWAY FROM THE DEVIL TOAD. IT DOESN'T LOOK LIKE IT, BUT IT COULD SWALLOW YOU WHOLE.
GULP!
CROAK!
ZZZ...
THERE YOU ARE! WITH YOUR PRECIOUS THREAD, I'LL WEAVE TUNICS THAT'LL MAKE ME LOOK LIKE A PRETTY PICTURE.
SILKWORMS

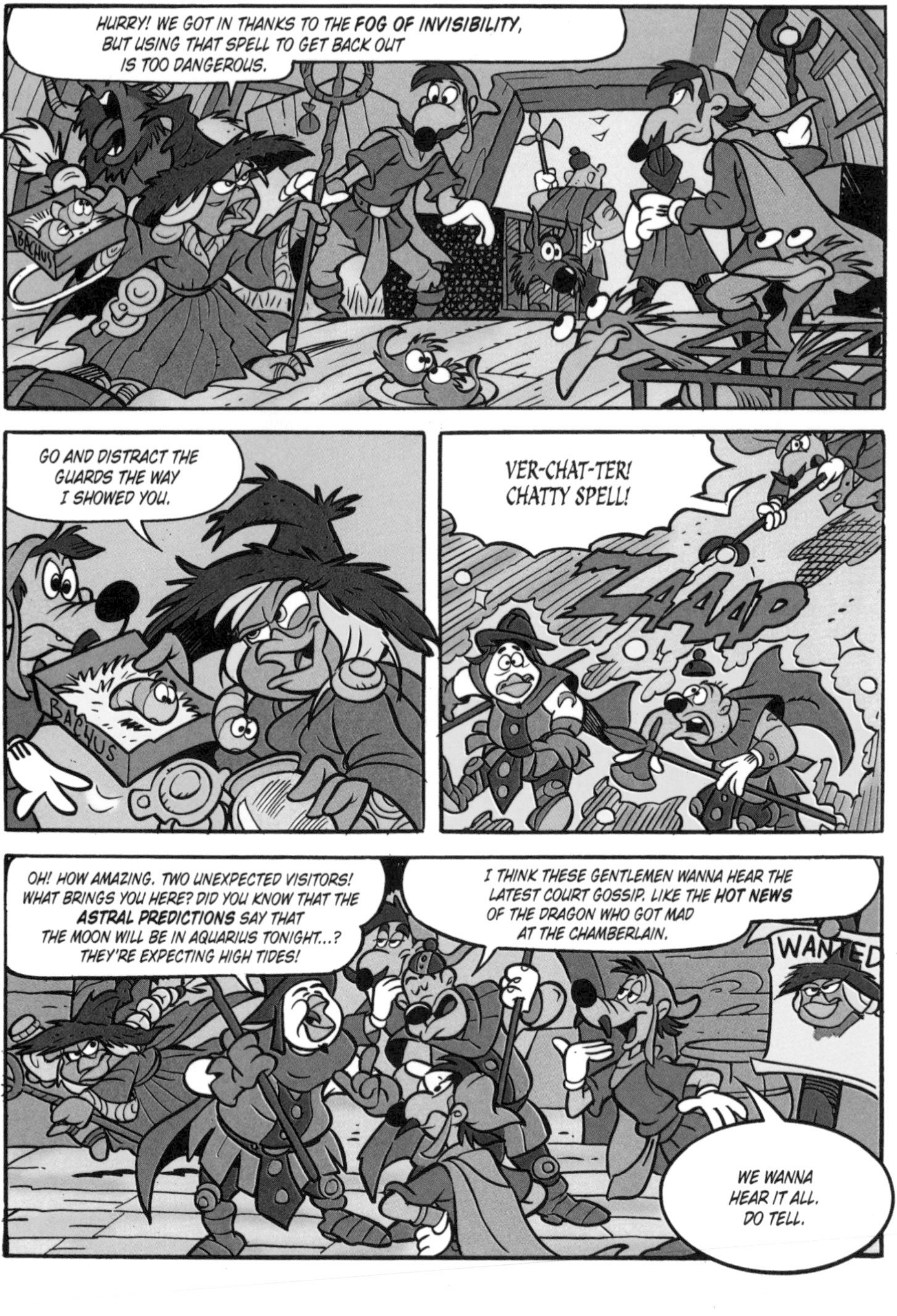
HURRY! WE GOT IN THANKS TO THE FOG OF INVISIBILITY, BUT USING THAT SPELL TO GET BACK OUT IS TOO DANGEROUS.
BACHUS
GO AND DISTRACT THE GUARDS THE WAY I SHOWED YOU.
BACHUS
VER-CHAT-TER! CHATTY SPELL!
ZAAAP
OH! HOW AMAZING. TWO UNEXPECTED VISITORS! WHAT BRINGS YOU HERE? DID YOU KNOW THAT THE ASTRAL PREDICTIONS SAY THAT THE MOON WILL BE IN AQUARIUS TONIGHT...? THEY'RE EXPECTING HIGH TIDES!
I THINK THESE GENTLEMEN WANNA HEAR THE LATEST COURT GOSSIP. LIKE THE HOT NEWS OF THE DRAGON WHO GOT MAD AT THE CHAMBERLAIN.
WANTED
WE WANNA HEAR IT ALL. DO TELL.

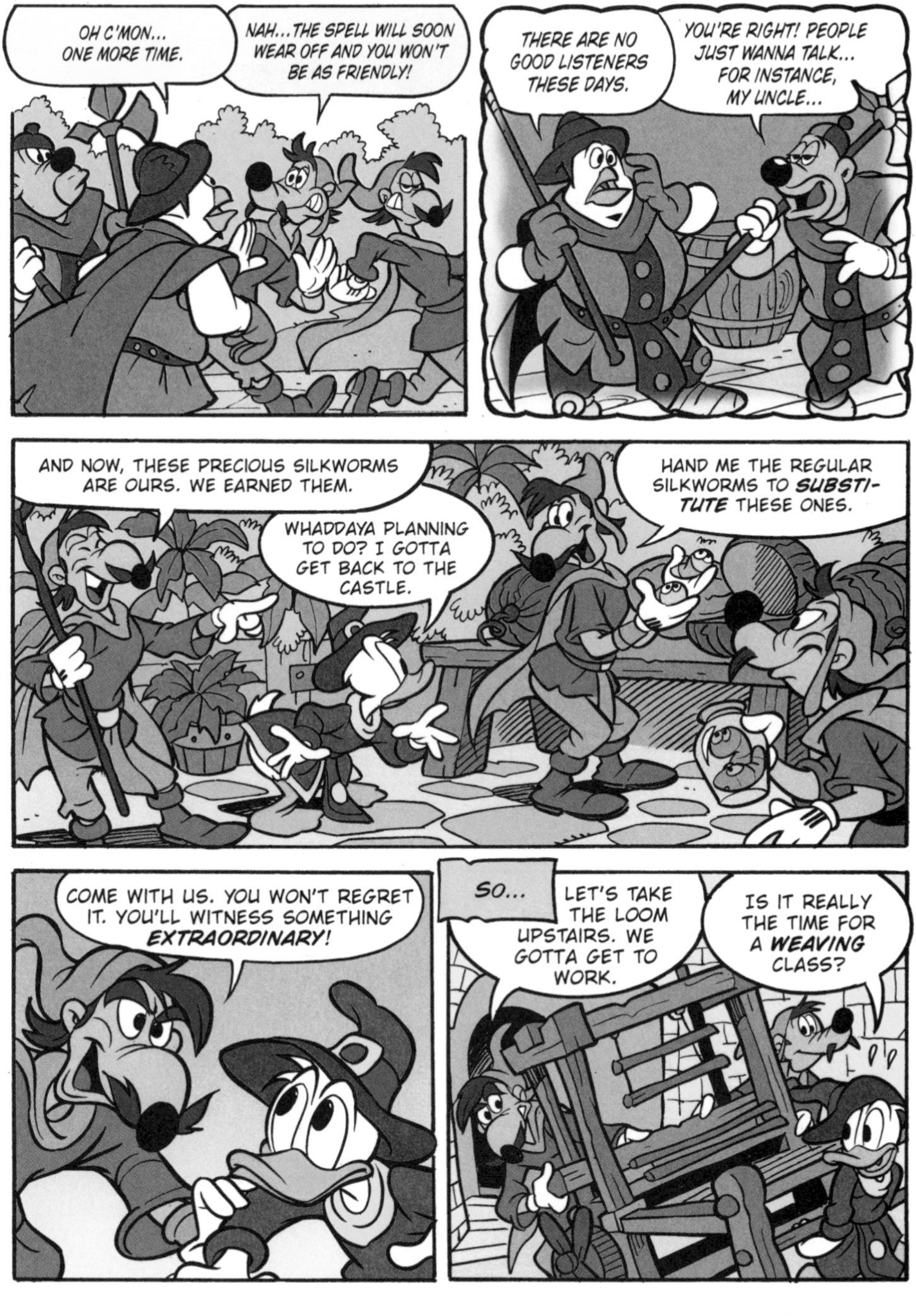
OH C'MON... ONE MORE TIME.
NAH...THE SPELL WILL SOON WEAR OFF AND YOU WON'T BE AS FRIENDLY!
THERE ARE NO GOOD LISTENERS THESE DAYS.
YOU'RE RIGHT! PEOPLE JUST WANNA TALK... FOR INSTANCE, MY UNCLE...
AND NOW, THESE PRECIOUS SILKWORMS ARE OURS. WE EARNED THEM.
WHADDAYA PLANNING TO DO? I GOTTA GET BACK TO THE CASTLE.
HAND ME THE REGULAR SILKWORMS TO SUBSTITUTE THESE ONES.
COME WITH US. YOU WON'T REGRET IT. YOU'LL WITNESS SOMETHING EXTRAORDINARY!
SO...
LET'S TAKE THE LOOM UPSTAIRS. WE GOTTA GET TO WORK.
IS IT REALLY THE TIME FOR A WEAVING CLASS?

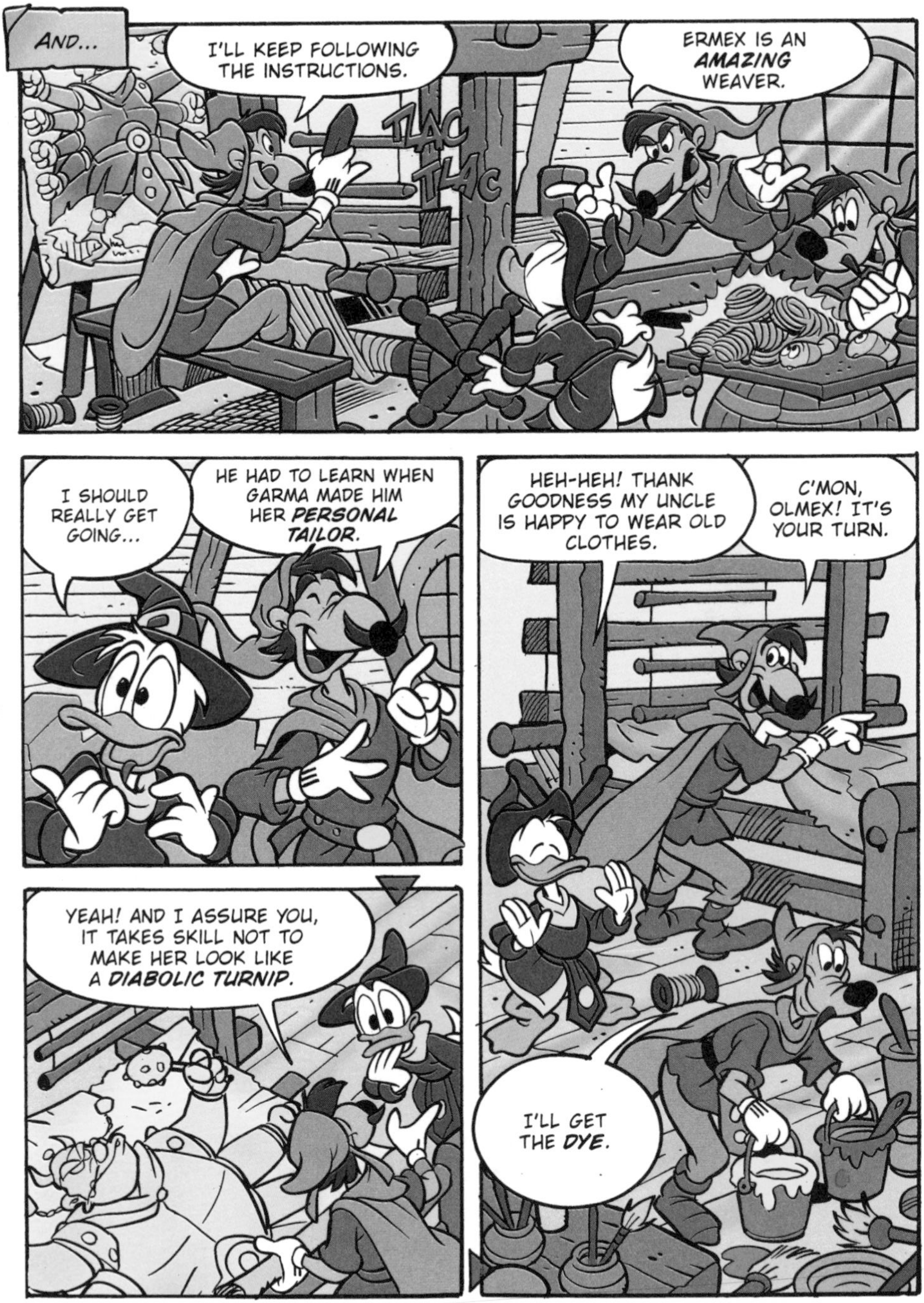
AND...
I'LL KEEP FOLLOWING THE INSTRUCTIONS.
TLAC TLAC
ERMEX IS AN AMAZING WEAVER.
I SHOULD REALLY GET GOING...
HE HAD TO LEARN WHEN GARMA MADE HIM HER PERSONAL TAILOR.
YEAH! AND I ASSURE YOU, IT TAKES SKILL NOT TO MAKE HER LOOK LIKE A DIABOLIC TURNIP.
HEH-HEH! THANK GOODNESS MY UNCLE IS HAPPY TO WEAR OLD CLOTHES.
C'MON, OLMEX! IT'S YOUR TURN.
I'LL GET THE DYE.

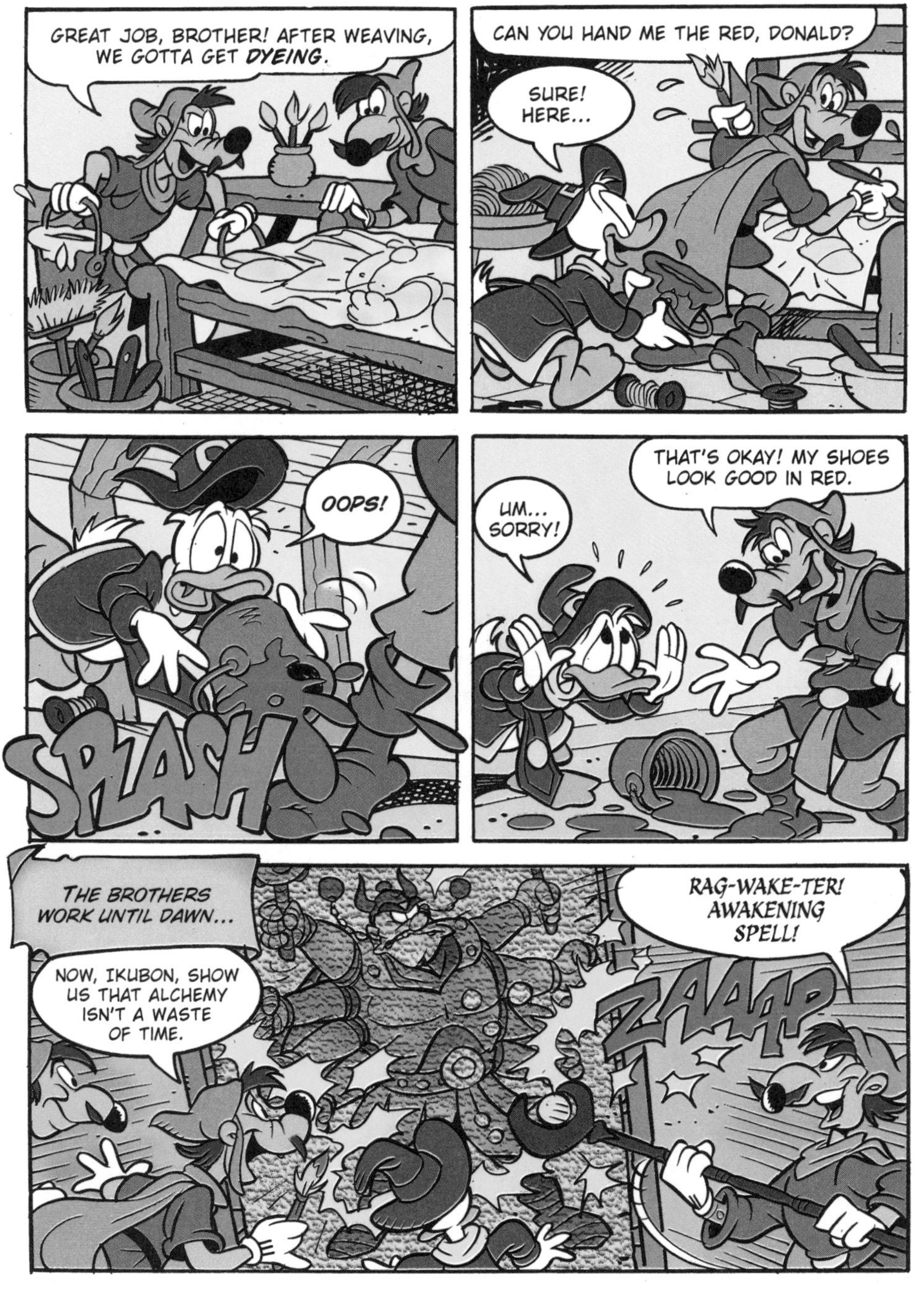
GREAT JOB, BROTHER! AFTER WEAVING, WE GOTTA GET DYEING.
CAN YOU HAND ME THE RED, DONALD?
SURE! HERE...
OOPS!
SPLASH
UM... SORRY!
THAT'S OKAY! MY SHOES LOOK GOOD IN RED.
THE BROTHERS WORK UNTIL DAWN...
NOW, IKUBON, SHOW US THAT ALCHEMY ISN'T A WASTE OF TIME.
RAG-WAKE-TER! AWAKENING SPELL!
ZAAAP

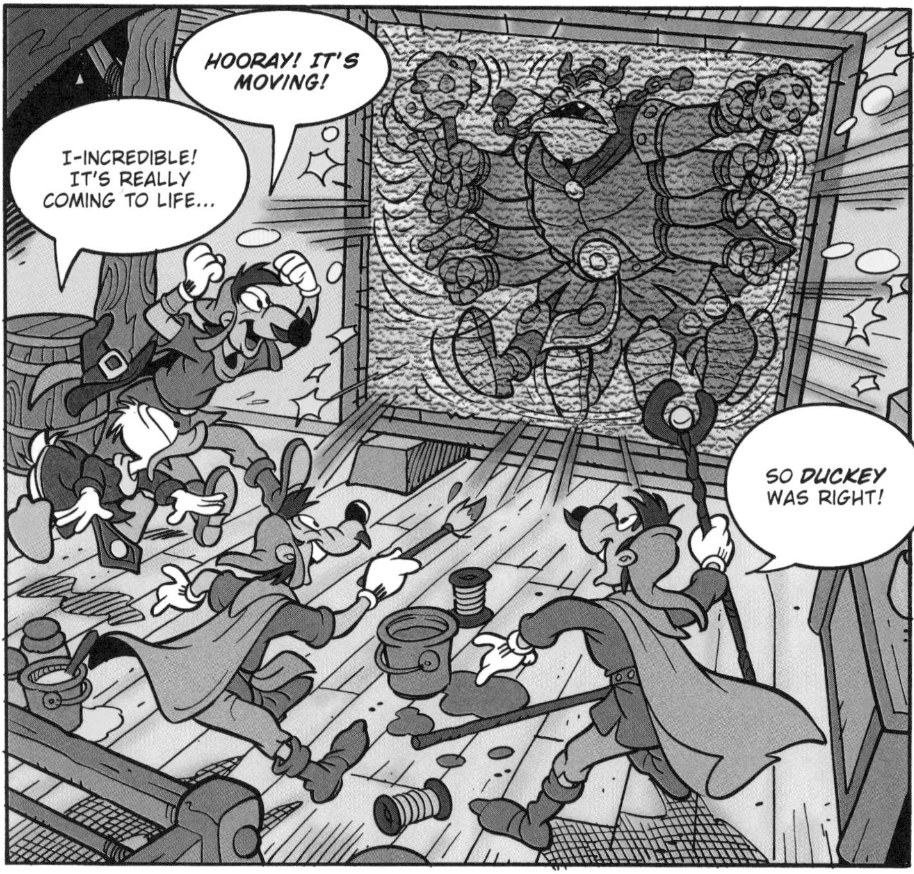
I-INCREDIBLE! IT'S REALLY COMING TO LIFE...
HOORAY! IT'S MOVING!
SO DUCKEY WAS RIGHT!

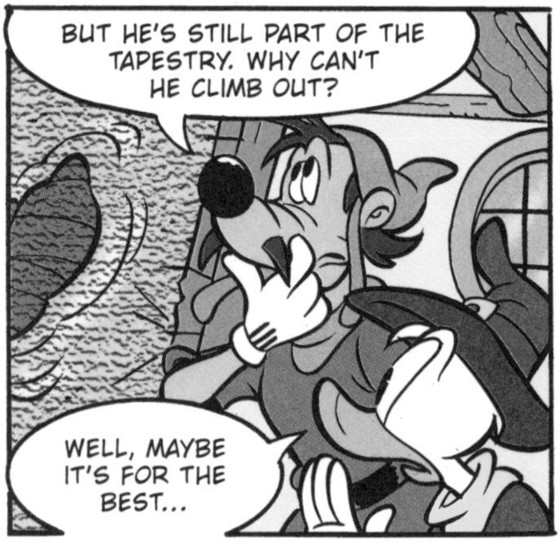
BUT HE'S STILL PART OF THE TAPESTRY. WHY CAN'T HE CLIMB OUT?
WELL, MAYBE IT'S FOR THE BEST...

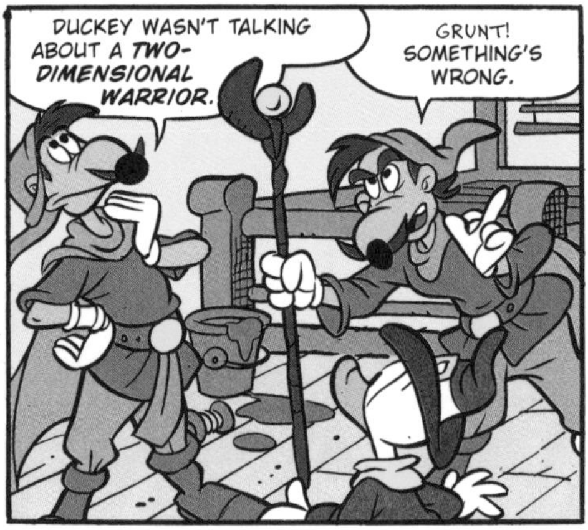
DUCKEY WASN'T TALKING ABOUT A TWO-DIMENSIONAL WARRIOR.
GRUNT! SOMETHING'S WRONG.

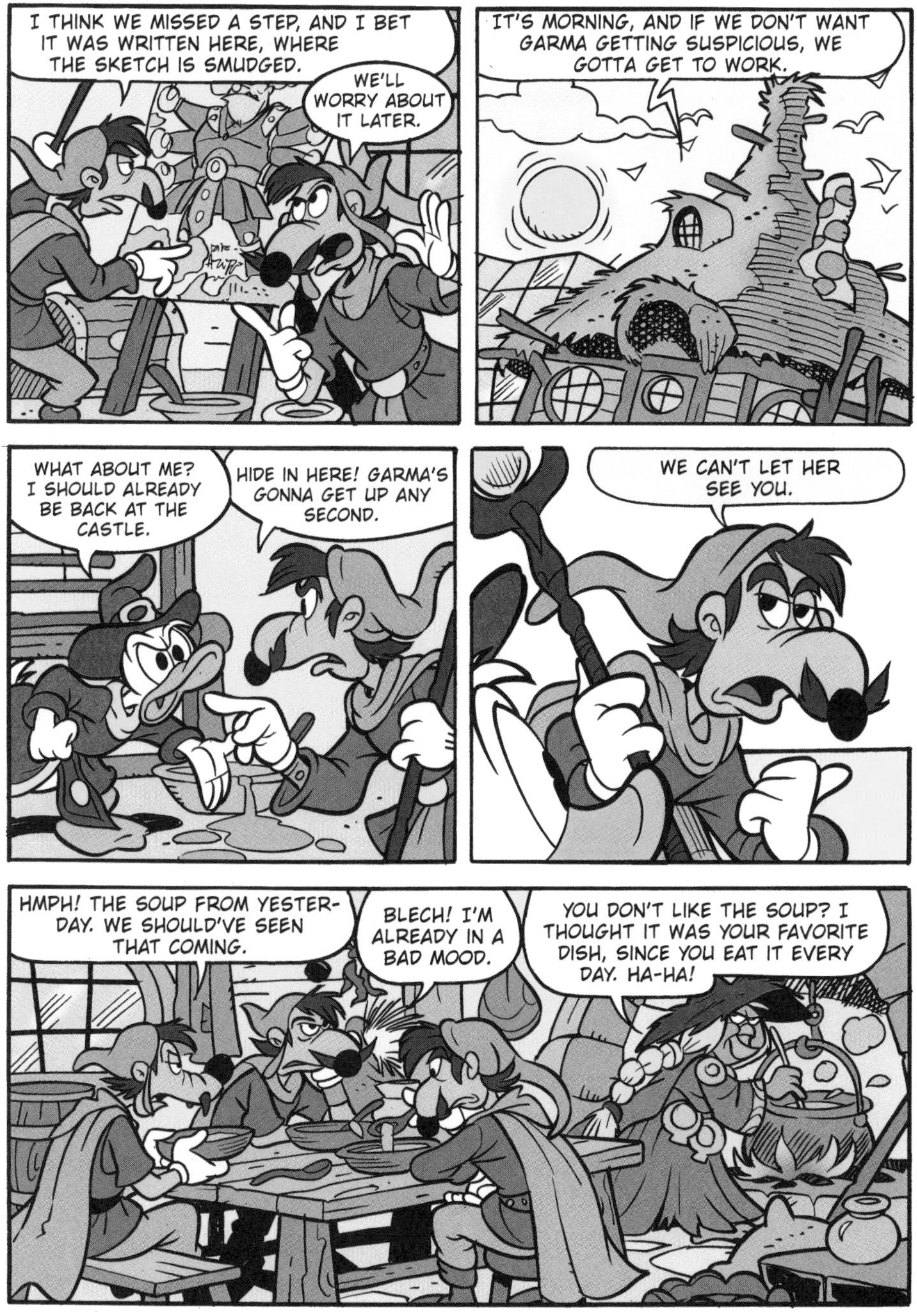
I THINK WE MISSED A STEP, AND I BET IT WAS WRITTEN HERE, WHERE THE SKETCH IS SMUDGED.
WE'LL WORRY ABOUT IT LATER.
IT'S MORNING, AND IF WE DON'T WANT GARMA GETTING SUSPICIOUS, WE GOTTA GET TO WORK.
WHAT ABOUT ME? I SHOULD ALREADY BE BACK AT THE CASTLE.
HIDE IN HERE! GARMA'S GONNA GET UP ANY SECOND.
WE CAN'T LET HER SEE YOU.
HMPH! THE SOUP FROM YESTER-DAY. WE SHOULD'VE SEEN THAT COMING.
BLECH! I'M ALREADY IN A BAD MOOD.
YOU DON'T LIKE THE SOUP? I THOUGHT IT WAS YOUR FAVORITE DISH, SINCE YOU EAT IT EVERY DAY. HA-HA!

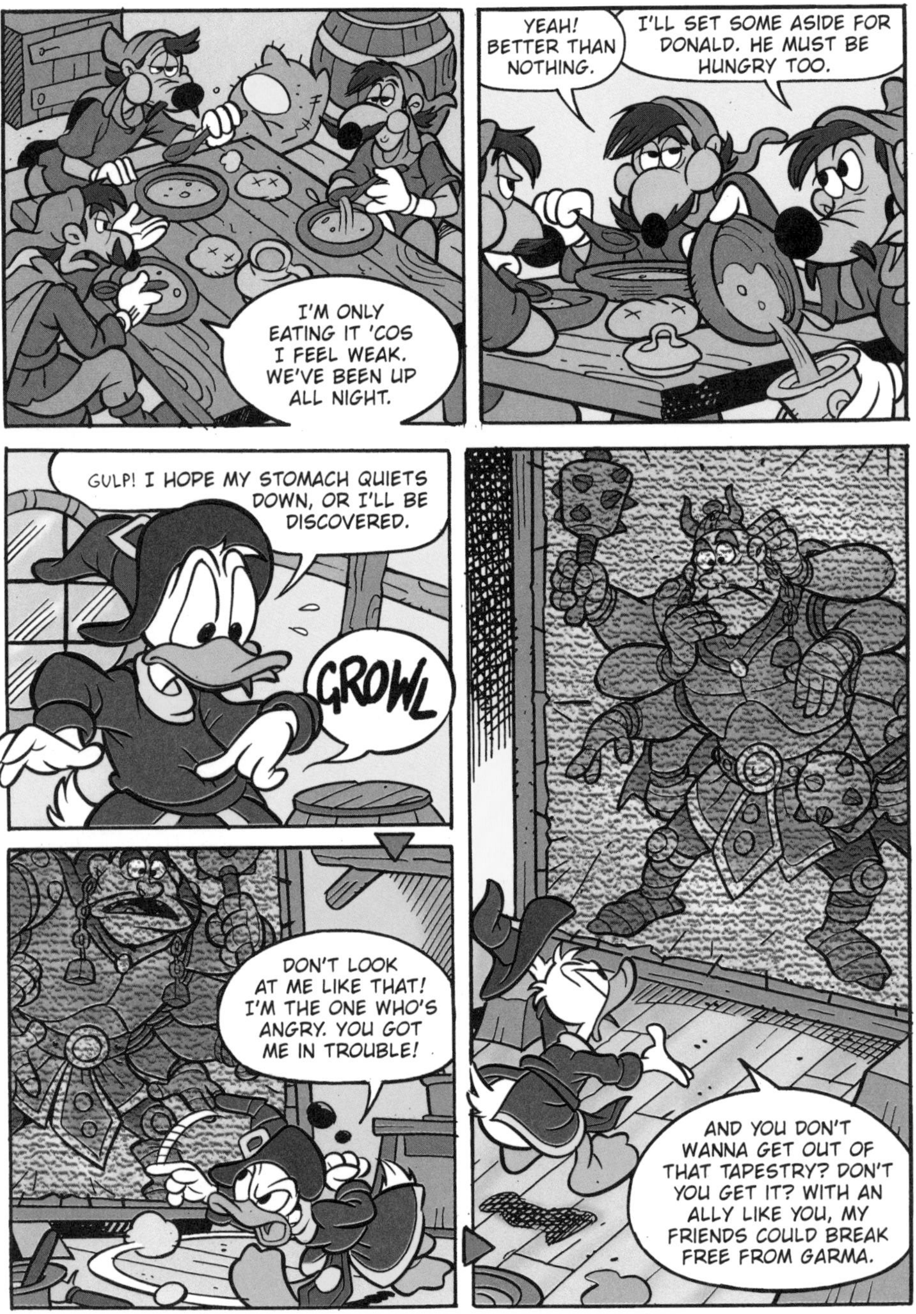
I'M ONLY EATING IT 'COS I FEEL WEAK. WE'VE BEEN UP ALL NIGHT.
YEAH! BETTER THAN NOTHING.
I'LL SET SOME ASIDE FOR DONALD. HE MUST BE HUNGRY TOO.
GULP! I HOPE MY STOMACH QUIETS DOWN, OR I'LL BE DISCOVERED.
GROWL
DON'T LOOK AT ME LIKE THAT! I'M THE ONE WHO'S ANGRY. YOU GOT ME IN TROUBLE!
AND YOU DON'T WANNA GET OUT OF THAT TAPESTRY? DON'T YOU GET IT? WITH AN ALLY LIKE YOU, MY FRIENDS COULD BREAK FREE FROM GARMA.

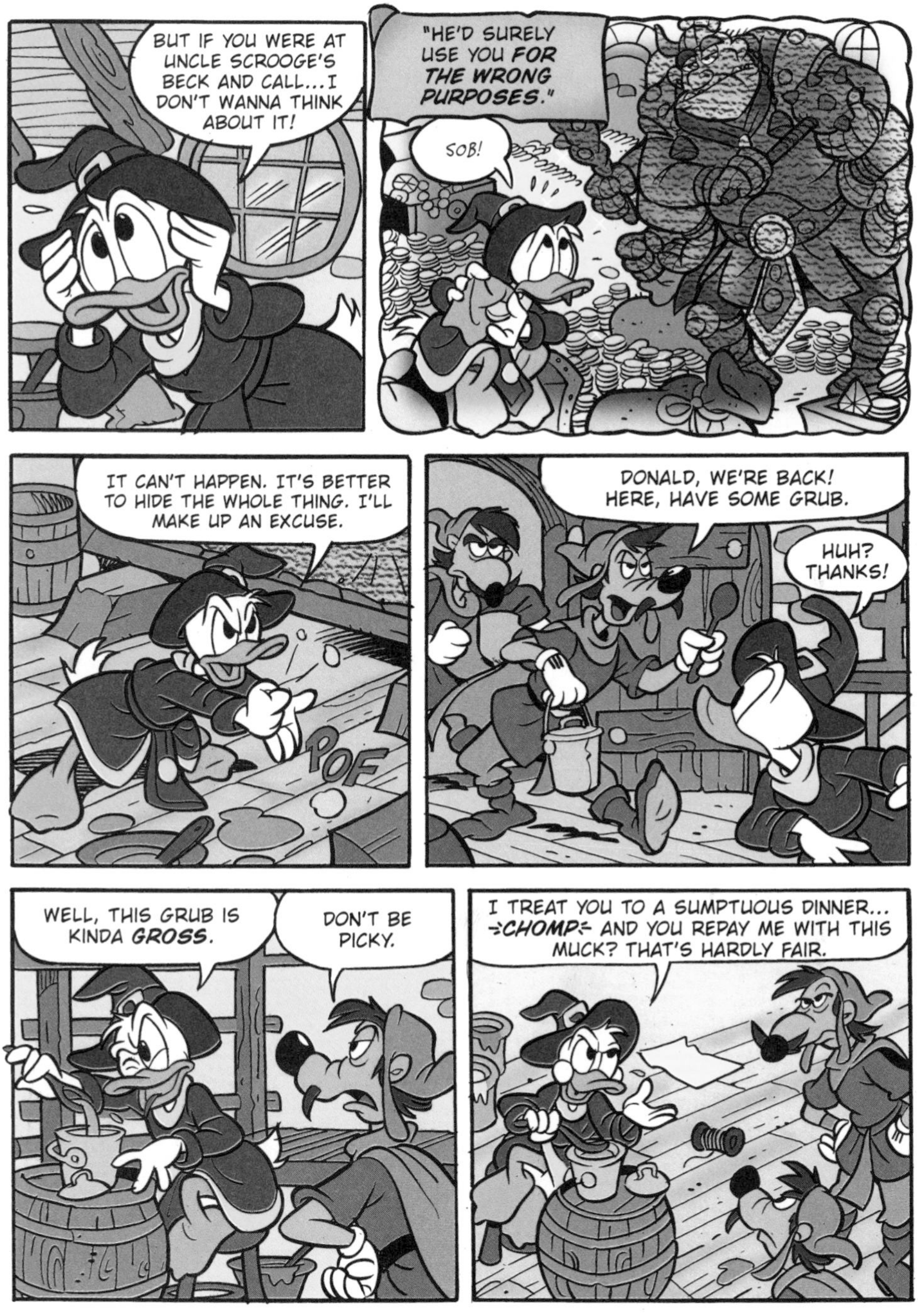
BUT IF YOU WERE AT UNCLE SCROOGE'S BECK AND CALL... I DON'T WANNA THINK ABOUT IT!
"HE'D SURELY USE YOU **FOR THE WRONG PURPOSES**."
SOB!
IT CAN'T HAPPEN. IT'S BETTER TO HIDE THE WHOLE THING. I'LL MAKE UP AN EXCUSE.
POF
DONALD, WE'RE BACK! HERE, HAVE SOME GRUB.
HUH? THANKS!
WELL, THIS GRUB IS KINDA **GROSS**.
DON'T BE PICKY.
I TREAT YOU TO A SUMPTUOUS DINNER... **CHOMP** AND YOU REPAY ME WITH THIS MUCK? THAT'S HARDLY FAIR.

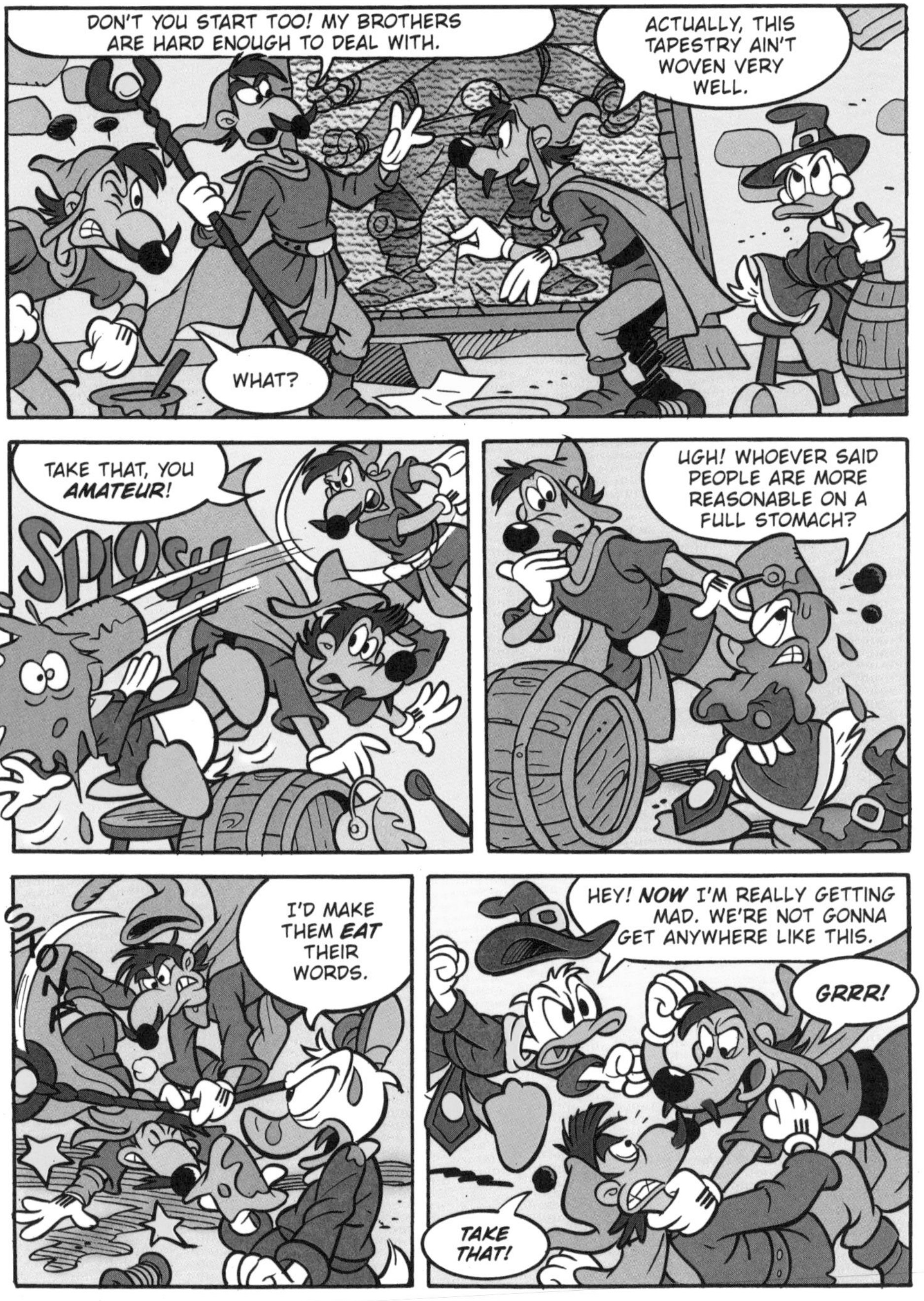

DON'T YOU START TOO! MY BROTHERS ARE HARD ENOUGH TO DEAL WITH.
ACTUALLY, THIS TAPESTRY AIN'T WOVEN VERY WELL.
WHAT?
TAKE THAT, YOU **AMATEUR**!
SPLOSH
UGH! WHOEVER SAID PEOPLE ARE MORE REASONABLE ON A FULL STOMACH?
I'D MAKE THEM **EAT** THEIR WORDS.
HEY! **NOW** I'M REALLY GETTING MAD. WE'RE NOT GONNA GET ANYWHERE LIKE THIS.
GRRR!
TAKE THAT!

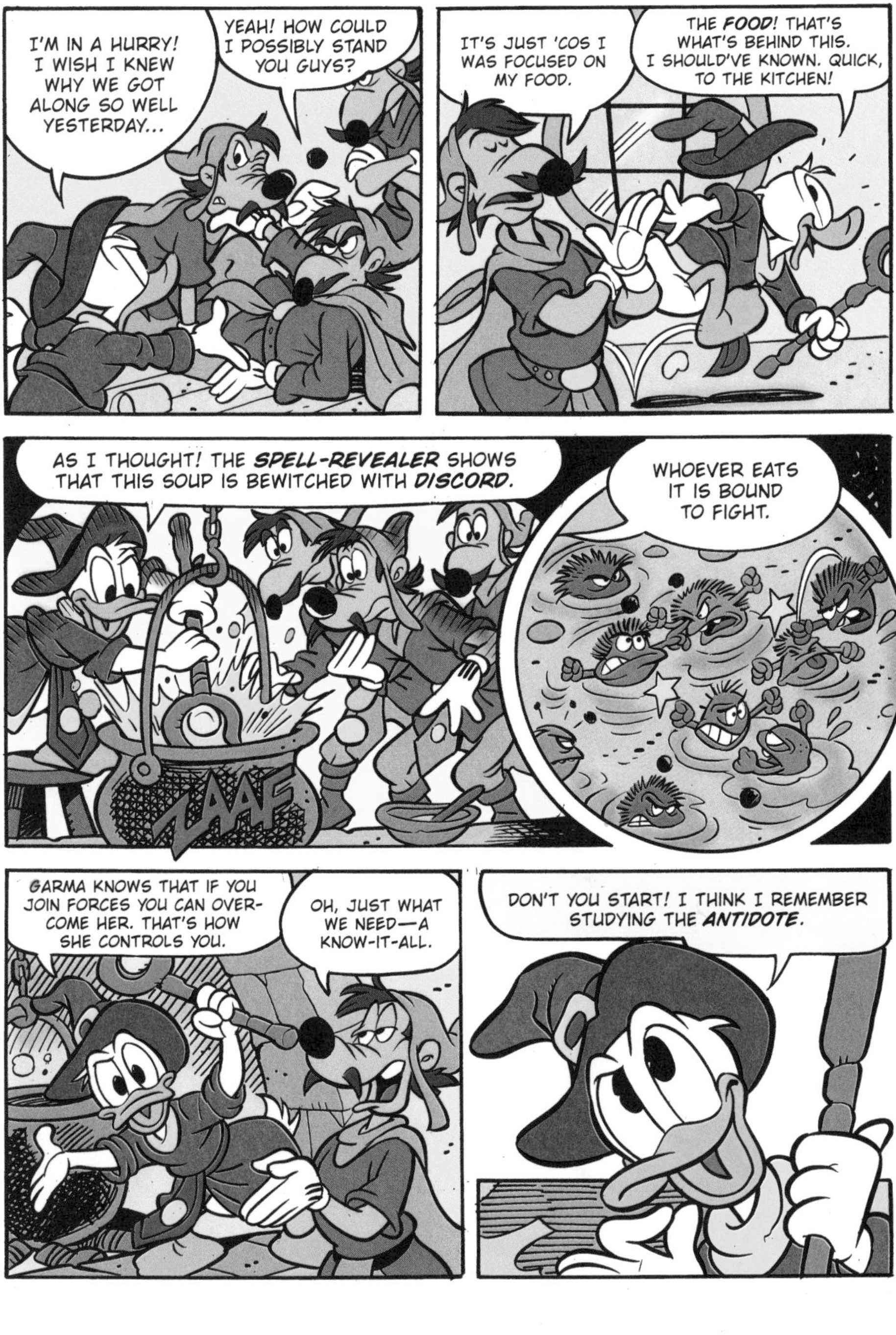

I'M IN A HURRY! I WISH I KNEW WHY WE GOT ALONG SO WELL YESTERDAY...
YEAH! HOW COULD I POSSIBLY STAND YOU GUYS?
IT'S JUST 'COS I WAS FOCUSED ON MY FOOD.
THE FOOD! THAT'S WHAT'S BEHIND THIS. I SHOULD'VE KNOWN. QUICK, TO THE KITCHEN!
AS I THOUGHT! THE SPELL-REVEALER SHOWS THAT THIS SOUP IS BEWITCHED WITH DISCORD.
WHOEVER EATS IT IS BOUND TO FIGHT.
ZAAF
GARMA KNOWS THAT IF YOU JOIN FORCES YOU CAN OVERCOME HER. THAT'S HOW SHE CONTROLS YOU.
OH, JUST WHAT WE NEED—A KNOW-IT-ALL.
DON'T YOU START! I THINK I REMEMBER STUDYING THE ANTIDOTE.

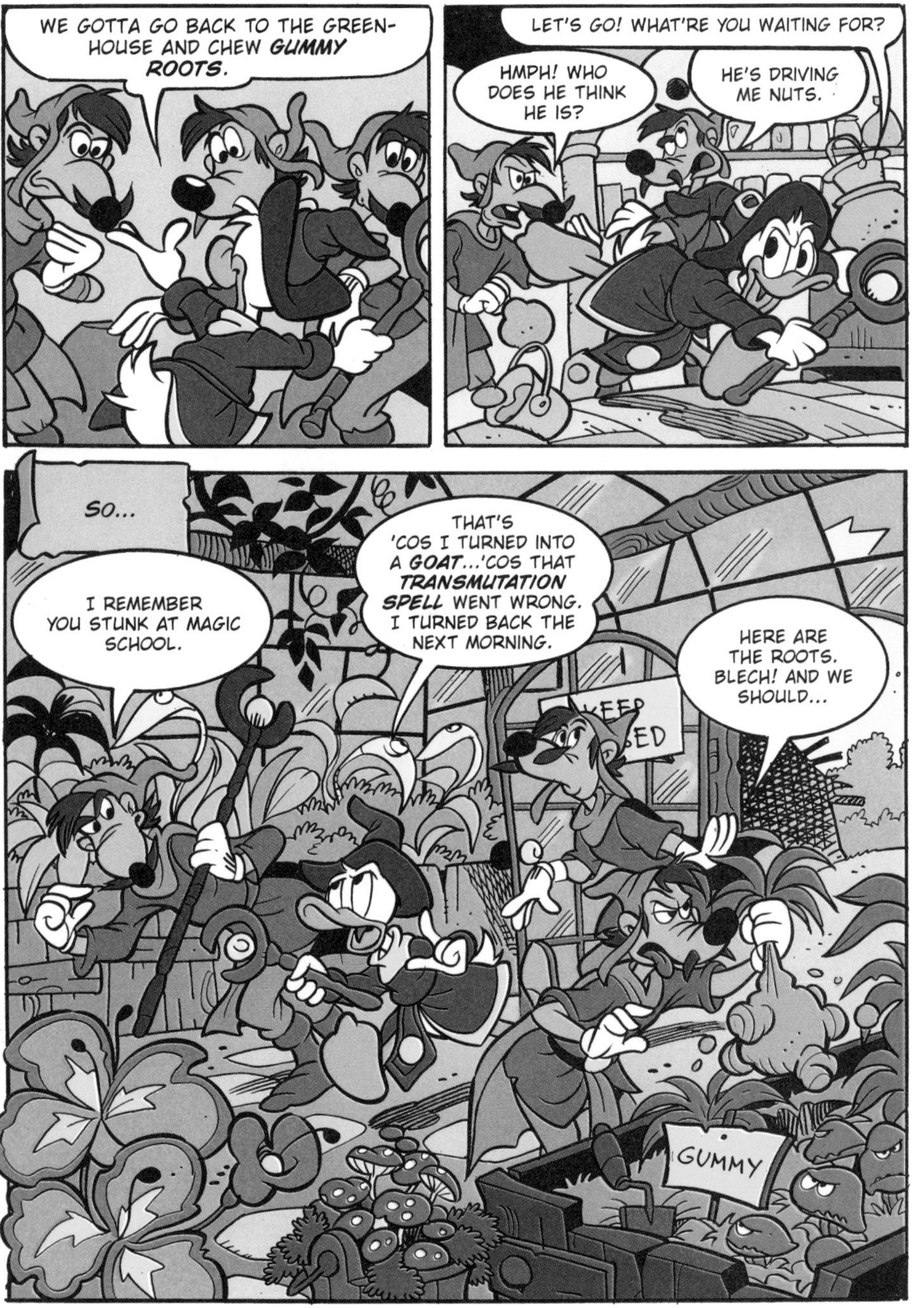
WE GOTTA GO BACK TO THE GREEN-HOUSE AND CHEW GUMMY ROOTS.
LET'S GO! WHAT'RE YOU WAITING FOR?
HMPH! WHO DOES HE THINK HE IS?
HE'S DRIVING ME NUTS.
SO...
I REMEMBER YOU STUNK AT MAGIC SCHOOL.
THAT'S 'COS I TURNED INTO A GOAT...'COS THAT TRANSMUTATION SPELL WENT WRONG. I TURNED BACK THE NEXT MORNING.
HERE ARE THE ROOTS. BLECH! AND WE SHOULD...
GUMMY

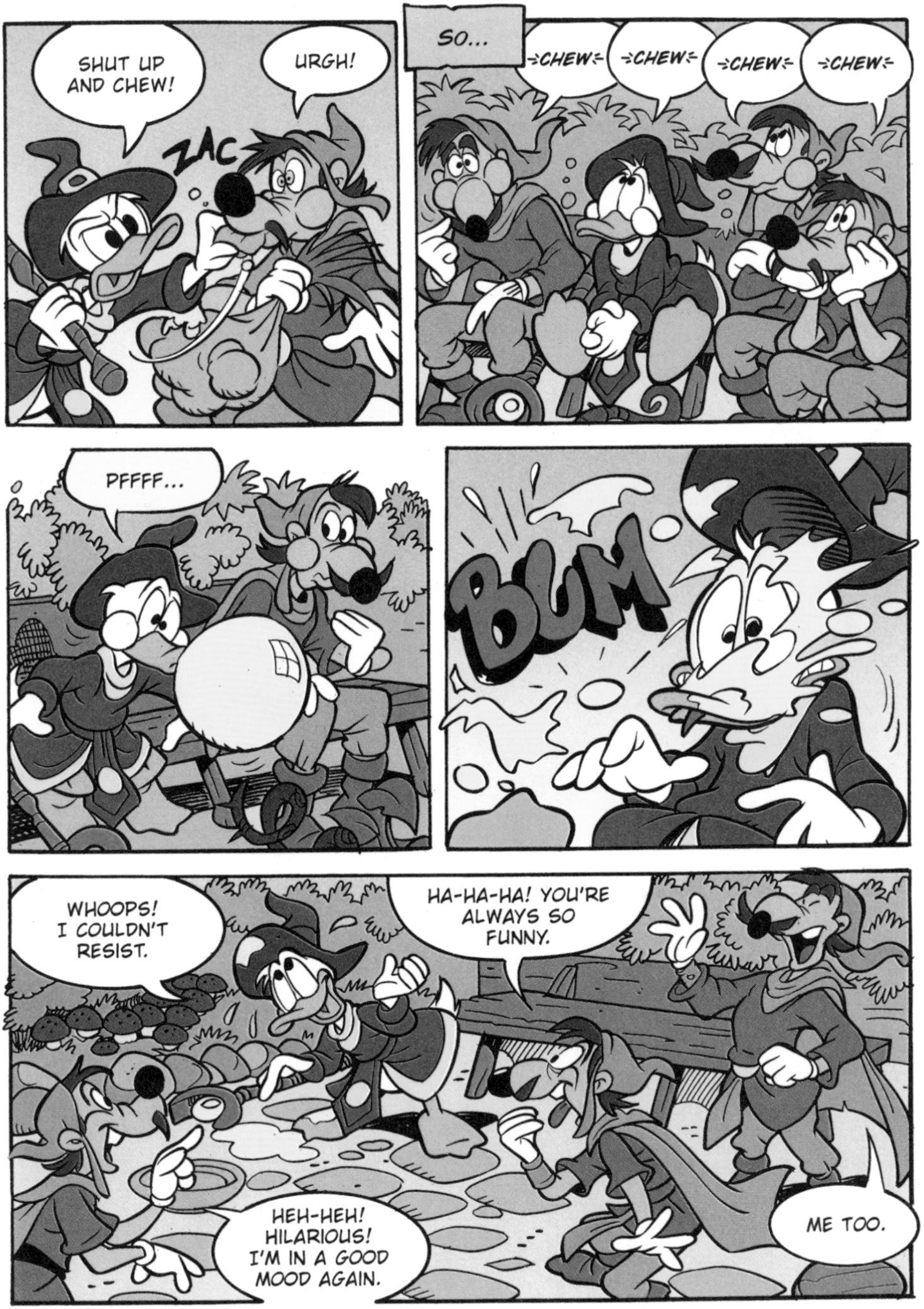
SHUT UP AND CHEW!
ZAC
URGH!
SO...
CHEW
CHEW
CHEW
CHEW
PFFFF...
BUM
WHOOPS! I COULDN'T RESIST.
HA-HA-HA! YOU'RE ALWAYS SO FUNNY.
HEH-HEH! HILARIOUS! I'M IN A GOOD MOOD AGAIN.
ME TOO.

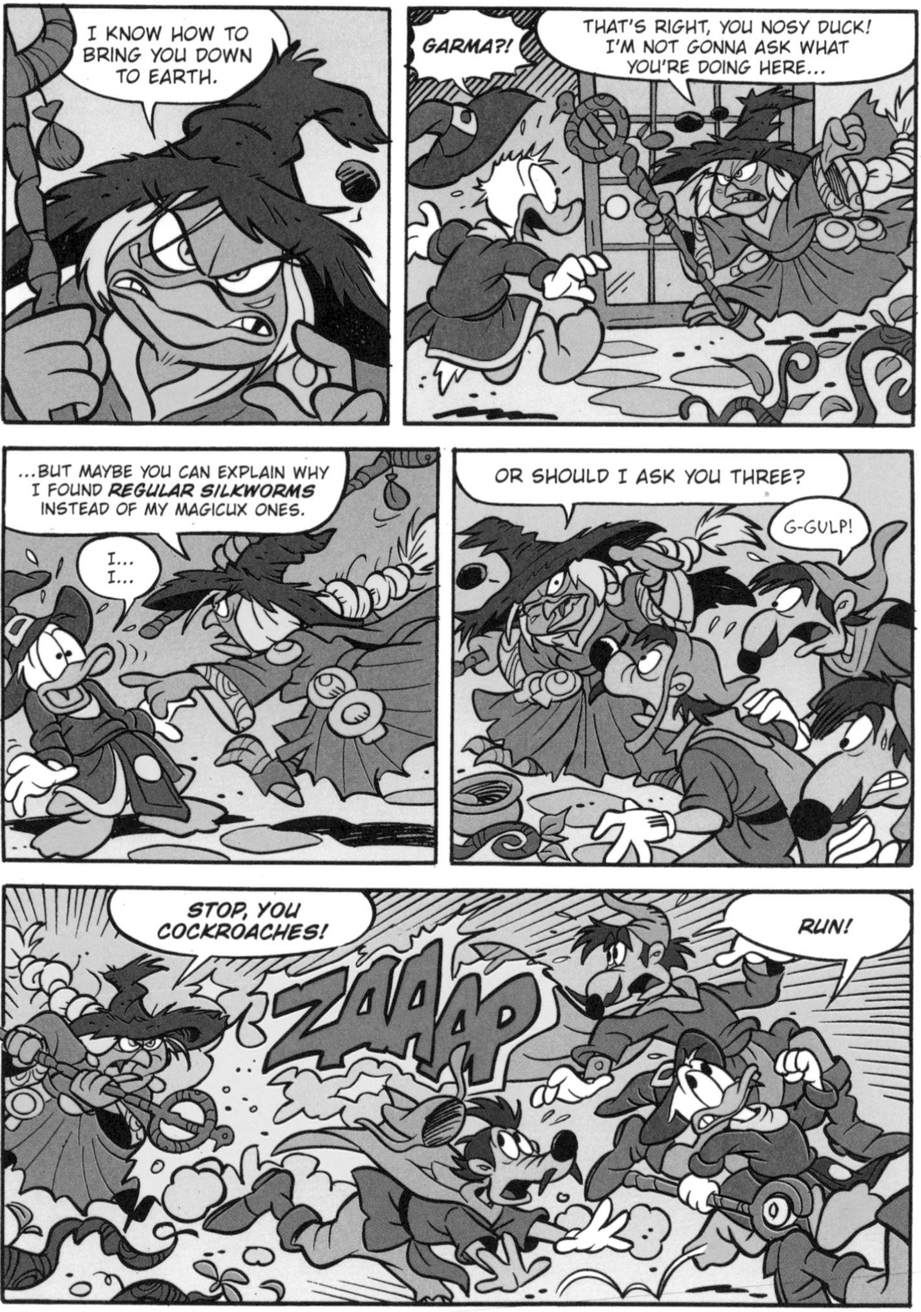
I KNOW HOW TO BRING YOU DOWN TO EARTH.
GARMA?!
THAT'S RIGHT, YOU NOSY DUCK! I'M NOT GONNA ASK WHAT YOU'RE DOING HERE...
...BUT MAYBE YOU CAN EXPLAIN WHY I FOUND **REGULAR SILKWORMS** INSTEAD OF MY MAGICUX ONES.
I... I...
OR SHOULD I ASK YOU THREE?
G-GULP!
STOP, YOU COCKROACHES!
ZAAAP
RUN!

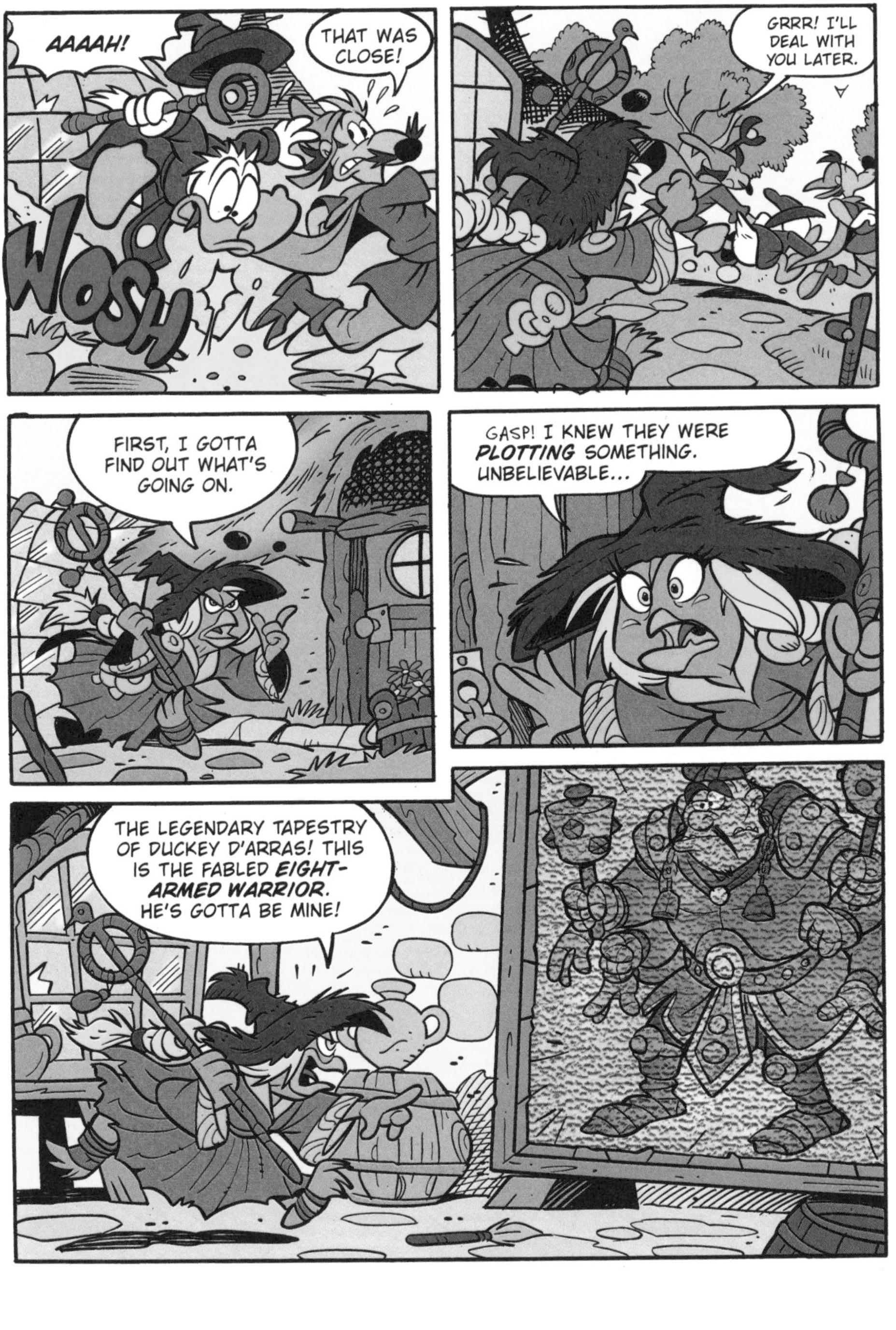
AAAAH!
THAT WAS CLOSE!
WOSH
GRRR! I'LL DEAL WITH YOU LATER.
FIRST, I GOTTA FIND OUT WHAT'S GOING ON.
GASP! I KNEW THEY WERE PLOTTING SOMETHING. UNBELIEVABLE...
THE LEGENDARY TAPESTRY OF DUCKEY D'ARRAS! THIS IS THE FABLED EIGHT-ARMED WARRIOR. HE'S GOTTA BE MINE!

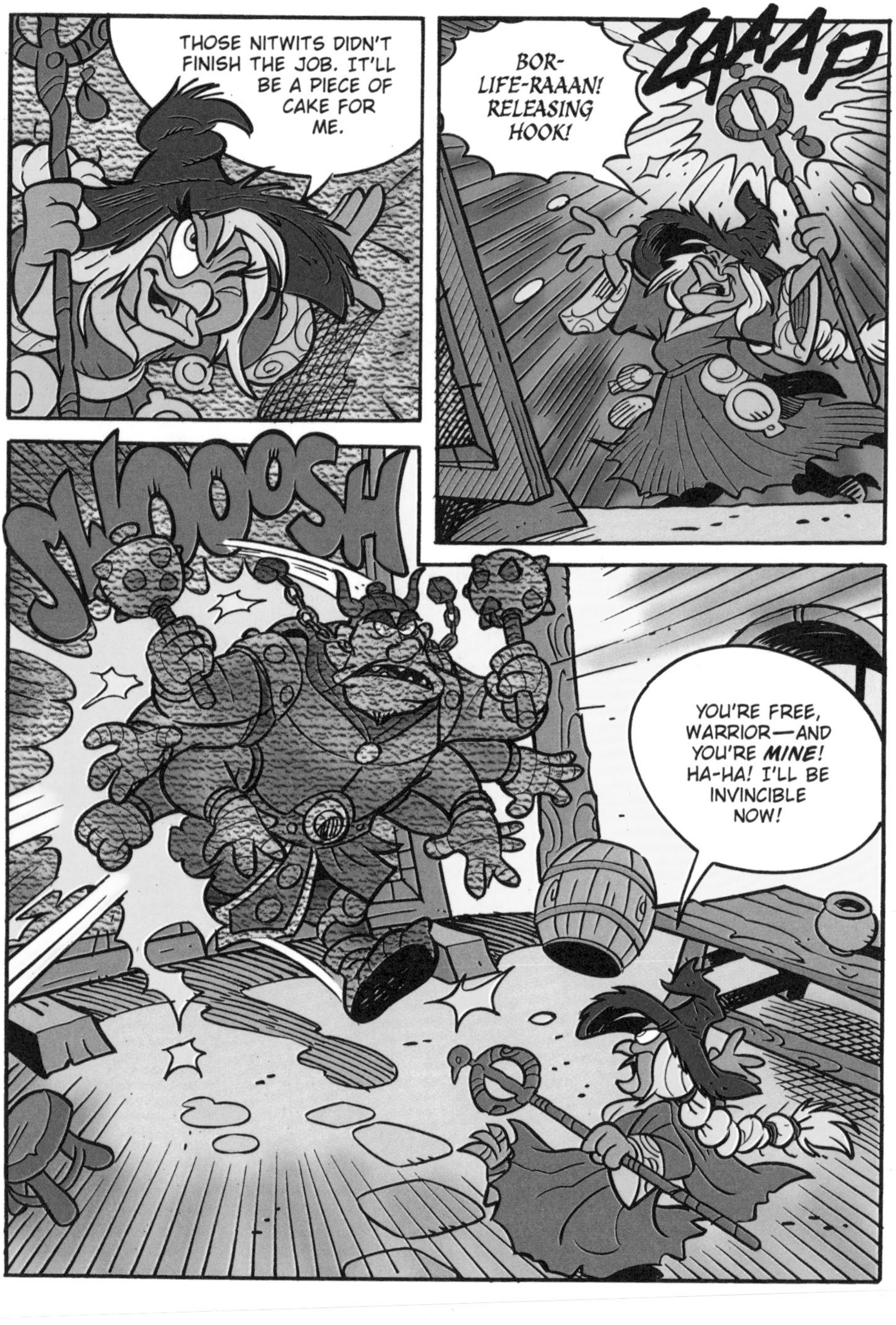
THOSE NITWITS DIDN'T FINISH THE JOB. IT'LL BE A PIECE OF CAKE FOR ME.
ZAAAP
BOR-LIFE-RAAAN! RELEASING HOOK!
SWOOOSH
YOU'RE FREE, WARRIOR—AND YOU'RE *MINE*! HA-HA! I'LL BE INVINCIBLE NOW!

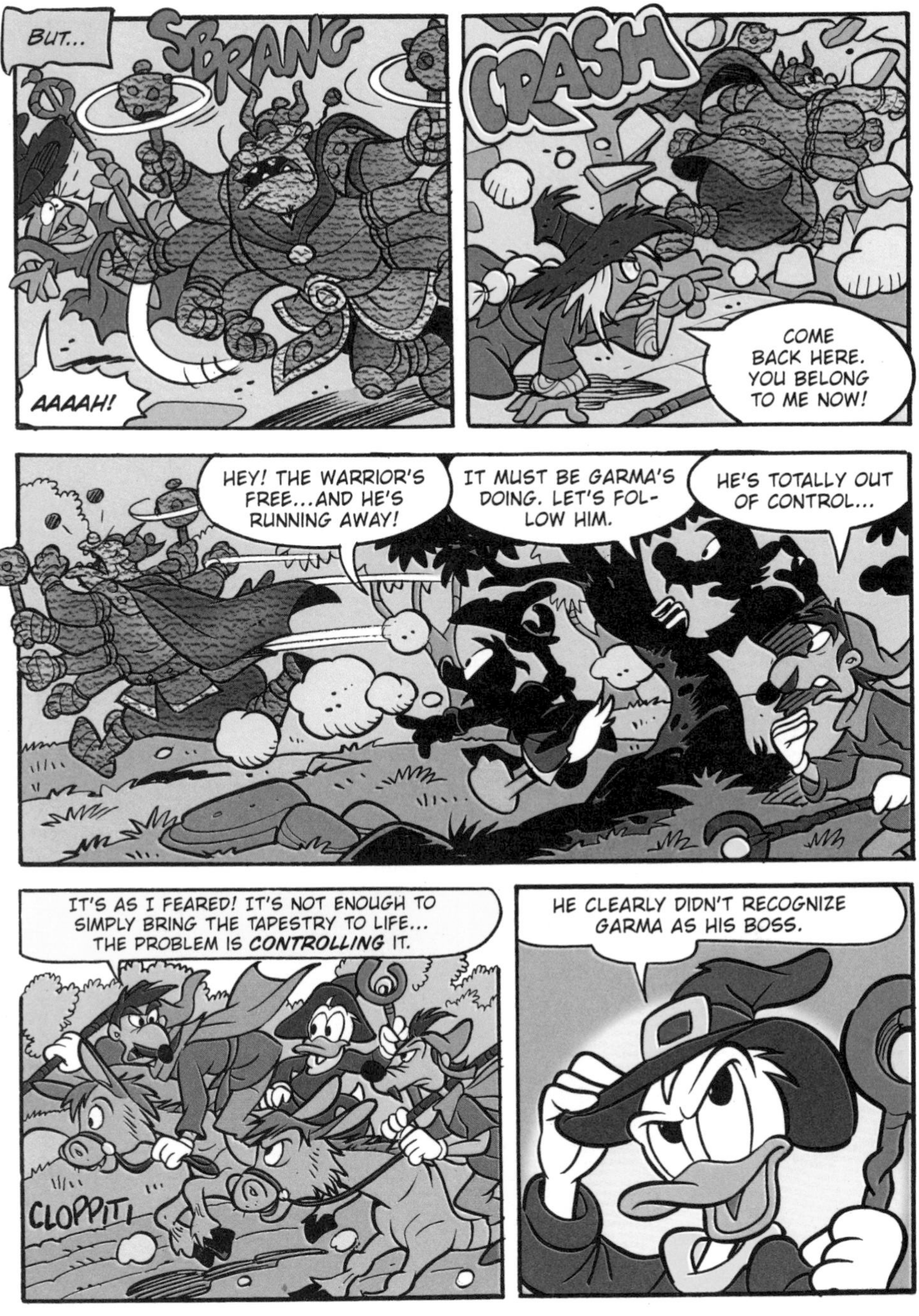
BUT...
SBRANG
AAAAH!
CRASH
COME BACK HERE. YOU BELONG TO ME NOW!
HEY! THE WARRIOR'S FREE...AND HE'S RUNNING AWAY!
IT MUST BE GARMA'S DOING. LET'S FOLLOW HIM.
HE'S TOTALLY OUT OF CONTROL...
IT'S AS I FEARED! IT'S NOT ENOUGH TO SIMPLY BRING THE TAPESTRY TO LIFE... THE PROBLEM IS CONTROLLING IT.
CLOPPITI
HE CLEARLY DIDN'T RECOGNIZE GARMA AS HIS BOSS.

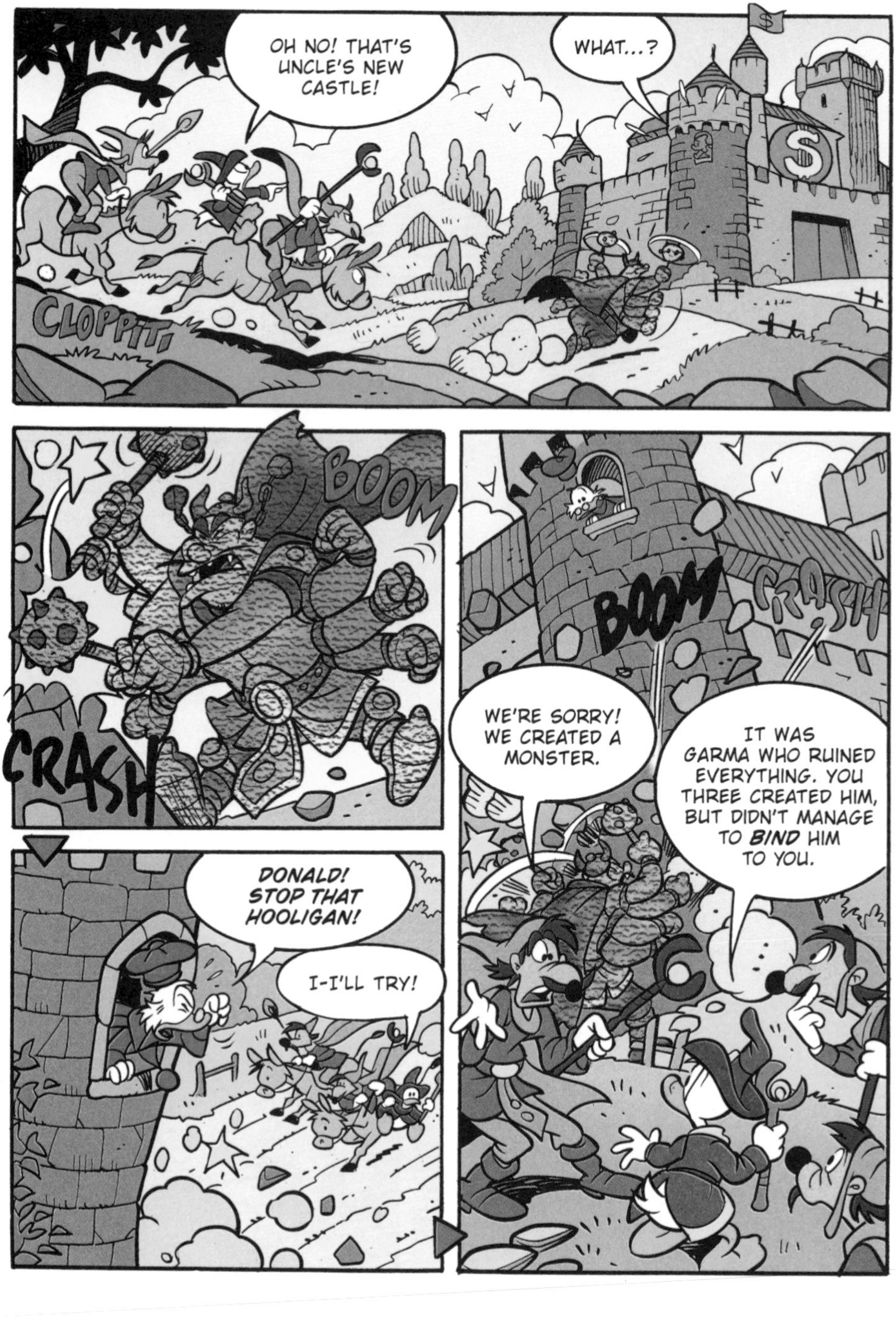
OH NO! THAT'S UNCLE'S NEW CASTLE!
WHAT...?
CLOPPITI
BOOM
CRASH
BOOM
CRASH
DONALD! STOP THAT HOOLIGAN!
I-I'LL TRY!
WE'RE SORRY! WE CREATED A MONSTER.
IT WAS GARMA WHO RUINED EVERYTHING. YOU THREE CREATED HIM, BUT DIDN'T MANAGE TO BIND HIM TO YOU.

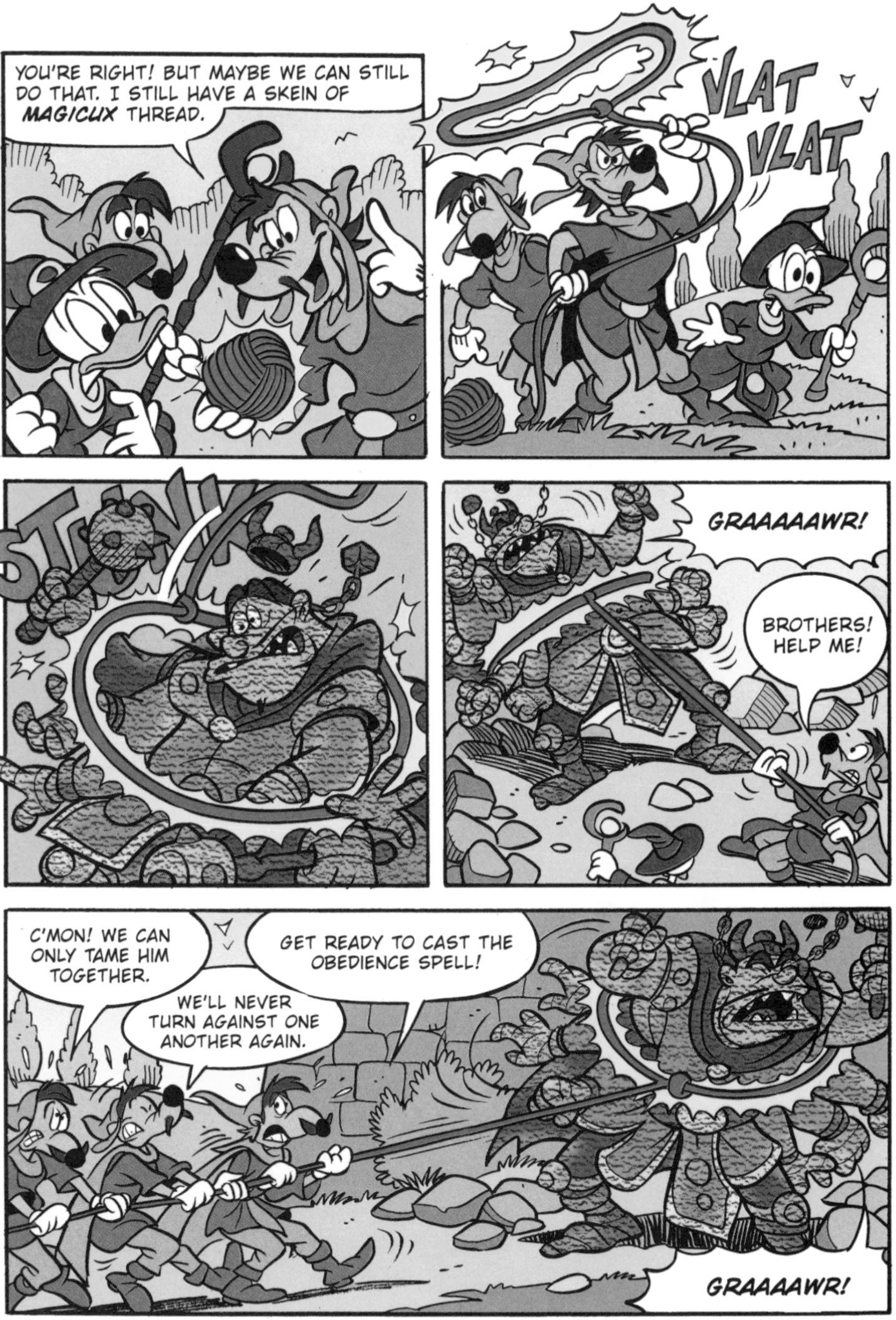

YOU'RE RIGHT! BUT MAYBE WE CAN STILL DO THAT. I STILL HAVE A SKEIN OF MAGICUX THREAD.
VLAT
VLAT
ST
GRAAAAAWR!
BROTHERS! HELP ME!
C'MON! WE CAN ONLY TAME HIM TOGETHER.
GET READY TO CAST THE OBEDIENCE SPELL!
WE'LL NEVER TURN AGAINST ONE ANOTHER AGAIN.
GRAAAAWR!

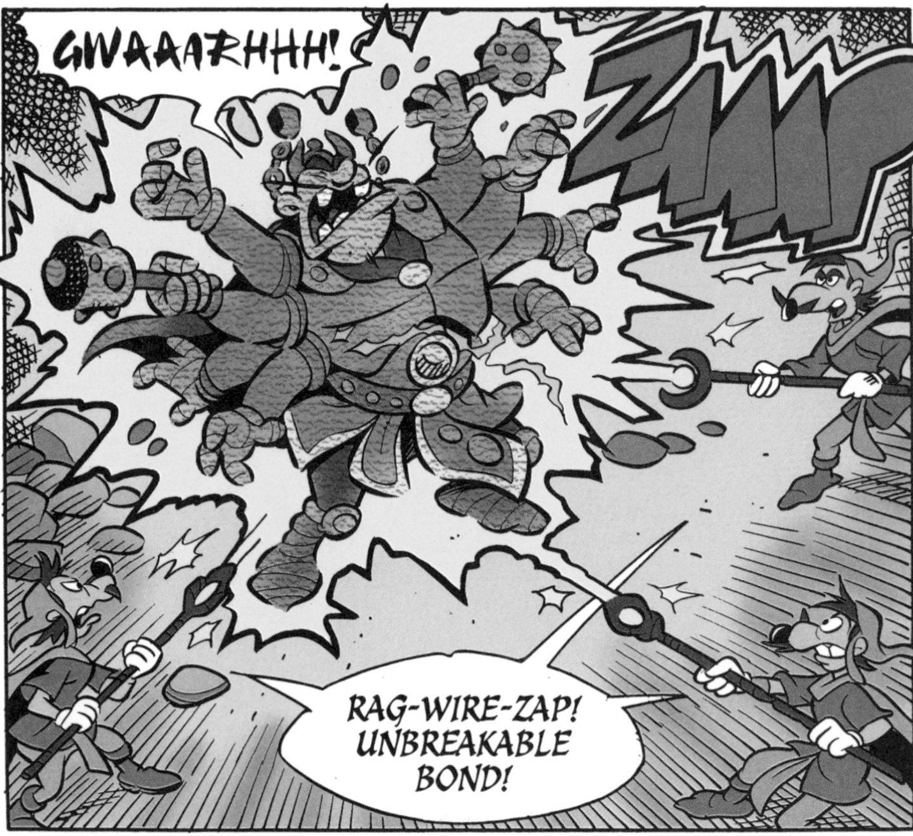
GWAAARHHH!
ZAAAP
RAG-WIRE-ZAP! UNBREAKABLE BOND!

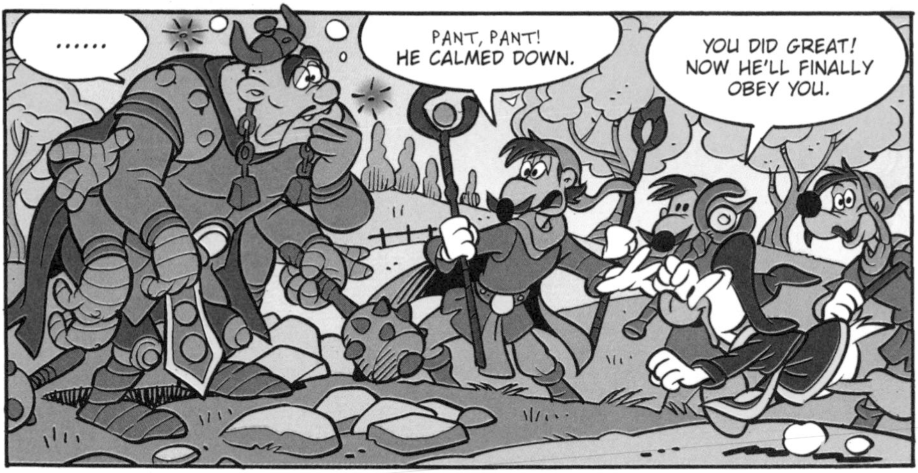
......
PANT, PANT! HE CALMED DOWN.
YOU DID GREAT! NOW HE'LL FINALLY OBEY YOU.

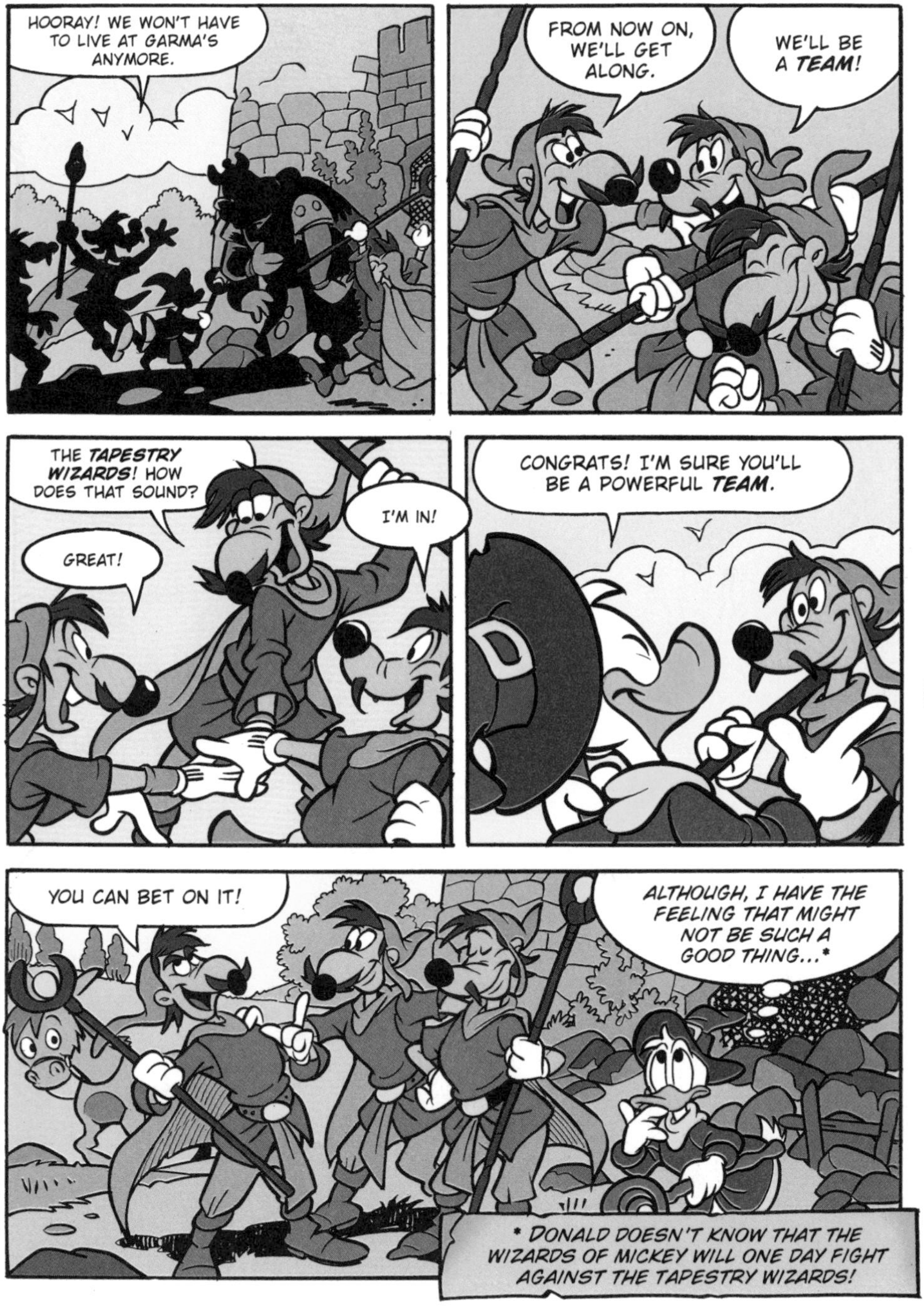
HOORAY! WE WON'T HAVE TO LIVE AT GARMA'S ANYMORE.
FROM NOW ON, WE'LL GET ALONG.
WE'LL BE A TEAM!
THE TAPESTRY WIZARDS! HOW DOES THAT SOUND?
GREAT!
I'M IN!
CONGRATS! I'M SURE YOU'LL BE A POWERFUL TEAM.
YOU CAN BET ON IT!
ALTHOUGH, I HAVE THE FEELING THAT MIGHT NOT BE SUCH A GOOD THING...*
* DONALD DOESN'T KNOW THAT THE WIZARDS OF MICKEY WILL ONE DAY FIGHT AGAINST THE TAPESTRY WIZARDS!

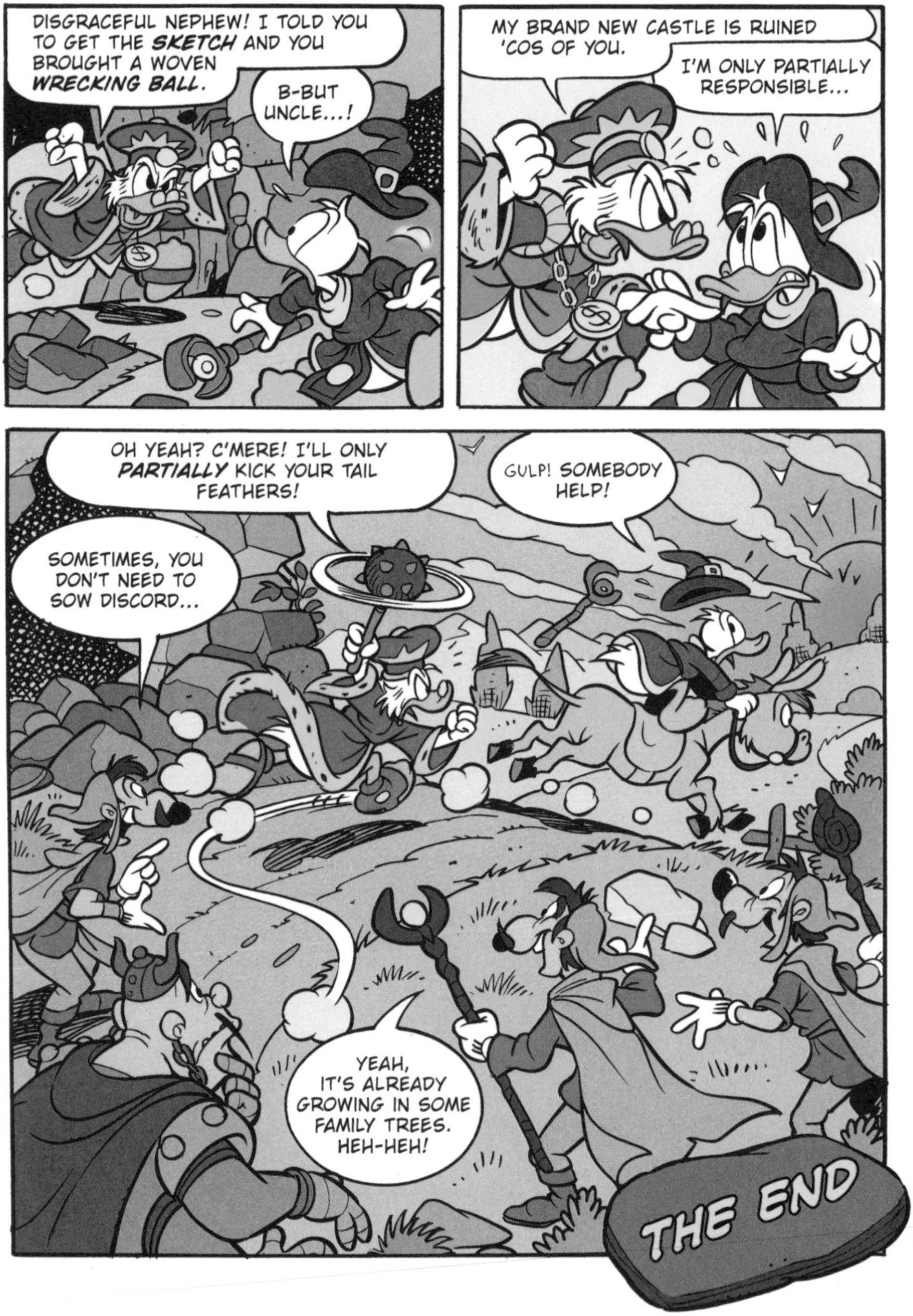
DISGRACEFUL NEPHEW! I TOLD YOU TO GET THE SKETCH AND YOU BROUGHT A WOVEN WRECKING BALL.
B-BUT UNCLE...!
MY BRAND NEW CASTLE IS RUINED 'COS OF YOU.
I'M ONLY PARTIALLY RESPONSIBLE...
OH YEAH? C'MERE! I'LL ONLY PARTIALLY KICK YOUR TAIL FEATHERS!
GULP! SOMEBODY HELP!
SOMETIMES, YOU DON'T NEED TO SOW DISCORD...
YEAH, IT'S ALREADY GROWING IN SOME FAMILY TREES. HEH-HEH!
THE END

Wizards of Mickey

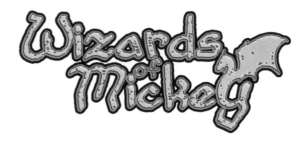

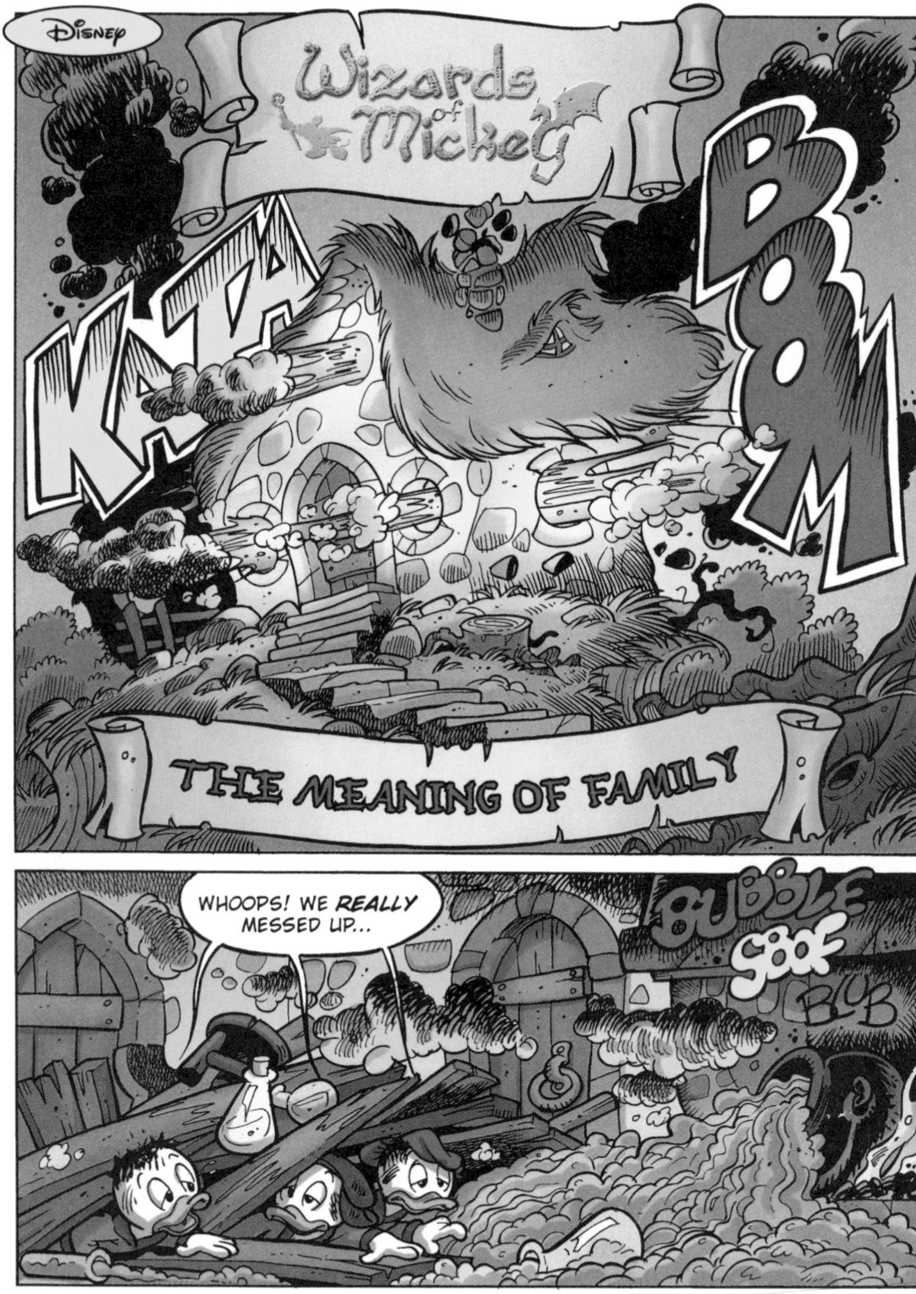
DISNEY
Wizards of Mickey
KA
BOOM
THE MEANING OF FAMILY
WHOOPS! WE *REALLY* MESSED UP...
BUBBLE
BLOB

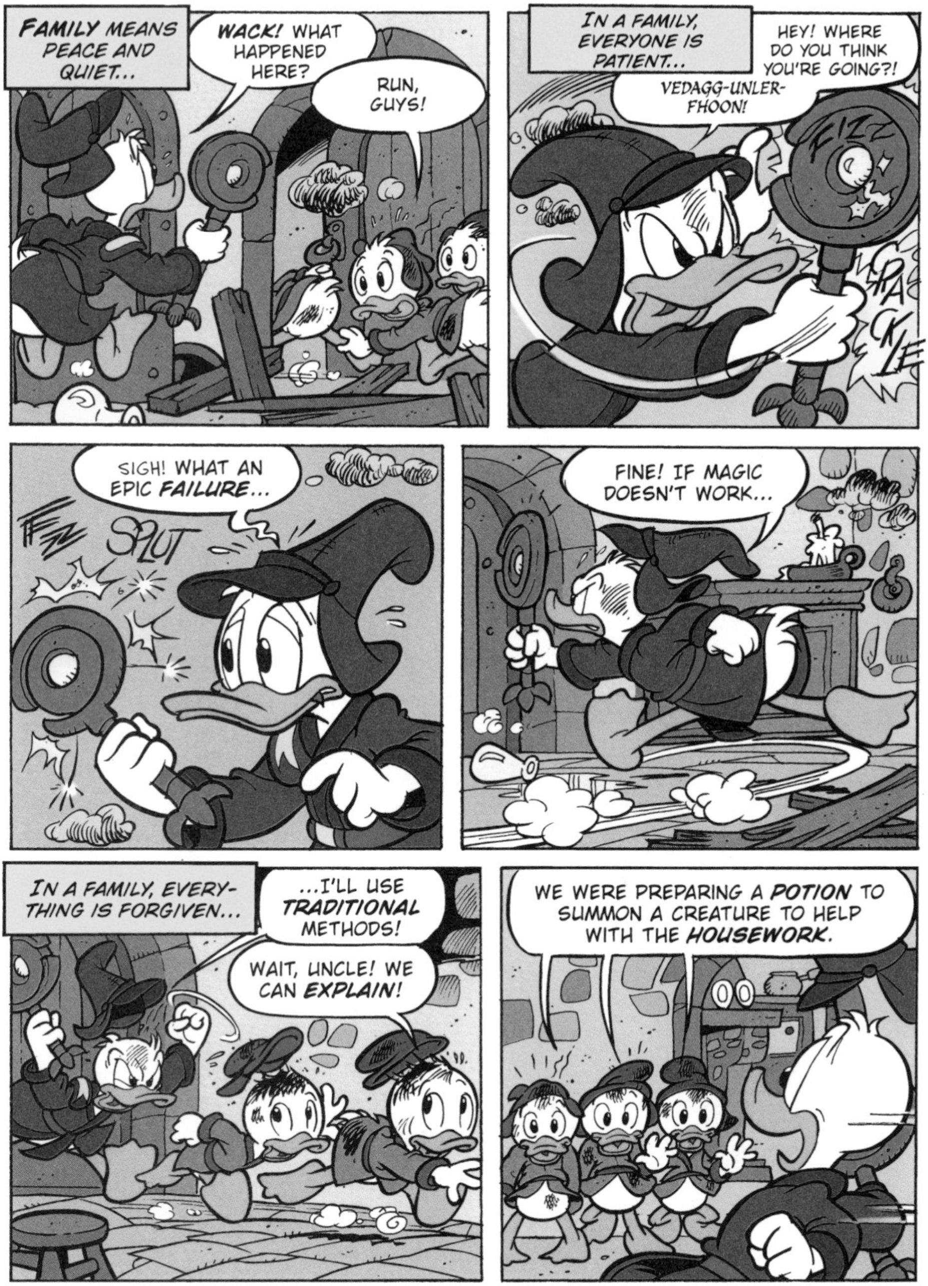
FAMILY MEANS PEACE AND QUIET...
WACK! WHAT HAPPENED HERE?
RUN, GUYS!
IN A FAMILY, EVERYONE IS PATIENT...
HEY! WHERE DO YOU THINK YOU'RE GOING?!
VEDAGG-UNLER-FHOON!
FIZZ
CRACKLE
SIGH! WHAT AN EPIC FAILURE...
SPLUT
FINE! IF MAGIC DOESN'T WORK...
IN A FAMILY, EVERYTHING IS FORGIVEN...
...I'LL USE TRADITIONAL METHODS!
WAIT, UNCLE! WE CAN EXPLAIN!
WE WERE PREPARING A POTION TO SUMMON A CREATURE TO HELP WITH THE HOUSEWORK.

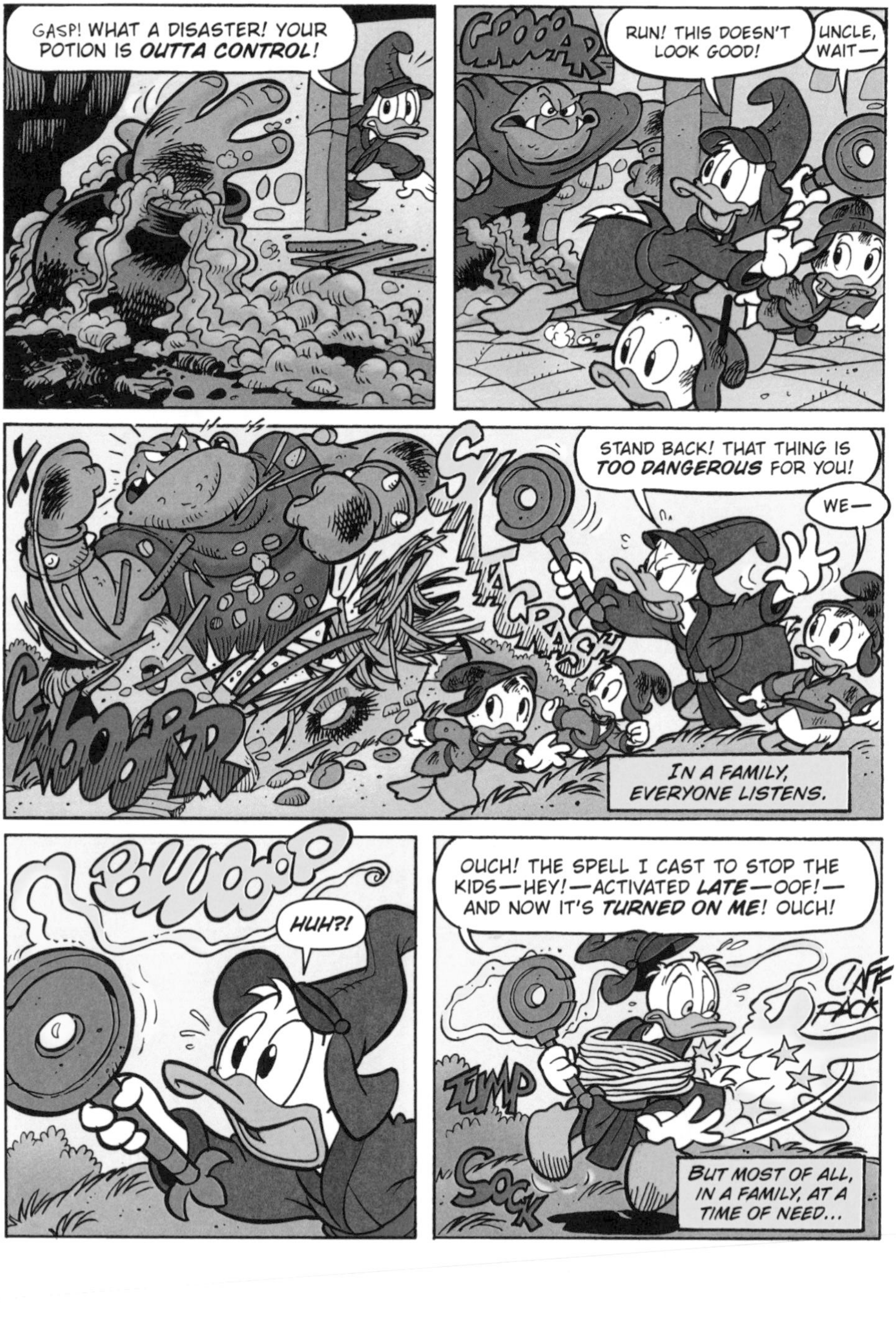
GASP! WHAT A DISASTER! YOUR POTION IS ***OUTTA CONTROL***!
RUN! THIS DOESN'T LOOK GOOD!
UNCLE, WAIT—
STAND BACK! THAT THING IS ***TOO DANGEROUS*** FOR YOU!
WE—
IN A FAMILY, EVERYONE LISTENS.
HUH?!
OUCH! THE SPELL I CAST TO STOP THE KIDS—HEY!—ACTIVATED ***LATE***—OOF!—AND NOW IT'S ***TURNED ON ME***! OUCH!
TUMP
SOCK
BUT MOST OF ALL, IN A FAMILY, AT A TIME OF NEED...

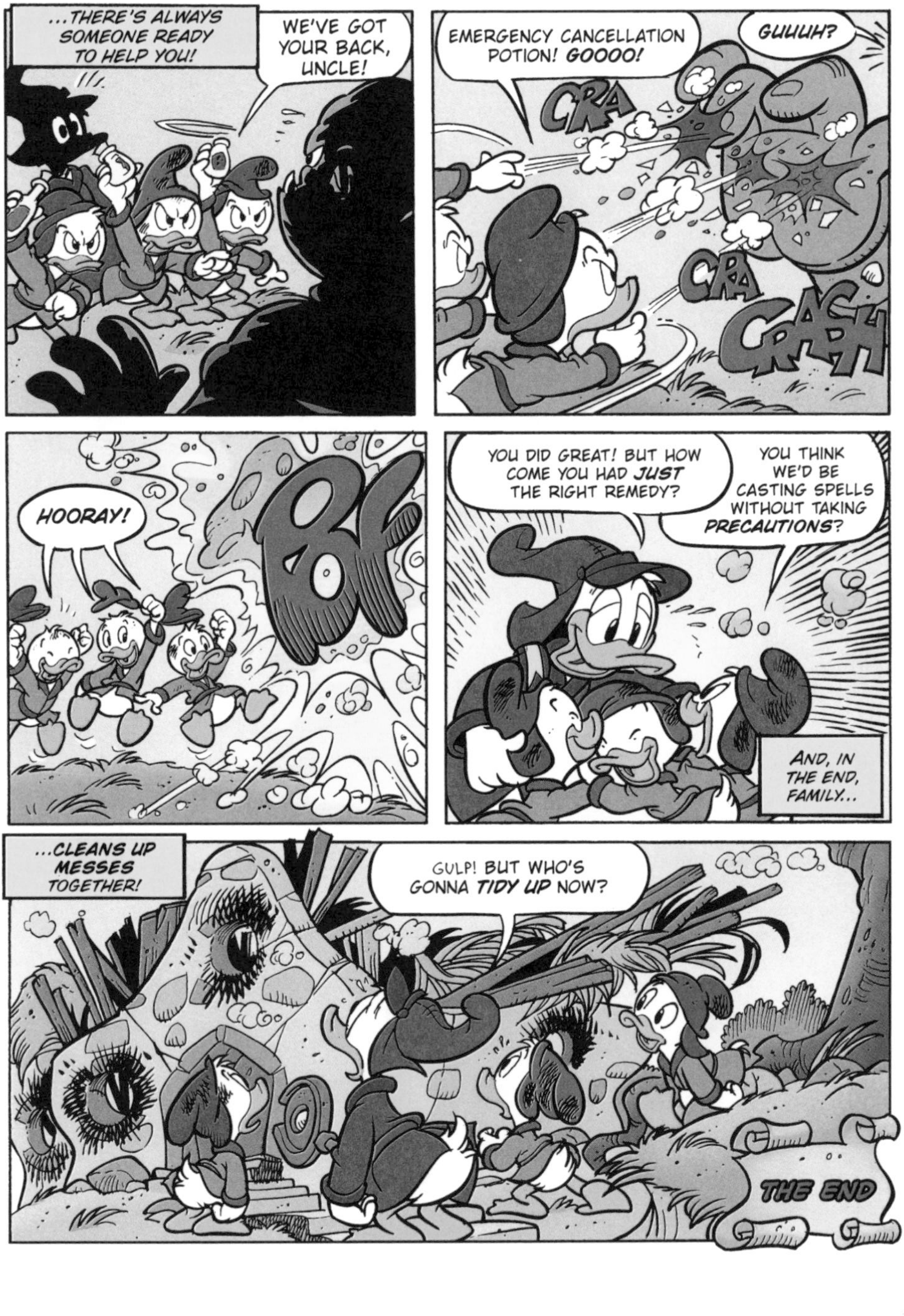
...THERE'S ALWAYS SOMEONE READY TO HELP YOU!
WE'VE GOT YOUR BACK, UNCLE!
EMERGENCY CANCELLATION POTION! GOOOO!
GUUUH?
CRA
CRA
CRASH
HOORAY!
POF
YOU DID GREAT! BUT HOW COME YOU HAD JUST THE RIGHT REMEDY?
YOU THINK WE'D BE CASTING SPELLS WITHOUT TAKING PRECAUTIONS?
AND, IN THE END, FAMILY...
...CLEANS UP MESSES TOGETHER!
GULP! BUT WHO'S GONNA TIDY UP NOW?
THE END

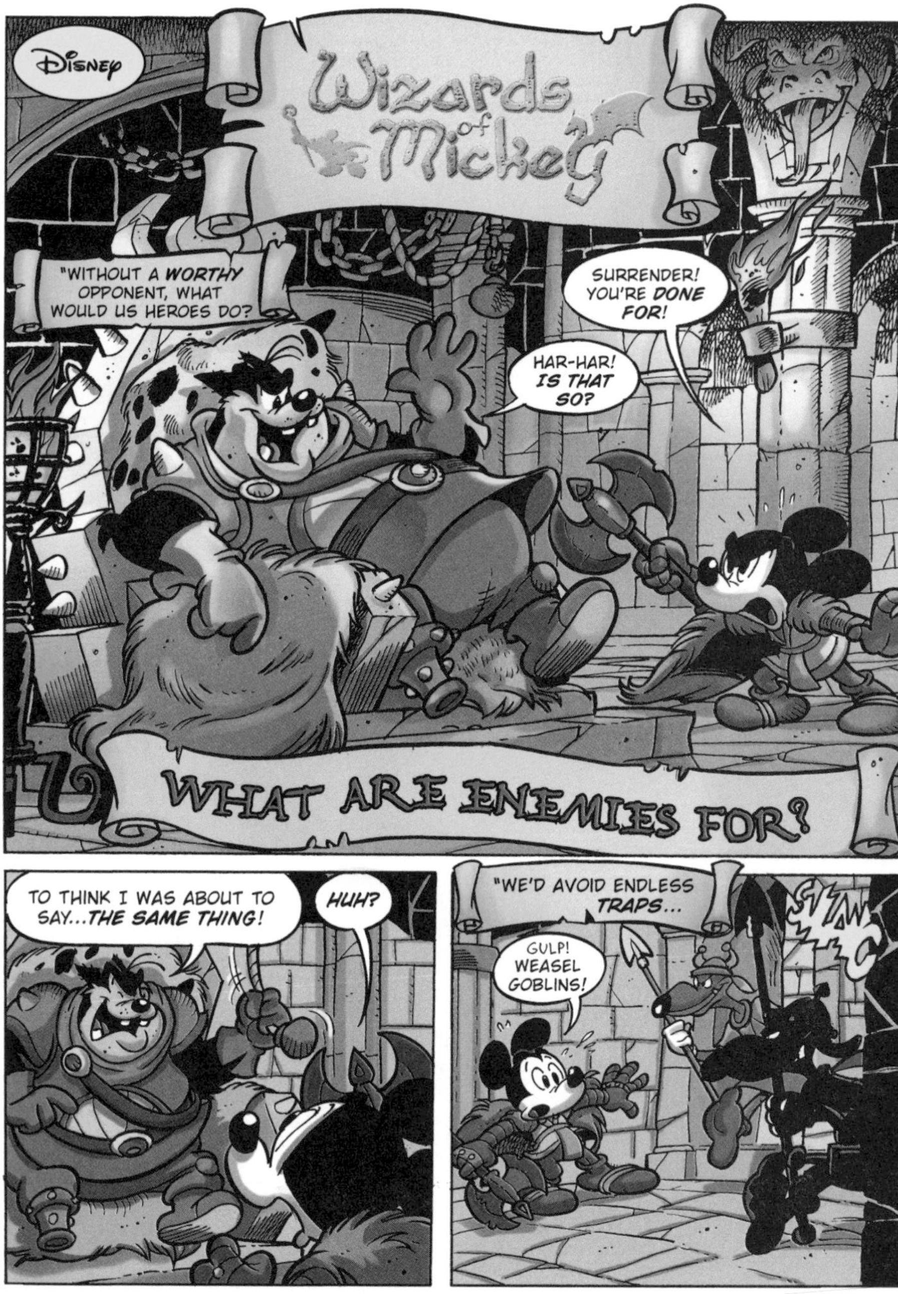

DISNEY
Wizards of Mickey
"WITHOUT A WORTHY OPPONENT, WHAT WOULD US HEROES DO?
SURRENDER! YOU'RE DONE FOR!
HAR-HAR! IS THAT SO?
WHAT ARE ENEMIES FOR?
TO THINK I WAS ABOUT TO SAY...THE SAME THING!
HUH?
"WE'D AVOID ENDLESS TRAPS...
GULP! WEASEL GOBLINS!

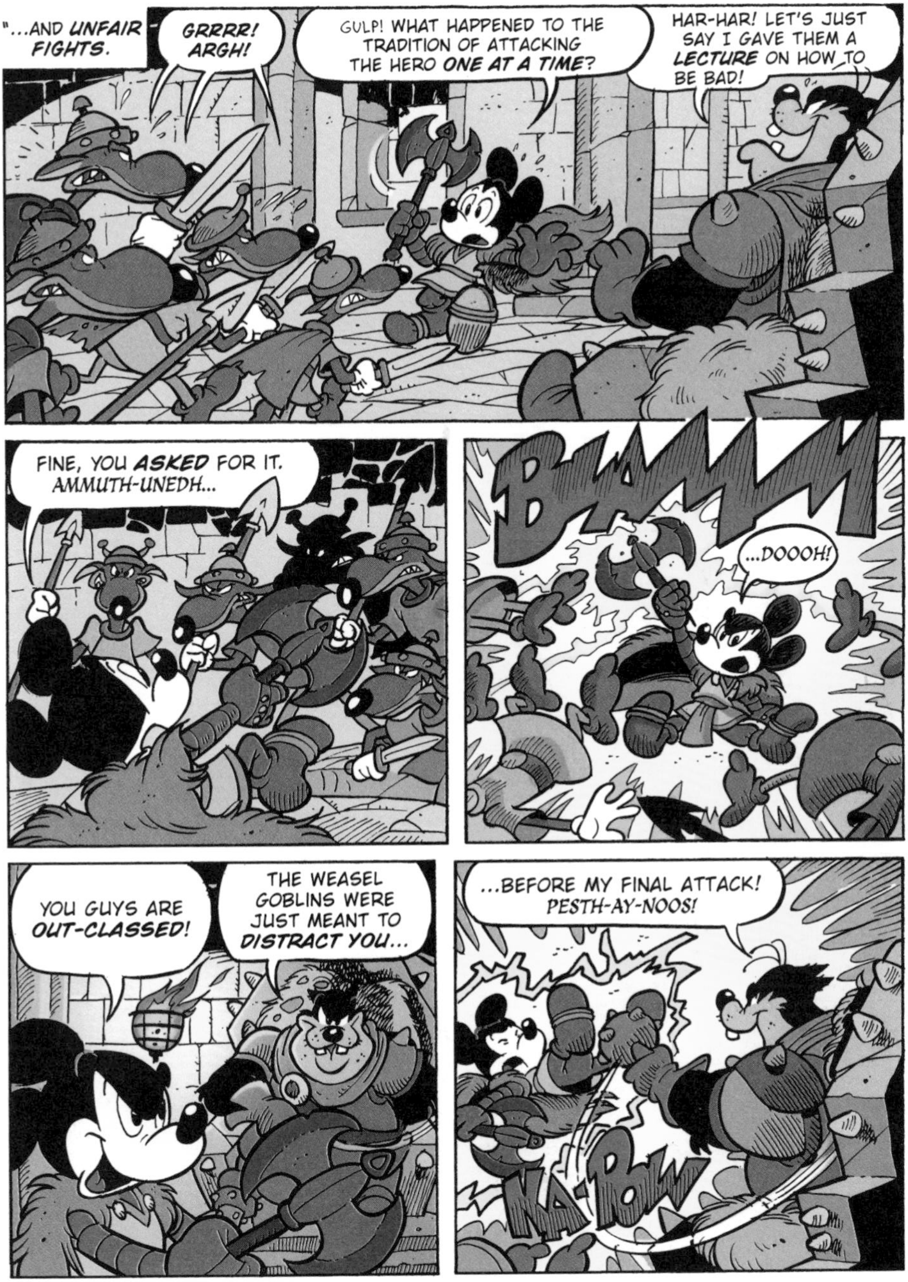
"...AND UNFAIR FIGHTS.
GRRRR! ARGH!
GULP! WHAT HAPPENED TO THE TRADITION OF ATTACKING THE HERO ONE AT A TIME?
HAR-HAR! LET'S JUST SAY I GAVE THEM A LECTURE ON HOW TO BE BAD!
FINE, YOU ASKED FOR IT. AMMUTH-UNEDH...
BLAMM
...DOOOH!
YOU GUYS ARE OUT-CLASSED!
THE WEASEL GOBLINS WERE JUST MEANT TO DISTRACT YOU...
...BEFORE MY FINAL ATTACK! PESTH-AY-NOOS!
KA-POW

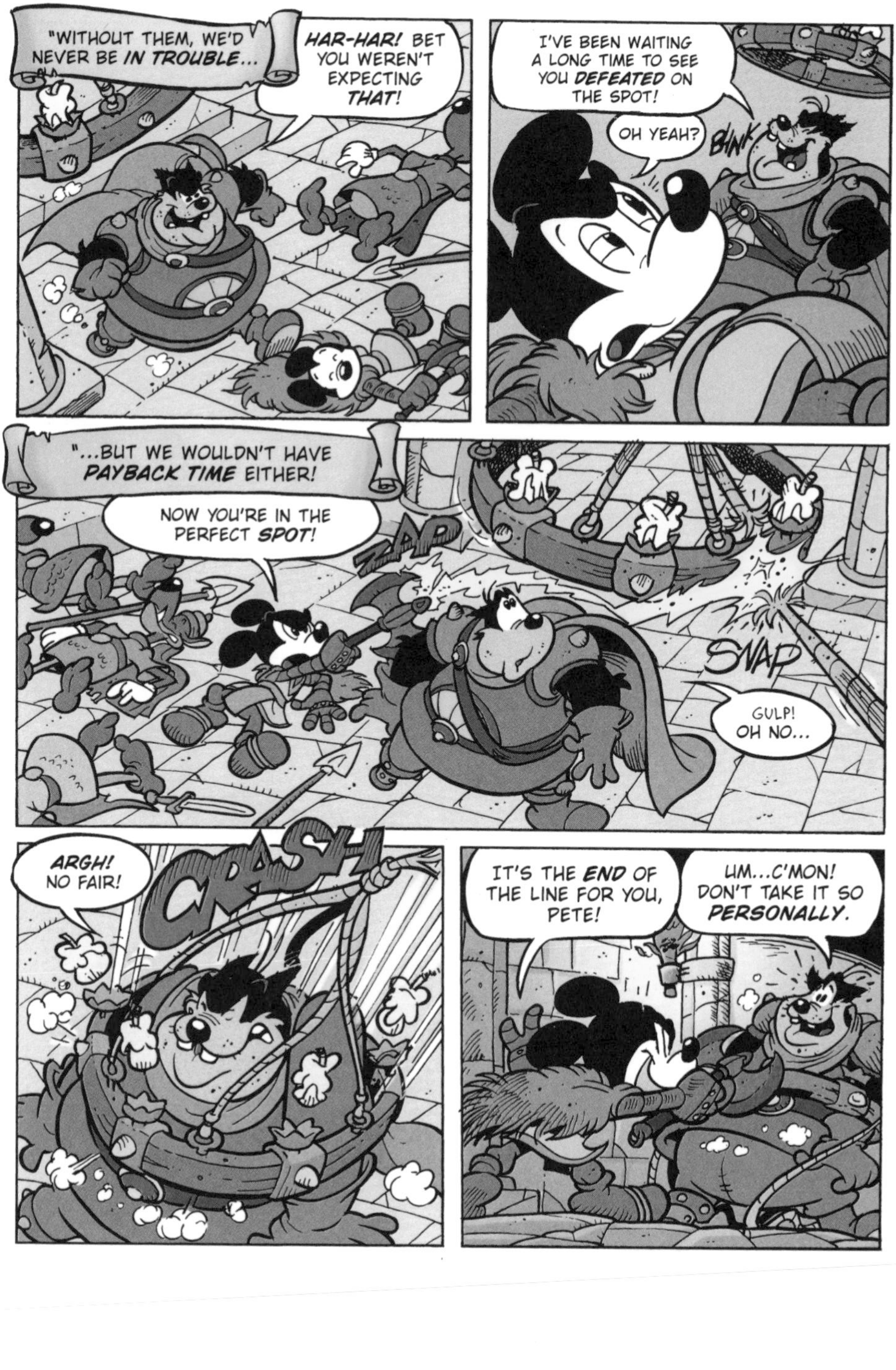
"WITHOUT THEM, WE'D NEVER BE IN TROUBLE...
HAR-HAR! BET YOU WEREN'T EXPECTING THAT!
I'VE BEEN WAITING A LONG TIME TO SEE YOU DEFEATED ON THE SPOT!
OH YEAH?
BLINK
"...BUT WE WOULDN'T HAVE PAYBACK TIME EITHER!
NOW YOU'RE IN THE PERFECT SPOT!
ZAP
SNAP
GULP! OH NO...
ARGH! NO FAIR!
CRASH
IT'S THE END OF THE LINE FOR YOU, PETE!
UM...C'MON! DON'T TAKE IT SO PERSONALLY.

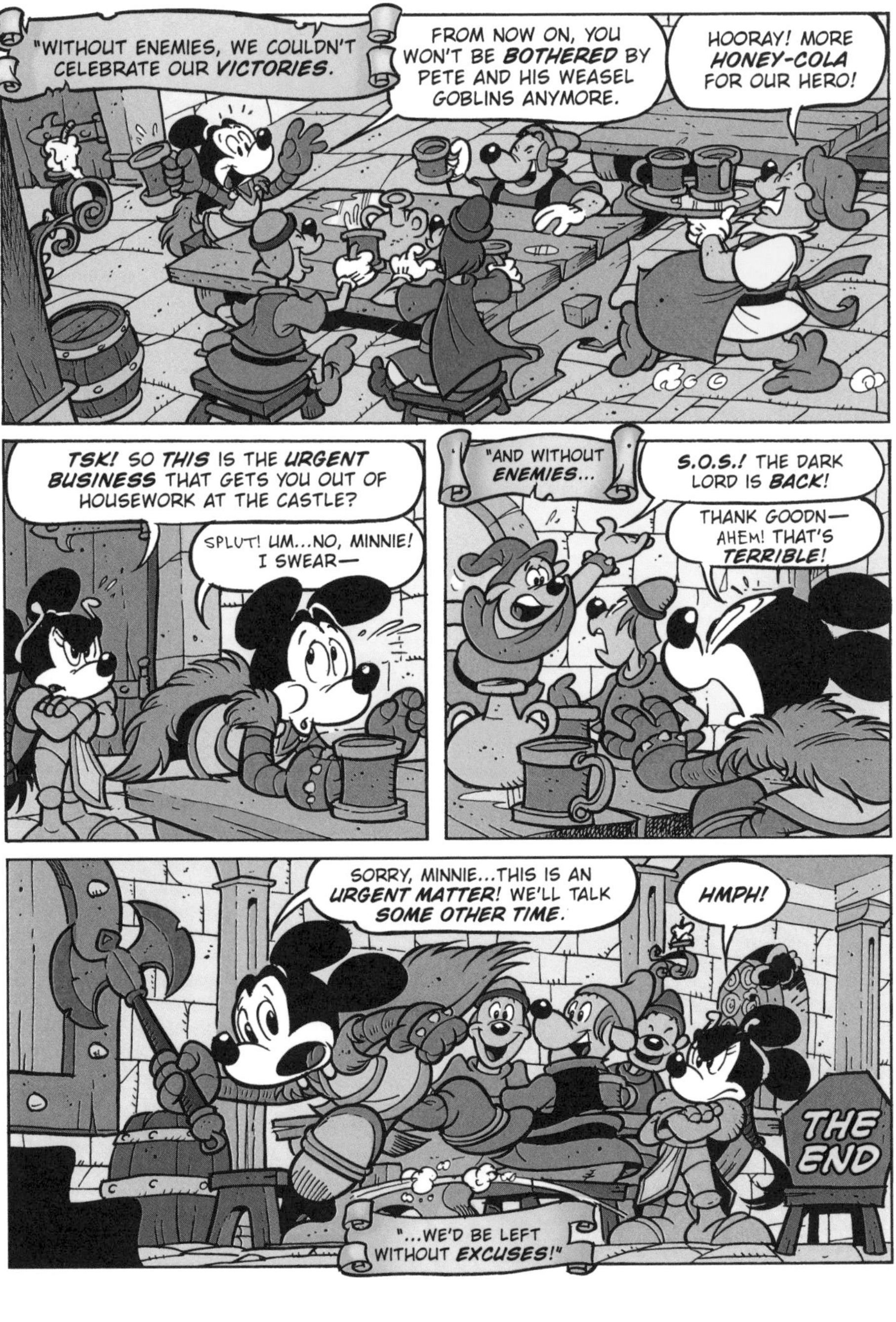
"WITHOUT ENEMIES, WE COULDN'T CELEBRATE OUR VICTORIES.
FROM NOW ON, YOU WON'T BE BOTHERED BY PETE AND HIS WEASEL GOBLINS ANYMORE.
HOORAY! MORE HONEY-COLA FOR OUR HERO!
TSK! SO THIS IS THE URGENT BUSINESS THAT GETS YOU OUT OF HOUSEWORK AT THE CASTLE?
SPLUT! UM...NO, MINNIE! I SWEAR—
"AND WITHOUT ENEMIES...
S.O.S.! THE DARK LORD IS BACK!
THANK GOODN— AHEM! THAT'S TERRIBLE!
SORRY, MINNIE...THIS IS AN URGENT MATTER! WE'LL TALK SOME OTHER TIME.
HMPH!
THE END
"...WE'D BE LEFT WITHOUT EXCUSES!"

Wizards of Mickey

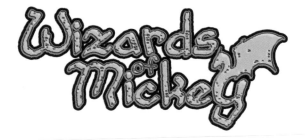

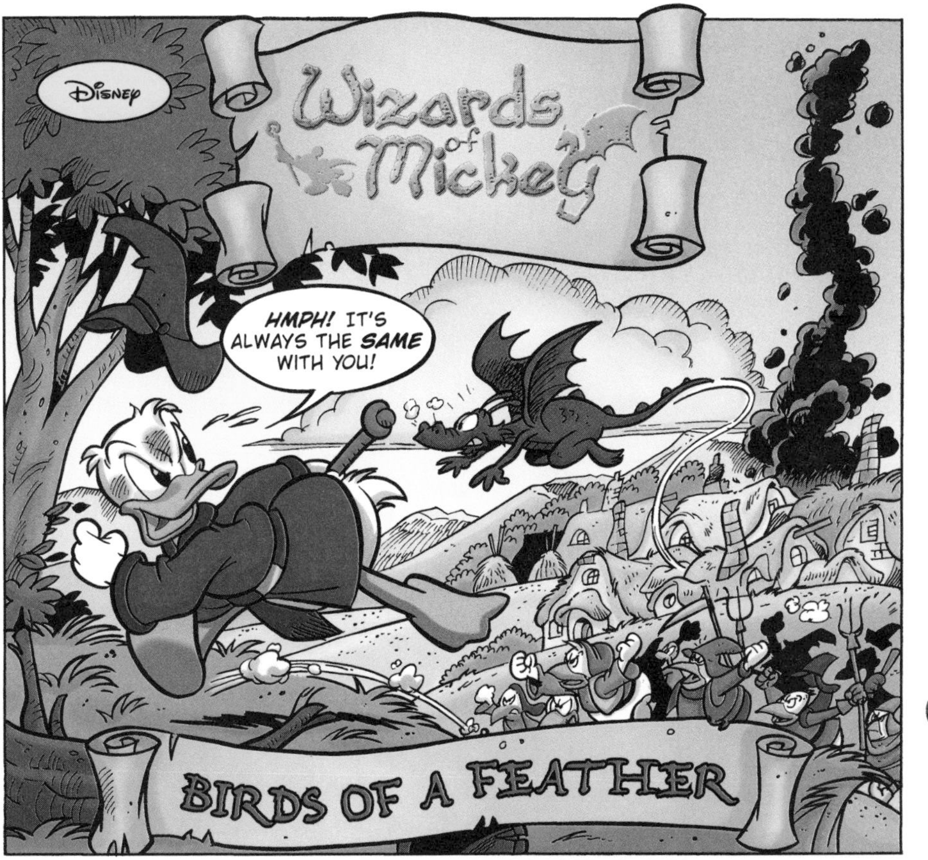
DISNEY
Wizards of Mickey
HMPH! IT'S ALWAYS THE SAME WITH YOU!
BIRDS OF A FEATHER

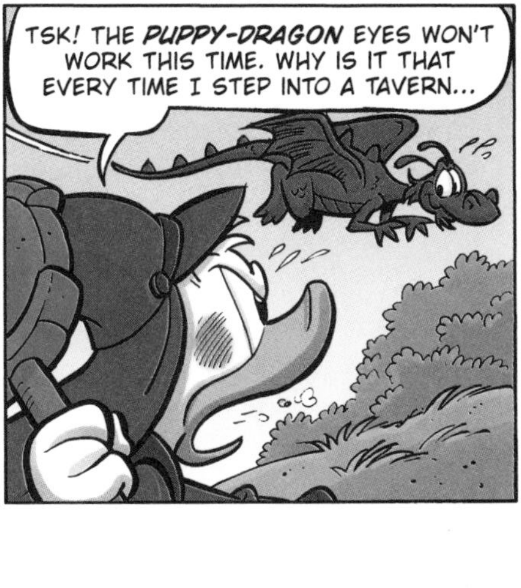
TSK! THE PUPPY-DRAGON EYES WON'T WORK THIS TIME. WHY IS IT THAT EVERY TIME I STEP INTO A TAVERN...

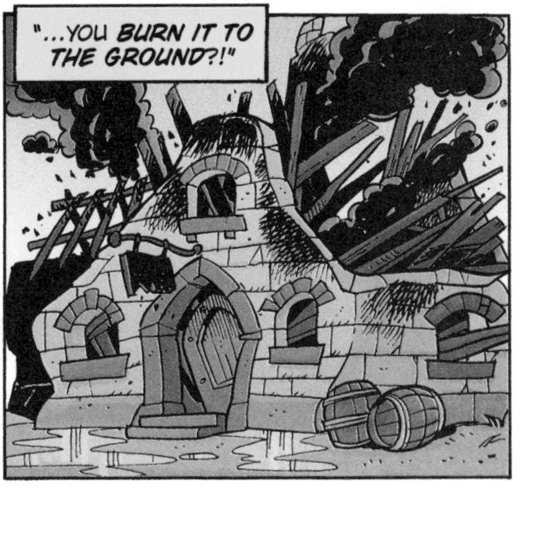
"...YOU BURN IT TO THE GROUND?!"

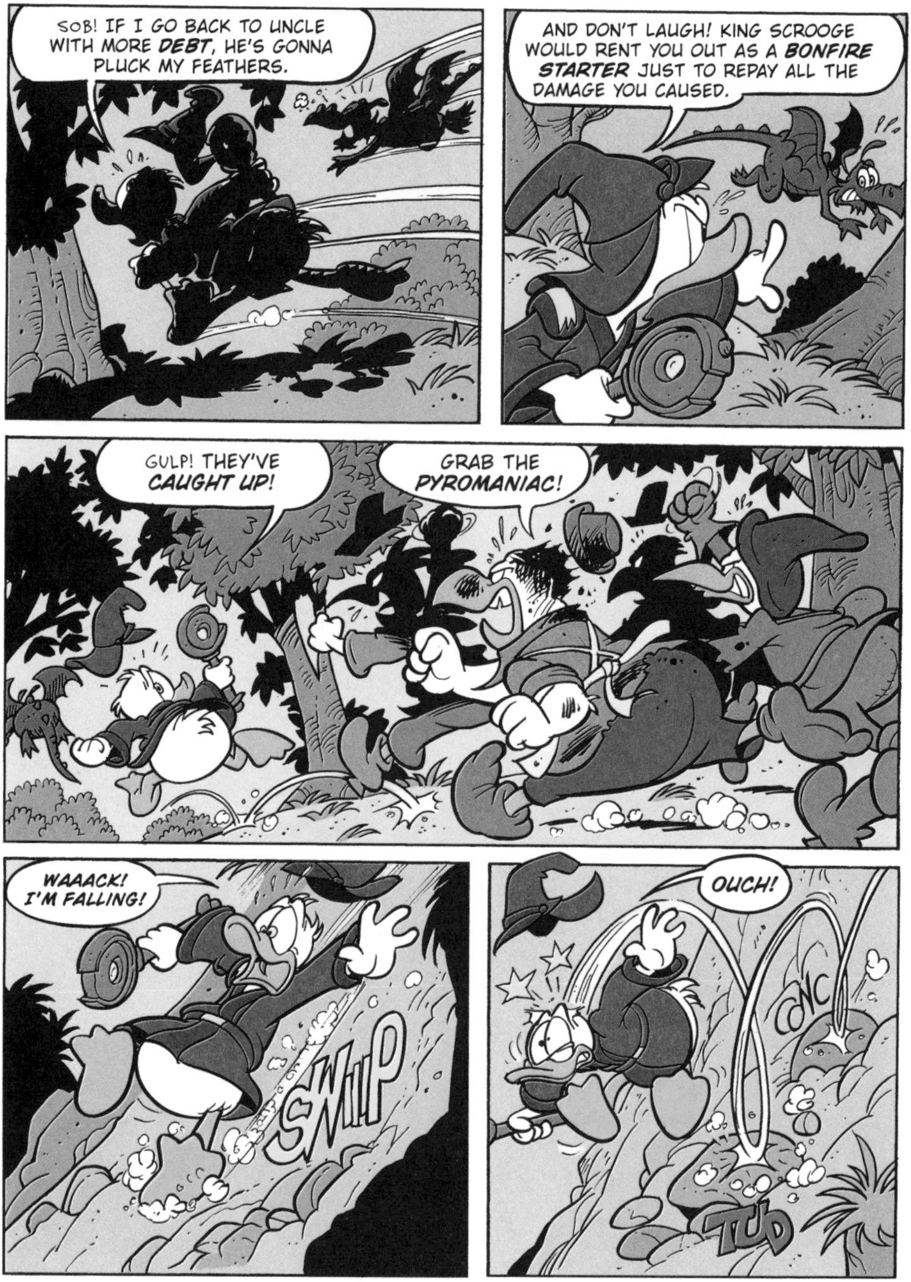
SOB! IF I GO BACK TO UNCLE WITH MORE DEBT, HE'S GONNA PLUCK MY FEATHERS.
AND DON'T LAUGH! KING SCROOGE WOULD RENT YOU OUT AS A BONFIRE STARTER JUST TO REPAY ALL THE DAMAGE YOU CAUSED.
GULP! THEY'VE CAUGHT UP!
GRAB THE PYROMANIAC!
WAAACK! I'M FALLING!
SWIIP
OUCH!
CONC
TUD

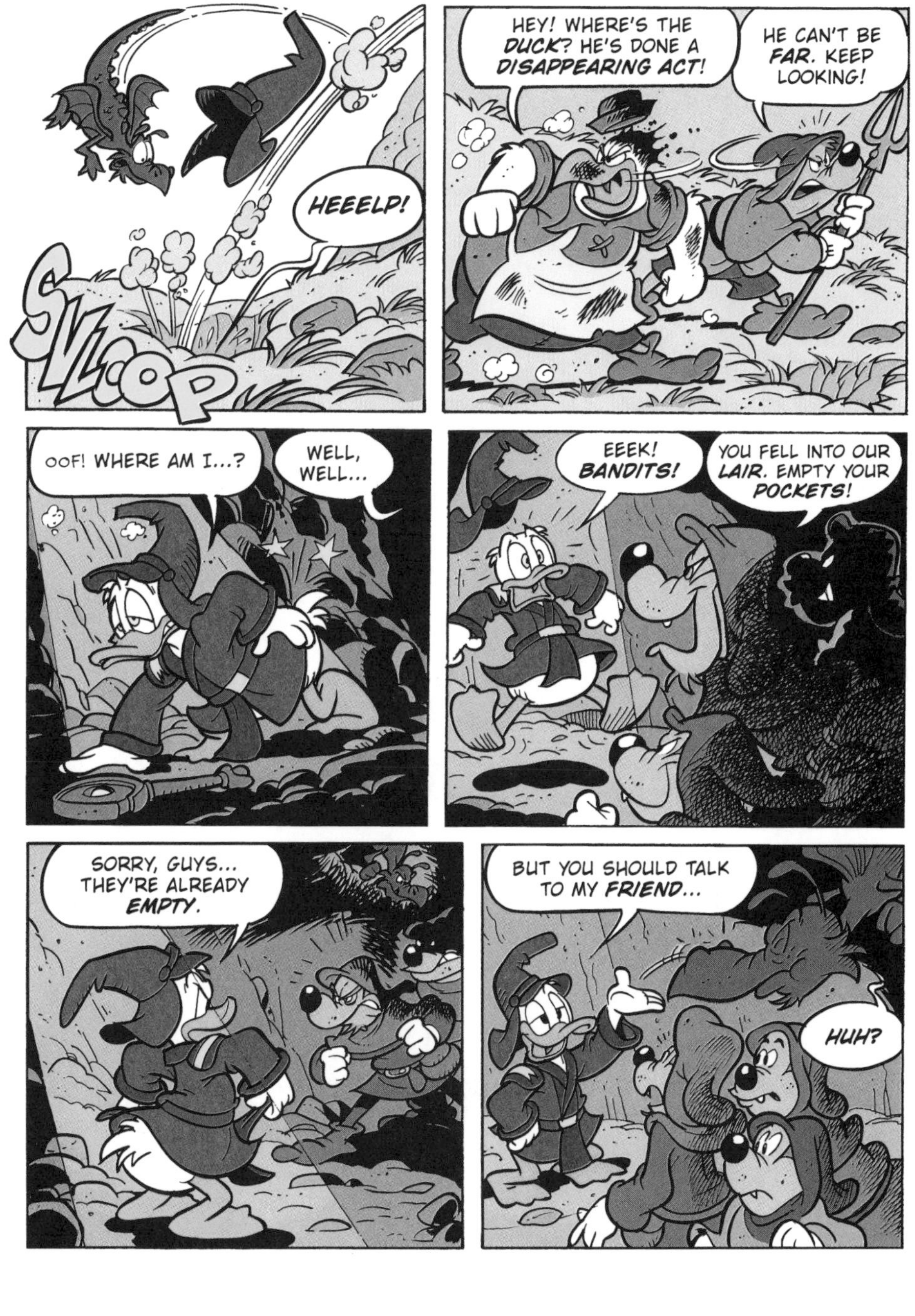
HEEELP!
SVLOOP
HEY! WHERE'S THE DUCK? HE'S DONE A DISAPPEARING ACT!
HE CAN'T BE FAR. KEEP LOOKING!
OOF! WHERE AM I...?
WELL, WELL...
EEEK! BANDITS!
YOU FELL INTO OUR LAIR. EMPTY YOUR POCKETS!
SORRY, GUYS... THEY'RE ALREADY EMPTY.
BUT YOU SHOULD TALK TO MY FRIEND...
HUH?

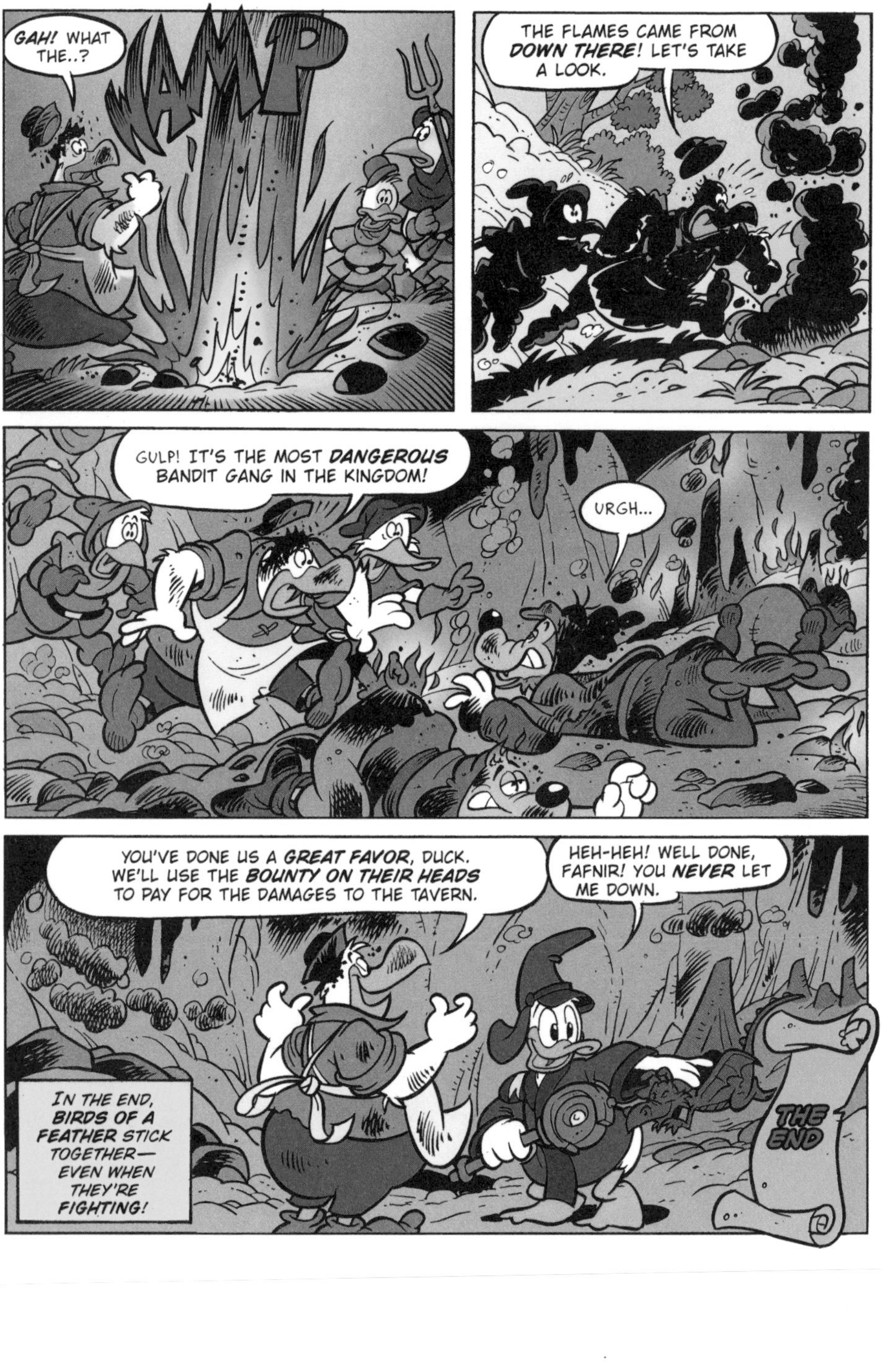

GAH! WHAT THE..?
WAMP
THE FLAMES CAME FROM DOWN THERE! LET'S TAKE A LOOK.
GULP! IT'S THE MOST DANGEROUS BANDIT GANG IN THE KINGDOM!
URGH...
YOU'VE DONE US A GREAT FAVOR, DUCK. WE'LL USE THE BOUNTY ON THEIR HEADS TO PAY FOR THE DAMAGES TO THE TAVERN.
HEH-HEH! WELL DONE, FAFNIR! YOU NEVER LET ME DOWN.
IN THE END, BIRDS OF A FEATHER STICK TOGETHER— EVEN WHEN THEY'RE FIGHTING!
THE END

Wizards of Mickey

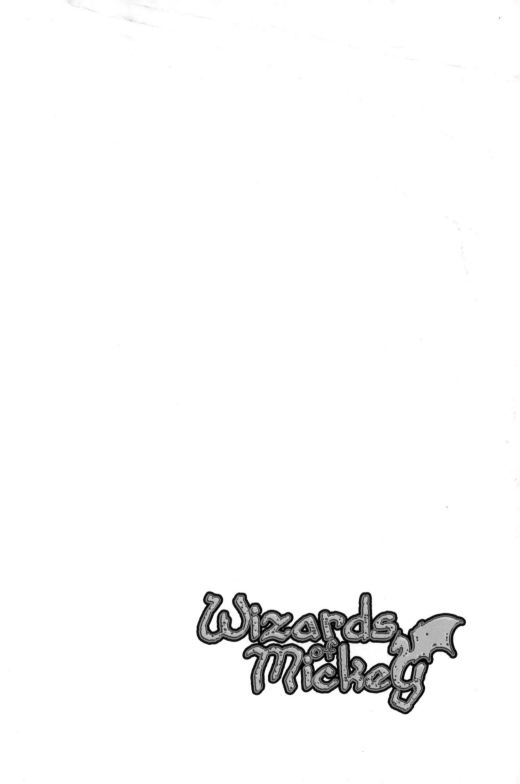

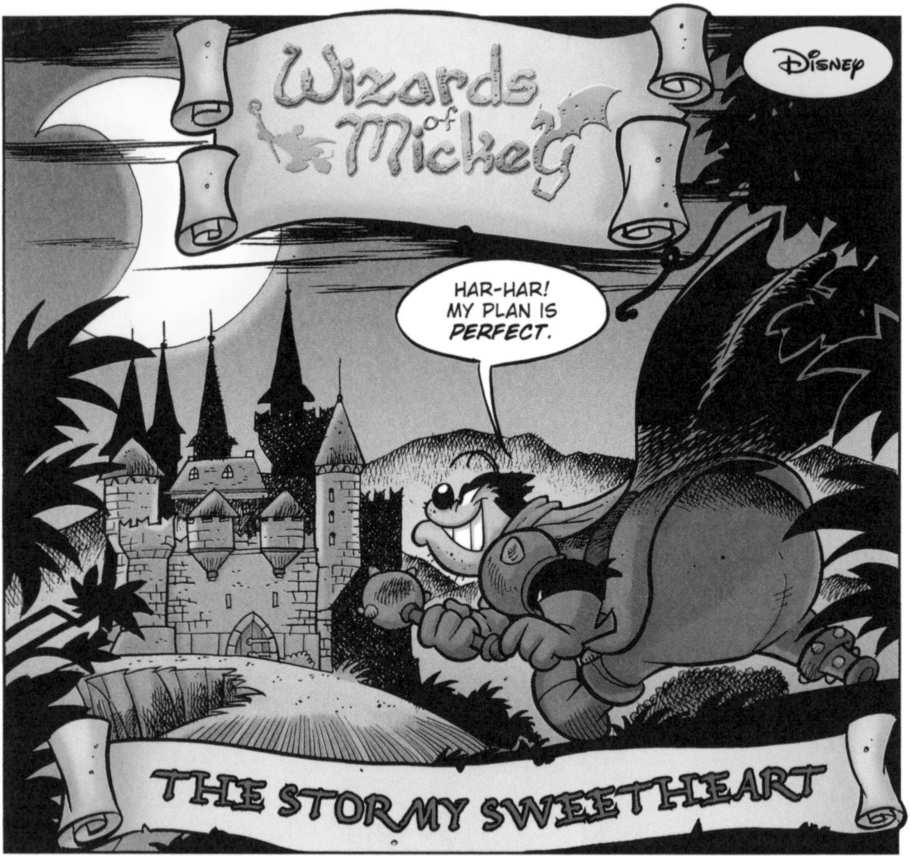
Wizards of Mickey
HAR-HAR! MY PLAN IS PERFECT.
THE STORMY SWEETHEART

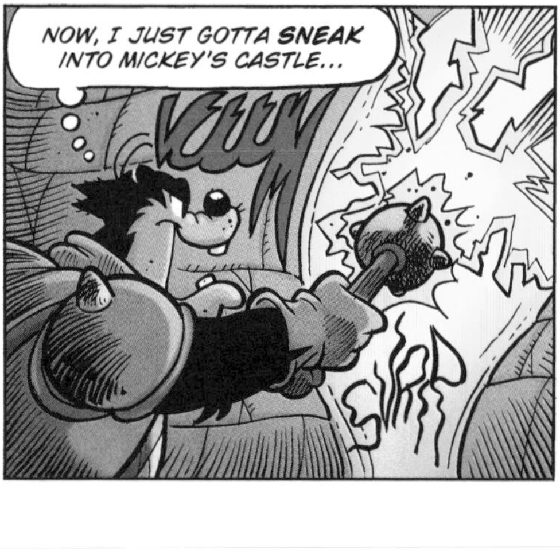
NOW, I JUST GOTTA SNEAK INTO MICKEY'S CASTLE...

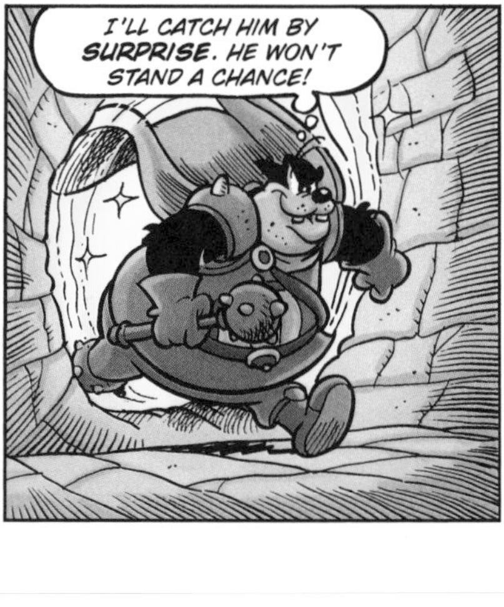
I'LL CATCH HIM BY SURPRISE. HE WON'T STAND A CHANCE!

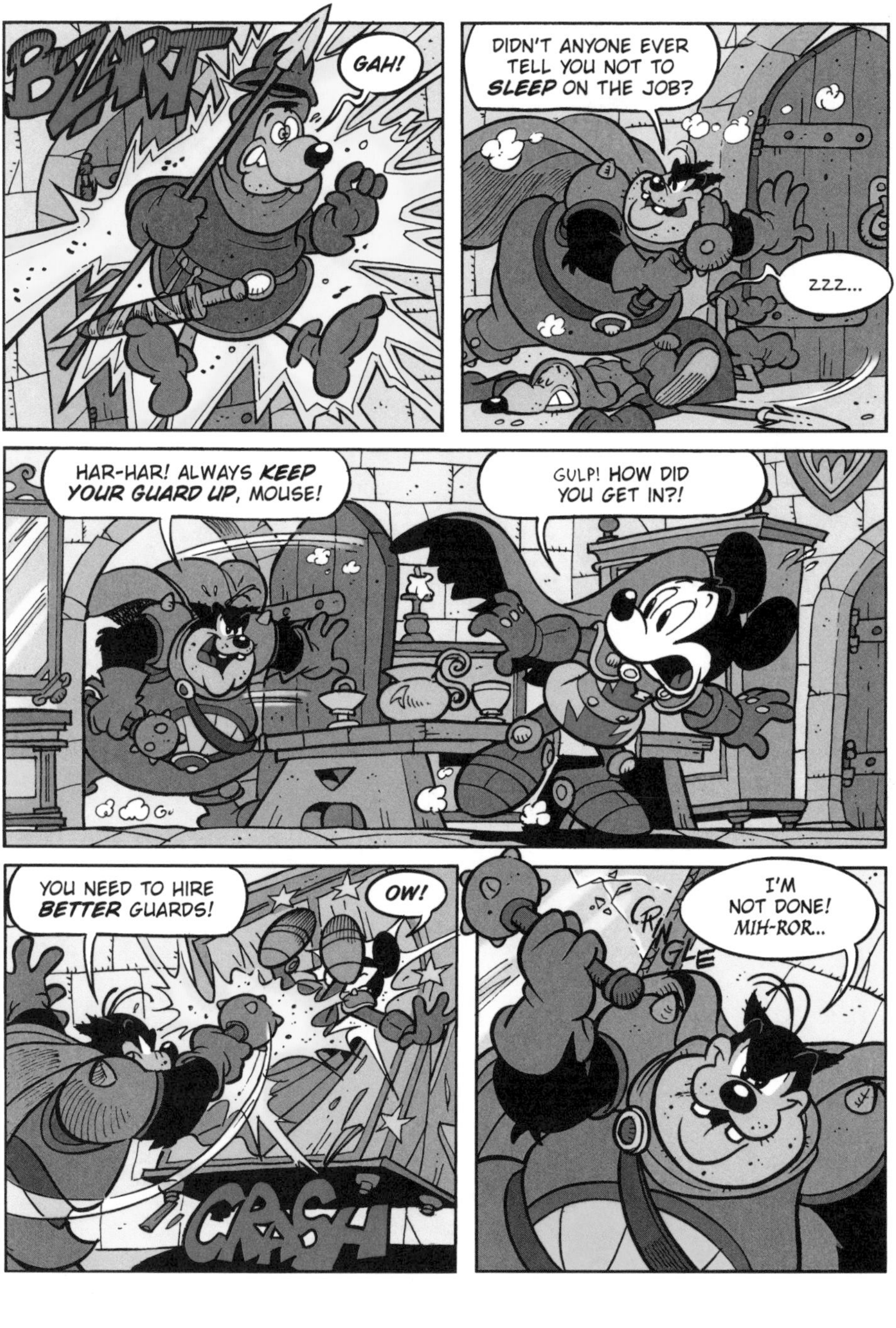
BZZAPT
GAH!
DIDN'T ANYONE EVER TELL YOU NOT TO SLEEP ON THE JOB?
ZZZ...
HAR-HAR! ALWAYS KEEP YOUR GUARD UP, MOUSE!
GULP! HOW DID YOU GET IN?!
YOU NEED TO HIRE BETTER GUARDS!
OW!
CRASH
CRINGLE
I'M NOT DONE! MIH-ROR...

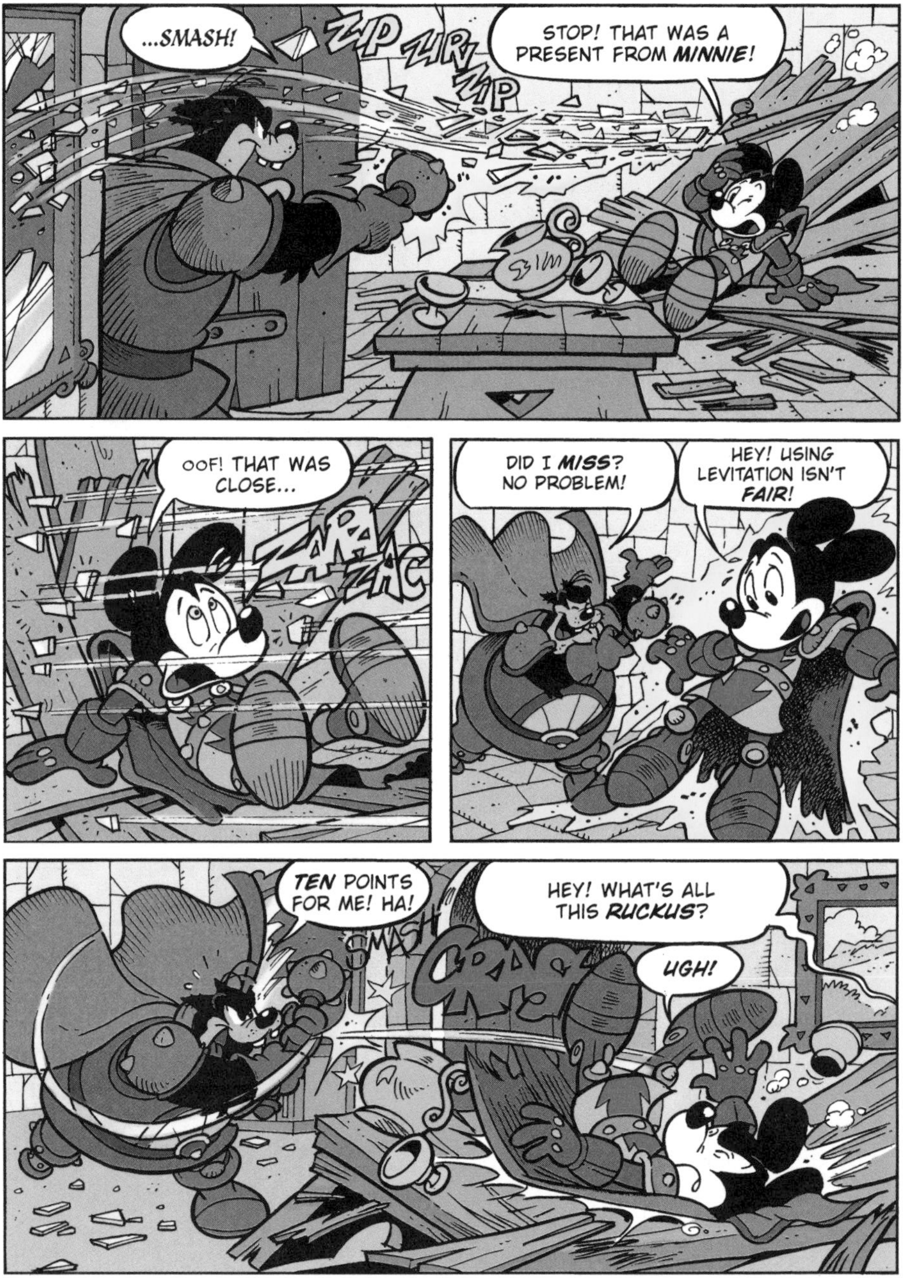
...SMASH!
ZIP ZIRR ZIP
STOP! THAT WAS A PRESENT FROM MINNIE!
OOF! THAT WAS CLOSE...
ZARAZAC
DID I MISS? NO PROBLEM!
HEY! USING LEVITATION ISN'T FAIR!
TEN POINTS FOR ME! HA!
SMASH
CRASH
HEY! WHAT'S ALL THIS RUCKUS?
UGH!

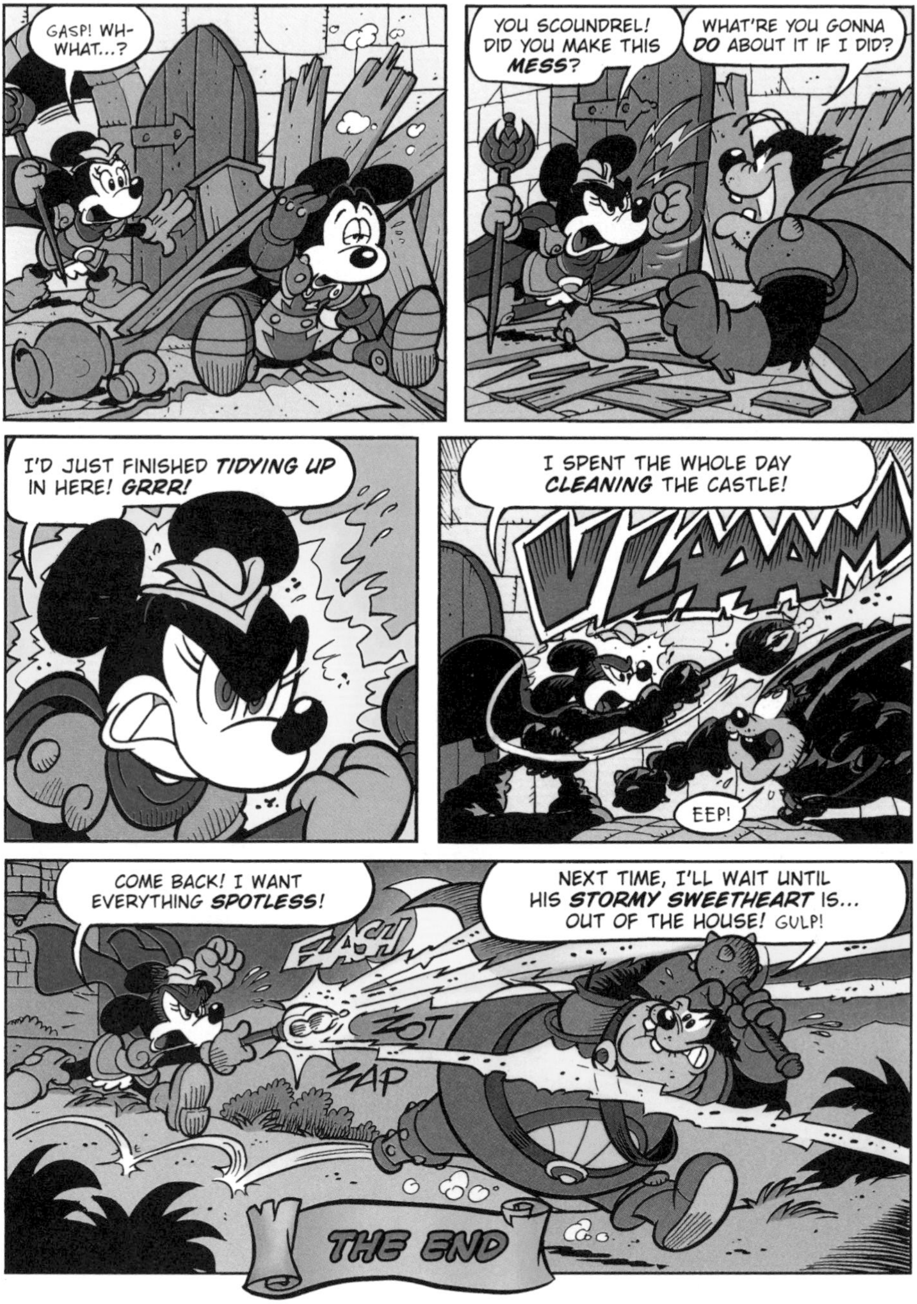
GASP! WH-WHAT...?
YOU SCOUNDREL! DID YOU MAKE THIS MESS?
WHAT'RE YOU GONNA DO ABOUT IT IF I DID?
I'D JUST FINISHED TIDYING UP IN HERE! GRRR!
I SPENT THE WHOLE DAY CLEANING THE CASTLE!
VLAAAM
EEP!
COME BACK! I WANT EVERYTHING SPOTLESS!
NEXT TIME, I'LL WAIT UNTIL HIS STORMY SWEETHEART IS... OUT OF THE HOUSE! GULP!
FLASH
ZOT
ZAP
THE END

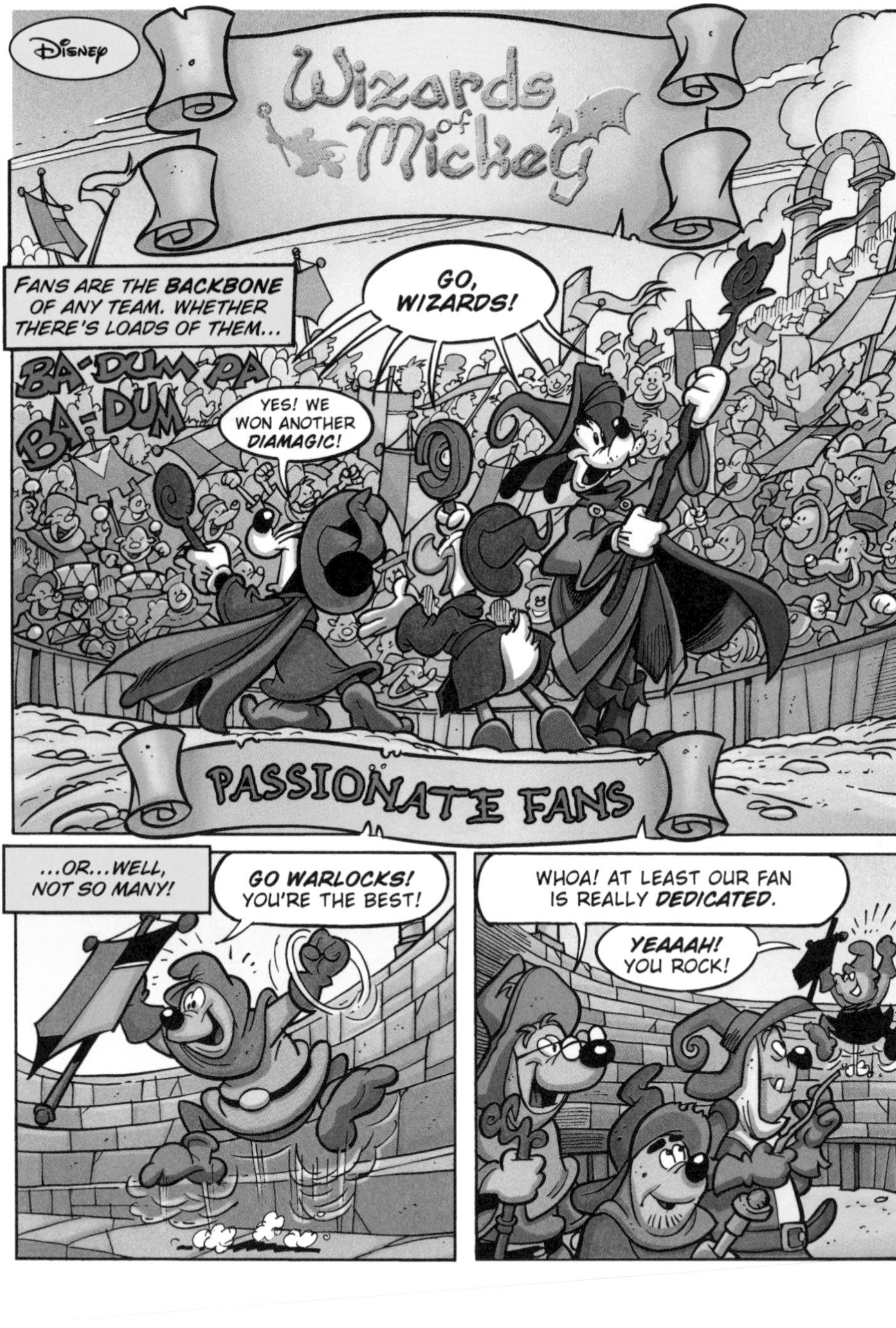
DISNEY
Wizards of Mickey
FANS ARE THE BACKBONE OF ANY TEAM. WHETHER THERE'S LOADS OF THEM...
GO, WIZARDS!
BA-DUM PA BA-DUM
YES! WE WON ANOTHER DIAMAGIC!
PASSIONATE FANS
...OR...WELL, NOT SO MANY!
GO WARLOCKS! YOU'RE THE BEST!
WHOA! AT LEAST OUR FAN IS REALLY DEDICATED.
YEAAAH! YOU ROCK!

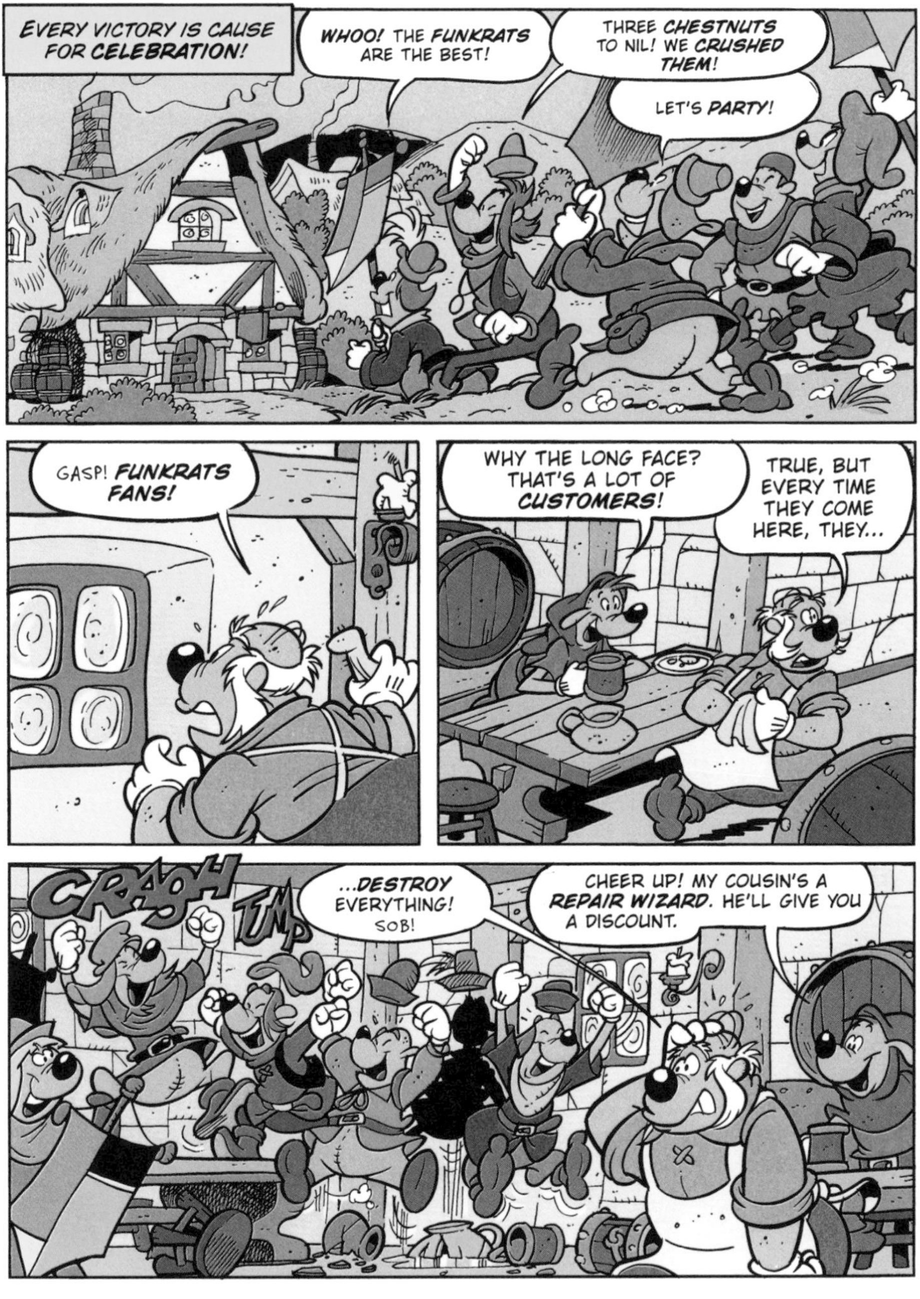
EVERY VICTORY IS CAUSE FOR CELEBRATION!
WHOO! THE FUNKRATS ARE THE BEST!
THREE CHESTNUTS TO NIL! WE CRUSHED THEM!
LET'S PARTY!
GASP! FUNKRATS FANS!
WHY THE LONG FACE? THAT'S A LOT OF CUSTOMERS!
TRUE, BUT EVERY TIME THEY COME HERE, THEY...
CRASH
TUMP
...DESTROY EVERYTHING! SOB!
CHEER UP! MY COUSIN'S A REPAIR WIZARD. HE'LL GIVE YOU A DISCOUNT.

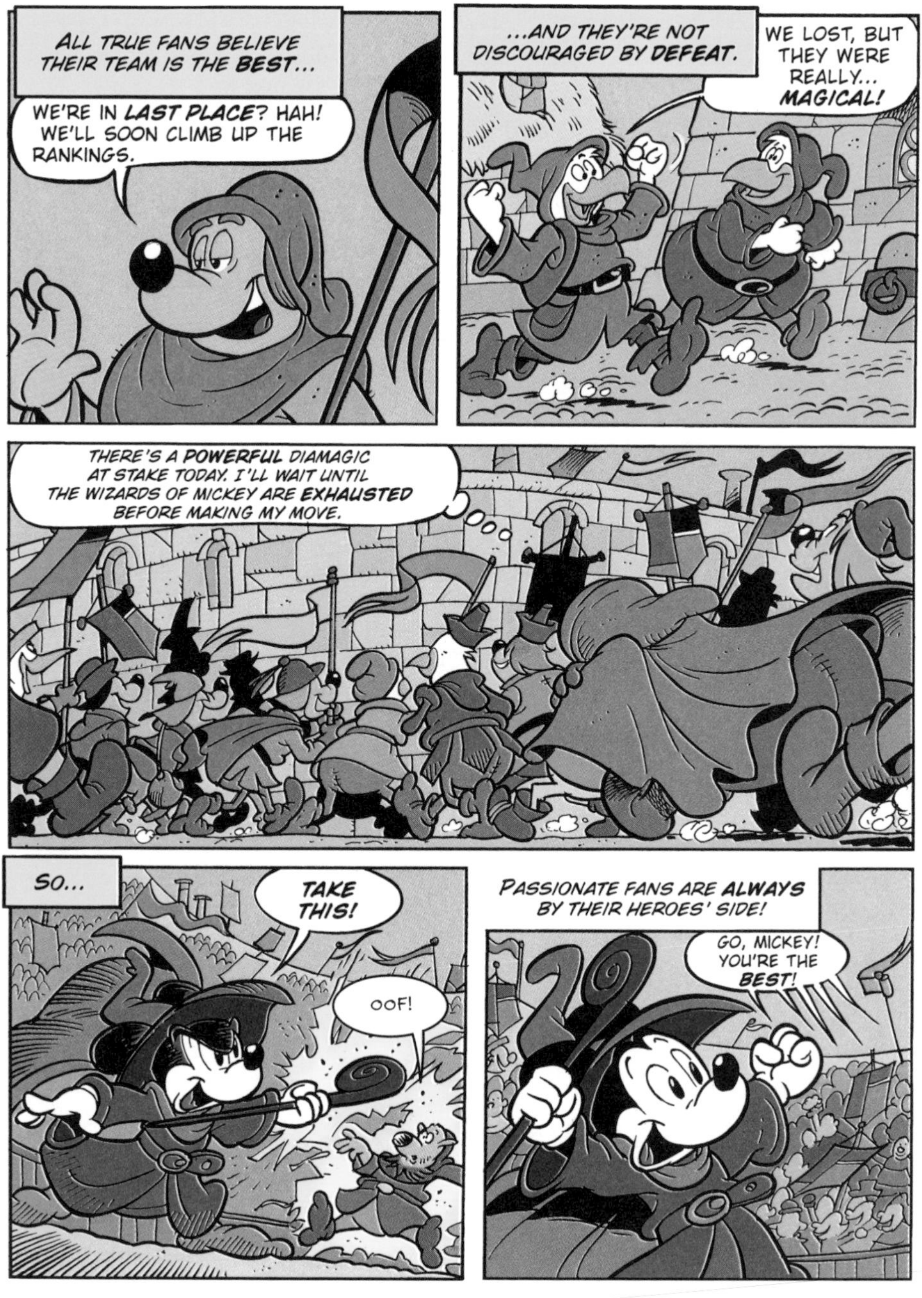
ALL TRUE FANS BELIEVE THEIR TEAM IS THE BEST...
WE'RE IN LAST PLACE? HAH! WE'LL SOON CLIMB UP THE RANKINGS.
...AND THEY'RE NOT DISCOURAGED BY DEFEAT.
WE LOST, BUT THEY WERE REALLY... MAGICAL!
THERE'S A POWERFUL DIAMAGIC AT STAKE TODAY. I'LL WAIT UNTIL THE WIZARDS OF MICKEY ARE EXHAUSTED BEFORE MAKING MY MOVE.
SO...
TAKE THIS!
OOF!
PASSIONATE FANS ARE ALWAYS BY THEIR HEROES' SIDE!
GO, MICKEY! YOU'RE THE BEST!

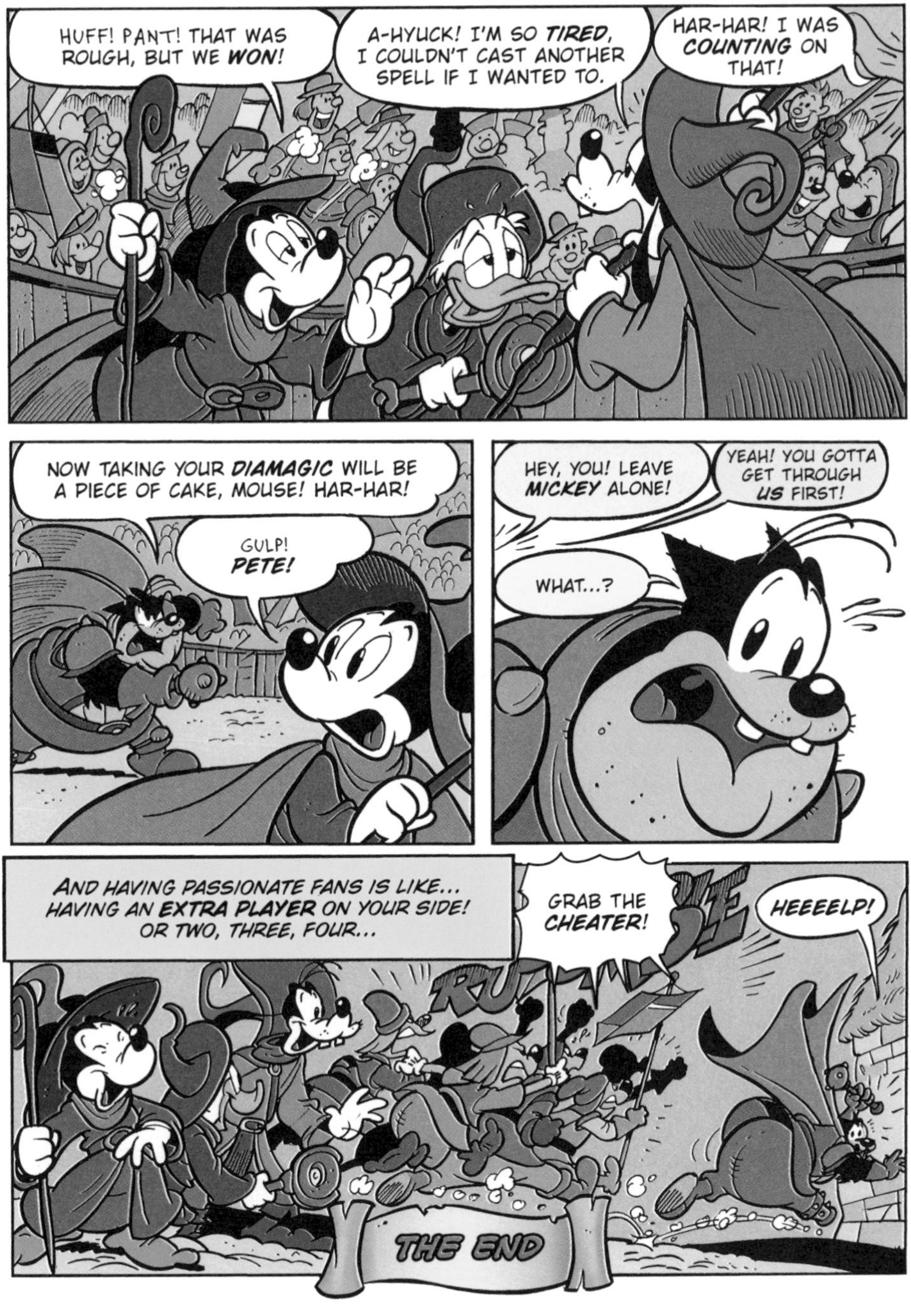
HUFF! PANT! THAT WAS ROUGH, BUT WE WON!
A-HYUCK! I'M SO TIRED, I COULDN'T CAST ANOTHER SPELL IF I WANTED TO.
HAR-HAR! I WAS COUNTING ON THAT!
NOW TAKING YOUR DIAMAGIC WILL BE A PIECE OF CAKE, MOUSE! HAR-HAR!
GULP! PETE!
HEY, YOU! LEAVE MICKEY ALONE!
YEAH! YOU GOTTA GET THROUGH US FIRST!
WHAT...?
AND HAVING PASSIONATE FANS IS LIKE... HAVING AN EXTRA PLAYER ON YOUR SIDE! OR TWO, THREE, FOUR...
GRAB THE CHEATER!
HEEEELP!
THE END

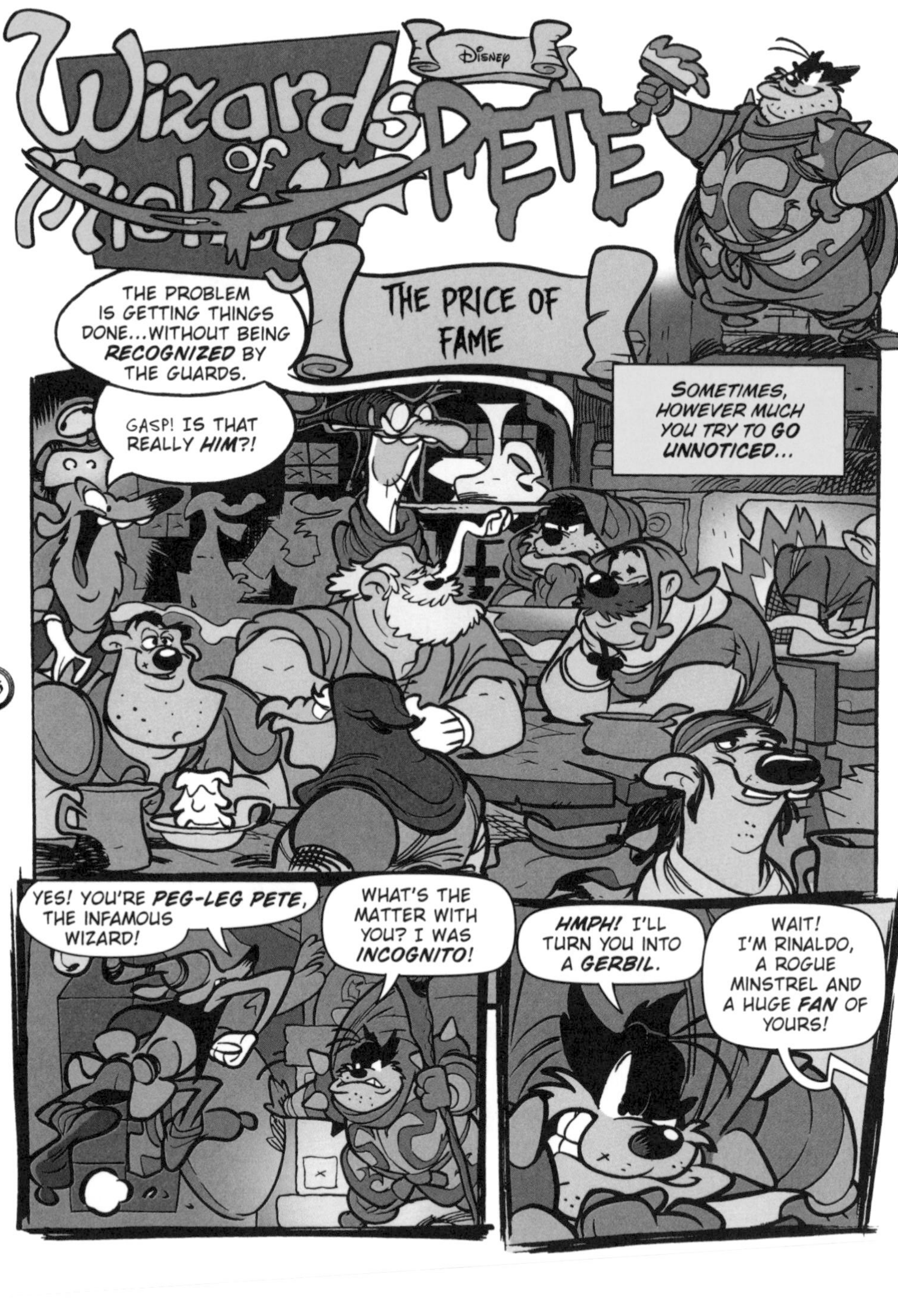
Wizards of Mickey
DISNEY
PETE
THE PRICE OF FAME
THE PROBLEM IS GETTING THINGS DONE...WITHOUT BEING RECOGNIZED BY THE GUARDS.
GASP! IS THAT REALLY HIM?!
SOMETIMES, HOWEVER MUCH YOU TRY TO GO UNNOTICED...
YES! YOU'RE PEG-LEG PETE, THE INFAMOUS WIZARD!
WHAT'S THE MATTER WITH YOU? I WAS INCOGNITO!
HMPH! I'LL TURN YOU INTO A GERBIL.
WAIT! I'M RINALDO, A ROGUE MINSTREL AND A HUGE FAN OF YOURS!

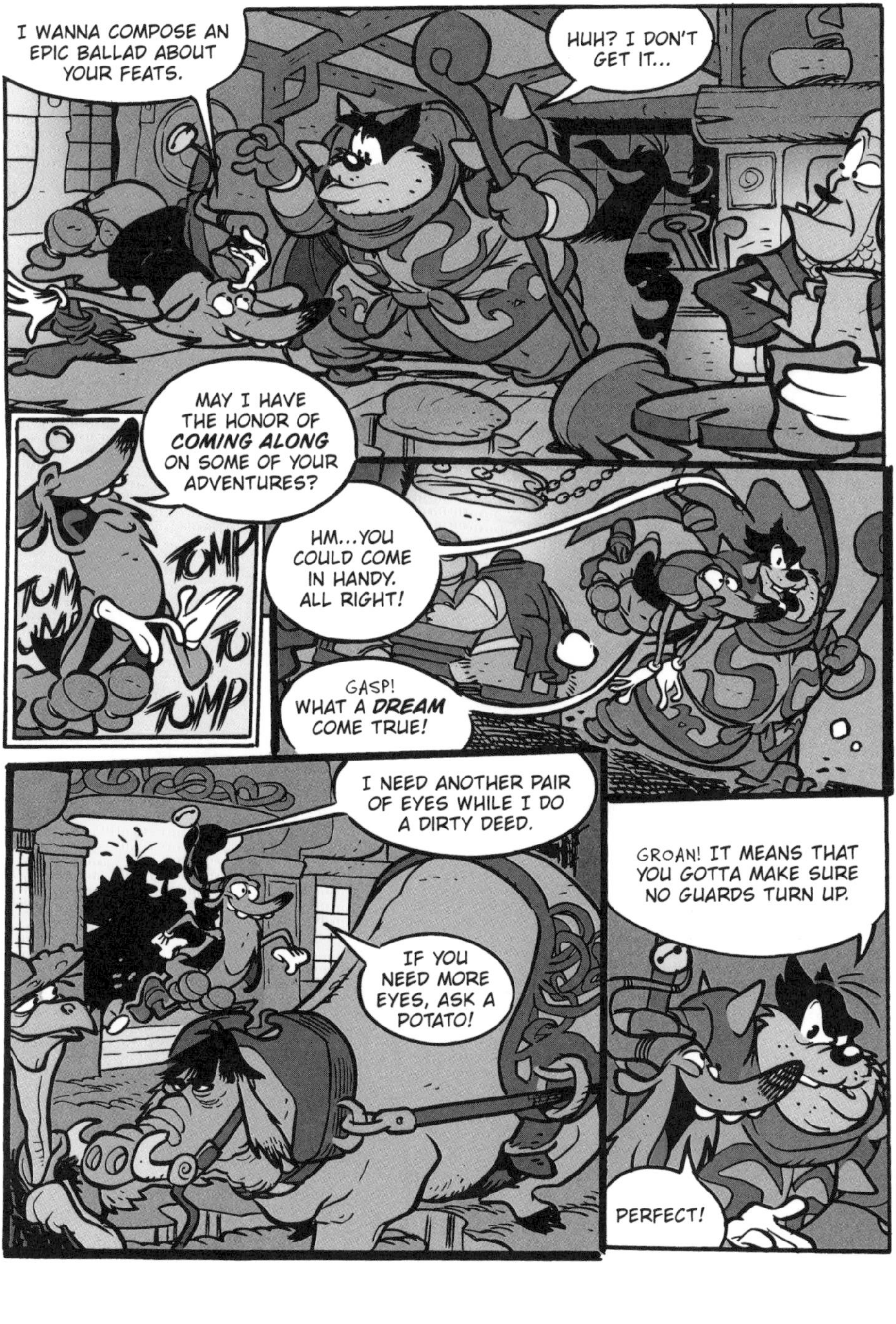
I WANNA COMPOSE AN EPIC BALLAD ABOUT YOUR FEATS.
HUH? I DON'T GET IT...
MAY I HAVE THE HONOR OF COMING ALONG ON SOME OF YOUR ADVENTURES?
TOMP
TUM
TUM
TU
TOMP
HM...YOU COULD COME IN HANDY. ALL RIGHT!
GASP! WHAT A DREAM COME TRUE!
I NEED ANOTHER PAIR OF EYES WHILE I DO A DIRTY DEED.
IF YOU NEED MORE EYES, ASK A POTATO!
GROAN! IT MEANS THAT YOU GOTTA MAKE SURE NO GUARDS TURN UP.
PERFECT!

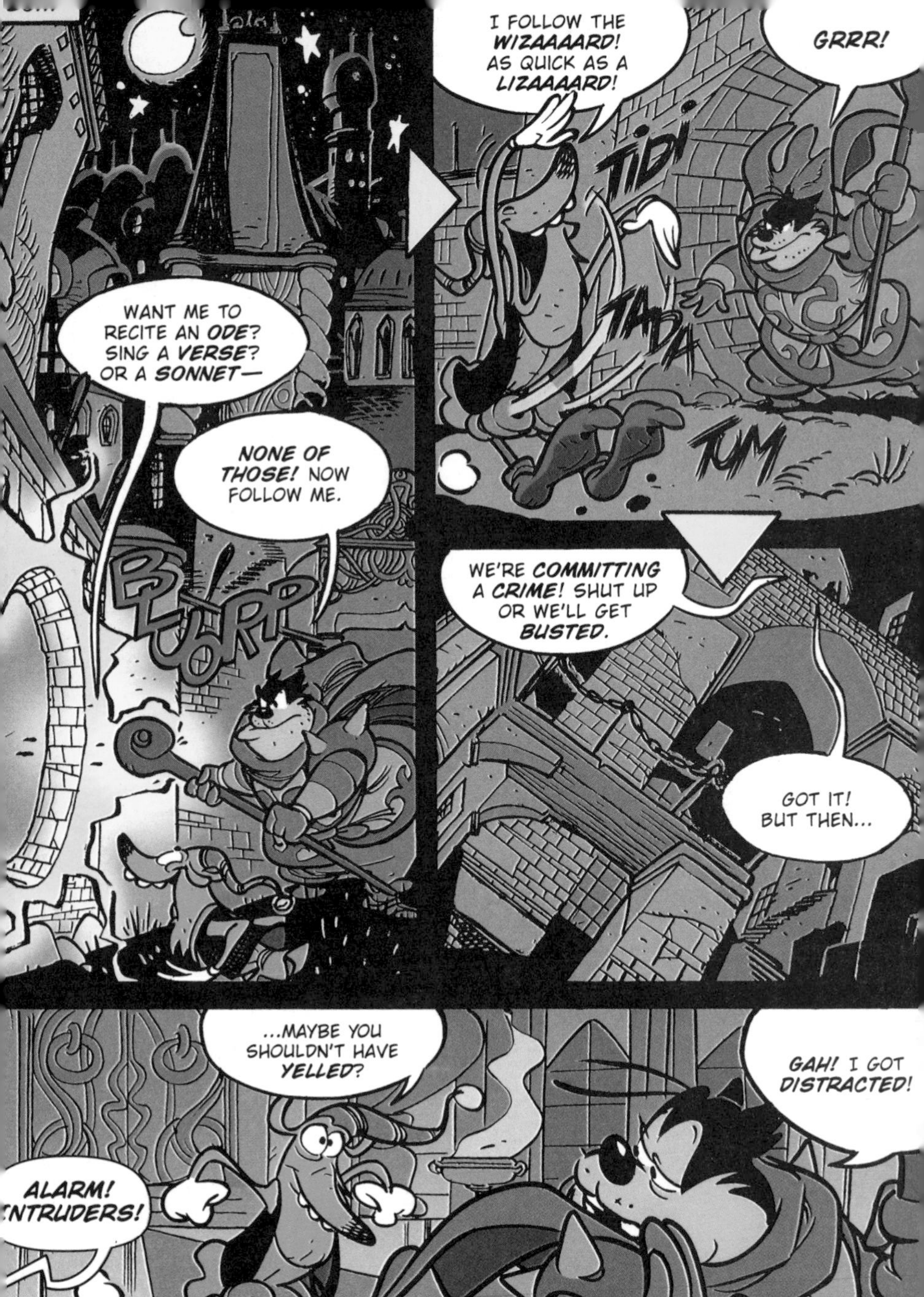

WANT ME TO RECITE AN ODE? SING A VERSE? OR A SONNET—
NONE OF THOSE! NOW FOLLOW ME.
BLURP
I FOLLOW THE WIZAAAARD! AS QUICK AS A LIZAAAARD!
GRRR!
TIDI
TADA
TUM
WE'RE COMMITTING A CRIME! SHUT UP OR WE'LL GET BUSTED.
GOT IT! BUT THEN...
...MAYBE YOU SHOULDN'T HAVE YELLED?
GAH! I GOT DISTRACTED!
ALARM! NTRUDERS!

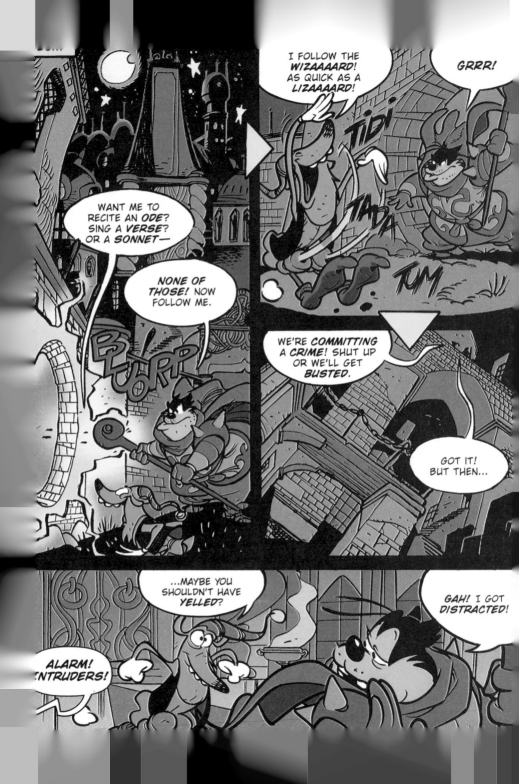

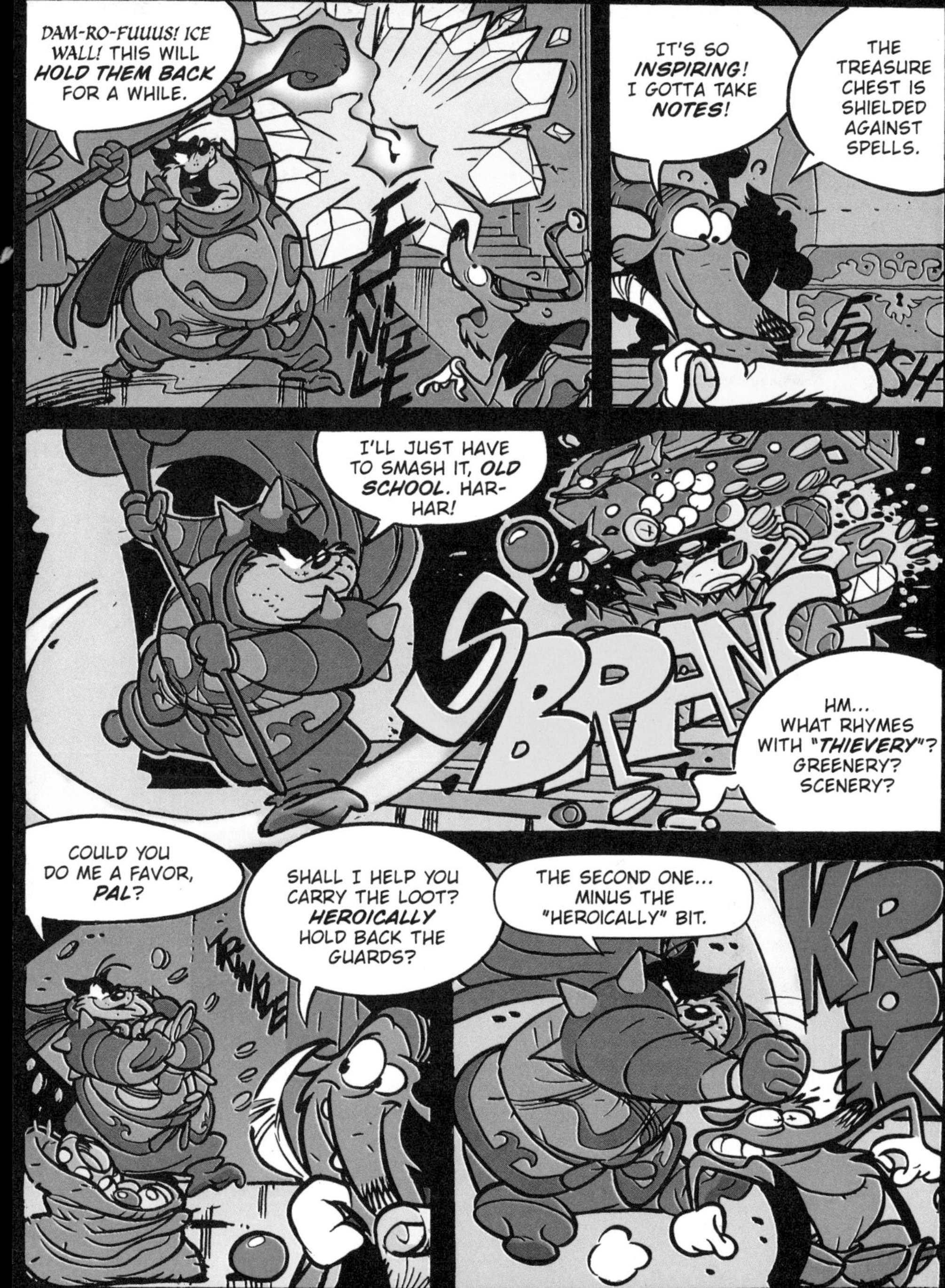

DAM-RO-FUUUS! ICE WALL! THIS WILL HOLD THEM BACK FOR A WHILE.
IT'S SO INSPIRING! I GOTTA TAKE NOTES!
THE TREASURE CHEST IS SHIELDED AGAINST SPELLS.
I'LL JUST HAVE TO SMASH IT, OLD SCHOOL. HAR-HAR!
SBRANG
HM... WHAT RHYMES WITH "THIEVERY"? GREENERY? SCENERY?
COULD YOU DO ME A FAVOR, PAL?
SHALL I HELP YOU CARRY THE LOOT? HEROICALLY HOLD BACK THE GUARDS?
THE SECOND ONE... MINUS THE "HEROICALLY" BIT.
KROK

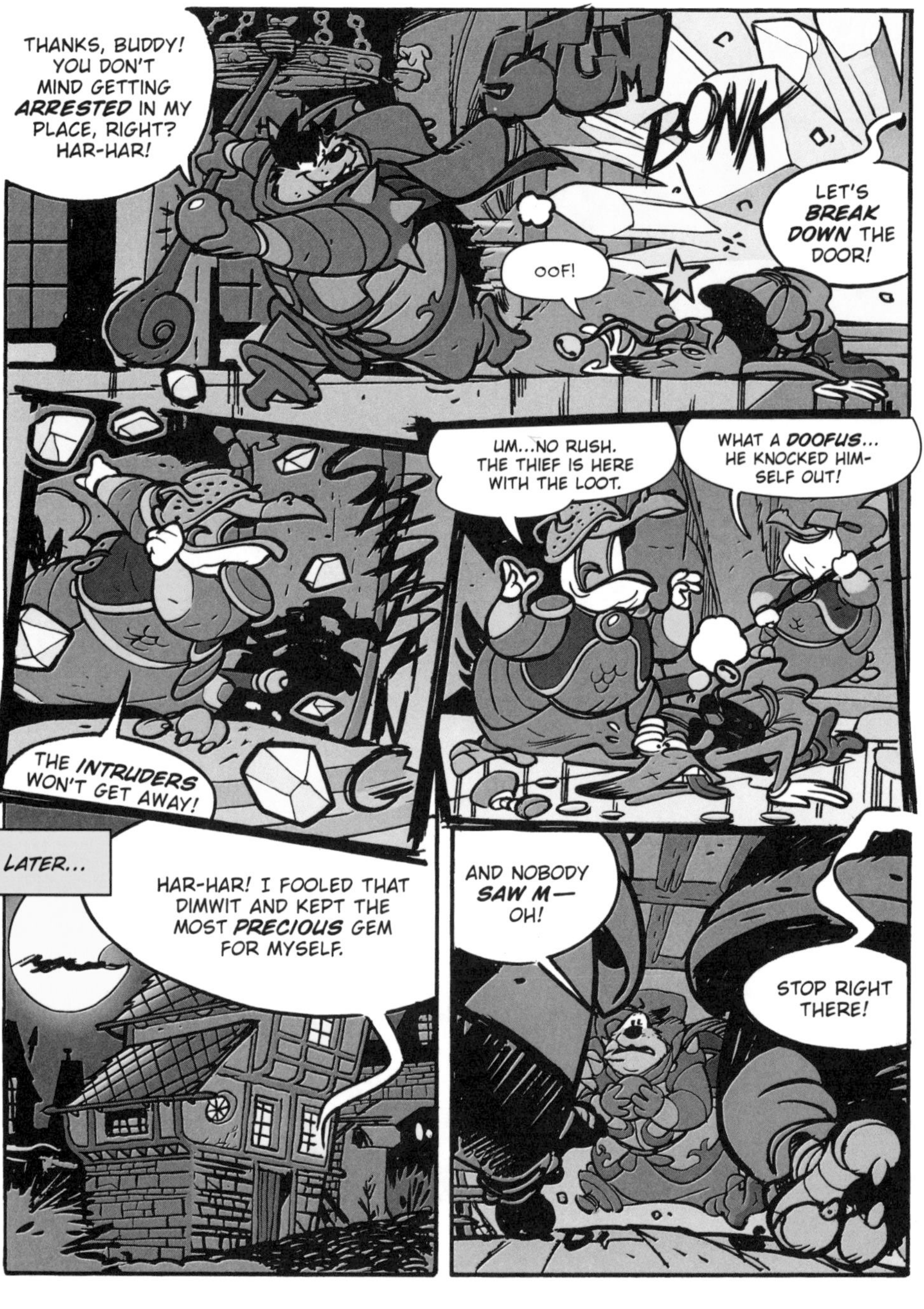
THANKS, BUDDY! YOU DON'T MIND GETTING ARRESTED IN MY PLACE, RIGHT? HAR-HAR!
STUM
BONK
LET'S BREAK DOWN THE DOOR!
OOF!
THE INTRUDERS WON'T GET AWAY!
UM...NO RUSH. THE THIEF IS HERE WITH THE LOOT.
WHAT A DOOFUS... HE KNOCKED HIM-SELF OUT!
LATER...
HAR-HAR! I FOOLED THAT DIMWIT AND KEPT THE MOST PRECIOUS GEM FOR MYSELF.
AND NOBODY SAW M— OH!
STOP RIGHT THERE!

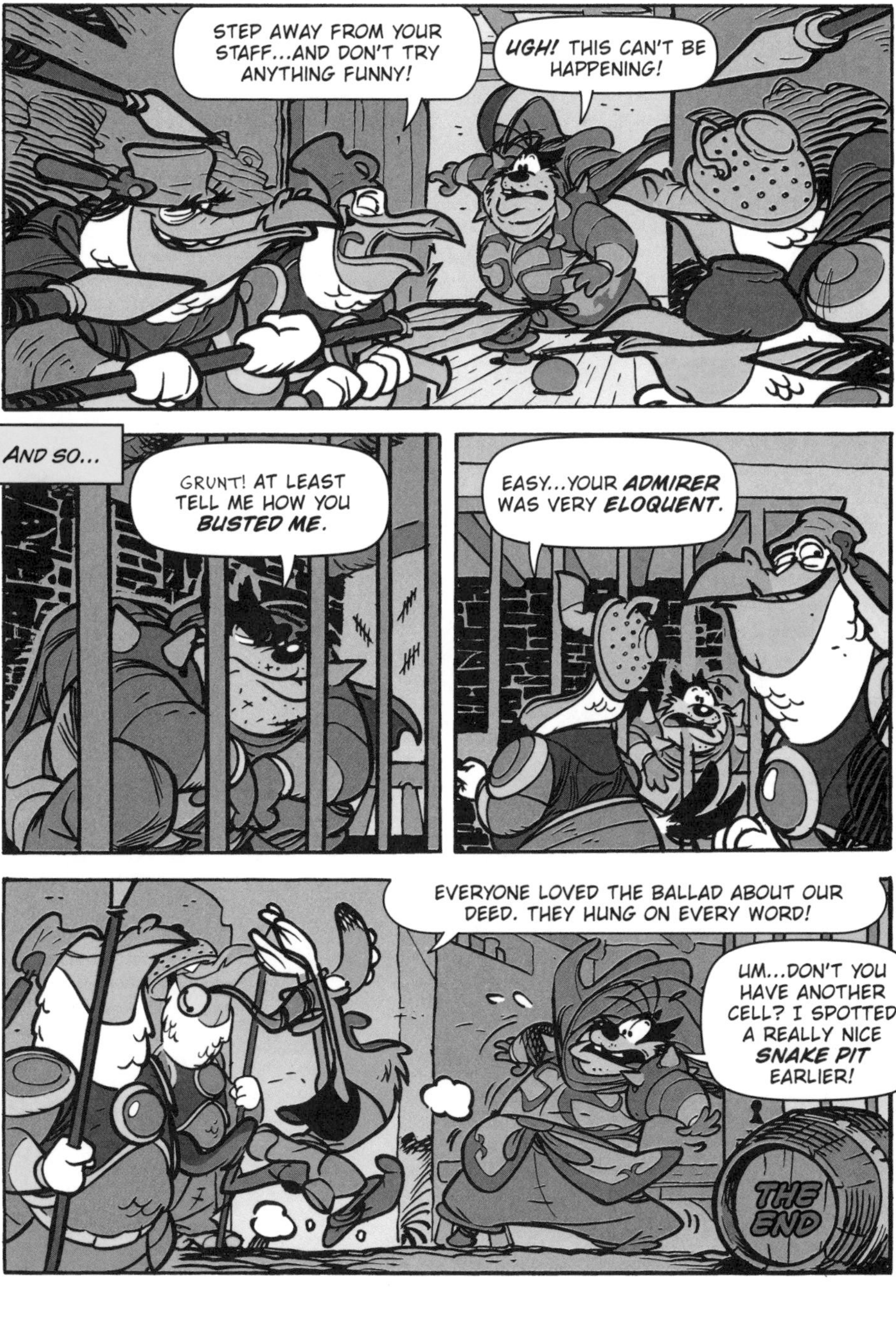

STEP AWAY FROM YOUR STAFF...AND DON'T TRY ANYTHING FUNNY!
UGH! THIS CAN'T BE HAPPENING!
AND SO...
GRUNT! AT LEAST TELL ME HOW YOU BUSTED ME.
EASY...YOUR ADMIRER WAS VERY ELOQUENT.
EVERYONE LOVED THE BALLAD ABOUT OUR DEED. THEY HUNG ON EVERY WORD!
UM...DON'T YOU HAVE ANOTHER CELL? I SPOTTED A REALLY NICE SNAKE PIT EARLIER!
THE END

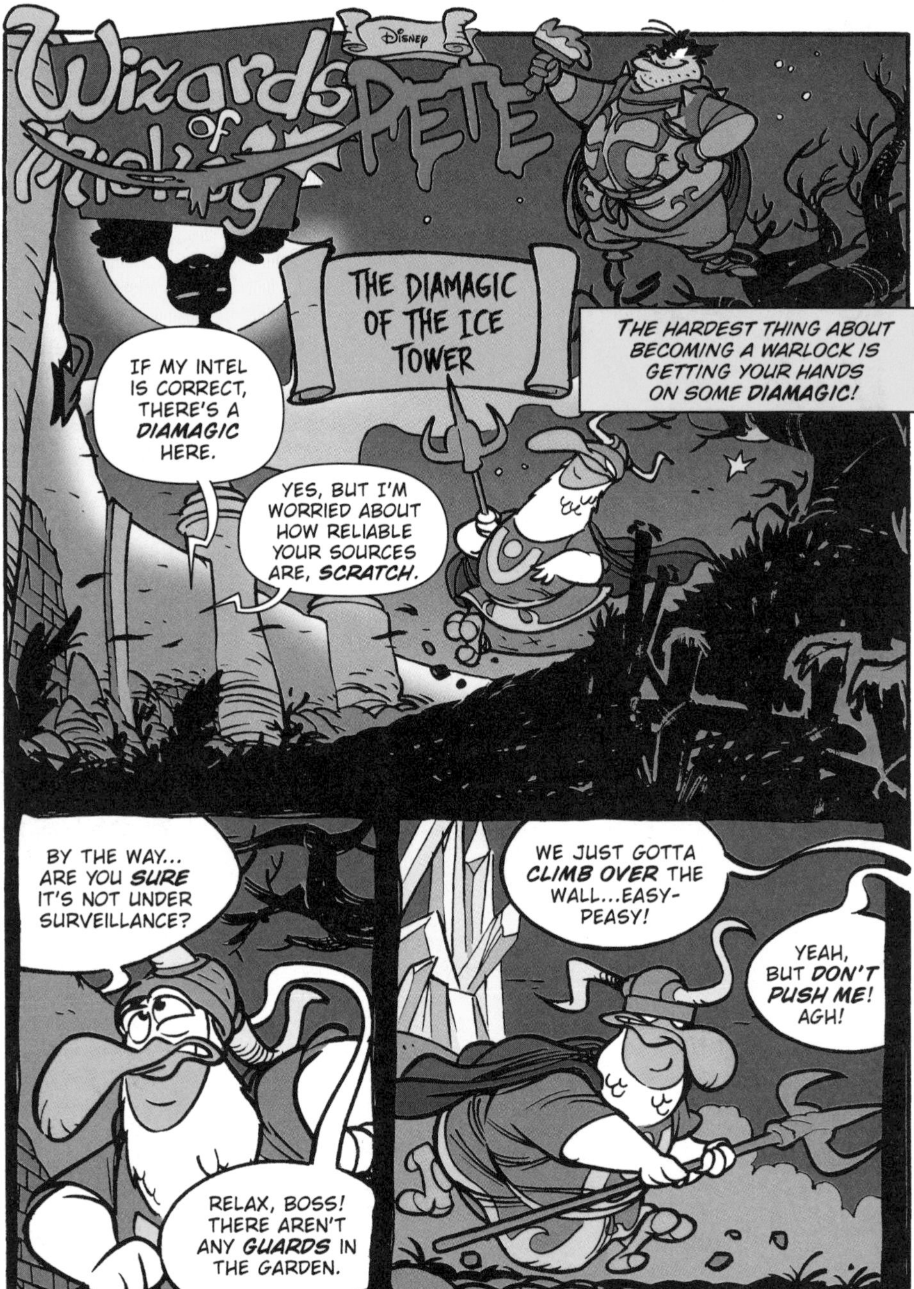
Disney
Wizards of Mickey
PETE
THE DIAMAGIC OF THE ICE TOWER
THE HARDEST THING ABOUT BECOMING A WARLOCK IS GETTING YOUR HANDS ON SOME DIAMAGIC!
IF MY INTEL IS CORRECT, THERE'S A DIAMAGIC HERE.
YES, BUT I'M WORRIED ABOUT HOW RELIABLE YOUR SOURCES ARE, SCRATCH.
BY THE WAY... ARE YOU SURE IT'S NOT UNDER SURVEILLANCE?
RELAX, BOSS! THERE AREN'T ANY GUARDS IN THE GARDEN.
WE JUST GOTTA CLIMB OVER THE WALL...EASY-PEASY!
YEAH, BUT DON'T PUSH ME! AGH!

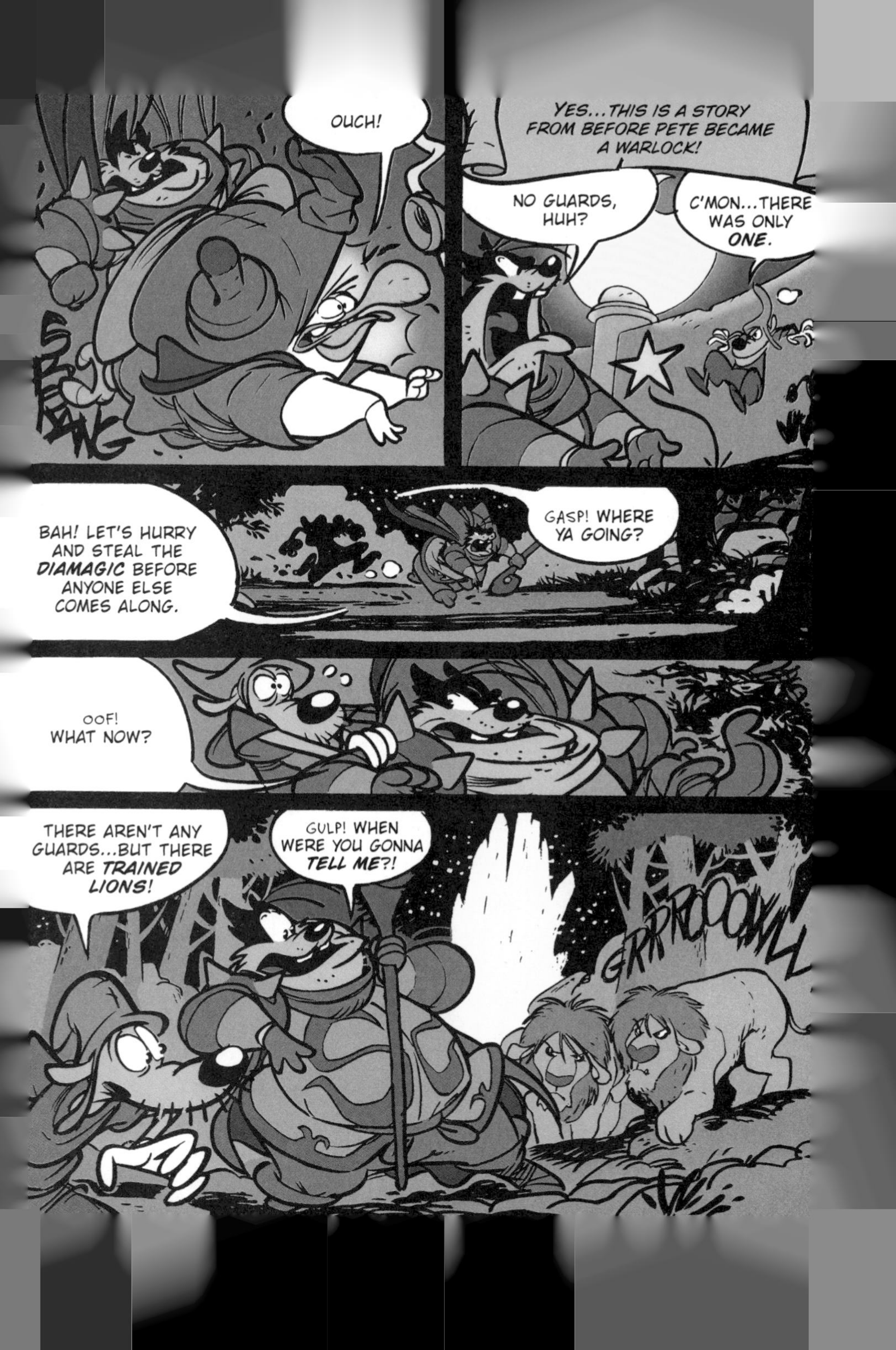
OUCH!
SPROING
YES...THIS IS A STORY FROM BEFORE PETE BECAME A WARLOCK!
NO GUARDS, HUH?
C'MON...THERE WAS ONLY ONE.
BAH! LET'S HURRY AND STEAL THE DIAMAGIC BEFORE ANYONE ELSE COMES ALONG.
GASP! WHERE YA GOING?
OOF! WHAT NOW?
THERE AREN'T ANY GUARDS...BUT THERE ARE TRAINED LIONS!
GULP! WHEN WERE YOU GONNA TELL ME?!
GRRROOOWL

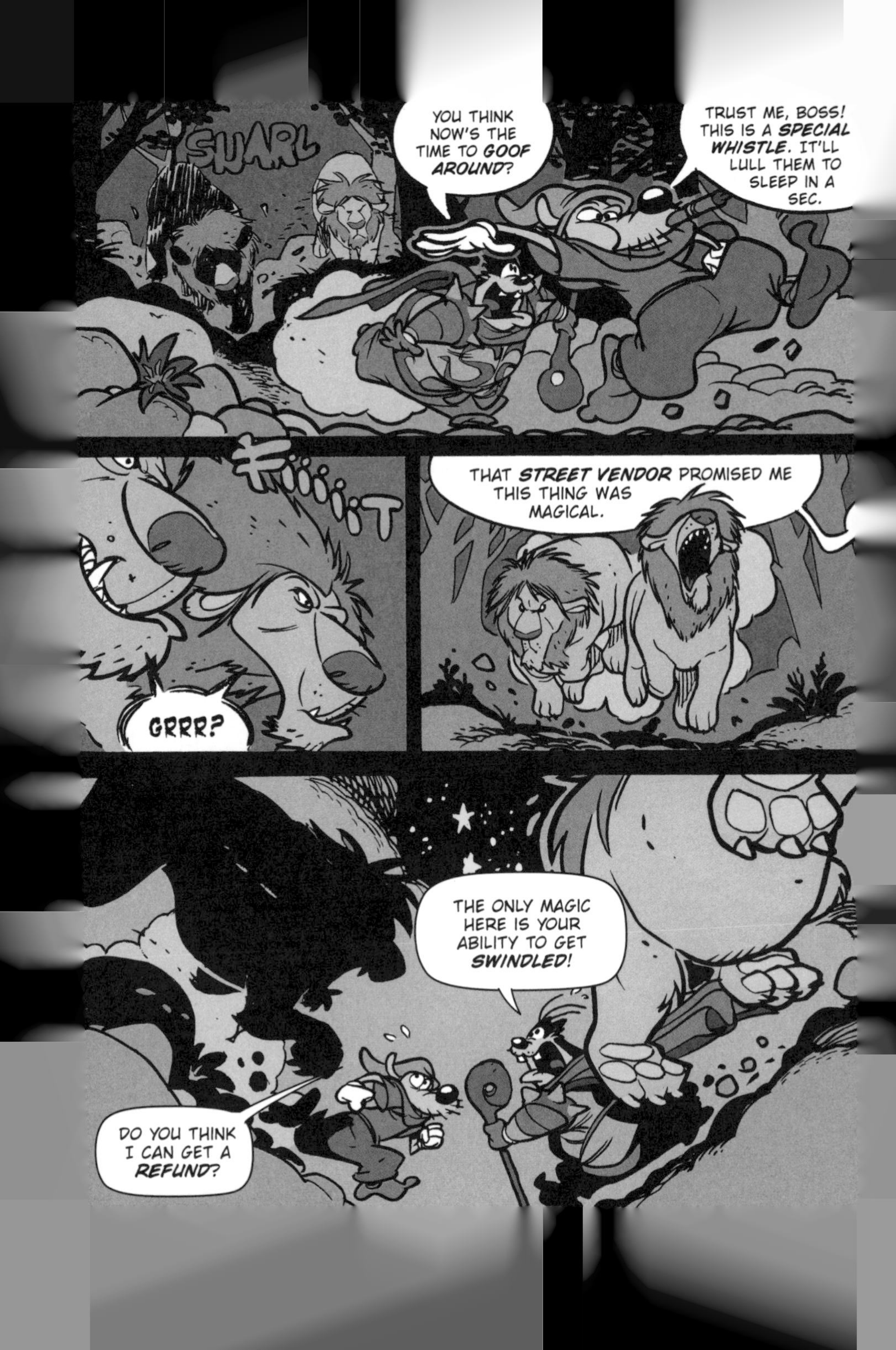
SNARL
YOU THINK NOW'S THE TIME TO GOOF AROUND?
TRUST ME, BOSS! THIS IS A SPECIAL WHISTLE. IT'LL LULL THEM TO SLEEP IN A SEC.
FIiiiiiIT
GRRR?
THAT STREET VENDOR PROMISED ME THIS THING WAS MAGICAL.
THE ONLY MAGIC HERE IS YOUR ABILITY TO GET SWINDLED!
DO YOU THINK I CAN GET A REFUND?

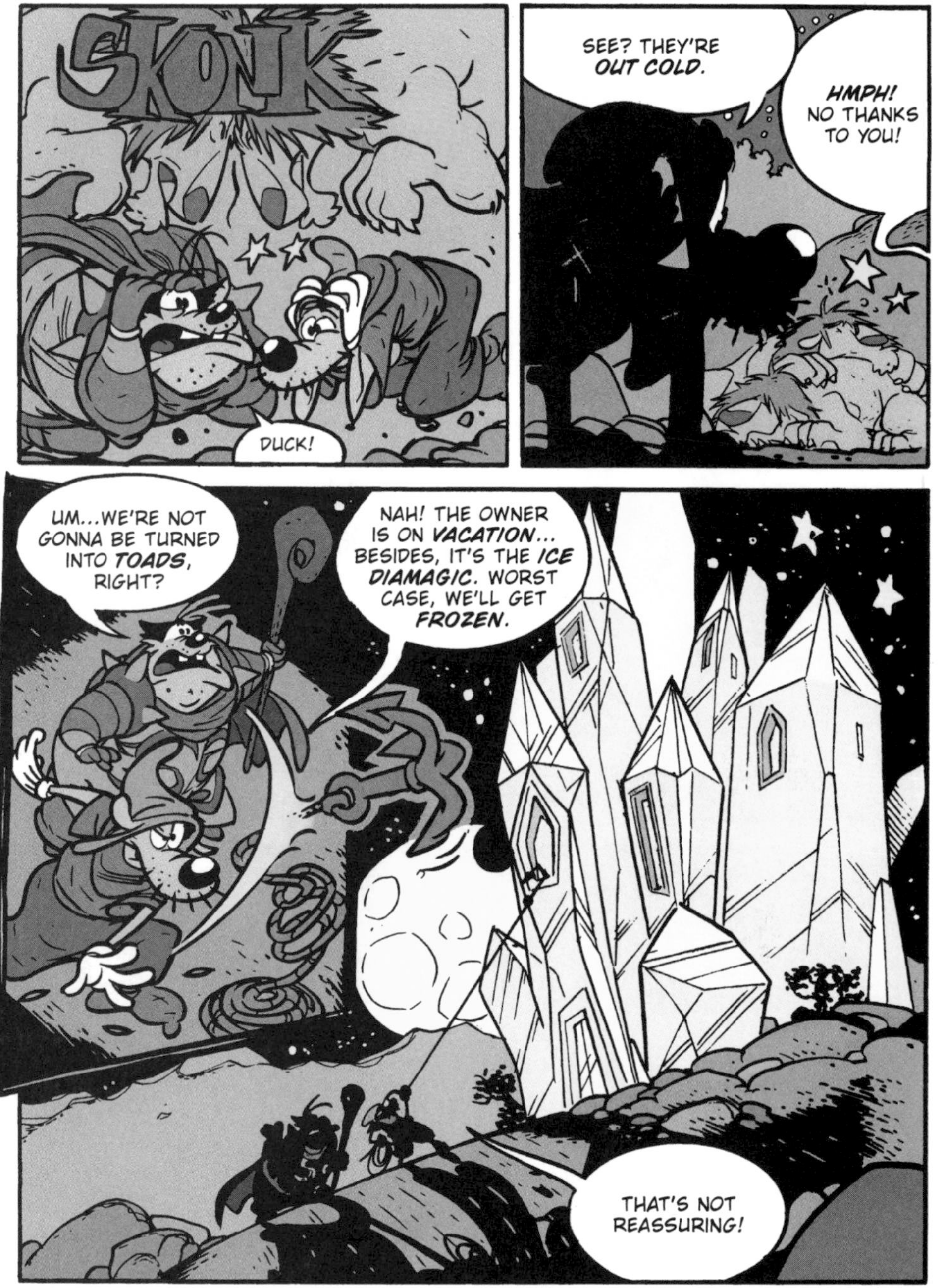
SKONK
DUCK!
SEE? THEY'RE OUT COLD.
HMPH! NO THANKS TO YOU!
UM...WE'RE NOT GONNA BE TURNED INTO TOADS, RIGHT?
NAH! THE OWNER IS ON VACATION... BESIDES, IT'S THE ICE DIAMAGIC. WORST CASE, WE'LL GET FROZEN.
THAT'S NOT REASSURING!

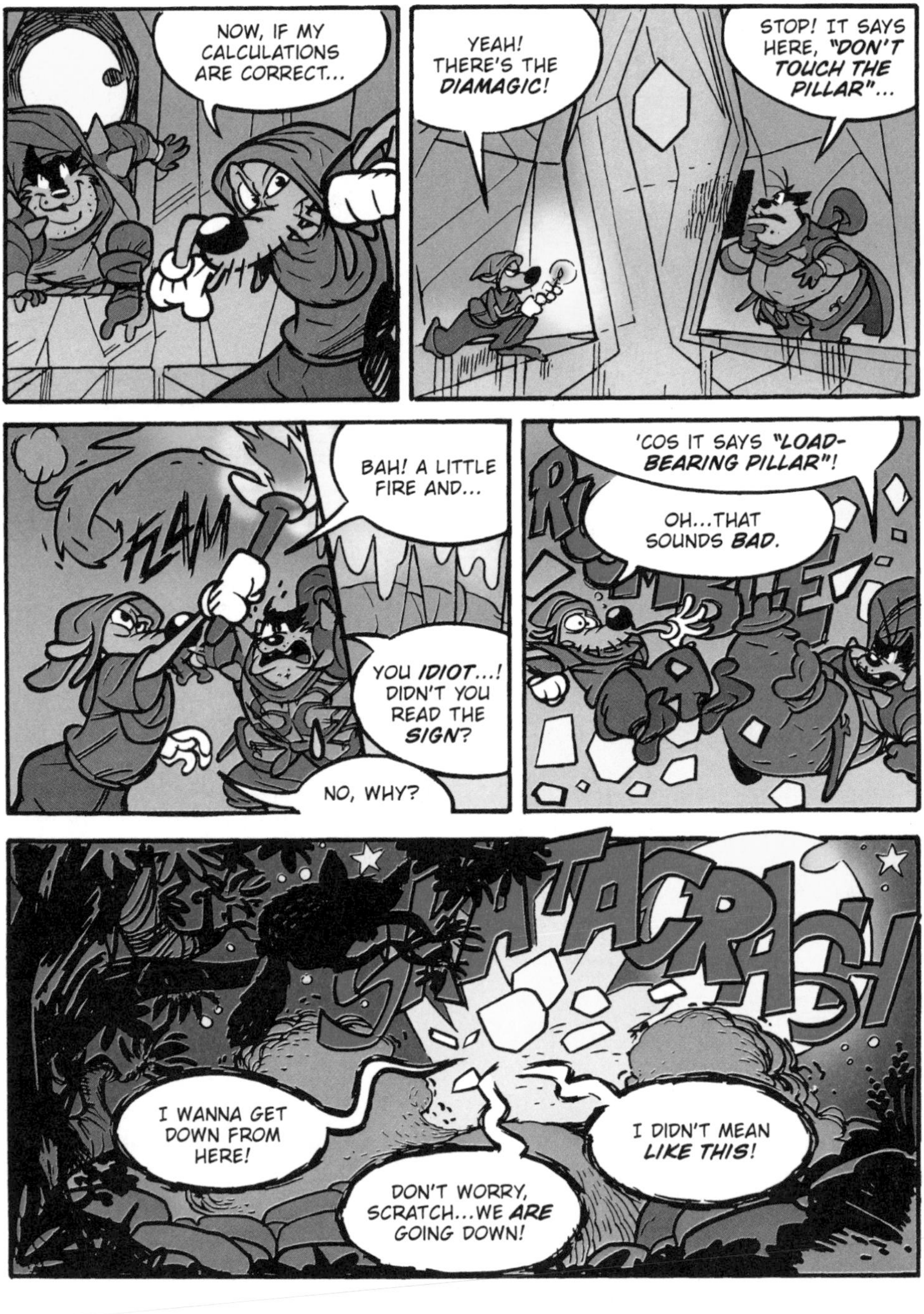
NOW, IF MY CALCULATIONS ARE CORRECT...
YEAH! THERE'S THE DIAMAGIC!
STOP! IT SAYS HERE, "DON'T TOUCH THE PILLAR"...
FLAM
BAH! A LITTLE FIRE AND...
YOU IDIOT...! DIDN'T YOU READ THE SIGN?
NO, WHY?
'COS IT SAYS "LOAD-BEARING PILLAR"!
OH...THAT SOUNDS BAD.
SMATACRASH
I WANNA GET DOWN FROM HERE!
I DIDN'T MEAN LIKE THIS!
DON'T WORRY, SCRATCH...WE ARE GOING DOWN!

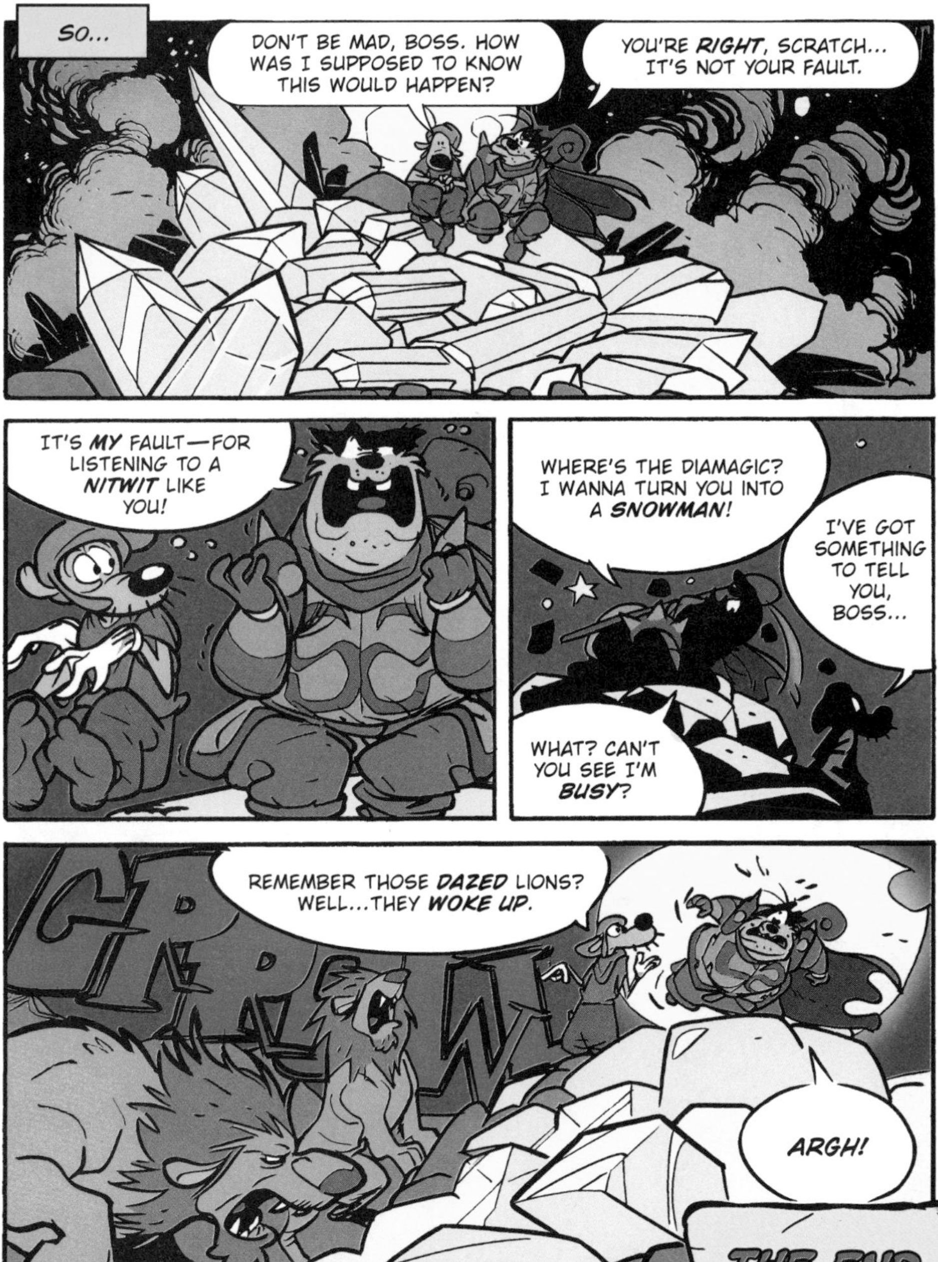
SO...
DON'T BE MAD, BOSS. HOW WAS I SUPPOSED TO KNOW THIS WOULD HAPPEN?
YOU'RE RIGHT, SCRATCH... IT'S NOT YOUR FAULT.
IT'S MY FAULT—FOR LISTENING TO A NITWIT LIKE YOU!
WHERE'S THE DIAMAGIC? I WANNA TURN YOU INTO A SNOWMAN!
I'VE GOT SOMETHING TO TELL YOU, BOSS...
WHAT? CAN'T YOU SEE I'M BUSY?
REMEMBER THOSE DAZED LIONS? WELL...THEY WOKE UP.
GRRROWL
ARGH!
THE END

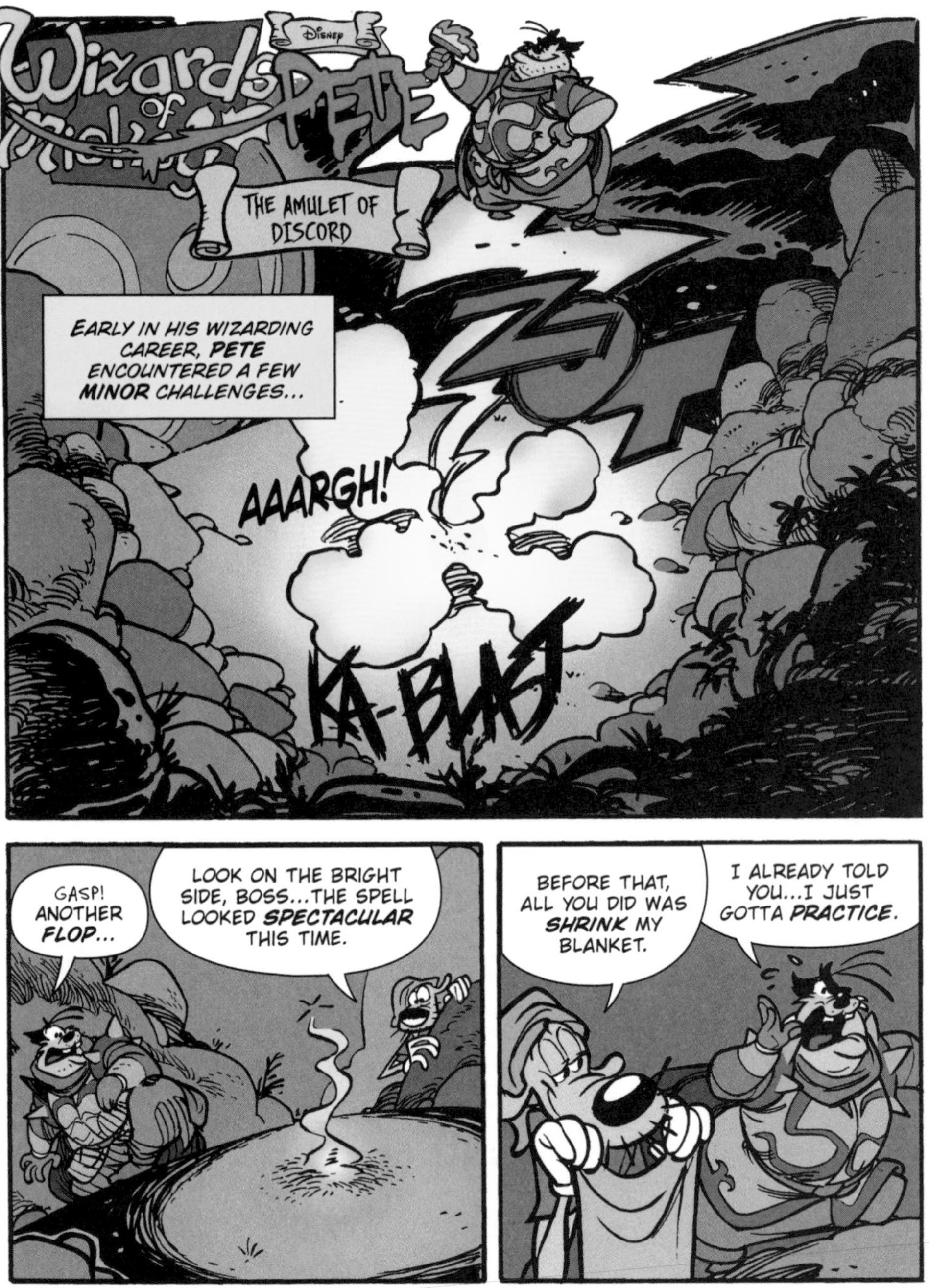

DISNEY
Wizards of
PETE
THE AMULET OF DISCORD
EARLY IN HIS WIZARDING CAREER, PETE ENCOUNTERED A FEW MINOR CHALLENGES...
ZOT
AAARGH!
KA-BLAST
GASP! ANOTHER FLOP...
LOOK ON THE BRIGHT SIDE, BOSS...THE SPELL LOOKED SPECTACULAR THIS TIME.
BEFORE THAT, ALL YOU DID WAS SHRINK MY BLANKET.
I ALREADY TOLD YOU...I JUST GOTTA PRACTICE.

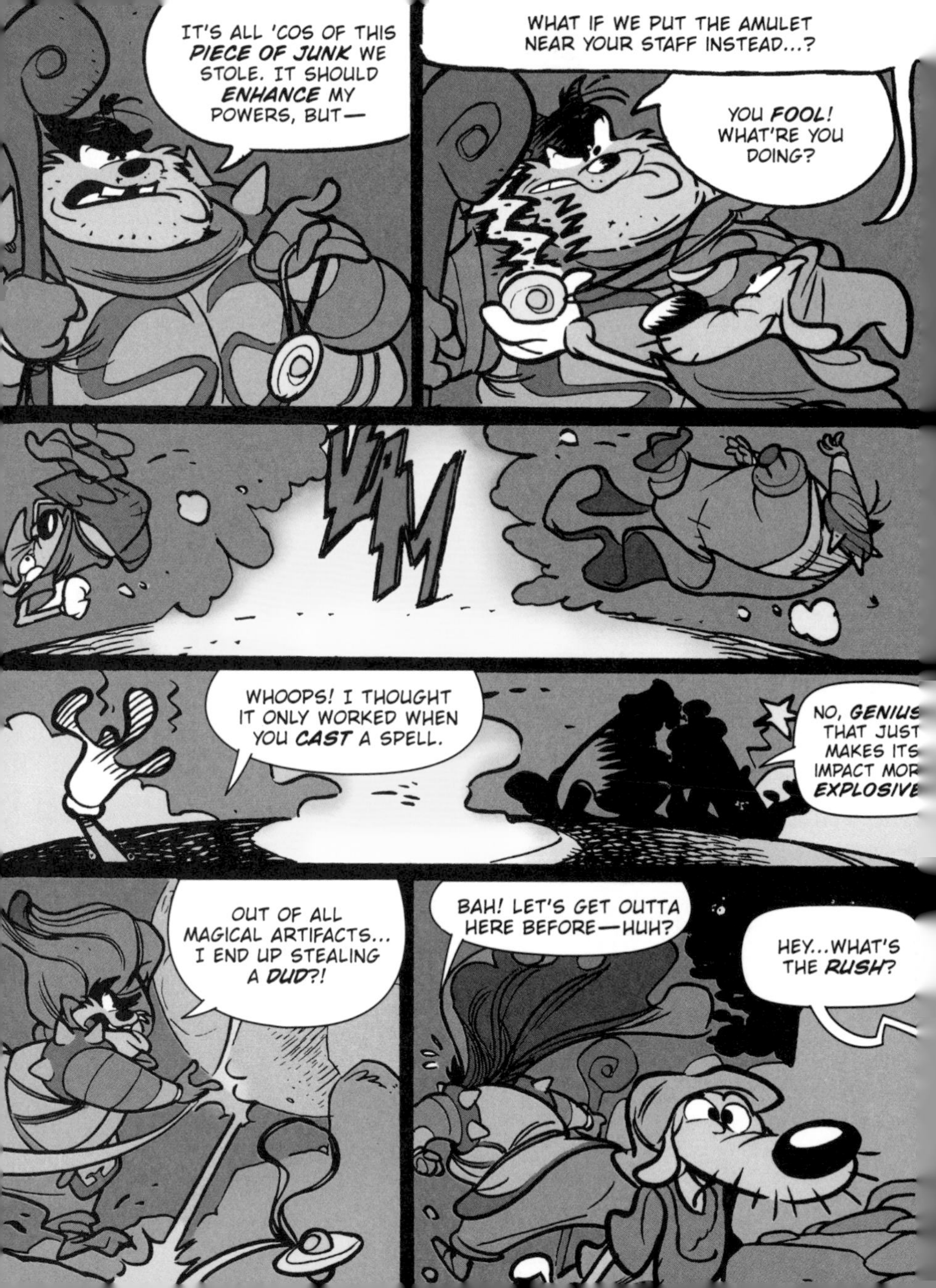

IT'S ALL 'COS OF THIS PIECE OF JUNK WE STOLE. IT SHOULD ENHANCE MY POWERS, BUT—
WHAT IF WE PUT THE AMULET NEAR YOUR STAFF INSTEAD...?
YOU FOOL! WHAT'RE YOU DOING?
WHOOPS! I THOUGHT IT ONLY WORKED WHEN YOU CAST A SPELL.
NO, GENIUS THAT JUST MAKES ITS IMPACT MOR EXPLOSIVE
OUT OF ALL MAGICAL ARTIFACTS... I END UP STEALING A DUD?!
BAH! LET'S GET OUTTA HERE BEFORE—HUH?
HEY...WHAT'S THE RUSH?

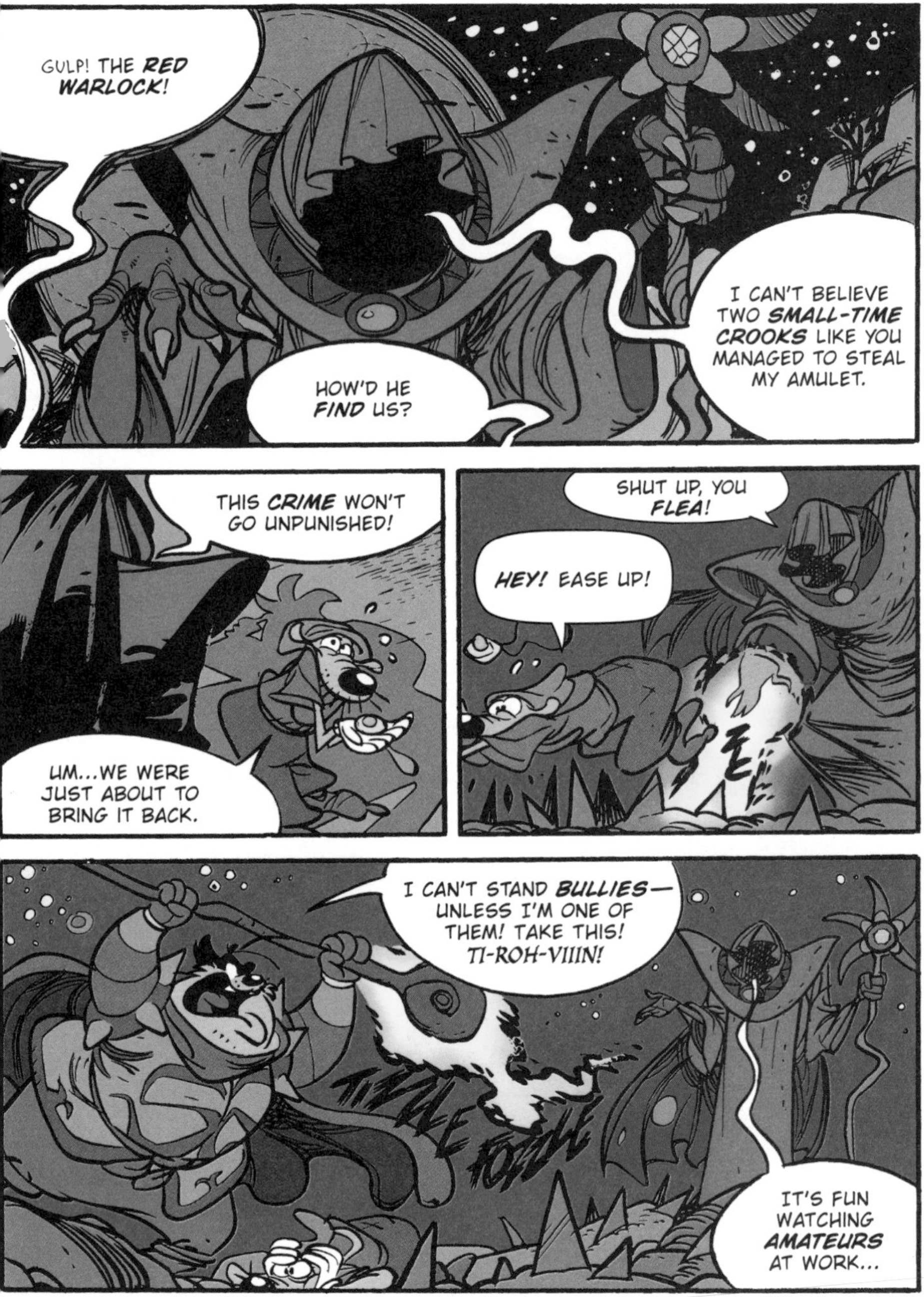
GULP! THE **RED WARLOCK!**
I CAN'T BELIEVE TWO **SMALL-TIME CROOKS** LIKE YOU MANAGED TO STEAL MY AMULET.
HOW'D HE **FIND** US?
THIS **CRIME** WON'T GO UNPUNISHED!
UM...WE WERE JUST ABOUT TO BRING IT BACK.
SHUT UP, YOU **FLEA!**
HEY! EASE UP!
I CAN'T STAND **BULLIES**— UNLESS I'M ONE OF THEM! TAKE THIS! *TI-ROH-VIIIN!*
IT'S FUN WATCHING **AMATEURS** AT WORK...

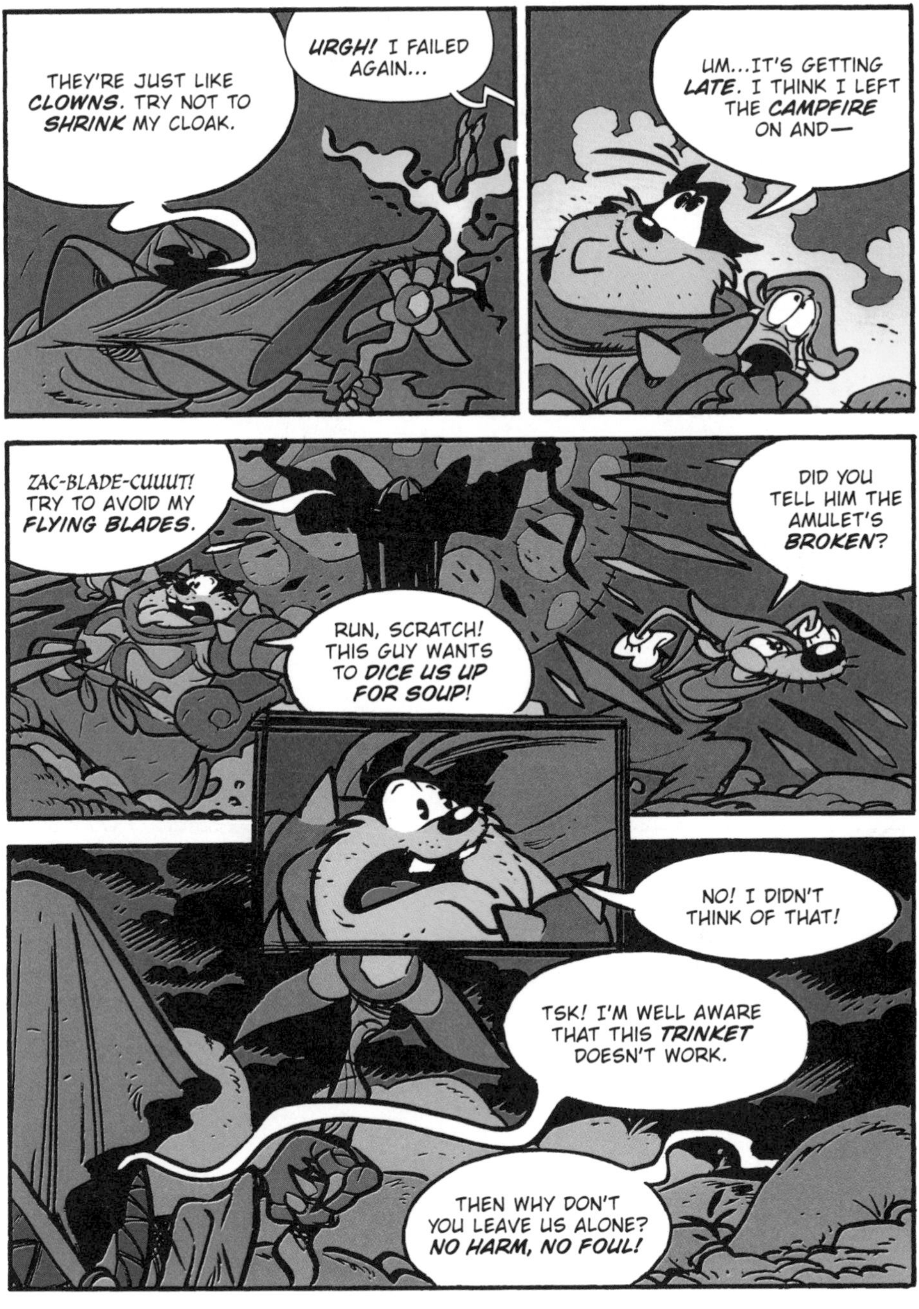
THEY'RE JUST LIKE CLOWNS. TRY NOT TO SHRINK MY CLOAK.
URGH! I FAILED AGAIN...
UM...IT'S GETTING LATE. I THINK I LEFT THE CAMPFIRE ON AND—
ZAC-BLADE-CUUUT! TRY TO AVOID MY FLYING BLADES.
DID YOU TELL HIM THE AMULET'S BROKEN?
RUN, SCRATCH! THIS GUY WANTS TO DICE US UP FOR SOUP!
NO! I DIDN'T THINK OF THAT!
TSK! I'M WELL AWARE THAT THIS TRINKET DOESN'T WORK.
THEN WHY DON'T YOU LEAVE US ALONE? NO HARM, NO FOUL!

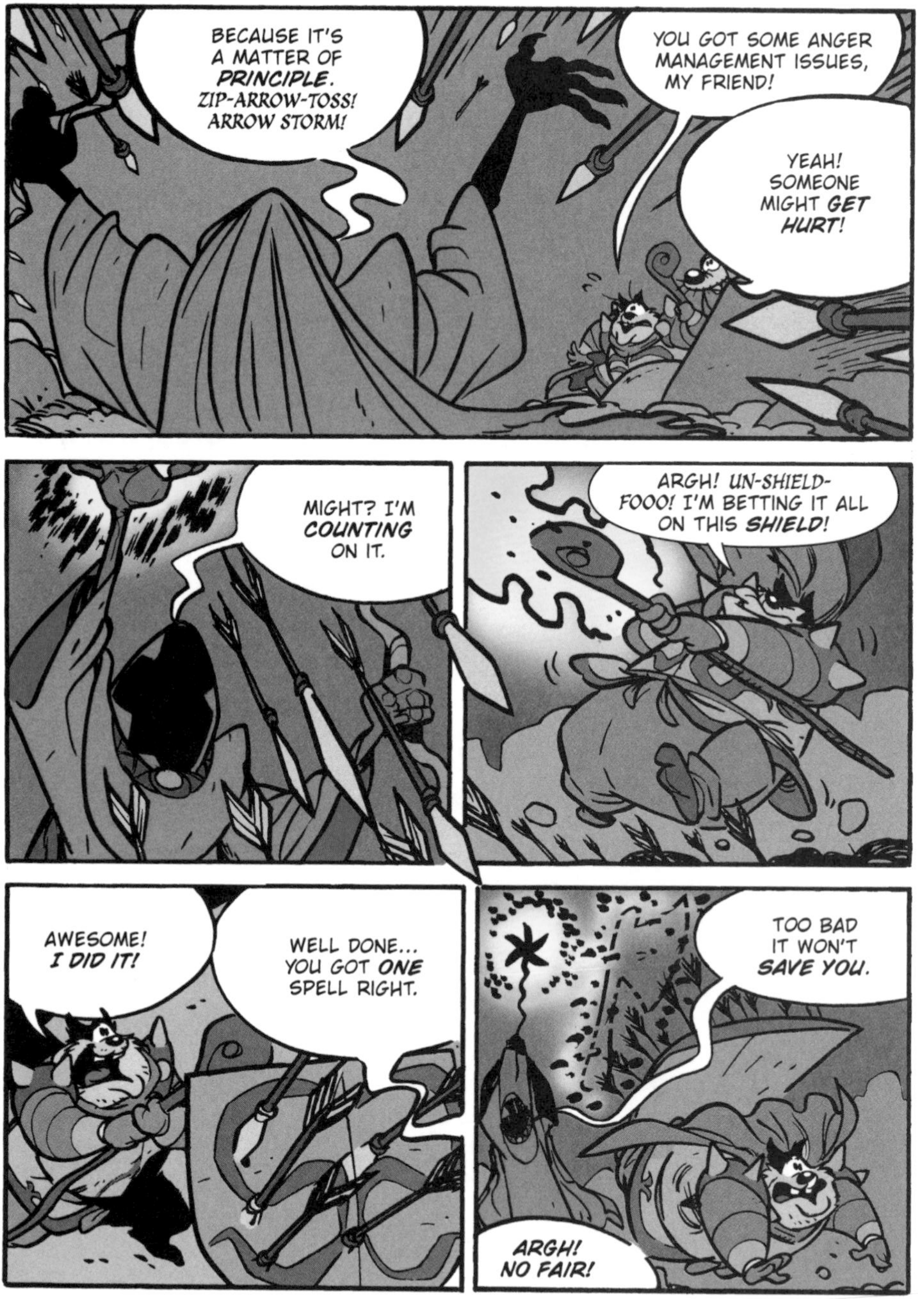
BECAUSE IT'S A MATTER OF PRINCIPLE. ZIP-ARROW-TOSS! ARROW STORM!
YOU GOT SOME ANGER MANAGEMENT ISSUES, MY FRIEND!
YEAH! SOMEONE MIGHT GET HURT!
MIGHT? I'M COUNTING ON IT.
ARGH! UN-SHIELD-FOOO! I'M BETTING IT ALL ON THIS SHIELD!
AWESOME! I DID IT!
WELL DONE... YOU GOT ONE SPELL RIGHT.
TOO BAD IT WON'T SAVE YOU.
ARGH! NO FAIR!

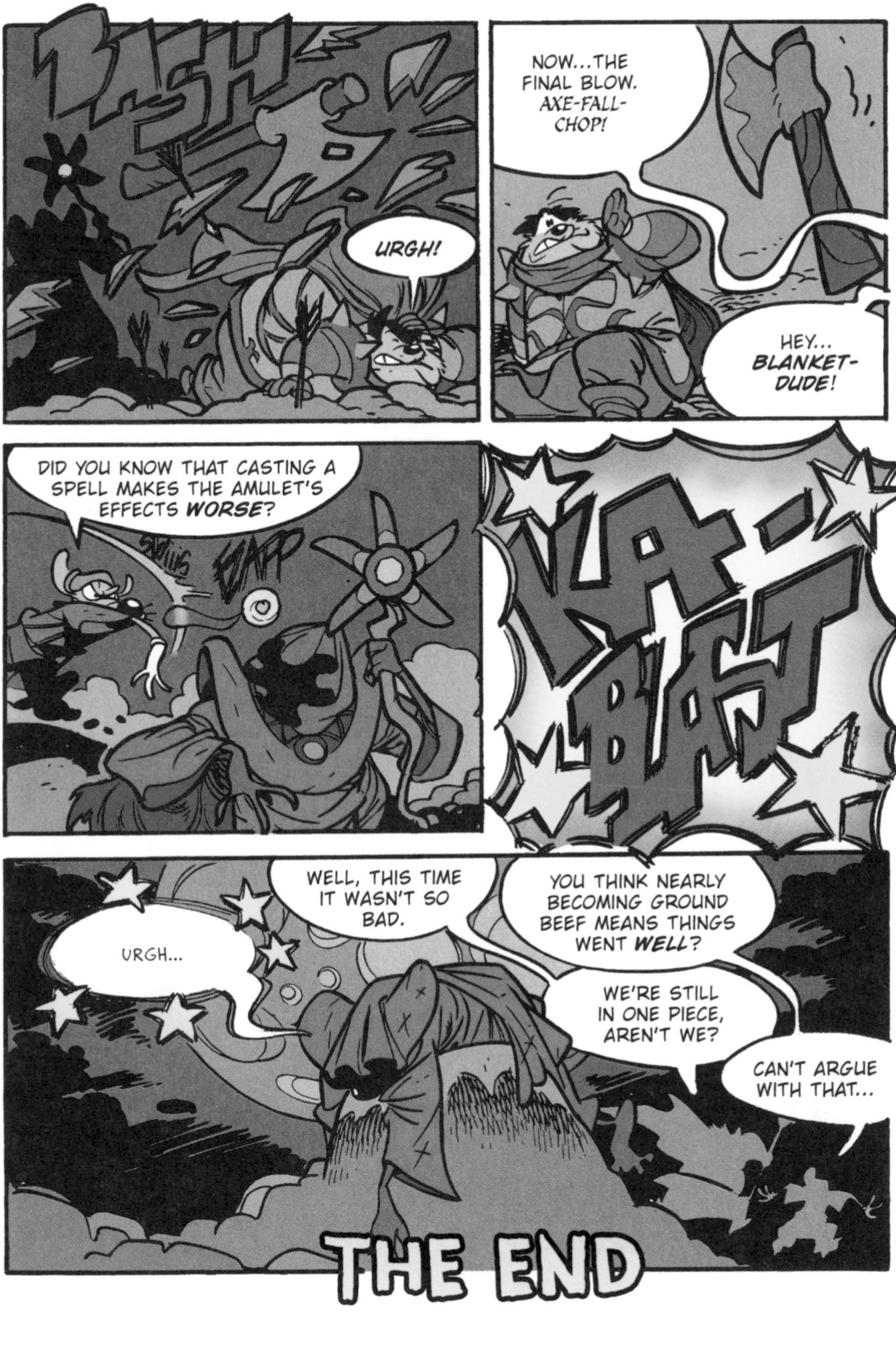
BASH
URGH!
NOW...THE FINAL BLOW. AXE-FALL-CHOP!
HEY... BLANKET-DUDE!
DID YOU KNOW THAT CASTING A SPELL MAKES THE AMULET'S EFFECTS WORSE?
KA-BLAST
URGH...
WELL, THIS TIME IT WASN'T SO BAD.
YOU THINK NEARLY BECOMING GROUND BEEF MEANS THINGS WENT WELL?
WE'RE STILL IN ONE PIECE, AREN'T WE?
CAN'T ARGUE WITH THAT...
THE END

Wizards of Mickey

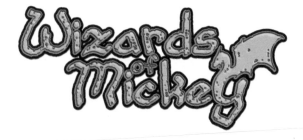

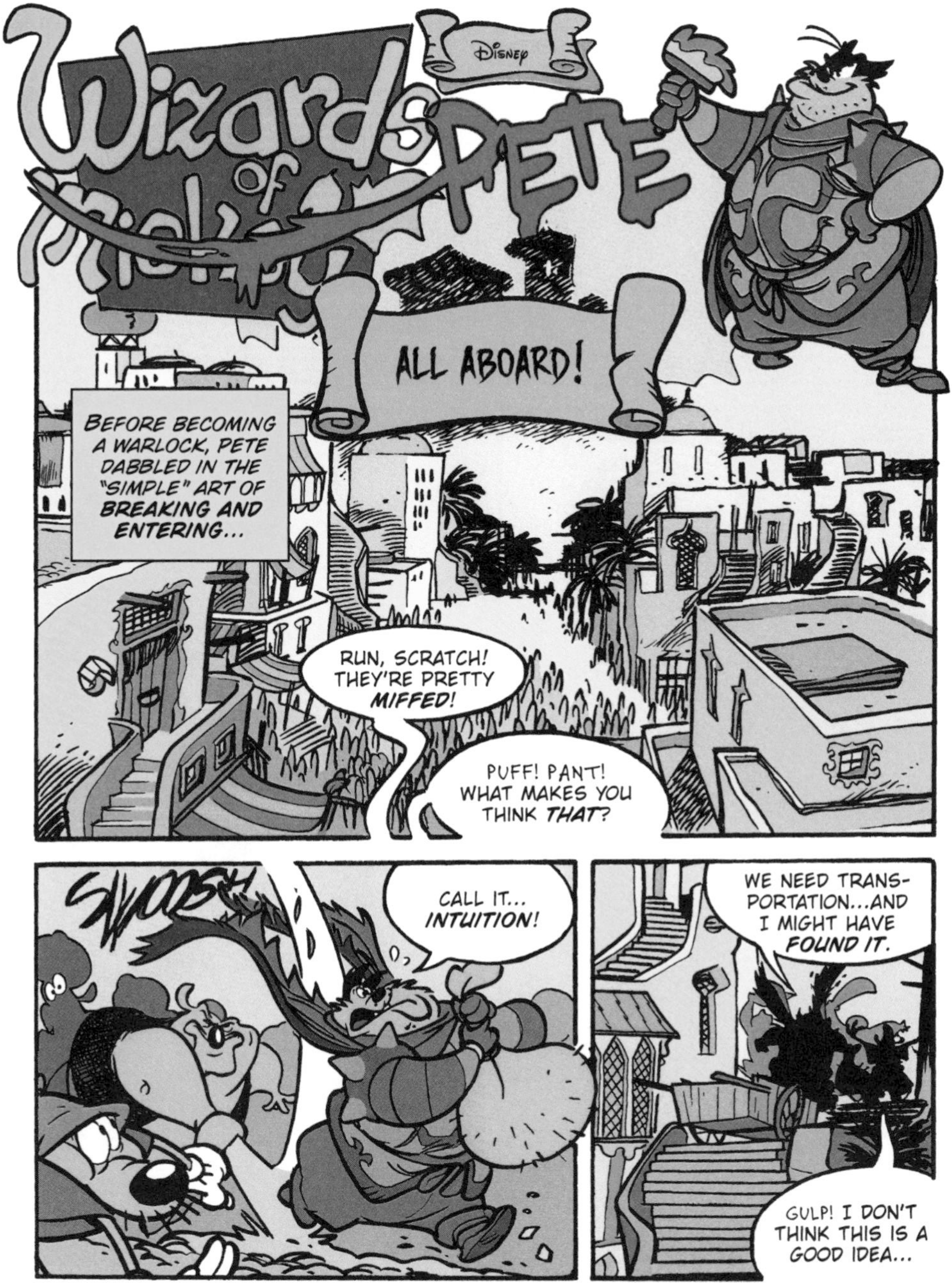
Disney
Wizards of Mickey
PETE
ALL ABOARD!
BEFORE BECOMING A WARLOCK, PETE DABBLED IN THE "SIMPLE" ART OF BREAKING AND ENTERING...
RUN, SCRATCH! THEY'RE PRETTY MIFFED!
PUFF! PANT! WHAT MAKES YOU THINK THAT?
SWOOSH!
CALL IT... INTUITION!
WE NEED TRANSPORTATION...AND I MIGHT HAVE FOUND IT.
GULP! I DON'T THINK THIS IS A GOOD IDEA...

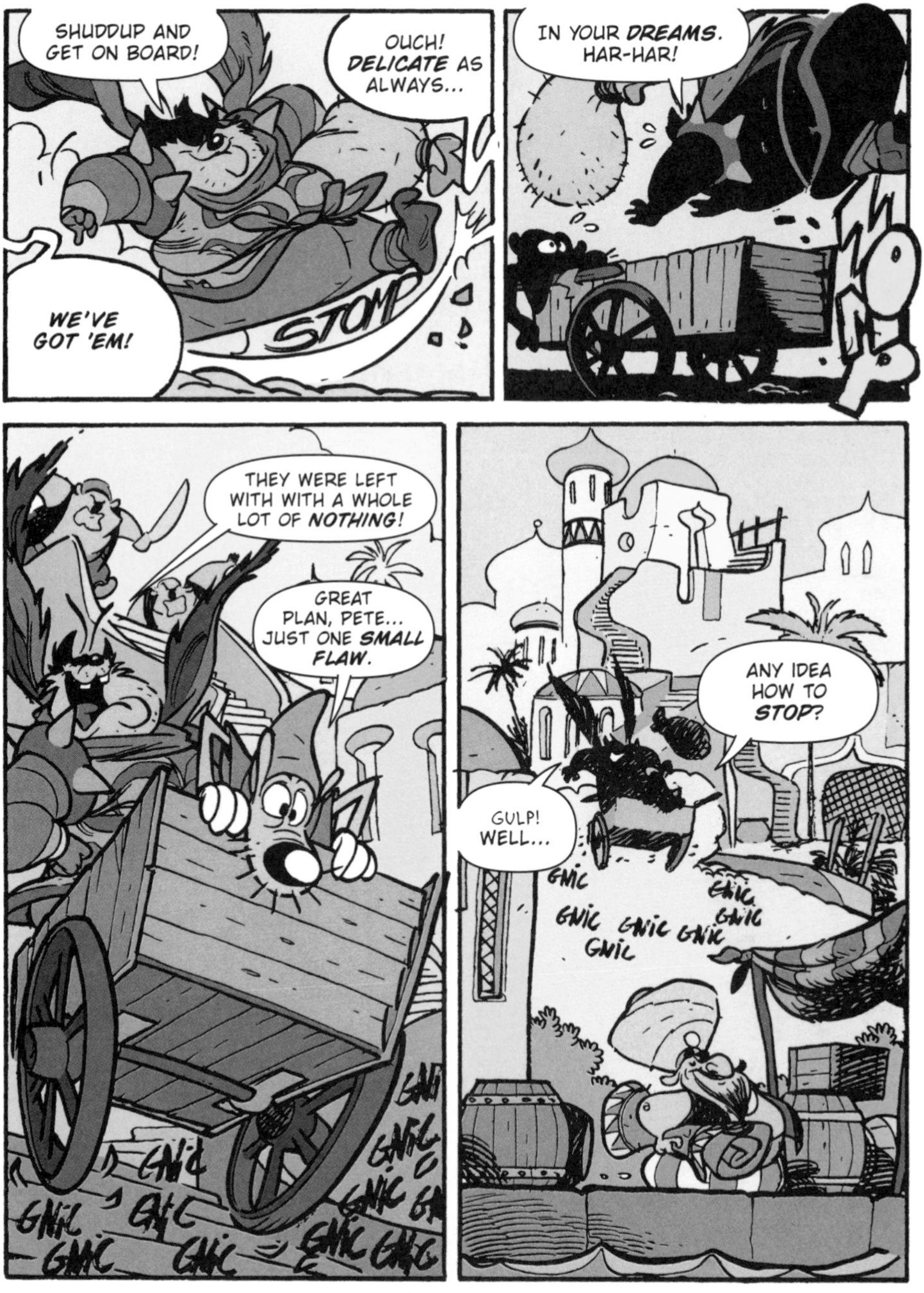
SHUDDUP AND GET ON BOARD!
OUCH! DELICATE AS ALWAYS...
WE'VE GOT 'EM!
STOMP
IN YOUR DREAMS. HAR-HAR!
THEY WERE LEFT WITH WITH A WHOLE LOT OF NOTHING!
GREAT PLAN, PETE... JUST ONE SMALL FLAW.
GNIC GNIC GNIC GNIC GNIC GNIC GNIC GNIC
ANY IDEA HOW TO STOP?
GULP! WELL...
GNIC GNIC GNIC GNIC GNIC GNIC GNIC

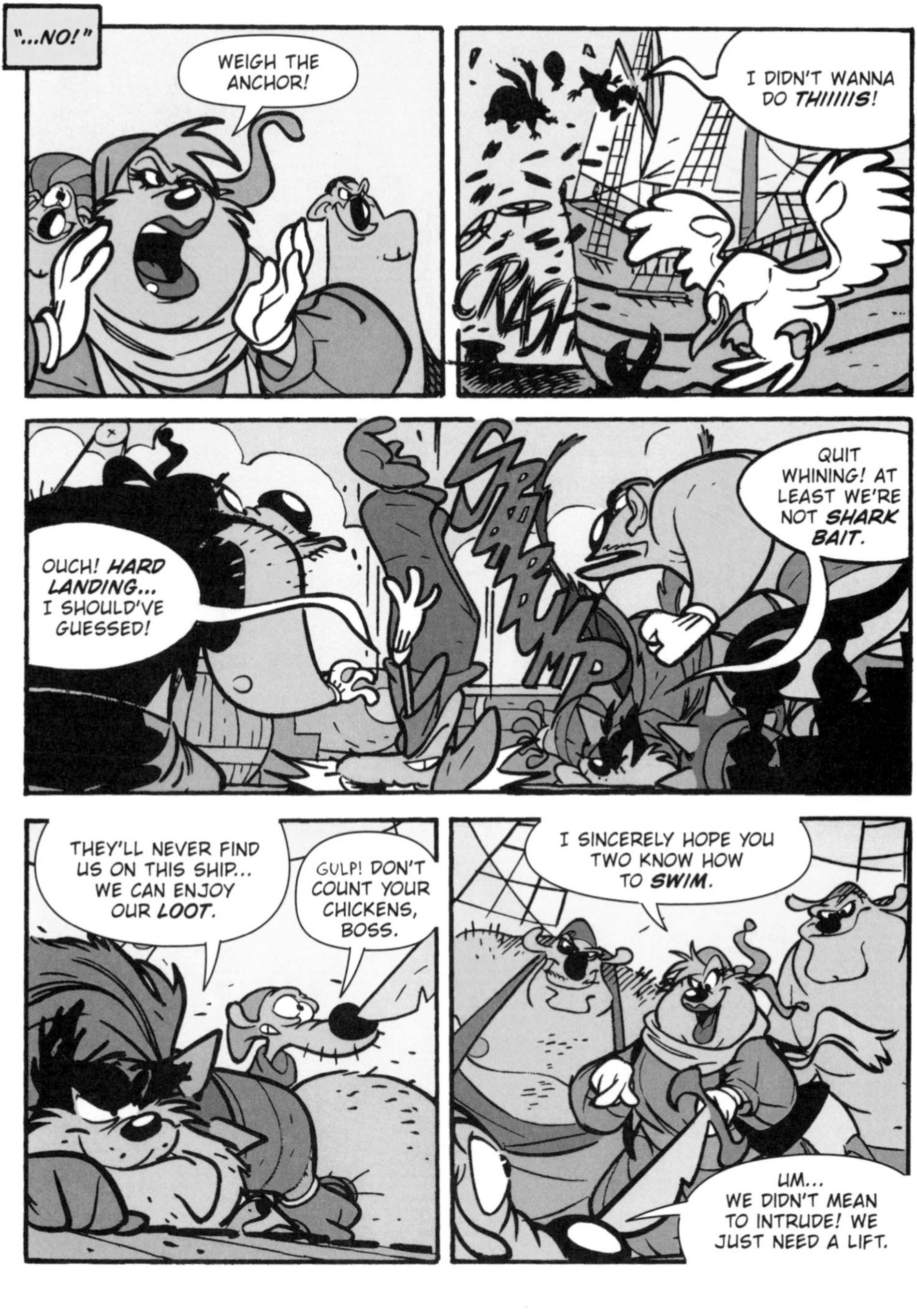
"...NO!"
WEIGH THE ANCHOR!
I DIDN'T WANNA DO THIIIIIS!
CRASH
OUCH! HARD LANDING... I SHOULD'VE GUESSED!
QUIT WHINING! AT LEAST WE'RE NOT SHARK BAIT.
THEY'LL NEVER FIND US ON THIS SHIP... WE CAN ENJOY OUR LOOT.
GULP! DON'T COUNT YOUR CHICKENS, BOSS.
I SINCERELY HOPE YOU TWO KNOW HOW TO SWIM.
UM... WE DIDN'T MEAN TO INTRUDE! WE JUST NEED A LIFT.

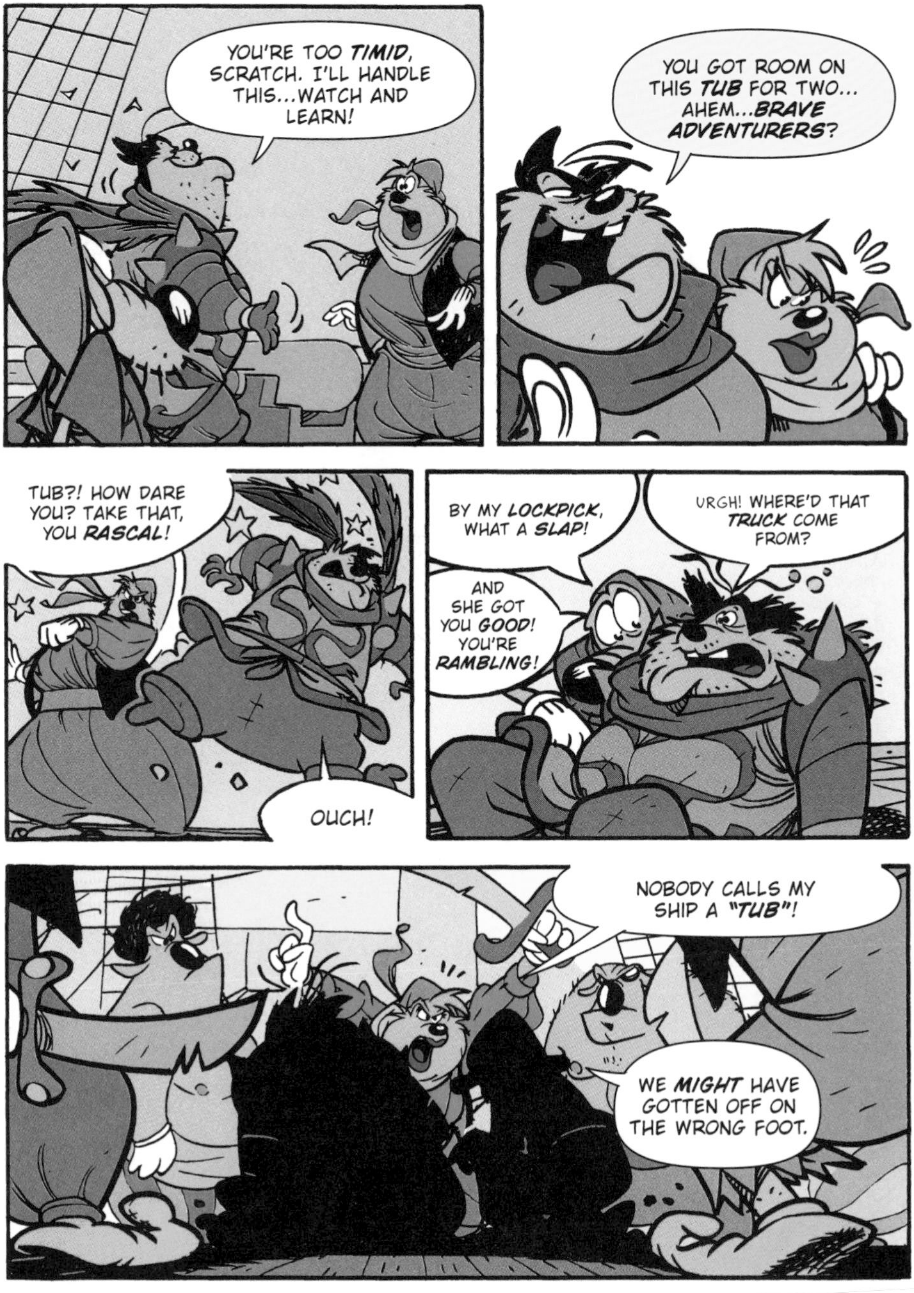
YOU'RE TOO TIMID, SCRATCH. I'LL HANDLE THIS...WATCH AND LEARN!
YOU GOT ROOM ON THIS TUB FOR TWO... AHEM...BRAVE ADVENTURERS?
TUB?! HOW DARE YOU? TAKE THAT, YOU RASCAL!
OUCH!
BY MY LOCKPICK, WHAT A SLAP!
URGH! WHERE'D THAT TRUCK COME FROM?
AND SHE GOT YOU GOOD! YOU'RE RAMBLING!
NOBODY CALLS MY SHIP A "TUB"!
WE MIGHT HAVE GOTTEN OFF ON THE WRONG FOOT.

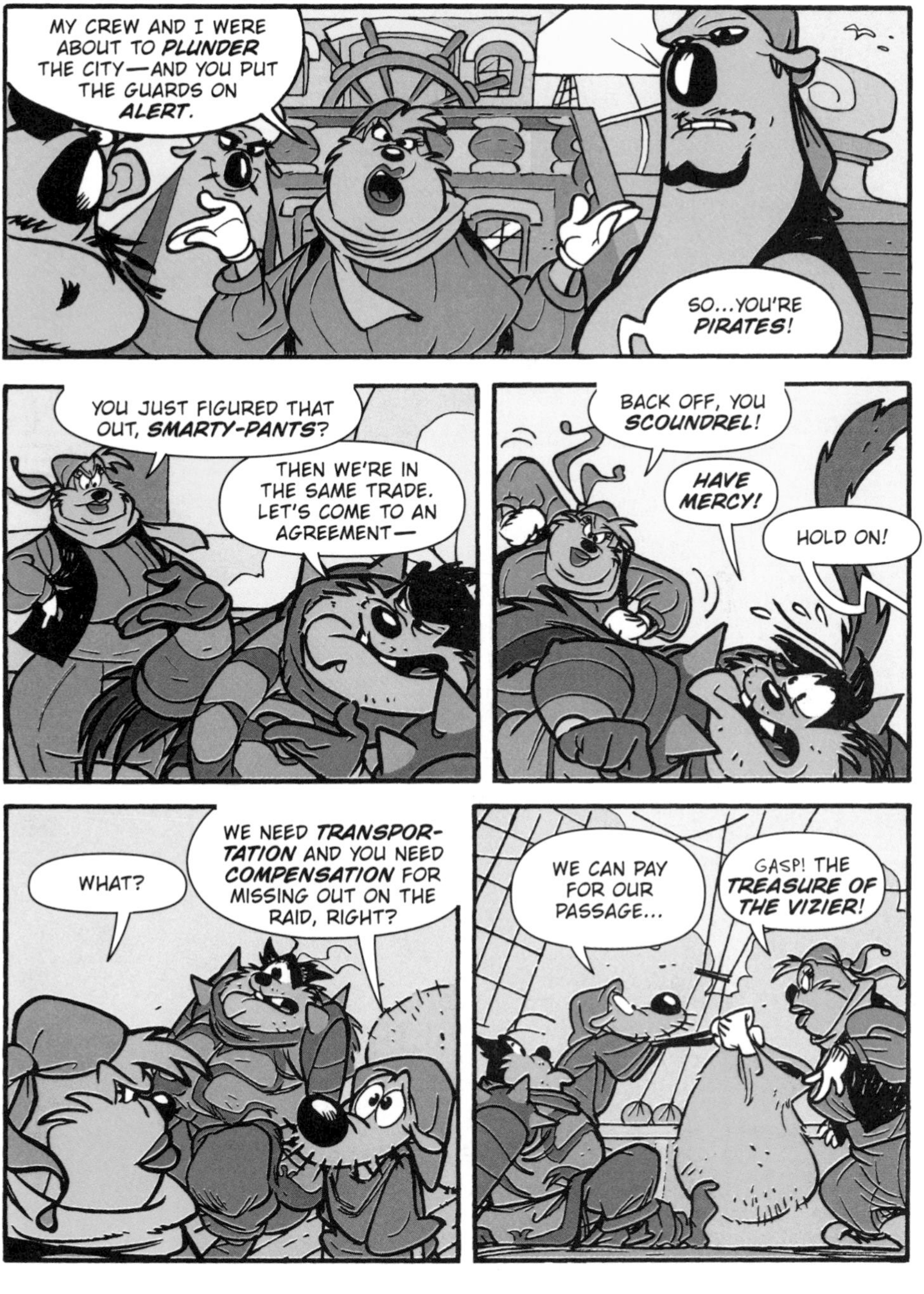
MY CREW AND I WERE ABOUT TO PLUNDER THE CITY—AND YOU PUT THE GUARDS ON ALERT.
SO...YOU'RE PIRATES!
YOU JUST FIGURED THAT OUT, SMARTY-PANTS?
THEN WE'RE IN THE SAME TRADE. LET'S COME TO AN AGREEMENT—
BACK OFF, YOU SCOUNDREL!
HAVE MERCY!
HOLD ON!
WHAT?
WE NEED TRANSPORTATION AND YOU NEED COMPENSATION FOR MISSING OUT ON THE RAID, RIGHT?
WE CAN PAY FOR OUR PASSAGE...
GASP! THE TREASURE OF THE VIZIER!

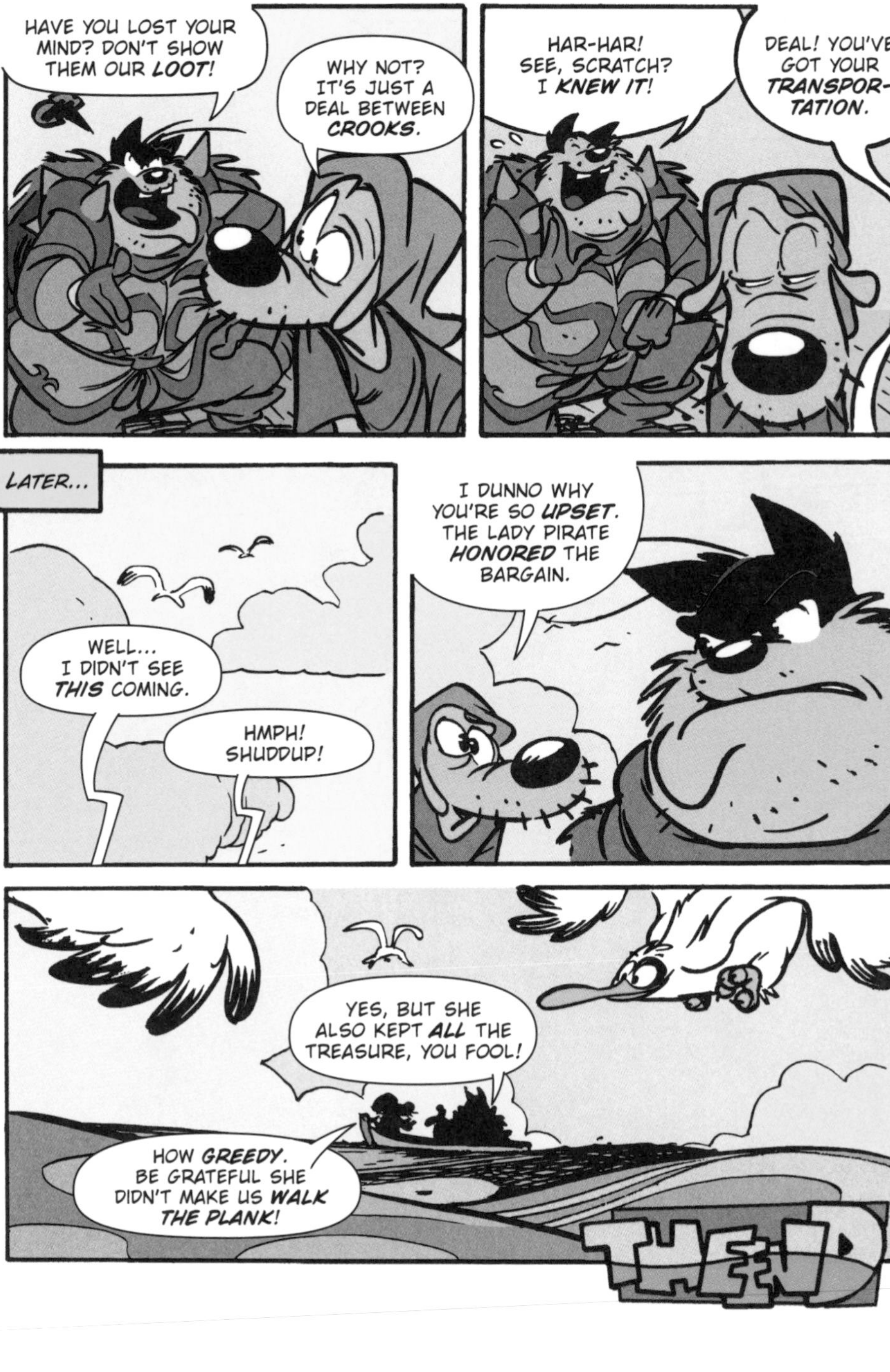
HAVE YOU LOST YOUR MIND? DON'T SHOW THEM OUR LOOT!
WHY NOT? IT'S JUST A DEAL BETWEEN CROOKS.
HAR-HAR! SEE, SCRATCH? I KNEW IT!
DEAL! YOU'VE GOT YOUR TRANSPORTATION.
LATER...
WELL... I DIDN'T SEE THIS COMING.
HMPH! SHUDDUP!
I DUNNO WHY YOU'RE SO UPSET. THE LADY PIRATE HONORED THE BARGAIN.
YES, BUT SHE ALSO KEPT ALL THE TREASURE, YOU FOOL!
HOW GREEDY. BE GRATEFUL SHE DIDN'T MAKE US WALK THE PLANK!
THE END

Wizards of Mickey

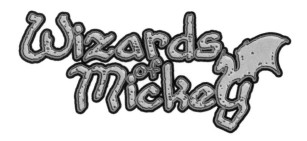

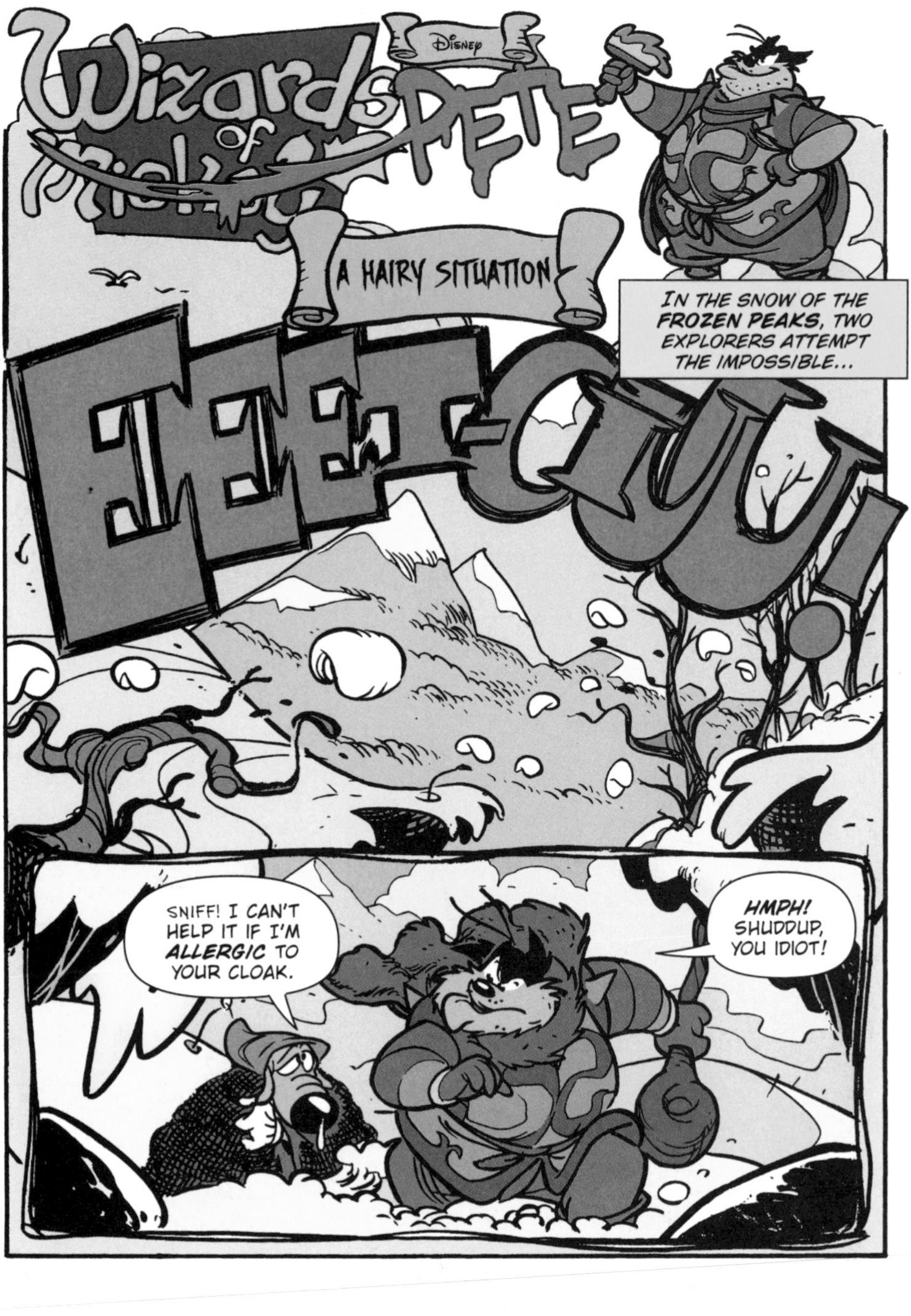

Disney
Wizards of Mickey
PETE
A HAIRY SITUATION
IN THE SNOW OF THE FROZEN PEAKS, TWO EXPLORERS ATTEMPT THE IMPOSSIBLE...
EEE-CHUU!
SNIFF! I CAN'T HELP IT IF I'M ALLERGIC TO YOUR CLOAK.
HMPH! SHUDDUP, YOU IDIOT!

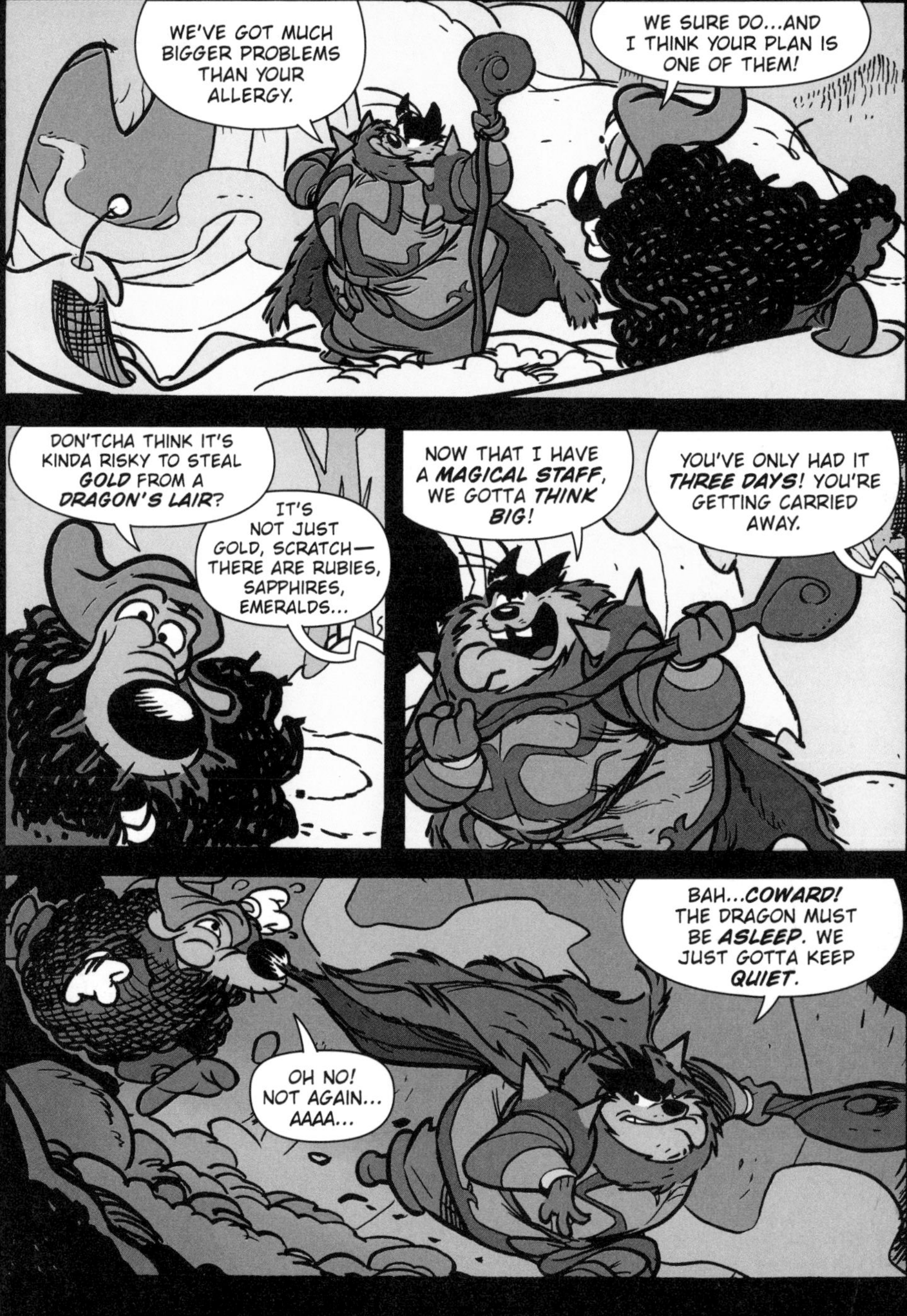
WE'VE GOT MUCH BIGGER PROBLEMS THAN YOUR ALLERGY.
WE SURE DO...AND I THINK YOUR PLAN IS ONE OF THEM!
DON'TCHA THINK IT'S KINDA RISKY TO STEAL GOLD FROM A DRAGON'S LAIR?
IT'S NOT JUST GOLD, SCRATCH—THERE ARE RUBIES, SAPPHIRES, EMERALDS...
NOW THAT I HAVE A MAGICAL STAFF, WE GOTTA THINK BIG!
YOU'VE ONLY HAD IT THREE DAYS! YOU'RE GETTING CARRIED AWAY.
BAH...COWARD! THE DRAGON MUST BE ASLEEP. WE JUST GOTTA KEEP QUIET.
OH NO! NOT AGAIN... AAAA...

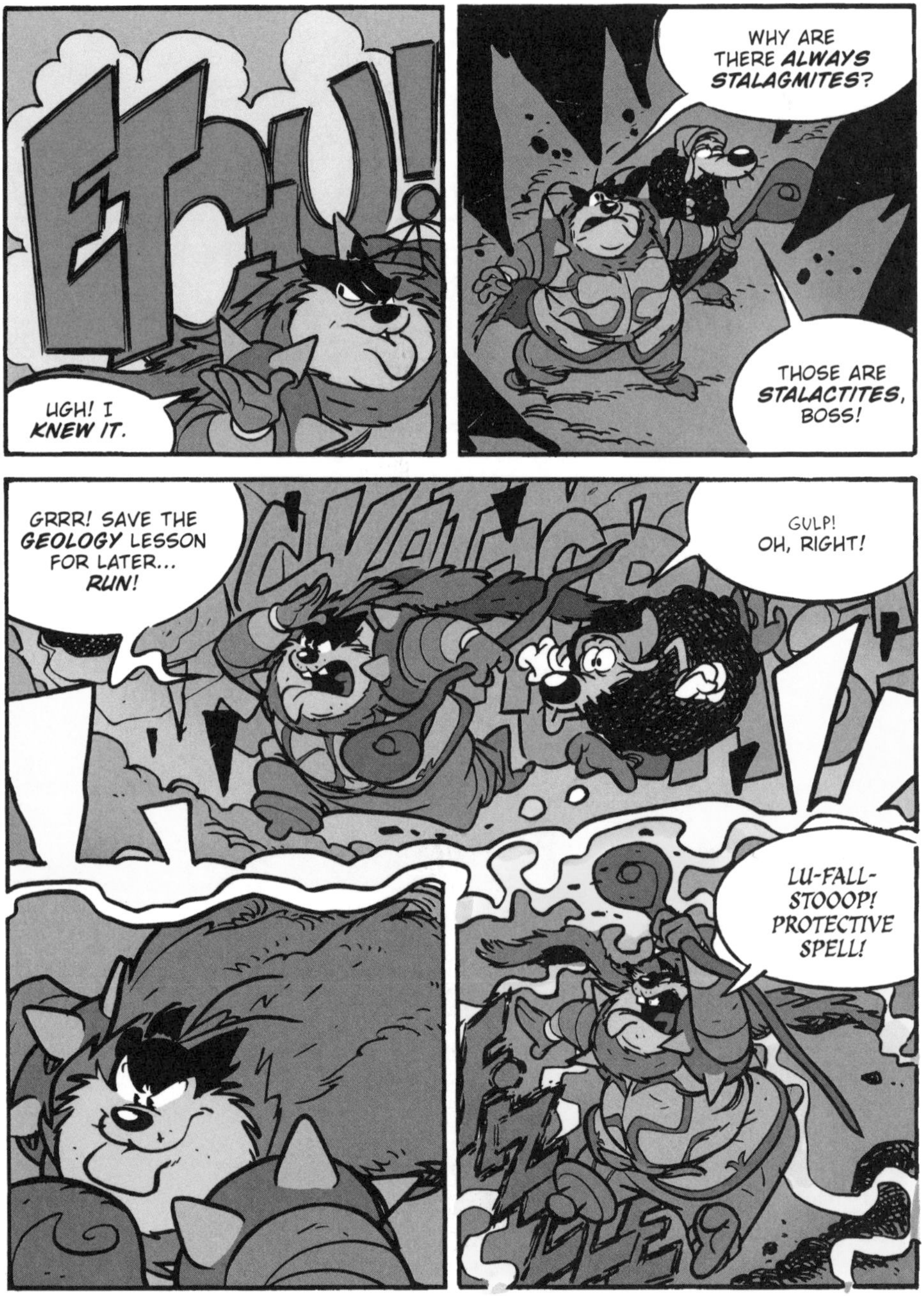
ETCHU!
UGH! I KNEW IT.
WHY ARE THERE ALWAYS STALAGMITES?
THOSE ARE STALACTITES, BOSS!
GRRR! SAVE THE GEOLOGY LESSON FOR LATER... RUN!
GULP! OH, RIGHT!
LU-FALL-STOOOP! PROTECTIVE SPELL!

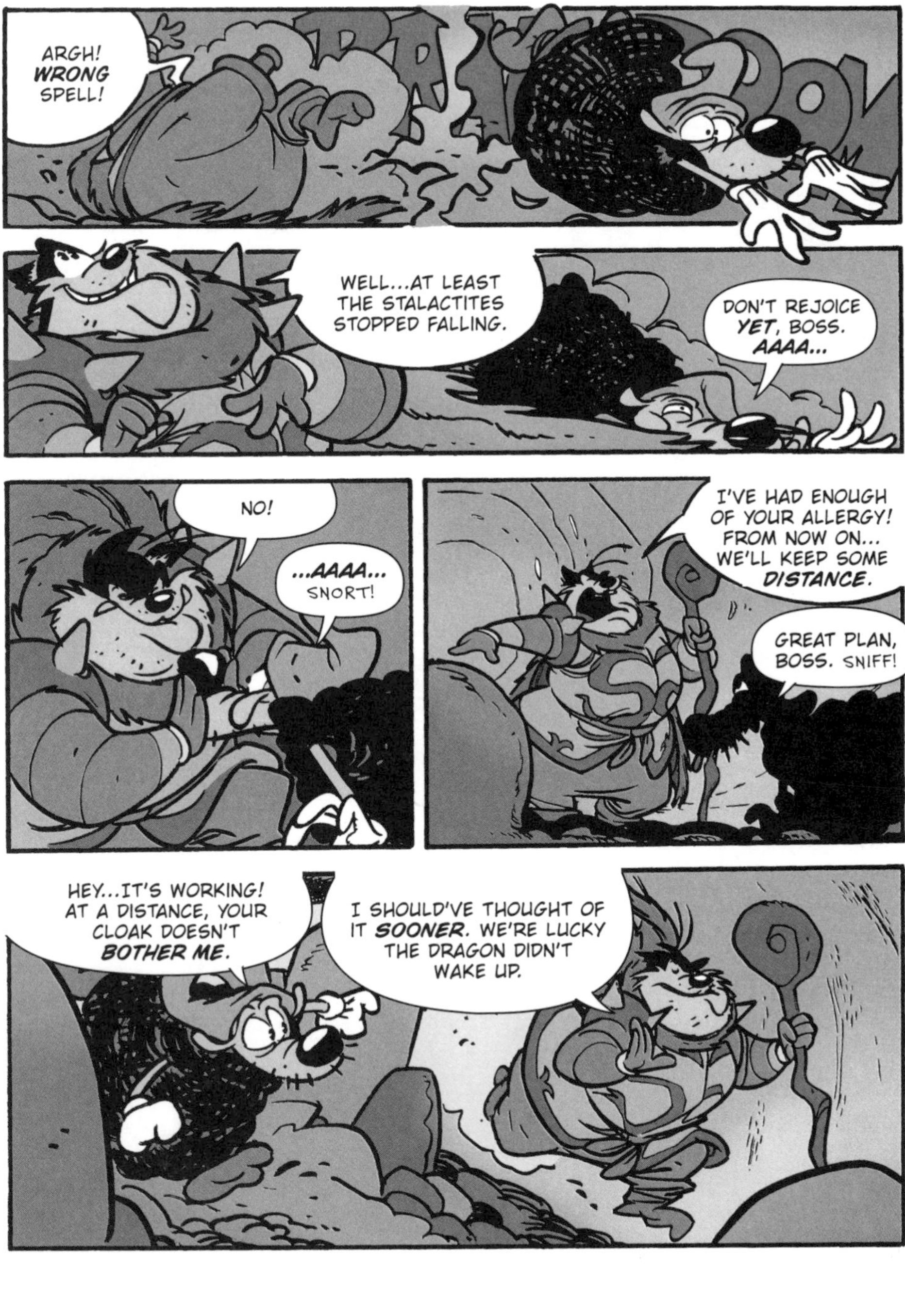
ARGH! **WRONG** SPELL!
WELL...AT LEAST THE STALACTITES STOPPED FALLING.
DON'T REJOICE **YET**, BOSS. **AAAA...**
NO!
...AAAA... SNORT!
I'VE HAD ENOUGH OF YOUR ALLERGY! FROM NOW ON... WE'LL KEEP SOME **DISTANCE**.
GREAT PLAN, BOSS. SNIFF!
HEY...IT'S WORKING! AT A DISTANCE, YOUR CLOAK DOESN'T **BOTHER ME**.
I SHOULD'VE THOUGHT OF IT **SOONER**. WE'RE LUCKY THE DRAGON DIDN'T WAKE UP.

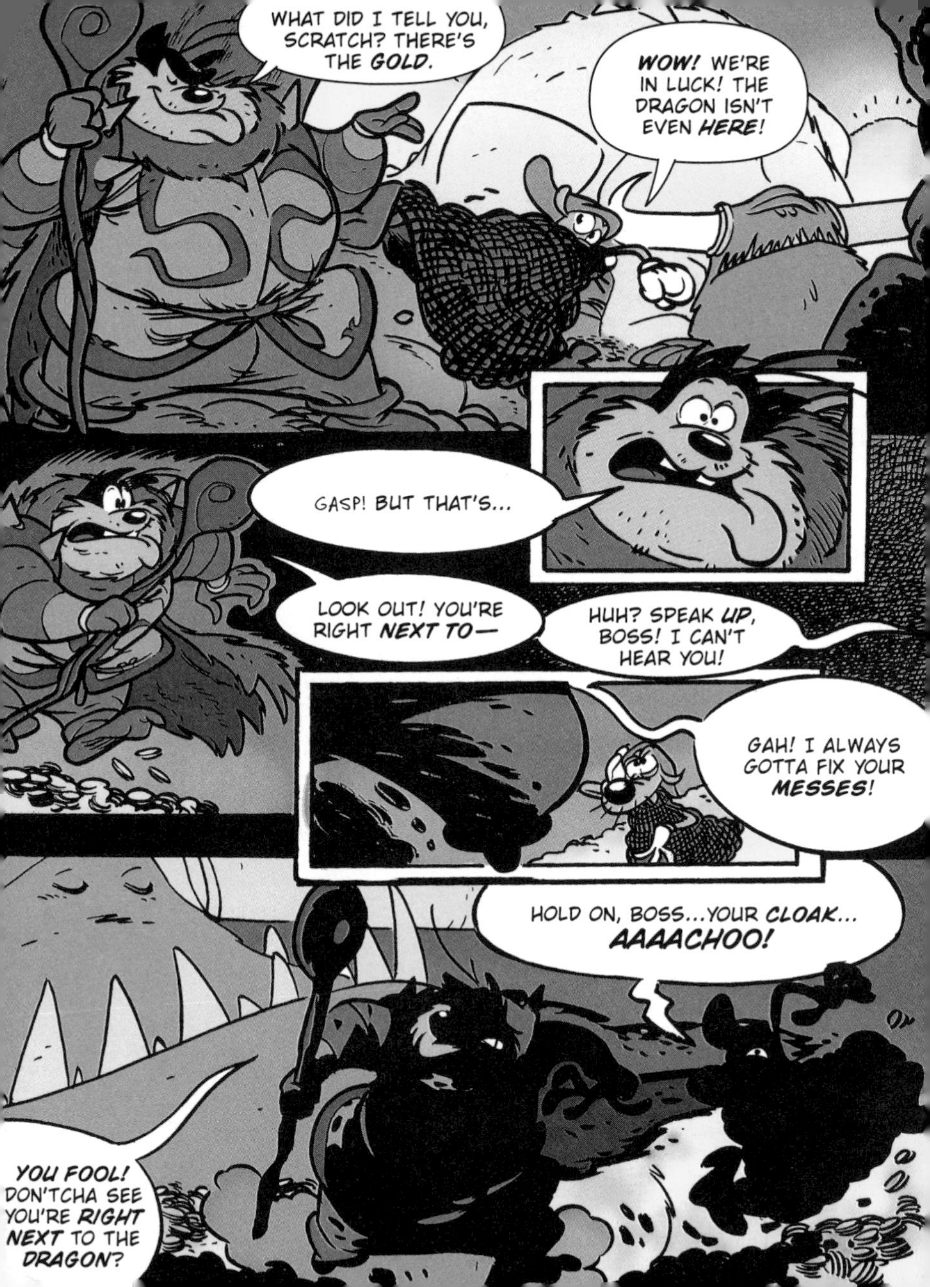
WHAT DID I TELL YOU, SCRATCH? THERE'S THE GOLD.
WOW! WE'RE IN LUCK! THE DRAGON ISN'T EVEN HERE!
GASP! BUT THAT'S...
LOOK OUT! YOU'RE RIGHT NEXT TO—
HUH? SPEAK UP, BOSS! I CAN'T HEAR YOU!
GAH! I ALWAYS GOTTA FIX YOUR MESSES!
HOLD ON, BOSS...YOUR CLOAK... AAAACHOO!
YOU FOOL! DON'TCHA SEE YOU'RE RIGHT NEXT TO THE DRAGON?

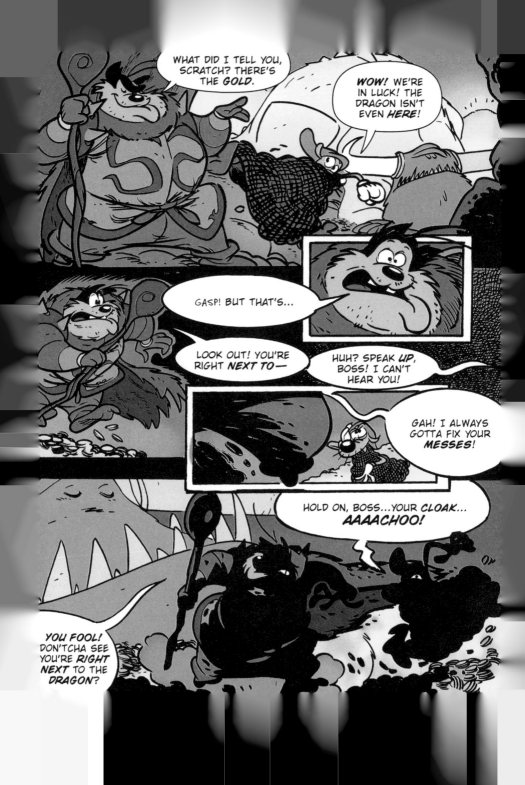

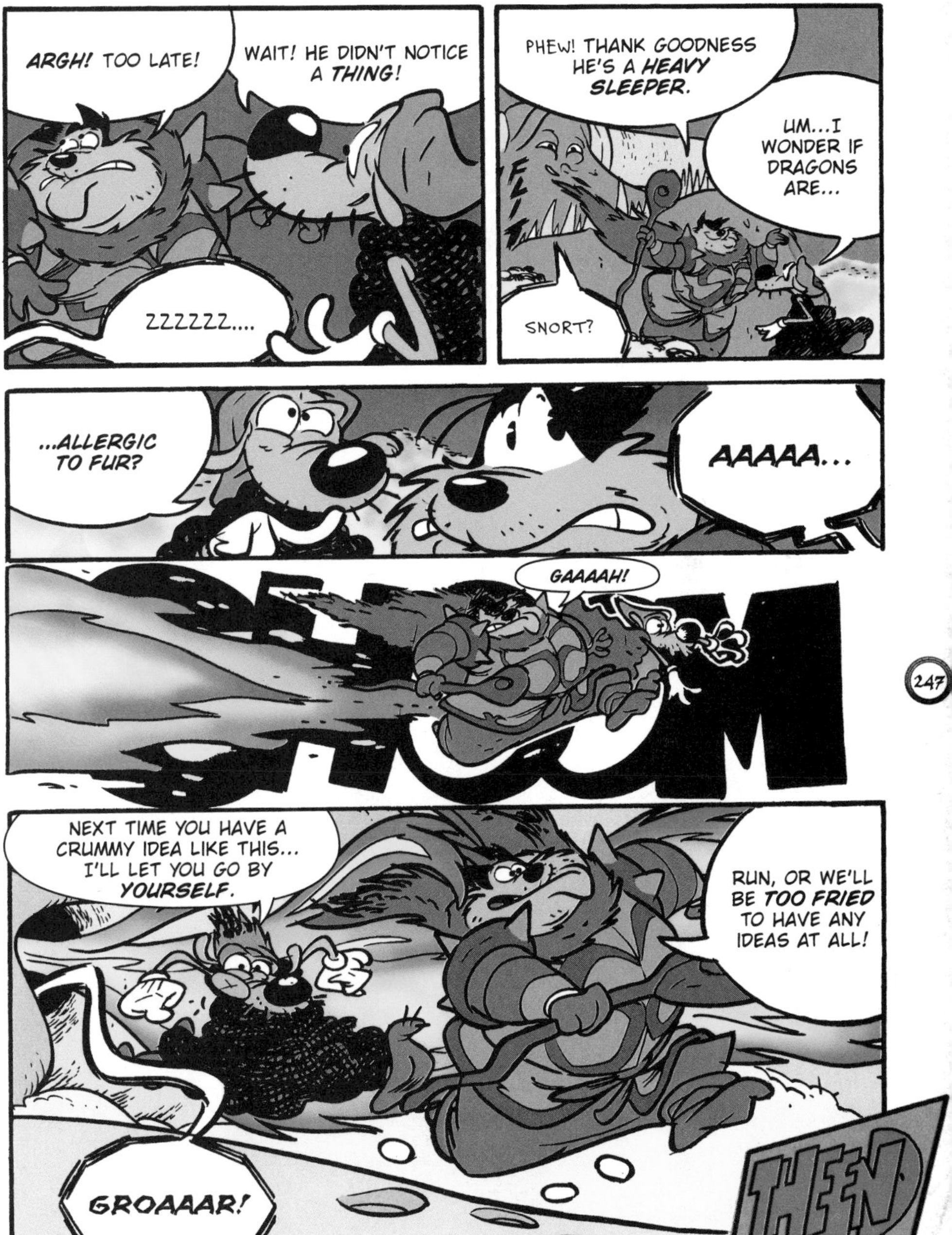
ARGH! TOO LATE!
WAIT! HE DIDN'T NOTICE A THING!
ZZZZZZ....
PHEW! THANK GOODNESS HE'S A HEAVY SLEEPER.
UM...I WONDER IF DRAGONS ARE...
SNORT?
...ALLERGIC TO FUR?
AAAAA...
GAAAAH!
NEXT TIME YOU HAVE A CRUMMY IDEA LIKE THIS... I'LL LET YOU GO BY YOURSELF.
RUN, OR WE'LL BE TOO FRIED TO HAVE ANY IDEAS AT ALL!
GROAAAR!
THE END

Wizards of Mickey

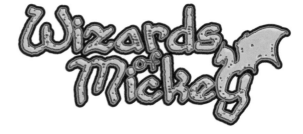

SEE YOU IN VOLUME 7!

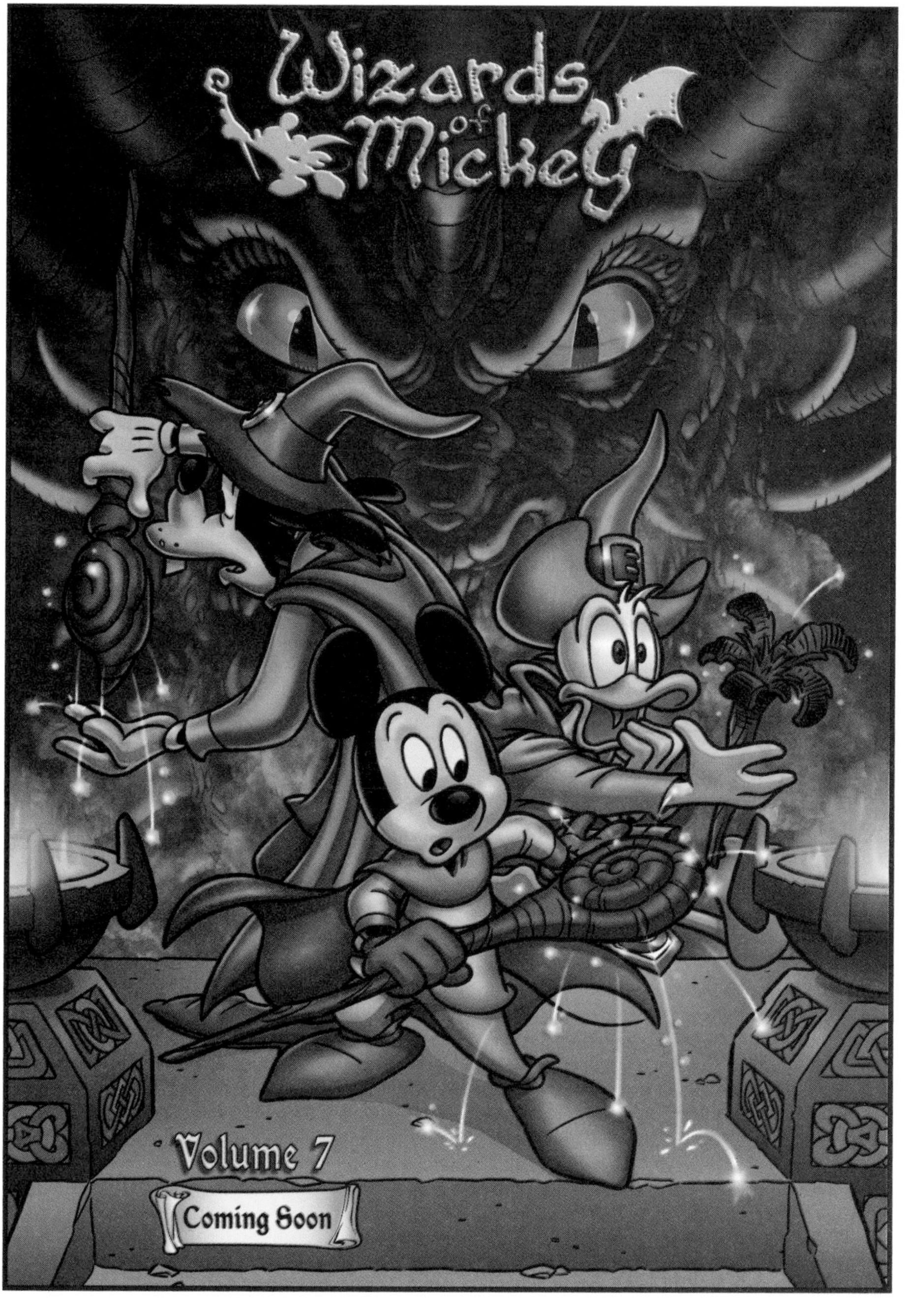
Wizards of Mickey
Volume 7
Coming Soon

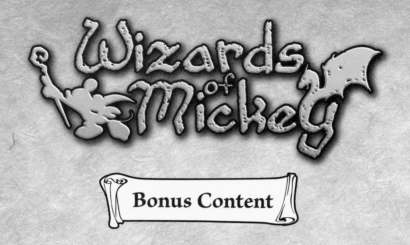

Wizards of Mickey

Bonus Content

From the pages of *Topolino*, a world famous Italian comic anthology featuring works from Disney, *Wizards of Mickey* stands out as one of the most iconic Disney comics.

It is our pleasure to share with you here some of the magazine artwork from those original issues on the following pages.

Enjoy!

TOPOLINO
IL GRANDE RITORNO DI
Wizards of Mickey
n.3285
€2,70*
TOPOLINO
Wizards of Mickey
6 storie INEDITE!
TOPOREPORTER: INCONTRO SEGRETO CON I MATES!

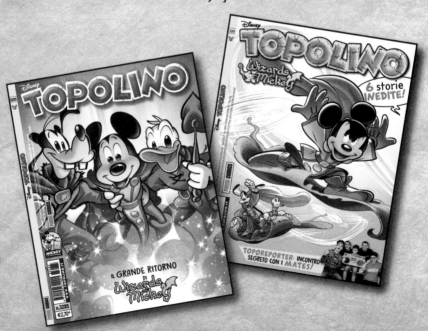

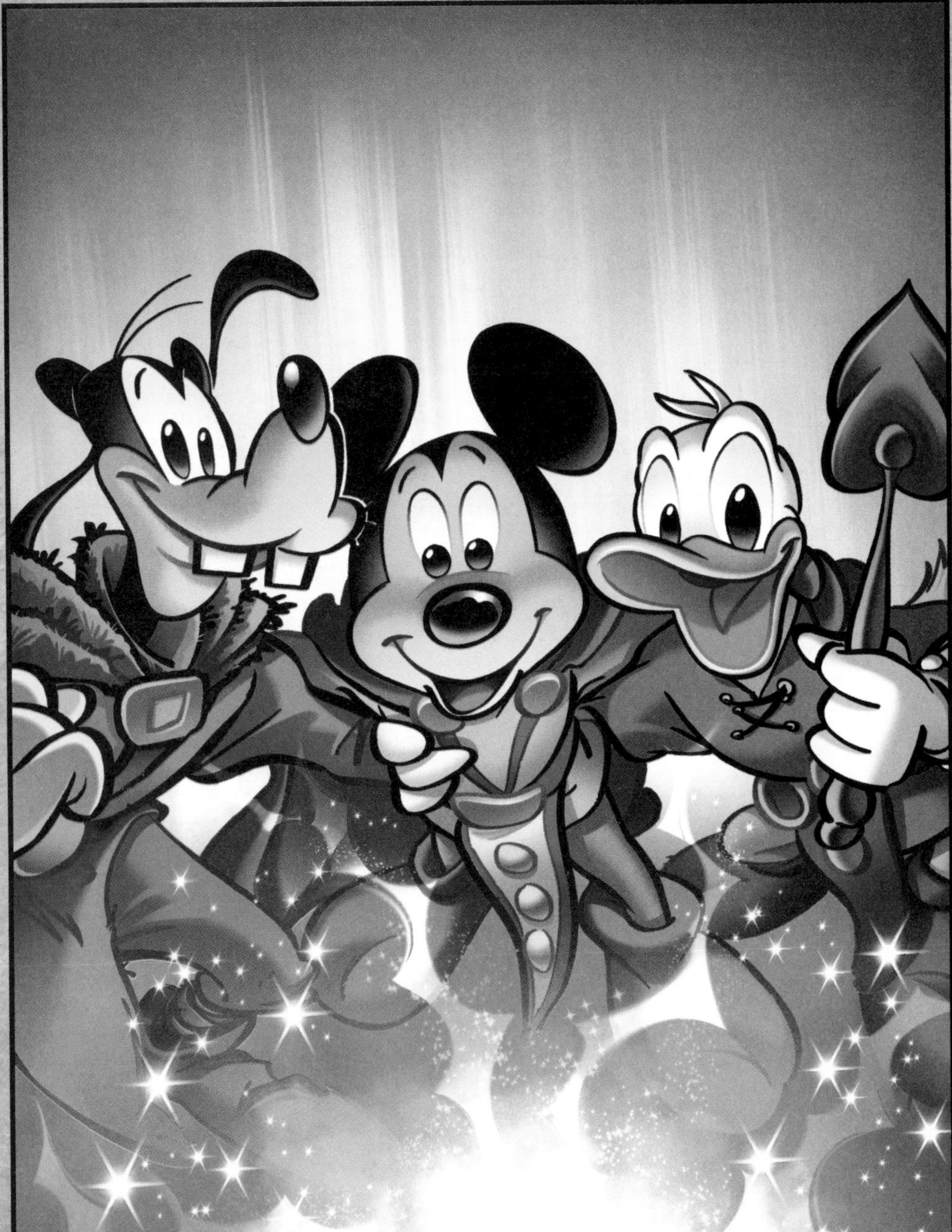

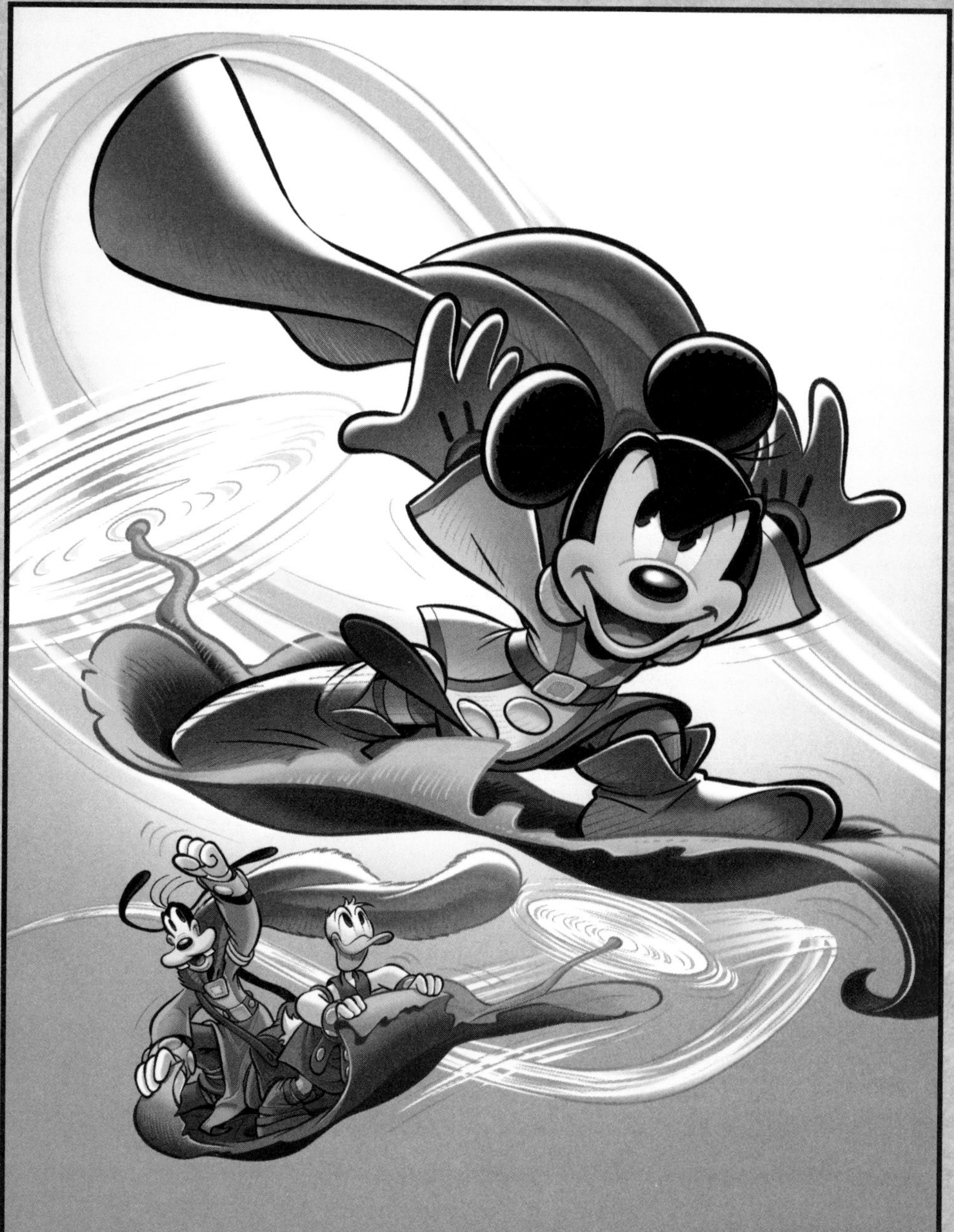

Wizards of Mickey

6

Wizards of Mickey, Vol. 6
© Disney Enterprises, Inc.

English translation © 2021 by Disney Enterprises, Inc.

JY
150 West 30th Street, 19th Floor
New York, NY 10001

Visit us at jyforkids.com
facebook.com/jyforkids
twitter.com/jyforkids
jyforkids.tumblr.com
instagram.com/jyforkids

First JY Edition: November 2021

JY is an imprint of Yen Press, LLC. The JY name and logo are trademarks of Yen Press, LLC.

Library of Congress Control Number: 2020944890

ISBNs: 978-1-9753-3844-2 (paperback)
978-1-9753-3845-9 (ebook)

10 9 8 7 6 5 4 3 2 1

LSC-C

Printed in the United States of America

Cover Art by Davide Cesarello
with colors by Andrea Cagol

Translation by Linda Ghio and Stephanie Dagg at Editing Zone
Lettering by Katie Blakeslee

OBERON
Story by Matteo Venerus
Art by Roberto Marini

ARENA
Story by Matteo Venerus
Art by Roberto Marini

DESTINY
Story by Matteo Venerus
Art by Roberto Marini

THE LOST LEGENDS
THE PLOT OF THREE
Story by Maria Muzzolini
Art by Alessandro Perina

SHORT STORIES
WIZARDS OF MICKEY
Story by Gabriele Panini
Art by Valerio Held

WIZARDS OF PETE
Story by Gabriele Panini
Art by Francesco D'Ippolito